THE ART
OF THE GLIMPSE

SINÉAD GLEESON's debut essay collection *Constellations: Reflections from Life* won Non-Fiction Book of the Year at the 2019 Irish Book Awards and the Dalkey Literary Award, and in 2020 was shortlisted for the Rathbones Folio Prize and the James Tait Black Memorial Prize. Her short stories have featured in several anthologies, including *Being Various: New Irish Short Stories* and *Repeal the 8th*. She has edited the award-winning anthologies *The Long Gaze Back: An Anthology of Irish Women Writers* and *The Glass Shore: Short Stories by Women Writers from the North of Ireland*, and is currently working on a novel.

THE ART
OF THE
GLIMPSE

100 Irish
Short Stories

CHOSEN BY

SINÉAD
GLEESON

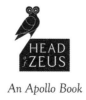

HEAD
of ZEUS

An Apollo Book

Head of Zeus Ltd
5–8 Hardwick Street
London EC1R 4RG
WWW.HEADOFZEUS.COM

THE ART OF THE GLIMPSE

100 Irish Short Stories

CONTENTS

INTRODUCTION

Whenever I am asked to edit an anthology, a wave of amnesia usually hits. It happened again when I was approached about compiling *The Art of The Glimpse*. While I cannot speak for other editors who've found themselves in this position, I confess to an ability to park all memory of what's involved: the workload, the volume of reading required, the time commitment, the setting aside of one's own writing, decisions about what to include, chasing copyright, clearances and permissions. If any editor, at any point before agreeing to take on such a project, actually remembered even a partial fragment of this madness, they'd say no. But anthologies have a distinct appeal of their own: the chance to resurrect lost writers, or familiar writers no longer widely known as much as they should be; to find writers who have gone out of fashion, or unpublished stories from the past. There is a certain satisfaction in being given an opportunity to showcase emerging work, of the canon opening up to new voices, some of whom have often been excluded from it in the past.

With such an undertaking, there are always issues – of space, omission, locating long-forgotten writers and physically finding copies of texts that are hard to track down. Agreeing to curate 100 stories has further complications: it's a substantial number of stories, but blessedly, it leaves scope to include a great variety of writers. And as this editor quickly discovered, such is the expansion of Irish writing that this leaves an anthologist spoilt for choice. Very quickly the numbers crept upwards and arrived at 100.

In the past I've noted that an anthology is an interesting means of taking the temperature of a nation. It's a way of indicating the concerns of contemporary authors and how they funnel those concerns into their fiction. The work of dead writers is also a kind of time capsule, poking one's head through the curtains of history to see what events, social concerns and politics were at play in the past.

This is the fourth anthology of Irish short stories I've edited, and my first for Head of Zeus. Two of the previous collections had a very specific aim: to highlight the voices of women, in *The Long Gaze Back: An Anthology of Irish Women Writers*, and its sequel, *The Glass Shore: Short Stories by Women of Northern Ireland*. Over the decades, anthologies had tended to ignore or include only a select handful of women. This has been widely cited as a combination of gate-keeping, of male editors not undertaking the necessary work to find other voices, and at the same time exhibiting a blindness to gender balance. Many women whose work deserves to be more widely read are included here: Margaret Barrington, Juanita Casey, Emma Cooke, Kathleen Coyle, Una Troy and Norah Hoult.

Unlike those all-female anthologies, this collection has no specific remit or premise. Head of Zeus laid down no thematic rules other than that the book was to be an anthology of 100 great already-existing Irish stories. They would not be commissioned for this book and would already have been published – or just about to be – elsewhere. The sheer size of such a book comes with its own limitations and a preference for shorter work. This anthology includes some shining examples of brevity: Mia Gallagher's 576-word 'The Lady, Vanishing' or Dermot Healy's 582-word 'Reprieve'.

It's always difficult to know where to start with such a selection, or how far back to go. Should it begin with a new century, like 1900? Or a seismic political moment such as the Act of Union in 1801, the convening of the first Republican Dáil in 1919, or the passing of De Valera's Constitution in 1937? The starting point here is in fact a story published in 1851, just after the catastrophic Famine of 1845–1849. Written by the Dublin-born Sheridan Le Fanu (1814–1973), it's ostensibly a story of violence and ghosts, but feels like an echo of the previous decade. Le Fanu's work focused intensely on the supernatural, and there are many ghosts – real and imagined – throughout this book.

The selection moves through the 19th, 20th and 21st centuries, and includes newer voices like those of Sally Rooney, Melatu Uche Okorie, Danielle McLaughlin and David Hayden. It includes classic writers like James Joyce, Elizabeth Bowen, and Frank O'Connor. There are writers you will reread fondly here, and (hopefully) many you've never encountered. This collection traces a long arc in Irish writing – through years of political conflict and the hegemony of the Catholic church, years when male voices were dominant and canonical inequality was the norm. This inequality has not only been about gender, but predicated on differences of class, of access to culture, and ethnicity.

The short story as a form transcends genre – it's particularly effective in horror and the supernatural (there are several examples in these pages), but *The Art of the Glimpse* also features comic writing, fables, experimental work, writing for young adults, crime, folklore, the surreal and satire.

As one would expect with any historical trawl through the Irish short story, there are themes present here that have been the bedrock of Irish writing: the tensions and violence of politics, poverty, emigration, families, mourning for the dead, sectarianism. These themes intersect easily and uneasily in several places: Neil Jordan's moving and complex love story takes place on the day of former President Eamon de Valera's funeral; in Bernard MacLaverty's 'Walking the Dog', there is confusion among political comrades over the religion of a potential victim.

Ireland has seen huge social and cultural shifts in the last decade – same-sex marriage and abortion have been legalised when they once seemed remote possibilities in a monotheistic, conservative culture. These and other changes have seeped into the collective consciousness of writers, allowing them to tackle themes of economic crisis, of class conflict, the experience of the marginalised Traveller community, racism and the very concept of identity and home, in stories by Kit de Waal, Oein DeBhairduin, Colm Keegan and Chiamaka Enyi-Amadi.

If some of the themes explored in these pages seem intrinsically Irish – or at least remind of us of certain familiar tropes of Irish writing – the book also pivots to subjects that are global and timeless: love, death, sexuality, desire, loss, abortion (in the story by Dermot Healy, for example) money, conflict, children, vocations and betrayal.

Here are stories of sex, infidelity, celibacy, sexual experimentation, from June Caldwell, Mary Costello and Claire Keegan. And here too is a more sexually ambiguous ending in an alternative version of Brendan Behan's story 'After the Wake', which has rarely been published. Queerness is represented by stories from the past when homosexuality was still illegal ('The Husband' by Mary Dorcey), and a sense of ease and exploration in Lucy Caldwell's 'Here We Are' and Emma Donoghue's 'Speaking in Tongues'.

Some of the writers here may surprise the reader by writing outside the frameworks we usually expect them to inhabit. Bram Stoker has become so typecast to readers as the author of *Dracula* that the hallucinatory comedy of 'A Young Widow' may catch them unawares. In a similar vein, no one thinks of Jennifer Johnston or Roddy Doyle as writers of supernatural stories, but that's what both have attempted with 'Trio' and 'The Pram' respectively. 'Holland Park' by Maeve

Binchy starts as a story of female friendship before the narrative shifts in very surprising ways.

Elizabeth Bowen, whose story 'Ann Lee's' is included here, called the short story 'a truly modern form'. Several writers have deconstructed the possibilities of shape and voice here, often in work that eschews linear narrative, such as Wendy Erskine, Keith Ridgway, Paul McVeigh, and Samuel Beckett in 'Ping'.

All anthologies are a miscellany, where writers who seem so distinct in style, genre and generation sit cheek-by-jowl. You may not admire every story in this collection, but you may find plenty to like, or a writer you've never heard of whose back catalogue you will want to track down. An anthology is a gift: a gathering of possibilities, and an opportunity to be converted into an avid completist of a writer's work that may have otherwise escaped you.

Irish writing continues to thrive and to challenge. It will evolve, and with it, the short story will continue to accommodate writers willing to stretch its boundaries. In the years ahead, we look forward to more recoveries of forgotten work, but also to more diversity, new voices and a willingness to experiment with this most versatile and malleable of forms.

SINÉAD GLEESON,
DUBLIN, 2020

THE QUEST

Leland Bardwell

Leland Bardwell (1922–2016) was a poet, novelist, short story writer, playwright, and co-founder of the literary magazine *Cyphers*. Her novels include *Girl on a Bicycle*, *That London Winter*, *The House* and *There We Have Been*. 'The Quest' appears in her story collection *Different Kinds of Love*.

W̲hat was I thinking about as I stepped off the train?

A black- (could be called raven-) haired infant?

A baby of about three weeks, a lusty, hungry demanding human being?

So what was this 'Charles'? An elongated baby? Lusty, demanding, never satisfied? One who changes women frequently, drives heavy, expensive cars?

A baby with long shins like a new-born foal.

Called Seán. Simple. Just Seán. No frills or attachments to the distaff side.

Seán then. But now 'Charles'. They changed the name. (And personality?)

And now a thirty-nine-year-old. Tall. Must be tall because of the shins. You can tell at three weeks.

It was a blowy day. Full of gusts, cold for August. There was a hint of cows and running water.

The platform was deserted. A tiny place, like a toy. The kind of station with just one apron, a tub of geraniums, a corrugated awning. To get to the other side one just walked across the line.

All around was England. Strange. I was alert from lack of sleep, everything sharp planes and angles as though the fields and farmhouses could be separated and reset in whatever pattern I wished. Except to the left where a row of houses peeped above trees. A solid row of tiled roofs and tall chimneys.

Twenty past. They mustn't be coming. What had the organisation said? 'You'll probably be met'? *Probably*?

So I wasn't met.

The crumpled piece of paper said, 3 Mill Lane, the village of Crowsfort. Yes, the cruciform legend read 'Crowsfort'.

Plough Monday. He'd been born on Plough Monday. Forty-eight hour labour. Narrow pelvis, they said. Parthenogenesis. No penetration. Peculiar.

We heard the first V2. The nurses had rushed to the window.

'A gas explosion,' they said, resuming their work.

Later, when we knew, we were frightened.

I left the platform, followed the path, found a closed-in lane, a lane bordered with trimmed box-hedge, the pebbles underfoot crunched like biscuit. It curled a little, narrowed, and there was an old fashioned stile into a graveyard.

The church was on the left. It had a Romanesque front, like the belly of a hen, and a short spire. Well, not a spire, really. Something more like the peak of a cap. A complacent little building quietly watching over the lichen-covered tombstones, the long grasses, even the primly landscaped area of more recent interments. Names like Hawsthorne, Towdie and Holmquist, Broadbent, Fairchild and one Smith, some sort of chief, he must have been, because many of his forebears were listed on the high memorial—a granite needle which raced skywards, baring their souls to the angels.

Afterwards there had been papers to sign. Yes, a very well-to-do couple. Educated and cultured also. He'll have a wonderful life. And I hadn't shed a tear. They expected me to cry. No. The long trauma was over. In three weeks I would be seventeen. And free.

Beyond the churchyard the vista opened up and I was in a road deep in chestnut trees. The houses to one side were quaint, pseudo-Elizabethan, with dormer windows that opened on a hinge, and curtains billowing out like different coloured tongues. At the end of the road I could see cars parked higgledy-piggledy with young women disgorging, calling to each other. Tiny children, pretty as butterflies, were being gathered up. They held out their offerings, plasticine figurines, dolls made from toilet rolls, pipe-cleaner animals, drawings in chalk.

As I neared them I could hear them talking. 'Say goodbye to Lena, Jenny, Paul.' 'Come on, Cherry, you'll see Austen tomorrow,' and Austen with a big black howl coming out of his stomach.

'Where is Mill Lane?' I asked a woman, a pretty, down-to-earth woman of about twenty-eight. She called out, 'Mill Lane, Peg? Know where Mill Lane is?'

No. No one knew Mill Lane. 'Must be the other side of town. You could ask in there. She's lived here all her life.'

She pointed to the only sad house. The house that needed paint, the garden that needed flowers.

I knocked. A voice called down from a window, 'Is that Rosie?'

'No,' I called back.

She appeared. A vexed face, uncared for as her garden. 'Thought you was Rosie.'

'Sorry. It's just…' She dragged me in. It was dim. She wheezed a little. 'What you want?'

'Please. I'm disturbing you. I only wanted to know…'

'This way.'

There was an absence of symmetry or sense to the room.

Settees and stools, all balding velvet, and old gold ruche, glass-topped tables, ornaments… Little blackmen in boats, gondolas, Hansel and Gretel houses, a cuckoo clock and a shepherd and shepherdess in filigree plastic.

'About time you come back.' Her hair looped down from a dusty ribbon. Dyed and dry as grass with the giveaway line of grey at the roots, it gave her lined face an operatic sadness, the melancholy of the ageing prima donna who goes for her last audition.

Agile as a grasshopper, she kneed aside the furnishing as she cut through the labyrinth, extracting a bottle—unmarked—from a sideboard near the fireplace.

''Ere luv.' She held out a tumbler, pouring one for herself.

Neat gin.

I let it in slowly. We both stood. Stared.

'3 Mill Lane,' I said. 'Could you direct me?'

'So you come back,' she repeated.

'Sorry. I'm not Rosie. Nan. Nan MacDonald. Looking for… a friend.'

'I'll go on,' I added. 'Won't disturb you any longer. Thank you for the drink.'

'You can't fool me.' My wrist in her hand felt the bones under the flesh, wobbling, silky like the skin of a frog. My business was elsewhere. Who was Rosie?

'So you'll leave me again?' She dropped my wrist, sat back in her chair, the thin arm holding the drink, the only thing that mattered then. 'Go, then.'

He had lain in a crib with a falciform awning. All pleated organdie, baby-blue, round the edges. That's what they sent to fetch him in. And boy did his dark eyes twirl and twirl and his small fists curl at the end of his long arms. His body was hard as a rock when he bawled and his face screwed up like a bitten apple.

I didn't go to him when he cried. Not always. Sometimes I picked him up and brushed his forehead with my lips if he quietened down. That's during the few weeks in the home. Miss Charity got angry when I lifted him. 'Leave them alone between feeds.' But I couldn't stand the racket. Although the Irish skivvy agreed with me. Grey and toothless as a herring, she'd reared ten, she said, 'And never let a one of them cry.'

The outside world hit me like a sheet, a grey sheet, billowing and blinding me. Breath came in and out as I ran, scorched my chest. I was in the main street. A street of closed shops, windows of flame in the evening sun. Snug grocers and fishmongers, hardware stores and old curiosity shops. Behind one window, velveteen dolls and bouncy balls and a marionette with bunches of golden hair and a Monroe pout hung in her complicated strings one arm lifted, one toe pointed as for a *pas de deux*. Her green tutu struck out each side like a miniature lampshade. At the end of the street, The Crown, a magnificent structure, with carriage lamps and gleaming oak doors, welcomed all comers with a warm smell of hops.

I went in.

They didn't let me meet the couple. It wasn't allowed then. They reassured me once more. When he had gone I played the tinny piano, a waltz by Chopin, a two-part *Invention* by Bach (The one in F major) until I was scolded and stopped. I wandered around. Snow had begun to patter outside. Soft stars on the window-pane. I pressed my nose against the glass, wanting to kiss and feel the clean cold on my lips. The building was cold and damp, a long hall with a refectory table. A table where we ate—all the fallen women—gabbling together, telling each other's story till we knew them off by heart. But it was empty then, no tin plates or cutlery, no clatter. Just the echoing of my steps on the stone floor.

I had to wait three days before I was released with an envelope in which a note said I was fit for work.

The beer took the taste of gin from my mouth. Middle-aged men greeted each other. The barmen called them 'Guv,' and treated all with cordial assurance. It had been a long coming. I was anxious. Someone told me where Mill Lane was. I ordered another beer.

I watched each man in turn. Could one be this 'Charles'? He had sent for me. He was expecting me, wanted to see me. Why, after so long? What had I agreed to come? I remembered 'Rosie'. That woman had expected Rosie, had thought I was Rosie. How long had she waited for Rosie? What had it to do with me?

The beer cooled my thoughts, blunted my nerve ends. Soon I would get up and go to Mill Lane.

The blood drained from me.

Charles had walked into the pub.

I ran to the ladies room, surprised I didn't look too awful, washed my face and hands, combed my hair, put on earrings, adjusted my black coat slightly off my shoulders, belt dangling, to appear casual, collected.

'Is that Charles?'

The man lifted his pint and put it on my table.

He was like my father, loose, dark, thick-browed, six foot perhaps. 'Nan,' he said. 'I knew you at once.' He looked at me oddly. I had said to my father, I'm going to England to work. He had looked at me oddly.

We walked in the dark, following the ball of orange light cast by his torch. I could feel grass underfoot eventually, his voice was amiable. He said he had just moved in, had been expecting me all evening, that his house was one of three tied cottages, and of course the mill had long since fallen into disuse.

'My parents bought this as a country retreat, but sadly never used it.' For once there was a mordant touch to his tones.

They had been killed in an accident last year, he told me.

Inside, two tiny rooms sloped to either side of the narrow hall. They were both empty of furniture except in one a few canvases were stacked against the wall facing inwards.

He stood tall in the bright, friendly, I thought beautiful, his dark hair waving over his sallow brow glowed blue like a crow's wing. 'I'll get two chairs,' he said.

Did he want me now his parents were dead? Uneasily I glanced at the backs of the canvases. What was he? A painter?

He brought food and plates of salad, interpreted my wonderings, said he had left his job to live here, had worked, oh yes for his 'pater'—a splendid man, botanist, scholar—his mother also, now he would retire permanently here. 'In the daylight you'll see it, it's infectious, you'll never want to leave it.' But… but…

Perhaps I learnt something of his ways as he talked, poking here and there into minor episodes of his childhood, schooldays, university.

'I lived with a girl for a while. We couldn't marry. Her husband refused to divorce her, threatened to take her child.'

He'd had no child of his own, no. They'd parted wishy-washy. Was he too good to be true? Too beautiful, too self-contained. Something niggled me. The dark must be there somewhere. The pictures? What was in the pictures?

The fact that I was famous didn't seem to bother him. He knew, remarked lightly he had read about me. (My most recent concert had been in Leningrad, had caused a stir, was widely covered.) It grew late. I asked about the canvases.

'I only paint to find out.' He turned the first. A view of Wicklow. Unmistakable. The big Sugarloaf the backdrop to the purples and browns of heather, bog; a ramshackle cottage, the centrepiece.

I had not thought of him as an artist of any kind. Not even a temptingly bad artist. This daub, so carefully copied from a photograph (probably), must be part of the dark side I was expecting he would expose sooner or later.

'Yes, I know,' he said seeing my look of consternation. 'It's awful, isn't it.'

'It's not so much that.' I was stuck for words.

'I copied it from a picture postcard.'

'Are the others all famous Irish views?' I asked limply.

'No. Worse. They are of women. Or rather one woman.' He let out a long breath like an 'AAAH', making no effort to turn the pictures round.

We sat for a while in silence. Although he had talked sporadically about himself, he made no effort to ask about my life. Time didn't seem to belong to him. Between babyhood and his fortieth year no time seemed to have passed at all. His life had been led in a field of shadows. My presence here was simply another shadow that would pass, leaving yet more shadows of a greyer hue.

The fire spat and flamed and he had sat down again and leant slightly forward, elbows on knees, hands occasionally stretched towards the heat. I found it uncomfortably warm and pushed my chair away. Then he got up. 'I'll show you,' he said.

One by one he turned the pictures round. The first was clearly a self-portrait, that is to say of a woman resembling himself. She had the same dark features and continental skin, the same narrow face and neat head. But there was something missing. The expression was empty, like one who is heavily drugged. The second somewhat similar except that he had tried to thicken the paint to give the impression of the ageing of the skin. The last two were increasingly horrific. Here the artist began to show some genuine talent—or if not talent, imagination—although once again they were clichés. The final picture, especially. In this she was represented as an old hag, the conventional witch, the epitome of evil.

He stood behind it now, glaring at me. 'You see I had to find out. They tried to shelter me, pampered me, gave in to my whims. They emptied me there.' He tapped his forehead.

'I didn't send for you until I'd finished this last one,' he continued.

It was as though he were trying to emulate evil, the evil he had tried to portray. The face had changed from polite to sour, the childish pout on his lips reminded me of the marionette in the window of the shop. He left the canvas and went into the kitchen, swaggering somewhat as he passed me.

Should I creep away, I wondered. But I didn't move, sat as though sculpted, another of his effigies. Didn't move until he came slowly out, the light dancing on the long blade of the kitchen knife, and then I jumped to my feet, backed against the wall, making myself an easier target if anything. But while he waved the knife in my direction he immediately began to hack at the canvas, tearing it across and across until finally he ripped it off its frame and threw it into the fire. Shreds of hair went chasing up the chimney and he stood and watched until the last ragged piece had faded into ash.

'Upon such sacrifices, my Cordelia, the gods themselves throw incense.' Did I say that out loud? I'm not sure. Anyway he went on staring into the fire. The logs had begun to die down, the black ash had quelled the flames, he kicked a piece of wood and a few sparks lifted to subside immediately. He turned to me. 'I told you, I just wanted to find out.'

'And have you?'

He made a metronomic movement with his head, his expression a melancholic void.

I picked up my bag.

'It's all in the travelling,' I said. 'Goodbye.'

I may have added, I'm booked into The Crown, or, if you're in Ireland, look me up.

I can't remember.

A LINGERING GUEST

Jane Barlow

Jane Barlow (1856–1917) was born in Clontarf in Dublin and grew up in Raheny. She was a classical scholar and one of the first women to be awarded a D. Litt from Trinity College, Dublin. She published three novels, six poetry collections and multiple collections of short stories, including the highly successful *Irish Idylls* (1892).

When Mrs. Van Herder died at her house on Marksville Avenue, New York, leaving a legacy of $100 to each servant who had been over three years in her employment, the Irish girl Rose Byrne could claim the bequest, having scrubbed the Van Herder floors for five long years; and ten minutes after she heard of her good fortune, she had firmly made up her mind what she would do with it: she would go home straightway. Home for Rose lay across the Atlantic, on the storm-beaten shore of the County Mayo, and a dozen twelve months had passed since she had seen it except in dreams. If the legacy had come sooner, she might, while waiting for the liner to sail, have spent much of her time and of her hundred dollars in the purchase of presents and clothes, wherewithal to glorify her rejoining of her family circle. But by now so many a precious stone had dropped out of that ring of hers, that she knew she would find only a few safe in its setting. An old grandmother and a married sister were all the near relations left to welcome her back. This, and the prudence learned from experience, made her preparations sober and thrifty. "I'm thinkin'," she said to herself, "that I'll do better to not be buyin' till I get home, for then I'll have a notion of what's wantin'. Buyin' things for them now is the same as puttin' the right keys into the wrong keyholes; there's naught amiss wid the keys themselves, only they won't open the locks. Them stores do be oncommon iligant, but sure I'll wait."

Rose, in fact, was thinking that the things most wanted at home would probably be quite common and not elegant at all; and when she reached Kilgowran, she very soon saw that her conjectures were even righter than she had expected them to be. Her grandmother's white-walled, brown-thatched cabin, which looked like a weather-worn mushroom on the wide, dark bog, was in reality still more poverty-stricken than it had seemed in her memory. Partly, perhaps, because those lofty and spacious chambers over seas, which you could fill with clearest brilliance by a twirl of your thumb, contrasted so strongly with this one dark little room, where the rafters slanted low above the uneven mud-floor, and the shadows among them were seldom disturbed by anything brighter than a stray flicker glancing from the hearth. Its mistress had been old and gaunt as long as Rose could recollect, and was now, of course, older and gaunter than ever. Her decrepit, broken-down aspect struck Rose painfully as they sat opposite one another, soon after the arrival, on small, rough creepy-stools, by the crumbling glow of the turf-sods. It was a sad thing, she thought, to see an infirm old woman so poorly off that she had to wrap herself in a ragged greatcoat as she crouched huddled up uneasily over her fire, which she stirred with a broken spade-handle. Rose reflected with some consolation that to provide "a dacint warm shawl" was certainly in her power; "any sort of comfortable armchair" might be, she feared, beyond her means.

Since Rose's last sight of it, however, old Mrs. Behan had added something to her little dwelling's scanty contents. Another grandchild, namely, the orphan daughter of her son Peter, a slip of a girl just growing up. Maggie Behan was now nearly of the same age that Rose Byrne had been when quitting the bog-land of Kilgowran, and she looked very much as her cousin had done a dozen troublesome years ago. And it was not long before Rose perceived that Maggie occupied the position of prime favourite which had formerly been her own. This, indeed, became apparent on the very first evening, despite Rose's temporary distinction as a newly returned traveller; and it was made unmistakably plain next morning, when Mrs. Behan declared to Rose her opinion that there had never been a one of them all who could hold a candle to little Maggie for good looks, though the Behans were always as handsome a family as any on the countryside. An impartial judge would have seen nothing more remarkable in Maggie's round, cheerful face than that pleasant freshness of early youth which Irish people call pig-beauty. So Rose understood well enough what was betokened by such extravagant praise. But she was not left merely to draw inferences. Their grandmother had a habit of expressing herself frankly, and accordingly she soon spoke her mind to Rose on this point. "Sure, now, you and me was always great, Rose, me dear," she said. "But little Maggie, the crathur, she's what the heart of me's fairly set on, and small blame to me, for her aquil wouldn't be aisy got. And, bedad, 'twas the same way ever; ne'er a word had I agin poor Norah, your mother, at all at all. But Pather was the lovely child—that's your poor uncle, Maggie's father— ay, indeed, I always had a wonderful wish for Pather."

Though it was scarcely in the nature of things that Rose should not feel somewhat aggrieved at finding herself thus superseded, circumstances helped her to take a philosophical view of the situation, saying to herself: "Why, it's only natural Granny'd think a deal of Maggie, that she's after bringin' up. And, sure, maybe the more she thinks of her the better, these times, for who else is there to be stoppin' along wid her and mindin' her, when she's gettin' so old and feeble?" Therefore as the days went past, Rose, keeping a watchful eye on significant trifles, was glad to see no lack on Maggie's part of helpfulness and affection. "She'll be well looked after," she thought, as she observed her young cousin's energetic "readying up" of the house-room, and good-humoured ways with the querulous old woman; and once she spoke some of these sentiments aloud.

Her grandmother and she had walked across the bog to eleven o'clock Mass at Kilgowran Chapel, and were sitting to rest in the August sun on the low dilapidated wall of the chapel-yard. Kilgowran burial-ground is a dreary, unrestful place, overlooked by the backs of several houses, and overgrown with tall green nettles and rusty brown docks. Among them the few gray stones, and the wooden crosses, plentier because cheaper, are sometimes nearly lost. These low, crookedly set crosses vary in hue from time to time, according to the different painting jobs that have been in progress thereabouts, as the leavings in a pot are often devoted to this purpose. A vivid canary was just then the prevailing colour. Mrs. Behan surveyed them musingly as she and Rose sat to wait for Maggie who had gone on a message; and she presently remarked: "I've no likin' for that yallery colour; it's as ugly as sin. If it was me, I'd sooner a deal have the pink one there is yonder over young Andy Fitz Simon. His father gave it a new coat the time he was doin' up Mr. Purcell's front palin's a while ago. But, sure, how would poor Maggie be stickin' up crosses or anythin' else over me, the crathur, thry her best?"

"Maggie's a very good girl," Rose said, to give the conversation a livelier turn. "I don't know what you'd do widout her."

But her commendation of her cousin, generally so eagerly taken up, had not the usual effect upon her grandmother. For instead of replying: "Ay, bedad," and launching out into complacent praises, Mrs. Behan answered firmly and gloomily: "I'd do first-rate; grand I'd do, if I got the chance." An unexpected response which surprised Rose considerably, but Maggie's arrival prevented comment or explanation.

In the course of the next week, Rose was again puzzled by some of her grandmother's sayings and doings. What perplexed her first was a marked disapprobation of the little purchases that she made for the benefit of the cabin and its occupiers. The sorely needed garments or utensils or groceries never had a reception more gracious than: "Well, now, yourself's the great gaby to be bringin' home all them conthrivances. 'Deed it's a pity to see you throwin' away your money on the likes of such ould thrash that nobody wants." More-over, Mrs. Behan's manner showed plainly that these protests were not merely polite disclaimers, but sincere utterances of her sentiments. Rose wondered and pondered without catching sight of any plausible reason. She well knew that none of her family had ever inclined towards excessive thrift either on their own or other people's account. Stranger still, Mrs. Behan began to let fall what sounded to Rose terribly like hints that she had outstayed her welcome, and had better end her visit. That this should have happened already, or in truth, could happen ever at all, was a bitter thought to Rose; and one night after her grandmother had been talking about the sailing of steamers from Queenstown, she felt so badly that she ate hardly a morsel at supper, and went to bed early, almost resolved to leave next morning. But thereupon Mrs. Behan had manifested such deep concern at these signs of indisposition, and had so bestirred herself to totter about, making tea and toast for the invalid, and scaring away intrusive hens whose crawking might disturb "her honey," that Rose found it for the time being impossible to harbour those grievous suspicions.

Then one evening on her return from the post-office, she found her grandmother alone in the kitchen. The old woman was stooping over the table upon which she had spread out the contents of Rose's large wash-leather purse. Perceiving herself detected, she attempted first to conceal her occupation with a corner of her shawl, and next to assume an unabashed demeanour, failing in a pitiable way that made Rose hasten to say gaily, accepting the scrutiny as a matter of course: "Well, Granny, it's fine and rich I am these times, amn't I?" And, restored to self-respect, Mrs. Behan spoke her mind without embarrassment. "Oh, bedad are you. But it's not very long before you won't be so. Five and ninepince you've spent since this day week. You might as well be lettin' on to keep a sup of wather in an ould sack. Never your fool's fut you set outside the door, but you'll throw away a couple of shillin's. Och, you needn't be offerin' to hide it; I see the parcel you have under your arm this minyit. And the end of it 'ill be that before we know where we are, the passage-money 'ill be gone. Look there," she said, pointing to the coins, which she had counted into two unequal heaps. "That's your fares on the steamer, and that other's all you have left for wastin': and it, by rights, you'll want to live on till you get places on the other side. But you'll keep it up, all I can do or say, till you'll not lave enough to take the two of yous over."

"The two of me, Granny?" Rose said. "Sure, the dear knows it's lonesome entirely I'll be goin' across, and what for in the world would I be payin' the double fares?"

"Where's Maggie?" said Mrs. Behan.

"*Maggie?!*" said Rose. "And now what would bewitch me to be takin' Maggie away, and she the only one you have to be doin' a hand's-turn for you over here?"

"Well enough I can be doin' meself all the hand's-turns I want," said Mrs. Behan. "What 'ud ail me to not? Haven't I got the hins? And I might be droppin' down off me standin' feet any minyit of the day, and then what 'ud become of little Maggie? It's the best chance for her whatever."

"Maggie'd be frettin' woeful if she was took away from you," said Rose. "Ne'er a fut she'd come, it's my belief, and anyhow 'twould be no thing to go do. I wouldn't be thinkin' of it at all."

They argued the point for a long time without change of opinion on either side, until at last Rose said: "Well, Granny, you know I'm goin' on Tuesday to stop awhile wid me sister up at Athbawn, so 'twill be time enough to talk about Maggie when I come back. There's no hurry." And in this adjournment Mrs. Behan had to acquiesce with what patience she could.

During her fortnight's visit to the struggling MacAteer family away up in Donegal, Rose considered the question much and anxiously, with the result that on her journey back to Kilgowran she was sometimes repeating in her mind a resolve at which she had reluctantly arrived. "I'll thry get a place in this counthry," she said to herself. "It's poor livin' and bad wages, and I well know the best way to lend them a helpin' hand is from across the wather. But how would Granny, the crathur, understand? And I'll promise her that if anythin' happens her, I'll take Maggie back wid me then to the States. Maybe that 'ill contint her."

But Rose never gave that promise. For when she reached the little brown and white cottage in the black bog, she found it more lonesome within than without; and running in affright to the Dohertys, its far-off nearest neighbours, she heard terrible news. Mrs. Doherty, looking scared and solemn, related how the evening after Rose left, Mrs. Behan had asked them to take in Maggie for a little while, as she herself was real bad, and going into Ballymoyle Infirmary. And how on that day week, when Jim Doherty had tramped over to enquire for her, he heard that she was dead and buried. "Took very suddint, the crathur, God be good to her," Mrs. Doherty said. "Or to be sure she'd ha' sent word by some manner of manes to poor Maggie that she set such store by, and that's sittin' here in desolation in the corner ever since, as quiet as a bird hunted out of its sivin sinses."

Maggie did indeed look so wan and woebegone that Rose's first thought was: "She'd never ha' been persuaded to come away wid me. If I had but known, I might have promised to take her safe enough, instead of to be vexin' poor Granny wid goin' against it; and I'd liefer than a great deal I had so." However, she was obliged to mingle active exertions with the regret that made them all dreary and wearisome. She could not afford to linger, lest her little fortune should actually, as poor Granny had dreaded, dwindle away, leaving her without the means of paying her cousin's passage. That Maggie must now accompany her was obvious, for "who else would be mindin' the girl?" and Maggie herself had apparently no wishes one way or the other. So Rose hastened to make their preparations before the waning fall became stormier winter, and the long amber rays, which seemed stooping to peer in under thatched eaves at little low windows, should be all lost among clouds and mist. One thing she did, gave some small consolation to Maggie and herself. She bespoke a wooden cross for their grandmother's grave from Jim Doherty, who was a great hand at carpentering. Jim at first made some demur about accepting the commission, on the grounds that he might be "bothered to find the right grave there promiscuous in the Union corner." But in the end he consented, and refused to take a farthing for it, and promised to paint it a fine strong pink, and if possible at all to set it in the proper place, though about this he still expressed doubts. So Rose entrusted Mrs. Doherty with the key of the deserted cabin till Mrs. MacAteer could take possession of its few effects, and she and Maggie said farewell to Kilgowran.

The cousins voyaged safely to New York, and were fortunate enough to get situations there in the same family. One day soon after Rose had reported their arrival to Mrs. Doherty at Kilgowran, she received an Irish letter, which she and Maggie read with bewildered amazement at first, and finally with almost incredulous joy. It was written by the Kilgowran schoolmaster, from the dictation evidently of more than one person, which made its style rather involved and obscure, as we may perceive: "Dear Rose, and Maggie, jewel machree, that has no call to be fritting all the while. Sure, now, Rose, you needn't be mad wid me, for the only plan I could contrive to get you out of it was to take off wid meself to the Infirmary as soon as I got your back turned, for then I well knew you wouldn't be long quitting yourself, and bringing little Maggie wid you. So I bid Jim Doherty let on I was the old woman they were after burying there on Friday. But afraid of me life I was lest he wouldn't have the wit to be telling you the right lies.—Dear Miss Rose Byrne, you can bear me witness that ne'er a word of truth I told you good or bad, except saying I couldn't tell the very place the grave was, and small blame to me for that same, when Herself is sitting here by her fire this minyit, and well able to be giving impidence as ever she was in her life. But I mean to let you know I didn't go back of my promise about the cross, no fear. A grand little one it is, and I have it painted as pink as a rose. Dear Miss Byrne, so when I brought it over to her now——" "The big *stookawn* he was to go do such a thing," Rose commented on reading this—"Nothing would suit her but I must stick it up for her on the wall alongside of her dresser, and an iligant appearance it has. I may say Mr. Gogarty the schoolmaster is in a great admiration of it altogether. [I am glad to state that I consider the cross a neatly made and tastefully constructed article.—J. G.] Indeed now, Rose, you were a very good girl to think of it, and there will I be keeping it, dry and convanient, till whenever I want it, plase God; and then Jim Doherty will see there will be no mistake about where it's put in the burying-ground. Sure the hins do be grand company to me. And Maggie alanna, you will be getting on finely in the States, and don't be lonesome, me jewel, for there do be no chances in Kilgowran. So no more at present from your grandmother Honoria Behan, and Jim Doherty."

"Well to be sure, but herselfs the great rogue, glory be to goodness," Rose said, when they had at last puzzled out the state of affairs. "And rightly she got the better of me that time, and quare fools she made of the two of us, that were frettin' ourselves distracted, and she just waitin' ready to flourish up out of her bed like an ould cricket hoppin', and back again wid her into her little house, as soon as she had us safely landed on board. But all the same it's wonderin' I am, Maggie, if she isn't apt to be lost entirely widout either of us."

"I'll save hard," said Maggie. "Wid such a power of wages it won't be a great while till I have enough to get back to her. Ah, Rose, dear, me heart's cold to think of her sittin' there wid that ould pink cross stuck up on the wall. But, plase God, that's where I'll find it yet when I get home to her; and then I'll not be long takin' it down."

And at the present time Maggie is saving hard, and the pink cross still bangs on the wall beside her grandmother's dresser.

STAND YOUR SKIN

Colin Barrett

Colin Barrett is the author of *Young Skins*, originally published by the Stinging Fly Press. Young Skins won the 2014 Frank O'Connor International Short Story Prize, the Rooney Prize for Irish Literature and the Guardian First Book Award. He is a 2018–20 Rolex Arts Protégé. His fiction has appeared in the *New Yorker*, the *Stinging Fly* magazine and *Granta*.

Bat is hungover. Bat is late. At the rear of the Maxol service station he heels the kickstand of his Honda 150 and lets the cycle's chrome blue body slant beneath him until its weight is taken by the stand. Bat dismounts, pries off his helmet—black tinted visor, luminescent yellow Cobra decal pasted to the dome—and a scuzzy cascade of dark hair plummets free to his ass.

Bat makes for the station's restroom. The restroom is little bigger than a public telephone box. Its windowless confines contain a tiny sink and cracked mirror, a naked bulb and lidless shitter operated by a fitfully responsive flush handle. There is not a single sheaf of bog roll anywhere.

A big brown daddy-long-legs pedals airily in the sink basin. Bat watches the creature describe a flustered circle, trapped. He could palm-splat the thing out of existence but with a mindful sweep of his hand instead sends it unscathed over the rim.

Bat gathers his mane at the nape, slinks a blue elastic band from his wrist and fashions a ponytail, as Dungan, his supervisor, insists. Bat handles his hair delicately. Its dense length is crackly and stiff, an inextricable nest of flubs, snarls and knots, due to the infrequency with which Bat submits to a wash.

Bat's head hurts. He drank six beers on the roof of his house last night, which he does almost every night, now. The pain is a rooted throb, radiating outwards, like a skull-sized toothache, and his eyes mildly burn; working his contact lenses in this morning, he'd subjected his corneas to a prolonged and shaky-handed thumb-fucking. A distant, dental instrument drone fills his ears like fluid. Hangovers exacerbate Bat's tinnitus.

He runs the H and C taps. Saliva-temperatured and textured water splurge from both. He splashes his face and watches the water drip like glue from his chin.

Bat was never a good looking lad, even before Tansey cracked his face in half, he knows that. His features are and always have been round and nubby, irremediably homely, exuding all the definition of a bowl of mashed-up spuds. His eyes, at least, are distinctive, though not necessarily in a good way; they are thick-lashed, purplishly-pupiled and primed glintingly wide. They suggest urgent, unseemly appeal. *You look constantly as if in want*, his old dear chided him all up through childhood. Even now she will occasionally snap at him— *what is it, Eamonn?*—apropos of nothing. Bat merely sitting there, watching TV or tuning his guitar or hand-rolling a ciggie for her.

Nothing, Bat will mutter.

You are a mutterer, Eamonn, the old dear will insist. *You always were*, she'll add, by way of implying she does not ascribe all blame for that to the boot to the face.

The boot to the face. Nubbin Tansey, may he rest in pieces. Munroe's chipper. Years gone now.

Bat jabs his cheek with his finger, pushes in. His jaw still clicks when he opens it wide enough.

Six separate operations, ninety-two percent articulation recovered and the brunt of the visible damage surgically effaced but for a couple of minute white divots in his left cheek, and a crooked droop to the mouth on that side. It's slight but distinct, the droop, a nipped outward twisting of the lip, an unhinging, that makes him look always a little gormless. Damage abides beneath the surface. Bat can feel by their feelinglessness those pockets of frozen muscle and inert tissue where the nerves in his face are blown for good.

Bat had been known as Bat for years, the nickname derived from his surname, Battigan, but after the boot and the droop a few smartarses took to calling him Sly, as in Sly Stallone. Sly didn't take, thank fuck; he was too entrenched in the town consciousness as Bat.

None but the old dear call him Eamonn now.

Bat palms more water onto his face, slaps his cheeks to get the blood shifting. The beers don't help of course, but the fact is the headaches come regardless, leadenly routine now. In addition there are the migraines, mercifully rarer though much more vicious, two-day-long blowouts of agonising snowblindness that at their worst put Bat whimpering and supine on the floor of his bedroom, a pound of wet cloth mashed into his eyesockets to staunch, however negligibly, the pain.

The doctors insist the head troubles have nothing to do with it, but Bat knows they are another bequeathal of the boot to the face.

He leaves the restroom and keys himself through the service door into the staff room. He deposits the bike helmet on the couch, unpeels his leather jacket, registers with a pulse of mortification the spicy whang peeling off his own hide.

On the staff-room counter he spies, amid a row of other items, a stick of women's roll-on; must be Tain's. He picks it up, worms his fist into each sleeve of his Maxol shirt and hastily kneads his pits with the spearminty-smelling stuff. As he places the roll-on back on the counter he notices a curled black hair adhering to the scented ball. He tweezes it off and flicks it to the floor.

Out front Dungan, the store manager, mans the main till.

Dungan is old. Fifties, sixties, whatever. He's the sole adult and authority figure in a work environment otherwise populated by belligerently indolent youngsters.

'Bat,' Dungan says.

'Yeah?'

'Take your particular timepiece. Wind the big hand forward fifteen minutes. Keep it there. You might show up on the dot once in your life.'

Humped above the cash register, Dungan resembles nothing so much as his own freshly revived corpse. His skin is loose and blanched, its pigmentation leached of some vital essence, and what remains of his thin grey hair is drawn in fraily distinct comb lines across his head, mortuary neat. His glasses are tinted, enshading the eyes. But you can tell Dungan is alive because the man is always snufflingly, sputteringly ill, his maladies minor but interminable; head colds, bronchial complaints and dermal eruptions hound him through the seasons' dims and magnifications.

'What needs doing?' Bat sighs.

Dungan looks over the rims of his glasses. The white of one eye is a blood-splatter of detonated capilleries.

'Sleeves. Sleeves, Bat. What did I say about sleeves?' He nods at Bat's arms. 'The tattoos can't be on display, lad. Plain black or white undershirts in future, please.'

'But everyone knows me,' Bat says.

'Professionalism is an end in itself,' Dungan opines. 'Now. There's six pallets of dry stock out back that need shelving and the rotisserie wants a scrub after that. We'll just have to try and keep you out of sight as much as we can.'

First break. Ten minutes. Bat is first out to the lot, peeling chicken-fat slicked marigolds from his hands. The lot is a three-quarters-enclosed concrete space done up to suggest a picnic area, where, the idea is, road-weary motorists can eat or stretch their limbs in what appears to Bat to be a rather bleak simulation of pastoral seclusion. There are rows of wooden tables and benches bolted into the cement (the obscenities carved into their lacquered surfaces only visible close up) and a ring-fenced aluminium wreck of a play area for children. Scruffy clots of weeds have grown up and died in the fistulas along the crumbling perimeter of the lot's paving. A mural painted onto the lot wall depicts a trio of cartoon rabbits in waistcoats and top hats capering against a field of green dotted with splotch-headed blue and red and yellow flowers. The untalented muralist had not been able to set the pupils of the rabbits' eyes into proper alignment, afflicting all three with various severities of cross-eye.

Bat perches atop the fat plastic lid of an empty skip, guzzles a Coke and regards the rabbits. The longer you look the more subtly crazed their expressions appear.

Presently Bat is joined by Tain Moonan and Rob 'Heg' Hegarty.

Tain is fifteen, Hegarty eighteen.

Both are summer recruits, and both will soon be finished up; Hegarty is returning to college in Dublin as a second-year computer science student and Tain will be heading into Junior Cert year in the local convent.

Hegarty ducks out into the morning air whistling a jaunty tune. He flashes a grin at Bat as he approaches, snaps a thin white spindle from his breast-pocket and sketches an elaborate bow as he proffers what turns out to be a perfectly rolled joint.

'Nice,' Bat snorts.

'Let's start the morning and kill the day,' Hegarty says.

Tain rolls her eyes.

'Alright Tain,' Bat says.

Tain only grunts. She studies Hegarty frankly as he crooks the joint between his lips, sparks his lighter and with a forceful, fish-face sucking motion pipettes a trail of purple smoke-wisps into the air.

'Busy out front?' Bat asks. Tain and Heg are on forecourt duty.

'Quiet enough,' Hegarty says, and passes the joint to Bat. Hegarty has a foot in height on Bat, a handsome, olive-oil complexion inherited from his half-Iberian mother, the wingspan and streamlined solidity of an athlete though he takes no interest in sports, and a pretty wad of crinkly black hair, like a black lad's. He's about the most laidback lad Bat has ever encountered; nothing fazes or riles him.

Tain hops onto the skip beside Bat, scoots over until she's right beside him. She picks up one of his unsheathed marigold gloves and tugs it down over her hand. She jabs Bat with her elbow, nods at the joint.

'Pass it on,' she says.

Bat gives her his best look of grown-up disapproval.

'This'll stunt your growth. Missy.'

'Listen to the voice of experience,' Hegardy says.

Tain rolls her eyes, sneers but declines a retort. She pulls her peroxided hair out of her face. The roots are grown out, black as jet. Bat gives her the joint. She takes it with her yellow gloved hand. A brief toke and she is immediately seized by a bout of convulsive coughing. Hegardy's eyes pop in delight and his mouth gapes in a mute O of impending hilarity. He leans in close so Tain can see. She swings a sneaker at his crotch, Hegardy bouncing backwards on his heels to elude the effort.

'Handle your shit, Moonan,' Hegardy barks in an American drill-sergeant voice.

'It's handled, dickhead,' Tain says, holding her throat and working out a few clarifying grunts. Composure restored, she begins to pick absently at the small red nub of a zit on her chin.

Bat looks from Tain to Heg. For the past three months Bat has watched these two smile, joke, snark, preen and goad each other, with escalating intensity, up until three weekends ago, when the tone of their exchanges changed abruptly. For a few days the two were terse, even clumsy in each other's company. Now, while things have relaxed into their original rhythm somewhat, their inter-actions possess an edge, a spikiness, that was previously absent. This worries Bat. Though Bat likes Hegardy, he is pretty sure the lad did something—and may perhaps still be doing something—with the schoolgirl. Because he likes Hegardy, Bat has shied from pressing the lad upon the matter, lest Hegardy admit he has in fact committed something perilously close to, if not in fact, full statutory rape. (Which is what it would be. Bat looked it up. With no little trepidation he ventured to the town library and at one of the terminal computers, hunched forward and glancing compulsively over his shoulder, googled what he considered the pertinent terms.)

'When's your last day?' Bat asks.

'Not till Sunday next,' Hegardy says, 'but college starts pretty much straight the week after. So I'm going to have a couple of going-away pints in The Yellow Belly this Friday. Don't say you won't be there. Bat.'

'This Friday?' Bat says.

'This Friday.'

Caught off guard. Bat is too brain dead to temporise; no excuse presents itself through the double-daze of residual hangover and incipient dope high. Bat no longer socialises in town; no longer socialises full stop. He does not want to tell Hegardy this, though doubtless Hegardy has an inkling.

'We'll see,' Bat says.

Tain is inspecting Bat's arm on her side.

'This one's boss,' she says, dabbing a yellow finger upon Bat's kraken tattoo, etched in the hollow of his forearm. It depicts a green squid-like monstrosity emerging from a bowl of blue water circumscribed by a fringe of froth, an oldtime ship with masts and sails encoiled within the creature's tentacles, about to be torn apart.

'Boss,' Bat says.

'Yeah,' Tain says. She traces a circle in the crook of his arm, and Bat feels a pinch as she nips with her fingers at his flesh.

'Ow.'

'You got good veins, Bat,' she says, then holds out her own arms for display. 'Big hardy cables of motherfuckers. You can't barely even see mine.'

Bat hesitates, leans in for a look. The down on Tain's arms glints in the morning light. Her skin is smooth and pale. Tain's right—her veins are barely there, detectable only as buried, granular traces of blue in the solid white of her flesh. There's a whiff of spearmint coming up out of her sleeve. Bat tries to ignore it.

'Why's that?' Bat says.

'Tain must have a condition,' Heg caws.

Tain ignores the sally.

'Look. Your veins are blue or green, whatever. But why's that, when your blood is red?' she says.

Bat thinks about this. 'That must be because of the lining or something. The veins' linings are blue and the blood runs red inside.'

'Blood ain't red,' Tain says. 'It turns red when it hits air, oxygenates. You know what colour it actually is?'

Bat shrugs. 'I'd be guessing, Tain,' he says.

'Bat's blood runs one shade,' Heg intones in a gravelly, film-trailer voice.

Bat looks from Tain to Heg and back.

'Black as night,' Tain growls in her version of the film-trailer voice.

Heg takes a final drag of the joint, drops it and sweeps it with his foot into a sewer grille, eliminating whatever tiny chance there might have been that Dungan would happen upon the incriminating butt and work out what it is they get up to out here—though that haggard bitch, as Tain refers to him, is nobody's idea of a deductive savant. Bat nods appreciatively. Heg is a thorough lad, cautious. Maybe he is not up to anything with Tain.

'Let's get back,' Heg says to Tain.

'Fucksake,' she mutters and pops herself off the skip. She heads in and Heg follows, turning at the last to catch Bat's eye.

'No, but come. It won't be the same otherwise.'

Dinner is boiled spuds, beans and frozen fish. Bat bolts his supper from a sideboard in the kitchen under the solemn surveillance of two bullet-headed eight-year-old boys. The boys are seated side by side by the opened back door, the old dear looming above them, wielding an electric razor and comb; the old dear cuts hair on the side, a home operation job, her clientele comprised mainly of the youngest offspring of her extended family.

Tonight's customers have the wide-spaced eyes and aggrieved, jutting mouths hereditary to the Minions. The Minions are cousins from the passed father's side, a clan notorious locally for its compulsive run-ins with the law and general ingenuity for petty civil dissension. Bad seeds, though Bat suspects the old dear is perversely proud of the association.

The old dear is shearing the boys simultaneously, in stages, not one after the other; she does the left side of one lad's head, then the other lad's left, then right/right, top/top and finally back/back. Kitchen towels are draped across the boys' shoulders and a tawny moat of chopped hair encircles their chairlegs. The back door is open so the old dear can smoke as she works, the draught escorting the smoke of her rollie out into the evening, away from the boys' lungs.

Above Bat's head a wall-mounted TV plays the Aussie soap *Home and Away*, but the boys' eyes do not leave Bat as he works at his dinner. The mane confuses little kids, who assume only women have long hair (and there's no woman in town with hair as long as Bat's). He's conscious also they may be eyeing the balky hydraulics of his jaw as he chews.

One of the boys slowly raises a hand, extends his forefinger and begins boring at a nostril, a movement that necessitates a slight shift in his posture.

'Don't be moving,' Bat says, 'or she'll have your lug off,' wrenching on one of his own earlobes for effect. 'She has a necklace of severed ears upstairs, made out of the lugs of little boys who wouldn't stay still.'

The lad stops boring but keeps his finger socketed in his nose. His eyes widen.

'That's not true,' the other lad puffs indignantly.

'Shut up the lot of you,' the old dear says, though of course she doesn't refute Bat's claim.

'What's your name?' Bat says to the lad who spoke.

'Trevor.'

A dim memory of a double christening, moons back, that Bat didn't go to. 'And that lad excavating his face beside you is JoJo, so.'

'Yeah,' Trevor says.

'And where's your mammy gone, Trevor?' Bat asks.

'The pub,' JoJo says.

'Is she out looking for a brother or sister for youse?' Bat says, grinning at the old dear as the boys look on, puzzled.

'Dearbhla,' the old dear sighs. 'Lord bless us and save us but you may not be yards off the mark there, Eamonn. HEADS DOWN,' she barks, and the Minion boys, perfectly in sync, fire their chins into their chests.

Bat smiles. They can be tough and they can be rough, but there's not a delinquent alive, budding or fully formed, the old dear can't crone into submission.

Before the roof and beers and bed, Bat hits the road. A night spin, deep into the countryside's emptinesses. The Honda is no power racer, but watching the dimpled macadam hurtle away beneath the monocular glare of his headlight, Bat feels he is moving too fast to exist; as he dips into and leans out of the crooks and curves of the road, he becomes the crooks and curves. A bristling silence hangs over the deep adjacent acres—the pastures, woodlands and hills sprawled out all around him. It goes up and up and up, the silence, and Bat can hear it, above even the hot scream of the engine.

His nerves are gently sparking by the time he lopes across the mossed asphalt shingles of the roof, cradling a sixpack. Bat plants his back against the chimney and drinks and drinks and waits for the moment the night becomes too cold, the air like a razor working itself to acuity against the strop of his arms; only then will he descend through the black square of his bedroom window.

The week rolls on. Friday night, the town centre. Bat in leathers, a pair of preliminary beers washed down to fortify the nerves. It's been a while. He parks the Honda in an alley by the AIB branch. Shadowed figures linger outside The Yellow Belly's entrance. Smokers. Bat approaches with his head lowered.

'Fuckin' Battigan. Bat,' a voice says, surprised.

'Man, Bat,' the other says.

'Lads,' Bat says. The lads are a bit younger than Bat; little brothers to those who would have been Bat's peers. One's a Connolly, spotty face like a dropped bolognese, the other's a barrelbodied, redheaded Duffy.

'Which Duffy are you?' Bat asks.

'Jamie,' the lad replies.

'Michael was in my class,' Bat says. 'We called him Scaldyballs.'

Connolly's face erupts in laughter. 'We call this cunt the same.'

'The ginger gene is dying out, so they say,' Bat informs Duffy, darkly.

Duffy braces his shoulders, looks at Connolly, who communicates something back with his eyes.

'What has you out anyway, Bat?' Connolly asks.

'Rob Hegarty's fucking-off-back-to-college do.'

'The brainboxes are off to brainbox land,' Connolly sighs, 'that time of year, I suppose.'

'Leaving us thick fucks to this dump,' Duffy scowls.

'Alright,' Bat says, stoppering the conversation. Inside he takes the couple of short steps up into the warm red heart of the bar. The main room is a long rectangle, half familiar faces eddying in its telescoped space. Some faces watch him; some don't.

Bat thinks: *I am here for Heg's fucking thing, so I'll go find Heg.*

Heg is at the farthest point at the rear of the bar. He is surrounded.

'Bat! Christ, good man!' Heg roars, and his companions' faces turn to take in Bat. Half a dozen lads Heg's age, and the same number in girls again. The girls; a dark-haired one stands by Heg. Cheekboned and smokily glowering, from her emanates a demeanour of regal peevishness, nose pinned up in the air. There is the briefest shift of light in her irises; she fixes Bat with the penetrating impersonality of a security camera. Bat drops his eyeline to the floor. He wants to hurl his body at her feet, repent his hideous pelt.

'Drink?' Bat squeaks, hoping Heg hears.

'C'mere... lads, you know this fuckin legend of a man,' Heg loafs an arm across Bat's shoulders. He's had a few, Heg, his gaze lolling and sliding like syrup as he tries to fix upon Bat.

'Na na na na na na na na, BAT MAN!!!' Heg roars. Bat winces, shucks off the dead weight of Heg's arm.

'Pint, Heg?' he says.

Bat cuts a paddling diagonal through the crowd, riding up along the polished grain of the counter like a drowning man gaining the shore. He actually grips the counter. He orders two pints—one for himself, one for Heg—and downs the first in a single ferocious engorgement. He slams the empty onto the counter as a head rush ignites behind his eyes; he sees sparks and a wavelet of nausea migrates from the middle of his face into the pit of his stomach. Bat orders another pint.

When he turns, a girl who looks like Tain is facing him.

It is Tain, in make-up, in a dress. Bat's eyes drop, in a skimming horizontal, compiling fugitive impressions before he can restrain himself. The dress is a shiny kind of silvery red thing, a square of absent material exposing a section of Tain's chest. The dress's hem ends midway down her thighs. Tain's legs are bare. Bat has never seen Tain's legs before. Her knees are miraculously, mundanely kneelike—blunt, knobby and flushed scaldingly red, as if in embarrassment at so public an exposure.

Bat gets a grip, forces eye contact with the girl.

'I know, I know,' Tain says mournfully. She's blushing.

She has a parcel wrapped in silver paper under her arm.

'Present for himself?' Bat says.

Tain holds it out and rotates it assessingly in her grip.

'Pretty gay of me, I think.'

'Why would it be gay?'

'It's...' She glances across at the crowd surrounding Heg. 'Who's that one with him?'

'Don't know,' Bat says. 'His sister, maybe?'

'Fuck, no, that's not his sister. Are you being funny? I've seen his sister, she's a trainee vet in London. That's not his sister.'

The dimensions of the parcel and the way it bends in a U shape as Tain tortures it in her grip—Bat guesses it's a book. Bat is no reader. His eyesight has always been poor; the other derivation of his nickname. He wears contacts now but as a kid he suffered for years, believing the scumbled, dripping appearance of text on a page was simply how words appeared to everyone. It seemed perfectly in keeping with the variform sadism of classwork that you had to try and prise sense from the unintelligible fuzz of type on a page. The teachers thought him thick—and Bat was thick—but it was only when some of the other kids dubbed him booksniffer on account of how close he put his face to the page that he realised something was up.

'What you get him?' Bat means the book.

'Has anyone else got him anything?' she says, still craning towards the group.

'I got him nothing other than this pint,' Bat says. 'And I'd offer you one but you're too young.'

Tain swivels, with slow decisiveness, back to Bat. She makes a fist and wedges it against her hip. 'Christ sakes just get me a vodka and lime, Bat.'

'In a tick,' he murmurs, lowering his head and shouldering back into the crowd, brimming pint in either paw.

Forty minutes later and Bat has put away three drinks to the group's single round. Tain is several bodies beyond his left elbow, stuck making small talk to a plump boy in black. The lad keeps placing and replacing on his ear the wire frame of his glasses. Most of the crowd are from out of town; Heg's college mates, dropped down for the weekend. The dark beauty, as still and mute as a hologram, must be one of them too, though the rest of the party ignores her as she ignores them, even Heg; that she has deigned to stand in his proximity is the only suggestion of any association between them. But then, Bat, too, has largely kept his trap shut, his conversational contributions amounting to timed groans and dry whistles as one or another anecdote winds to its climax. They are all talking about and around college, the communal life they share there; the talk is an involved braid of in-jokes and contextual nuggets and back references. Bat feels doltish—too big, too bluntly dimensioned, a thickset golem hewn from the scrabbled, sodden dirt of Connaught. His jaw throbs—the teeth set into his jaw throb.

Heg is drunk, his expression adrift in some boggy territory between gloating and concussed. Abruptly the hologram substantiates itself—the tall beauty leans in and begins kissing Heg most vociferously on the mouth. He kind of writhes around in her grip. A girl with an overbite breaks into a braying laugh. Bat gently shoulders his way out of the group and wheels off towards the jacks. His nape bristles; he feels the drag, like a faint current, of someone's attention and turns. Tain scowling, in hot pursuit.

She still has the present, jammed down into her handbag.

'I feel like a wanker,' she says.

'*Don't*,' Bat says. 'Heg has us all just standing around like gobshites.'

A hand on Bat's shoulder. He flinches.

'Fuck me, man, how's it going?'

Bat's grip tenses around a phantom pint. He gulps. But it's only Luke Minion. As it goes Luke is one of the more congenial strands of that brood of cousins. Luke has always had time for Bat; was witness to the boot to the face.

'Well, Luke.'

'It's been an age, lad.'

'Yeah.'

'Who's this?' Minion asks of Tain, an amused curl to the lip.

'I work with her. Tain. This is Luke.'

'You're still out with the Maxol crowd.'

'It's a living,' Bat says.

'It is,' Minion says through his teeth. He runs a hand through his crow-coloured cowlick of a widow's peak. Most of the Minions are stocky and solidly hipped. Luke is rangy, with clear grey eyes. Last Bat heard the man was running up mountains; there was talk of a sponsored tackle of Kilimanjaro. It never happened. Before that Luke had been living in a mobile home on the furthest acre of his family's farmplot. He'd had a Czechoslovakian girl and a baba stowed away there for a while, but one day the pair woke up and the baba was dead.

'What you at these days?'

Minion's eyebrows rise, 'Bits and pieces.'

'In the Minion fashion,' Bat says, hearing the old dear in his tone.

'This guy,' Luke says to Tain. 'You ever hear tell of how he wound up with that face?'

Tain looks to Bat.

Bat wonders if she can read the total misery in his visage.

'No,' she says brightly, looking more like a child, in her densely daubed mask of make-up, than ever before.

'Yeah,' Luke says, 'sure you're only a young one.'

'Hitting the jacks,' Bat says, his throat going tight, like he's just swallowed a plum gourd.

The nausea has resurfaced in the other direction, a roiling ball of unpleasantness bubbling out of his gut. His mouth waters, and he tastes a flash of blood. He wipes his mouth with his sleeve. His head is sore; his head is always sore. The headaches tune down to a vestige, but they never truly go.

The drinking doesn't help, Bat thinks, *but it does help.*

As he slams open a cubicle door the possibility of throwing up seems fragilely close. He gropes the door shut behind him. A pitifully loud retch doubles him over; nothing follows but a gutty hock, a hot trickle of bile. Bat retches until it plops from his lips into the jacks' waiting mouth.

There in the cubicle, unbidden, floats up the remnant of a dream; a recurring dream. Bat knows intuitively, though this is the first time he has consciously recalled recalling it. The dream remnant is merely this, like a random, unfinished scene from a film: Bat is Bat, but in a different body. A Dungan-like body, wasted and bowlegged, older perhaps, though perhaps not. Certainly frailer, flimsier, and he, dream-Bat, is walking around what must be this town. It's just a street, an undistinguished strip of concrete paving flanked by generic buildings—and he's wearing a mustard-seed suit. That's what his mother—in the dream—calls the suit. The suit does not fit. It's several sizes too large and the superfluous material billows and flumps comically around his limbs. And in the dream all Bat is doing is walking around and around and crying and crying and somewhere to the back of him—he can't precisely tell—his old dear's voice pursues him like a vindictive raincloud, saying *change the medication, change the medication.*

How long has he been having this fucking dream, he wonders?

And then his thoughts turn to the boot to the face; the last thing Bat himself recalls of that night was staggering through the door of Munroe's takeaway with a hunger in his belly, his head down and headphones in, music blaring and scrolling through his playlist to see what song was cued up next. He woke up in hospital. The culprit was a five-foot-two sparkplug went by Nubbin Tansey, and Luke Minion was there, saw it all unfold.

And now Tain is outside. Tain is on a stool by the bar, waiting for Bat to return. Bat squinches closed his eyes.

How long have I been having this fucking dream?

*

Tain is on a stool and Minion, expert bar-grift, has inveigled her into buying him a drink—the first she's ever ordered in a bar. The barlad didn't look at her twice as she put in the round. It makes Tain feel pathetically proud of herself. She's on her fourth vodka and lime and has no more money. The odour of limes—spiked and soured by the gelid see-through spirit—is all she can smell. She's watching Minion—the lad finicks with his stool, skims his palm round the lip of the seat like he's searching for the sweet spot. Finally he hoists himself into position. He looks at her and launches in.

'It must've been up on the heels of four on a Saturday morning, Munroe's being one of the few eateries still open at that hour so it was fairly packed. I was queuing at the counter, hangover already coming on, waiting on a kebab and batter burger. Nubbin Tansey was up on one of the table tops, making a holy fucking show of himself. Now Tansey was a shortarse but he was built through; physique of a jockey on steroids. He was well oiled, as we all were, looking wild and dishevelled, his shirt hanging off him, buttons all burst off. Doc Martens scuffing the Formica as he whelped out a furious jig. His boys were crowing him on—there were five or six of them, big rowdy units—and the Turkish lads behind the counter weren't going to risk stepping in, though good old Saleem, the manager, was threatening to call the pigs if Tansey didn't get the fuck down fairly lively. Tansey, bald since seventeen to go with the height deficiency, was amped up, face gone red and every veineen in his skull popping, a solid wall of perspiration coming right off him and fizzing in the fluorescence as he jigged and jigged. Nervous little cheers coming up from all corners of the takeaway, hoping he'd stop. Then Tansey started out with these karate moves, firing the legs out and chop sockying the air, which brought up further cheers. He was moving fair graceful for a man as scuttered as he was. And then he stops, a tacky sling of spit flapping from his chin. He wipes the spit and says to the boys, 'I'm taking the head, THE HEAD, off the next cunt comes through that door,' and points at the entrance, a good six feet away from the edge of the table-top he's prancing on. Another cheer at Tansey's declaration, though this time only from his boys. And for a while that was that, there was this little spell, thirty seconds, where everything got quiet, even Tansey seemed to be winding down. He'd gone into a squat and was sharing a private chuckle with one of his boys when the doorbell jingles, the jingle letting everyone know there's a body coming through, and I saw the shock of jet hair, the leather jacket and Bat's battered runners. Not a chance to say nothing. Not that I believed, I suppose, that Tansey was actually going to follow through on his boast; shite talk and no follow through, I had it diagnosed. But the bell jingles, and in steps Bat, oblivious that he was the next cunt, elected by fate, and without a hesitation, without even stopping to see who he was going for, Tansey up and leapt. It was some fuck of a leap, credit to the lad, his leg straight as a rod leading his body, clearing that six feet and stoving slap bang into the side of Bat's head. Cleanest connect of a jaw you'll ever see. Bat sent flying like a rag doll. Spun and flung. He smacked the wall and bounced back up off the floor and then down again in a buckled heap. And Tansey—Tansey landed perfectly on his feet. Some young wan had let out a scream but now there was no noise except for Tansey's breathing. His eyes were lit, in a marvel at what he'd done. No noise but the air heaving in and out of him, and Bat facedown in a sprawl of hair and blood. Every last cunt there must've thought he was dead. I did.'

'Nubbin Tansey,' Tain says. 'I don't know him.'

'You wouldn't,' Minion says. He was actually inspecting his nails now. 'He's dead. Been dead three years.'

'How'd he die?'

'Rigged a rope round the crossbeam in his folks shed and—' Minion takes his feet up off the floor. He hitches each shoe into the bottom rung of his stool and leans forward until the stool tips over. He fires out the feet to land standing, twists and catches the stool before it clatters to the ground.

'Jeez,' Tain said. She has placed the silver parcel flat on the counter and is now steadily picking away at a bit of sellotape on the wrapping.

'No, no,' Minion insists. 'None of that. Tansey—he was one of those ones with nothing good in him. He was a fucking headcase. Paranoid, devious, a temper he couldn't turn down. Would kick the shit out of you at the drop of a hat—and I mean *you*. The mother of his kid wouldn't let him see the baby—he beat her to a pulp, cracked a bottle over her skull. He was one of them couldn't stand being in his own skin, and couldn't stand the rest of us neither.'

Tain takes a sip of her vodka and lime.

'Saddening?' Luke Minion says.

Tain bunches her lips together, shakes her head.

'Did Bat not get the guards on him?'

'The mother wanted to, and half the Minion clan wanted to kill the lad, they were just waiting on Bat's say so. But Bat never said nothing, didn't even press charges. Tansey was one of them ones in and out of the county court every other day anyway—another stint wouldn't have bothered him. There was a manner of settlement—the Tanseys footed the bill for the surgery Bat had to have after. But that was it, as far as retribution went, on Bat's side. You're his friend, aren't you?'

'Yes,' Tain says.

'You know him, then. I used to pick on him a lot when we were kids.

We all did. And if I wanted an excuse I could say he was the type that asked for it, or didn't know how not to ask for it. Slap him in the face nine times and he'd come right back for number ten.'

There's a silence. Luke turns out from the bar, angles a sidling look at Tain.

'What age are you?' Luke says.

'Eighteen.'

'You with Bat?' he says, and flicks a brutal gesture with one hand.

Tain colours. 'It's… it's nothing like that.'

'Well,' Luke drawls, 'we could go somewhere and have you just sit on my face for an hour?'

'What the fuck,' Tain blurts, then bursts out laughing.

Minion cackles.

'Just a suggestion,' he says and offers a trivially unfussed shrug of the shoulder.

Tain looks towards Heg's party. The dark beauty has collapsed in a despicably graceful heap on Rob, who can't help but look like the smuggest prick in the world.

'That fella then, is it?' Minion said.

'Huh,' Tain says.

'That curly-headed faggot with the ride welded to him. He's what has you doleful. I can see.'

He has his hand now on her thigh, up under the hem and on the bare flesh.

'If it helps, this'll be nothing other than meaningless,' he says.

So when Bat emerges from the jacks he stomps back towards Tain and this is what he sees; Minion, wrapped round her, mouth on hers. She's rolling her shoulders in tandem to Minion's impassioned flinchings, though there's something mechanistic and barely controlled in her reciprocation. It looks coercive, Bat thinks sadly, but with a kind of concluding satisfaction. Tonight was a mistake, emphatically so, and this display of frankly felonious lechery is a fitting cap. Bat waggles the big stupid shovels of his hands.

Last words present themselves.

He could say: *Bye Heg, thanks for nothing, hope you and your fucking college buddies got a good laugh out of tonight.*

He could say: *Why Tain, why be that fucking pathetic, you're cleverer than that, and you're cleverer than Heg too.*

But he'll say nothing, of course. His jaw throbs. It throbs with nothing. All he wants is a drink, but he can get that at home.

Bat puts the head down, hair enfolding him like a screen, and leaves the humans to the humans.

*

In the lane where his bike is parked Bat runs a hand round the inside of the helmet to make sure no kids have pissed in it or stuck it with chewing gum. The helmet's grotty foam lining slips tight as a callipers round his head. Ignition and Bat takes a moment to listen: the engine's rumble, overlapping with its own echo, crashes like surf back off the lane's narrow walls.

On the way home he zips by the Maxol station and for the fuck of it he does a lap of the premises. He slows to a stop out back. In the scanty, grained moonlight and with his iffy sight he can still just about decipher the trio of painted rabbits on the wall. He thinks of the stoic mania of their botched gazes and it is unnerving, now, to consider them presiding over the bleak emptiness of the lot, night after night after night.

Bat realises he is silently mouthing Tain's name over and over.

At home the old dear is in the dark, in the sitting room, TV light the only illumination. In repose, half asleep, her face looks embalmed. It is not a restful expression. She has a wool blanket clutched up to her throat.

'I can smell you from the hallway,' she says.

'Thanks, Ma,' Bat says. In the kitchen he pulls a sixpack from the fridge.

He cracks one open, wolfs it down. Around him Bat can hear the incessant creaking of the house fixtures, like a field of ice coming apart in increments. A draught runs from several accesses and converges in the kitchen, frigidly whistling by Bat's ear. He hears the fretful scrawlings of rats behind the walls, under the pipes....

'How was the town?' the old dear asks.

'Fine,' Bat groans.

'I bet it was.'

'Who'd you see?'

'Luke Minion. Couple of work folk. Hegarty, the Moonan girl. Saw Peter Donnelly's youngest, Danny Duffy.'

'Sounds like they were all out, so.'

When Bat does not answer she says, 'Was it alright?'

'I survived,' Bat says.

The *pksssh* of a can's tab getting popped. The old dear shifts in her seat. She listens to her son's effortful ascent, the lumbering clop of each step up the squeaking stairs and then the succession of fainter percussive pulses travelling the sitting-room ceiling as he moves from the landing into, and then across, his bedroom. She's sure she can hear the shunt of the window and then he is out and up onto the roof; though she must make this assumption on faith.

She has dreams of him falling, of Eamonn letting himself fall. She has dreams of his bike leaving the road, his body a red rent along the macadam of some bleak country lane and the massive, settling silence afterwards. This is what a mother must do: preemptively conjure the worst-case scenarios in order to avert them. She never considered or foresaw that little shit Nubbin Tansey and his boot, and *he* happened. She cannot make that mistake again.

There is a part of her that hates her son, the enormous, fatiguing fragility of him.

She watches the TV and listens, without intentionally listening, for the creak and thud of his return through the window. On the TV her favourite host and his guests. Entire passages of conversation slip by. She falls asleep and jolts abruptly to, not knowing she's been asleep.

The TV screen is extinguished, a minute blue dot levitating in its dark centre. The draught whistles, far above her, through the black; there is no noise and it is dark everywhere. For a long moment she does not know who she is, or where she is. When it comes back to her, she calls out for her son.

MEN ARE NEVER GOD'S CREATURES

Margaret Barrington

Margaret Barrington (1896–1982) was born in Malin, Donegal, and was a writer and journalist who contributed to *The Bell* and various newspapers. Her short story 'Village Without Men' appeared in her story collection *David's Daughter, Tamar* which was published posthumously in 1982. It also features in *The Glass Shore: Short Stories by Women from the North of Ireland*.

You could watch him with delight as he walked up the hill to the paddock beyond the village where he kept his horses. For he had the beautiful artless walk of a man whose whole body acted in concert, whose muscles lay easily on his bones; the quick, light step; the long, slenderly boned legs; the narrow waist and hips; the flat, wide-shouldered back; the arms overlong. As you watched him, you would think that Almighty God had, for once, created the perfect man.

Yet when Jerry MacAvoy turned round and you saw the faint melancholy of his light blue eyes, you could not help but laugh. With that sardonic humour of which He alone is capable, the Creator had clapped on him the face of the clown; that face with the large gashed mouth, the small, separated teeth, the widely spaced round eyes, the bulbous nose and harsh colour which from the earliest ages has moved men to irrepressible mirth. Its bare melancholy creates no answering melancholy. Its tragedy must be borne alone.

Perhaps in compensation, as is so often the case, his nature bore out the semi-divine mask. Of an evening, in Delahunty's bar, he was the best possible company. The men who gathered there listened with shining eyes to his shrewd wit, his ready answers and laughed with loosened girth. They savoured their drink the better for his company, their blood flowed more easily, the lurking, dark shadows of their minds dissolved. They carried home to their gloomy houses, to their too familiar beds, something of the poetry of his humour.

He was lucky, too, in his wife, Anna, a lighthearted girl who could forget the comedy of his face in the delight of his body, and knew that no other woman ever would. With happiness in her heart she left him free and attended to the humdrum business of the butcher's shop. He liked his glass, he liked to dance, he liked a pretty girl as well as another, but her only rival was the mare, Janetta.

It was his custom when he attended the markets to buy cattle, to keep his eyes open for some likely young horse to break and train and then sell to some English visitor over for the hunting. In this way he found Janetta. She was younger than he would have liked. She had not yet lost the furry tail nor the coltish movements of extreme youth. But something in the way she nuzzled up to him, nipped his sleeve and then started away, attracted him. Indeed she never quite lost this coltishness, even when she put on strength and beauty.

When he went to the paddock and called her, she would come running, only to stop dead just beyond the reach of his outstretched hand. Then, skittishly, she would toss her mane, flatten her ears in pretended anger, sidestep and circle around him while he coaxed, wheedled and called her endearing names. 'Hey, Janetta! Come here, ye beauty, ye darlin', ye lovely whoore!'

It was no use. She never answered his pleading. Only when he turned his back on her and walked towards the gate, she followed, her soft nose nibbling his coat, her hot breath on his neck.

But when he threw his leg across her back, he was her master: when his long thighs clipped her sides, she was docile and quiet. Her body answered every movement of his, was of one rhythm with his. No other horse had given him such pleasure; no other horse ever made him feel so much a man.

Then he would slap her with the flat of his hand and shout to her and though the words he spoke were the same, they were no longer pleading, no longer coaxing, but strong, triumphant: 'Yup, Janetta! Up, girleen! Up, my lovely whoore!'

She had one bad fault. It arose indeed from her very strength, her lightness, her skittishness. She flew her banks. And this in the Irish countryside, with its sunk ditches and uneven levels, is not only a bad fault, but a dangerous one. It took Jerry a long time to cure her. He raised the bank in the paddock until he forced her to alight and change her feet. He drove her close into ditches before he let her rise. At last it seemed that she was cured.

A new curate came to the village. He arrived in a fine new motor-car, a present from an adoring mother, a well-to-do widow who owned a grocery store and public house in the next county. The women liked young Father Tracy, for his youth, for his holy air which was nothing more than a fixed stare, and for the wild sermons he preached condemning sin. Father Mooney, the parish priest, now falling into years, had almost ceased to worry about sin, taken up as he was with his ageing digestion. Hardly a Sunday passed now without Father Tracy showing them, in all its allure, the rosy path to Hell. Dances without proper supervision of the clergy, drink, cards, horse-racing, women's clothes and illicit love-making, all came under the scourge of his tongue. They trembled while they listened. So near they were to losing their immortal souls.

The men said nothing one way or another until Father Tracy asked for 'oat-money'. The parish was a large one. It straggled up the glen and over the mountainside. The former curate had gone around it on an old nag. Once a year he had asked for contributions of oats or money to feed the horse. Those who had oats sent a bag and those who had none gave a little money, according to their means. Willingly given since the priest was poor. And now here was Father Tracy asking for 'oat-money' to buy petrol for his car.

The men discussed the matter in Delahunty's bar. The general opinion was that it was nothing more than a piece of impertinence to ask for 'oat-money' for a car.

'Ah, he's greedy,' said Jerry. 'And greed in man or beast is deplorable. It makes for a big belly and no staying power.'

'He's young and strong, let him walk,' shouted the Growler, a large, ferocious man who prided himself on his scholarship. 'Let him practise Christian humility and walk.'

'God save ye!' said Jerry. 'How could the likes of him walk? Barrin' the disgrace of puttin' one foot in front of the other in the sight of his parishioners, the man's bad on his feet. He'd likely fall down and break his knees.'

'Ye take it too lightly, Jerry,' shouted the Growler again. 'Far in a way too lightly. Here he comes to this place and from the talk he lets out of him, ye'd think he'd landed in Sodom and Gomorrah. Ye'd think we did nothin' the livelong day and all the dark hours of the night but dance and drink, put money on horses and ruin women. Do we never do a stroke of work? Is this the one plague-spot in Holy Ireland?'

'Ah, God help him!' said Jerry with a sad shake of his head. 'If the poor divil only knew. All the trouble in this parish happens on the road home from evenin' devotions.'

And Jerry looked so serious and so comical that the men all laughed until the drink sang in their heads.

Dan Byrne clapped Jerry on the back and asked when he had last been to evening devotions.

'I am in everything the Church's man,' Jerry answered and lifted his pint in salutation.

'You don't mean to tell me, Jerry,' said the Growler, 'that ye're goin' to give in? The Church in this country is getting altogether too graspin'. If we don't resist, they'll be takin' the shirts off our backs next.'

'Growler,' said Jerry. 'Have a care. Think of yer immortal soul, hoverin' on the brink of destruction. What the hell does yer shirt matter? That car is goin' to get its oats.'

Two days later Father Tracy tried in vain to start his car. He took out the plugs and cleaned them, tickled the carburettor, poured kettles of hot water into the radiator. Not a stir. The engine was as dead as mutton. When he had exhausted his small store of mechanical knowledge and his temper, he sent for a mechanic. Someone had poured about a stone of oats into the petrol tank.

There wasn't any doubt, the men agreed, but that Jerry MacAvoy was a great card.

From that day Father Tracy's car seemed to suffer from the world's spite. Not a week passed but something went wrong. Father Tracy learned with fury and amazement all the misfortunes that could happen to a car. Then for a whole week he was kept at home by the disappearance of the battery.

No one knows, even now, after four years, who was the first to lay hands on that battery. Only one fact has emerged and that is that everyone in the village had it at one time or another, in his possession. It had apparently moved from one house to another without human agency and was finally discovered, completely exhausted, by Father Tracy himself, on the steps of the church.

This time Father Tracy acted. The head of each household was summoned to appear at the District Court to answer the charge of purloining Father Tracy's battery. And since Father Tracy was a fanatical Gaelic enthusiast, the summonses were served in both English and Gaelic.

'The English,' said Jerry that night in Delahunty's bar, 'is to show us what we're in for in this world and the Irish is to strike terror into our immortal souls.'

The Growler looked up. He was sitting at the back of the bar, poring over the summons with the help of O'Growney's grammar and Father Dineen's dictionary.

'There are three mistakes in the Irish,' he said triumphantly. 'Three mistakes. What do ye think of that? What are we payin' for?'

'Make a careful note of them, Growler,' said Jerry. 'Be ye sure to point them out to Saint Peter. For very shame, then, he'll maybe let us pass.'

'And but this is no joke,' said Dan Byrne, the shoemaker. 'Here we are, one and all, summonsed. We've got to do somethin'.'

What I want to know,' said Jim Doyle, 'is how in the Holy Name he got to know the whereabouts of the battery?'

'Abuse of the confessional,' said the Growler. 'The women runnin' to dear Father Tracy wit' their little sins. God forgive them! It's time their wings was clipped.'

'Don't be talkin', Growler,' said Jerry, with some impatience. Who in hell would be bothered to confess a battery? Sure it wouldn't be hard to find out all about it seein' it was sittin' open to the public view, in every house in the place.'

'Still and all,' said the Growler, nodding his head, 'This is tyranny and no mistake.'

'Well the way I look at it,' said Delahunty from the other side of the bar, 'it would be a shockin' scandal if it came to court. Bad for all of us.'

Delahunty was a silent man who rarely mixed in disputes of any kind. Also he was the only one not involved in this affair.

'Bad for all of us, for the village, for business. Best thing to do is to settle the matter right now.'

'We can't stop it,' said the Growler. 'Even so be that we're willing, we still couldn't. Only Father Tracy can do that.'

'Ye never know,' said Delahunty, 'where these things will stop once they begin.'

Jerry MacAvoy put down his glass on the counter.

'Ye're right,' he said. 'I tell ye what. I'll go along to Father Mooney and get him to talk sense into his curate.'

Jerry found the old priest, wrapped up in a blanket and bending miserably over the fire. He was suffering from one of his 'attacks'. On the table beside him sat a tall glass of brandy and water which he sipped almost continuously. From time to time he would place his hand on his stomach and look around in agony. The brandy and nature struggled within him and then up would come the wind in an explosive, resounding belch.

'I'm sorry to see ye like this, Father Mooney,' said Jerry.

The words sounded unpleasantly in Father Mooney's ear. He looked sharply at Jerry. Was the man laughing at him, insinuating maybe that he'd been drinking? It was not a favourable beginning.

'It's onions,' said the parish priest savagely. 'That one puts onions into everything she cooks, knowin' full well they bring on heartburn.'

'Do they now?' said Jerry. 'That's bad.' His mind searched for comfort. 'But they do say that a raw potato'll put things right in next to no time.'

The priest looked wildly at Jerry. His eyes went red with rage. Jerry's face, with its look of comic innocence, infuriated him. The man was sitting there and deliberately making a mock of him, the parish priest, to his face, in his own house.

'Do—you—want—to—kill—me,' he gasped. Again the sudden eruption which stopped further speech.

'Oh, well I suppose it's only talk,' said Jerry. 'Never havin' been taken that way myself, I don't rightly know.'

Now if Jerry had only been able to produce some harrowing disorder from which he suffered from time to time, all might have been saved. But to come here, and boast of rude health, and laugh at a suffering man, was more than flesh and blood could endure.

'I suppose,' Father Mooney snapped, 'ye're here on some errand or other. Har'ly to enquire about my health.'

'That's so, Father. It's about this affair of Father Tracy's battery. Ye see how it is. We don't want the matter to come up in court. 'Twould look bad for everybody concerned and nothin' gained either way. Father Tracy's young and hot-headed and we thought you, havin' the interest of the village at heart, could maybe head him off.'

Father Mooney glared at Jerry.

'I'll have ye remember, first of all, that it's har'ly your place to criticize a priest. It's the great vice of this age, irreverence, lack of proper respect for those set in authority. Then let me say that Father Tracy has my full approval— mark ye—full approval. It's time and so it is that this place learned proper humility and decency. Ye think ye can make a mock of yer clergy—but mark my words—' Here Father Mooney was obliged to seize the glass of brandy and water. He swallowed at least half the contents at a gulp and again looked around in puzzled anguish.

'Ah but, Father, can't ye see. 'Twas one of the young chizzlers that done it. You know, one of the young lads, not knowin' any better.'

'And don't ye see, Jerry MacAvoy, it's your place to chastise your children; to teach them while they're young proper respect for authority. Else they'll grow up no better than their fathers. For thirty years I've wrestled with this parish, in kindness and patience. Now look at ye—and look at me.'

'Now, Father, a word from you—'

'I'll not say it, Jerry. I won't say it. I won't hinder Father Tracy in the course he has taken. Indeed he has my full encouragement, my full approval.'

Whether it was that Jerry hated going back to the men in Delahunty's with such an answer, he who was known among them for his persuasive tongue, or whether it was the priest's anger which infected him, or whether he just needed this to turn him against the petty tyranny of everyday life, no one could say. His kind, comical face twisted with anger. He no longer looked funny. He looked downright ugly.

'Is that your last word?' he asked.

'My last word.'

The parish priest leaned back in his chair.

'Well then, hear mine. From now on till the day you're carried feet foremost into it yourself, I'll never set my foot past the door of any church, nor support it in any way, nor give as much as one ha'penny to it or its works.'

'That, Jerry MacAvoy, will be your loss, not God's. And remember that pride is one – of – the – seven – deadly—'

Again Father Mooney's outraged digestive tract seized control. He held his stomach in agony and just as the belch sounded loud and clear, bringing a short relief, Jerry added: 'Sins.'

He took his hat from the table and went out.

Next Sunday there was a notable number of absentees from mass. But the rebellion was short-lived. Pressure from the women, habit and fear drove most of them back. Soon they were all back except the Growler and Jerry MacAvoy.

Janetta's fame began to spread when it became known that Jerry was going to ride her at the point-to-point. Sam Gill, the vet, dropped in on Jerry on his way home from a case and had a look at the mare. Jerry saddled her and led her up to the paddock. Gill watched her as she cleared the sticks, light as a bird. Then Jerry put her at the bank. He pushed her in fairly close before he let her rise. Up she went, changed her feet with the agility of a cat and came down, breathing as easily as a child. Gill passed in under her neck to listen and then shouted his praise.

'You've a winner there, Jerry. But you've got a bit too much condition on her.'

'She's a hunter, not a race-horse. It'll come off.'

'Ah, she's a beauty and no mistake. She'll win the Grand National yet. Ye'll get a good price for her, Jerry.'

Jerry shook his head.

'No, but I'll win a good few races wit' her. And I'll jump her at the Show.'

He unfastened the girth and lifted the saddle. Standing beside the mare, he stroked her glossy hide, murmuring to her, praising her. Then slowly his strong fingers pressed on the point in her back where the hair divides. She shivered and trembled. A light shudder passed through her limbs. Slowly she turned her head and her dark eyes looked softly at Jerry.

'Hell,' said Gill. 'She's like a woman.'

'Only she doesn't laugh at my mug.' And Jerry's mug looked so wistful and so comical as he spoke, that Sam Gill burst out laughing and laughed all the way home.

One day Father Tracy met the Growler in the street and Father Tracy thought it the time and place to reason with him concerning his absence from mass. The Growler, whose endurance was being sorely tried by his wife's nagging, lost his temper. In beautifully rounded periods, he told Father Tracy what he thought of him, as a man and a priest, what the village thought of him, the townland, the barony, the country, Ireland and the world. He cast aspersions on Father Tracy's truthfulness, honesty and sanity. He insinuated that Father Tracy's female ancestry could not well bear examination and that in the interests of posterity it was a very good thing that he had been priested.

Father Tracy turned pale and trembled with anger.

'Do you realize,' he shouted, 'that you are speaking to a priest of God? Do you realize that I could exercise my power and at this instant turn you into a stone?'

'I don't believe a word of it,' answered the Growler. 'But so be it that ye could, I hope someone would come by and pick me up and throw me at ye.'

The case came up before District Justice Beattie. Even after fifteen years' experience of courts and witnesses, Mr. Beattie could scarcely make head or tail of the matter. There was a flood of half-perjury, at which the Irish are past masters, cross statements, insinuations, scandalous references, red herrings and irrelevant detail. After listening patiently for three and a half hours, he dismissed the case and bound the defendants over to keep the peace. It was, in a way, a victory.

Soon after, the Growler, worn down by his wife's prayers and nagging, turned up shamefacedly at mass.

When Father Mooney spoke to Anna about Jerry, he got his answer.

'I have never interfered wit' him, never questioned his comin's or goin's and I won't begin now. I can only pray for him.'

And then she said something queer, very queer from a good religious girl like Anna. 'God,' she said, 'is har'ly the same as us. He can make allowances, for men are never His creatures.'

Jerry laughed when Father Mooney took him to task.

'I'll go back, Father,' he said, 'the day they carry you feet foremost through the church door. Now isn't that a nice puzzle for ye. By rights ye should die, here and now, to save my soul.'

It was likely that the idea of the dance was brought forward by Father Mooney in the first place as a distraction. Jerry's rebellion was being commented on too generally and, since he was liked, a certain admiration for the stand he was making had grown up among the bolder spirits. Father Mooney, with the help of Mrs. Delahunty, decided to get up a dance to raise funds for the new parish hall. It was planned to take place the night of the point-to-point races. Then, if Jerry's horse won, as seemed more likely, well you never knew. God had strange ways of bringing back his own and it was well known that Jerry had never missed a dance.

Then, the night before the races, the night before the dance, the Bishop died. Everyone thought that now the dance would be put off. Not the races, though. Even piety has its limits.

After long consultation with Father Tracy and then with Mrs. Delahunty, who had ordered the food and drink, Father Mooney announced that since the dance was for such a good object, it would take place. He was sure the Bishop himself would have insisted. Indeed, it seemed, after due repetition, that the Bishop, on his dying bed, had insisted. What was more likely, as Jerry MacAvoy took care to point out, was that Mrs. Delahunty, a hard, close-fisted woman, had insisted there and then on Father Mooney paying for the food. The drink would, of course, keep.

Jerry sat easily on Janetta's back. But the devil himself was in the mare that day. She cast a nervous, uneasy eye at the crowd which yelled and shouted in the field and an occasional tremor, a light sweating of the flanks, told that she was nervous. Jerry rode through the people, speaking to this one and that, showing off his mare.

She made a bad start. But once underway, she went along quietly and obediently, answering the pressure of his knees, the tone of his voice. She had never moved more lightly, never before gathered her strength together in this way, so that the ground moved under her as if with no effort on her part. She rose, sweetly, to the first fence and then settled down. A point-to-point is run, not with the jockeying of the race-track, but hell-for-leather all the way. Jerry called to her, called her 'his sweet girl, his darlin', his lovely whoore', and it was as if joy and love moved her. She gave every ounce. Three quarters of the way home, she had left the field behind.

Then the sunk ditch, and Jerry did not remember in time. In the very joy of her heart, Janetta rose, cleared the bank and all Jerry's skill could not save her. She came down and rolled over. Jerry had the cunning to roll clear.

When he pulled her up, she stood trembling. Quickly his hands searched for a broken bone, a strained tendon. She seemed alright. The field thundered past. But Jerry forgot the others, forgot the race, on which he had laid far too much money, forgot everything but Janetta. He slung his coat over her back and walked her slowly home.

When he led her into the stable she turned her head and looked at him. Her dark eyes were so full of anguish that he cried out. His hands caressed her tenderly and he found himself shouting, shouting that she must not die, must not leave him. Anna had already sent for Sam Gill.

Gill was cool and business-like. The mare had a twisted gut. A painful accident but not necessarily fatal.

'Ah, don't worry, Jerry. I'll save her. She'll be as right as rain in a week. Ye'll ride her yerself at the Show and I'll be along to see ye. Keep up yer heart, man.'

Jerry, half crazed with misery, kept following Gill about, in and out of the stable, into the kitchen and back again, watching every movement, watching his hands as they touched the mare. And each time that Jerry entered the stable, Janetta turned her eyes towards him and trembled as if beseeching him to free her of this terrible pain.

'For God's sake, man,' said Gill in exasperation, 'Get out of my way. Go to bed. Go and get drunk but get from under my feet.'

Jerry didn't go back to the house. He stood leaning against the stable wall. From there he could see the dance hall, lit up, see the dark forms of the dancers as they passed the windows, hear the shrill tones of the fiddle, the gay shouts of the men. He muttered curses on them, strong, hard curses, spit through his teeth. He swore he would never dance again.

At dawn the dance broke up and Jerry went back to the stable. Gill was standing, wiping the sweat from his forehead with his bare forearm. He was so tired that he could scarcely stand. He turned irritably on Jerry.

'Will ye get out,' he said. 'Ye're no more use than an old woman.'

Jerry paid no heed. He looked at Janetta. The mare's anguished look was like a knife in his heart. He turned away, went into the kitchen and took down his gun. Roughly he pushed Gill aside and shot her. Then, without saying a word, he went back into the house, and throwing his arms across the kitchen table, wept like a child.

That was how Anna found him in the morning.

She would have liked to weep herself. But someone had to attend to the pigs, milk the cow, turn her out to pasture, get the breakfast, attend to the children. It was ill to speak to a man when his heart was sore.

Anna always blamed herself for not being in the shop when Father Mooney came in. Jerry was there cutting up a side of beef and she had thought it best to leave him alone. She hurried in when she heard the priest's voice and with terrified eyes saw Jerry standing there, the chopper in his hand.

'We thought to see you at the dance last night, Jerry,' Father Mooney was saying cheerfully, as if there was nothing but happiness in the world. 'You that's so fond of dancing and having a good time. It was most enjoyable, I can tell you, most enjoyable. Still, we missed you.'

Jerry grinned. He had never in all his life looked so comical, Anna thought, the way his eyes were red from crying, his wide mouth swollen.

'What, Father?' he said. 'Me go to a dance and the Bishop dead?'

Anna sighed. Better, far better, for the sake of his immortal soul, that he had brained the priest.

THE GIRLS AND THE DOGS

Kevin Barry

Kevin Barry is the author of three novels and three story collections. His work appears in the *New Yorker*, *Harpers*, the *Stinging Fly* and elsewhere. He has been translated into sixteen languages. He also writes plays, screenplays and essays. He lives in County Sligo.

I was living in a caravan a few miles outside Gort. It was set up on breeze blocks in the yard of an old farmhouse. There were big nervous dogs outside, chained. Their breathing caught hard with the cold of the winter and the way the wind shuddered along their flanks was wretched to behold. I lay there in the night, as the dogs howled misery at the darkness, and I doted over a picture of my daughter, May-Anne, as she had been back in the summertime. I hadn't seen her in eight months and I missed her so badly. I was keeping myself well hidden. Things had gone wrong in Cork and then they went wronger again. I had been involved with bringing some of the brown crack in that was said to be causing people to have strokes and was said to have caused the end altogether of a prostitute lad on Douglas Street. Everybody was looking for me. There was no option for a finish only to hop on a bus and then it was all black skies and bogger towns and Gort, finally, and Evan the Head waited for me there, in the ever-falling rain, and he had his bent smile on.

'Here's another one I got to weasel you out of,' he said. And me without the arse o' me fuckin' kecks, 'ay?'

He jerked a thumb at a scabby Fiesta that wore no plates and we climbed into it and we took off through the rain, January, and we drove past wet fields and stone walls and he asked me no questions at all. He said it was often the way that a fella needed a place and he would be glad to help me out. He said that I was his friend after all and he softened the word in his mouth – friend – in a way that I found troubling. It was the softness that named the price of the word. He said things could as easily be the other way around and maybe someday I would be there to help him out. We turned down a crooked boreen that ran between fields left to reeds and there were no people anywhere to be seen. We came to the farmhouse and the smile on the Head's face twisted even more so.

I never promised you a rose garden, he said.

You would have hardly thought it held anyone at all but for the yellow screams of children escaping the torn curtains and the filthy windows. Evan said he had rent allowance got for the house on account of his children. He had bred six off Suze and a couple off her sister, Elsie. These were open-minded people I was dealing with. At least with regard to that end of things. We went inside and the kids appeared everywhere, they were shaven-headed against the threat of nits, and they were pelting about like maniacs, grinding their teeth and hammering at the walls, and the women appeared – girlish, Elsie and Suze, as thin as girls – and they smirked at me in a particular way over the smoke of their roll-ups: it is through no fault of my own that I am considered a very handsome man.

'Coffee and buns, no?' said Evan the Head, and the girls laughed.

The house was in desperate shape. There were giant mushroomy damp patches coming through the old wallpaper and a huge fireplace in the main room was burning smashed-up chairs and bits of four-be-two. The Head wasn't lying when he said I'd be as well off outside in the caravan. He brought me to it and I was relieved to get out to the yard, mainly because of the kids, who had a real viciousness to them.

Now of course the caravan was no mansion either. The door's lock was busted and the door was tied shut with a piece of chain left over from the dogs and fixed with a padlock. The dogs were big and of hard breeds but they were nervous, fearful, and they backed away into the corners of the yard as we passed through. Evan unlooped the chain and opened the door and with a flourish bid me enter.

'Can you smell the sex off it?' he said, climbing in behind.

'Go 'way?'

'Bought it off a brasser used to work the horse fairs,' he said. 'If the walls could talk in this old wagon, 'ay?'

It had a knackery look to it sure enough. It was an old sixteen-footer aluminium job with a flowery carpet rotten away to fuck and flouncy pillows with the flounce gone out of them and it reeked of the fields and winter. There was a wee gas fire with imitation logs. Evan knelt and got it going with his lighter.

'Get you good an' cosy,' he said. 'You any money, boy-child?'

'I've about three euro odd, Ev.'

'Captain of industry,' he said.

The gas fire took and the fumes rose from it so hard they watered my eyes. I asked was it safe and he said it'd be fine, it'd be balmy, it'd be like I was on my holidays, and if I got bored I could always pop inside the house and see if young Elsie fancied a lodger.

'For her stomach,' he said.

I am not lying when I tell you there was a time Evan the Head was thought to be a bit of a charmer. He was from Swansea originally and sometimes in his cups he would talk about it like it was a kind of paradise and his accent would come through stronger. I had known him five years and I would have to say he was a mysterious character. I had met him first in a pub on Barrack Street in Cork called the Three Ones. It wasn't a pub that had the best of names for itself. It was a rough crowd that drank there and there was an amount of dealing that went on and an amount of feuds on account of the dealing. There had been shootings the odd time. I was nervous there always but Evan was calm and smiling at the barside and one night I went back to the flat he had in Togher and I bought three sheets of acid off him at a good price – White Lightnings, ferocious visuals – and he showed me passports for himself that were held under three different names. I was young enough to be impressed by that though I have seen quarer sights since, believe me. Evan used to talk about orgies all the time. He would go on and on about organising a good proper orgy – 'ay? – and he told me once about an orgy in a graveyard in Swansea that himself and an old girlfriend had set up and that's when he started taking down Aleister Crowley books about the occult and telling me he suspected I might be a white witch.

Magick, said Evan, should be always written with the extra 'k'.

I emptied out my bag in the caravan – it held just a few pairs of boxer shorts and T-shirts and trackie pants. I had little enough by way of possessions since Fiona Condon had turfed me out, the lighting bitch. I had not arranged to collect my stuff. I would not give her the satisfaction, her and her barring order, and I was dressing myself out of Penney's. She hadn't let me near my daughter; I hadn't seen May-Anne since that day in early summer I had taken her out to the beach at Garrettstown. Evan watched me as I unpacked my few bits and I felt by his quietness that he was sorrowful for me. At least I hoped that was what the quietness was.

'Have you any food, Ev?' I said.

'You not eaten?'

I told him I'd made it from Cork on the strength of a banana and a Snickers bar.

'Poor starving little wraith,' he said.

He said I could come in later. He said there would be a pot of curried veg on the go. And that was the way our routine began. I would come in, the evenings, and I would be fed, and I would watch TV for a while and help with burning the four-be-twos before going and dry-humping Elsie on a mattress in a back room that smelled of kid piss and dried blood.

Elsie the third night told me that she loved me.

Now Elsie to this day I do not believe had original badness in her. It was just that she could be easily led and her sister had badness in her sure enough and as for Evan, well.

I said, the third night:

'But Elsie you're fleadhin' Ev and all, yeah?'

'What's fleadhin'?' she said.

'Fuckin',' I said. 'It's a Cork word for fuckin'.'

'Business o' yours how?' she said.

Elsie and Suze were from Leeds – Leeds-Irish – and they had people in south Galway. Their father had been put away for knocking their mother unconscious with the welt of a slap hammer and they turned up on the doorstep of the Galway cousins and they were turned away again lively. Their eyes were too dark and their mouths were too beautiful. They were the kind of girls – women – who look kind of dramatic and unsafe. They were at a loose end arsing around Galway then, fucking Australians out of youth hostels and robbing them, and they met Evan the Head in the Harbour Bar, was the story, when there still was a Harbour Bar, before the Galway docks was all cunts in pink shirts drinking wine. Evan was loaded at that time having brought in a trawler full of grade-two resin from Morocco – he came into Doolin with it, bold as brass, stoned as a coot in the yellow of his oilskins – and that was ten years back and if one of the sisters wasn't up the spout off him since, the other was.

'Evan an' me is over,' said Elsie, 'but I'm not sayin' he isn't a wonderful father.'

At that moment there was the loud cracking sound of wood snapping – *shhlaaack!* – which meant that Evan the Head had lain a length of four-be-two along the bottom steps of the stairs and taken a lep at it from the banister. He was a limber man and he enjoyed breaking up the firewood in this way.

See him perched up on the banister, with the weird grin on, and he eyeing just the spot where he wanted to crack the wood – then the wee lep.

In Cork I had seen Suze sure enough, lumbering under children and dope smoke on the couch of the Togher flat, but I had never seen Elsie though I had heard her, once, in a far room, crying.

'Does Suze love him still do you think?'

'No,' said Elsie, 'but he has the spell on her, don't he? I can beat the spell.'

So it was – so simple – that we became a kind of family that January in the old farmhouse outside Gort. But of course I could not say I was ever entirely comfortable with the situation. I kept going out to the caravan at night, to be alone for those cold hours, for my own space and to think of May-Anne, to look at her photograph, and to listen to the dogs, the strange comfort of them. Elsie thought this was snobbish of me. She wanted me to stay with her on the mattress. And Evan the Head said he agreed with her, and Suze agreed, and that was the start of the trouble.

But I'm getting ahead of myself. I want to tell you about Elsie and what she looked like when she came. She wouldn't allow me to put it inside because there'd been complications with the last child she'd had bred off her for Evan and she didn't want another kid happening. I said fine to that. I have never been comfortable with being a father. I love May-Anne – my dotey pet, I always call her – but it makes me frightened just to think of her walking around in the world with the people that are out there. See some of the fuckers you'd have muttering at the walls down around the bus station in Parnell Place, Cork. You'd want a daughter breathing the same air as those animals?

'Get in there!' Ev cried from the hallway into the back room where Elsie and I lay on the mattress. 'Get in!'

When she came Elsie had a tic beneath her left eye – at the top of her cheek there was a fluttering as if a tiny bird was caught beneath her skin. The dry-humping made me feel like a teenager again but not in a good way. We lay there – a particular night – with Elsie's tic going, with me all handsome and useless, and Evan leapt on the four-be-twos off the banister, and the eight mad kids bounced off the ceilings and bit each other and screamed, and the wind howled outside, and the wretched dogs cried a great howling in answer to the wind, and then Suze was at the door, and she said:

'Why don't we make this interestin'?'

Yes it started like that – the trouble – it started as a soft kind of coaxing. Sly comments from Suze and sly comments from Evan the Head. And I got worried when the winter stretched on, the weeks threw down their great length, the weeks were made of sleet and wind, and it became February – a hard month – and the sly comments came even from Elsie then. She was easily led and bored enough for badness. I started to feel a bit trapped in this place and I thought about moving on but I had nowhere to go and no money to get there. Given the way things had turned out in Cork, I would be shot or arrested if I went back, no question. I missed May-Anne so badly but I thought the best I could do for her was to keep myself safe until the troubled times had passed over.

Then, late one night, Evan the Head came into the yard – I heard him hiss at the dogs – and without so much as a knock he was in the door of the caravan and he sat on the foot of my fold-out bed. He lit a candle and I saw him by its soft light. He had his twisted smile on. First words he said to me:

'Suze is the better comer.'

'Go 'way?'

'Know what a geyser is?'

'I do, yeah.'

'That's Suze if she's in the form. You see she's got one eye a dark brown and one a dark, really dark green?'

'Yeah, kinda…'

'Yeah kinda noticed that, 'ay? Did you, boy?'

'Yeah.'

'Yeah well that's a good sign,' he said, 'for a comer.'

I did not reply because I did not like the way he was smoking his roll-up. The hard little sucks on it and his eyes so deep-set.

'She's inside,' he said.

I said nothing.

'I said she's waitin' on you, boy. Are you goin' to keep her waitin'?'

'Ah please, Ev.'

'You don't want to get that lady riled. Suze? Not a good plan, boy-child. I said you don't get that fucking lady riled.'

'Evan, look, I've the thing with her sister, haven't I?'

He stood then – he loomed in the candlelight – and the words that came were half spat, half whispered:

'You'll get in that fucking house and you'll fuck my wife and you'll fuck her sister or you'll get the fuckin' life taken out of you, d'ya hear me, boy?'

'Evan get out of the caravan, please!'

He leapt up on the bed then and he danced about and he laughed so hard. And he kind of poked at my head with his feet, kind of playful, as if he was going to stamp me, but he let it go, he stood down, and he left without another word. Then I heard him turn the padlock on the chain outside.

They kept me locked in the caravan for days and nights I quickly lost the count of. The windows were rusted shut and could not be squeezed back and I was so weak because they brought me no food and no water. I was in a bad state very quickly. The dogs outside I believe sensed that I was weakening, that I was dying, and they called to me. We were held on the same length of chain. In the daytime the girls came and whispered through the door to me – awful, filthy stuff that I would not repeat, for hours they whispered – and I knew that Elsie hadn't the better of the spell anymore. Evan came by night and he crawled over the roof of the caravan and he made little tapping noises. I roared and cried myself hoarse but there was no one to hear me out there and after a few days I was slipping in and out of a desperate weird sleep – full of sour, scary dreams, like bad whiskey dreams – and I felt the cold of the fields come into my bones and once in the afternoon dusk I woke from a fever to find Evan the Head outside a window of the caravan and in each of his arms he held a child to look in at me, and I knew it was the first time ever that I had seen those children calm. I have never had religion or spiritual feelings but lying there in the caravan in the farmyard outside Gort I knew for sure there was no God but there was surely a devil.

But if I gritted my teeth against the fear and kept my eyes clamped tightly shut, the sweats would seem to ease off for a while and I would see clearly my day on the beach with May-Anne, at Garrettstown, in the summer. It was a windy, blustery day, but the sea and the sand made us high, we were soaring, and we ran about like mad things on the beach. Afterwards, before the bus back to town, I bought her a 99 at a seaside shop. The shop had all sorts of beach tat for sale and she asked me about the pork-pie hats that said 'kiss-me-quick'.

'What's kiss-me-quick?'

'It's just a seaside thing,' I, said. 'An old saying. From England I think.'

'Kiss-me-quick kiss-me-quick kiss-me-quick,' she said it in a duck's voice from a cartoon and I pecked her on the cheek, really quickly, peck peck peck, and I nuzzled the nape of her neck – she squealed.

I don't know how many days I had been locked in the caravan when I crawled the length of it one morning and under the sink found two tins of Campbell's Cream of Tomato Soup from years ago, probably – from the days of the brasser I would say. I opened them and I drank them cold and if I did not come to life exactly it felt as if my thoughts came for a short while in a clearer, more realistic way. Then I went to the closet to throw up.

I hated to use the chemical toilet in there because of the smell but I had no choice – my gut heaved and emptied itself. I wrapped myself around the tiny plastic loo, tears streaming. I saw then that the spillage over the years had worked away at the floorboards beneath. They were rotten to the extent that some had been replaced with a piece of ply.

I waited until the night. Elsie and Suze had come out just once in the afternoon to whisper their filth at me, and Evan had on the roof for a while made his tap-tappings and I believed he was working at some kind of spell – something from an Aleister Crowley book, maybe; magick – and when he went away I waited, waited, until all in the farmhouse was darkness and quiet, and there was just the feeling of the dogs outside.

I unhooked the chemical loo and lifted it clear and the ply beneath came loose so easily it was unreal, it was like wet cardboard in my hands. The hole I quickly made was no more than two, two and a half foot wide but that was enough to squeeze through, and I scraped past an axle, and I was crawling along the wet ground of the yard then beneath the caravan. All of the dogs huddled close to the ground and peered at me, oh and their eyes – so yellow – were livid, but they made not a sound, they were quiet as the air was cold.

I wriggled out from beneath the caravan and sat with my back to it to ease the beating of my heart. No lights came on in the farmhouse and the dogs in perfect silence watched me as I found the strength to walk to the Fiesta and climbed into it. I lifted off the panel for the wires to come loose and I knew well enough which wires to rub together.

I was no more than halfways down the crooked boreen when the lights came on in the farmhouse and there were roars and screams and the sound of doors and footsteps and with my eyes pinned ahead I steered along till the boreen gave onto road and I missed the verge and the tyre ripped on rocks but I kept going hard into the night. The way the ripped rubber of the tyre slapped along the back road had a rhythm to it – three beats, again and again and again – and I heard it as kiss-me-quick, kiss-me-quick, and I drove it until the screaming of the voices – oh May-Anne – and all that was behind me had faded – my sweetheart, my dotey – to nothing, just nothing at all, and I was at a high vantage suddenly and beneath me, on a plain, were the lights of Gort.

PING

Samuel Beckett

Translated from the French by the author

Samuel Beckett (1906–1989) was a novelist, playwright, poet and translator. He left Ireland for France, where he lived for most of his life, and much of his later work is bilingual. His best-known work includes *Waiting for Godot*, *Krapp's Last Tape*, and his prose works *Watt* and *Malone*. Beckett was awarded the Nobel Prize for Literature in 1969.

All known all white bare white body fixed one yard legs joined like sewn. Light heat white floor one square yard never seen. White walls one yard by two white ceiling one square yard never seen. Bare white body fixed only the eyes only just. Traces blurs light grey almost white on white. Hands hanging palms front white feet heels together right angle. Light heat white planes shining white bare white body fixed ping fixed elsewhere. Traces blurs signs no meaning light grey almost white. Bare white body fixed white on white invisible. Only the eyes only just light blue almost white. Head naught eyes light blue almost white silence within. Brief murmurs only just almost never all known. Traces blur signs no meaning light grey almost white. Legs joined like sewn heels together right angle. Traces alone uncover given black light grey almost white on white. Light heat white walls shining white one yard by two. Bare white body fixed one yard ping fixed elsewhere. Traces blurs signs no meaning light grey almost white. White feet toes joined like sewn heels together right angle invisible. Eyes alone uncover given blue light blue almost white. Murmur only just almost never one second perhaps not alone. Given rose only just bare white body fixed one yard white on white invisible. All white all known murmurs only just almost never always the same white invisible. Bare white body fixed ping elsewhere. Only the eyes only just light blue almost white fixed front. Ping murmur only just almost never one second perhaps a way out. Head naught eyes light blue almost white fixed front ping murmur ping silence. Eyes holes light blue almost white mouth white seam like sewn invisible. Ping murmur perhaps a nature one second almost never that much memory almost never. White walls each its trace grey blur signs no meaning light grey almost white. Light heat all known all white planes meeting invisible. Ping murmur only just almost never one second perhaps a meaning that much memory almost never. White feet toes joined like sewn heels together right angle ping elsewhere no sound. Hands hanging palms front legs joined like sewn. Head naught eyes holes light blue almost white fixed front silence within. Ping elsewhere always there but that known not. Eyes holes light blue alone uncover given blue light blue almost white only colour fixed front. All white all known white planes shining white ping murmur only just almost never one second light time that much memory almost never. Bare white body fixed one yard ping fixed elsewhere white on white invisible heart breath no sound. Only the eyes given blue light blue almost white fixed front only colour alone uncover. Planes meeting invisible one only shining white infinite but that known not. Nose ears while holes mouth white seam like sewn invisible. Ping murmurs only just almost never one second always the same all known. Given rose only just bare white body fixed one yard invisible all known without within. Ping perhaps a nature one image same time a little less blue and white in the wind. White ceiling shining white one square yard never seen ping perhaps away out there one second ping silence. Traces alone uncover given black grey blurs signs no meaning grey light almost white always the same. Ping perhaps not alone one second with image always the silence. Given rose only just nails fallen white over. Long hair fallen white invisible over. White scars invisible same white as flesh torn of old given rose only just. Ping image only just almost never one second light time blue and white in the wind. Head naught nose ears white holes mouth white seam like sewn invisible over. Only the eyes given blue fixed front light blue almost white only colour alone uncover. Light heat white planes shining white one only shining white infinite but that known not. Ping a nature only just almost never one second with image same time a little less blue and white in the wind. Traces blues light grey eyes holes light blue almost white fixed front ping a meaning only just almost never ping silence. Bare white one yard fixed ping fixed elsewhere no sound legs joined like sewn heels together right angle hands hanging palms front. Head naught eyes holes light blue almost white fixed front silence within. Ping elsewhere always there but that known not. Ping perhaps not alone one second with image same time a little less dim eye black and white half closed along lashes imploring that much memory almost never. A far flash of time all white all over all of old ping flash white walls shining white no trace eyes holes light blue almost white last colour ping white over. Ping fixed last elsewhere legs joined like sewn heels together right angle hands hanging palms front head naught eyes white invisible fixed front over. Given rose only just one yard invisible bare white all known without within over. White ceiling never seen ping of old only just almost never one second light time white floor never seen ping of old perhaps there. Ping of old only just perhaps a meaning nature one second almost never blue and white in that much memory henceforth never. White planes no traces shining white one only shining white infinite but that known not. Light heat all known all white heart breath no sound. Head naught eyes fixed front old ping last murmur one second perhaps not alone eye unlustrous black and white half closed long lashes imploring ping silence ping over.

AFTER THE WAKE

Brendan Behan

Brendan Behan (1923–1964) was born in Dublin and grew up in working-class Crumlin. He is better known as a dramatist, producing several plays, but also wrote autobiographical fiction including *Borstal Boy* and *Confessions of an Irish Rebel*. *After the Wake*, a collection of twenty-one shorter prose stories was published posthumously in 1981.

W hen he sent to tell me she was dead, I thought that if the dead live on – which I don't believe they do – and know the minds of the living, she'd feel angry, not so much jealous as disgusted, certainly surprised. For one time she had told me, quoting unconsciously from a book I'd lent him, 'A woman can always tell them – you kind of smell it on a man – like knowing when a cat is in a room'.

We often discussed things like that – he, always a little cultured, happy, and proud to be so broad-minded – she, with adolescent pride in the freedom of her married state to drink a bottle of stout and talk about anything with her husband and her husband's friend.

I genuinely liked them both. If I went a week without calling up to see them, he was down the stairs to our rooms, asking what they'd done on me, and I can't resist being liked. When I'd go in she'd stick a fag in my mouth and set to making tea for me.

I'd complimented them, individually and together, on their being married to each other – and I meant it.

They were both twenty-one, tall and blond, with a sort of English blondness.

He, as I said, had pretensions to culture and was genuinely intelligent, but that was not the height of his attraction for me.

Once we went out to swim in a weir below the Dublin Mountains. It was evening time and the last crowd of kids too shrimpish, small, neutral cold to take my interest – just finishing their bathe.

When they went off, we stripped and, watching him, I thought of Marlowe's lines which I can't remember properly: 'Youth with gold wet head, through water gleaming, gliding, and crowns of pearlets on his naked arms'.

I haven't remembered it at all, but only the sense of a Gaelic translation I've read.

When we came out we sat on his towel – our bare thighs touching – smoking and talking.

We talked of the inconveniences of tenement living. He said he'd hated most of all sleeping with his brothers – so had I, I'd felt their touch incestuous – but most of all he hated sleeping with a man older than himself.

He'd refused to sleep with his father which hurt the old man very much, and when a seizure took his father in the night, it left him remorseful.

'I don't mind sleeping with a little child,' he said, 'the snug way they round themselves into you – and I don't mind a young fellow my own age'.

'The like of myself,' and I laughed as if it meant nothing. It didn't apparently, to him.

'No, I wouldn't mind you, and it'd be company for me, if she went into hospital or anything,' he said.

Then he told me what she herself had told me sometime before, that there was something the matter with her, something left unattended since she was fourteen or so, and that soon she'd have to go into hospital for an operation.

From that night forward, I opened the campaign in jovial earnest.

The first step – to make him think it manly, ordinary to manly men, the British Navy, 'Porthole Duff', 'Navy Cake' stories of the Hitler Youth in captivity, told me by Irish soldiers on leave from guarding them; to remove the taint of 'cissiness', effeminacy, how the German Army had encouraged it in Cadet Schools, to harden the boy-officers, making their love a muscular clasp of friendship, independent of women, the British Public Schools, young Boxers I'd known (most of it about the Boxers was true), that Lord Alfred Douglas was son to the Marquess of Queensbury and a good man to use his dukes himself, Oscar Wilde throwing old 'Q' down the stairs and after him his Ballyboy attendant.

On the other front, appealing to that hope of culture – Socrates, Shakespeare, Marlow – lies, truth and half-truth.

I worked cautiously but steadily. Sometimes (on the head of a local scandal) in conversation with them both.

After I'd lent him a book about an English schoolmaster, she'd made the remark about women knowing, scenting them as she would a cat in a dark, otherwise empty room.

Quite undeliberately, I helped tangle her scents.

One night we'd been drinking together, he and I, fairly heavily up in their rooms.

I remember when he'd entered and spoken to her, he said to me: 'Your face lights up when you see her'. And why wouldn't it? Isn't a kindly welcome a warming to both faith, and features?

I went over and told her what he'd said.

'And my face lights up when I see yours,' she said, smiling up at me in the charming way our women have with half-drunk men.

The following morning I was late for work with a sick head.

I thought I'd go upstairs to their rooms and see if there was a bottle of stout left that would cure me.

There wasn't, and though she was in, he was out.

I stopped a while and she gave me a cup of tea, though I'd just finished my own down below in our place.

As I was going she asked me had I fags for the day. I said I had – so as not to steal her open store, as the saying has it – and went off to work.

She, or someone, told him I'd been in and he warned me about it the next time we were together. He didn't mind (and I believed him) but people talked, etc.

From that day forward I was cast as her unfortunate admirer, my jealousy of him sweetened by my friendship for them both.

She told me again about her operation and asked me to pray for her. When I protested my unsuitability as a pleader with God, she quoted the kindly, highly heretical Irish Catholicism about the prayers of the sinner being first heard.

The night before she went into hospital we had a good few drinks – the three of us together.

We were in a singing house on the Northside and got very sob-gargled between drinking whiskey and thinking of the operation.

I sang *My Mary of the Curling Hair* and when we came to the Gaelic chorus, '*siúil, a ghrá*' ('walk, my love'), she broke down in sobbing and said how he knew as well as she that it was to her I was singing, but that he didn't mind. He said that indeed he did not, and she said how fearful she was of this operation, that maybe she'd never come out of it. She was not sorry for herself, but for him, if anything happened her and she died on him, aye, and sorry for me too, maybe more sorry, 'Because, God help you,' she said to me, 'that never knew anything better than going down town half-drunk and dirty rotten bitches taking your last farthing'.

Next day was Monday, and at four o'clock she went into the hospital. She was operated on on Thursday morning and died the same evening at about nine o'clock.

When the doctor talked about cancer, he felt consoled a little. He stopped his dry-eyed sobbing and came with me into a public-house where we met his mother and hers and made arrangements to have her brought home and waked in her own place.

She was laid out in the front room on their spare single bed which was covered in linen for the purpose. Her habit was of blue satin and we heard afterwards that some old ones considered the colour wrong – her having been neither a virgin nor a member of the Children of Mary Sodality.

The priest, a hearty man who read Chesterton and drank pints, disposed of the objection by saying that we were all Children of Mary since Christ introduced St. John to our Lady at the foot of the Cross – Son, behold thy Mother; Mother, behold Thy Son.

It is a horrible thing how quickly death and disease can work on a body.

She didn't look like herself, any more than the brown parchment-thin shell of a mummy looks like an Egyptian warrior; worse than the mummy, for he at least is dry and clean as dust. Her poor nostrils were plugged with cotton-wool and her mouth hadn't closed properly, but showed two front teeth, like a rabbit's. All in all, she looked no better than the corpse of her granny, or any other corpse for that matter.

There was a big crowd at the wake. They shook hands with him and told him they were sorry for his trouble; then they shook hands with his and her other relatives, and with me, giving me an understanding smile and licence to mourn my pure unhappy love.

Indeed, one old one, far gone in Jameson, said she was looking down on the two of us, expecting me to help him bear up.

Another old one, drunker still, got lost in the complications of what might have happened had he died instead of her, and only brought herself up at the tableau – I marrying her and he blessing the union from on high.

At about midnight, they began drifting away to their different rooms and houses and by three o'clock there was only his mother left with us, steadily drinking.

At last she got up a little shakily on her feet and, proceeding to knock her people, said that they'd left bloody early for blood relatives, but seeing as they'd given her bloody little in life it was the three of us were best entitled to sit waking – she included me and all.

When his mother went, he told me he felt very sore and very drunk and very much in need of sleep. He felt hardly able to undress himself.

I had to almost carry him to the big double bed in the inner room.

I first loosened his collar to relieve the flush on his smooth cheeks, took off his shoes and socks and pants and shirt, from the supply muscled thighs, the stomach flat as an altar boy's, and noted the golden smoothness of the blond hair on every part of his firm white flesh.

I went to the front room and sat by the fire till he called me.

'You must be nearly gone yourself,' he said, 'you might as well come in and get a bit of rest.'

I sat on the bed, undressing myself by the faint flickering of the candles from the front room.

I fancied her face looking up from the open coffin on the Americans who, having imported wakes from us, invented morticians themselves.

OVER AND DONE WITH

Claire-Louise Bennett

Claire-Louise Bennett is the author of *Pond*. Her fiction and essays have featured in many publications, including *gorse*, the *White Review*, *Harper's Magazine*, *Frieze*, *Artforum*, the *New York Times* and *Vogue Italia*.

The winds hereabouts had worked up such a remarkable storm it made the news in the neighbouring country and so one morning I awoke to enquiries from my family, my father to be precise, about how I was faring. I said I was very snug indeed, which was no exaggeration, and I added that since my house is tucked into a hollow it is reasonably sheltered and altogether quite safe. Then I said sometimes I worried that a tree might fall upon it because I didn't want to reassure my father too much and thereby dispense with his concern entirely. I asked him of course what it was like there and he said it had just been very windy, just that. I've been up since five thirty, he said, which was no great surprise to either of us because his new children are supremely young and he told me in fact that the girl just then was eating a gingerbread man. Later on that day, or perhaps it was the following afternoon, I went out onto the driveway and not unlike the method by which an oystercatcher grazes the shoreline I bent down here and there to collect the many sticks and branches that had broken off during the storm—which kept up, on and off, for about a week I should think.

Hard to tell this time of year how long anything is going on for and for that reason I took it upon myself to intervene now and then, such as when, just two days after Christmas, I avouched enough was enough and promptly took down the decorations. I didn't have a tree, just some things arranged along the mantel, holly and so on, but since it's a large mantel it is something of a feature and therefore very noticeable and I'd made it particularly resplendent and was first of all very pleased with how it all turned out. Even so, it quickly became oppressive actually and the holly itself almost sort of evil, poking at the room like that with its creepy way of making contact with the air, no I didn't like it one bit so a week went by and then it was all got rid of in a flash. The holly I flung directly into the fire beneath, and it was a young fire because this happened even before breakfast and as such the impatient stripling flames went crazy with the holly, consuming it so well, so pleasingly —I was enormously pleased in fact and shoved in branch after branch even though the flames were becoming really tall and very bright and the holly gasped and crackled so loudly. That's right, suffer, I thought, damn you to hell—and the flames sprouted upwards even taller and brighter and made the most splendid gleeful racket. Burn to death and damn you to hell and let every twisted noxious thing you pervaded the room with go along with you, and in fact as it went on burning I could feel the atmosphere brightening. I won't do it again, I thought, I won't have it in the house again. And I recalled the sluggish misgivings I'd felt when the man took the money out of my hand and held up a tethered bundle of muricated sprigs for me to somehow take hold of in return. Standing there, with this dreadful trident, while his young son manoeuvred a small hand around a grim bag of change. The whole thing was sullied and I remember at the time feeling faintly that I should just leave it but then I located the cause of that regrettably irresolute sensation to an area in me where snobbery and superstition overlap most abominably and I chided myself for being so affected and fey—what are you some sort of overstrung contessa I thought—certainly not, then wish them well and get going. And off down the street I bobbed, yet, anachronistic feelings of pity and repulsion notwithstanding, I had a very clear sense of having succumbed to something I was not entirely at ease with and it was at that moment perhaps that the first pair of red eyes partly opened and considered me with age-old contempt.

The sticks, in case you wondered, make very good kindling of course and I thought it a good idea to collect a nice lot of them before any rain fell and made them damp and less inclined to combust. It was a nice thing to do anyway—going about the driveway like that, picking up sticks, was a nice thing to do. In I came, two or three times, and deposited bundles of sticks into the basket in front of the shorter bookcase. It surely was the afternoon by then and the atmosphere had really brightened, everything was good and nice again because of all that wonderful fluttering industriousness that keeps everything buoyant and encompassed. I'm referring primarily to the birds of course who had naturally always been there. During those two days that are decorously ceded to Christmas whenever I looked out at them it was not the same thing in the least as when I look at them on all the other days, and so, though I'd only done what I took to be the bare minimum, I acknowledged that I probably didn't ought to have gone along with the putative festivities at all this year, even to the slightest degree. And anyway, you do it or you don't— all I'd managed to bring about with my reluctant tinkering was a subtle yet agitating distortion. One has to have illustrated links with the fair to middling ranks of reality I should think in order for something like Christmas to really work out otherwise it just seems odd and sort of accusatory and one feels turbulent and extrinsic and can't wait for it all to slump backwards into its shambolic velvet envelope and shuffle off down the hill.

No doubt about it, Krampus was in tow this year, and when I looked at my lovely sticks piled so neatly in the basket in front of the shorter bookcase it seemed not for the first time something of a lapse indeed that I don't possess the first idea of how to go about casting a spell. Just say a few words, I said, as the sticks are burning, but that wouldn't be right at all and anyway what words would I say and I'm sure they should rhyme now and then at the very least and I'm hopeless at making up rhymes. It doesn't matter actually because it's all over with and there's no trace of anything now. Besides, there's never any need of course for me to be messing about with twigs and verses and chants on account of the fact that my technique for moving matters along is really quite advanced by now. I'm quite sophisticated in all sorts of ways you see and hardly ever need to dwell upon anything. That's right, I don't go into things too deeply any more—as such, when they ask, and they will ask, how it all went, and had I a nice day, I shall say it went just fine, thank you, I had a very lovely day indeed. On its own that's a little pacified perhaps and might well be considered evasive and could, thereby, be misconstrued, so I'll do my bit and say a few tantalising words about the dinner itself—we had pheasant, I'll say. One apiece. Wrapped in thick rivulets of streaky bacon and the whole thing gussied up with such deliciously tart and exuding redcurrants. Oh how nice, they'll say, was it nice? Oh yes, I'll say, it wasn't bad—tender overall, but perhaps a little dull in places. Is that so, they'll say, do you think you'd have it again? Sure, I'll say, sure I'll have it again. Though next time I'll do it slightly differently. Next time I'll break the bugger's backbone and do him in the pan.

HOLLAND PARK

Maeve Binchy

Maeve Binchy (1939–2012) was an Irish journalist, novelist, play-wright and short story writer. Her novels – including bestsellers *Light A Penny Candle* and *Circle of Friends* – have been translated into thirty-seven languages and sold more than 40 million copies world-wide. Many of her stories have been successfully adapted for film and television.

E veryone hated Malcolm and Melissa out in Greece last summer. They pretended they thought they were marvellous, but deep down we really hated them. They were too perfect, too bright, intelligent, witty and aware. They never monopolized conversations in the taverna, they never seemed to impose their will on anyone else, but somehow we all ended up doing what they wanted to do. They didn't seem lovey-dovey with each other, but they had a companionship which drove us all to a frenzy of rage.

I nearly fainted when I got a note from them six months later. I thought they were the kind of people who wrote down addresses as a matter of cour-tesy, and you never heard from them again.

'I hate trying to recreate summer madness,' wrote Melissa. 'So I won't gather everyone from the Hellenic scene, but Malcolm and I would be thrilled if you could come to supper on the 20th. Around eightish, very informal and everything. We've been so long out of touch that I don't know if there's anyone I should ask you to bring along; if so, of course the invitation is for two. Give me a ring sometime so that I'll know how many strands of spaghetti to put in the pot. It will be super to see you again.'

I felt that deep down she knew there was nobody she should ask me to bring along. She wouldn't need to hire a private detective for that, Melissa would know. The wild notion of hiring someone splendid from an escort agency came and went. In three artless questions Melissa would find out where he was from, and think it was a marvellous fun thing to have done.

I didn't believe her about the spaghetti, either. It would be something that looked effortless but would be magnificent and unusual at the same time. Perhaps a perfect Greek meal for nostalgia, where she would have made all the hard things like pitta and humus and fetta herself, and laugh away the idea that it was difficult. Or it would be a dinner around a mahogany table with lots of cut-glass decanters, and a Swiss darling to serve it and wash up.

But if I didn't go, Alice would kill me, and Alice and I often had a laugh over the perfection of Malcolm and Melissa. She said I had made them up, and that the people in the photos were in fact models who had been hired by the Greek Tourist Board to make the place look more glamorous. Their names had passed into our private shorthand. Alice would describe a restaurant as a 'Malcolm and Melissa sort of place', meaning that it was perfect, understated and somehow irritating at the same time. I would say that I had handled a situation in a 'Malcolm and Melissa way', meaning that I had scored without seeming to have done so at all.

So I rang the number and Melissa was delighted to hear from me. Yes, didn't Greece all seem like a dream nowadays, and wouldn't it be foolish to go to the same place next year in case it wasn't as good, and no, they hadn't really decided where to go next year, but Malcolm had seen this advertisement about a yacht party which wanted a few more people to make up the numbers, and it might be fun, but one never knew and one was a bit trapped on a yacht if it was all terrible. And super that I could come on the 20th, and then with the voice politely questioning, would I be bringing anyone else?

In one swift moment I made a decision. 'Well, if it's not going to make it too many I would like to bring this friend of mine, Alice,' I said, and felt a roaring in my ears as I said it. Melissa was equal to anything.

'Of course, of course, that's lovely, we look forward to meeting her. See you both about eightish then. It's not far from the tube, but maybe you want to get a bus, I'm not sure...'

'Alice has a car,' I said proudly.

'Oh, better still. Tell her there's no problem about parking, we have a bit of waste land around the steps. It makes life heavenly in London not to have to worry about friends parking.'

Alice was delighted. She said she hoped they wouldn't turn out to have terrible feet of clay and that we would have to find new names for them. I was suddenly taken with a great desire to impress her with them, and an equal hope that they would find her as funny and witty as I did. Alice can be eccentric at times, she can go into deep silences. We giggled a lot about what we'd wear. Alice said that we should go in full evening dress, with capes, and embroidered handbags, and cigarette-holders, but I said that would be ridiculous.

'It would make her uneasy,' said Alice with an evil face.

'But she's not horrible, she's nice. She's asked us to dinner, she'll be very nice,' I pleaded.

'I thought you couldn't stand her,' said Alice, disappointed.

'It's hard to explain. She doesn't mean any harm, she just does everything too well.' I felt immediately that I was taking the myth away from Malcolm and Melissa and wished I'd never thought of asking Alice.

Between then and the 20th, Alice thought that we should go in boiler suits, in tennis gear, dressed as Greek peasants, and at one stage that we should dress up as nuns and tell her that this was what we were in real life. With difficulty I managed to persuade her that we were not to look on the evening as some kind of search-and-destroy mission, and Alice reluctantly agreed.

I don't really know why we had allowed the beautiful couple to become so much part of our fantasy life. It wasn't as if we had nothing else to think about. Alice was a solicitor with a busy practice consisting mainly of battered wives, worried one-parent families faced with eviction, and a large vocal section of the female population who felt that they had been discriminated against in their jobs. She had an unsatisfactory love-life going on with one of the partners in the firm, usually when his wife was in hospital, which didn't make her feel at all guilty, she saw it more as a kind of service that she was offering. I work in a theatre writing publicity-handouts and arranging newspaper interviews for the stars, and in my own way I meet plenty of glittering people. I sort of love a hopeless man who is a good writer but a bad person to love, since he loves too many people, but it doesn't break my heart.

I don't suppose that deep down Alice and I want to live in a big house in Holland Park, and be very beautiful and charming, and have a worthy job like Melissa raising money for a good cause, and be married to a very bright, sunny-looking man like Malcolm, who runs a left-wing bookshop that somehow has made him a great deal of money. I don't *suppose* we could have been directly envious. More indirectly irritated, I would have thought.

I was very irritated with myself on the night of the 20th because I changed five times before Alice came to collect me. The black sweater and skirt looked too severe, the gingham dress mutton dressed as lamb, the yellow too garish, the pink too virginal. I settled for a tapestry skirt and a cheap cotton top.

'Christ, you look like a suite of furniture,' said Alice when she arrived.

'Do I? Is it terrible?' I asked, anxious as a sixteen-year-old before a first dance.

'No, of course it isn't,' said Alice. 'It's fine, it's just a bit sort of sofa-coverish if you know what I mean. Let's hope it clashes with her décor.'

Tears of rage in my eyes, I rushed into the bedroom and put on the severe black again. Safe, is what magazines call black. Safe I would be.

Alice was very contrite.

'I'm sorry, I really am. I don't know why I said that, it looked fine. I've never given two minutes' thought to clothes, you know that. Oh for God's sake wear it, please. Take off the mourning gear and put on what you were wearing.'

'Does this look like mourning then?' I asked, riddled with anxiety.

'Give me a drink,' said Alice firmly. 'In ten years of knowing each other we have never had to waste three minutes talking about clothes. Why are we doing it tonight?'

I poured her a large Scotch and one for me, and put on a jokey necklace which took the severe look away from the black. Alice said it looked smashing.

Alice told me about a client whose husband had put Vim in her tin of tooth powder and she had tried to convince herself that he still wasn't too bad. I told Alice about an ageing actress who was opening next week in a play, and nobody, not even the man I half love, would do an interview with her for any paper because they said, quite rightly, that she was an old bore. We had another Scotch to reflect on all that.

I told Alice about the man I half loved having asked me to go to Paris with him next weekend, and Alice said I should tell him to get stuffed, unless, of course, he was going to pay for the trip, in which case I must bring a whole lot of different judgements to bear. She said she was going to withdraw part of her own services from her unsatisfactory partner, because the last night they had spent together had been a perusal of *The Home Doctor* to try and identify the nature of his wife's illness. I said I thought his wife's illness might be deeply rooted in drink, and Alice said I could be right but it wasn't the kind of thing you said to someone's husband. Talking about drink reminded us to have another and then we grudgingly agreed it was time to go.

There were four cars in what Melissa had described as a bit of waste land, an elegantly paved semi-circular courtyard in front of the twelve steps up to the door. Alice commented that they were all this year's models, and none of them cost a penny under three thousand. She parked her battered 1969 Volkswagen in the middle, where it looked like a small child between a group of elegant adults.

Malcolm opened the door, glass in hand. He was so pleased to see us that I wondered how he had lived six months without the experience. Oh come on, I told myself, that's being unfair, if he wasn't nice and welcoming I would have more complaints. The whole place looked like the film set for a trendy frothy movie on gracious modern living. Melissa rushed out in a tapestry skirt, and I nearly cried with relief that I hadn't worn mine. Melissa is shaped like a pencil rather than a sofa; the contrast would have been mind-blowing.

We were wafted into a sitting-room, and wafted is the word. Nobody said 'come this way' or 'let me introduce you' but somehow there we were with drinks in our hands, sitting between other people, whose names had been said clearly, a Melissa would never mutter. The drinks were good and strong, a Malcolm would never be mean. Low in the background a record-player had some nostalgic songs from the Sixties, the time when we had all been young and impressionable, none of your classical music, nor your songs of the moment. Malcolm and Melissa couldn't be obvious if they tried.

And it was like being back in Andrea's Taverna again. Everyone felt more witty and relaxed because Malcolm and Melissa were there, sort of in charge of things without appearing to be. They sat and chatted, they didn't fuss, they never tried to drag anyone into the conversation or to force some grounds of common interest. Just because we were all there together under their roof... that was enough.

And it seemed to be enough for everyone. A great glow came over the group in the sunset, and the glow deepened when a huge plate of spaghetti was served. It was spaghetti, damn her. But not the kind that you and I would ever make. Melissa seemed to be out of the room only three minutes, and I know it takes at least eight to cook the pasta. But there it was, excellent, mountainous, with garlic bread, fresh and garlicky, not the kind that breaks your teeth on the outside and then is soggy within. The salad was like an exotic still-life, it had everything in it except lettuce. People moved as if in a dance to the table. There were no cries of praise and screams of disclaimer from the hostess. Why then should I have been so resentful of it all?

Alice seemed to be loving every minute of her evening, she had already fought with Malcolm about the kind of women's literature he sold, but it was a happy fight where she listened to the points he was making and answered them. If she didn't like someone she wouldn't bother to do this. She had been talking to Melissa about some famous woman whom they both knew through work, and they were giggling about the famous woman's shortcomings. Alice was forgetting her role, she was breaking the rules. She had come to understand more about the Melissa and Malcolm people so that we could laugh at them. Instead, she looked in grave danger of getting on with them.

I barely heard what someone called Keith was saying to me about my theatre. I realized with a great shock that I was jealous. Jealous that Alice was having such a nice time, and impressing Melissa and Malcolm just because she was obviously not trying to.

This shock was so physical that a piece of something exotic, avocado maybe, anyway something that shouldn't be in a salad, got stuck in my throat. No amount of clearing and hurrumphing could get rid of it and I stood up in a slight panic.

Alice grasped at once.

'Relax and it will go down,' she called. 'Just force your limbs to relax, and your throat will stop constricting. No, don't bang her, there's no need.'

She spoke with such confidence that I tried to make my hands and knees feel heavy, and miracles it worked.

'That's a good technique,' said Malcolm admiringly, when I had been patted down and, scarlet with rage, assured everyone I was fine.

'It's very unscientific,' said the doctor amongst us, who would have liked the chance to slit my throat and remove the object to cries of admiration.

'It worked,' said Alice simply.

The choking had gone away but not the reason for it. Why did I suddenly feel so possessive about Alice, so hurt when she hadn't liked my dress, so jealous and envious that she was accepted here on her own terms and not as my friend? It was ridiculous. Sometimes I didn't hear from Alice for a couple of weeks; we weren't soul mates over everything, just long-standing friends.

'... have you had this flat in the City long?' asked Keith politely.

'Oh that's not my flat, that's Alice's,' I said. Alice was always unusual. She had thought that since the City would be deserted at weekends, the time she wanted a bit of peace, that's where she should live. And of course it worked. Not a dog barked, not a child cried, not a car revved up when Alice was sleeping till noon on a Sunday.

'No, I live in Fulham,' I said, thinking how dull and predictable it sounded.

'Oh I thought...' Keith didn't say what he thought but he didn't ask about my flat in Fulham.

Malcolm was saying that Alice and I should think about the yachting holiday. Keith and Rosemary were thinking about it, weren't they? They were, and it would be great fun if we went as a six, then we could sort of take over in case the other people were ghastly.

'It sounds great,' I said dishonestly and politely. 'Yes, you must tell me more about it.'

'Weren't you meant to be going on holiday with old Thing?' said Alice practically.

'That was very vague,' I snapped. 'The weekend in Paris was definite but the holiday... nothing was fixed. Anyway weren't you meant to be going to a cottage with your Thing...?'

Everyone looked at me, it was as if I had belched loudly or taken off my blouse unexpectedly. They were waiting for me to finish and in a well-bred way rather hoping that I wouldn't. Their eyes were like shouts of encouragement.

'You said that if his wife was put away for another couple of weeks you might go to their very unsocialistic second home? Didn't you?'

Alice laughed, everyone else looked stunned.

Melissa spooned out huge helpings of a ten thousand calorie ice-cream with no appearance of having noticed a social gaffe.

'Well, when the two of you make up your minds, do tell us,' she said. 'It would be great fun, and we have to let these guys know by the end of the month, apparently. They sound very nice actually. Jeremy and Jacky they're called, he makes jewellery and Jacky is an artist. They've lots of other friends going too, a couple of girls who work with Jeremy and their boy friends, I think. It's just Jeremy and Jacky who are... who are organizing it all.'

Like a flash I saw it. Melissa thought Alice and I were lesbians. She was being her usual tolerant liberated self over it all. If you like people, what they do in bed is none of your business. HOW could she be so crass as to think that about Alice and myself? My face burned with rage. Slowly like heavy flowers falling off a tree came all the reasons. I was dressed so severely, I had asked could I bring a woman not a man to her party, I had been manless in Greece when she met me the first time, I had just put on this appalling show of spitely spiteful dikey jealousy about Alice's relationship with a man. Oh God. Oh God.

I knew little or nothing about lesbians. Except that they were different. I never was friendly with anyone who was one. I knew they didn't wear bowler hats, but I thought that they did go in for this aggressive sort of picking on one another in public. Oh God.

Alice was talking away about the boat with interest. How much would it cost? Who decided where and when they would stop? Did Jeremy and Jacky sound madly camp and would they drive everyone mad looking for sprigs of tarragon in case the pot au feu was ruined?

Everyone was laughing, and Malcolm was being liberated and tolerant and left-wing.

'Come on Alice, nothing wrong with tarragon, nothing wrong with fussing about food, we all fuss about something. Anyway, they didn't say anything to make us think that they would fuss about food, stop typecasting.'

He said it in a knowing way. I felt with a sick dread that he could have gone on and said, 'After all, I don't typecast you and expect you to wear a hairnet and military jacket.'

I looked at Alice, her thin white face all lit up laughing. Of course I felt strongly about her, she was my friend. She was very important to me, I didn't need to act with Alice. I resented the way the awful man with his alcoholic wife treated her, but was never jealous of him because Alice didn't really give her mind to him. And as for giving anything else... well I suppose they made a lot of love together but so did I and the unsatisfactory journalist. I didn't want Alice in that way. I mean that was madness, we wouldn't even know what to do. We would laugh ourselves silly.

Kiss Alice?

Run and lay my head on Alice's breast?

Have Alice stroke my hair?

That's what people who were in love did. We didn't do that.

Did Alice need me? Yes, of course she did. She often told me that I was the only bit of sanity in her life, that I was safe. I had known her for ten years, hardly anyone else she knew nowadays went back that far.

Malcolm filled my coffee cup.

'Do persuade her to come with us,' he said gently to me. 'She's marvellous really, and I know you'd both enjoy yourselves.'

I looked at him like a wild animal. I saw us fitting into their lives, another splendid liberal concept, slightly racy, perfectly acceptable. 'We went on holiday with that super gay couple, most marvellous company, terribly entertaining.' Which of us would he refer to as the He? Would there be awful things like leaving us alone together, or nodding tolerantly over our little rows?

The evening and not only the evening stretched ahead in horror. Alice had been laying into the wine, would she be able to drive? If not, oh God, would they offer us a double bed in some spare room in this mansion? Would they suggest a taxi home to Fulham since my place was nearer? Would they speculate afterwards why we kept two separate establishments in the first place?

Worse, would I ever be able to laugh with Alice about it or was it too important? I might disgust her, alarm her, turn her against me. I might unleash all kinds of love that she had for me deep down, and how would I handle that?

Of course I loved Alice, I just didn't realize it. But what lover, what poor unfortunate lover in the history of the whole damn thing, ever had the tragedy of Coming Out in Malcolm and Melissa's lovely home in Holland Park?

SCAPHISM

Blindboy Boatclub

Blindboy Boatclub is a comedian, musician, satirist, writer, activist, podcaster and one half of the Rubberbandits. His debut collection of stories, *The Gospel According to Blindboy* (2017), was a bestseller and a second collection, *Boulevard Wren* appeared in 2019. His weekly podcast reaches over 1,000,000 listeners monthly. The pilot of his forthcoming BBC docu-comedy series was longlisted for a BAFTA.

The way the bottom of his jeans used to soak up the piss from the floor of the jax would bring on that metallic taste on my tongue that I get before an epileptic fit. Every fucking Thursday after darts. He'd have those navy denims that you get in Guiney's, with all the unnecessary stitching around the thighs and the arse. They made him look like a giant toddler with a dirty nappy. Every Thursday, lads. Fat Macca and Ernie Collopy would be going head to head in a vicious tourney of darts. It was always the two of them in the final. Ernie would have went professional if it wasn't for women and liquor. Fine men.

Without fail though, this other fucking eejit would be over for his first drop of Harp. He'd drink it in this servile way, where we could all see his teeth through the pint glass. He'd drink his pint like the pint was telling him to drink it rather than him telling the pint to get drank. Then off to the jax he'd go, and come back out with an inch of piss on the boot-cut cuffs of his Guiney's jeans. I couldn't go near my porter, because I'd be transfixed by the cuffs of his pants. I'd watch a centimetre of cold piss on denim creep up and darken his trousers. Capillary action: the ability of a liquid to flow in narrow spaces without the assistance of, or even in opposition to, external forces like gravity. I'd stare at that exact definition on the screen of my Samsung, to try and achieve a sense of control over the situation.

By 10.15 p.m., he'd be on Harp number two, and a pack of scampi fries would be ordered. 10.25 p.m. and he was back into the jax for his second piss. Two inches of dark wet navy up his leg at this point, lads. Other people's piss, he's wearing the feculence of every man in this pub up his fucking leg. Get different trousers, man ta fuck. The heel of his black leather Gola tackie would sometimes trap the bottom cuff of the pants leg, so he'd be standing on the end of his own pants. It would squelch, there'd be grains of sand on the soggy denim, from fucking where? No sand in the jax of this pub.

By 11.20 p.m., the third piss would be had. He'd be half-cut, leaning against the bar, belly hanging out of the cardigan. And the piss, boys, the piss would be six inches up his shin. Capillary action, sucking up piss, contradicting Newtonian physics. He never even noticed, and that's what would hurt the most, he didn't even know what was happening to his own leg. Art Naughton and Julie Slattery would notice, coz I'd see them staring, but they'd just fall back into their sherries. I'd try to catch their eyes, maybe get some backup, sort this out. A mutiny. But no. Cowards.

At 11.45 p.m. or thereabouts, the piss would be threatening his upper shin. That's when the taste of metal would arrive in my mouth, like I'd licked a nine-volt battery, followed by a burnt almond sensation and finally bad eggs. When the room would lose its place in time and shapes no longer made sense, that's how I knew I was having the epileptic fit. I'd come around after, and Packie Willie the barman would have tonic water and ice for me with a slice of lemon in it. All that citrus and effervescent quinine would see me right and bring me back. Every Thursday, lads, swear to fuck, every Thursday.

No one took notice anymore. No one knew why I'd droop into a fit, no one talked to me about it. No one knew it was because of that stupid bollocks and the capillary action of the piss on his floppy Guiney's denim. At 12.10 a.m., she'd come in off the night shift, Anne, and stroll over to him. He'd have the Grand Marnier and sparkling water waiting for her at the bar-top, and she'd lean in and fucking kiss him, and the leg of her Garda uniform would rub off the shin of his capillary-action piss-pants. Every Thursday.

When Anne came in, it meant the doors got locked and Art Naughton and Julie Slattery could take out their pack of Major and smoke indoors like it was 1985. Packie Willie would turn on the Sanyo behind the counter with the six-changer disc tray. Deacon Blue, Jimmy Nail, Showaddywaddy, Prefab Sprout, Thomas Dolby, The Style Council, The Communards, Wham, Kajagoogoo, the solo efforts of Lamar from Kajagoogoo. He'd start dancing with his elbows, and the belly over the belt, and the top of his arse on show, squelching piss-britches on the wood floor that had eight generations of varnish and was black. She'd dance alongside him, with one of Julie Slattery's Majors sticking out of her mouth, clapping her hands like Daryl Hall, looking at him into the eyes. Acting like myself and herself hadn't been married for eighteen years.

I'd sit up, looking at the screen of my Samsung. The battery would go at three, so I'd read the back of a packet of King crisps. At around 5.30 a.m., we'd all clear out. Barney Shanahan would collect them in the taxi, and I'd walk home. Every Thursday, lads. In the winters, I'd walk home in the pitch black, not a hint of light. I'd click my tongue like a bat, that way I'd hear a lamp-post if it was near. The sound would bounce back at me. When it's November dark, the slip on the ground underneath, you've to dance with it or it'll crack you open. The cold has such bitter presence that you can feel your way through it, it has rises and lumps. You can sense the lukewarmth of a hedge, the trail that a panting fox leaves, a little band of clammy air that you can grab like a rope and use it to drag your way up a bóithrín. In the summer, it'd be bright, I hated that, there's too much pomp and show to summer mornings. When it's winter and dark, you can get properly acquainted with your journey. You get its honesty, you get to know its fears, its intentions. There's areas of the Limerick countryside that can't be trusted purely on grounds of personal integrity. These are where people fall into ditches, or drown in bogs. The area charms that person into their death, it's never accidental. I've walked them all with no eyes.

I'd arrive back to the cottage at around eight in the morning. No keys, I'd leave the hall door wide open to confuse the tinkers. That's when I'd be able to relax and have the first drink. I'd be away from the pressures of the pub and the piss-britches. I keep the bottles of Tyskie on the window where they'd be cold. This particular Friday morning, I couldn't find the opener. I scanned my belongings to see which one I was willing to risk breaking to open the cap off. Not my Samsung, not the remote, not my lighter, fuck it, it's my only one, not Anne's hair straightener that she never collected. So I ripped the curtain-pole off the wall. Seven foot long, some fulcrum on it. I jammed the bottle of Tyskie in between two cushions on the couch with a heavy encyclopaedia holding it in place, and opened it with the curtain-pole from the other side of the room. Popped off in two seconds, lads, what did I say? Fucking fulcrum. I haven't got a master's in physics for nothing.

I had a fine lump of smelly sock hash that I got off the Costellos from Pallasgreen. Hums like black pudding when you burn it into the Rizla. I continued with the Tyskies until *Judge Judy* came on the television. She was talking to young ones who couldn't stop spending money and getting into debt. I'd been meaning to ring Anne's piss-trouser boyfriend for the best part of two years. I'd been meaning to tell him that I hoped himself and Anne would have good fortune in all their future endeavours. The Samsung was charged, and something about this particular episode of *Judge Judy* gave me the courage to ring his number, so I fucking did, lads.

The phone was ringing, he answered, he was talking to me. I was going to tell him about the epilepsy, tell him how silly it was that I'd be getting fits over his piss-pants, and how I'd get so upset when himself and Anne kissed while dancing to the solo efforts of Lamar from Kajagoogoo. We'd all laugh about it. Maybe I'd call over for dinner some night. Fuck it, maybe I'd dance with the two of 'em next Thursday. I'd smoke Julie Slattery's Majors too, and clap like Daryl Hall with Anne and high-five himself. We'd all head back to their gaff in Barney Shanahan's taxi, drink Grand Marnier, have a devil's threesome, why not? Breakfast, dinner and toast.

But I didn't. I told him that I'd developed stage three cancer of my oesophagus and needed to clear the air. I asked him to meet me by the river in Plassey where we could fish for perch together. In fairness to him, he had no qualms about this and felt fierce sorry for me. I don't have stage three cancer in my oesophagus at all though, lads. I left the house with an open Tyskie in either fist. I'd no fishing rod, so when I made it as far as Castleconnell, I dropped into the Spar for a ball of twine, a naggin of Huzzar for the rest of the journey, a litre of milk and a squeezy bottle of honey shaped like a gay bee. At Castletroy, I found a branch of oak and inserted the twine onto the end of it. Threw it over my shoulder. At the University of Limerick, I asked a girl to give me one of her earrings. She lashed it straight over, not a bother, fair play to her. I put that on the end of the twine like a hook. I had the bones of a fishing rod on me, lads.

When I got to the bank of the Plassey River, he was there. Daycent enough rod he had too, got it in Aldi the last time they had a fishing sale, not that bad at all. Big welcoming smile on him, as I got closer, he doled out his fat hand in friendship. When I could smell his breath, I wrapped the twine around his neck and didn't stop pulling until his eyes closed. He lay flat on the sandy Plassey riverbank, sleepy boy. Gorgeous evening. There's a pond a small bit upriver, with stagnant water, near a little island, very quiet. I carried him up into my arms, pure cradling like, and went there. I tore the fucking ridiculous Guiney jeans off him, first port of call, and lobbed them in the river where they'd never give me another fit again. I found three old logs, hollow boys, great for floating. One under his back, tied his fat belly to that, one above his head with hands bound, and same with the feet. Getting great mileage out of the Castleconnell twine. Gas-looking cunt, balls naked, tied up to the logs, like a bachelor at his stag do in Liverpool. Some craic.

He woke up when I was rubbing the picnic honey all over his balls and arse. Roaring and shouting he was, so I started pouring the honey down his throat, we wouldn't get disturbed that way. Flaked a litre of milk over him too. This is the best bit though, lads. I gently floated him out into the middle of the pond. Logs doing their job at buoyancy, feeling proud of myself. Very still water, so it was nice and calm. There he was, drifting out, not one move on him. Eyes up to the sky. Mad bastard. It was midday, so the horseflies were having a great time with the honey all over his goolies.

Now, I know what ye're thinking. What class of sick bastard comes up with this type of stuff? Who'd do this to their ex-wife's new lad? But they've been doing this for years, especially to adulterers. It's called scaphism. Perfectly legitimate method of execution. Look it up on yer Samsungs. The Persians invented it. The flies will bite as he floats on the pond. The longer he floats, the more he'll shit and piss. This will bring more flies. Give it a day, and they'll lay their eggs. The maggots will hatch, and he'll still be alive, floating gently on his back. All tied up. The underside of him will get nice and putty-like in the water, and fat pike will take schkelps out of his calves, trying to eat the worms. Maggots eating into him too, only the soft wet bits though, like the mouth, the dick, the eyes, the nose, the ears, the arse. The maggots will accumulate so much that they'll cut off blood flow, causing early gangrene to set in.

Don't blame me, lads – blame the ancient Persians for inventing the slowest and cruellest method of death known to humanity. You'd think methods like that get lost in the flow of time, forgotten in barbarism. But they don't, because time doesn't flow, it creeps capilliarily up the universe's leg, ignorant of Newton's laws, slow and unnoticed by the weak, bringing the dark stain of retribution with it. I gaze up at the heavens, and they gaze back, in boot-cut jeans and black leather shoes.

ANN LEE'S

Elizabeth Bowen

Elizabeth Bowen (1899–1973) was the author of eleven novels and multiple short story collections, including *The Demon Lover and Other Stories* and *Ivy Gripped the Steps and Other Stories*. Her work was frequently concerned with Anglo-Irishness, wartime life and post-war London, and she wrote many acclaimed ghost stories. Bowen also published several works of non-fiction.

Ann Lee's occupied a single frontage in one of the dimmer and more silent streets of south-west London. Grey-painted woodwork framed a window over which her legend was inscribed in far-apart black letters: 'ANN LEE – HATS.' In the window there were always just two hats; one on a stand, one lying on a cushion; and a black curtain with a violet border hung behind to make a background for the hats. In the two upper storeys, perhaps, Ann Lee lived mysteriously, but this no known customer had ever inquired, and the black gauze curtains were impenetrable from without.

Mrs Dick Logan and her friend Miss Ames approached the shop-front. Miss Ames had been here once before two years ago; the hat still existed and was frequently admired by her friends. It was she who was bringing Mrs Dick Logan; she hesitated beneath the names at the street corner, wrinkled up her brows, and said she hadn't remembered that Ann Lee's was so far from Sloane Square Station. They were young women with faces of a similar pinkness; they used the same swear-words and knew the same men. Mrs Dick Logan had decided to give up Clarice; her husband made such a ridiculous fuss about the bills and she had come to the conclusion, really, that considering what she had to put up with every quarterday she might have something more to show for it in the way of hats. Miss Ames, who never dealt there, agreed that Clarice *was* expensive: now there was that shop she had been to once, Ann Lee's, not far from Sloane Street—

'Expensive?' Mrs Dick said warily.

'Oh well, not cheap. But most emphatically worth it. You know, I got that green there—'

'O-oh,' cried Mrs Dick Logan, 'that *expressive* green!'

So they went to find Ann Lee.

It was an afternoon in January, and their first sensation was of pleasure as they pushed open the curtained door and felt the warm air of the shop vibrate against their faces. An electric fire was reflected in a crimson patch upon the lustrous pile of the black carpet. There were two chairs, two mirrors, a divan and a curtain over an expectant archway. No hats were visible.

'Nice interior!' whispered Mrs Logan.

'Very much *her*,' returned Miss Ames. They loosened their furs luxuriously, and each one flashed sidelong at herself in a mirror an appraising glance. They had a sense of having been sent round on approval, and this deepened in the breast of Mrs Logan as their waiting in the empty shop was prolonged by minute after minute. Clarice came rushing at one rather: Mrs Logan was predisposed to like Ann Lee for her discreet indifference to custom. Letty Ames had said that she was practically a lady; a queer creature, Letty couldn't place her.

'I wonder if she realizes we're here,' whispered Letty, her brows again faintly wrinkled by proprietory concern. 'We might just cough – not an angry cough, quite natural. You'd better, Lulu, 'cause you've got one.'

Mrs Logan really had a slight catarrh, and the sound came out explosively. They heard a door softly open and shut, and the sound of feet descending two or three carpeted steps. There was another silence, then close behind the curtain one cardboard box was placed upon another, and there was a long, soft, continuous rustling of tissue paper. One might almost have believed Ann Lee to be emerging from a bandbox. Then the curtain twitched, quivered, and swung sideways, and some one gravely regarded them a moment from the archway. 'Good afternoon,' she said serenely, and 'Good afternoon.'

Her finger brushed a switch, and the shop became discreetly brilliant with long shafts of well-directed light.

'I've come back again,' Miss Ames brought out a shade dramatically, and Ann Lee nodded. 'Yes, so I see. I'm glad, Miss Ames. I had expected you.' She smiled, and Mrs Dick Logan felt chilly with exclusion. 'And I've brought my friend, Mrs Dick Logan.'

Ann Lee, with delicately arched-up eyebrows, turned to smile.

She was slight and very tall, and the complete sufficiency of her unnotice-able dress made Mrs Dick Logan feel gaudy. Her hands were long and fine, her outspread fingers shone against her dress – on a right-hand, non-committal finger she wore one slender ring. Her face was a serene one, the lips a shade austere, and her hair was closely swathed about her head in bright, sleek bands. There was something of the priestess about her, and she suffered their intrusion with a ceremonial grace. She was so unlike Clarice and all those other women, that Mrs Logan hardly knew how to begin, and was gratified, though half-conscious of a solecism, when Miss Ames said, 'My friend would like so much to see some hats. She's rather wanting two or three hats.'

Ann Lee's eyes dwelt dispassionately on Mrs Logan's face. She looked questioningly at the eyebrows and searchingly at the mouth, then said with an assumption that barely deferred to her customer, 'Something quiet?'

Something quiet was the last thing Mrs Logan wanted. She wanted something nice and bright to wear at Cannes, but she hardly liked to say so. She put forward timidly, 'Well, not *too* quiet – it's for the Riviera.'

'Really?' said Ann Lee regretfully – 'how delightful for you to be going out. I don't know whether I have – no, wait; perhaps I have some little model.'

'I rather thought a turban – gold, perhaps?'

'Oh, a *turban*—? But surely you would be more likely to find what you want out there? Surely Cannes—'

This made Mrs Logan feel peevish. Even if a person did look like a Madonna or something, it was their business to sell a hat if they kept a shop for that purpose. She hadn't followed Letty quite endlessly through those miserable back streets to be sent away disdainfully and told to buy her hats in France. She didn't care for shopping on the Riviera, except with her Casino winnings; the shops expected to be paid so soon, and Dickie made an even worse fuss when he saw a bill in francs. She said querulously:

'Yes, but haven't you got anything of that sort? Any goldish, sort of turbany thing?'

'I never have many hats,' said Ann Lee. 'I will show you anything I have.'

Lulu glanced across at Letty, breathing more deeply with relief at this concession, and Letty whispered, as Ann Lee vanished momentarily behind the curtain: 'Oh, she's always like that; like what I told you, queer. But the *hats*, my dear! You wait!'

When Ann Lee returned again carrying two hats, Mrs Logan admitted that there had indeed been something to wait for. These were the hats one dreamed about – no, even in a dream one had never directly beheld them; they glimmered rather on the margin of one's dreams. With trembling hands she reached out in Ann Lee's direction to receive them. Ann Lee smiled deprecatingly upon her and them, then went away to fetch some more.

Lulu Logan snatched off the hat she was wearing and let it slide unnoticed from the brocaded seat of the chair where she had flung it and bowl away across the floor. Letty snatched off hers too, out of sympathy, and, each one occupying a mirror, they tried on every single hat Ann Lee brought them; passing each one reverently and regretfully across to one another, as though they had been crowns. It was very solemn. Ann Lee stood against the curtain of the archway, looking at them gently and pitifully with her long pale eyes. Her hands hung down by her sides; she was not the sort of person who needs to finger the folds of a curtain, touch the back of a chair, or play with a necklace. If Mrs Logan and her friend Miss Ames had had either eyes, minds, or taste for the comparison, they might have said that she seemed to grow from the floor like a lily. Their faces flushed; soon they were flaming in the insidious warmth of the shop. 'Oh, *damn* my face!' groaned Miss Ames into the mirror, pressing her hands to her cheeks, looking out at herself crimsonly from beneath the trembling shadow of an osprey.

How could Lulu ever have imagined herself in a gold turban? In a gold turban, when there were hats like these? But she had never known that there were hats like these, though she had tried on hats in practically every shop in London that she considered fit to call a shop. Life was still to prove itself a thing of revelations, even for Mrs Dick Logan. In a trembling voice she said that she would certainly have *this* one, and she thought she simply must have *this*, and 'Give me back the blue one, darling!' she called across to Letty.

Then a sword of cold air stabbed into the shop, and Lulu and Letty jumped, exclaimed and shivered. The outer door was open and a man was standing on the threshold, blatant in the light against the foggy dusk behind him. Above the suave folds of his dazzling scarf his face was stung to scarlet by the cold; he stood there timid and aggressive; abject in his impulse to retreat, blustering in his determination to resist it. The two ladies stood at gaze in the classic pose of indignation of discovered nymphs. Then they both turned to Ann Lee, with a sense that something had been outraged that went deeper than chastity. The man was not a husband; he belonged to neither of them.

The intruder also looked towards Ann Lee; he dodged his head upwards and sideways in an effort to direct his line of vision past them. He opened his mouth as though he were going to shout; then they almost started at the small thin voice that crept from it to say 'Good evening.'

Ann Lee was balancing a toque upon the tips of her fingers, an imponderable thing of citron feathers, which even those light fingers hardly dared to touch. Not a feather quivered and not a shadow darkened her oval face as she replied, 'Good evening,' in a voice as equably unsmiling as her lips and eyes.

'I'm afraid I've come at a bad moment.'

'Yes,' she said serenely, 'I'm afraid you have. It's quite impossible for me to see you now; I'm sorry – I believe that hat is *you*, Mrs Logan. I'm sorry you don't care for black.'

'Oh, I do like black,' said Mrs Logan unhappily, feasting upon her own reflection. 'But I've got so many. Of course, they do set the face off, but I particularly wanted something rather sunny looking – now that little blue's perfect. How much did you…?'

'Eight guineas,' said Ann Lee, looking at her dreamily.

Mrs Logan shivered and glanced vindictively towards the door. Ann Lee was bending to place the toque of citron feathers on the divan; she said mildly over her shoulder, with one slight upward movement of her lashes, 'We are a little cold in here, if you don't mind.'

'Sorry!' the man said, looking wildly into the shop. Then he came right in with one enormous step and pulled the door shut behind him. 'I'll wait then, if I may.' He looked too large, with his angular blue cloth overcoat double-buttoned across the chest, and as he stuffed his soft grey hat almost furtively under his arm they saw at once that there was something wrong about his hair. One supposed he couldn't help it waving like that, but he might have worn it shorter. The shoes on his big feet were very bright. Fancy a man like that... Lulu allowed a note of injury to creep into her voice as she said, 'I beg your pardon,' and reached past him to receive another hat from Letty. The shop was quite crowded, all of a sudden. And really, walking in like that... He didn't know what they mightn't have been trying on; so few shops nowadays were hats exclusively. He didn't see either herself or Letty; except as things to dodge his eyes past – obstacles. The way he was looking at Ann Lee was disgusting. A woman who asked eight guineas for a little simple hat like that blue one had got no right to expose her customers to this.

Letty, her hair all grotesquely ruffled up with trying-on, stood with a hat in either hand, her mouth half open, looking at the man not quite intelligently. One might almost have believed that she had met him. As a matter of fact, she was recognizing him; not as his particular self but as an Incident. He – It – crops up periodically in the path of any young woman who has had a bit of a career, but Ann Lee – really. Letty was vague in her ideas of Vestal Virgins, but dimly she connected them with Ann. Well, you never knew... Meanwhile this was a hat shop; the least fitting place on earth for the recurrence of an Incident. Perhaps it was the very priestliness of Ann which made them feel that there was something here to desecrate.

Ann Lee, holding the blue hat up before the eyes of Lulu, was the only one who did not see and tremble as the square man crossed the shop towards the fireplace and sat down on the divan beside the feather toque. He was very large. He drew his feet in with an obvious consciousness of offence and wrapped the skirts of his overcoat as uncontaminatingly as possible about his knees. His gaze crept about the figure of Ann. 'I'll wait, if you don't mind,' he repeated.

'I'm afraid it's no good,' she said abstractedly, looking past him at the toque. 'I'm busy at present, as you can see, and afterwards I've orders to attend to. I'm sorry. Hadn't you better—?'

'It's four o'clock,' he said.

'*Four o'clock!*' shrieked Lulu. 'Good God, I'm due at the Cottinghams!'

'Oh, don't go!' wailed Letty, whose afternoon was collapsing. Ann Lee, smiling impartially, said she did think it was a pity not to decide.

'Yes, but eight guineas.' It needed a certain time for decision.

'It's a lovely little hat,' pleaded Letty, stroking the brim reverently.

'Yes, it's pretty,' conceded Ann Lee, looking down under her lids at it with the faintest softening of the lips. They all drew together, bound by something tense: the man before the fire was forgotten.

'Oh, I don't know,' wailed the distracted Mrs Logan. 'I must have that little black one, and I ought to get another dinner-hat – You know how one needs them out there!' she demanded of Miss Ames reproachfully. They both looked appealingly at Ann Lee. She was not the sort of person, somehow, that one could ask to reduce her things. There was a silence.

'It is four o'clock!' said the man in a bullying, nervous voice. They jumped. 'You did say four o'clock,' he repeated.

Ann Lee quite frightened the two others; she was so very gentle with him, and so scornfully unemphatic. 'I'm afraid you are making a mistake. On Thursdays I am always busy. Good evening, Mr Richardson; don't let us waste any more of your time. Now, Mrs Logan, shall we say the blue? I feel that you would enjoy it, though I still think the black is a degree more you. But I daresay you would not care to take both.'

'I'll wait,' he said, in a queer voice. Unbuttoning his overcoat, he flung it open with a big, defiant gesture as he leaned towards the fire. 'Oh, the toque!' they screamed; and Ann Lee darted down and forwards with a flashing movement to retrieve the frail thing from beneath the iron folds of the overcoat. She carried it away again on the tips of her fingers, peering down into the ruffled feathers; less now of the priestess than of the mother – Niobe, Rachel. She turned from the archway to say in a white voice, her face terrible with gentleness, 'Then will you kindly wait outside?'

'It's cold,' he pleaded, stretching out his hands to the fire. It was a gesture: he did not seem to feel the warmth.

'Then wouldn't it be better not to wait?' Ann Lee softly suggested.

'I'll wait today,' he said, with bewildered and unshaken resolution. 'I'm not going away today.'

While she was away behind the curtain, rustling softly in that world of tissue paper, the man turned from the fire to look round at the contents of the shop. He looked about him with a kind of cringing triumph, as one who has entered desecratingly into some Holiest of Holies and is immediately to pay the penalty, might look about him under the very downsweep of the sacerdotal blade. He noted without comment or emotion the chairs, the lustrous carpet, Mrs Logan's hat, the ladies, and the mirrors opposite one another, which quadrupled the figure of each lady. One could only conclude that he considered Miss Ames and Mrs Logan as part of the fittings of the shop – 'customers' such as every shop kept two of among the mirrors and the chairs;

disposed appropriately; symbolic, like the two dolls perpetually recumbent upon the drawing-room sofa of a doll's house. He stared thoughtfully at Miss Ames, not as she had ever before been stared at, but as though wondering why Ann Lee should have chosen to invest her shop with a customer of just *that* pattern. Miss Ames seemed for him to be the key to something; he puzzled up at her with knitted brows.

'Perhaps it would be better for us to be going?' said Miss Ames to Mrs Logan, her words making an icy transition above the top of his head. 'I'm afraid it's difficult for you to decide on anything with the place crowded and rather a lot of talking.'

Mrs Logan stood turning the blue hat round and round in her hands, looking down at it with tranced and avid eyes. 'Eight – sixteen – twenty-four,' she murmured. 'I do think she might reduce that little toque. If she'd let me have the three for twenty-two guineas.'

'Not she,' said Letty with conviction.

The man suddenly conceded their humanity. 'I suppose these are what you'd call expensive hats?' he said, looking up at Mrs Logan.

'Very,' said she.

'Several hundreds, I daresay, wouldn't buy up the contents of the shop, as it stands at present?'

'I suppose not,' agreed Mrs Logan, deeply bored – 'Letty, when *is* she coming back? Does she always walk out of the shop like this? Because *I* call it... I shall be so late at the Cottinghams, too. I'd be off this minute, but I just can't leave this little blue one. Where'll we get a taxi?'

'First corner,' said the man, rearing up his head eagerly. 'Round on your left.'

'Oh, thanks,' they said frigidly. He was encouraged by this to ask if they, too, didn't think it was very cold. Not, in fact, the sort of weather to turn a dog out. 'I'm sorry if I've inconvenienced you any way by coming in, but I've an appointment fixed with with Miss Lee for four o'clock, specially fixed, and you can imagine it was cold out there, waiting—' The rustling of the paper ceased; they thought the curtain twitched. He turned and almost ate the archway with his awful eyes. Nothing happened; the sleek heavy folds still hung down unshaken to the carpet. 'I've an appointment,' he repeated, and listened to the echo with satisfaction and a growing confidence. 'But I don't mind waiting – I've done so much waiting.' 'Really?' said Miss Ames, in the high voice of indifference. Determined that she must buy nothing, she was putting her own hat on again resignedly. 'She's bound to be back in a jiff,' she threw across reassuringly to Lulu, who sat bareheaded by a mirror, statuesquely meditative, her eyes small with the effort of calculation.

'I don't suppose either of you ladies,' said the man tremendously, 'have spent so much time in your whole lives trying on clothes in shops of this kind, as I've spent outside just this one shop, waiting. If any more ladies come in, they'll just have to take me naturally, for I'm going to sit on here where I am till closing time.'

Miss Ames, fluffing her side hair out in front of the mirror, repeated 'Really?' bland as a fish.

'I'm quite within my rights here,' said he, looking down now with approval at his feet so deeply implanted in the carpet, 'because you see, I've got an appointment.'

'There was no appointment, Mr Richardson,' said Ann Lee regretfully, standing in the archway.

Mrs Dick Logan, catching her breath, rose to her feet slowly, and said that she would have all three hats, and would Ann Lee send them along at once, please. It was an immense moment, and Miss Ames, who knew Dickie, thought as she heard Mrs Logan give her name and address in a clear unfaltering voice that there *was* something splendid about Lulu. The way she went through it, quarter-day after quarter-day... Miss Ames glowed for their common femininity as she watched her friend pick up yet another hat and try it on, exactly as if she could have had it too, if she had wished, and then another and another. Ann Lee, writing languidly in an order-book, bowed without comment to Mrs Logan's decision. And Letty Ames couldn't help feeling also that if Ann Lee had wished, Lulu would have had that other hat, and then another and another.

Mrs Logan stooped to recover her own hat from the floor. Ann Lee, looking down solicitously, but making no movement to assist her, meditated aloud that she was glad Mrs Logan was taking that little black. It was so much *her*, to have left it behind would have been a pity, Ann Lee couldn't help thinking.

As they gathered their furs about them, drew on their gloves, snapped their bags shut, and nestled down their chins into their furs, the two ladies glanced as though into an arena at the man sitting on the divan, who now leaned forwards to the fire again, his squared back towards them. And now? They longed suddenly, ah, how they longed, to linger in that shop.

'Good afternoon,' said Ann Lee. She said it with finality.

'Good afternoon,' they said, still arrested a second in the doorway. As they went out into the street reluctantly they saw Ann Lee, after a last dim bow towards them, pass back through the archway so gently that she scarcely stirred the curtains. The man beside the fire shot to his feet, crossed the shop darkly, and went through after her, his back broad with resolution.

There were no taxis where they had been promised to find them, and the two walked on in the direction of Sloane Street through the thickening fog. Mrs

Dick Logan said that she didn't think she dared show her face at the Cotting-hams now, but that really those hats were worth it. She walked fast and talked faster, and Miss Ames knew that she was determined not to think of Dickie.

When they came to the third corner they once more hesitated, and again lamented the non-appearance of a taxi. Down as much of the two streets as was visible, small shop-windows threw out squares of light on to the fog. Was there, behind all these windows, some one waiting, as indifferent as a magnet, for one to come in? 'What an extraordinary place it was,' said Mrs Logan for the third time, retrospectively. 'How she ever sells her things…'

'But she does sell them.'

'Yes.' She did sell them, Mrs Logan knew.

As they stood on the kerbstone, recoiling not without complaints from the unkindness of the weather, they heard rapid steps approaching them, metallic on the pavement, in little uneven spurts of speed. Somebody, half blinded by the fog, in flight from somebody else. They said nothing to each other, but held their breaths, mute with a common expectancy.

A square man, sunk deep into an overcoat, scudded across their patch of visibility. By putting out a hand they could have touched him. He went by them blindly; his breath sobbed and panted. It was by his breath that they knew how terrible it had been – terrible.

Passing them quite blindly, he stabbed his way on into the fog.

CONCERNING VIRGINS

Clare Boylan

Clare Boylan (1948–2006) worked as a journalist and author until her death at 58. She published three short story collections – *Nail on the Head*, *That Bad Woman* and *Concerning Virgins* – and eight novels, including *Holy Pictures* (1983), *Last Resorts* (1984), *Black Baby* (1988) and *Home Rule* (1992).

These things no longer matter because the house is gone and the people are dead but ghosts only settle when they have got over their surprise and history shows that concerns last longer than matter.

An old man, Narcissus Fitzgall, lived with his two daughters in a house called Herons' Peep on the edge of the water in County Wicklow. It had been built on a hill above the river but appeared, from the inside, to be suspended in water. Water dappled its ceilings with luminous shadow and moved in spotted motion behind the curtains. It gushed darkly underneath the bedroom windows and vanished in a silver trail miles away, between lacy wands of ash. Where the river ended the sea began. There was a stretch of marsh fed by seawater and wild birds nested in giant reeds. Beyond this was a little shingle beach on which to stand in the wind and listen to the soft crumple of the waves and a tempting chatter like glass-beaded curtains as the tide dragged its dead water back across the stones.

The house and its steeds and its birds and its reeds seemed made for pleasure but Narcissus Fitzgall was not a happy man. 'I need a wife,' he sighed. 'God grant me a wife. Sweet suffering souls!' – he damaged his gouty foot upon the martyred rump of a favourite hound – 'it ain't as if I want a cook or a beauty – only a wife.'

He did not need a wife to care for him. His two daughters, Blanche and Grace, served the old man with silent loyalty. They were aged somewhere between thirty and forty and looked as if they had been washed too frequently – and he detested them.

Although he insisted absolutely on purity in women his personal preference was for a woman you could whack on the behind, whose breasts grew lax in their moorings after champagne and claret. As he grew older his days were poisoned by the constant filial presence. They had developed a preserved look as they began to dry out as if they would live, rustling and dispirited, for ever.

He did not need a wife to soothe his passions. Fancy these days was an irksome intruder whose name he sometimes could not remember. When the need arose, a young scullery maid made less of a compliment and could be dismissed if she grew argumentative. He needed a wife to give him a son. Time was running out. His body had grown unreliable. It had lost interest in his will and seemed embarked on an excavation for its own skeleton, neglecting to send blood to his extremities or to digest the fat of game or the esters of old alcohol. Unless he could soon put a squalling heir to the breast of a woman who bore his name, he must go to his grave in the horrible knowledge that Herons' Peep would fall to the busy, timorous fingers of his daughters.

For all its beauty, Herons' Peep was not a feminine estate. It was a man's house. Unlike most Irish houses, which look stern on the outside and graceful within, it showed all its gentleness in its face. Inside it was handsome but harsh. The uncovered floors answered the stamp of boots. Grates were vast marble maws where whole trees were splintered and consumed. The sofas had been built big enough for a horse or a hound to sleep on, and they did if they liked. Plumbing, when it came, was a series of thunderous geysers and gullets that caused many a superstitious maid to leap from her seat believing she would be sucked down to the very floor of the ocean below. There were no flowers, no little lamps nor Venice glass. Gilt-framed shepherdesses and darling little painted dogs did not sentimentalize the walls. The kitchen was the very pit of hell, enlivened only by a bright patter of gore from the dripping corpses of the day's sporting slaughter. The river alone was allowed to indulge in female whim, making her music softly on the ceilings – a solitary clemency for many a stolen maid.

In the early days visitors were shocked by the severity of the house and put it down to the lack of a woman's touch. The little girls heard the whispers and assumed this responsibility. As soon as they were able, they hoarded lengths of fabric in their room, begged from neighbours or bought in parish sales, and sewed up assortments of curtains.

Their father locked them in the nursery and fed them boiled rabbit for a week. When they were released, thin and faintly green, they had turned an old velvet ballgown into a set of frilly cushions for a sofa. In spite of Fitzgall's fury they persisted for it seemed as vital to them as salvation to leave the mark of their gender. As little girls deafened by paternal wrath they would hide and cry for their mother. Now when he raged at them they lay down on their beds or stole his spirits and returned gaunter and more enduring. Their nervous fingers never ceased in dainty toil. Although the old man used their finest work to blow his nose or rub down his dogs, the house was sinking under a creeping infection of embroidered samplers.

One day when he was seventy-five he decided that since God would not trouble to send him a spouse, he must get one for himself. He had exhausted his store of charm, influence and menace with all the women in the county, so he resorted to a wise old woman who lived in the local village of Rathwillow and who did a bit of hairdressing in her spare time.

'I need a wife,' he told her.

'What sort of a wife?' She studied him most acutely, as if measuring him up for a suit or a coffin.

'A drudge, a bag, a bat, a hag – any wife so long as she has in her the makings of a boy.'

She kept looking at him, making no comment but holding his eye as if awaiting some response from himself. At length she turned away and observed: 'I knew a man wanted a ferret an' he put a notice in a periodical.' For this, he had to give her a guinea.

All the same, he did advertise for a wife, withholding his name and that of his estate, for he was not a popular man – merely describing himself as handsome, unfettered and rich and offering a box number for reply. After that he had only to add his small requirement in the woman who would fulfil him.

He had been married once to a very beautiful girl called Alice Clements. She was demure and pure as a swan. He went to great efforts to lay claim to her, thundering about the countryside on hunters, shooting pheasants and peasants, spending most of his money on Herons' Peep so that his brothers were left with bare tracts of land to build on. He took her to Paris for her honeymoon and gave her all her heart's desire, and she had treated him abominably. She gave birth to two daughters and showed no repentance. When the younger of the girls was only two she jumped into the river, leaving him in his prime with a house of motherless daughters – and no son.

He sought another wife as soon as possible. He had exhausted his store of sentiment on Alice and formulated more economical styles of wooing.

Sometimes he simply canvassed the parents of an intended with his financial statements. Oddly, the response was poor. He lowered his sights to the landless gentry but even their luckless female tribes resisted him. He offered his fortune to poor, pure peasant girls but they fled into convents or painted their faces with the scars of smallpox. He could not understand it. He was a man of substance; handsome – the blood a bit too close to the skin and the brow too beetling, but a good feast for a hungry virgin.

At first he wondered if he had transgressed the narrow boundaries of county form by resuming courtship a month after his bereavement but a crueller truth emerged. His wife's ghost spoke against him. It was said he had driven her to her death. Her pallid spirit came back dripping from the deep and called him callous – he, who had lavished his fortune upon her and expended his best energies in bringing her to bliss.

When he married chaste Alice, he meant her to become his amorous master-work, his private whore. Naturally she had repulsed the passionate sieges of his courtship. He could not have married her otherwise. He perceived all virtuous wives as irresistible hypocrites who enjoyed the joke of public modesty and twinkled for their husbands like the stars by night. He introduced his bride to his symphony of connubial themes, inspired by the most expensive houses of London and in the arms of plump, intuitive girls of fifteen, and she gazed at the water-patterned ceiling. Her lips, obediently fastened to where he directed them, moved ticklishly in prayer.

So deep was Alice's resistance that Narcissus Fitzgall could not resist it. Instead of leaving her alone to be a good wife and mother, he persisted over the years in tormenting her with different systems of arousal. Rumour has it (but whoever believes such things?) that at length he brought a serving wench to their bed to demonstrate the true nature of female response. Alice lay mute in muslin cap and shift until, at a point where he was unable to give her his attention, she leaped from the sheets with a small mew, went downstairs with her candle and slipped into the river.

A little bitterness is fitting to the victim of a tragedy. 'How do we look, Father?' said his two young daughters twelve years later as they prepared for their first dance in gowns cut down from the remnants of their mother's wardrobe. 'The woods would be very silent if only the nightingale sang,' their papa sadly smiled. All the same they did well at parties – well enough to make him suspect that some young scoundrels had their minds intent on robbing his female property of their only worthwhile asset. He had no interest in his daughters but he had ambitions for them. He wanted them to marry well. There were good estates within riding distance where advantageous connec-tions might be made for the son he would eventually get. The girls looked fair enough. They had no wens or marks and were growing pretty little figures. All he had to do was keep them safe until they were old enough to marry. He forbade them further dances and banned visitors from the house. He locked up his daughters and had men with dogs patrol his grounds. The girls attempted to smuggle out notes and make secret trysts and gnawed noblemen limped about the county to testify to the fact that they had once been attractive, as Narcissus Fitzgall's dogs had once been vicious.

Fitzgall was getting old. He had forgotten that in order for men and women to marry they have first to meet. Memory had flung out the souvenirs of courtship – the teas and dances and rides and picnics, spread over with lace and perfume and roses and manners, laid under with a thunderous compression of lust.

The girls met no one. Lace flew from their nervous fingers and their lips grew pale. They read and walked and stitched and stitched and took little nips of tonic wine. By the time they were deemed of marriageable age, they already had the look of spinsters. Wicked rumour flourished once more, enclosing them like a wall of brambles. Why had the Fitzgall girls been locked up for years and years? It was said they suffered from the phrensy, that their mother had jumped in the river to quench her candle when the moon was full and had left her orphans a legacy of queerness in the head. When Narcissus Fitzgall put them up with a fair dowry there were no bidders. He was enraged and blamed his daughters for plainness, resenting them more with each sparrow's foot that left its tiny print beneath their downcast eyes.

It was indecent that no man had married them, that he should have to bear the brunt of their unflowered withering. One only put up with older women because of the children they had borne, as an example of virtue to those maturing young. It was insupportable that his lovely, adventurer's house might one day fall to his unclaimed daughters.

Now that he had taken measures to prevent this, he might have grown kinder, but as he awaited a response to his advertisement for a wife, the old man became very odd indeed. Sensing an end to his detestable dependence, he grew spiteful and rash.

He filled the sherry bottle, where he knew the girls helped themselves to secret refreshment, with vinegar, and put hare's blood in the port decanter. He employed a poor thing in the village to make up a series of samplers stitched to his direction and disposed them through the house. He found Grace standing rigidly in front of the one that read: 'If hell is a well of whiskey, oh, death where is thy sting?' Blanche was being timidly sick in the bathroom after an appalling sip from the port decanter.

The poor girls knew nothing of his plans and were alarmed to hear him croaking with cruel laughter in the night. 'Tea, Papa?' Bravely they crept up beside his bed.

'Leave the poor teapot in peace!' he roared at them. 'You have a spinster's preoccupation with little pissing spouts.'

When he had frightened them away he returned to his amusement of imagining the procession of applicants for his marital favours – the lonely, the ugly, the fat. He thought he might choose a very fat one. He enjoyed imagining the hulking brute of a son they would make and what sport he would have with his decrepit siblings. His daughters would flee to some chilly wing of the house where he need never look at them but could, when he remembered, dispatch milquetoast or a little thin soup.

Disappointingly, this pleasure was deferred. When he went to collect his post there was nothing but a begging letter from a widow, pleading for a fragment of his fortune in order to feed her children. After three weeks had passed with no single answer, he consulted the wise woman again.

'Did you maybe set your sights too high?' she wondered.

'I asked for nothing,' he protested, 'not looks, not charm, not money! See!' He handed her a copy of his notice and she read it, her gnarled face slowly unravelling to reveal a blackened pit of mirth. 'You wanted jam on your egg and no mistake,' she cackled, and read aloud: 'Handsome, landed gent of considerable means seeks virgin bride of childbearing age.'

'What proposal could be more modest?' he begged.

'God bless you, sir, and saving your presence, you black-hearted oul' black-guard – with curs like yourself around, where do you expect to find a virgin?'

'Silence, hag! I'll have your head,' Narcissus Fitzgall was infuriated by her impudence.

'Why not, so, since you had my maidenhead more than fifty years ago – not that you'll remember – and that of every other poor girl who had neither man nor money to protect her.

'Forget about virgins now, sir. Look out for a nice widow lady who'll give you a son without even troubling you to father it.'

'The mother of my son must be a virgin.' The old man remained stubborn.

'Give me another guinea,' she said.

He put the money in her hand and she transferred it to her corset and slowly began to write. 'Old man, solvent, wishes to make contact with maiden lady in desperate circumstances, view to matrimony and mutual advantage.'

There were desperate women then as there are desperate women now and always will be. When next he went to inspect his mail a couple of letters awaited him. Having passed the previous month in disappointment he felt exhilarated, spoilt for choice. He determined that one of the authors would be his bride no matter how dire her circumstance, how horrible her impediment. Bad breath would not stand in his way, nor apoplexy nor skin blackened by mercury poisoning, he vowed as he tore open his post and scanned the spin-sterish script of two virgins who pleaded to become 'Yours truly…'

When the girls found him he had begun to go brittle and the letters were locked into a mortified grasp. They stooped solicitously to their father's corpse. With barely a glance at one another and only the mildest of sighs, they retrieved their very private correspondence.

THE MORNING AFTER THE BIG FIRE

Maeve Brennan

Maeve Brennan (1917–1993) was born in Dublin but moved with her family to the US as a teenager. She published almost forty stories in the *New Yorker*, and is the author of two short story collections, *The Springs of Affection* (originally *In and Out of Never-Never Land*) and *The Rose Garden*, as well as a novella, *The Visitor* and *The Long-Winded Lady: Notes from the New Yorker*.

From the time I was almost five until I was almost eighteen, we lived in a small house in a part of Dublin called Ranelagh. On our street, all of the houses were of red brick and had small back gardens, part cement and part grass, separated from one another by low stone walls over which, when we first moved in, I was unable to peer, although in later years I seem to remember looking over them quite easily, so I suppose they were about five feet high. All of the gardens had a common end wall, which was, of course, very long, since it stretched the whole length of our street. Our street was called an avenue, because it was blind at one end, the farthest end from us. It was a short avenue, twenty-six houses on one side and twenty-six on the other. We were No. 48, and only four houses from the main road, Ranelagh Road, on which trams and buses and all kinds of cars ran, making a good deal of noisy traffic.

Beyond the end wall of our garden lay a large tennis club, and sometimes in the summer, especially when the tournaments were on, my little sister and I used to perch in an upstairs back window and watch the players in their white dresses and white flannels, and hear their voices calling the scores. There was a clubhouse, but we couldn't see it. Our view was partly obstructed by a large garage building that leaned against the end wall of our garden and the four other gardens between us and Ranelagh Road. A number of people who lived on our avenue kept their cars in the garage, and the people who came to play tennis parked their cars there. It was a very busy place, the garage, and I had never been in there, although we bought our groceries in a shop that was connected with it. The shop fronted on Ranelagh Road, and the shop and the garage were the property of a red-faced, gangling man and his fat, pink-haired wife, the McRorys. On summer afternoons, when my sister and I went around to the shop to buy little paper cups of yellow water ice, some of the players would be there, refreshing themselves with ices and also with bottles of lemonade.

Early one summer morning, while it was still dark, I heard my father's voice, sounding very excited, outside the door of the room in which I slept. I was about eight. My little sister slept in the same room with me. "McRory's is on fire!" my father was saying. He had been awakened by the red glare of the flames against his window. He threw on some clothes and hurried off to see what was going on, and my mother let us look at the fire from a back window, the same window from which we were accustomed to view the tennis matches. It was a really satisfactory fire, with leaping flames, thick, pouring smoke, and a steady roar of destruction, broken by crashes as parts of the roof collapsed. My mother wondered if they had managed to save the cars, and this made us all look at the burning building with new interest and with enormous awe as we imagined the big shining cars being eaten up by the galloping fire. It was very exciting. My mother hurried us back to our front bedroom, but even there the excitement could be felt, with men calling to one another on the street and banging their front doors after them as they raced off to see the fun. Since she had decided there was no danger to our house, my mother tucked us firmly back into bed, but I could not sleep, and as soon as it grew light, I dressed myself and trotted downstairs. My father had many stories to tell. The garage was a ruin, he said, but the shop was safe. Many cars had been destroyed. No one knew how the fire had started. Some of the fellows connected with the garage had been very brave, dashing in to rescue as many cars as they could reach. The part of the building that overlooked our garden appeared charred, frail, and empty because it no longer had much in the way of a roof and its insides were gone. The air smelled very burnt.

I wandered quietly out onto the avenue, which was deserted because the children had not come out to play and it was still too early for the men to be going to work. I walked up the avenue in the direction of the blind end. The people living there were too far from the garage to have been disturbed by the blaze. A woman whose little boy was a friend of mine came to her door to take in the milk.

"McRory's was burnt down last night!" I cried to her.

"What's that?" she said, very startled.

"Burnt to the ground," I said. "Hardly a wall left standing. A whole lot of people's cars burnt up, too."

She looked back over her shoulder in the direction of her kitchen, which, since all the houses were identical, was in the same position as our kitchen. "Jim!" she cried. "Do you hear this? McRory's was burnt down last night. The whole place. Not a stick left… We slept right through it," she said to me, looking as though just the thought of that heavy sleep puzzled and unsettled her.

Her husband hurried out to stand beside her, and I had to tell the whole story again. He said he would run around to McRory's and take a look, and this enraged me, because I wasn't allowed around there and I knew that when he came back he would be a greater authority than I. However, there was no time to lose. Other people were opening their front doors by now, and I wanted everyone to hear the news from me.

"Did you hear the news?" I shouted, to as many as I could catch up with, and, of course, once I had their ear, they were fascinated by what I had to tell. One or two of the men, hurrying away to work, charged past me with such forbiddingly closed faces that I was afraid to approach them, and they continued in their ignorance down toward Ranelagh Road, causing me dreadful anguish, because I knew that before they could board their tram or their bus, some officious busybody would be sure to treat them to my news. Then one woman, to whom I always afterward felt friendly, called down to me from her front bedroom window. "What's that you were telling Mrs. Pearce?" she asked me, in a loud whisper.

"Oh, just that McRory's was burnt to the ground last night. Nearly all the cars burnt up, too. Hardly anything left, my father says." By this time I was being very offhand.

"You don't tell me," she said, making a delighted face, and the next thing I knew, she was opening her front door, more eager for news than anybody.

However, my hour of glory was short. The other children came out – some of them were actually allowed to go around and view the wreckage – and soon the fire was mine no longer, because there were others walking around who knew more about it than I did. I pretended to lose interest, although I was glad when someone – not my father – gave me a lump of twisted, blackened tin off one of the cars.

The tennis clubhouse had been untouched, and that afternoon the players appeared, as bright and immaculate in their snowy flannels and linens as though the smoking garage yard and the lines of charred cars through which they had picked their way to the courts could never interfere with them or impress them. It was nearing tournament time, and a man was painting the platform on which the judge was to sit and from which a lady in a wide hat and a flowered chiffon dress would present cups and medals to the victors among the players. Now, in the sunshine, they lifted their rackets and started to play, and their intent and formal cries mingled with the hoarse shouts of the men at work in the dark shambles of the garage. My little sister and I, watching from our window, could imagine that the rhythmical thud of the ball against the rackets coincided with the unidentifiable sounds we heard from the wreckage, which might have been groans or shrieks as the building, unable to recover from the fire, succumbed under it.

It was not long before the McRorys put up another garage, made of silvery corrugated-metal stuff that looked garish and glaring against our garden wall; it cut off more of our view than the old building had. The new garage looked very hard and lasting, as unlikely to burn as a pot or a kettle. The beautiful green courts that had always seemed from our window to roll comfortably in the direction of the old wooden building now seemed to have turned and to be rolling away into the distance, as though they did not like the unsightly new structure and would have nothing to do with it.

My father said the odds were all against another fire there, but I remembered that fine dark morning, with all the excitement and my own importance, and I longed for another just like it. This time, however, I was determined to discover the blaze before my father did, and I watched the garage closely, as much of it as I could see, for signs that it might be getting ready to go up in flames, but I was disappointed. It stood, and still was standing, ugly as ever, when we left the house years later. Still, for a long time I used to think that if some child should steal around there with a match one night and set it all blazing again, I would never blame her, as long as she let me be the first with the news.

LEITRIM FLIP

June Caldwell

June Caldwell's short story collection *Room Little Darker* was published in 2017 by New Island Books and in 2018 by Head of Zeus. Her novel *Little Town Moone* is forthcoming from John Murray. She is a prize-winner of the Moth International Short Story Prize and lives in Dublin.

I would never tell a hound like that I'd done it on purpose. You can't predict the 'switch' and though he seemed more cuddly-do than spanky-don't, the army background was a clincher. It was also the only time that I'd get to test him properly in all this, the juncture where I cradled the dynamism, not him. Oh he hadn't managed to keep his eyes open wide enough at all. Like most men, he'd stupidly underestimated me. I dumped him before we'd begun to see how he'd jerk and crawl. He texted back quite surprised with a simplistic 'I understand'. I hadn't expected that smack of humanity, it made me feel contrite, for a nanosecond. Then I considered he may have done it on purpose to achieve the desired effect, to manipulate. He was a Dom after all. It was the first day we'd met in person. He'd be discarded hours later for being a mindless superficial twat. And a hypocrite. I couldn't stomach a man inside me who hadn't the ability to think things through beyond the half-baked one-dimensional. Stick your fucking brain in me first before you stick your cock in! Truth is, I wanted to see how he'd react given that he'd be playing me like this in my role as a sub into the near future. I wanted to witness how he'd jump, psychologically. It's hard to find people on those kinky websites who'd go the whole hog. I was also just out of a long-term relationship and I felt like fucking men over big time. Could I bear being back in that grimy white work van of his horsing through the streets of Dublin with my huge tits bobbing and the lyricism of his voice swinging around his Adam's apple like a Satanic hammock? 'You think so slave, can I stop you there, have you any idea what you're whittling on about, are you totally clueless, have you any notion of the world you've stepped into?' Mouth mouth mouth. He really didn't shut the fuck up. There was hilarity in it too, but a lot of latent aggression for sure. The wanker thought he was so smart. An ex-Marine no less. All that vicious training, all that

PTSD, all that crying alone in stone bathrooms in foreign places with too much sand.

When we got to the hotel room he was anything but smart, flying around in a Dickensian mania (Mr Bumblefuck). He had his gut unselfconsciously splayed in full view and his leather play kit glory-holing itself on the dressing table where the slick menus and tourist bumf usually sit. The words were farting from his ginger gob, doing a very good bluebottle impression he was, buzzing to the bathroom, then back out again – 'Oh, see, I like you slave, you're just my type' – circling the bed with a creepy half-smile, back to the bathroom again, talking like a pirate turkey stuffed with amphetamines. Then the runny shite came, endless diarrhoea sentences as he tried to get a grip on what he was actually doing. Was he capable of squirming into the dark at all? Though as I'd soon learn, the one thing he could do without having to concert direct himself with hot air was tie me up. To tie my hands behind my back shrewdly and roughly (and even then he lost the key, still stuck in the handcuff, the gobshite!) and there I was with his fat cock in my mouth hurting my jawbone. My carefully applied whore-red lipstick smudging all over this stranger's pasty skin, the idea of having to chomp on it interminably until he shot a bad diet-load down my gullet. To be totally fair it was a nice sensation being restricted in movement with his warm flesh in my gob like that, a first for me. I felt properly submissive in this moment. Up down up down slurp slurp all around trying to use my mouth to piston and position him so I could make him 'orgasm'. He was enjoying that I couldn't quite manage it, laughing at me, chortling, so cheap to do that but I understood the effortless humiliation in it for him. Two-pissholes-in-the-snow blindfold cemented on which meant I genuinely couldn't see a damn thing. Not one of those sex shop synthetic pieces of crap but a proper patch-per-eye medieval yoke which he'd bound very tight. My arms were really hurting yanked behind like that; I hadn't bothered telling him I had back problems caused by the fucked-up hips and afterwards of course he'd blame the fat. A brute like him doesn't wait around for explanation. 'You nearly had me there slave but you let it go!' he announced. 'Fuck's sake I almost came!' As if I was supposed to read his twitches like a basket of braille bundled by the cottage fire. I moaned loud for him to remove the cuffs from behind my back. My tits were preventing me from grabbing his cock and working it with my hands and tongue simultaneously so we could get out of this kip he'd booked and pour some pints down us like he'd promised. When he released me I grabbed hold of him like a boat part I'd no interest in but had to rough-house to get on with the boating holiday regardless. 'You nearly had me there again, fuck's sake slave get a move on!' I wondered how much the sound of his own voice could stop him from coming. Even his cock must be totally sick of hearing him.

I imagined him at home fighting at the dinner table with his Debenhams-clad wife. She'd be good-looking enough given that he's a big ego. Good-looking in the conventional sense of looking OK in a swimsuit for her age, but a head like a horse, with too much make-up splattered all over. I could imagine him swinging the breeze not letting her away with a stray consonant during arguments. Sitting room bully. Bedroom bulldozer. The only way she'd be able to get her own back would be to stop fucking him, which is probably why he was here with me. He'd be one of those slow-release tormentors who could be sappy when convention required (important calendar dates: anniversaries, Valentine's Day, Mother's Day). His need for control a driving force both blinding him and shoving him forward.

He came then, suddenly, with a screamy shudder. A small spurt of what tasted like leftover sweet 'n' sour from a drunken weekend's Chinese takeaway. His balls were properly deflated, hanging like empty sacks of rice. Thank God that bit was over. He pulled me up and unbuckled the blindfold. Sunlight pissed all over me. He'd no interest in throwing me over the bed and riding me hard which he'd been threatening to do on email for days. No, it was now all about him and the pursuit of city centre hooch. Can't even remember if he bothered to use the crop or flogger on me at that stage, despite my heavy hints by coyly mauling his trade tools through my fingertips every time I tiptoed by where they rested, redundant. There was just one crafty moment where I felt he had more power than me; when he grabbed my hair unexpectedly from behind and flung me down on the bed. The weight of his physicality pinning me there, face scraped in the cheap cotton of the over-washed duvet, the feel of his harsh breath behind me, the strength of his arms. I wanted to shout, 'Keep going soldier boy, keep going!' but he was too interested in getting out into a shite pub up around Camden Street somewhere. I'd see more of his masterly skill later, but for now it rested pretty in his emails where he'd write sexy shit like, 'Next time slave, I'm going to introduce you to subspace, it's about time you became acquainted.' That excited me. I'd read a lot about it. Seemed wholly technical, like a Master or a Sir would need proficiency and artistry to get you there. To empty tingly endorphins into your system via the fever-burn of the whip. Taking you to a megalopolis of filthy sensation beyond the blandness of a naff hotel room. Beyond where you'd ever thought of going on your tod. A euphoric place only a pervert could perfectly locate on the mind map. 'You'll be tied to the door frame,' he informed me. 'You'll dance to the music as the crop sings. You'll be whipped all over too, hard. I've never met a cheekier submissive. I'll bring ear defenders, the type we used on the ranges. There'll be no safe word allowed for punishments. Be prepared slave, you will not be able to sit for a week.' I'd asked how he knew when a sub reached this fabled place. 'When she stops dancing,' he said. 'When she's no longer able to wriggle at all.' Jesus, that turned me on. The manky idea of total compliance. Unhooking me from the straps fastened to the top of the door after I'd stopped twisting and flailing, dropping me into his big animal arms; that first embarrassing tinge of intimacy. Though for now he was still a stupid wanker with no idea he'd be dumped in the morning as a display of my power. Instead of saying 'do you want to play soldier boy, then let's fucking curtain-raise for real', I turned to him when he asked was I ready to vamoose and softly replied, 'Yes Master, I'm ready.'

In a cage in a kitchen in a farmhouse in Leitrim. Master pacing the ground with hairy belly hanging. Bog all room. Caught for days on end. Hours fleecing hours. 'Grab that fucking bag slave, if I push your arse right up to the bars, stretch your arms out, grab the bastarding thing, pull the handles in, slide it over, from under that chair there, I've a taser in the bag, I'll do the bastards.' Then what? We're still locked in a cage, with the pair of them pleasantly electrocuted and still no fucking escape. 'Your fault, this,' he says, crawling over my legs, bashing against my hips. 'Fuck's sake give me some room!' Master is always prepared for these things, what with being a soldier. Except he's not. 'It wasn't my idea to meet up with them,' I remind him. The husband feeding us from Pedigree Chum bowls while the wife saunters in and out in a pink babydoll chemise filming on her smartphone every half hour or so. Jewelry, watches, bags, coats, play kit, shoes, underwear, taken, gone, confiscated. Ceiling cameras scattered around. Streaming a live feed to a website. Fuck knows what pervs are watching. Twice a day the husband enters in a leather gimp mask, fully concealed, raining down with rivets. Brass padlock on the mouthpiece. 'Nommm nommm,' he says. Wearing nothing but a harness with mickey pouch. Bull whip in hand. Lashes the cage bars, long noisy cracks. Grunts through his gag. The wife laughs; sweet chuckle of a librarian who's stumbled across a chalky first edition and can't help but wet her knickers. 'Be good doggies now,' she says. 'And there'll be special treats later.' Makes husband a Cup-a-Soup. Mushroom. I am ravenous. The smell is intoxicating. We squash to the very back where the patio door is. Husband moves to whip the sides. Eventually the tip of the whip reaches our skin inside. 'Fuck's sake, I'll knock your block off as soon as I get out of here, I'll shit in your wife's eyes, I'll snap her legs, pull one off, beat you with it.' Master needs to calm. It just makes them laugh all the more. He keeps winking at the husband like they're both supposed to know something. 'Can you put some briquettes in the range?' I ask, I plead, I stare at the wife, I beg. 'It's freezing cold in here, please.' She looks pissed off. 'That's no way to address me,' she says. 'How should I address you?' Master hands me the laminated instruction sheet from yesterday, or the day before? Address Kennel Owners As Follows: 2 'woofs' for a request, 3 for the litter tray, 2 small whimpers for a toy, full bark for collar and leash…' It goes on. 'Woof woof,' I say. Master pulls the back of my hair, knocking me to the ground from the hind legs position.

George's Street, Dublin, on a steely Friday night in citrine taxi light when we get together again after the first hotel meet. 'You have to taste the guacamole in this place, it's like nothing I've ever put my filthy tongue on. They use whole lime skins and whatever way they mash it all up, it's phantasmagoric…' Big words irk him. He's wearing a fat priest black polo neck and some shite corduroy pants (couldn't call them trousers). 'I don't want no poncy place slave, all that nouveau cuisine bollix, give me steak and chips, that's me sorted.' We ramble through the heavy door and I immediately nab a waiter to secure us two stools at the bar for the next hour and a half. You can't book a table in this place; I knew that'd be nothing but botheration for Master. The only other restaurant we'd been to before, he complained like fuck from the off: the cramped table top; the lack of hot spice; the tepid temperature of the curry. Commanded me to the toilet so he could bellyache without the presence of a weakminded woman looking on. 'It better be good slave, this is your city, not mine.' I recommended the Taco Laguna: stir-fried Iberico pork with summer vegetables in a lettuce cup. I thought it might appeal to his virile carnivore. I loved the music in this place, clatter of eighties tunes on a loop, banging loud. 'A lettuce cup, are they having a fucking laugh?' There were twelve 'rules' he'd given me and only two I abided by. 'I'm not shaving "from the neck down" to be hairless. It's ridiculous, way too much effort, especially if I only see you twice a month,' I said. 'Have you any idea how long it takes to shave a snatch totally bald? It's worse than plucking a Christmas turkey. Housewives gave up that shit in the seventies when supermarkets spun modern.' I ordered the Roast Gambas: Pico de Gallo, guacamole and crema queso in a taco shell. He wasn't impressed at the €17 price tag. 'Are you going to pay for this slave?' Well, given that he was the self-confessed Commandant in Charge, I assumed he'd get the bill. 'You're not wearing the collar either, did you think I hadn't noticed?' I refused to wear the thick worn-leather neckband with the cattle ring on the front. It was vile. Dog-like. Or worse. Bison-like. Or worse. I wanted a decent sterling silver band, discreet, not particularly noticeable. 'Don't you get this? You do as you're told slave. You leave all the decisions to me, you obediently follow instructions, ALL of them.' My boyfriend, The Narcissist, only recently walked. I missed him like mad even though we hadn't humped for three years and all was rotten in our State of Denmark. I used to munch here with him, holding hands under the table, superfluity of life plans over frozen margaritas. We'd buy a small cottage in Stoneybatter when my parents snuffed it. Get the attic converted into a double sleeping platform with a ladder so his kids could stay. Tile the backyard, fling it with plants. Pay the €5k for a gorgeous white wood burner in the sitting room. He'd be sickened at this new inroad. He'd want to protect me from noxious kink. 'This is not you love. You're way too sensitive for this shit.' Ah but I'm not. Didn't we learn so much about our repressed selves by that traumatic parting? 'I feel so mentally crazed so much of the time, I just want someone to take me in hand, to show me how to behave,' I'd tell him. 'You know? Not take any crap, knock some of the meanness out of me I feel with the pressure at home.' His navy eyes, his lovely face, his endless love that died like a pig. 'Ask one of those prats for some napkins slave, this tack is runny as fuck.' On Master goes. 'See those cheeky messages you send me on KIK all the time telling me that I'm a deadhead from a rubbish high-rise in Glasgow who can only spell phonetically, I hope your arse is able to cash the cheque for that?' I'd already explained I was an 'alpha submissive', a different hybrid to the pain sluts and gormless kneelers. 'That first night we met,' he says. 'We got pissed and you dumped me. You do know you're going to have to be severely punished for that?' They stroll in two seconds later, pre-arranged: Malcolm and Sarah from Leitrim. Master shakes the husband's hand, kisses her sloppily on the cheek. 'Game on,' he says, all happy out. She scoops up the last of the tortilla chips, lathering them in precious guacamole. Tall and slim. He's tall and creepy. Twenty minutes later we're on our way to Leitrim in a white Hiace. Out on wide roads where growers set up spud stalls as soon as the bad weather kicks in. Maris Pipers, Roosters, Queens. 'You're pretty,' the wife says. 'Big porno boobs.' Thistles scratch the car windows too fast. In the retina of a running rabbit there's an ache for warmth but it'll never arrive. 'You're nice too,' I say, not knowing what I'm really supposed to elucidate back. Two and a half hours later we arrive at a dirt track too lurid to be a boreen. The house sits on its own scrubland with an abandoned boat stuck on its side filled with compost. No lights. No neighbours. No salvation.

Saturday or Sunday in early glow as Lord Canine and Mrs Mutt are nowhere. Certain moments are elementary, so simple they become eternal. Photons of electromagnetic radiation travel forty-five billion years to reach earth and we're still only at the stage where microwave ovens are modern. With these moments of clarity we learn to value tiny things... chronology makes everything solid and strong. That's what I'm telling myself. We're fuck all on the grand scale. Master has only recently (within the last few weeks) admitted it has all gone very wrong. Intended as a coaching exercise on compliance for me. His stomach is deflated. There are large sores on his legs; hag's faces painted in dangerous red. When I look at them I remember the first satsuma I scoffed in school in 1974, digging my fingernails into the scabrous skin, smelling and tasting the miniscule bursts that shot out onto my chin. He's not speaking much. I too have lost weight, but am feeling hopeful. During the day I take turns crouching on each bum cheek, still plump enough to supply some cushion at least. If I press up against the front of the bars I can stretch my legs partially lengthways the full width. Up out and over the cluttered window pane full of dusty toby jugs, the honeysuckle French kisses the sunlight, bowing to our subjugation. Panicles of whorled branches, purplish-brown, prised open, spreading in fruit. Tufted grass with creeping rhizomes. I've never felt happier scoring the different colours in the sky, diffracted through the air. Here, a field of phantom cattle clump about joylessly scaring the púca that once leapt on a local man's back. We were given a handbook of local legends as our only reading material. The man, who is forever nameless, managed to stab the entity with a penknife and throw it to the ground. When he returned the following day he found a wooden log with a knife-sized hole along one side. 'What was it like fighting in the Falklands?' I ask Master. He doesn't answer straight away. The only avenue of punishment left. 'There was logic to it,' he replies. He hasn't taken the beatings well, sobbing for hours, refusing to communicate or look at me. Squashed into the furthest corner, throwing up some gobbledygook at an absent wife. 'When I get back I'll get the gas boiler serviced love, I'm sorry I've been away so long.' Unlike me, when I reach the puddle of tears, no longer feeling a thing – when Lord Canine uses the really thick rattan cane – it purges every bristle of stress, setting me up for the whole of the next day. Our bodies are deeply marked in thick purple stripes. Skin on my thighs broken open a number of times. Pain so excessive and profound, I pass out cold.

In they saunter with a group of five rubber gimps. One doused in duck yellow from head to toe. His rotund vacuum-packed belly and peaked hat a delight in a way. Master whimpers dejectedly. 'Here are our precious doggies!' Mrs Mutt says, pulling out wooden chairs to form a neat row for the spectators to get comfortable. I immediately fall on all fours, turning fast in manic circles so they can see the butt plug with fawn fur tail wagging devotedly. 'Woof woof woof woof!' I say. I've perfected a deep meaningful growl that represents not aggression but cute little playing sounds to please my owners abundantly. 'Isn't she a joy!' one of them in a black and white Victorian maid outfit declares. 'Totally smashing!' says another in a gas mask. God knows what rural hills and crannies they slipped down from for a few lost hours. If they've emerged from the stinking steam of packed dairy sheds or if they've run out of Rosewood French doors in architecturally designed contemporary bungalows facing strategically southwards. 'What breed is she?' someone else asks. Master flings me a stingy look, very like the first time I climbed into his van and he told me to prepare for a journey like no other. 'She's a Dandy Dinmont Terrier, cheerful nature. He's the opposite, Golden Retriever we'd great hopes for, but he won't even mount her anymore.' Lord Canine piles stray wood into the range. His fetish flippers smacking the ground as he carefully plops about. 'Are the bold doggies hungry? Do the bold doggies want some succulent strips of beef? Have the bold doggies done pee pees on the floor?' I leap up and tear at the first piece of overcooked meat flung, licking the residue of grease pearls dripping down the fortified steel billets. It's twenty years since I've eaten animal flesh but endurance has taught me to accept every small gift graciously. We're no longer fed from bowls since Master began attacking in rabid fits. Mealtimes triggering his prey drive. As if deep in his medulla oblongata he knows to bite a human moving too quickly. I hear his stomach rumbling like distant thunder muttering imperfectly from the purl of clouds. It's unlikely I'll be able to date a normal bloke after all this is over. I've thought about this a lot. Sitting in a heaving sports bar in Dame Street all faux giddy when Manchester United score a goal. All that droll macho nonsense. When escape comes, whether in three months, eight or a year, I will recall all these particulars. 'We're never getting out,' Master says. I'm shocked his army training hasn't served him in more callous or mercenary ways. He really is a depressed moron. 'It can't be that far to the N4,' I've told him, numerous fucking times. 'Remember we only beetled off the main road for a few kilometres to get here.' Even if it was a miserable day with flea fogs of rain obstructing vision in every direction… when our cage is being cleaned and one of them makes the systematic error of turning away for a microsecond, we'd bolt. Once, Master grabbed me by the throat when I described this very scenario, banging my head so hard Mrs Mutt tore in from the sitting room hurling hot tea at his snout causing incalculable torment. 'Whoever picks us up on the main road eventually will hear us yelping like we've never been able to yelp before.' Master bangs his rump against the padlock to get attention.

All five stand up in a splodge of vibrant PVC blushes, making their way to the bars so the rest of the room is concealed from our view. They bend over us, all whoop and holler, pulling at the cage so it tips slightly. We topple about as if inside ferry kennels on top deck on a stormy day. I know exactly what to do. I fling myself on my back and open my legs wide. Two paws scrunched up over clamped breasts, head hanging to the side for a champion view. With the temperature rising I begin to pant heavily, sweating like mad. I make it achingly clear for Master there's only one option left to cool me down, to cool us all down. It rests solely with him now to do his thing and get enough oxygenated blood back into this ecosystem. I pant even more to seal the deal. After it's over we'll curl tightly together, snuggling into well deserved sleep. Free to run at breakneck speed along the most beautiful sweep of beach. Tearing up lumpy dips of sand so relentlessly our tails stop wagging and our legs collapse under the weight of yummy ecstasy. Running, scampering, sprinting, until nothing we've ever been through before matters.

HERE WE ARE

Lucy Caldwell

Lucy Caldwell was born in Belfast. She is the multi-award-winning writer of three novels, several stage and radio dramas, and two collections of short stories (*Multitudes*, Faber, 2016, and *Intimacies*, Faber, 2020). She is also the editor of the anthology *Being Various: New Irish Short Stories* (Faber, 2019).

The summer is a washout. Every day the heavens open, and the rain comes down; not the usual summer showers with their skittish, shivering drops but heavy, dull, persistent rain; true *dreich* days. The sky is low and grey, and the ground is waterlogged, the air cold and damp, blustery.

We don't care. It is the best summer of our lives.

We go to Cutters Wharf in the evenings because nobody we know goes there. It's an older crowd, suits and secretaries, some students from Queen's. Usually we sit inside, but one evening when the clouds lift and the rain ceases, we take our drinks out onto the terrace. The riverfront benches and tables are damp and cold, but we put plastic bags down and sit on those. It isn't warm, but there is the feeling of sitting under the full sky, that pale high light of a Northern evening, and there is the salt freshness of the breeze coming up the Lagan from the lough.

After we leave Cutters Wharf that night, we walk. We walk along the Lagan and through the Holylands: Palestine Street, Jerusalem Street, Damascus Street, Cairo Street. We cross the river and walk the whole sweep of the Ormeau Embankment. The tide is turning, and a two-person canoe is skimming downriver, slate grey and quicksilver.

When we reach the point where the road curves away from the river, the pale evening light still lingers, so we keep walking, across the Ravenhill Road, down Toronto Street and London Street and the London Road, Rosebery Road and Willowfield Drive and across the Woodstock Road and on, further and further east until we are in Van Morrison territory: Hyndford Street and Abetta Parade, Grand Parade, the North Road, Orangefield.

There are times in your life, or maybe just the one time, when you find yourself in the right place, the only place you could possibly be, and with the only person.

She feels it too. She turns to me. 'These streets are ours,' she says. 'Yes,' I say. 'Yes, they are.' And they were. The whole city was.

She was a celebrity in our school, in the way that some girls are. She was the star musician and always played solos at school concerts and prize days and when a minor royal came to open the new sports hall. One year in the talent contest she played the saxophone while another girl sang 'Misty'. They didn't win – some sixth-formers who'd choreographed their own version of 'Vogue' got more votes – but they were the act you remembered. She wore a white suit and sunglasses, but it wasn't that: it was the way she bent over her instrument and swayed, as if it was the most private moment in the world.

It was a few weeks later that her mother was killed. She was out jogging when a carful of teenage joyriders lost control and careened up onto the kerb. They didn't stop: if they had stopped, or at least stopped long enough to ring an ambulance, she might have survived. As it was, she died of massive internal haemorrhaging on a leafy street in Cherryvalley, less than a hundred metres from her home. Her husband was a local councillor and so it made the headlines: the petite blonde jogger and the teenage delinquents.

Her entire class went to the funeral, and the older members of the orchestra, too. I was only a second year and had never even spoken to her, so I just signed the card that went round. She didn't come to practice for several weeks, and there were rumours that she had given up music for good. You'd look for her in the corridors, her face pale and thin with violet bruises under the eyes.

Then, one day, she was there again, sitting in her usual place, assembling her clarinet, and if the teacher was surprised or pleased to see her he didn't let on, and none of the rest of us did either.

She smiled at me sometimes in orchestra practice, but I knew she didn't know who I was. I was two years below, for a start, and she had no way of knowing my name because the music teacher called all three of us flutes 'Flutes'. She smiled because he would make silly mistakes, telling us to go from the wrong place or getting the tempo wrong, and there'd be exaggerated confusion in the screeching, bored, lumbering ranks while he flustered and pleaded and tried to marshal a new start. People were cruel to him, sometimes even to his face. She never was: she just smiled, and because of the way the music stands were laid out I happened to be in the direction of the smile.

I used to say her name to myself sometimes. Angie. Angela Beattie.

What else? She cut her own hair – at least that's what people said, and it looked as if it could be true, slightly hacked at, although the mussed-up style made it hard to tell. Her father was a born-again Christian – he belonged to a Baptist church that spent summers digging wells in Uganda or building schools in Sierra Leone – and when our school joined up with another in West Belfast to play a concert at St Anne's Cathedral she wasn't allowed to take part because it was a Sunday, even though it would be in a church, even though it was for peace.

There was so little I knew about her then.

In the summer term of fourth year, everyone took up smoking, or pretended to. The school was strange and empty that time of year, the Upper Sixth and Fifth Form on study leave, the Lower Sixth promoted to prefects and enjoying their new privilege of leaving the grounds at lunchtime. It was ours to colonise. We linked arms and ducked behind the overgrown buddleia into the alley behind the sports hall, boasting that we needed a smoke so badly we didn't even care if anyone caught us.

The day they did, it was raining and so we weren't expecting it, but all of a sudden there they were, coming down the alleyway, one at each end. I was holding one of the half-smoked cigarettes, and I froze, even as all the others were hissing at me to chuck it away.

The prefect walking towards me was Angie.

I could feel the flurry as those with cigarettes or a lighter scrambled to hide them and others tore open sticks of chewing gum or pulled scarves up around their faces, but only vaguely, as if it was all happening a very long way away.

Angie stopped a couple of metres away. My hand was trembling now. 'Oh my God,' I heard, and, 'What are you at?' and, 'Put it out, for fuck's sake.' But I couldn't seem to move.

Angie looked at me. The expression in her eyes was almost amused. Then, ignoring the nervous giggles and whispered bravado of the others, she took a step forward and reached out for the cigarette. Her fingers grazed mine as they took it from me. She held it for a moment then let it fall to the ground, crushed it with her heel. She looked me in the eye the whole time. I felt heat surge to my face. 'You don't smoke,' she said, and then she said my name.

I felt the shock of it on my own lips. I hadn't known she knew it: knew who I was. She gazed at me for a moment longer in that steady, amused, half-ironic way. Then she said to the other prefect, 'Come on,' and the second girl shouldered past, and they walked back the way Angie had come.

'It's not cool, girls,' she called, without turning round. 'You think it is, but it's not.'

There was silence until they'd turned the corner. Then it erupted: 'What the fuck,' and, 'Oh my God,' and, 'Do you think she's going to report us?', and, 'I am so dead if they do,' and, 'What is she like?', and then, 'Do you reckon she fancies you?' It was the standard slag in our school, but out of nowhere

I felt my whole body fizz, felt the words rush through me, through and to unexpected parts of me, the skin tightening under my fingernails and at the backs of my knees.

'Wise up,' I made my voice say, and I elbowed and jostled back. 'It's because of the music. My lungs will be wrecked if I carry on smoking. I actually should think about giving up,' and because we were always talking about having to give up, the conversation turned, and that got me off the hook, at least for the moment.

For the rest of term, I agonised over whether to stop hanging out with the smokers at lunch or whether to keep doing it in case she came back. In the end, I compromised by going behind the sports hall as usual but not inhaling so I could say with all honesty, if she asked, that I didn't smoke any more.

My days became centred around those ten minutes at lunchtime when I might see her again. I would feel it building in me in the last period before lunch, feel my heart start to flutter and my palms become sweaty. But she didn't raid the alleyway again. There was nowhere else I could count on seeing her: orchestra practice had ceased in the last weeks of the summer term – the Assembly Hall was used for examinations and there were too many pupils on study leave anyway – and the sixth-form wing, with their common room and study hall, were out of bounds to fourth-years.

I passed her in the corridor once, but she was deep in conversation with another girl and didn't notice me. On the last day of term, I saw her getting into a car with a group of others and accelerating down the drive, and that was that.

The summer holidays that followed were long. My father, a builder, had hurt his back a few months earlier and had been unable to work so money was tight: there wasn't even to be a weekend in Donegal or a day trip to Ballycastle. The city, meanwhile, battened down its hatches, and I was forbidden to go into town – forbidden, in fact, from going further than a couple of streets away from our house. All my friends who lived nearby were away; I was too old to ride my bike up and down the street or play skipping games like my younger sister.

'Why don't you practise your flute?' my mother would say as I sloped endlessly about the kitchen. Normally I'd roll my eyes, but as the days stretched on I found myself doing it. I didn't admit to myself it was because of Angie Beattie, but as I practised I couldn't help thinking of her. When you first learn the flute, you're told to imagine you're kissing it. Now, every time I put my mouth to the lip plate, I thought of her. I'd think of her mouth, the curve of it. I'd think of the times I'd watched her at the start of orchestra practice, how she'd wet the reed of her clarinet and screw it into place, test it, adjust it, curl and recurl her lips around the mouthpiece. I'd let my mind unfurl, and soon I'd think other things too, things that weren't quite thoughts but sensations, things I didn't dare think in words and that afterwards left me hot and breathless and almost ashamed.

I got good at the flute that summer. When school started up again, the music teacher noticed. He kept me back after the auditions and found me some sheet music, asked me to learn it for the Christmas concert. Then he said he'd had a better idea and rummaged in his desk some more. A sonata for flute and piano, he said – we were short on duets. Angie Beattie could accompany me.

'She might not want to,' I said.

'Nonsense,' he said.

I don't remember much about the first few lunchtime practice sessions we had together. Each one, before it happened, seemed to loom, so inflated in my mind I almost couldn't bear it, then, when it was happening, rushed by. At first I could barely meet Angie's eye: it was mortifying, the extent to which I'd thought about her, let myself daydream about her, and more. But the music was difficult – for me, at least, which made it hard work for her as my accompanist – and that meant there was no time to waste; we needed to get straight to work. After the first week I found I was able to put aside, at least when I was actually with her, the memory of the strange summer's fantasies. But sometimes, late at night, I'd be consumed for an instant with an ache that seemed too big for my body to contain.

One evening, we stayed late practising after school, and, completely out of the blue, she invited me back to her house for dinner. My heart started pounding as I tried to say a nonchalant yes. I'd imagined her house, the rooms she lived in, so many times; I'd imagined so often a scenario in which she might ask me back there. I phoned my mum from the payphone in the foyer, and then we walked back together, down the sweep of the school's long drive, through the drifts of horse chestnut and sycamore leaves in the streets, swinging our instrument cases. There was mist in the air, and, as we turned off the main road, the taste of woodsmoke from a bonfire in a nearby garden.

The Cherryvalley streets were wide and quiet, thick with dark foliage, lined with tall, spreading lime trees. It was all a world away from my street, its neat brick terraces and toy squares of lawn, the gnomes and mini-waterfall in our neighbour's garden that I used to love and show off to schoolfriends before I realised they weren't something to be proud about. Cherryvalley seemed to belong to somewhere else entirely – a different place, or time.

'It's nice around here,' I said.

She glanced at me. 'D'you think so?' There was something in her expression I couldn't read, and I remembered – of course, too late – that her mother had died here, maybe on this very street, or the one we just walked down. The streets felt not quiet but ominous then, the shifting shadows of the leaves, the plaited branches.

'I meant,' I said, flustered, 'the streets have such pretty names.'

She didn't reply, and I tried to think of something else to say, something that would show I was sorry, that I understood. But of course I didn't understand, at all.

We walked on in silence. I wondered what had made her ask me back and if she was already regretting it.

The Beatties' house was draughty and dark. Angie walked through, flipping on light switches and drawing the curtains. I thought of my house, the radio or the TV or often both on at the same time, my mum busy cooking, the cat always underfoot.

Angie made me sit at the kitchen table, like a guest, while she hung my blazer in the cloakroom and made me a glass of lime cordial, then hurried about getting dinner ready. She turned on the oven and took chicken Kievs from the freezer, lined a baking tray with tinfoil, boiled the kettle to cook some potatoes, washed lettuce in a salad spinner and chopped it into ribbons. I had never, I realised, imagined how her home life actually worked. I felt shy of this Angie – felt the two years, and everything else, between us.

When Mr Beattie got back, he looked nothing like the man you used to see shouting on TV or gazing down from lamp-posts. He was tall and thin and washed-out-looking; his shoulders were stooped, and his hair needed cutting. He shook my hand, and I found myself blurting out, 'My dad used to vote for you.' It was a lie: my dad never bothered to vote, and my mum, even though Dad teased her about it, only ever voted Women's Coalition.

I felt Angie looking at me, and I felt my neck and face burning. 'Good man,' Mr Beattie said. 'Every vote counts. These are historic times we're living through.'

'And history will judge us,' I heard myself say. I have no idea where it came from. The car radio, probably, the talk show Mum always had on and always turned off. Mr Beattie blinked, and Angie burst out laughing.

'Indeed,' he said. 'Indeed.'

'He likes you,' Angie said, when Mr Beattie had left the room. 'He really likes you.'

I wasn't sure what there had been to like, but before I could say anything, she said, 'If he talks about church, don't say you don't go.'

'Okay,' I said. 'Why not?'

'Oh,' she said. 'It's just more trouble than it's worth.'

When everything was ready and the three of us sat down at the table, Mr Beattie bowed his head and clasped his hands and intoned a long grace. I looked at Angie halfway through, but she had her head bowed and her eyes closed too. I took care to chime in my 'Amen' with theirs.

As we ate, Mr Beattie asked questions about school, about music. Often Angie would jump in with an answer before I had a chance, and I couldn't work out if it was for my benefit or her father's. When he asked what church I went to, Angie said, 'She goes to St Mark's, don't you?'

'St Mark's Dundela,' Mr Beattie said.

'That's right,' Angie said.

'That's the one,' I said. St Mark's was where our school had its Christmas carol service, the only time of year my family ever set foot in a church, and only then because I was in the choir.

'Good, good,' Mr Beattie said, and I made myself hold his gaze. All that nonsense was just hocus-pocus, is what my dad liked saying. Once, when some Jehovah's Witnesses knocked on our front door and asked if he'd found Jesus, my dad clapped his forehead and said, 'I have indeed, down the back of the sofa, would you believe?' My sister and I had thought it was the funniest thing ever.

'St Mark's Dundela,' Mr Beattie said again. I started to panic then, trying to remember something, anything about it. But he didn't ask any more. 'C. S. Lewis's church,' was all he said, and I smiled and agreed.

The meal seemed to go on for ever. The St Mark's lie had made me feel like a fraud, but it wasn't just that: the whole situation was putting me on edge. Angie was more nervous than I'd ever seen her. In fact, I couldn't think of a time when I had seen her nervous, not when she confronted the smokers, not even before a solo. *I must be doing everything wrong,* I thought. I had the horrible feeling, too, that Mr Beattie could see through me, or, worse, could see into me, into some of the things I'd thought about his daughter.

For dessert there was a chocolate fudge cake, from Marks & Spencer, shiny and dense with masses of chocolate shavings on top.

'Dad has a sweet tooth, don't you, Dad?' Angie said. She cut him a slab of cake, and they grinned at each other for a moment. 'We used to have chocolate cake for dinner sometimes, didn't we?' she said. 'Or cheesecake.'

'Strawberry cheesecake,' Mr Beattie said.

'We reckoned,' she said, turning to me, 'that because it had cheese in it it was actually quite nutritious.'

'A meal in a slice,' Mr Beattie said.

'Protein, fat, carbohydrate and fruit,' she said, turning back to him.

'A perfectly balanced plate,' he said, and they smiled that smile again, intimate, impenetrable.

When the meal was finally over, Mr Beattie said, 'Well, after all this talk of the duet, you must give me a concert.'

Without looking at me, Angie said, 'Another time, Dad, we're both played out today,' and I knew she was embarrassed of me. I felt tears boil up in my eyes, and I stood up and said I needed the toilet. I took as long as I could in there, soaping and rinsing my hands several times over, drying each finger. I'd say I had homework, I decided. I'd say my mum didn't like me being out after dark. Both of these things, I told myself, were true.

When I told Angie that I had to go, she looked at me, then looked away. 'Oh,' she said. 'Right.'

Mr Beattie brought my blazer from the cloakroom and said he'd see me to the door. 'It's nice to see Angie bringing a friend back,' he said. 'I look forward to hearing this duet of yours one of these days.'

The whole way home, I felt a strange, fierce sense of grief, as if I'd lost something – a possibility, something that wouldn't come again.

After that, I avoided her, concert or no concert. I went with the smokers at lunch, half-daring her to come and find me, half-dreading it. Thursday and Friday passed without my seeing her. An awful weekend, then Monday and Tuesday, and on Tuesday afternoon I knew I had to skip orchestra practice. On Wednesday she came to the mobile where my class did French, in the middle of a lesson, and said to the teacher she needed to speak to me. She was a prefect, and it was known that we were both musical; the teacher agreed without any questions.

The shock and relief and shame of seeing her coursed through me, and I had to hold onto the desk for a moment as I stood up. As I followed her out of the classroom and down the steps and around the side of the mobile, I couldn't seem to breathe. 'How long are you planning on keeping this up?' she said.

'I don't know,' I said. I could see her pulse jumping in the soft part of her neck. A horrible, treacherous part of me wanted to reach out and touch it.

'Angie,' I said, and from all of the things that were whirling in my head I tried to find the right one to say.

The trees and glossy pressing shrubs around us were thrumming with rain. All the blood in my body was thrumming.

'Look at me,' she said, and, when I finally did, she leaned in and kissed me. It was brief, only barely a kiss, her lips just grazing mine. Then she stepped back, and I took a step back too and stumbled against the roughcast wall of the mobile. She put out a quick hand to steady me, then stopped.

'Oh God, am I wrong?' she said. 'I'm not wrong, am I?'

Two weeks later, in my house this time, a Saturday night, my parents at a dinner party, my sister at a sleepover. In the living room, in front of the electric fire, we unbuttoned each other's shirts and unhooked the clasps of each other's bras. Then our jeans and knickers: unzipping, wriggling, hopping out and off. We kept giggling – there we were gallivanting around in my parents' living room in nothing but our socks.

'Here we are,' she said, as we faced each other, and my whole body rushed with goosebumps.

'Are you cold?' she said, but I wasn't. It wasn't that, at all.

Afterwards, we pulled the cushions off the sofa and lay on the floor, side by side. After a while we did start to shiver, even with the electric fire turned up fully, but neither of us reached for our clothes, scattered all over like useless, preposterous skins.

'We're like selkies,' she said, 'like *Rusalka* – do you know the opera?' and when I said I didn't, she stood up and struck a pose and sang the water nymph's song to the moon, she told me later, and I jumped to my feet and applauded, and we started giggling again, ridiculous bubbles of joy.

'Here we are,' she said again, and I said, 'Here we are,' and that became our saying, our shorthand. Here we are.

All love stories are the same story: the moment that, that moment when, the moment we.

We were we through Christmas, and into the spring. It was so easy: the music had been the reason, and now it was our excuse. We used one of the practice rooms each lunchtime and sometimes after school, and no one questioned it. Sometimes we'd play, or she'd play and I'd listen, or we'd both listen to music, and sometimes we'd just eat our sandwiches and talk. I'd go to hers after school, although I never quite felt at ease there, and I preferred it when we'd go for drives in her car, up the Craigantlet hills or along the coast to Holywood. I drifted from my friends, and she from hers, but the music practice hid everything.

And then we had the summer and we were freer than ever, completely free, and I lied blithely to my parents about where I was going and who with, using a rotating cast of old friends, and neither of them ever cottoned on, and I assumed it was the same for Mr Beattie too.

I don't want to think about the rest of it: the evening he finally confronted us, walked right in on us. I don't want to give any room to the disgust or the revulsion, to the anger and the panic that followed, and the tears, our tears, our wild apologies, when we should have been defiant, because what was there, in truth, for us to be apologising for, and to whom did we owe any apology?

'I have to do it,' she kept on saying. 'I'm all he's got. It won't change anything. But I have to do it.'

That winter, my English class studied Keats. I wrote a whole essay, six, seven sides, on the final stanza of 'The Eve of St Agnes'. 'And they are gone: aye, ages long ago / These lovers fled away into the storm.' In the stanza before, the lovers are gliding like phantoms into the wide cold hall and the iron porch where the Porter lies in a drunken stupor. His bloodhound wakes and shakes its flabby face but doesn't bark. The bolts slide open one by one, the chains stay silent, and the key finally turns, then, just as they think they've made it, the door groans on its hinges. You think it's all over for them, but then you read on, and you realise they've slipped away, out of your hands, before your very eyes, a miracle, a magic trick, a wormhole to another place, another time, where no one can ever follow.

The teacher kept me after class. She didn't believe I'd written it, at least not alone. I opened my lever arch and showed her my notes. Page after page after page in my crabbed, self-conscious writing. Ending rights the focus, I'd written, does not leave us in too cosy a glow but reminds us of age/decay/coldness of religious characters. I left this part out: I finished my essay with the lovers escaping. We talked about the real ending, Keats's ending, and we talked about his drafts of the ending, some of which were printed in the footnotes of the cheap Wordsworth edition.

'You've really thought about this,' she said. 'You've really taken this to heart.' I started to cry. 'Oh dear,' the teacher said, and she found me a tissue from a plastic pouch in her desk drawer, and she came round and sat on the front of her desk and asked if there was anything I wanted to talk about. I shook my head and held out my hand for my essay, and I wondered how much she knew, or guessed, my whole body liquid with shame.

*

I looked her up on the Internet just once, some months ago, on impulse, spurred by the Marriage Equality march in Belfast. It instantly felt too easy, too much. She'd never made it as a solo or even an orchestral musician, but she was a music teacher – and she was married; she and her husband ran a small music school together in Ayrshire. There were pictures of them both on the website, taking group lessons, conducting ensembles, standing with students of the most recent Woodwind Summer School. She was still whippet thin, no make-up, choppy hair. He looked younger than her: Doc Martens and skinny jeans, spiky hair, an earring. I clicked from one picture to the next. I don't know why I was so taken aback. I was engaged, after all. Engaged, happily engaged, and about to buy a flat. I just had never imagined it for her.

A memory came to me: one time in Ruby Tuesday's, or The Other Place, one of the studenty cafés across town in South Belfast where you could sit and eke out a mug of filter coffee for a whole evening. We'd said I love you by then – maybe for the first time, or maybe very recently; we were huge and important and giddy with it, with all of it, with us. I felt as if my blood was singing – that sparks were shooting from me – that everything I touched was glowing.

I could have done anything in those weeks. I could have run marathons or swum the length of the Lagan or jumped from a trapeze and flown. And yet I was happy, happier than I thought it was possible to be, just sitting in a cafe, talking. We sat in that café and talked about everything and nothing, talked and talked, and we were us. I remember that; I couldn't get over that. The room and everything in it: the scuffed wooden booths, the chipped laminate tables, the oversized menus, the fat boys in Metallica T-shirts and Vans at the table beside us, the cluster of girls across the way still in their school uniforms, the waitress carrying a plate of profiteroles, the rain on the window, the yellow of the light – it seemed a stage set that had been waiting our whole lives for us and at last we were here.

The waitress at the table, splashing more coffee into our mugs: 'Anything else I can get for yous, girls?' and we say, 'No, thank you,' in unison, then burst out laughing, at nothing, at all of it. For all the waitress knows, for all anyone knows, we're just two students, two friends, having an ordinary coffee.

'I want to tell her,' I say. 'I want to stand up and tell everyone.' And for a moment it seemed as if it might just be that simple: that that was the secret. 'I don't want us to have to hide,' I went on. 'I want to tell everyone: my parents, your dad, everyone. I want to stand in front of the City Hall with a megaphone and shout it out to the whole of Belfast.'

Suddenly neither of us was laughing any more.

'I wish we could,' she said.

We were both quiet for a moment.

'When you were older,' I said, thinking aloud, 'you could team up with a male couple, and the four of you could go out together, and people would assume, assume correctly, you were on a double-date. Only the couples wouldn't be what they thought.'

I was pleased with the idea, but she still didn't smile. 'Hiding in plain sight,' she said.

'You could live together,' I went on, 'all in one big house, so your parents wouldn't get suspicious. If you had to, you could even marry.' I started laughing again as I said it.

'No,' she said, and she was serious, more than serious – solemn. She reached out and touched one finger to my wrist and all of my blood leapt towards her again. 'We won't need to,' she said. 'By then we'll be free.'

That night, I walked the streets of East Belfast again in my dreams. Waking, the dream seemed to linger far longer than a mere dream. *These streets are ours.* I was jittery all day, a restless, nauseous, over-caffeinated feeling. I could email her, I thought, through the website. I wouldn't bother with pleasantries or preliminaries, I'd just say, 'There we were. Do you remember?'

THE WEE GRAY WOMAN

Ethna Carbery

Ethna Carbery (1864–1902) was a writer, poet, journalist, editor and co-founder of the women's nationalist organisation Inghinidhe na hÉireann. With Alice Milligan, she co-edited *The Shan Van Vocht*, which published some of James Connolly's first political writing. She is best known for *The Four Winds of Erinn*, *In the Celtic Past* and a short story collection, *The Passionate Hearts*.

His cabin stood by the side of a burn into which the sally-trees drooped from either side, making a thick fringe of green that met overhead and cast dappled shadows on the clear water when the sun stood high and fierce in the heavens. Little ripples broke in white bubbles around the stones that made the crossing-places, and the speckled trout darted like tiny silver spears through their haunts below the overhanging banks.

It was a tranquil, lonely spot; eerie, too, in the autumn twilight, when the slow-creeping mists rose up from the bog for miles around, and many were the tales told of an evening, by the folk living on the high land, of lights that flashed all over the bog at the very moment that Jamie Boyson set his candle in his cottage window to guide the Wee Gray Woman up the rugged loaning to her seat in the chimney corner.

Once it happened that the wild young fellows of Glenwherry came in the dead of night to play a trick on Jamie. They stole over the stepping-stones of the burn and noiselessly reached the one-paned window, half hidden by thatch, in which the light gleamed. A red turf fire blazing on the hearth lit up the interior of the old man's kitchen; it shone on the battered ancient dresser, and on the store of carefully-kept delf that had been his mother's. For Jamie had the name of being cleanly and thrifty in his ways. The hearth was carefully swept, the flat stones at front and sides whitened by a practised hand, and no ragged streaks wandered over the edges on to the clay floor beyond. A three-legged stool stood in front of the fire, placed there for the convenience of the unearthly visitant who, Jamie said, came nightly to sit and rest herself by the *greesaugh* until the black cock should crow in the rafters above the settle-bed, invariably awaking him at the same moment that the Wee Gray Woman got warning to leave. That was why he could never get a right look at her, he lamented. Sometimes he opened his eyes in time to see the flutter of her gray cloak as she passed out of his door, and once he caught a gleam of red. It was a red hood she wore, not like anything that mortal ever saw before, but just as if a big scarlet tulip had been crushed down over her head with all the leaves sticking out round her face. And his blood always curdled when she gave a cry going over the threshold, as if she was being dragged away into some dreaded torment from which she had had a respite.

"It would break the heart in yer breast to hear it, just for all the work like the whine of a dog when there's death aroun'," he would say.

But no one could get him to commit himself as to a theory about the comings and goings of the Wee Woman. Whether he fancied her a friendly denizen of fairyland, or a poor wandering ghost dreeing her purgatory for her own sake or the sake of some one loved and living, the inquisitive people of the bog-side could never learn, yet night after night the hearth was swept, and the stool placed that she might have her rest until dawn broke in a flame of gold and pale chilly green over the hill-tops.

So the ghostly story spread, as such stories will, through the country, finding by turns sympathiser and sceptic alike, who yearned, though fear of the super-natural kept most of them away, for a peep through Jamie's window before the black cock gave the signal. But the young fellows from Glenwherry, daring and mischievous as they were, had made up their minds to solve the mystery, and nothing daunted, holding their breath steadily, they drew close to the little window, and out of the thick blackness of the last night-hour glared into the haunted kitchen.

The firelight flickered fitfully at first, so that their eyes, half blinded with the darkness, saw nothing save shadows; then, suddenly, a gleam shot from the heart of the dying turf, and showed a vision that drove them back from the window, saddened and ashamed.

It was only the old man asleep in his settle-bed, his thin, wrinkled profile outlined like a cameo against the background of dark wood, and the patient old hands, that were so gentle and capable, folded upon his breast, as when he had lain down to sleep.

After that the Wee Gray Woman might come and go, without dread of being watched for, or disturbed, and among the Glenwherry lads Jamie found a set of stalwart partisans, whose judgment in his favour dare not be gainsaid.

He was not altogether devoid of occupation and amusement in his lonely existence. The little one-roomed cabin was tidy as a woman might have kept it. And though he harboured neither cat nor dog, during one winter at least— the severest winter known for many years in that locality—he had a pet, and the pet was a cricket. Imported from a neighbouring fireside, he had trained it with the utmost patience and skill until the diminutive dusty-looking object learned to jump out from behind the big pot in the chimney-corner at his call. The story of his having accomplished such a marvel scarcely gained credence; it was not to be compared to that of his ghostly guest; but the country children cherished it and repeated it in wide-eyed wonder, when they gathered round their elders' knees before the unwelcome bedtime; while the more superstitious asserted that it was the Wee Gray Woman come to bide with Jamie Boyson by day in another guise. It certainly looked uncanny enough, hop-hopping over the floor, chirruping in a shrill, faint treble to his deeper intonation, and, when he lifted it, creeping into the shelter of his hand, as a home bird might that has known and loved and trusted in the kind guardianship.

But once upon a time Jamie Boyson had need of neither ghost nor cricket for company. That was in the days of his early manhood, when, stalwart, supple, and strong, he led the boys of Crebilly to victory on many a hard-fought field of a Sunday, proving himself a champion to be proud of, in throwing the shoulder-stone, and wielding the *camán* against the athletic Glenwherry lads, with big Dan O'Hara at their head. Then, where was his equal to be found at dance or christening? Why, half the girls in the country were in love with him, and hopelessly, too, as they learned to admit to their own sad hearts, that fluttered so uncomfortably under the Sunday 'kerchiefs when he passed, his black head erect, and his shoulders squared like a militia major's, without a look at one of them, up the chapel aisle to his seat next his mother in the old family pew.

The family pew held something else besides his mother; something the very sight of which was enough to bring the red blood in a rush to the roots of his curly dark hair, and make his heart almost leap out of his breast for gladness; something that was small, and fair, and blue-eyed, half-hidden behind his mother's ample form, and scarcely lifting her white lids from the beads she was passing through her fingers.

She was no stranger to him; he had many opportunities of watching her pale sweetness by his own fireside at night, without embarrassing her with that burning gaze of his under the disapproving eyes of all the congregation; but he was wont to say to himself, as a sort of justification that little Rosie at her prayers taught him more about heaven and holiness than the priest could do with all his preaching.

His brother Hugh used to joke him often and often about his fancy for the little orphan girl whom his mother had saved from the poorhouse, and Jamie's brow would glow with the angry red that warned Hugh's tongue to stop, and the laughter to die out of his merry brown face. There were only the two of them left to his mother, and one took little Rosie into his life as a sister, while to the other she, whom the country lads in general had called "a poor, pale wisp o' a thing", became his all, his world, his gateway of Paradise. How the love for her grew up in his heart was a mystery to him. Perhaps it took root when as a little child—the evening she came home to them—she laid her flaxen head on the bashful lad's broad shoulder and would not be parted from him until sleep stole on her unawares and released the tiny hands from their grasp on his strong ones. Or perhaps it came later as he learned to watch delightedly her deft, gentle household ways, and heard her crooning to herself over her flowering, in the rare leisure moments the active, bustling mother allowed.

There was an old song he was very fond of singing about "Lord Edward"— an old song she loved to listen to—and he was always sure of a grateful glance from the shy eyes, when of a winter's night he favoured the little circle around the hearth of Lisnahilt with the stanzas set to an air that was very popular in the district:—

"The day that traitors sold him an' enemies bought him,
The day that the red gold and red blood was paid;
Then the green turned pale and trembled Like the dead leaves in autumn.
An' the heart an' hope of Ireland in the cold grave was laid.

"The day I saw you first, with the sunshine fallin' round ye,
My heart fairly opened with the grandeur of the view;
For ten thousand Irish boys that day did surround ye.
An' I swore to stand by them till death, an' fight for you.

"Ye wor the bravest gentleman an' the best that ever stood,
An' yer eyelids never trembled for danger nor for dread,
An' nobleness was flowin' in each stream of your blood—
My blessin' on ye day and night, an Glory be your bed.

"My black and bitter curse on the head an' heart an' hand
That plotted, wished, an' worked the fall of this Irish hero bold,
God's curse upon the Irishman that sould his native land,
And hell consume to dust the hand that held the traitor's gold."

Sometimes tired with the day's hard work, she would rest her head against the wall with a low sigh of weariness. She must often be tired, he thought; those little feet had run about so nimbly since early morning, and the little red hands had washed and baked, without a moment's pause; but, please God, that would be all ended soon, when his wife should reign over a home of her own, and he had taken her into the shelter of his strong arms for evermore.

Yet no word of this crossed his lips, though the desire that filled his heart beat like a strong ceaseless wave within his breast, giving him an almost unbearable pain, and he never dreamt but that she knew. In the very effort to control himself, his voice was, curiously, harsh when he spoke to her; and while the poor child trembled at the rude accents, her faltering reply aroused in the big, tender-hearted fellow a wild feeling that was half exquisite pity, and half hate. Ah! if he had only spoken then, the grim tragedy of his life might have been spared him.

One bleak night in autumn a sound outside drew him to the door, and opening it, he stood listening.

"John Conan's calves are in the clover-field," he said; "go and put them out."

Rose lifted her timid blue eyes to him questioningly.

"Do you hear me?" he asked.

"But I'm afraid," she murmured; "it's so dark, an'—" He pointed his finger to the open door and the black stormy night outside.

"Go," he repeated fiercely, turning to his chair, and lifting his pipe off the shelf, and the girl passed into the darkness without another word.

What madness was on him that he had spoken to the little girl, and sent her on such an errand? he asked himself when she had gone. He had been conscious of a strange, sore sensation all day, since at Crebilly Fair, that forenoon, Tom M'Mullan had proposed a match between her and his son Jack, one of the wildest young scamps in the whole countryside, and the unreasoning jealousy grew and grew until he had wreaked his pain in vengeance on his poor Rosie's unoffending head.

"Oh! amn't I the queer, ungrateful fool," he muttered, "to trate the wee lass this way."

An hour passed, he waiting every moment to hear her footfall on the threshold, and his mother speculating comfortably that she had gone in for a gossip to John Conan's. At last he could bear his regret and the suspense no longer, and went out to seek her.

It was only a step or two to the clover-field, and reaching the low stone wall he called to her eagerly in the darkness. The startled calves, still enjoying their forbidden banquet, lowed back in answer.

He vaulted the gate, every step of the way familiar to him by night as by noon, and called anxiously and long. Then he remembered his mother's surmise, and turned across the field to Conan's.

There was no little Rosie sitting with the laughing girls grouped together in the corner, over a quilting frame, and in response to his husky demand a couple of Conan's young sons volunteered to accompany him on his search— Hugh, his brother, being away for the night in a market town many miles off.

He walked on, quickly, in the direction of the bog, guided only by his intimate knowledge of the treacherous path that wound like a serpent across the marshy windswept surface. He heard the small waves beat against each other with a faint sad sound, while overhead not one solitary star glimmered, to light his heart with hopefulness. Through the terrible night, and into the dawn, his frantic search continued, calling her name in a hoarse agony that wrung the souls of those who heard him.

"Rosie, Rosie, my little girl, it's Jamie's callin'. Ah! come, can't ye, an' don't be hidin' there. Don't ye hear me darlin', it's Jamie, an' the supper's waitin' on us. Let Conan's calves go—they're always a trouble to somebody, but *you* come home. Here, take my han'"—stretching out his arms into the empty shadows—"take it, love, an' don't be afeard, nothin' can touch ye, pulse o' my heart, when I'm beside ye, Rosie! Rosie!"

And so on through the dreary hours, over the wild bogland, his voice rang in pitiful entreaty, until jagged streaks of golden red flamed like trailing banners in the East, and the birds, wide-awake, took up in a chorus, clear-tongued and grateful, the morning song; but alas! for him, whose song-bird had flown afar, and for whom the dawn henceforth should hold no radiance, nor the rose-flushed mellow evening any passion.

Yet his frantic cry broke in upon the happy choir, and the blackbird and thrush, from hedge and beechentree, watched him staggering home in the sunshine, murmuring through lips that scarcely knew the words they uttered— "Rosie, Rosie, girl dear, come home."

Some hours later a turf-cutter, crossing the burn to his work, caught a gleam of something bright under the cold running water. It was little Rosie's fair head lying against the stones in the shade of the drooping sallytrees, whither through the darkness, blinded by her sorrow, she had wandered to her death.

Jamie Boyson aged suddenly after that. When the friends of his boyhood had grown into sturdy, middle-aged men, strong and hearty, he was already old, with a gloom upon him that no smile was ever known to lighten. In time, when his mother died, and Hugh had married, he grew unable to bear the sound of children's chatter through the rooms where he had once hoped to see his own little ones at play, and came to live his life alone in the cabin by the burnside, from whence he could watch the very spot where poor Rosie's gentle head had lain under the clear cold ripples.

So the country folk, noting his absent dim blue eyes, and wandering talk about the Wee Gray Woman, grew to believe that it was little Rosie's ghost come to bear him company until the call should sound for him, and his broken and desolate heart should find peace.

That was many, many years ago; and, perhaps, they have met long since in heaven, where Jamie Boyson, young, and straight, and strong again, with all the bitterness gone from his heart, has taken little Rosie in his arms and told her the truth at last.

CHILDREN'S CHILDREN

Jan Carson

Jan Carson is a writer and community arts facilitator based in East Belfast. She has published a novel, *Malcolm Orange Disappears* and short story collection, *Children's Children* (Liberties Press), a micro-fiction collection, *Postcard Stories* (Emma Press). Her novel *The Fire Starters* was published by Doubleday in 2019. It won the EU Prize for Literature for Ireland 2019.

They met, by arrangement, at the rock that looked like a rabbit from one side and the Empire State Building from the other. She had never ventured further north and knew it only as a rabbit. He knew nothing of the south. The rock had been a skyscraper to him for as long as he could remember.

She was the last and he was the last. All the other young ones had left for the mainland with the notion of becoming beauty therapists or PhD students. The pair of them were leftover children, too fat and faithful to consider leaving. They did not dream remembering dreams, nor indulge themselves in ambition. They felt physically ill if they went so much as a single day without encountering the ocean. They knew nothing more than the placid seasons of their parents and grandparents: up with the sun, down with the cows, and television for all those needs which could not be grown or hauled—sleek gilled and flappering—from the sea.

They were leftover children, set aside for such a time as this. Tomorrow they would be married for the good of the island, both northern and southern sides. They understood what this meant and could picture themselves tomorrow evening, in good clothes, with music. Yet, when they tried to imagine one month later, drinking tea and making up a stranger's bed, they could not alight upon anything more concrete than the details: shoelaces, crockery, the caustic smell of Lifebuoy soap on an unfamiliar sink.

They understood entirely but had not been given a choice. The arrangement was a simple mathematical equation; if more people were not soonly made, there would be no one left to keep the island afloat. They would marry for the good of everyone, themselves included. Little thought had been given to what would happen after their marrying. Questions such as which side of the island they might settle on, or who their children would marry, or where they would eat their Christmas dinner when Christmas made its annual appearance, had not been considered.

The rock marked the exact midpoint of the island, seven foresty miles from the northern shore and a similar, open-fielded seven from the opposite coastline. The island was long and puckered like a section of intestine, recently unravelled. It was drenched in the winter and barely dry by the time summer had folded into autumn. Each year it lost ten to twenty stones of weight as, one by one, and occasionally in couples, the young ones caught the ferry to the mainland and never returned. Bolstered by this newfound lightness the island's tideline had receded by three centimetres in the last decade. This extra pinch of pebbly sand was widely attributed to global warming. The islanders rested easy, convinced that they, and they alone, were riding high while the rest of the world sunk on the whim of a polar icecap.

The islanders were a staunch and meaty breed, shock-haired, handsome and raised on short-loan classics from the library boat which visited once a month on a Wednesday. They lived in either the north or the south. Even those who hovered around the midlands, like small children toeing the bonfire's edge, knew exactly which side of the line they laid their heads on. On the island you were north or you were south, or you left for the mainland. The east and west were not to be considered. They remained geographical afterthoughts, as inconsequential as a pair of open brackets. Once, in the 1970s, a half mile of the east coast had unhooked itself and floated off to Lanzarote or some such sunny place. No one had noticed or particularly cared, for the peripheral directions had remained unimportant so long as north had stayed north and south had continued to dominate the southern extremities.

All the island's children had been formed from the same sandy soil and sprouted annually, in metric units, towards the same sap-grey sky. They spoke the same words, darkly set, and drunk from the same slow river, rising as it did in the north, and fumbling southwards through fields and forests in pursuit of the motherless ocean. When it rained, as it every day did, it was the same cloud sulk which settled on all their pitched roofs, their swing sets and off-road vehicles, the same rain which coaxed the lazy turnips out of the island's muck-thick belly and into their soup pots.

The people were consistent as common spades, on either side of the border. Yet, it was unheard of to point these similarities out to an islander currently resident. In 1973, a young fella who'd come to make a documentary film had been drowned by the feet and posted home in envelopes for claiming it was sheer stupidity to split the island while the same sort of people lived on either side of the border. The islanders could not so much as look in a puddle for noting just how different they were from their neighbours across the border. They prided themselves on variegated eyebrows, specialist cuisine and sporting activities peculiar to their own backyards. Even a throwaway comment from a visiting mainlander, such as, 'Do all the good folk on this island have the same lovely shade of hair?' or 'Youse ones on the island are fairly good at the old boatbuilding, are you not?' could turn an islander purple with indignation. No true southerner wished to be mistaken for an eejit from the north. Neither did the northerners wish to exhibit habits or haircuts distinctly associated with the south.

As she approached the rock, she recognised him. He was shorter than his photograph but the moustache was familiar, also the furious eyebrows. And, if she was not greatly mistaken he was wearing the same faded polo shirt he'd worn the day his picture had been taken.

He'd never seen her before, in person or print, but as she was the only woman in a field of trees, rocks and twitchetty sheep, he rightly assumed her to be his wife.

'Are you she?' he asked.

She nodded. Her hat crept up her forehead and came to rest like a dollop of cream on the peak of her crown. She was pretty enough, like a lady on local television, but not the sort you'd see in the movies.

Are you he?' she asked.

'I am for sure,' he replied.

The sound of him was all through his nose and strained, exactly like her Uncle Mikey from the north, who she'd only heard on the telephone and once in person, as a small child, at her grandmother's funeral.

'I brought sandwiches,' she said, and he wondered if they put the same things in their sandwiches on the other side of the island.

He'd heard from his brother Paul, who lived on the mainland now, that they buttered their sandwiches with mayonnaise in the south. This was probably just rumouring though. Ever since the island had split in two, like a pair of book pages parting, all sorts of stories had crept backwards and forwards across the border: the northerners kept their old ones in with the chickens; the folks of the south did not believe in dentists or even toothbrushes; they had not yet got satellite television or even microwave ovens in the north. As children they'd passed these rumours round the primary playground, gently, gently with cupped hands and lowered voices. They were too old for such nonsense by the time they arrived at big school. Big school was a Portakabin in the corner of the primary playground, with proper-sized toilets and a set of encyclopaedias preaching leather-bound reason from the topmost shelf of the bookcase. In light of histories as definite as Martin Luther King, the Battle of Hastings and also the Holocaust, it was ludicrous to believe sheer fluff and speculation. Yet the rumours were too delicious to let go of entirely.

'Here,' she said, 'have a ham sandwich.'

She unpeeled the tinfoil for him and passed the naked sandwich across the border. They sat down on the grass. She on her side, he on his. He pressed the two pieces of bread together and mayonnaise oozed out between the crusts.

'There's mayonnaise on this here sandwich,' he cried. 'Are youse mad over there in the south?'

'Youse can talk, putting red sauce in your tea; most disgusting thing I ever heard.'

'We do not.' But there was no way of proving this without a teapot.

They ate their sandwiches in silence. The mayonnaise nearly made him boke but he didn't want to put her off before they were even married. She watched him eating. The way the saliva caught in the corners of his mouth, like cuckoo spit stretching with every bite, turned her stomach. She was not used to people eating with such animal enthusiasm but she tried not to stare. When they were married she would start into his manners, teach him how civilised people approached an eating table.

'So, are you up for this then?' he asked.

'I suppose so.'

'Happy enough with what you're getting?'

'I'm sure you're in the same boat as me. I'd always planned on wedding one of our sort.'

'Desperate times, eh?'

'Are you saying I'm ugly?'

'Course not, sweetheart. You're definitely not the worst-looking woman on this island. It's just, I think neither of us would be doing this if there was anybody left on our own side.'

'Anybody else at all.'

'Still it's for the good of the island isn't it? We've to make a wee sacrifice for the auld ones.'

'We do indeed, sure haven't they always put us first?'

They fell to talking, he and then she, describing at length the very many exotic things which existed on their sides of the island: tall trees in the north and a man with seven fingers in the south, five kinds of ale on her side of the line and five completely different, but similarly potent, draughts on his.

The sound of him was a Continental holiday against the boredom. She found herself goosebumpling up and down her forearms, much afraid and also excited.

The sound of her was a shotgun far away and not quite threatening.

They were all but ready to cross the border, to skip the priests and get on with the good act of marrying, when the future sneaked out like a stifled fart.

'Your side or mine?' he asked.

She feigned grace and offered to move north for the sake of her husband's kin. (This was a lie of sorts, lovingly told and masking her desire to live, for the first time beneath trees, with foxes, in the company of singing folk.) He countered her lies with his own. He would move south, first for the good of his wife, then for the prospect of open fields and fresh milk and the lion's slice of morning sun.

They could not settle upon a side, for the land changed shape the moment you crossed the border. Ten minutes before their wedding day they realised that the island was asking more of them than they could ever manage.

'If we both move north, we'll upset the balance and tip the island into the sea,' he explained, holding her little hand coldly across the border.

'And if we settle in the south, things will be skewed in that direction,' she cried, 'never mind what'll happen when we start having the weans.'

'The weight of us combined could ruin everything.'

They unclasped, hands coming apart like two ends of an ancient necklace. She sat cross-legged in the south and he watched the dawn descend upon the northern face of the rock. They held their silence reverently and wondered if they loved the island enough to be neither north nor south, foreigner or familiar, but rather a brave new direction, balanced like a hairline fracture in the centre of everything.

ONE WORD

Juanita Casey

Juanita Casey (1925–2012) was a poet, playwright and novelist. Her poetry collections include *Hath the Rain a Father?* and *Horse by the River and Other Poems*. She published two novels and two plays, one of which was produced by the Abbey. Her story in this collection originally appeared in the anthology *Cutting the Night in Two*.

I am not a cruel woman, cried Miss Judith Dannaher. I love God's animals! But if I catch one of those bloody asses in my garden again I'll break all their bloody legs, Lord save us, like sticks for me fire.

Miss Dannaher kicked her own ass in the chest, and felt some measure of relief.

It was all his fault, that whoring Jimmy, roaring off at all hours of the day and night and attracting the rest of his outlaw band off the sand dunes and into her domains.

The times she had to go after the limb of Satan too, looking all over the place and up the roads for him when he broke his hobbles and was away with the nine others of his unspeakable tribe.

The nine belonged to various neighbours around, but having either broken out or been turned away, the nine lived off their wits and other people's gardens and occasionally would be caught up and press-ganged into work again for a few hours.

The long ears of them would scissor together at Miss Judith Dannaher's approach, the rain dropping off their thick pelts and pearling their whiskers as they hunched beneath the few shrubs and thorns around the Maiden's Tower, and she dare not utter the murder within her lest the whole lot take fright and whisk off up the road again. Only when it rained could she catch the wretched Jimmy with any ease, as all the asses were loth to move out from the shelter of the bushes.

Once she had him though. O once she had him. I'll knock shite out of yez, she'd choke hoarsely and mentally murder him all over in various delightful ways until she got him home, when knock shite out of him she did.

Sunshine on the other hand meant that long, soul-destroying saunter behind them all, pretending she didn't really want Jimmy at all and was just out for her health. Apoplexy quietly swelled within her as they moved step to her step, just in front, just out of grab, with their black tricorne eyes looking back at her and their tails demurely switching. By the Holy God, she would clench. By the Holy God...

Two or three interesting hours could pass thus in gentle ambulation, while bees visited clover and cinquefoil and campion, and the breeze curled the frills of the asses' manes and caressed her hissing brow.

But if there was a wind, then goodbye to the asses and goodbye to Jimmy as they carolled and brayed, bucked and buffeted each other in a mad race to the sea, an ancient, disturbing spirit under their matted hides, and the wildness of swift Asia in their changed eyes. They became, for a short day, the inheritors of ruined Nineveh, the swift ones of Nimrod, the fierce runners of the deserts. Along the strand, matching strides with the waves, wheeling to confront the walker on the sands with the long, burning stare over the civilisations to their green time before men.

When the sea-grasses hummed and whistled and when the winds came, they lifted their scarred and heavy heads. They were the inheritors of the Khamsin and the Sirrocco. They were the Seers.

On these days, the wind also got into Miss Judith Dannaher's head, and she gave up and went to bed with a fierce migraine, which pounded and drummed as though all Jimmy's four hooves were, for once, kicking hell out of her.

With the occasional and begrudging help of the ever-reluctant Jimmy, Miss Judith Dannaher tilled the soil of her few acres, saved a little frantic hay, moved her hens' houses around her own cabin in an uproar of hens, oaths, and the total disarray of both herself and Jimmy, carted a variety of useful and useless agricultural products about, buried the cart and Jimmy at intervals beneath vast, steaming dollops of cow manure, and the same trio went shopping with the odour of sanctity adhering with the bits of straw to all three.

On these expeditions, Miss Judith Dannaher tugged, beat, swore, kicked, and wished the most interesting amendments upon the creeping Jimmy, but on the return journey nothing could hold him as he tore for home and freedom with his mouth pulled back to his ears and the cart and Miss Judith Dannaher yawing and gybing behind him like a boat in a following sea. Whoa, whoa, ye whore, I'll knock shite out of yez was the battle-cry of this ill-assorted equipage as it shaved corners, the village bus, slow children and old Mr Fintan Maloney on his crutches, and joyous dogs pursued its course with hopes of receiving a flight of sausages from one of its better rebounds.

Upon unharnessing the now demure and extinguished Jimmy, Miss Judith Dannaher would apply her arm, voice, and boots to him, and a fury of dust would erupt as she beat and whacked his hide like a carpet.

Miss Judith Dannaher lived on one side of the Maiden's Tower, and the brothers Johnny and Jimmy O'Neill lived on the other. Between their cabins ran a stream, and over the stream a plank bridge, and behind them a tangled patchwork of small fields and miniature forests of scrubby oaks, thorns and ash. In front lay the Burrows, mile upon mile of sand dunes, and in front of these a swish down on to the white miles of strand and the moody sea.

Miss Judith Dannaher's fields contained, as well as the occasional Jimmy, three old cows and three young heifers, her hens, some geese and a few ducks, and a tethered community of nanny goats, all spinsters like Miss Judith Dannaher and with therefore not a drop of milk between them.

The fields of Johnny and Jimmy O'Neill contained but themselves, some blackberries and fungi at the right seasons, and the brothers O'Neill let them get on with it.

The Maiden's Tower was a long pinnacle of stone, mushroom-capped with small square inlets to keep arrows out of spying eyes and was a fair example of the old round tower of Irish history. Legend and history however ran a race with truth, and all deadheated.

The Maiden had watched her Captain sail away on the tides of spring and whiled away the time and her heart's desire by building the Tower to his memory and to his return. Which he never did. That the Maiden chose to erect a peculiarly phallic edifice did not go unnoticed among the unsophisticated of the region, and private additions and ramifications to the Maiden's tale abounded in every family.

Every morning the brothers O'Neill arose and breakfasted without one word between them, and they both stalked down to their boat and its nets on the estuary shore. With long, deliberate strides they heroned down the shingle together, each one to his own task in the boat, moving together and each other like pieces in a jig-saw.

All day they rowed and netted at the river mouth close by, slow yet deft, unhurried yet quick enough, and without one word between them.

A lorry came out from the town each day to buy whatever catch they and the other scattered fishermen of the area might bring in, but on days of wind and white water the day began as usual with their Trappist breakfast, but no fishing could be attempted, and so Johnny and Jimmy O'Neill would stare at the sea from either side of the plank bridge, and without one word between them. Then Johnny would take the track over the Burrows, and Jimmy would follow the frothy tideline beside the sea, and a few hundred yards apart they would stalk the three miles into Coneytown village and bend into Barney Hagan's within a bootfall of each other. Seated on opposite sides of the Vandyke interior, they would drink time and the sea into an opacity of oblivion without one word between them and return under the moon and the flying clouds and the spit of the rain, Johnny taking the track over the black

Burrows, and Jimmy following the luminous tideline beside the sea, a few hundred yards apart and so blind, so deaf, and so dumb that they could not, had they wanted to, have uttered one word between them. At the cabin, at which they arrived within each other's shadows, they unbooted and undressed to their combinations and, turning their backs to each other, fell asleep to the thunder of the surf and of their own snores.

Their lives, in this manner, had creaked apart and together down the same rut like the hub of a loosening wheel since the year of 1916 when Johnny joined the British Navy and Jimmy remained at home at his nets. In those days Miss Judith Dannaher had been as a lily in her fields, a shy wild violet of the Burrows. She and Johnny were to marry on his return from the wars. But one day she thought of the other bereft and languishing Maiden, decided a bird in the hand was better than an absent heart, and settled in its absence for Jimmy.

There was no haste, as Miss Judith had her farm and Jimmy his fish, and the rain and the sun and the winds rolled the seasons around them. Until, suddenly, there was Johnny. And from that one day the brothers O'Neill rethreaded the hole in their lives and went on with their netting as before, but now without one word between them. Miss Judith, after a suitable period of furious lament, rethatched her cabin, made herself a new apron, shot her father's old donkey, and bought a new one, a black jack she named Johnny, and out of which, for the next twenty-three years, she knocked shite.

Over the years she lost both her beauty and her old father and gained very little else but a whetstone of a temper upon which she honed her tongue.

On the day of the Second World War, Miss Judith lost her asinine fiancé in a plot of cabbages behind Michael Murphy's shed, ballooned with the bloat and upturned like a small, black currach with his four legs as stiff at each corner as bedposts.

A few days later Miss Judith, advertising, became engaged to the equally black-hearted Jimmy, then a winsome three-year-old with a shiny coat, and they settled into their mutual years of deadlock and checkmate, with Miss Judith knocking shite out of Jimmy as she had out of the late Johnny.

Thus the ordered years passed. They rolled by the brothers O'Neill with the porpoises of summer and the westerlies of winter, their wordless days punctuated by the flap of soles and bass, mullet and pollock on the boards of the boat at their feet. Their years of snapping congers, of turbot heavy as anchors, of fatuous skate and of quicksilver sprats, and of the rainbow leap of the salmon and the strange ungodliness of the huge angler fish with its mantrap jaws and its ventral parody of hands.

The years bloomed and seeded and withered too for Miss Judith Dannaher, with the harebells and the froggy marsh flowers, the mossy gates which opened her days into one field from another, and the faded finality of the grained back door shutting out the night's black paw. The days of unborn calves and ice on buckets, of geese on the high wind of Christmas, and of a striped snail on summer's rosetted wall.

The years of thistledown and blown spindthrift, the years of mustardseed.

The years changed, and to those who say there is no change their changeling lives must suffer the strangest of them all.

Like leaves, one falls on a bright day of frost, and the other is left for the night wind. One drifts to the wet grass, and one remains to tap in the sunlight.

It is a slow pavane, and yet those that are left say how swift is the end, how unexpected, how terrible. They cannot see the unravelling of the net, the break in the web, the turning of the inexorable kaleidoscope to bring about a new pattern, the new enigma.

On a December day, Miss Judith Dannaher closed all her windows and wedged the doors, fed her stock, and made up her fire. There could be no work until the sheeting rain and savage wind eased.

The hens peered out of their houses at the roar, and the tucked cows shivered at the closed door of their byre.

The wind flung the sand off the beach, and the sea ran against the sullen river's push, and they fought each other into a great, toothed, lionheaded wall of grey water.

The brothers O'Neill were caught up as their boat scraped ashore, and they were rolled in their black oilskins under its sucking arch like peas down a drain. The wind caught the ghosts of two words and tore them into infinity.

O Judith, cried Johnny.

O Judith, cried Jimmy.

In the dim cabin Miss Judith Dannaher had fallen asleep by her bright fire.

In a hollow of the whistling Burrows nine grey asses and one black with a broken hobble sheltered against the driving sand, patiently enduring the stinging fury of the wind with the humble acceptance of martyrs.

On the strand the whirling paper shell of a sea-urchin blew against a white branch of driftwood and disintegrated in a puff of fragments.

Her head settling further down on to her chest, Miss Judith Dannaher exhaled a strangled snore, and the light ashes of her dead fire stirred and fluttered on the cold hearth.

BEATRICE

Evelyn Conlon

Evelyn Conlon is a short story writer, novelist and anthologist, described as one of Ireland's truly original voices. She has written about capital punishment, famine, secret lives, the double standard, borders, sex and lies. Her work is widely anthologized and translated, most recently into Chinese and Tamil. She lives in Dublin and is a member of Aosdána.

Maybe it was the day that had caused it. A warm, over-generous June fifteen hours. The sky had been full of sun. The sort of day you are afraid to commit to memory in case it disappears. Beatrice Sherry had spent it being unbearably happy for no reason at all. Well, that is if you think fresh air so tasty it can be swallowed and such sun, such sun, no reason at all.

All these days now, she thought about what it might have been that caused it and how it happened. It was easier that way, blaming or thanking some vague it. Surely no one would expect her to say that she had done it herself, had landed herself here. Ah, but she had. She had stood beside him deliberately at the end of the night; they had been introduced casually as happens at aimless parties flung together on holiday evenings in the west of Ireland. She found herself beside him, oh yes, found herself, then a waltz came on, I don't waltz, he said, I'll teach you, she said, and when she moved closer to get into the dance position a warm shiver whistled up to her head, making it feel light. There was blood everywhere carousing, carousing through her veins. She didn't teach him to waltz, and next thing they found themselves at the door, ah yes, found themselves, he supposedly going – it would be easier to test the thing now – she supposedly staying.

Beatrice held the door open for him, as if it was her house, which it wasn't; they each moved about one-eighth of one inch closer to the other, just enough to ensure that they could not then draw back. And no one knew whose mouth was drinking whose. They found themselves in his place (at least, he had a key) and they stripped each other slowly, rubbing their bare skin together, their tongues resting inside each other's mouths, or sucking ferociously, or gently licking. Her breasts felt sharp and brazen against him, she lowered her mouth and kissed his nipples. They hardened so readily he was shocked. They touched as much as they could stand, held each other's faces in their hands, and then pulled the breath from each other in one ecstatic coming that left them near tears and bewildered. They couldn't bear to take their arms from around their bodies.

But morning had to come. They slipped away – he to work, she to more holiday – afraid to say a word. She was terrified, because surely nothing could ever be the same again, nothing, day nor night nor season, nor logic nor sense. The day was Thursday. She went back to her mechanical drawing job the following Monday. They had met once again. On Friday his wife had joined him. It hadn't, after all, been his place, he had the key to his friend's flat for when he was working in these parts. Even this became an intimate revelation. Because it was the weekend, and such a beautiful one, his nurse wife was joining him to spend it by the sea. What sea? Beatrice had forgotten the Atlantic behind her. Her husband, R, joined her also and as far as she could remember, they talked normally.

On Saturday at a quarter past five Beatrice managed a quick hour in the pub. From the newsagent's she had spotted Him at the door, pecking his wife goodbye, she who was obviously on the way to the beach. Beatrice told her husband, with unmannerly haste, that she was going to head off alone for a walk. She wouldn't be long. He said ok. Beatrice followed Him into the back bar. 'Oh goody,' he said. 'I like furtive women.' They did not strip each other in the pub because you have to be careful about these things. She stayed one hour and left quickly when she saw her, by now perplexed, husband walking past the window.

THE NEXT YEAR

I packed and met my friend in the Pembroke for lunch. She knows, so she gave me this diary as a joke so I can record the best and the worst, as if I would. I have ten days, in the middle of which R will join me for the weekend. R, my husband, don't, don't hassle me. The train went through the usual places, which should have been settling but wasn't. Will this throw my whole life into a sickening chaos? I have to hope that it won't; I have to hope that it will. That's why it would be better not to find out. Will we be able to speak to each other, will we be able to talk to each other? But first of all, will I be able to speak at all and will I give it away by not being able to do anything but stammer and swallow? Or should I say, will he like me as much as I like him? I wish the train journey was over. I have one definite arrangement but the rest may be torture for me. I may become a sixteen-year-old un-woman waiting to be wanted. Ah no! He is not cruel. Hopefully. I don't have to mean 'hopefully'. I don't believe that men you sleep with once then become cruel. Why, why am I thinking this nonsense then? I spend the rest of the journey seeing him seeing me.

My B&B is quite all right. Passed the day being nervous. I am to meet him at six o'clock. That will give us time. I wish it was five to six. It's only four.

I went to the pub at three minutes to six and he wasn't there of course, so I went to the toilet and spoke out loud to myself as if I was talking to him. If you do that to me I will die. Honestly I will. I knew that I should have been saying, if you do that to me I will kill you, but that's not what came out. Went down again. Sat at bar, with my back to the door, in a delighted nervous mess. He came in and I couldn't look, my eyes burned so much. My face took on a life of its own. I smiled, then I looked. He thought I looked lovely and he meant that it was great to see me and I knew why I was there. He didn't touch me and I thought I would split open for the want of his skin. Then it dawned on me that he thought it was his prerogative to touch me first. We talked through an hour – he has had it with marriage, houses, monogamy. Up to his neck, he says. Up to those beautiful balls of yours, I would have thought, if I hadn't been too polite. I was less worried by marriage than he, less immersed in its pointlessness. As he got gloomier I realised that I thought of mine as the state of having or being an identical twin. I suppose that meant mine wasn't working. We were thinking, too, like people who were not with each other, so we had brandy. I got down from my stool to pay for it, which was not necessary, and touched his leg accidentally as I sat back up. That released us from a dreadful wondering, wondering whether the lives we'd just described could possibly be ours and if so how had we let them happen. One touch and we were free. We couldn't wait to finish the brandy. The man beside me didn't want his wife to hang up her coat, fur, on the back of the door. Anyone could lift it, he said. She was needled. She was out for a drink, she reminded him, and couldn't give a fuck about the coat.

They went to 'his' place. He said he had the key and stayed there when he was working around here. His friend who owned it was away a lot, mostly in Belfast doing a course in Peace Studies in…

'Yes, you told me,' she said intimately.

He looked surprised, wary almost. He couldn't remember telling her.

'Last year.'

'Oh yes.'

She didn't have an orgasm, which was very unlike her, she could usually have one just thinking. A blessing perhaps, or maybe not. She tried to get him to help her, which was new to her. He was reluctant. He got up from the bed quickly and said, 'You women are always so superior, holding back.'

She could have said one of many things. Touchy, aren't we? might have sufficed as the kindest one of them. What she said was, 'Just you wait until the next time.' That relaxed him. He wanted to go back to the pub, so they went.

Morning came as if it and they had been together for ever. But he left, mid-sentence, to go to work, leaving the oddest non-arrangement hanging between them. She could ring him up at half four and then he'd see how he was fixed.

I went to the newsagent's, bought a book and waited in the B&B. And waited some more. I read, pausing now and then, jolted by remembrance. I have just eaten and it is now four o'clock. I can ring him soon. Can. Am allowed to. Dear me, what a long way down. I tell myself that I am not nervous, that instead I have a quiet glow. Not an ecstatic one, a quiet one. I'm thinking about my real life at the moment and, because this glow is part of it, it's not so bad. But I'm not confident that he will want to see me tonight. Yet he looked so sorry when I said that R was going to join me, genuinely sorry, I blushed it was so obvious. And he rang his friend to let him know that 'we' were there, not just him. He didn't have to do that, it was definitely showing off. Would it be better if it were after half four? But uncertainty has its own thrill. 'I'll be finished here at half five. You could meet me and we could drive up to this other job that I have to check before we decide what to do.' We. 'Fine,' I say, knowing in my heart that I'm too old, too good, too bright, or too something, to be so grateful.

I see the church clock on my way, oh no, oh no, my watch is slow. Will I ever see him again? Ever? Surely he won't have waited, surely he won't, but he had. I would never have had the nerve to be late, I never do, but maybe it was no harm to have kept him wondering, as long as it has turned out all right. Drove to his job, I sat in his car outside, for a minute I imagined that I had been married to him for years. He came out and said, 'Do you want one of the best pints of Guinness in Ireland?' 'Yes,' I said. But I wish to God I knew whether we will go to bed or not. He has the control, this is how he likes it, he's not the sort to like it otherwise. I will have to wait. First, call at the flat. He jumps out of the car, 'Right. Immersion on, water flowers, will be with you in a minute.' Water flowers! That's telling me something, I wish I knew what. 'Now for the Guinness.' He smiles at me, innocently. I'm confused.

*

We walked speedily to the pub. Somewhere after too much drink he hints that we might. I'm nearly sober enough to realise that it is a hint and to wish he had said it earlier, but nearly drunk enough to get mad. My passion has been stopped from too much careless yo-yoing. We go back, he has a bath, we do. He raises my legs too high, I cannot feel him properly inside like that, I cannot find a touching place for my head. I cannot think this way. I do not care. Am I afraid? I cannot talk to him, he would sniff at my words. Talk would be too personal for him, he is on top. Then he gave me a scarf that he used to wear to the dole when life was not so good. 'Here,' he said, 'have this.' Yes, rolled off the bed, off me, let's be precise, and handed me a silk scarf that was sitting on the top of his overnight bag. 'Wear it, it will look lovely on you.' He has left me somewhere I'm not used to being. I say something which makes him laugh a lot, I cannot remember what it was, even as he laughs I have forgotten. However, I am glad that I can make him laugh. Eventually I leave and go back to my booked accommodation. He did not ask me to stay, he wants to see me tomorrow. I am glad to get into a bed on my own. Will I try it again? Of course I will.

Beatrice and he spent three evenings together, each one organised at the last minute. That shouldn't have mattered but it did, it piled up indignity.

On the fourth day, R arrived. He and Beatrice went for a drive, after he had consulted the map. They had a drink and she insisted on talking about this man she had met yesterday, she couldn't help it. He says he can't possibly support the Provos any more. That he used to, although he never believed in war. Now he simply can't. R says sarcastically, 'Looks like they've lost a valuable ally, a supporter who didn't believe in war. Must have suffered from a lot of agonised dissonance.' She says, 'Forget it.' He says, 'No, come on, tell me why the man can't, any more.' 'Enniskillen,' she says. 'But that happened ages ago, did the man hear about it late?'

R is alert and watchful. She had better be careful. But she drinks more and talks about people reaching the edge and about the ferocious pleasure that unacceptable behaviour can bring to a person. She talks too much and gives out bits of information but R doesn't notice or pretends not to. Maybe he's saving it up. Next morning R and Beatrice make an unembarrassed coupling, easy as a kiss. It's what they do sometimes, help themselves to each other. R went back to Dublin at the appointed time, leaving an open sea behind him.

*

Spent the day checking myself. Why am I doing this? To hear myself described in a new way, that's it. In both words and involuntary sounds. I enjoy the agony? I remember the exact sound of his moan when I kissed him. I want to find new explanations, I don't need words for emotions that I don't know, but for the rest, yes. I want to hear him say confidentially to the barman as he asks, too late, for a carryout, 'Ah, we only see each other twice a year', and to another, 'My wife likes lots of ice'. We have no past, will have no future, we will be bigger, brighter than any regrettable thing. But yet it's only my part in it because I have no intention of telling him. He would think that I was trying to get us involved. I have no perception of him hearing me. My dear.

Beatrice also spent some moments trying not to think of his wife and her own husband. It was easier not to think of R. In the end she took the easy way out and flippantly forced herself to think that if they weren't doing the same thing, it wasn't her fault. She didn't mean it but, as an excuse, it would do for now, now being the time before consequences.

I rang him to arrange where we would meet. He mentioned DB's, where we had met before. He said, 'You know where that is?' 'As if I could forget,' I said, with silver in my voice. 'Silly girl,' he said in a downturned tone. Again, I had left myself open for that. I felt like saying, Who the fuck do you think you are? but I didn't.

(Later when I told him what I had wanted to say he smiled deliciously. 'I expected that,' he said. Ah! so he is wanting someone open and vulnerable, who will wince, against whom he will appear ever, ever so strong. I was also silly enough to ask if he had ever brought anyone else to this flat. He said, in a high voice, 'I've had the key for eighteen months.' That was just a fleeting something in me, a wish for one little thing from him.)

I turned up at DB's with all my stuff. I had decided to presume, now R had been and gone, that I would stay for the rest of the time with him, or else I had decided to be reckless, I don't know. He twitched when he saw my bag. A man sat with us, a friend of his whom he'd just bumped into. He was waiting for a woman to turn up and it was quite obvious that she wasn't going to. He was downcast. My man didn't look too upbeat about his woman – me – who had. The night was spent, used up, talking to this stood-up man.

We left the pub. He said crossly, 'I'll carry that', taking my bag from me. If I'd insisted that I do it myself, my voice might have wavered, such was the humiliation, embarrassment. I wanted to say, Look, I am... whatever, and I don't usually turn up to stay uninvited but I thought that in the circumstances... But when we got outside the pub he crooked his arm and beckoned me to link him. I put my arm in and found myself holding tight. 'Now,' he said, satisfied. I was afraid of such fickleness. He turned the key; I dropped my link because it felt too familiar, let my hand fall into the cold. He turned from the open door and picked it up as if it was his.

He fussed around the settee, the table, making me comfortable, sensing my unease... And then he said, 'First I must ring my wife.' The flat had two large windows, both of them dirty. There was an opening between the bedsitting room and the kitchen, supposedly making separate rooms. I went to the kitchen and tried not to hear but I felt like a keyhole-listener as surely as if I'd had my back bent and my ear pressed. I couldn't see out the window. I raged to myself – talk to your heart's fucking content with some boring stood-up thirty-three-year-old, and as for ringing up your wife, stop trying to impress me. I bet you have the year loaded up with planned weekends, otherwise the two of you would go mad looking at each other. I bet you have ducks flying up your sitting room wall, I bet your bathroom is painted pink or powder blue, I bet you think the alcove at the top of the chipboard built-in cupboard is a feature, in fact that's why the two of you bought the house. I bet you moved out the furry animals from the back window of the car just for me. But worst of all, none of this is my business. Nothing about you is my business.

The extremity of my pathetic gratefulness in the face of his sourness was about to blow up. I simply could not listen any longer, nor could I bear to know that I knew what he would say to me if I tried to explain, and that before he had it said I would have forgiven him. In truth, I would have liked to have said goodbye, to put his elbows into my hands and kiss him on the mouth. I wrote a quick note 'Sorry I couldn't stay. See you sometime'. I let myself out quietly and was booked into the nearest B&B before he had got off the phone, I bet. I curled up in bed like an armadillo. All night I heard the sound of seagulls out there being plaintive, scratching the sky as if it was glass. If only it was winter I might be blessed with a quiet body. If the fires were lit in rooms, they might take some of the heat out of me.

Beatrice had to wonder for a while why she had done it. There had been the lush devouring, the agile taste of mouths in the morning, long arched fingers moving slowly in the right places. She knew what it hadn't been; she would not have held him just for the sake of holding him. As well as that, she said in conversation, 'yes indeed' when really she meant 'no'. She had never smiled at him without knowing that she was doing it; she would never have told him the truth. But surely there was no need for him to demolish it so completely.

In time Beatrice got her imagination to mend the holes in her understanding. She knew he had loved her passion when it opened, as is necessary, but he had also found it unacceptable, too un-innocent. I even guided his hand, she thought. Not only that, she had switched the light back on after he had turned it off. And she had kept her eyes wide open. Wider. Oh, why not take the blame myself, she thought, days cannot do things of their own accord. It was worth it to remember herself in a straight blue dress, a zip from the top to three-quarters way down, a slit from the bottom to join the zip. Even in the dark she liked new cities.

THE YEAR AFTER THAT

Went away to my town with R. The water in the sea, for that, after all, is all it is, was white with cold.

A FAMILY OCCASION

Emma Cooke

Emma Cooke (1935–2015) was born in Portarlington and was the author of several novels, *A Single Sensation* (1981), *Eve's Apple* (1985) and *Wedlocked* (1994). This story is taken from her only short story collection, *Female Forms*, published by Dublin's Poolbeg Press in 1980.

It was a Tuesday afternoon and the family was coming to tea. The parlour in "Sunnyside" was fragrant, polished, waiting. Mrs. Lee's chair stood, with its cushions nicely plumped, beside the wireless. In the fireplace a small flame licked its way around a sod of turf. The black marble clock on the mantelpiece coughed and struck three.

The Girls, Dodo and Polly, were home from England on their annual holiday. They had travelled from London on the previous Friday. They were upstairs getting ready. Dodo had filled the cut-glass vase on the bookshelf with roses and carnations. A posy of pansies, pinks and forget-me-nots stood on the pedestal table by the window.

Mrs. Lee was in bed having her afternoon nap; dreaming that she was bringing the children on a picnic and that Polly and Dodo, who were unaccountably grown up, had taken Beattie away in the pram.

Lucy was in the kitchen counting the iced fancies that had been sent over from the confectionery. If Beattie brought all her brood, which of course she would, they were going to be short of a cake. She sighed and opened the box with the sponge sandwich in it. She cut a slice and added it to the plate of buns. She would do without her own slice. The act of self-sacrifice replaced her annoyance with a warm little glow. Now to start the potato cakes. She had just enough time.

At half past three Lucy untied her apron and put it away, looked into the small mirror beside the cupboard, patted her hair into place and went into the parlour. Her mother was already sitting down wearing the new black cardigan that The Girls had brought home.

Polly and Dodo appeared, elegant in pin-striped suits, tailored blouses and immaculate ties. Polly looked at the clock. "Nearly time," she said. She and Dodo lit cigarettes. Lucy took one as well. She only smoked when The Girls were home on holidays; by herself it felt wicked.

Mr. Lee looked at them from his photograph on the mantelpiece. He had taken it himself – two years before he died. Now that she was in her thirties the resemblance between himself and Dodo was very pronounced.

Peg arrived before their cigarettes were finished. She swept in all twitters and gaiety, her two children, Barbara and Stanley, following shyly behind her. Like The Girls, she had a neat figure, sallow skin, dark glossy hair. But her style was softer. Her hair was permed and today she wore a dress of navy blue and white striped material with a little floppy bow at the neckline.

"My goodness. She's all dolled up, isn't she, Polly?" said Dodo.

"Chase me Charlie!"

"Look who's talking," cried Peg, "you're very swanky yourselves."

Lucy watched them, thinking how close Peg and The Girls had always been. She hoped that Beattie wouldn't be too late. Beattie was so disorganised.

"How are Barbara and Stanley?" asked Polly.

The children hung their heads.

"Stanley, button your blazer," said his mother.

"And Barbara has her school uniform on," Lucy pointed out.

Barbara was brought forward to show The Girls her brown coat, the special pleat in the front of her gym slip, the zip pocket, the cream blouse.

She stood like a dummy, trying to hold onto the feeling of superiority that her first year away from home had given her. But it drained away under her aunts' scrutiny, leaving her as vulnerable as a snail without a shell.

"How do you like Dublin?" Polly inquired.

"She loves it," said her mother.

"Ever get lonely?"

Barbara shook her head.

"Good girl."

"Are you fond of each other?" asked Dodo, who knew very little about children. Barbara and Stanley nodded. The women turned away from them with a sense of duty done, and began to talk all at once.

"Can we go and play?" Stanley called shrilly to his grandmother. Mrs. Lee nodded and they escaped to the garden.

The hands of the church clock stood at five past four. Beattie shoved and pushed the children past the gate. They always wanted to stop and look at the tombstones. Organ music pealed inside. A funeral march. Mr. Watson practising. Someone must be sick.

'We're late for Grannie, Barbara and Stanley will be there already," said

Beattie. She had a stitch in her side from rushing and the new corset. She was sorry now that she had left the baby with Mrs. Green. She could have put Michael and Dickie up on the pram.

"Hurry, hurry, hurry!" she puffed. Mr. Everard stood at the door of his shop. Hands behind his back, eyes half closed, not a speck on his white tennis shoes. Nothing to do except watch the world go by. Everyone except herself seemed to have time to spare.

"I want to see Barbara," said Yvonne, who was the same age.

"Good," said Beattie. Over the bridge and round the corner. They were nearly there. Surely the children had been a lot tidier when they left the house, thought Beattie. Sometimes she wished that she was like Peg, with only two. She wondered how she was going to last the afternoon in her corset. At least it might keep Dodo from noticing that she was pregnant again.

Last summer, when she was home, Dodo had called up one afternoon and sat through a complete ironing session; talking about England, and theatres and friends that she had made, while Beattie tried to fold sheets and dresses so that the torn parts would not show. Before she left she placed a brown paper parcel on the kitchen table, saying cryptically, "I don't want to interfere."

Beattie opened it as soon as Dodo had gone. It contained a book called "Planned Parenthood". Beattie had been annoyed at first. But then, knowing Dodo, she giggled at the funny side of it. She put the book on the top shelf of the wardrobe where Seamus would not find it. It was still there, gathering dust.

The children waited for her on the front step of "Sunnyside". The door was always on the latch and she pushed it open.

"Yoo-hoo!" she called.

An echoing call came from the parlour. She went in, the children straggling after.

"Ah! Beattie – at last!" said Mrs. Lee.

"And all the chick-a-beatties," added Polly and Dodo in unison.

"One, two, three, four, five—" counted Dodo.

"Six is with Mrs. Green," Beattie said quickly.

"—six, seven, all good children go to heaven." Dodo crinkled her grey eyes.

"The whole family, Beattie. How lovely." Auntie Jane, who wasn't really an aunt, was there because The Girls were home.

"Not quite, Auntie Jane," Beattie said.

"Goodness me, I lose count," said Auntie Jane, wafting lavender water with every gesture.

"I knew you were here, I smelt you through the door," five-year-old Dickie told her triumphantly. The Girls smothered their laughter.

Beattie caught his arm. She could have murdered him. "Tell Auntie Jane you're sorry," she demanded.

Dickie looked at the carpet. "Sorry," he whispered. He wondered why it was rude of Auntie Jane to smell so pretty. He liked it. There was a short pause to let his apology register. Then Mrs. Lee said, "Barbara and Stanley are in the garden."

The children tumbled out of the room. The Girls clapped their hands over their ears in mock dismay.

"Go easy!" Beattie yelled. "Sorry Mother," she added automatically.

Lucy stood up. "I think I'll put the kettle on," she announced, "Frank will be over from the shop soon."

"Can I help?" asked Peg.

"Thank you dear, but I know where everything is," Lucy said apologetically.

So do we all, thought Beattie, sitting down on the sofa beside Auntie Jane. Everything in "Sunnyside" had been kept in exactly the same place as far back as she could remember, down to the chocolate egg on the top shelf of the bookcase. It had been there since she was a little girl. A present from cousins in America. She remembered, when she was small, wishing and wishing that her mother would take off the cellophane wrapping and divide it up. Let them see what it tasted like. But she never did. It must be mouldy by now.

The women settled down to a comfortable chat about the things that had happened during the past year. Frank came from the shop and when he went back to sit in his office, Desmond, the younger brother, arrived.

"I suppose it's all gone," he said when he came in.

"Every scrap," said Polly.

"I'll go and squeeze the teapot." Lucy bustled out to collect the pile of potato cakes that she had been keeping warm for him.

Desmond leaned back and rubbed his waistcoat after he had eaten six. "Well that's more like it," he said.

"Do you remember the day that we went on the picnic down the river and you gobbled up all the buns? You must have been about five years old," Polly asked him.

"How many were there?" he prompted her.

"Twelve!"

"Oh my!" said Auntie Jane, her eyebrows nearly touching the brim of her hat.

Desmond guffawed – then, "Do you remember the time that Frank gave Peg a carry on his motor bike and her knitted skirt caught in the wheel?" he said.

The memory convulsed the room.

Dodo took over. "How about when Lucy fell down the grating in the church aisle?"

"I was going in to do the flowers for the Harvest Festival."

"And Percy Ward had lifted the grating back to get down to the furnace."

"The rector had to come and help pull her out."

"Lucky she's well padded."

The stories were told, one voice taking up the thread from another. Beattie shifted on the sofa. A bone from her corset was killing her. The room seemed very warm.

In the garden the children played their annual game of pelting each other with the small, unripe apples that had fallen off the trees. This year Barbara and Yvonne were the targets. They crouched in the greenhouse waiting for a chance to make a dash for the big laurel hedge.

"I'm getting a new coat," whispered Yvonne as they peered out through the tomato plants.

"I'm learning ballet," said Barbara.

"What's that?"

"Dancing, of course."

"Oh!" They both tried to look nonchalant.

"Everyone learns—" Barbara was interrupted by a volley of ammunition from the enemy, who had decided to try a surprise attack.

"Come on!" They clasped hands and ran squealing through the doorway.

She was going to die. Here on Mother's sofa – after all they had done for her – in return for their tolerance – she was going to, at last, as they had always expected her to, commit a final, unforgivable breach of taste. Sweat drenched her armpits. She tried to smell it, distending her nostrils, her lungs aching for a whiff of some antidote to Auntie Jane's lavender.

"Do you really, Beattie? Imagine." Auntie Jane was looking at her in amazement.

"Oh yes." She bared her teeth at them, but nobody seemed to notice anything strange. What on earth were they talking about? The melodeon? It was quite true. She did lock herself into the kitchen and play it for half an hour after she had put the children to bed. Yes, if someone was still crying when she stopped she attended to them. She sat there nodding while the family recounted the details.

"Young people are marvellous nowadays," gushed Auntie Jane.

A miscarriage would be worse than dying. Think of the mess. Poor Lucy would have to do all the work. But she couldn't have a miscarriage with Desmond still in the room. Mother would never allow it. If she was dying they'd have to send for Seamus – and the priest. They'd never think of the priest and Seamus would have a fit. She hoped Seamus wasn't drinking today. She'd have to make her last confession in her mother's parlour. Oh God!

"It's your own personal decision, Beatrice." That's what her father had said. He had been a just man. He used to stop her on Sunday mornings when they met. Walking opposite directions to church. Both of them alone. Lucy was the only other churchgoer in "Sunnyside" and she got up for eight o'clock. Seamus always went to last Mass.

"Good morning, Beatrice."

"Good morning, Father."

"Are you all well?"

"Yes, thank you."

They might have been heads of state exchanging credentials. It often struck her as comical. But he wasn't a man for frivolity.

She felt dizzy. She wished that she was in her own house. She wished that they could afford to get their wireless fixed and then she wouldn't need the melodeon. Seamus had taught her to play it when they were courting. She wished—.

Wails, reaching a crescendo as they approached the sittingroom, halted the conversation.

"Oh dear!" Peg half rose to her feet. The Girls blew long spirals of cigarette smoke. Lucy got up anxiously.

"Some naughtiness, they're as wild as young goats," said Mrs. Lee, looking accusingly at Beattie. Desmond hid his grin behind a handkerchief as Lucy hurried from the room.

"I'll help her," Beattie said. She wrenched herself out of her agony. The pains went through her heart as she stood up. But she made it to the door, only knocking a bowl of flowers to the ground on the way.

It was not the end of the world after all. Barbara's uniform was a bit muddy and Yvonne had a nasty scrape on her cheek.

"What were you doing in the hedge anyway?" asked Lucy, brushing away at Barbara's brown serge. Beattie had rushed upstairs muttering something incoherent.

"Playing," they said vaguely.

Beattie came into the kitchen and took a sheet of brown paper from the pile in the left-hand cupboard.

"What's that for?" Lucy asked.

"A secret," Beattie replied airily. She hurried out again and they heard her singing "ta-ra-ra-boom-de-ay" as she climbed the stairs.

"What's she doing?" asked the little girls.

"Goodness knows." Lucy shook her head. There was never any accounting for poor Beattie.

In the bathroom Beattie wriggled out of her corset. It was a hideous pink thing with numerous laces and silver eyelets. If Seamus saw her in it he'd have a fit. She rolled it up in the brown paper and hurled it high onto the top shelf of the hot press; back behind the eiderdowns and winter curtains. A surprise for Lucy when she found it.

She stood in the middle of the bathroom floor and felt herself relax and expand, like a flower about to bloom. It was marvellous. Funny to think that she was a grown woman. She remembered the time when her chin was only a few inches higher than the rim of the bath. Sometimes the whole thing seemed preposterous – the children, babies, Seamus.

Funny how she had met Seamus. He had drifted into a social in the Parochial Hall. A stranger in town. Not knowing that he was trespassing. Masquerading under false colours at a Protestant dance. He had been sent to work in the region by the Turf Board. Everyone had been delighted to see a new young man turn up. When the rector's wife came over and introduced herself the truth dawned on him. He decided to bluff it out. It would make a good story for the lads.

Beattie had been standing near him at suppertime.

"Jesus!" The expression had surprised her. She had turned round to find Seamus standing staring at a sandwich as if it was about to explode.

"What's wrong?" she asked.

"What day is it?" he murmured.

She looked at the clock. It was after midnight. "I suppose it's Friday," she said.

Seamus looked at her in horror. "And I'm eating meat," he said. He often said later that the first thing that had attracted him to her was that she was such a good sport.

They danced together for the rest of the evening, the offending sandwich tucked away in Beattie's handbag. That was a joke that she had kept to herself. In the end it hadn't been funny at all.

A button like a little gum drop rolled down her dress and rested against her shoe. It was followed by another.

"Beattie," a voice called anxiously, "where are you?"

Beattie stooped and picked them up. Lucy would have a needle and thread. Dodo was outside on the landing. "For heaven's sake, Beattie, what are you doing?" Beattie held out her hand. "Look!" she said.

Dodo peered at the buttons, then at Beattie's gaping dress, then at her flushed face.

"Oh Beattie," she said, "you're not—"

Beattie nodded her head. "I am."

"Honestly, you're hopeless." Dodo looked at her with concern. "I get worried about you," she went on, "when I come home and see you with all those children, and that man—" she broke off. "Can't you do anything? Can't you be more careful?" she asked in a dry, matter of fact tone.

"No," said Beattie, "we're not allowed." There was no point in going into all the details, but when she said it out like that, to her sister, it seemed ridiculous.

As they stared at each other Beattie felt a soft flutter in her stomach. It was the baby. The first time that she had felt it moving. She placed her hand protectively against her body. "I'll be alright," she said, "keep your fingers crossed."

"Wait," ordered Dodo. She went into her bedroom and came out carrying a cardigan. "Put that on, it will keep you covered. ' She placed it gently across Beattie's shoulders.

They linked arms as they went downstairs. In the parlour everybody turned expectantly towards them.

"What's up?"

"We thought you were lost!" the family exclaimed.

"Beattie burst her buttons," Dodo announced. And the way that she said it made it sound so comical that they all began to laugh.

THE AWAKENING

Daniel Corkery

Daniel Corkery (1878–1964) was a writer and academic, who published novels, poetry, criticism and four collections of short stories.
Several of his plays were produced by the Abbey Theatre in Dublin.

I

Ivor O'Donovan knew it was Ted Driscoll had called him: raising himself
above the edge of the bunk he was just in time to see him manoeuvring
that bear-like body of his through the narrow little hatchway, to see the
splintery shutter slap to behind him. At the same moment he heard the Captain
clearing his throat. The bunk opposite was his, and now Ivor saw him, all
limbs, mounting awkwardly yet carefully over the edge of it. What between
the sprawling limbs, the ungainly body and the hovering shadows above them,
the place was narrowed to the size of a packing case. The timber work of the
cabin had become so dark with the smoke of the stove that neither shadows
nor limbs seemed to stir except when their movements were sudden and jerky.
Ivor soon heard the Captain gathering his oil-cloths from the floor with one
hand while with the other he dragged at the bunk where the cabin boy was
sleeping; this Ivor knew, for as he sat up he caught the familiar words:

"Come on, come on; rouse up; they'll be waiting."

The Captain he then saw disappear through the toy-like hatchway.

Ivor O'Donovan himself with a stifled groan descended lifelessly from the
bunk to the floor. He drew on his sea boots—they had been his father's—drew
his oil-cloths about him and in turn thrust his hand into the warm pile of
old coats and sacking in which the sleeping boy was buried. He shook him
vigorously: "Come on, come on; they'll be waiting," he said, and then hurried
aloft into the drizzling darkness and took his place with the others.

The tightness that he felt on his brain from the moment Ted Driscoll had
roused him seemed natural, not unexpected; nevertheless he groaned to recollect the cause of it. Now, however, as he settled down to his night's work,
planted in the darkness there at the gunwale, braced against it, facing the
Captain, the dripping fish-laden incoming net between them, he noticed that
the tightness had somehow slackened, was still loosening its grip of him, so

much so that he had some fear that it would again suddenly pounce on him with its first heat and violence.

Ted Driscoll and Tom Mescall were forward at the windlass; beyond them the boy, bending down, was coiling the rope they passed to him.

It was very dark. Everything was huge and shapeless. Anchored as she was, tethered besides, clumsy with the weight of dripping fish-spangled net coming in over the gunwale, the nobby was tossed and slapped about with a violence that surprised him; flakes of wet brightness were being flung everywhere from the one lamp bound firmly to the mast. Yet the night was almost windless, the sea apparently sluggish: there must be, he thought, a stiff swell beneath them. What most surprised him, however, was to find himself thinking about it. That evening coming down the harbour, he would not have noticed it. The whole way out, his back to the sea, he had stood upright, his feet set wide apart, his hands in his belt, glum, silent, gazing at the cabin boy who, sprawled upon the deck, was intent upon the baited line he had flung over the stern. But as far as Ivor was concerned that patch of deck might have been free to the sun: his own anger, his passion, was between him and the world. That afternoon he had waited for Chrissie Collins for two hours. At the very start he knew, he *knew*, so at least he had told himself she would not come. For all that he had gone hot and cold, again and again, while waiting for her. He had broken from the spot impulsively: a moment later he had trailed back again, giving her one more quarter of an hour to make good in. Then when his rage was at the peak, hurrying down to the jetty, he had suddenly caught sight of her, all brightness, stepping briskly up the hillside, the schoolmaster walking beside her, as eager as herself. Her head was bent, her eyes were fixed on her dainty toe-caps, and she was listening complacently to the schoolmaster's blather. Only that he should have to tear through the village and it filled with the gathering crews, he'd have told her what he thought of her.

With his eyes downwards on the sprawling limbs of the boy, he had indulged, as if it were the only thing for a man to do, the heat of the passion that that one glimpse of her had aroused in him.

Now, ten hours later, braced against the timbers, swaying and balancing, freeing the net, freeing the rope, grabbing at the odd dog fish, the odd blob of seaweed, the tangle of seawrack, flinging them all, as they came, far out, clear of the rising meshes—he was puzzled to contrast his present indifference with his stifling anger of the afternoon. Yet he was not pleased with himself. This calming down of his seemed like a loss of manhood. His mind could not, it appeared, stay fixed on the one thought. He found himself noticing what he had never noticed before—how the mackerel, entangled in the meshes, would catch the light of the worried lamp and appear just like a flight of shining steel-bright daggers hurtling by him from gunwale to hold. Never to have noticed so striking a thing before, how curious! But had the Captain ever noticed it? He glanced shyly at the aged face opposite him and started, for the Captain, he saw, had had his eyes fixed on him, all the time, perhaps! And Ivor recalled, reddening slightly, that also that afternoon while lost in his own passionate thoughts he had caught him observing him with the self-same silent gravity. Why should he do it? He was Captain. But the boat was his, Ivor's; and one day when he was somewhat older, and when his mother was willing to trust him, he would sail it. But this was unfair, he felt, for the Captain, this Larry Keohane, had been ever and always his father's dearest friend and shipmate, had sailed with him till he was drowned, had indeed been with him that very night; and afterwards he it was who had undertaken the management of the boat for them; and in such a way that not a penny of the fish money had ever gone astray on them. Later on, now two years ago, he had taken Ivor on board as one of the crew, and taught him whatever he now knew of sailoring and deep sea fishing. There was surely plenty of time yet for thinking of playing the Captain. Besides, the selling of the fish was trickier work than the catching of it. His eyes fell on the claw-like hands of the Captain, they were twisted with rheumatism, and a flood of kindly feeling for this grave and faithful friend suddenly swept over him with such power that he found his own hands fumbling at the net without either skill or strength in them. To glance again at the Captain's face he did not dare.

"Up, boys, up!" he impulsively cried to the windlass men as if to encourage them. In the clinging darkness, although the drizzle was becoming lighter and lighter, he could make out only the shapeless bulk of themselves and the windlass: two awkward lumps of manhood rising and falling alternately, their sou'westers and oil-cloths catching some of the flakes of the wet brightness that were flying around everywhere. 'Twas curious work, this fishing. Like a family they were, confined in a tiny space, as far almost from the other boats as they were from the houses on the hills where the real families were now huddled together in sleep. The real families—each of them was different from the others. Tom Mescall's was the most good-for-nothing in the whole place. Others had quite nice houses, clean and well-kept. But most strange of all was it to have him, Ivor, thinking of such things, his head calm and cool (and he thereupon grabbed a huge dog-fish from the passing net and with a gesture deliberately sweeping sent it far out into the splashing darkness).

II

The work went on and on and Ivor could not help all kinds of thoughts from crossing his brain, nor help noticing the onward rush of them. The dragging of the net was done in silence, no one speaking until they each and all were sure that they had had a fairly good catch, and that all the nets were heavy. Ivor then was aware that some dull and lifeless conversation was passing to and fro between the men at the windlass. He was hailed suddenly by one of them, Ted Driscoll: "Look where Leary is, east."

Far off, east, Ivor saw a tiny light. As he watched it the other voice came through the darkness, half speaking, half calling:

"'aith then he wouldn't be long swinging on to the Galley in there."

"Is it Leary, do you think?" Ivor asked the Captain, and he was answered: "'Tis like the place he'd be."

Ivor then sent his gaze ranging the sea noting the disposition of the boats. They were far off, nearly all of them. Some were miles beyond Galley Head. Others were away towards the west. Here and there a pair of lights seemed to ride close together, only seemed, however, while an odd one, like Leary's, played the hermit in unaccustomed waters. Far to the west the great light of the Fastnet every few moments threw a startling beam on the waters and, quenching suddenly, would leave a huge blackness suspended before their very eyes, blinding them. He noticed how, little by little, the timid lamps of the fishing fleet would in time manage again to glimmer through that darkness. He bent himself once more on the work, thinking over and over again what a curious way they had of making a living. On the land at this time of night every one of the houses was a nest of sleep—chilly walls mid warm bedding. After all Chrissie Collins was a farmer's daughter, a small hillside farmer, a "sky" farmer. Farm houses had ways of their own. Fishermen also had ways of their own. The next time he met her he would hold his head as high as hers.

The dragging went on and on. The unending clanking of the windlass, the wet mass of the net, the grip of his feet on the narrow way between gunwale and hold while the boat tossed and tugged, the sudden flashes of the lamp, the long silences of them all, the far-off lonely looking fights of the other anchored nobbies and ketches, the bold startling blaze of the Fastnet, and above all the stream of shining daggers sweeping by—for the first time in his life he reckoned up the features of the fisherman's calling, and felt some sort of pleasant excitement in doing so, as if he had heard some good news or come upon some unexpected treasure. He could not understand it.

When the last of the nets was in they tidied the decks, pitching the seawrack into the sea. He heard the Captain say to Driscoll, whose head was bent down on the confused mass of fish and net in the hold: "Good, and a fair size too. I'm very glad."

"I'm very glad," repeated Ivor in his mind, wonderingly, yet feeling that the words fitted in. He noticed Driscoll and Mescall, their arms hanging heavily after their night's work, their sea boots lumping noisily along the deck, going aft to the little cabin, making down the hatchway without a word. The boy had gone down previously. The waft of the smell of boiling fish, of boiling potatoes, that came from the smoke pipe told of his toil below. To Ivor it was very welcome. He was hungry; and besides they would presently all meet together round the little stove, "I'm very glad," he whispered, not knowing why. And the smoke, he saw, was like a lighted plume rising from the top of the iron pipe.

The Captain drew closer to him. He took the fragment of pipe from his mouth and, smothering the glowing bowl in his fist, pointed sou'west:

"'Tis Casey that's going in."

"Is it?" Ivor said, also picking out the one craft in all the far-scattered fleet that had got under weigh that—very slowly, for there was scarcely a breath of wind—was making for the land.

"Maybe 'tisn't," the Captain then said.

"I'm sure 'tis him all right," Ivor said, though he was not sure at all.

They stood side by side following with their eyes the distant slow-moving fight. There was scarcely a morning that some boat or other did not hoist sail the moment their catch was made and hasten in. There was always some special reason for it. And the other craft, every one of them, would make guesses at the boat, as also at the cause of her lifting anchor in such haste. The others were content to make the pier any time before the buyers had received from other fishing ports and from Dublin itself their morning telegrams fixing the day's prices. Ivor thought how it was nearly always something having to do with the real household, with the real family, that brought a fisherman to break that way from the fishing grounds before the others. Sickness, or the necessity for some early journey, or the emigrating of a son or daughter. "I remember your father, one time we were out, and far out too, south the Galley, ten mile it might be, how he called out and we not ready at all: 'That'll do, boys, we'll make in.'"

The Captain's quiet husky voice stopped, and Ivor wondered if that was all he had to say; but the tale was taken up again:

"That was twenty-two years ago this month."

Ivor was once more astray, he could not find reason in the words.

"Yes," he said, quietly.

"That night he expected a son to be born to him; and he wasn't disappointed."

Ivor knew that he himself was the child that on that night came into the world; but what kept him silent was the Captain's gravity. Such matter among them had always been a cause for laughter. Ivor was nevertheless glad that the Captain had spoken seriously; for all that, fearing to betray his own state of mind, he answered:

"That's not what's taking Casey in anyhow."

The Captain did not seem to hear.

"All night long," he said, "I'm thinking of things that I saw happen out here on these waters for the last fifty-four years."

Ivor raised his head in astonishment. Why should such recollections have set the Captain examining him the whole night long?

"Strange things," the Captain resumed, "strange voices, sad things too, very sad, things that should not happen."

After all, the Captain was in the humour for spinning a yarn, that was all. But, instead of the yarn, the Captain, scanning the sky, merely said:

"'Tis going south; the day will be fine, very fine."

Ivor too felt a slight stir in the air, and from the hatchway Driscoll called them down.

"With God's help 'twill be a fine day," the Captain said once more, throwing the words over his shoulder as they moved aft, one behind the other, sauntering along in their heavy sea boots.

III

The air in the cabin was reeking with the smell of fish and potatoes, and so thick with fire smoke and tobacco smoke that one could hardly make things out. There was hardly room for the five of them there. The boxes they sat on were very low and the men's knees, on which they held the plates, seemed to fill the whole space. One felt the warmth against one's face like a cushion. Yet Ivor welcomed it all—the heat, the smell of the good food, the close companionship—not alone for the comfort it all wrapped him round with but for the memory it raised in him of those many other nights on which he had experienced it, his body as cold as ice and his fingers unable to move themselves. The others were already eating lustily and noisily.

"Not too bad, not too bad," he cried out cheerily, planting himself between Driscoll and Mescall, just because they were head to head and nose to nose in earnest argument. They took no notice of him, continuing it still across his very face. Driscoll, who was the simplest of them, was showing how Mrs. O'Connor, the shopkeeper who supplied them with all and sundry, had done him out of two and elevenpence, and Mescall, who, in spite of his harum-scarum wife and family, was their merrymaker, was explaining how she had tried the same trick with him and how he had laid a trap for her and caught her—a trap so clever that Driscoll had no idea how it worked or how by using it he could recover his two and elevenpence. The boy was heard plunging vessels in a bucket of water. All the time the Captain held his peace, and Ivor, noticing it, glanced at him, wondering if he were still recalling what he had seen happen on the fishing grounds during his long lifetime upon them.

Leisurely yet ravenously the meal went on, and when they thought of it, or at least so it seemed, first Mescall and then Driscoll, who had had no sleep till then, threw off their sea boots and disappeared into the darkness of the bunks. In the same haphazard way Ivor, the Captain, and the boy returned to the deck.

IV

At last they had her moving: her sails were flapping, coming suddenly between their eyes and the dazzling flood of light outwelling from sea and sky. When they filled, when she settled down, Ivor heard the Captain say in a voice that sounded unusual:

"I suppose I may as well go aft."

Unable to account for the words Ivor answered in mere confusion of mind:

"'Tis better, I suppose," as if the matter was not quite clear.

Silently the Captain went aft to the tiller, and Ivor, as was his custom, threw himself on the pile of rope in the bow: there was no more to be done. He felt the streaming sun, into which a benign warmth was beginning to steal, bathing his body from his hair down. After the work of the night, after the food, a pleasant lassitude, as thick as his thick clothing, clung to him. The cabin boy was already fast asleep on the deck, cuddled up like a dog, his face buried in his arms. Ivor felt sleepy too, yet before he yielded to it, he recalled the memory of the handful of them, cut off from all other company, working silently in the drizzling darkness, the tossing lamp momentarily flashing in their eyes and lighting up their dripping hands. He recollected too the rise and fall of the awkward bodies of the two men at the windlass, the clanking of the axle, and the uncompanioned boy beyond them working away in almost total darkness. Clearer than all he recalled the flight of glittering spear heads sweeping by between himself and the Captain. Then also the group in the smoky cabin, the hearty faces, the blue and white plates, the boy plunging the vessels in the water. How different from what was now before his eyes! The sea was wide, wide; the air brisk, the seagulls screaming, quarrelling, gathering in schools, dashing at the transparent crests of the waves or sweeping in great curves to the east, the west, everywhere, their high-pitched cries filling the air with a rapture that opened the heart and at the same time alarmed it. Yes, very different, yet his pictures of the night time—the groups silently working in the darkness, the gathering in the little cabin—these were dearer to him just now than the bright freshness of the morning. He recalled the unexpected words of the Captain—"I'm very glad."

At last the drowsiness that he would keep from him overpowered him.

He awoke to find the boy's hand timidly unclutching his shoulder:

"Himself wants you."

Rising up he caught the Captain's eyes resting upon him with a calmness that surprised him, that disturbed him. He went aft.

"You're wanting me?"

"Sit down there, Ivor, there's a thing I have to say to you." Fearing some reference to Chrissie Collins, some questioning, some good advice, Ivor sat down without a word. The Captain blurted out:

"Ivor, boy, 'tis time for you to sail what belongs to you."

As he spoke his hand lifted from the tiller—an instinctive giving up of office. Instantly however it fell upon it again. Ivor perceived the action with his eyes, not with his mind, for the words had sent a thrill of delight through his whole body. Everything he had been noticing that night of nights was in that overwhelming sensation—the darkness, the clanking windlass, the shining fish, the cabin, the seagulls, everything—but he caught hold of himself and said:

"But, Lar, why that? Why that?"

"Because 'tis time for you."

"But why so? 'Tisn't how you're going from us; what's after happening?"

"Nothing. Nothing. Only all the night I'm thinking of it. 'Tis the right thing. Herself is at me too. If there's a touch of wind in the night, she don't sleep a wink."

"Oh! If the boat goes we all go."

"You can't talk to them like that. Anyway 'tis right. 'Tis your due. We got on well, Ivor. Them that's gone, they deserved as much. We done our best, all of us."

"Lar, 'tis better wait till my mother hears of it."

"If you wouldn't mind I'd give you Pat to be in my place. He'd be better for you than a stranger."

Again that thrill of delight went through him. He thought at once if the Captain had not offered his son, a stranger would have to be brought into the boat, one of those unlucky creatures perhaps who had given the best of their lives sailoring the wide world over, creatures who were not trustworthy, who had bitter, reckless tongues, who destroyed the spirit of goodwill in any boat they ever got footing in. That danger the Captain had put aside. There was therefore a clear way before him, and a boat's crew after his own heart.

"I'm thankful, Lar, and herself will be thankful; but what will you be doing with yourself?"

A little smile grew upon the Captain's face, and both of them raised their eyes to scan the hillsides they were approaching. In the sun which now lay thick upon their brown-green flanks, nestling in the zig-zag ravines they saw the little groups of houses where the fishermen lived. Some of the cottages, snow-white, faced full in the eyes of the morning, sunning themselves. Others were turned aside, still asleep in the shadows, catching a bright ray only on chimney head or gable.

"Wouldn't I want to sit in the sun and smoke my pipe as well as another? That will do, Ivor. Ted's coming up. He's after smelling the land. In the evening I'll fix up with your mother."

V

It was a Saturday morning. That night and the next they would all sleep in their own houses, not in the boats.

In the evening the Captain went to Ivor's house, and, as he said himself, fixed things up with his mother. Then he shook hands with them all, with Mrs. O'Donovan, Ivor, his two sisters, and his young brother, who was only a boy. He then set off up the hill for his home.

Afterwards, standing up before the bit of glass nailed against the wall, Ivor stood shaving himself. His heart was blazing within him, his cheeks burning, for the Captain had been speaking his praises, and all his people had been staring at him.

It had been a day of uninterrupted sunshine, and now a bright heaven, slow to darken itself, although the sun had been a long time sunken, darkened to blackness every ridge, bush, tree clump, roof and gable that stood against it. On the roads and fields it still threw down a persistent glow; and Ivor went in and out the doorway praying for the dusk to thicken. In the midst of the Captain's praise of him he had felt a burning desire to see his boat once again with his own eyes, to be sure it was still there at the pier, where, with scores of others, it was fastened. He wanted to feel the tiller beneath his right hand—that above all. And yet he would not care to have any of his neighbours see him doing so. Nightfall was never so slow in coming. At last, however, with a yearning look at the still livid sky he set off down the path towards the roadway. He could gambol, he could sing, only that at the same time he had thoughts of the heavy responsibility that in future would rest upon him. He strove to calm himself, to walk with the appearance of one who had no other business than to breathe the cool air of the evening. He knew there would be groups of men still in the public-houses as well as along the sea wall; and these he wished to escape.

Before entering the village he vaulted over the wall, descended the rocks, and made along by the edge of the waters. At a point beyond the farthest house he climbed on to the road again, and, more assured, made towards the deserted pier. At its extreme end, almost, his *Wildwood* was moored. The pier itself, the debris on it, the fish boxes, the ranks of barrels—as well as all the conglomeration of boats along its sheltered side—the whole had become one black mass sharply cut out against the livid waters of the harbour. On a standard at its very end a solitary oil lamp, as warm in colour as the waters were cold, was burning away in loneliness. Towards it, and as quietly, almost as stealthily as if on a guilty errand, he steered his way. He was glad when the piles of barrels so obstructed the view that no one could spy him from the road. Doubtless the news was already abroad; by now the men were surely all speaking about it; as for himself, it was very strange coming at the time it did, coming, without expectation, at the tail-end of the night when for the first time he knew what it was to be a true fisherman. He was glad Chrissie Collins had her schoolmaster. It left himself as free as air. And thinking the thought he breathed in the pleasant coolness of the night, yet could not, it seemed, gulp down enough of it. Glad of the darkness, of the loneliness, he suddenly threw out his two arms wide apart, stretching them from him, and drew the keen air slowly and deliciously through his nostrils. And breathing still in the selfsame manner went forward a few steps. Then suddenly, he saw a figure, outlined against the tide, seated on some fish boxes, gazing silently at the nobby for which he himself was making! He knew it was the Captain. His arms fell and he stood quite still.

"Oh!" he said, in a sudden stoppage of thought. He turned stealthily and retraced his steps, fearful of hearing his name cried out. But nothing was to be heard except his own careful footfall; and before he reached the road again he had recovered himself. It surely was a sad thing for Larry Keohane to have his life drawing to an end. Why was it that nothing can happen to fill one person with happiness without bringing sadness and pain to somebody else? Yet the Captain, he remembered, that evening in his mother's house had been quite cheerful, had told them how glad he was that they had made quite a good catch on his last night, and what a peaceful night it had been! And what a fine boat the *Wildwood* was; and how happy he was to be leaving her in hands that would not treat her foully; indeed he could well say that he was flinging all responsibility from his shoulders; and that was a thing he had been looking forward to for a long time. And saying that, he had gone from them cheerily and brightly. Yes, yes, but here surely was the real captain, this seaman staring at his boat.

Ivor waited, sitting on the wall in the darkness, for a long time. At last he heard the slow steps of the old man approaching, saw him pass by—saw him very indistinctly for the darkness, yet knew that he had his hand covering his pipe in his mouth and his head on one side, a way he had when he was thinking to himself. He waited until the footsteps had died away up the hillside; then he rose to resume his own quest towards the nobby. He found he could not bring himself to do so. He did not want to do so.

With slow lingering steps, with stoppings and turnings, at last he too began to make towards his home. His head was flung up, almost flung back. More than once he told himself that he didn't ever remember the sky to have been so full of stars. Somehow he felt like raising his hand towards them.

SLEEPING WITH A STRANGER

Mary Costello

Mary Costello's short story collection, *The China Factory*, was nominated for the Guardian First Book Award. Her first novel, *Academy Street*, won the Irish Book Awards Book of the Year and was shortlisted for the International Dublin Literary Award, the Costa First Novel Award and the EU Prize for Literature. *The River Capture* (2019) is her second novel.

He left behind the warm waters of the bay, the seaweed, the blue of the Burren. He swam in a current of his own and hovered, like a skydiver in the dark. He would swim out far, underwater, to the Continental Shelf. He no longer felt man, but marine. He had a need to reach the depths, to glide to the silent darkness and feel the cold brush of luminous sea creatures.

When he came up for air he was blinded by the sun. He turned his head and saw the yellow diving platform and the concrete roof of the changing shelter, saw that he had barely moved beyond the rocks. In the distance the sun glinted on a car roof moving along the Prom. He swam back in and hoisted himself up onto the path, dripping seawater, his body tight and sinewy and vigorous again.

It was October. The morning was bright, cold. In the shelter he dressed and wrung out his swimming trunks. He combed his hair and felt himself coming back to the world. Mona would be in the kitchen at that moment, clearing away the breakfast things. In a while she would leave the house and take the Knocknacarra bus into town for her Saturday morning coffee and then, later, lunch with friends. He took his bag and began the walk to his car. He felt a slight uncertainty since leaving the water, as if the day was not to be trusted. A woman in dark clothes and long hair walked ahead of him, looking out to sea. He turned his head to the same angle and followed a wave until it merged with the grey water in the bay. As he drew close to the woman he felt a faint quickening. He came level and turned his face to hers. Their eyes met and she looked away quickly. She was not who he thought she was.

*

Mona had left a note on the counter to say she'd be gone all day. She and her friends—all teachers—would linger over lunch and wine and talk of school and family, and the longing for retirement. Mona kept herself well and looked a decade younger than her sixty years. She read novels and played bridge and together they went to the theatre and concerts and occasionally had friends over for dinner. He poured a glass of water and sat at the table with the house silent around him. He licked his forearm and tasted salt and remembered when he was a child how his father placed mineral licks in fields and sheds to ease the craving in calves. They might dement themselves licking the rungs of gates otherwise. He looked around the kitchen, delaying the moment when he would go upstairs to his desk and sift through notes and begin his report on a whole-school evaluation he'd completed that week. He no longer cared for his work. He would like to be devoted to one thing but had never found that thing. He looked out the window. They had lived in this house for twenty-eight years. Mona was a twin and one night in bed she spoke into the dark. 'If I ever die, you must marry my sister,' and he swore that he would, that he would seek out only those bearing the greatest likeness to her. It had felt like a pact. But she did not die and her sister went to Australia. One morning, soon after, she walked into the kitchen and stood in a pool of light under the yellow cabinets and told him she was pregnant. They had children because they could not be childless; childlessness would have amplified the loneliness of marriage.

In mid-morning the nursing home in Athlone called to report on his mother's condition. She had Alzheimer's and had been winding down for years and now there was cause for concern. He drove east out of the city on the new motorway. He had driven the roads of the county for twenty-five years as a primary schools' inspector, heading deep into the countryside each morning, past fields with stone walls, and cows being driven home for milking, through sleepy villages an hour before anyone rose. In late spring sheep huddled behind walls, bleating for their lambs, and the lambs, newly weaned, cried out their own terrible lament from nearby sheds. Once, he stopped and stood on the raised verge of the roadside looking over a wall at them, listening to their plaintive bleating. He sat into his car and drove on. How long, he wondered, before the ache of a ewe disappears?

He looked at the land beyond the motorway, at a tree on a hill, a cow, the dome of the sky. He wondered about the existence of these things—a tree, an animal, an insect. He wondered if theirs was any greater, any happier, than his own. He would have liked to talk about these things but it was too late now. He could not broach such things with Mona. They had not made love in a year. He remembered the woman on the Prom earlier, gazing out to sea like the woman at the end of a pier in a film he'd once seen. He saw lone women everywhere. One morning over twenty years ago he had passed a helmeted girl on the roadside. Her motor bike was parked and she was leaning over a dead fox. A few miles further on he arrived at the local school and as he walked up the path with the principal, the girl arrived and he turned and saw her unzip her jacket and remove the helmet and shake her hair free. Her name was Grace. He sat under a map of Ireland at the back of the classroom, observing her. He listened as she told the children that she had passed a dead body on the road. She had touched it, she said, and it was warm. A family of cubs would go hungry that day. All morning she moved among the children and bent her head close to theirs and whispered in their ears. Sometimes she smiled at him and they exchanged little knowing looks. She wore jeans and a white shirt. Her limbs were young, strong, unscarred, her body with its whole sensual life before it. He said her name in Irish, *Gráinne*, and at the end of the lesson he asked, What did you want to be when you were small? I wanted to be everything, she said.

Mona would be in the restaurant by now, settling herself in her seat, lifting out her reading glasses to study the menu. She was not without her mystery. She had a bridge partner, a school colleague named Tim. He thought of them at the card table at night, and the looks that must pass between them. He remembered once watching a TV programme about rock climbing, and how climbing partners grow to read each other's minds, to comprehend each other in some deep silent way.

In the nursing home his mother's mouth was open, like the little beak of a fledgling. Sometimes on his visits a terrified look would cross her face when he entered her room. He said her name, Mother. Her frame was shrunken and the veins and arteries were visible on the undersides of her arms. Her slippers sat neatly on the floor by the radiator. A nurse came and stood beside him and spoke softly. 'The doctor saw her earlier. Her lungs are not good… he doesn't think there's much time left.' He felt his mother's hand. When his father lay dying, his hands and feet and nose, the extremities, had grown gradually colder. His mother had kept touching them, as if temperature, and not hours or minutes, was the measure of time. Soon after his death she herself began to fade. She filled the electric kettle with milk and was frightened by rain. She began to sing the songs of Jeanette MacDonald and Nelson Eddy. She remembered what he had just said, but not the thing before. He thought of her brain as being littered with a hail of tiny holes, like the spread of buckshot.

*

That spring, years ago, he found excuses to revisit the girl in the classroom. He was touched by her youth and her sympathy. He hoarded up thoughts of her and as he drove home, he let them suffuse him. He would remember her little cough, or the way she forgot he was there and absent-mindedly put her head in her hands at her desk. On the final observation day he sat at the back of her class again, drafting his official report. When he looked up, her eyes were on him, unsmiling, looking deeply into him.

At the end of the day, with the pupils dismissed, he invited her to sit.

'You have a bright future ahead of you,' he said.

'Thank you.'

'This job is temporary. Jobs are scarce. Do you have something else lined up?'

She gave a slight shrug. 'No, not really. I'm going to Dublin for the summer. A few us are taking a house there, we're going to try some street theatre.'

He smiled and indicated that she should continue.

'I don't know if we'll even survive. We have high hopes! We'll probably be forced back into the classroom in September.' Her eyes were green. Her neck was smooth and white. 'Long term, though, we'll probably go to America.'

He cleared his throat, and moved his papers about. 'Really? To teach?'

She tilted her head a little. 'Mmm, I don't know… maybe… I want to go to New York for a while, hang out there, you know, live through four seasons in the city.' Her eyes were lit up. 'Anyway if I do go it'll be with the gang. There's a community drama programme we're hoping to get onto. America's great for that kind of thing. I had a job there last summer. The people are different, they're very… trusting. I met a poet at a bus stop one day… he talked to me like he knew me my whole life.'

Under the cuffs of her shirt her wrists were narrow and white. He had a glimpse of her future. She would always hear the cries of men and children.

'So you're off to the Big Apple for a wild time then!'

'Oh, I wouldn't say that, I wouldn't say "wild". I don't even drink.'

'No?'

'No. Don't get me wrong. I used to. I just don't like what it can do.'

Suddenly he felt reckless. 'What can it do?'

She blew out slowly and her fringe lifted in the stream of air. 'Well… I'd be afraid of losing control. I might end up falling down on the street… getting run over by a bus… sleeping with a stranger.'

Down the corridor a door slammed. Then there was silence. He thought she might hear the terrible commotion inside him. He picked up the report and handed it to her. 'I don't usually do this,' he said.

She read the page silently and then left it down. 'Thank you,' she said in a whisper.

He began to tidy his pages. His hands were trembling. He was aware of time slipping violently by.

'There's a job coming up in a school not far from here… ' He could not look at her so he leaned down for his bag. 'I know the principal, he's a friend… if you were interested…' He searched for the right words. 'You'd be a great asset to the school.'

They looked at each other. He saw her absorb the implications of the offer, and then her eyes softened with too much understanding, and it was unbearable.

'Of course, you may not want to stay around,' he said. 'From what you've said…'

He had almost lost the run of himself. He had become a small raw thing.

'Well… thank you. But if I do stick with teaching it'll probably be in Dublin.'

Driving back to the city that evening he grew distraught. Mona would never know the depths of him. He would die a faithful husband. They were bound together by the flesh of three sons and the dread of loneliness. That night he stood before a mirror. He thought he could hear the sound of his pulse fading. Every morning after that, at every daybreak, something slipped away. He drove along city streets in the evenings and stared at the backs of girls and women. Her name, her face, hovered behind his eyes. He went down to the strand on summer nights with the city lights at his back and stripped off and rolled out with the waves. He worked long hours and drove his sons hard at their studies and sports and exhausted everyone around him, and some days Mona turned on him with bitter, baffled eyes and he knew they had passed some milestone and there was no turning back.

His mother did not open her eyes. He drew the window blind down halfway, and waited. She lay supine before him, the torso, the bones that had borne the freight of her life, sunken in the bed. A girl with a plain wide face carried in a lunch tray and he smiled weakly and shook his head. She returned a few minutes later and, without a word, placed a cup of tea and two biscuits in front of him. This simple act moved him greatly.

In the late afternoon he walked outside and sat on a wooden bench and texted Mona. He dialled his sister's number and then instantly cancelled it. He wanted the day, and the death if it occurred, to himself. He walked around the back and stood on the edge of the lawn looking down at the Shannon. Pleasure cruisers were tied up at a small marina on the far side. Further along the bank there was a new hotel, like a large white cube, with huge windows. The water was calm; the reeds made the river seem patient. He leaned against a tree and looked up at the steel railway bridge high above the water. Just then the Dublin train nosed into view and crossed the bridge and, out of the blue, he remembered Grace again.

He had come upon her, unexpectedly, just three years before, when he had been addressing a teachers' conference in Maynooth. The crowd was large and during the morning coffee break, he turned to leave his empty cup on the long table and there she stood, no more than four feet away, calmly considering him. They were instantly recognisable to each other. Her hair was longer, darker, with a stripe of grey at the front, like a badger's. The stripe marked her out as different, changed, afflicted. *We are the same now*, he thought, *you have caught up*.

'I am forty,' she said, 'and married.' She crossed her hands on her lap. A great happiness had entered him the moment she sat into his car. He could not explain the closeness he felt to her. He was driving towards the city, blind, resolute. He thought of all the car journeys, all the years of remembrance. They floated along the quays in the late afternoon sun. He drove into an underground car park and they climbed concrete stairs and when they emerged out onto the street she let him take her hand. They entered a hotel, and up in the room he stood at the window and looked down at the street. Then he turned and crossed the floor and laid his head on her lap. They did not speak. He felt like a man in a novel—silent, obsessed, extreme in his love. He thought of this moment as his last chance, his only chance, and he felt everything—the past, the future—become almost obliterated by it.

'Tell me your life,' he whispered. The room was still warm from the day's heat. Soon, outside, the light would fade.

She smiled. 'A man broke my heart, once,' she said quietly.

'Your husband?'

'No. Another man. In America… an actor. I met my husband when I came back.' She gave a little laugh. 'He insists on loving me… I will never have children.'

'I'm sorry.'

She stroked his hair.

'Did you get over him? The American guy?'

She looked past him. 'When I came back I stayed at my mother's. I used to walk the lanes. It was summer then. One evening I took her car and drove for miles. When I returned I parked in the local churchyard, at the back, under the yew trees. I thought, This is where people come on summer evenings to do away with themselves. But I just sat there. I was so pierced… I thought we were predestined.'

She took his hand and led him to the bed. She removed his shoes. The charge was immense. The light in the room had changed and he was reminded of summer evenings in childhood when daylight vanished and a certain kind of sadness fell on him. She raised her face to him, her throat, the tender place on her temple that he wanted to touch. He saw her eyes, saw that something in her had been extinguished. Who did this to you? he wanted to say. He took her in his arms and covered her with his whole body, with the soles of his feet. 'Go deep,' she whispered.

They lay side by side looking up at the ceiling. He heard the rumble of the city in the distance. She had made him feel vast. He had to hold back words, thoughts, search for other words that might bear their weight. He remembered something from the radio that day, about how the skies are full of old junk, thousands of space shuttles and old Russian satellites that break up and fall to earth as debris. Pieces the size of a family car could come crashing down on one's house. He turned to tell her this. Her eyes were on him, full and moist and desolate.

'He only liked the beginnings of things,' she whispered. 'He used to hit me… He was so broken. It made me love him more.'

Twilight came. He had an urge to carry her to the car and drive off with her. Gradually, beside him, he felt her grow remote. She stepped from beneath the sheet and crossed the room. The light came on in the bathroom and the door closed softly. Then the shower was running. He looked at the shapes in the room, the TV screen, the lamps, the armchairs. He waited a long time. He knew then that she wanted him gone. He rose and dressed and went down in the lift, his legs barely able to ferry him. Out in the evening he felt sick in his stomach. The orange streetlights made everything eerie. He drove along empty streets where the trees hung low. He did not know his way out of the city. He stopped and sat in a café under harsh lights and stared at his reflection in the plate-glass window. He thought of her back in the hotel room, sitting in front of the mirror, brushing her hair in long, even strokes.

The horizon turned black as he drove west. He imagined forks of lightning striking the road, lighting up the way ahead. He opened the window and cold air streamed in and he accelerated hard and closed his eyes for a few seconds. It did not matter if he never reached home. He knew what awaited him, what had to be got through. He knew the water in the bay and every city street and every tree on his road. He knew his own driveway and the front door where his key fitted and the sound of his step on the stairs and the smell of the warm sheets rising to meet him. He pictured himself sitting on the edge of the bed, his weight sagging as he bent down and removed his shoes. He thought how such small things—untying shoelaces, undressing—or the thought of such things, could unhinge a man.

Lights were coming up across the river, on the marina, in the hotel, and soon they would rise from the town and reflect on the water. He felt a little chill. He crossed the damp grass and went inside. They had put a small table in his mother's room, with a white cloth and a crucifix and two lighted candles. A nurse came in and lowered the lights. He listened to his mother's breath, shortening. He laid his fingers on her pulse and rested them there and felt himself weaken in a moment of terrible tenderness, of mercy. He felt it in his arms, *caritas*, a love for her greater now than at any moment in his whole life. Suddenly, she opened her eyes wide and stared, petrified, at something at the foot of the bed. He whispered *Momma* and moved to that spot and for one long beautiful moment he thought she was back, and that it was all a mistake and in the next moment she would sit up and be whole again, and elated. But her eyes looked through him, seeing something beyond him.

The building was quiet. He thought he should whisper something in her ear. Her lungs were rattling, filling up with liquid, drowning like weighted sacs. Soon they would be full. When it happened, when the moment arrived, her little breaths petered out in one long exhalation, and he held his own until it ceased.

He sat there for a long time feeling it was neither day nor night. Something remained, drifting in the room. She had been long gone before tonight, long exiled. He had lived in an exile of his own too, in recent years. He closed his eyes now. Mona had made his home. She had made his children, inside her. He turned his head to where his mother's slippers sat on the floor. The sight of them, their patient waiting, moved him. He bent down and took them on his lap and put a hand inside each one. His heart began to pound. He had given Mona the whole of his life, the days, the hours, the quotidian. Every single day, but one. She would have him beyond this life too. Their bones would lie in the same grave and lean against each other and calcify in the earth together. What more could she want? What more could he give?

He was still for a long time. He did not know if this moment counted for everything or almost nothing. He drove west into the night. On the radio a piano was playing, single high notes, marvellous and pure, like the ringing of delicate bells. Their tinkle, their ambulation, tapped on his soul and made it soar.

THE VOCATION

Kathleen Coyle

Kathleen Coyle (1886–1952) was born in Derry, and later moved to the UK with her family. Coyle published thirteen novels – including *A Flock of Birds* and *Morning Comes Early* – children's stories and a memoir. Despite only one published short story collection, she made a living in later life contributing fiction to women's magazines in the US.

The day was sunless. The air lay in great sheets of shadow between the mountains. Here and there in the distance a farm shone like a white envelope. Now and then a goose or gannet rose up out of the shadows into a sky that resembled a tract of grey unchartered water. The Madon farm was higher than any other and backed by the higher level of the bogs which made a dark thread between the unearthly earth and sky. Catherine Madon came out to the doorway, and, holding her hand across her eyes, stared down the road. She listened. She heard the far-away beat of the Atlantic; it made the solitude seem immense. The cries of birds tinkled through it, the burr of the chain clock behind her ran out and back. Her heart was heavy—heavy as the landscape, and as clear. Only a few hours ago Hilary, her son, had gone down that roadway which she now scanned for her husband. Son and husband, husband and son, said the pendulum. Time passed; Hilary had gone away to be a priest. A nightcoming herd of cattle stood out on the thread of bog. The outline of the beasts was blocked and solid, a great roan and white swivelled mass, suddenly still. They did not seem real. They swelled out on the patch of sky behind like phantoms, then moved on. Her breath became regular again. The crooked, limping figure of Mooney the herd followed them into the dip and vanished. She continued to stand there until she saw Simon come into sight. He was walking beside the mare. Although they were too far away for her to see she was aware of the slack reins linking him to the mare. He would throw them over the hame when he came to the gate. It would only take him a few minutes to unyoke her. She waited, waited.

'There's a raw December clank in the air.'

His voice startled her, spun towards her like a flat stone flung on the silence. She had forgotten him, thinking of Hilary. The meaning of Hilary tormented her. The exultation had escaped. It was wrung out of her as the light was being wrung out of the day. 'Aye,' she answered. She saw the gaunt form of his face, the hollows where his eyes burned across the dusk to her. His voice filled her with wonder—wonder and pain. How would he take it? What would he do to her? To the boy he could do nothing.

It seemed to her that in that moment her spirit fled from her body and became greater than herself, gigantic like the cattle in the twilight. She became gigantic, a colossal woman spreading cloaked arms across the parted mountains. Life lay in her folds, gathered, hidden, witnessing. Simon went into the byre. The steam spired up through the half-door and joined the mist over the midden. She went indoors.

She stirred the Indian meal, put bowls down on the table. The vision of Margaret Mary Alacoque became alive above the mantelshelf in the reaching firelight. 'Dear Sacred Heart of God!' she said slowly, mechanically as the echo of a prayer that had suffered too much repetition. She moved her fingers up and down the age-polished pot-stick in her hand. The peat crumpled, blazed, and died. Hilary was in the train now, his brooding face held against the pane, his eyes asking questions. The place where she stood cried the emptiness that he had left.

Simon clamped in in his heavy boots. 'That's a night...' he said, 'that'd set a man running.'

'With a fear in it?' she asked. She wanted to keep her back to him, but she had to turn. Lip-deep she said: 'Simon!' There was a cross of courage in her soul.

He put his arms round her, his face close. Her lips were drawn into his beard, mute, meeting his. They had been married for eighteen years and she still gave herself to him with passion. She rested in his embrace, waiting, seeing Hilary go down the road without once looking back.

It came at last: 'Where's the lad?'

She pressed her fingers in upon his shoulder and then her hands went loose, quiet. 'He's gone!'

'Gone! Gone where?'

'He's gone away.'

'What d'ye mean?' he demanded sharply, freeing her.

'He's gone, Simon....' He looked so foolish, heavy as a great boot, emptied and standing dead on the floor. Before him she took the past ten years of their three lives and showed him what he had been too blind to see. He had not wanted to see. The moment was divisional, breaking them like a piece of burning turf into a thousand sparks. She remembered another such moment 'He's gone, Simon, to be a priest.'

'A priest!'

Everything upright went down in him. Some sorrow found its level. For the first time in her life she felt that he had the power to know her. It chilled all pity and mercy. Her strengths became weaknesses. It was she who cried out, hurt, 'Oh, don't you see, the son, Simon? Ye never read him. He was bound to be this... a priest.'

'It's you that's done it!' he cried out in anger, mad with her. 'You've always been calling him off the fields, one'd think there was contamination on them, there couldn't be a grain grown that you'd let him love. You'd twist it in him, poisoning him, Kate. From the very start you'd made up your mind about him, telling him those yarns about Savronola and that saint that had the trick of catching the fishes, and the queen with her bib full of roses... poetry it was... you had him....'

'Poetry!' a sigh parted her lips and turned into a smile that set her face alight in the glow of the hearth.

'Aye, Kate, poetry. Many's the time I sat listening to the two of you, thinking he was young and the manhood yet to spring in him. I knew well what you were after and I paid no heed... I was set certain that he'd turn one day and change on you, love God like a man, love Him everywhere...'

'Everywhere?'

'Aye, in everything.'

'God is everywhere,' she said stupidly, arguing against what she did not clearly perceive in his meaning.

He laughed at her. A dark bitter laugh that defeated her more than words. It had been coming so gradually for years that now when it had actually happened he felt in those first minutes that it had happened long ago. He moved, and on the other side of the table put his hands down and looked at her. 'Ye'd think, woman, that I did not believe in God?'

'You never pray!'

'Prayer! Litany after litany, chittering like mice, crumbs....'

'Don't ye dare...' she stopped him, 'mock at prayer.'

'I'm not mocking.'

'Ye are.'

'I'm no mocker.' He came back into the firelight and repeated it. 'I'm no mocker, but by God! Catherine, don't ye see what ye've done? Ye've robbed me, ye've stolen my son.'

She was afraid. She said, stretching out towards logic as towards a weapon, 'He is my son, too.'

'And ye've given him to God. Ye've given him up, ye've sent him away, you made him go. It's taken all his life time to do it.'

'You can't rob God,' she answered, still clutching the weapon.

'No! No! No! Fool, Catherine! But you can rob the land, you can rob the heart of man in God's face...' He stammered and his voice broke, hoarsened, 'I mind the days, the hours... I've lifted him out of the growing corn, out of the flax... the blue field... he has them eyes... blue...'

'Don't!' she set the word in a screech, low, smothered. He was heaping the emptiness upon her and she could not bear it. She loved her son. She loved this man who was ranting against her, breaking her. She wanted Hilary, wanted him back. God could wait for his coffin. In her soul was treachery to God. It was Simon who was making a traitor and a coward of her.

'Ye ruined him. Ye ought to have had a daughter, a girl'd have quietened ye, satisfied your woman's way of wanting sacrifice.'

'How,' she asked, demented with what he was saying to her, 'could I have sacrificed a girl?'

'The way all women are sacrificed. All they need is for Life to take them.'

'Oh dear, dear Heaven!' she moaned, groped for a chair and sat on it. She put her hands to her face. She had felt so strong before he had come in, spiritually greater than he, supported by her faith, by prayer, and Hilary had said: 'I'll pray in the train that he won't take it so badly, that he'll understand.' He was understanding in a way that she had not expected. He was making her feel that she had cheated him, herself, and, and God. She sought for reason. 'I asked you a year ago... the son asked you...'

'And what did I say?'

'You said no.'

'Aye, it meant that. You were so set on the idea that you wanted nothing out of my meaning but a yes or no. He said to me, the boy... you were standing watching him as though the fact that he had come out of your womb gave you a greater right than mine to him... he said:

"I've been thinking that I've got a vocation to be a priest."

"That ye've got a vocation, my lad," I answered, "I can well believe, but be careful before you tie a trade on it."'

She remembered heavily, full of stupor, the anger with which she had blamed him for calling it a trade to serve God. She was sitting still, now, with her hands locked on her apron. The apron spread around her making a great volume of white before the fire. She looked at him. He was sitting back on the table, hulkily in his dark, clumsy Sunday clothes; his legs were stuck out, his arms folded and a fist held up awkwardly against his cheek. She thought of the tobacco-smell of his mouth. She felt little before him, lost without Hilary. It was as though Hilary had taken her strength with him. While he had been there it had burned bright as a candle on an altar and she had not feared Simon.

'What do you think I tilled that land for, reclaiming those lower fields year after year? What do you think I cared for?' She did not speak. 'You and me—what do we need?' She was still silent. 'My God! Kate, a couple of acres'd raise all we'd eat!' He had never laid numb hands on a frost-plough without thinking that he was doing it for his son. And now? Now when he had begun to believe, this last year, that he'd got the boy on the road to be a fine farmer… this! Only this very day Flynn Flaherty had bespoke him for one of his daughters. He thought of his son begetting other sons and, suddenly, the storm went free in him, volcanic: 'D'ye know what ye've done? D'ye know? It's worse than castration…'

She stood up as though to ward off his speech, to keep it from reaching her. She stood still, saying nothing, and with her hands locked.

'D'ye know?' he repeated.

Beyond him, escaping his power over her, she thought of Hilary, as she thought of him thousands of times, saying mass; washing his sanctified fingers in the acolyte's cruet, and below him the congregation spread as a fan before the mystery. Around them in the shadowy kitchen gathered all the days of toil in her life, days of love, and nights crowned with blessed sleep or wrought with vigilance. Her life had been hard and bare as a rock but strong. It had known the wind and the rain and pain. But no pain like this.

He was joined to her there in the thoughts that possessed her for he said: 'You, Catherine, you know what the body needs. It has its needs; think, woman, think, don't ye mind all it has meant….'

He seemed to shake before her, and then she saw that he was trembling— and that his arms were outstretched. She opened to him then, hiding nothing: 'Och, Simon! I mind it all. I forget nothing, but I always hid the thing that never said yes in me, never was eased. It was that…all that…all that I gave to God and… Simon! Simon! It was grander… grander than love itself, but it did not come often… it was rare…'

'Sure I know it. I know all about it.' He pushed her away. Then he turned and took her into his arms again for he saw that she was weeping: 'It's the God in us, Kate, in all of us.'

His hold, the tone of his voice assured her—made her loyal to God. 'Then I done right! I… I only magnified the Lord!' Blessed be she who doth magnify the Lord.

'As sure as ye're standing here on his hearth-stone Catherine Madon, ye've robbed your son.'

'I couldn't help it, it was stronger'n me. It was stronger than anything I could do against it, Simon.'

Her helplessness quelled the rage in him, modified it into self-communion. He didn't feel so grand himself. Coming up the road the freezing stillness had maddened him. He had taken the whip, ready to lash out at the mare. He had drawn it back again, ashamed of himself. And the strange thing was that everything had gone well with him that day. He'd got a top price for his sheep and sold Kate's butter to a dealer from the Port of Salon and he'd brought her home a sack of sharps and a sack of fine white flour. He had got Hilary's watch from the watchmaker's. Into the silence he said: 'I've got the son's watch.'

And when he said that she broke in his arms and sobbed aloud.

'Och! Ye're a real fool,' he said tenderly. For the first time in his life he knew and felt the fatigue that comes before death. The cheat of Life reached him.

'Can't we call him back? He's gone with Father Martin the Dominican. He's gone to the monastery at Kingsbride.'

'Kingsbride!'

His laugh seemed terrible to her, impure. 'Simon!'

'No! No!' he answered fiercely. 'He's gone now. They've got him. He'll never be the same. It's worked in him for years and it'll take years to work it out, and by then it'll be too late. He's spoilt for the life of men, spoilt, if he came back they'd put a name on him....'

Some girl would have loved him all the wilder for that. 'I hope to God no woman ever loves him after he's ordained.' And he thought that his son was a fool to have been so secret with him. It was his mother's doing. The boy was only seventeen. What did he know? He began to blame himself for shutting out the boy, for laughing at him when he thought now, it would have served him better not to have laughed. He remembered an incident that had occurred at one of the last Lenten stations. The priest had put the mass-stone on an old sideboard that was propped with wedges of wood where the feet ought to have been. The wedges had shifted and the sideboard had tilted forward, flinging open the doors, and a piece of cheese had rolled out. He had laughed fit to split his sides. Hilary had not laughed. He had looked at him as the innocent look at the insane. He had filled with anger against the boy and mocked him. He had wanted to knock the softness out of him. He realised now that it was no use. The lad was too full of dreams and visions. The broodiness of his mother and the mountains had got him. Over Catherine's shoulder he spat into the fire. They were fools the two of them—to rear a son and sacrifice him. But it was he who was the greater fool.

Catherine moved out of his arms. She had stopped crying. Smooth as the polish on a stone she felt the finality of her son's going. The polish would grow, the smoothness shine brighter in the years to come. She had willed this with all her nature. And now her nature was dead.

It would never again be the same between her and Simon. Hilary would come between them, betwixt their love for one another—the priest, the prayer. 'It'll be grand,' she said steadily, 'to have him praying for us.' She lifted the stick off the plate and put it in the pot and began to stir.

'Grand… and the crops rotting on us.'

She prayed silently, striving for unity with her son in spirit.

'And soon we'll be rotting ourselves… the grass'll be as green as ever.'

Every day now, he'd be saying a bitter thing like that, putting the mark slowly on her. The hands and feet of Christ were pierced. She turned, the pot in her hands ready to empty into the bowls. She spoke, crushing the words out: 'Man, don't ye believe?'

'Believe!' He saw the grief in her eyes, stagnant. It took the edge off his voice, made it reasonable. 'I believe. I believe, Kate, more than you. I believe that God gave the earth.'

She put the pot back on the hob. He took his spoon, dipped it into the milk in the bowl before him and began to eat, hungrily, as a man eats when he comes home from market.

Reaching up to the chimney-shelf Catherine Madon lit the tallow candle. The pointed yellow flame steadied into brightness against the German print of Margaret Mary Alacoque and illuminated the smooth child-like face with the saintly eyes, and spread to the rays of the exposed Divine Heart.

Behind her Simon said, brutishly, his mouth full, 'But, by God, Kate, he was a damned skunk to go off like that without a word to his father!'

He who leaves not father and mother… for my sake. Give him strength, she prayed, guard him! She saw the boy's dark face, the beauty of his mouth… give him strength! She looked at her husband with contained, wide eyes. She said not a word. But within her she knew beyond all argument that Hilary had had to go like that. 'It'll be a great day for us when he'll be saying his first mass.'

'Aye, a great day!' The Judgment Day. The Resurrection. 'A great day,' he repeated. It would be the end of much. Quickly, as though it had begun to choke him, he rose from his food and went to the door, opened it, and stood there staring down the valley of darkness. He was taking it in at last. His son had gone away, out of the house, forever. He was without a son. He was a man toiling in the fields that would outlast him, in earth that would smell as sweet to another generation. The priest in his son would, in its turn, turn to the same ashes. Earth to earth. The despair of life burdened his soul. He stood there, thinking, asking wisdom of desolation.

'Come in,' Catherine begged. She had not sat down and was staring at his back with a sort of stupid sympathy, feeling sorry that the blow had fallen upon him like this. She could have stood his anger better. 'Come in, Simon!'

He heard, but he did not turn. He pitied her. He hated what she had done. He hated her, for she had something that he had not—conquest. God, he thought viciously, was kinder to women in affairs of this sort. They seemed able to live close to those were absent. He strode out into the swelling darkness, and his eyes lost the sense of the lighted room that he had left, he felt that Hilary was lost to him, lost in the darkness. Once upon a time God had arrested the sacrifice. He had called out of the burning bush. God might still do something… but Catherine! Catherine was there, and she, he knew would relight any faggot.

A SWIM

Elizabeth Cullinan

Elizabeth Cullinan (1933–2020) was a typist at the *New Yorker* (typing up John Updike manuscripts) before penning two short story collections (23 stories were published by the *New Yorker*) and two novels, *House of Gold* (1970) and *Change of Scene* (1982). Her work centred on working-class Irish-Americans, Catholicism and women keen to avoid the lives their mothers had.

The day was doubtful, more like two different days competing for possession of the narrow beach. Over the sand, the sky was blue and perfect, but a long, solid gray cloud was drawn up out over the water, and though it seemed to hang still, it was slowly advancing, like another tide, on the sunny shore. A good crowd was settled there on Portmarnock Strand, but most of the little groups had stayed close to the three broad concrete steps leading down to the beach. There was an air of indifference about them, and that, along with the way everyone was dressed, made it seem as if they had not so much gone to the beach as found themselves there. The men were in business suits, shoes and socks, neckties. Some had hats. The women wore suits, or dresses with coats or layers of sweaters, and shoes and stockings. Here and there people who were just about to go into the water or had just come out stood around in bathing suits that were, without exception, old-fashioned and unattractive, faded and creased (kept from year to year, always good enough, each new season, for the occasional use they'd receive). There was a sharp east wind, and the beach was studded with half-finished forts and dry trenches the children had abandoned for games that would keep them warm. Those with sixpence could ride on the little donkey, down near the water, and the lucky ones hopped and shouted and ran races as they waited in line. Another line, mostly adults, had formed outside a big blue tent that was pitched in the center of the crowd. In front of the tent were tables with cups and saucers, sugar bowls, teaspoons, pitchers of milk. Beside the flap was an enormous red-crayon sign: TEA.

The big green doubledecker Dublin bus came to a stop in front of the three concrete steps, and a young man jumped off. He was dressed in the same way as the people on the beach but much more carefully than any of them. There was a sharp crease in the trousers of his blue serge suit, and his tie was neatly knotted under the collar of an immaculate white shirt. The girl who was with him could, just as she was (full red tweed skirt, black sweater, Aran cardigan), have taken a part in *The Playboy of the Western World*, but Bernadette Shea was not even Irish. She was American, and she had never been swimming in Ireland, and as she swung down from the bus and turned to look at the beach, she burst out laughing.

Nothing there seemed funny or strange to Jim Delaney, who came from Killorglin, a town in Kerry. "What's wrong?" he asked her.

"Everybody's so dressed up!" When they met in front of the G.P.O. in Dublin, she wondered why he'd worn his second-best suit, vest and all, just to go to the beach, but it had seemed tactless to ask, just as it was tactless, she realized now, to have laughed. "I feel out of place," she said, turning the joke on herself.

"There's no sunbathing in Ireland," he said, "sure there's not."

"Doesn't anyone wear beach clothes?"

"You're thinking of the French Riviera." He bent over to take off his shoes and socks.

"No, I'm not," she said. "I'm thinking of home." His feet were narrow, with high arches and slender toes, and they reminded her (just as the look in his light brown eyes did, and his pale, fine, straight reddish blond hair, and the way he walked) of how vulnerable he was. She was vulnerable, too, but her appearance hid it better than his. She had a pretty face, black hair, and not a bad though not a really good figure.

"There must be marvelous beaches in America," he said as they began to make their way through the clusters of people.

"Oh, there are," she said, "but next to the beach there's always a huge parking lot, or rows and rows of bungalows." Or bathhouses. For some reason, she didn't say it out loud. Instead, she looked around for a place to change. The tent was the only possibility, but surely, she thought, everyone didn't undress in the same place. She was glad she had worn her bathing suit under her clothes; even more glad when they came alongside the tent and she saw the sign. "Tea!" she cried.

"A cup of tea is nice after a swim."

She burst out laughing again, and again tried to cover up. "At home," she said, "they sell awful things at the beach. Hot dogs and ice cream and beer." Two men raced by, heading for the water. There was something sad and embarrassing about their old-fashioned bathing suits, and Bernadette looked away. "When I was little I was always getting sick at the beach."

"Look now," he said, drawing her attention back to the men, who had reached the water's edge and stopped there, hugging their sides against the wind. "There're some bathing togs."

What would *he* wear, she wondered. The same as those men? Would his skin have that same delicate, milky whiteness? Probably, and she'd have to pretend she didn't notice. She was as careful as if she were in love with him, but her care was meant to make him see what she had seen right away, that the advantage she appeared to have was only superficial. She had set out to show him her worst side, all her shortcomings, and she had put herself at his disposal, seeing him as often as he wanted but trying to avoid, whenever she could, the formalities that would give their meetings a conventional design. She made no effort to look her best with him, never wore her best clothes, never wore perfume. She tried never to criticize him, or disagree with him, or blame him, or bring about any other test of strength that, with the liability of his love, he would have to fail. And when they went out she often arranged to meet him, not have him call for her or take her home, or she'd suggest that they see each other of an afternoon rather than an evening, or in some thoroughly neutral setting, like the National Library. Above all, she never mentioned other places she went, with other people. But after a while there were none. Other attachments ended, but this one survived—survived her not loving him and, later on, his falling in love with someone else. Not only did it survive that threat, it flourished on account of it, for one evening he told her about the other girl, who the night before, as on many other occasions, had left him for good. After that, their evenings were devoted to the other affair, planning his strategy, analyzing his mistakes, celebrating his victories. He would call her up to talk of it, sometimes late at night after he left the other girl home. Once he appeared on her doorstep at eight o'clock in the morning. She had just got up. She drew the tweed cover up over the rumpled bedclothes of the divan, made some coffee, and then sat huddled by the gas fire while he paced back and forth across the room, tracing again and again, through the faded roses in her carpet, the undeviating course of his love, from bad to worse. That time, he said, she'd saved his life, but the half attention she'd given him that morning, even the full attention of all the other times, added up to very little as far as she was concerned. In her opinion there was only one thing she had done for him. He never mentioned it and neither did she, but she knew he often used her as a trump card that would help him gain the upper hand—she was, as she pictured it, the mysterious American friend whom he cared for in a way the other girl would not have understood. To her surprise, Bernadette had caught herself out in a kind of resentment of that role, but still, she was more relieved than resentful. People figured in each other's lives in ways they couldn't predict. They had met, she decided, so that she could help him bring this affair to a successful conclusion. But that hadn't happened. He had been unsuccessful, and the other girl had really gone away, leaving them no longer conspirators, but no longer, either, what they'd been at first. They were more like friends, but still, more than friends. Her concern for him had turned to real affection, and his love, once removed now, had become sufficiently abstract for him to speak of it openly with her, as though it involved persons other than themselves. "You were always the stronger," he said. And another time: "Only for your charity. I'd have been pretty desperate about you." And then, speaking of herself and the other girl: "I always knew that you were by far the finer person." That she should have come out on top struck Bernadette as dangerous, and made her wonder if it might be better to stop seeing him, but when she thought it over that seemed impossible. It was no longer the point. There was no point at all now, only that they had met and continued to meet and that they were so alike. The relationship had a kind of sadness, he'd once said, but the sadness was his, not hers. To her it seemed as if they had come on something new in the way of human feeling, something vague and yet very demanding but, to the extent that it was demanding, also rewarding, something that had no name, no objective, and that gave them nothing to go by, only each other's wishes, which, as their only guide, they were obliged to study carefully, testing and trying each to be sure it was true, and not just the desire on the one hand to please and on the other to be agreeable.

"I thought we'd try what it's like up in the dunes," he said. "That is, if you think it might appeal to you."

"Whatever you'd like."

"Maybe you'd rather not climb up there. It's pretty steep."

"I don't mind that," she said.

"Which would you prefer, then, down on the beach or up in the dunes?"

"I suppose the view would be nice up there."

"It would," he said.

"And that was your first idea."

"Will we try the dunes so?"

"All right," she said.

The sand on the beach was packed solid from the dampness, but the sand of the dunes was soft, and at a touch it spilled down treacherously. He went first, catching hold of the long grass and digging his feet in as he climbed, to make steps for her, and at the top he reached over and grabbed her by the wrist to hoist her up.

In back of the dunes were meadows that stretched as far as the eye could see, with cattle grazing there behind a barbed-wire fence. The spread of green and the lazy movements of the animals made the whole scene less austere, though at the same time it seemed lonely up there. They were hidden from the crowd near the concrete steps, and if other people were in the other dunes there was no telling, for each was deep and private.

"That's Howth," he said, pointing to where the coastline formed a steep bluff.

Bernadette glanced at the hill (they'd climbed it one bleak day back in early autumn), then she turned back to the beach. Nowhere, not on that straight stretch of sand, nor in the dunes, nor in the fields behind them, had she found what she was looking for, and finally she asked him. "Where do you change?"

"Here."

"In front of everyone?"

"Who's to see?"

It made her uneasy. "In America," she said, "it's against the law to change your clothes on a public beach."

"That's funny." He took off his coat and turned his back to her.

He was undressing right there, beside her. It was a long time since he'd made her nervous, but as she turned away to face the water she remembered how in the beginning she had often been that and more, been almost afraid, as though his love, which she'd encouraged him to cheat, would, somehow or other, get its own back. Besides, he was uncompromising by nature, and the exception he'd made with respect to his love for her was so out of character that that day at Howth, looking out over the sheer cliff, listening to the screeching of the gulls, she'd even wondered if he might not take it into his head to push her off. "There are signs all over the place"—she had to clear her throat—"'No disrobing in public.'"

"And have you to pay to get undressed?"

"Unless you wear your suit under your clothes. That's what I did today."

"In that case," he said, "you're very slow."

From the tone of his voice, she could tell he'd finished changing. She unzipped her skirt and dropped it to the ground; then she turned around. He was bent over his clothes, folding them neatly. His body was thin, but it was well filled out, and though his skin, which seemed to give off a rich, sweet smell, was very white, it had a density that made it look rosy, not milky. He stood up and turned around, and she saw that his woolen bathing suit was very presentable—not like American trunks but still not like the dated suits they'd seen. More of a Continental style, though less brief than that.

"Hurry up," he said. Without another word, he dashed down the side of the dune, raced across the beach, and ran into the water. It was low tide, and he had to wade far out before the water was deep enough for him to flop down. Bernadette watched for a moment as he started paddling awkwardly, his head held stiff and high; then she picked up her bathing cap and slid down the side of the dune.

When she was alone, her impressions would expand and fill out with a freedom that the responsibility of his company sometimes kept in check, and as she crossed the narrow beach its strangeness began to be mildly exhilarating. The wind on her back and arms and legs was gentler than it had seemed when she was dressed, and, now that she was barefoot, the hard-packed sand felt more like a sidewalk than a beach—a sidewalk with a tide line for a curb and a gutter strewn with shells and stones and stiff strings of seaweed. She picked her way through the dry crust to the water's edge and stopped there, among the gulls and sandpipers. The water was gray there at the edge, but farther out it was a cloudy green, and, near the horizon, dark blue. Here and there the wind raised whitecaps that rode nearly as far as the shore before they dropped again to ripples that broke against her ankles, and then, as she began to wade out, against the calves of her legs, against her knees, against her thighs. When she finally plunged in, the shock of the cold took her breath away, but she began to swim hard and kept on until she came up beside him. His hair was plastered to his head. His eyes were clear and relaxed.

"You're a good swimmer," he said.

"It took me forever to learn." Ridiculously, her exhilaration had turned to shyness.

"When I was five years old, my father tossed me out of a boat one day."

"What did you *do*?"

"I learned to swim."

"I learned to swim in a heated, indoor pool."

"You ought to be able to make it over to England," he said, "with that kind of training."

"I was the worst one in the class."

"I don't believe it."

"I was," she said. "I was perfectly happy just pretending I could swim. Like this." She took a few steps along the spongy floor of the sea, moving her arms in the breast stroke.

"I used to do that, too," he said.

"You did? Do you suppose all children do?"

"Most likely," he said. "Can you float?" The serious way he spoke, and the serious way he lay down on the water, made Bernadette remember how different this lonely place with its rudimentary pleasures was from American beaches where people did handstands, played volleyball, rode surfboards through an ocean full of waves, or simply lay in the hot sun. And only by making a joke of it could she throw off the feeling of sadness that the sight of the bare beach ahead gave her.

"With my training," she said, "of course I can float." Lying down beside him, Bernadette was suddenly ashamed of whatever it was—something brash in her character, some artificiality—that led her to keep drawing obvious distinctions, making pointless comparisons. "Let's have a race," she said, jumping up again. It was too *cold*. *That* much was true. "Get on your mark!"

"I'd be no match for you," he said. "With your training."

"Get set!"

"All right. Go!" He shot out ahead, kicking up a spray that drenched her. She had to move out of his wake before she could start after him, but when she did, in no time at all she'd caught up and then, though she'd meant to let him win, left him behind. The splashing in back of her died down. She stood up and turned around, squeezing the water out of her bathing suit, to find him floating, eyes closed, arms outstretched.

"I guess I'm the winner," she said.

He opened one eye. "What else did you expect?"

The one-eyed look gave his face a sharp expression that made Bernadette feel she'd been put in her place. Had she been showing off? The eye closed, and when the look of disapproval was gone it was hard to believe it had ever existed.

"This is more my speed," he said.

Overhead, the solid gray cloud had broken apart and faded, and the loose clouds that had begun to drift across the sky were almost white, though they threw freezing, black shadows over the water. Bernadette shivered. It was no kind of a day to be in swimming, and she was sorry now she hadn't told him that when he called. "In America," she should have said, "no one would go for a swim in weather like this." But she hadn't said that. "Today?" she'd asked him, and she hadn't corrected him when, taking her question to mean today, as opposed to, say, tomorrow, he'd said, "Today, this afternoon." He was not as good at guessing her thoughts as she was at guessing his, and though that hadn't ever bothered her before, she found it irritating to have to realize now that he was enjoying himself so he was hardly aware of her presence, much less that she was cold and uncomfortable. She sank down out of the wind, into the water; then on an impulse she jackknifed under. His pale body shone ahead of her, bright and blurry, no more than seven strokes away, she figured, as she closed her eyes and began pushing toward him. The cold made her head ache, but she finished the full seven strokes and then put out her hand. Nothing was there. Her eyes opened, then her mouth, her nose. Her head filled with sea water, and in a panic she surfaced, not under him but beside him.

He was standing up, watching a couple back on the shore, a girl who stood at the water's edge, shrieking, as the boy who was with her dipped his hands in the water and splashed her over and over again. "That's fine sport going on there."

Bernadette opened her mouth to answer and instead started coughing.

"Are you cold?"

She nodded. Salt water drained, with a bitter taste like nose drops, down into her throat.

All at once his face was anxious. "We'd best go in," he said.

"So soon?" His concern had filled the space between them with an image so miserable—pale cheeks, bloodshot eyes, bleary smile—that in spite of herself she had to protest, "We've only just got wet."

"That's all you want to do," he said, "in this climate."

The clouds were darkening the beach now, but people were still arriving. As she toweled herself dry, up in their windy gallery, Bernadette watched a family, mother and father and two little girls, settle down on the sand, spreading out a tartan blanket in a direct line with their place in the dunes. "What can they be thinking of," she said, "coming now, with that sky."

"You're as well off here as anyplace else, in a shower."

She combed her soaking wet hair behind her ears and tied a scarf over her head; then she drew on her skirt and sweater.

"Aren't you going to take off that wet suit?" he said.

"I have nothing else to put on."

"If you like you could have my vest."

The offer was so odd that she stopped to consider it, only to reject it right away. "I don't think it would help," she said. What she needed was an overcoat. No, something more basic than that. She watched him pick up his bundle of clothes; then, enviously, she turned back to the beach. Off in the distance a man was driving golf balls, and the white speck traveling across the sky caught her eye, though she lost it again as it blended with the gray bulk of Howth. Where was the path across it, she wondered, and where was the village at the end? Distance and the dull day had hidden them both, the dirt path winding up over the hill and the houses huddled at the bottom—in the dark as she remembered them, with windows of light, for though it had been mid-afternoon that day when they'd set out to climb the headland, by the time they reached the town night had fallen. The streetlights had guided them down to the front, and from there they'd turned up a lane that ended in a flight of crooked stone steps squeezed between two buildings. They'd climbed the crooked steps to the top and crossed the street to an old pub where, he'd promised her, they would have prawns for supper, served on two pieces of buttered bread. Inside the pub it was hardly any warmer than outside, and the first thing he did was order two small Jameson's; then they took the drinks over to a table near the electric fire. After the first few sips, the whiskey began to make her warm and comfortable, and she felt the color come to her cheeks. The evening had turned out happily, and there'd been others like it—evenings at Mooney's on Harry Street, where there was a bartender who looked like James Joyce, and at the pub on Sussex Road, near the Canal, which they had called the little pub, until the night there was a fight there and he was hit on the head with a bottle, and then they called it the low pub. Evenings at Jammet's, the beautiful, old-fashioned Dublin restaurant, and evenings at the Palace Grill, where people up from the country went for their tea—bacon, egg, and sausage, tea, bread and butter. During the fall they met twice a month at the State Cinema in Phibsboro for the showings of the Film Society; then through the winter and spring they watched for French and Italian pictures they might want to see that would come to the theaters on the quays, the Astor and the Corinthian. All those times, all of them aimless and happy, troubled her as they came to her now, as though buried in her memory they'd grown to a size that her mind could no longer comfortably contain.

"That was refreshing, wasn't it?" He had dressed quickly and was standing beside her.

"It was," she said.

"Though it's a pity the sun went in."

"Yes."

"My guess is it'll come out again."

But if anything, she thought with a shiver, it looked more like rain than ever.

"Are you cold?"

"A little."

"We'll lie down in the dune so," he said. "That'll be shelter from the wind."

As they stretched out, side by side, his sense of well-being and her discomfort bred a silence that soon became awkward. Down on the beach the two little girls, in their bathing suits now, were running and splashing each other at the water's edge, while the mother and father, wrapped in towels, were changing their clothes. Finally Bernadette said, "I don't see how they do it without dropping something."

"Isn't it strange," he said, "that in a place like America, where it's so free, there have to be special places for undressing."

"It's just a custom," she said. "Like driving on the right-hand side of the road."

"But they talk of the Irish being prudish, and yet you could strip right out in public here and no one would pay the slightest heed."

"What does that prove?"

"Nothing, Bernadette. I only meant it was strange."

"Maybe they're just indifferent."

"Maybe."

For the second time in half an hour, the second time ever, she thought she had caught sight of a flaw in his feeling for her, and as the silence closed over them again, it occurred to her that behind the perfect approval she had, she saw now, come to count on there might exist criticism, not of the failings she had shown him but of others she had unconsciously tried to hide, from him and perhaps even from herself. Unsettled and unsure, the wet bathing suit prickling her skin, she rolled over onto her back. "You know what?" she said after a moment.

"What?"

"I think I just felt a drop of rain."

He sat up and raised his palm to the air. "I don't feel any thing," he said. "But here, put my coat on in case it comes down."

"You'll get soaked in your shirt-sleeves."

He took off the blue serge coat and held it out. "Take it," he said. "Don't be foolish."

Foolish was what she felt as she slipped her arms into the sleeves; foolish and, worse still, helpless, bound by conditions she herself had laid down for a situation that she seemed to have misjudged. "That's a whole lot better," she said, though it was no better at all. The coat was just another layer of insulation. Under the wet bathing suit, her body was like ice, and she thought she could feel a dull pain across her back and shoulders. *Catch your death of cold.* There was a solid truth locked inside the old saying, she realized, as she turned it over in her mind. You could catch pneumonia and be gone in a flash. *She went very quickly.* How many times had she heard that expression? "Jim," she said suddenly, "I think I *will* have to take off this bathing suit. I'll spread it out and try to get it dry."

"Good," he said. "And let me give you my vest."

"What good would *that* do?" She looked to see if he'd noticed the sharpness in her voice, but he had picked up a stone and was turning it over in his hand, examining it.

"You need something," he said. "Those bathing togs won't be dry for hours, and you could get rheumatism sitting around on a day like this."

Bernadette could see his watch. It was three o'clock, and he appeared to be by no means ready to leave. If she were to hold out, she had to have something on besides her sweater and skirt. And not his vest. She knew what she needed. She would have to ask him. But how? Quickly, she thought. Without thinking about it. "Listen," she said, "would you lend me your underwear?"

"That's what I said. My *vest.*"

She stared at him, and then, out of some advertisement or a display in a shopwindow, the word explained itself. His vest was his undershirt. "I thought you meant your waistcoat," she said.

"Not at all!" He loosened his tie and reached down under the collar of his shirt to show her.

"In America—" she began to explain, but he wasn't listening.

"Wait here," he said. "I'll throw you the things."

She watched him stride across the dunes, and when he dropped down out of sight she began to take off the damp sweater, then the skirt, then the wet bathing suit. Crouched there, she heard him call, and she looked over the edge of the dune.

"Here you are!"

The clothes landed just beyond her reach. As she put out her arm to get them, she noticed a play of light on the green fields; she raised her head to the sky and saw that the clouds were drifting inland. "Thank you!" she called back to him. The sun was coming out. The afternoon was taking on new life.

"I'll meet you down on the beach!"

It came to her then, as though at his suggestion. There was no need for them both to stay, no need to watch the points pile up against her. Marveling that it hadn't occurred to her sooner, she saw that the thing to do was separate.

The sun glittered on the water, picking out points of light on the crest of every ripple, but the beach was hardly any different from what it had been in shade, for the wind was still strong, and it thinned the sunlight to a hard brightness that had no heat in it. But, dressed and dry again, Bernadette felt quite warm as she stepped over to the edge of the dune.

He stood near the base, his feet planted far apart on the flat sand, his hands clasped behind his back and his head set squarely, as though he were confronting the horizon with a glance as level as its own. Even from behind, the pose suggested an absorption that Bernadette hated to break into, and yet she didn't want, either, to take him by surprise. Still undecided, she put one foot over the side of the dune, but she was too close to the edge, and the soft sand gave way. She slipped and let out a cry that made him turn quickly.

"Take your time," he called.

But it was too late. The long grass was tangled, like netting, and the shells and stones embedded in the sand scraped the soles of her feet and kept her from getting her footing. She skidded all the way down to the bottom.

"Did you hurt yourself?"

"No," she said, brushing the sand from her clothes. "I'm all right." But the plunge had shaken her. Her legs were wobbly as they set out in the direction they'd come from, and she felt less able to make the break she'd planned, though being more difficult it became all the more necessary. "I was sure I felt a drop of rain before," she began.

"That's the Irish weather for you," he said. "No day complete without that drop of rain."

"All the same, I think I've had enough fresh air for today."

"Would you like to leave?"

"If you don't mind."

"Whatever you say, only I had an idea a cup of tea might be nice."

"I'll walk you as far as the tent," she said, "then I'll go get the bus."

"On your own?"

"I thought you might want to stay."

"Why would I do that?"

She saw from his astonishment that the idea that had served her so often in their complicated world was preposterous here in this setting where everything was simple and natural and what it seemed to be. "It's still early," she suggested.

"I've had enough myself," he said. They had reached the outskirts of the crowd and he turned around, facing the dunes as though taking his leave of them. "I was afraid you might have caught a chill back there, but seeing as you're all right—"

Over his shoulder Bernadette saw the bus draw up across the road from the concrete steps, and all at once, as desperately as a moment before she had longed to leave, now she longed to stay. "I was afraid I had, too," she said. If they could stay, if they could go back and explore the farthest reaches of that long strip of sand, it seemed to her they might recover this day and, with it, all the other days that had suddenly become so precious. "My blood felt like ice water." She laughed up at him, but he looked away, turned around.

"There's the bus!" he said.

The few passengers dropped down and dispersed, some toward the beach, others along the road. "We'll never make it," she said.

"Let's run for it."

In the quick decision, reached easily and alone, she felt once more the force of those secret reservations, like money put aside, that his love had allowed, perhaps even urged, him to keep against a day like this when a combination of circumstances, some in his favor but more in her disfavor, would double his resources and make him, at last, self-sufficient. He started off across the sand, and there was nothing for her to do but take off after him, zigzag through the crowd, up the concrete steps, and across the street. But the bus was not quite ready to leave. They had a good few minutes to climb on board and settle down, and then, minutes to spare.

"I think it's as well to go now," he said.

"Yes," she said, "I guess it is."

"There's no use taking chances."

"No, there isn't."

The bus driver climbed in and sat down behind the wheel. The conductor hopped on at the rear.

"We'll come back again."

Bernadette looked out the window. There were the people dressed in their street clothes. There was the blue tent billowing in the wind. There was the donkey patiently walking along the shore. She wouldn't see them again with him, for she knew he wouldn't ask her. They were out of place here. They were less than what they seemed to be.

"Later on in the summer we'll give it another try."

"Will we?" she said.

It was clear from his look of dismay that he knew what she meant, but she had struck the truth so lightly that he could pretend she hadn't touched it at all.

"We will," he said quickly, "toward the end of August.

The water'll be warmer then. We'll start out in the morning and maybe bring a lunch. That is," he added, "if it'd please you."

All along they'd been outside the truth, just as they'd been outside love, and now the truth, like love, would not let them in. She nodded. "If it would please you," she said.

THE YEW TREE

Tharsp Sharko

Oein DeBhairduin

> **Oein DeBhairduin** is an educator, poet, folk herbalist and an avid
> archivist of Traveller tales, sayings, retellings and historic exchanges.
> He manages an education centre, is vice-chair of the Irish Traveller
> Movement, a council member of Mincéir Whidden, a board member
> of several local Mincéirí action groups and a key custodian of Tome
> Tari, the Indigenous Traveller Language Group.

*I spent a lot of my childhood in graveyards. Not in a morose way, but in the
way that many people from the Traveller community spend time in graveyards. Travellers often don't have a permanent place in life, so when we die,
we mark the ground with a stone to show we were there.*

*We visit for funerals, of course, and the quarter mass. We also visit the
graves of loved people on birthdays, on grief days, on high holidays and when
the extended family come to town. Every relative, every loved one, every
kindred friend is remembered. We go to graveyards to be among those who
stand on the edge of our shared experiences, when dreams remind us of them
and sweetly sung songs invoke their memories, keeping them alive in stories
of how they were and where they exist on the wiry brambles of ancestry.*

*All those free and able, settled or Traveller, whose hearts were light enough
to carry them through the streets of Tuam always went for the quarter mass
on 6th June, St Jarlath's feast day. We don't willingly go to sorrowful places
with a heavy heart in case the carrying of it would mire us to that place.*

*There is the old graveyard and the new graveyard and, in the centre, a large
space filled with unmarked famine graves. We would gather in the middle,
packed tight although the graveyard is huge, as if tied together by invisible
strings.*

*In the west of the old graveyard, there is a grey sandstone memorial cemented
into the wall, which is marked with no Traveller's name but it is for Travellers,
remembered and forgotten, buried in unmarked graves and unnamed places
in the Tuam graveyard and across the world.*

Unbaptised and nameless Traveller children were usually buried in uncon-secrated ground, in the cradle of ancient sites, lisheens, near holy monuments, blessed wells and other sacred places. On rare occasions, Traveller children could be buried in the consecrated soil of the graveyard, which would other-wise have been barred to them for having neither name nor the grace of baptismal waters. Those who had recently lost a friend, relative or neighbour, could lay their still children at the feet of the deceased. The little baskets would be tenderly carried to their rest in known and trusted arms. In many of the graves of Ireland, at the feet of those who journeyed before us, sleep swaddled children, safe in the care of kind-hearted custodians.

In this graveyard, not far from my family home, stands a scattering of tall yew trees, beaten by age, weather and the waves of grief they have endured from all that pass by them. I recall admiring them as a child, those beautiful solemn figures rooted throughout the sacred space. The high, cold, grey, stone walls and dark iron gates mark the boundary lines between the place of the dead and that of the living.

One year, although we went in June, it felt like an autumn morning, still, clear, crisp and cold, but the warmth of the people brought the reminder of the rising days of summer. I remember asking my father later that day about the yew trees and being told about where they were said to come from and why they are almost always found in graveyards.

Many years ago, on a date not recalled exactly, distant enough to be forgotten but recent enough to still be spoken about, there was a young Mincéir féin, newly married, with a beautiful child and a home filled with so much love and care that dawn brought only joy and twilight no quarrels.

He worked the markets and she spun lace, and the bonny-hearted lackeen left laughter in her footsteps and smiles in her wake. His hands were rough but gentle, accustomed to hard work, and hers, light and nimble, fingertips calloused from the tatting of fine silken lace.

They lived for some years knowing only the glow of shared kindness and hopes of a bright future. One year, however, in the depths of winter, their home was visited by a quick fever and all three were struck by it. Their limbs were heavy and smouldering like the charred branches of the campfire, their laboured breaths like its strangled smoke. By the second day the wife and child had succumbed to it. On the third day, the young man recovered and woke to their loss. His legs were weakened, soft like willow, his pale face awash with sweat like cold winter dew, bleached of charm and warmth. He was bereft and gripped by the loss of his loved ones. His body felt as heavy as dark, moist peat trodden on by innumerable feet, gushes of agony deep-knit in his bones when he moved, his once strong being as fragile and jagged as broken eggshells.

After the funeral he stayed by their grave until the night had passed and a fresh dawn was breaking on the horizon. His friends came and brought him home, welcoming him back to the world of the living with company and light conversation, poitín to soothe his heart and good food to rekindle the embers of his wounded spirit.

The next day the man returned to the graveyard until his friends came and, again, brought him home. Each day the pattern repeated. The man would rise from his bed and wander to the graveside, the day would pass and in the stillness of the night his friends would seek him out and bring him home.

Soon he refused to return home, shunning his friends, staying in the grave-yard to watch over the grave of his lost ones. He stood, a solitary and bewildered figure, his once bright future in ashes. The man had neither north nor south, nor the track of the road back to who he had been.

Over time his skin became cracked and darkened by the sun, rain and gale. His hair became tangled with twigs, feathers and spiders. As the days passed, he grew colder and fixed, rigid and unmoving. Even his voice, once warm in speech, had changed to a mumble of light creaks and crackles. His clothes withered and grew green with mildew and moss, and his tears, still sharp with loss, were red round droplets against his cracked skin.

His toes, knowing the earth beneath his feet so very well, grew long and twisted, reaching down to the familiar spot and rooting him to the place. His toenails, coiled and gnarled, clawed through the soil and stone, snapping the tangled tendrils in the dank earth beneath the quiet topsoil of the graveyard.

What had once been daily visits, a heartfelt pilgrimage of remembrance and connection, had become the loss of coming home, and he became something else. What stood at the graveside was no longer the shape nor shade of the kind man, the good husband, the doting father, but instead a figure of cracked bark-like skin, green spines from age and red berries from the tears that still spilled from him.

In the lock of his grief the man had become the first ever yew tree.

This tale reminds me that grief can bind us into a rigid loss if we stand in it for too long. If we become unmoving, unexploring of the world and unwanting of the company and kindness of others, we too risk becoming the lonely yew in the graveyard, so lost in our own grief, that we lose ourselves.

THE BEAUTIFUL THING

Kit de Waal

Kit de Waal is a UK Midlands-based award-winning novelist. She was born in Birmingham to an Irish mother and Caribbean father. Her debut, *My Name Is Leon*, won Kerry Group Irish Novel of the Year 2017. Her second novel, *The Trick to Time*, was longlisted for the Women's Prize for Fiction 2018. *Becoming Dinah*, her YA novel, was published in 2019.

I met my father in 1969 when I was ten, I don't mean we were estranged; he lived with us, I saw him everyday. But one evening, at the kitchen table, while he polished his heavy winter boots, he started talking about coming to England and the day he got off the boat and I saw then he had a life that stretched back before I was born. So that's how I met him and this is what he told me.

My father and Judas were sitting in the bar on Moon Street, a long airless room, shuttered from the heat. My father drained his warm, half-share of beer and pushed the glass away.

'We going then Judas? You sure?'

Judas smiled.

My father wanted someone keen for adventure and for the long trip to England so he shook hands with Judas and went his way. They would stick together, make a go of it, send money back and one day, come home themselves with cash in their pockets and a tale to tell. There was three weeks to wait before the ship sailed and time enough to see if Judas would change his mind like he'd changed it so many times, when they were children, when they climbed into the sweet shop, grabbed what they could, pledged their silence and ran. But Judas told. They were beaten and disgraced, the uneaten sweets restored to the shop. And Judas earned his name. By the time he was twenty-eight his treachery was almost forgotten.

My father had left Antigua before. He was nineteen when he took the boat to Florida to cut sugar cane in The Glades for five dollars a day. He picked oranges in Pahokee, living in a shack with twenty other men and then worked his way slowly north through the plantation fields of Georgia and Alabama where a black man took his life in his hands every time he stepped on the street. He laboured in the sawmills and lumberyards of The Carolinas, heaving and hauling something or other all the way to New York City where he felt his first winter.

'New York was bright like a summer's day,' he said 'but cold like ice water.'

He was a warehouse hand in a grain store, loading unwieldy bags of rice and corn in East Flatbush.

'Them bags was heavy as a dead man. You had to wear gloves or the cloth would tear the skin of your palms. Disease would get in and before you know it, you can't work and that is worse than sickness. If you are sick, it only last a few days.

Anyway, you take your two hands like this and you grab the sack like you're a caveman and you just found a wife.'

He threw the wife over his shoulder.

'Now you have to make a pile over in the corner.'

He pointed to the far side of the kitchen and stumbled towards it and threw the invisible sack down.

'By the afternoon, all you want is your bed. All you want is to stop. All you want is the easy job the white man gets. But you're not white and you have your cavewoman on your shoulder, and you have a mother in Antigua with diabetes. So you make your pile grow, hour after hour you make it grow and to make the time pass you start racing yourself. Then you race the clock, then you race the man next to you.

'It's a game now and you find a little fun in it and you're shouting at each other and people are running bets. 'Lofty to win,' they say because I'm gone six foot by now. The other guy is from Dominica where they grow small but tough. It's not easy but I'm in front and everyone's watching, cheering. Then the foreman comes over, a Puerto Rican who thinks he's better than us. He's a black man still, but he's light skinned and we are dark. Anyway, he tells us to stop. There's noise now. My blood is hot; the sweat is on my back. My sacks are high but the Dominican's sacks are wide and this race means everything to me. It means I'm good for something and I can come out on top. I can't stop. I can't.

'Then the white boss comes. Now it's different. He takes his time, walks slow, everything stops. The man comes right up to me and stands so close I feel the heat from his cigar. He shakes his head and calls me jiggaboo.

'Jiggaboo,' he says 'we don't need boys that can't take orders. I thought you would have known how to take orders, jiggaboo. Thought it would be in your blood.'

My father twisted his feet into his boots and stood up. The laces trailed on the kitchen floor as he walked to the stove. He took two cups from the shelf and made cocoa for us both, three sugars for me, four for himself. If I knew then that the sugar would kill him, I might have said something but I was ten years old and I was angry with the white man and wanted my father to box him down.

But instead he cut us each a slice of fruitcake and ate his slowly with his eyes closed.

'Did you fight him, Dad?'

'No,' he said after a while. 'He sacked me. Told me to get out. Right there, in front of the others. Gave me half an hour to leave. I picked up my money, just a few dollars. In a week I was back home sitting on that stool in Moon Street making plans with Judas.'

Some of this I'd heard before; my father, twenty days on the ship, getting colder and colder, with bad food and good company, marking time on a bed as narrow as a prison bunk waiting to see the Motherland.

'We didn't think of ourselves as foreigners. She was our Queen too. You believed those things then. You believed you belonged somewhere. But then again, we heard the stories. Black people being called names, getting spat on, things like that. We heard someone got attacked and robbed in London town but we knew him as a drinker so thought it must have been a bar room fight. We hoped. We had to hope. Well, anyway when we are coming in to dock, me and Judas get dressed up in our best clothes. You have to make a good impression.'

My father stood up.

'First,' he said, 'a good trilby, pulled down at the front, like so. Next, an overcoat, brand new, heavy, gabardine.'

He smoothed down the lapels, undid the imaginary belt and showed me inside.

'Now,' he said 'my suit,' and the light came into his eyes. 'When you are tall, and you will be tall, nothing can beat a good suit. It was dark grey, mohair and wool. And then a white cotton shirt and a red tie in a Windsor knot.'

My father turned around so I could admire his outfit. He winked.

'I was slender then so you have to use your imagination.'

He looked down at his feet.

'I was wearing spats. I saved up for months. Spats was all the fashion in America. Black shoes with a white leather front, buttons up the side. Lovely.'

He bent down and tied his bootlaces.

'Boat after boat was arriving from the West Indies, from Jamaica, Barbados, St. Lucia. I was just one more black man standing on the dock looking for work. But we had an address in Manchester for a job and a room and there were other men going the same way, a couple of women as well. Good looking women.'

He winked again.

'We walked off the boat in a big group, all together, and they showed us into a Customs room. We had our passports ready, British passports.'

He made a noise with his tongue against his teeth, a long hiss. I knew what it meant.

'We were coloureds to them. We were blackies. And they asked us a whole lot of questions about where we were going and how much money we brought and things like that. Eventually we got out on to the street. People were staring at us. Stopping and pointing, white men in gangs looking at me and Judas and the rest of us. We heard more names, worse ones, 'nigger', 'monkey', 'wog'. We had to get to the bus station quickly, we had to get away. So we started walking. I didn't like it. At least in America there were black men on the street, you didn't stand out so much. But here? And then, the more I looked, the more I noticed something. Nobody had on spats.'

He looked down at his feet.

'All the English men had on black shoes or black boots, plain black, lace up. Like these.'

He shook his head and sighed.

'And there is me in my ten dollar spats. I looked different. I looked wrong. I stopped walking. I can't do it. I can't go all the way to Manchester looking like this. I can't change the colour of my skin but I can change my shoes.'

He pointed in the distance.

'There it was, a shoe shop. I say to Judas, 'Come Judas. Come with me into that shop so I can buy a new pair of shoes'.

The others kept going and Judas looked at me. He looked at the little shoe shop and the white men standing on the corner and he shook his head. 'No, Lofty. I'm staying with the others,' he said. He walked away. Turned the corner. Gone. I was on my own.'

I pictured Judas, the fat man with the easy smile who came to our house every Christmas, played dominoes with my father, balanced his glass of rum on the arm of the chair.

'What happened, Dad?' I said raging inside.

'I let him go. Judas, Judas he doesn't change, even now. Anyway, I walked into the shop. There was an old man and a woman, must have been his wife and some customers. 'Yes?' said the man. I pointed at the black shoes in the window and told him I needed a pair in a size 10. Everyone was looking at me. I didn't even put down my case and there was no price on the shoes. I was spending the money I had brought to live on. I was thinking all the time, 'Get out Lofty, what you doing?' But the man brought me the shoes. 'These are twelve and nine, sir,' he said and pointed to a chair. I didn't know he meant the price. I thought he brought me odd sizes but I just sat down on the little chair. And then you know what happened?'

'What, Dad?'

The woman comes over to me and she kneels down. She takes off my spats and she put on one black shoe. She laces it and then she does the same again. When she looks up at me, she is smiling. 'How does that feel, sir? she says. 'Is that alright?'

My father had his arms crossed and his head high. His eyes were closed and he was smiling.

'A white woman at my feet, treating me with respect. 'Is that alright, sir?' she said. It was a beautiful thing.'

He was silent for some time. I could hear him breathing.

'What happened to the spats, Dad? Have you still got them?'

'No, no,' he said. 'I left them with the lady. She collected things for the poor. We had a good conversation. She shook my hand when I left and said 'Good Luck.'

'She was nice, wasn't she, Dad?'

'Yes,' he said. 'A good woman.'

He put on his bus jacket and badge and squeezed the knot of his tie. I passed him his flask and his bag and he sighed as he put it over his shoulder. As we walked together to the front door, he shouted upstairs to tell my mother he was gone and then looked at me.

'Be good,' he said.

He shook my hand for the first time and held it a while.

'And don't be angry. If you look, you will always find a beautiful thing.'

From the doorstep I watched him go. I saw him hunch and shiver, check his watch, turn up his collar and heard above his soft whistle, the ringing of his boot-tips on the wet English street.

SPEAKING IN TONGUES

Emma Donoghue

> **Emma Donoghue** was born in Dublin and now lives in Canada. She writes for stage and screen as well as page, but is best known for her novels, which include *Room* (Hughes & Hughes Irish Novel of the Year, Booker-shortlisted and adapted into an Oscar-nominated film) *Akin*, *The Wonder*, *Frog Music*, *The Sealed Letter*, *Life Mask* and *Slammerkin*.

'Listen,' I said, my voice rasping, 'I want to take you home but Dublin's a hundred miles away.'

Lee looked down at her square hands. I couldn't believe she'd only spent seventeen years on this planet.

'Where're you staying?' I asked.

'Youth hostel.'

I mouthed a curse at the beer-stained carpet. 'I've no room booked in Galway and it's probably too late to get one. I was planning to drive back tonight. I have to be at the office by nine tomorrow.'

The last of the conference goers walked past just then, and one or two nodded at me; the sweat of the *céilí* was drying on their cheeks.

When I looked back, Lee was grinning like she'd just won the lottery. 'So is it comfortable in the back of your van then, Sylvia?'

I stared at her. It was not the first time I had been asked that question, but I had thought that the last time would be the last. She was exactly half my age, I reminded myself. She wasn't even an adult, legally. 'As backs of vans go, yes, very comfortable.'

The reason I got into that van was a poem.

I'd first heard Sylvia Dwyer on a CD of contemporary poetry in Irish. I'd borrowed it from the library to help me revise for the Leaving Cert that would get me out of convent school. Deirdre had just left me for a boy, so I was working hard.

Poem number five was called 'Dhá Theanga'. The woman's voice had peat and smoke in it, bacon and strong tea. I hadn't a notion what the poem was about; you needed to know how the words were spelt before you could look them up in the dictionary, and one silent consonant sounded pretty much like another to me. But I listened to the poem every night till I had to give the CD back to the library.

I asked my mother why the name sounded so familiar, and she said Sylvia must be the last of those Dwyers who'd taken over the Shanbally butchers thirty years before. I couldn't believe she was a local. I might even have sat next to her in Mass.

But it was Cork where I met her. I'd joined the Queer Soc in the first week, before I could lose my nerve, and by midterm I was running their chocolate-and-wine evenings. Sylvia Dwyer, down from Dublin for a weekend, was introduced all round by an ex of hers who taught in the French department. I was startled to learn that the poet was one of us – a 'colleen', as a friend of mine used to say. Her smooth bob and silver-grey suit were intimidating as hell. I couldn't think of a word to say. I poured her plonk from a box and put the bowl of chocolate-covered peanuts by her elbow.

After that I smiled at her in Mass once when I was home in Shanbally for the weekend. Sylvia nodded back, very minimally. Maybe she wasn't sure where she knew me from. Maybe she was praying. Maybe she was a bitch.

Of course I had heard of Lee Maloney in Shanbally. The whole town had heard of her, the year the girl appeared at Mass with a Sinéad O'Connor head shave. I listened in on a euphemistic conversation about her in the post office queue but contributed nothing to it. My reputation was a clean slate in Shanbally, and none of my poems had gendered pronouns.

When I was introduced to the girl in Cork she was barely civil. But her chin had a curve you needed to fit your hand to, and her hair looked seven days old.

On one of my rare weekends at home, who should I see on the way down from Communion but Lee Maloney, full of nods and smiles. Without turning my head I could sense my mother stiffen. In the car park afterwards she asked, 'How do you come to know that Maloney girl?'

I considered denying it, claiming it was a case of mistaken identity, then I said, 'I think she might have been at a reading I gave once.'

'She's a worry to her mother,' said mine.

It must have been after I saw Sylvia Dwyer's name on a flyer under the title DHÁ THEANGA/TWO TONGUES: A CONFERENCE ON BILINGUALISM IN IRELAND *today that my subconscious developed a passionate nostalgia for the language my forebears got whipped for. So I skived off my Saturday lecture to get the bus to Galway. But only when I saw her walk into that lecture theatre in her long brown leather coat, with a new streak of white across her black fringe, did I realize why I'd sat four hours on a bus to get there.*

Some days I have more nerve than others. I flirted with Sylvia all that day, in the quarter hours between papers and forums and plenary sessions that meant equally little to me whether they were in Irish or English. I asked her questions and nodded before the answers had started. I told her about Deirdre, just so she wouldn't think I was a virgin. 'She left me for a boy with no earlobes,' I said carelessly.

'Been there,' said Sylvia.

Mostly, though, I kept my mouth shut and my head down and my eyes shiny. I suspected I was being embarrassingly obvious, but a one-day conference didn't leave enough time for subtlety.

Sylvia made me guess how old she was, and I said, 'Thirty?' though I knew from the programme note that she was thirty-four. She said if by any miracle she had saved enough money by the age of forty, she was going to get plastic surgery on the bags under her eyes.

I played the cheeky young thing and the baby dyke and the strong silent type who had drunk too much wine. And till halfway through the evening I didn't think I was getting anywhere. What would a woman like Sylvia Dwyer want with a blank page like me?

For a second in that Galway lecture hall I didn't recognize Lee Maloney, because she was so out of context among the bearded journalists and wool-skirted teachers. Then my memory claimed her face. The girl was looking at me like the sun had just risen, and then she stared at her feet, which was even more of a giveaway. I stood up straighter and shifted my briefcase to my other hand.

The conference, which I had expected to be about broadening my education and licking up to small Irish publishers, began to take on a momentum of its own. It was nothing I had planned, nothing I could stop. I watched the side of Lee's jaw right through a lecture called 'Scottish Loan-Words in Donegal Fishing Communities'. She was so cute I felt sick.

What was most unsettling was that I couldn't tell who was chatting up whom. It was a battle made up of feints and retreats. As we sipped our coffee, for instance, I murmured something faintly suggestive about hot liquids, then panicked and changed the subject. As we crowded back into the hall, I thought it was Lee's hand that guided my elbow for a few seconds, but she was staring forward so blankly I decided it must have been somebody else.

Over dinner – a noisy affair in the cafeteria – Lee sat across the table from me and burnt her tongue on the apple crumble. I poured her a glass of water and didn't give her a chance to talk to anyone but me. At this point we were an island of English in a sea of Irish.

The conversation happened to turn (as it does) to relationships and how neither of us could see the point in casual sex, because not only was it unlikely to be much good but it fucked up friendships or broke hearts. Sleeping with someone you hardly knew, I heard myself pronouncing in my world-weariest voice, was like singing a song without knowing the words. I told her that when she was my age she would feel the same way, and she said, Oh, she did already.

My eyes dwelt on the apple crumble disappearing, spoon by spoon, between Lee's absentminded lips. I listened to the opinions spilling out of my mouth and wondered who I was kidding.

By the time it came to the poetry reading that was meant to bring the conference to a lyrical climax, I was too tired to waste time. I reached into my folder for the only way I know to say what I really mean.

Now, the word in Cork had been that Sylvia Dwyer was deep in the closet, which I'd thought was a bit pathetic but only to be expected. However.

At the end of her reading, after she'd done a few about nature and a few about politics and a few I couldn't follow, she rummaged round in her folder. 'This poem gave its name to this conference,' she said, 'but that's not why I've chosen it.' She read it through in Irish first; I let the familiar vowels caress my ears. Her voice was even better live than on the CD from the library. And then she turned slightly in her seat, and, after muttering, 'Hope it translates,' she read it straight at me.

> *your tongue and my tongue*
> *have much to say to each other*
> *there's a lot between them*
> *there are pleasures yours has over mine*
> *and mine over yours*
> *we get on each other's nerves sometimes*
> *and under each other's skin*
> *but the best of it is when*
> *your mouth opens to let my tongue in*
> *it's then I come to know you*
> *when I hear my tongue*
> *blossom in your kiss*
> *and your strange hard tongue*
> *speaks between my lips*

The reason I was going to go ahead and do what I'd bored all my friends with saying I'd never do again was that poem.

I was watching the girl as I read 'Dhá Theanga' straight to her, aiming over the weary heads of the crowd of conference goers. I didn't look at anyone else but Lee Maloney, not at a single one of the jealous poets or Gaelgóir purists or smirking gossips, in case I might lose my nerve. After the first line, when her eyes fell for a second, Lee looked right back at me. She was leaning her cheek on her hand. It was a smooth hand, blunt at the tips. I knew the poem off by heart, but tonight I had to look down for safety every few lines.

And then she glanced away, out the darkening window, and I suddenly doubted that I was getting anywhere. What would Lee Maloney, seventeen last May, want with a scribbled jotter like me?

I sat in that smoky hall with my face half hidden behind my hand, excitement and embarrassment spiralling up my spine. I reminded myself that Sylvia Dwyer must have written that poem years ago, for some other woman in some other town. Not counting how many other women she might have read it to. It was probably an old trick of hers.

But all this couldn't explain away the fact that it was me Sylvia was reading it to tonight in Galway. In front of all these people, not caring who saw or what they might think when they followed the line of her eyes. I dug my jaw into my palm for anchorage, and my eyes locked back onto Sylvia's. I decided that every poem was made new in the reading.

If this was going to happen, I thought, as I folded the papers away in my briefcase during the brief rainfall of applause, it was happening because we were not in Dublin surrounded by my friends and work life, nor in Cork cluttered up with Lee's, nor above all in Shanbally where she was born in the year I left for college. Neither of us knew anything at all about Galway.

If this was going to happen, I thought, many hours later as the cleaners urged Sylvia and me out of the hall, it was happening because of some moment that had pushed us over an invisible line. But which moment? It could have been when we were shivering on the floor waiting for the end-of-conference céilí band to start, up, and Sylvia draped her leather coat round her shoulders and tucked me under it for a minute, the sheepskin lining soft against my cheek, the weight of her elbow on my shoulder. Or later when I was dancing like a berserker in my vest, and she drew the back of her hand down my arm and said, 'Aren't you the damp thing.' Or maybe the deciding moment was when the fan had stopped working and we stood at the bar waiting for drinks, my smoking hips armouring hers, and I blew behind her hot ear until the curtain of hair lifted up and I could see the dark of her neck.

Blame it on the heat. We swung so long in the *céilí* that the whole line went askew. Lee took off all her layers except one black vest that clung to her small breasts. We shared a glass of iced water and I offered Lee the last splash from my mouth, but she danced around me and laughed and wouldn't take it. Up on the balcony over the dance floor, I sat on the edge and leaned out to see the whirling scene. Lee fitted her hand around my thigh, weighing it down. 'You protecting me from falling?' I asked. My voice was meant to be sardonic, but it came out more like breathless.

'That's right,' she said.

Held in that position, my leg very soon began to tremble, but I willed it to stay still, hoping Lee would not feel the spasm, praying she would not move her hand away.

Blame it on the dancing. They must have got a late licence for the bar, or maybe Galway people always danced half the night. The music made our bones move in tandem and our legs shake. I tried to take the last bit of water from Sylvia's mouth, but I was so giddy I couldn't aim right and kept lurching against her collarbone and laughing at my own helplessness.

'Thought you were meant to be in the closet,' I shouted in her ear at one point, and Sylvia smiled with her eyes shut and said something I couldn't hear, and I said, 'What?' and she said, 'Not tonight.'

So at the end of the evening we had no place to go and it didn't matter. We had written our phone numbers on sodden beermats and exchanged them. We agreed that we'd go for a drive. When we got into her white van on the curb littered with weak-kneed céilí dancers, something came on the radio, an old song by Clannad or one of that crowd. Sylvia started up the engine and began to sing along with the chorus, her hoarse whisper catching every second or third word. She leaned over to fasten her seat belt and crooned a phrase into my ear. I didn't understand it – something about 'bóthar,' or was it 'máthar'? – but it made my face go hot anyway.

'Where are we heading?' I said at last, as the hedges began to narrow to either side of the white van.

Sylvia frowned into the darkness. 'Cashelagen, was that the name of it? Quiet spot, I seem to remember, beside a castle.'

After another ten minutes, during which we didn't meet a single other car, I realized that we were lost, completely tangled in the little roads leading into Connemara. And half of me didn't care. Half of me was quite content to bump along these lanes to the strains of late-night easy listening, watching Sylvia Dwyer's sculpted profile out the corner of my right eye. But the other half of me wanted to stretch my boot across and stamp on the brake, then climb over the gear stick to get at her.

Lee didn't comment on how quickly I was getting us lost. Cradle snatcher, I commented to myself, and not even a suave one at that. As we hovered at an unmarked fork, a man walked into the glare of the headlights. I stared at him to make sure he was real, then rolled down the window with a flurry of elbows. 'Cashelagen?' I asked. Lee had turned off the radio, so my voice sounded indecently loud. 'Could you tell us are we anywhere near Cashelagen?'

The man fingered his sideburns and stepped closer, beaming in past me at Lee. What in god's name was this fellow doing wandering round in the middle of the night anyway? He didn't even have our excuse. I was just starting to roll the window up again when 'Ah,' he said, 'ah, if it's Cashelagen you're wanting you'd have to go a fair few miles back through Ballyalla and then take the coast road.'

'Thanks,' I told him shortly, and revved up the engine. Lee would think I was the most hopeless incompetent she had ever got into a van for immoral purposes with. As soon as he had walked out of range of the headlights, I let off the hand brake and shot forward. I glanced over at Lee's bent head. The frightening thought occurred to me: *I could love this girl.*

The lines above Sylvia's eyebrow were beginning to swoop like gulls. If she was going to get cross, we might as well turn the radio back on and drive all night. I rehearsed the words in my head, then said them. 'Sure who needs a castle in the dark?'

Her grin was quick as a fish.

'Everywhere's quiet at this time of night,' I said rather squeakily. 'Here's quiet. We could stop here.'

'What, right here?'

Sylvia peered back at the road and suddenly wheeled round into the entrance to a field. We stopped with the bumper a foot away from a five-barred gate. When the headlights went off, the field stretched out dark in front of us, and there was a sprinkle of light that had to be Galway.

'What time did you say you had to be in Dublin?' I asked suddenly.

'Nine. Better start back round five in case I hit traffic,' said Sylvia. She bent over to rummage in the glove compartment. She pulled out a strapless watch, looked at it, brought it closer to her eyes, then let out a puff of laughter.

'What time's it now?'

'You don't want to know,' she told me.

I grabbed it. The hands said half past three. 'It can't be.'

We sat staring into the field. 'Nice stars,' I said, for something to say.

'Mmm,' she said.

I stared at the stars, joining the dots, till my eyes watered.

And then I heard Sylvia laughing in her throat as she turned sideways and leaned over my seat belt. I heard it hissing back into its socket as she kissed me on the mouth.

When I came back from taking a pee in the bushes, the driver's seat was empty. I panicked, and stared up and down the lane. Why would she have run off on foot? Then, with a deafening creak, the back doors of the van swung open.

Sylvia's bare shoulders showed over the blanket that covered her body. She hugged her knees. Her eyes were bright, and the small bags underneath were the most beautiful folds of skin I'd ever seen. I climbed in and kneeled on the sheepskin coat beside her, reaching up to snap off the little light. Her face opened wide in a yawn. The frightening thought occurred to me: I could love this woman.

'You could always get some sleep, you know,' I said, 'I wouldn't mind.' Then I thought that sounded churlish, but I didn't know how to unsay it.

'Oh, I know I could,' said Sylvia, her voice melodic with amusement. 'There's lots of things we could do with a whole hour and a half. We could sleep, we could share the joint in the glove compartment, we could drive to Clifden and watch the sun come up. Lots of things.'

I smiled. Then I realized she couldn't see my face in the dark.

'Get your clothes off,' she said.

I would have liked to leave the map-reading light on over our heads, letting me see and memorize every line of Lee's body, but it would have lit us up like a saintly apparition for any passing farmer to see. So the whole thing happened in a darkness much darker than it ever gets in a city.

There was a script, of course. No matter how spontaneous it may feel, there's always an unwritten script. Every one of these encounters has a script, even the very first time your hand undoes the button on somebody's shirt; none of us comes without expectations to this body business.

But lord, what fun it was. Lee was salt with sweat and fleshier than I'd imagined, behind all her layers of black cotton and wool. In thirty-four years I've found nothing to compare to that moment when the bare limbs slide together like a key into a lock. Or no, more like one of those electronic key cards they give you in big hotels, the open sesame ones marked with an invisible code, which the door must read and recognize before it agrees to open.

At one point Lee rolled under me and muttered, 'There's somewhere I want to go,' then went deep inside me. It hurt a little, just a little, and I must have flinched because she asked, 'Does that hurt?' and I said, 'No,' because I was glad of it. 'No,' I said again, because I didn't want her to go.

Sylvia's voice was rough like rocks grinding on each other. As she moved on top of me she whispered in my ear, things I couldn't make out, sounds just outside the range of hearing. I never wanted to interrupt the flow by saying, 'Sorry?' or 'What did you say?' Much as I wanted to hear and remember every word, every detail, at a certain point I just had to switch my mind off and get on with living it. But Sylvia's voice kept going in my ear, turning me on in the strangest way by whispering phrases that only she could hear.

I've always thought the biggest lie in the books is that women instinctively know what to do to each other because their bodies are the same. None of Sylvia's shapes were the same as mine, nor could I have guessed what she was like from how she seemed in her smart clothes. And we liked different things and took things in different order, showing each other by infinitesimal movings away and movings towards. She did some things to me that I knew I wanted, some I didn't think I'd much like and didn't, and several I was startled to find that I enjoyed much more than I would have imagined. I did some things Sylvia seemed calm about, and then something she must have really needed, because she started to let out her breath in a long gasp when I'd barely begun.

Near the end, Sylvia's long fingers moved down her body to ride alongside mine, not supplanting, just guiding. 'Go light,' she whispered in my ear. 'Lighter and lighter. Butterfly.' As she began to thrash at last, laughter spilled from her mouth.

'What? What are you laughing for?' I asked, afraid I'd done something wrong. Sylvia just whooped louder. Words leaked out of her throat, distorted by pleasure.

At one point I touched my lips to the skin under her eyes, first one and then the other. 'Your bags are gorgeous, you know. Promise you'll never let a surgeon at them?'

'No,' she said, starting to laugh again.

'No to which?'

'No promise.'

When Sylvia was touching me I didn't say a single one of the words that swam through my head. I don't know was I shy or just stubborn, wanting to make her guess what to do. The tantalization of waiting for those hands to decipher my body made the bliss build and build till when it came it threw me.

There was one moment I wouldn't swap anything for. It was in the lull beforehand, the few seconds when I stopped breathing. I looked at this stranger's face bent over me, twisted in exertion and tenderness, and I thought, Yes, you, whoever you are, if you're asking for it, I'll give it all up to you.

In the in-between times we panted and rested and stifled our laughter in the curve of each other's shoulders and debated when I'd noticed Lee and when she'd noticed me, and what we'd noticed and what we'd imagined on each occasion, the history of this particular desire. And during one of these in-between times we realized that the sun had come up, faint behind a yellow mist, and it was half five according to the strapless watch in the glove compartment.

I took hold of Lee, my arms binding her ribs and my head resting in the flat place between her breasts. The newly budded swollen look of them made my mouth water, but there was no time. I shut my mouth and my eyes and held Lee hard and there was no time left at all, so I let go and sat up. I could feel our nerves pulling apart like ivy off a wall.

The cows were beginning to moan in the field as we pulled our clothes on. My linen trousers were cold and smoky. We did none of the things parting lovers do if they have the time or the right. I didn't snatch at Lee's foot as she pulled her jeans on; she didn't sneak her head under my shirt as I pulled it over my face. The whole thing had to be over already.

It was not the easiest thing in the world to find my way back to Galway with Lee's hand tucked between my thighs. Through my trousers I could feel the cold of her fingers, and the hardness of her thumb, rubbing the linen. I caught her eye as we sped round a corner, and she grinned, suddenly very young. 'You're just using me to warm your hand up,' I accused.

'That's all it is,' said Lee.

I was still throbbing, so loud I thought the car was ringing with it. We were only two streets from the hostel now.

I wouldn't ask to see her again. I would just leave the matter open and drive away. Lee probably got offers all the time; she was far too young to be looking for anything heavy. I'd show her I was generous enough to accept that an hour and a half was all she had to give me.

I let her out just beside the hostel, which was already opening to release some backpacking Germans. I was going to get out of the car to give her a proper body-to-body hug, but while I was struggling with my seat belt, Lee knocked on the glass. I rolled down the window, put *Desert Hearts* out of my mind, and kissed her for what I had a hunch was likely to be the last time.

I stood shivering in the street outside the hostel and knocked on Sylvia's car window. I was high as a kite and dizzy with fatigue.

I wouldn't ask anything naff like when we were likely to see each other again. I would just wave as she drove away. Sylvia probably did this kind of thing all the time; she was far too famous to be wanting anything heavy. I'd show her that I was sophisticated enough not to fall for her all in one go, not to ask for anything but the hour and a half she had to give me.

When she rolled down the window, I smiled and leaned in. I shut my eyes and felt Sylvia's tongue against mine, saying something neither of us could hear. So brief so slippery, nothing you could get a hold of.

THE HUSBAND

Mary Dorcey

Mary Dorcey is an Irish poet and fiction writer. Her story collection *A Noise from the Woodshed* won the Rooney Prize for Irish Literature. Her six books of poetry – most recently, *New and Selected* – and three works of fiction are researched internationally from the USA to Asia. A life-long activist for gay and women's rights, she is completing her new novel *Mother, Daughter, Lover*.

They made love then once more because she was leaving him. Sunlight came through the tall Georgian window, it shone on the blue walls, the yellow paintwork, warming her pale, blonde hair, the white curve of her closed eyelids. He gripped her hands, their fingers interlocked, his feet braced against the wooden footboard. He would have liked to break her from the mould of her body; from its set, delicate lines. His mouth at her shoulder, his eyes were hidden and he was glad to have his back turned on the room; from the bare dressing-table stripped of her belongings and the suitcase open beside the wardrobe.

Outside other people were going to mass. He heard a bell toll in the distance, a man's voice drifted up 'I'll see you at O'Brien's later', then the slam of a car door and the clatter of a woman's spiked heels hurrying on the pavement. All the usual sounds of a Sunday morning rising distinct and separate for the first time in the silence between them.

She lay beneath him, passive, magnanimous, as though she were granting him a favour, out of pity or gratitude because she had seen that he was not after all, going to make it difficult for her at the end. He moved inside her body, conscious only of the sudden escape of his breath, no longer caring what she felt, what motive possessed her. He was tired of thinking, tired of the labour of anticipating her thoughts and concealing his own.

He knew that she was looking past him, over his shoulder towards the window, to the sunlight and noise of the street. He touched a strand of her hair where it lay along the pillow. She did not turn. A tremor passed through his limbs. He felt the sweat grow cold on his back. He rolled off her and lay still, staring at the ceiling where small flakes of whitewash peeled from the moulded corners. The sun had discovered a spider's web above the door; like a square of grey lace, its diamond pattern swayed in a draught from the stairs. He wondered how it had survived the winter and why it was he had not noticed it before. Exhaustion seeped through his flesh bringing a sensation of calm. Now that it was over at last he was glad, now that there was nothing more to be done.

He had tried everything and failed. He had lived ten years in the space of one; altered himself by the hour to suit her and she had told him it made no difference, that it was useless, whatever he did, because it had nothing to do with him personally, with individual failing. He could not accept that, could not resign himself to being a mere cog in someone else's political theory. He had done all that he knew to persuade, to understand her. He had been by turns argumentative, patient, sceptical, conciliatory. The night when finally, she had told him it was over he had wept in her arms, pleaded with her, vulnerable as any woman, and she had remained indifferent, patronising even, seeing only the male he could not cease to be. They said they wanted emotion, honesty, self-exposure but when they got it, they despised you for it. Once, and once only, he had allowed the rage in him to break free; let loose the cold fury that had been festering in his gut since the start of it. She had come home late on Lisa's birthday, and when she told him where she had been, blatantly flaunting it, he had struck her across the face, harder than he had intended so that a fleck of blood showed on her lip. She had wiped it off with the back of her hand, staring at him, a look of shock and covert satisfaction in her eyes. He knew then in his shame and regret that he had given her the excuse she had been waiting for.

He looked at her now, at the hard pale arch of her cheekbone. He waited for her to say something but she kept silent and he could not let himself speak the only words that were in his mind. She would see them as weakness. Instead, he heard himself say her name, 'Martina,' not wanting to, but finding it form on his lips from force of habit: a sound; a collection of syllables that had once held absolute meaning, and now meant nothing or too much, composed as it was of so many conflicting memories.

She reached a hand past his face to the breakfast cup that stood on the bedside table. A dark, puckered skin had formed on the coffee's surface but she drank it anyway. 'What?' she said without looking at him. He felt that she was preparing her next move, searching for a phrase or gesture that would carry her painlessly out of his bed and from their flat. But when she did speak again there was no attempt at prevarication or tact. 'I need to shower,' she said bluntly, 'can you let me out?' She swung her legs over the side of the bed, pushing back the patterned sheet, and stood up. He watched her walk across the room away from him. A small mark like a circle of chalk dust gleamed on the muscle of her thigh; his seed dried on her skin. The scent and taste of him would be all through her. She would wash meticulously every inch of her body to remove it. He heard her close the bathroom door behind her and a moment later, the hiss and splatter of water breaking on the shower curtain. Only a few weeks ago she would have run a bath for them both and he would have carried Lisa in to sit between their knees. Yesterday afternoon he had brought Lisa over to his mother's house. Martina had said she thought it was best if she stayed there for a couple of weeks until they could come to some arrangement. Some arrangement! For Lisa! He knew then how crazed she was. Of course, it was an act—a pretence of consideration and fair mindedness, wanting it to appear that she might even debate the merits of leaving their daughter with him. But he knew what she planned, all too well.

He had a vision of himself calling over to Leinster Road on a Saturday afternoon, standing on the front step ringing the bell. She would come to the door and hold it open, staring at him blankly as if he were a stranger while Lisa ran to greet him. Would Helen be there too with that smug, tight, little smile on her mouth? Would they bring him in to the kitchen and make tea and small talk while Lisa got ready, or would they have found some excuse to have her out for the day? He knew every possible permutation, he had seem them all a dozen times on television and seventies' movies, but he never thought he might be expected to live out these banalities himself. His snort of laughter startled him. He could not remember when he had last laughed aloud. But who would not at the idea that the mother of his child could imagine this cosy Hollywood scenario might become reality?

When she had first mentioned it, dropping it casually as a vague suggestion, he had forced himself to hold back the derision that rose to his tongue. He would say nothing. Why should he? Let her learn the hard way.

They would all say it for him soon enough: his parents, her mother. The instant they discovered the truth, who and what she had left him for, they would snatch Lisa from her as instinctively as they would from quicksand. They would not be shackled by any qualms of conscience. They would have none of his need to show fine feeling. It was extraordinary that she did not seem to realise this herself; unthinkable that she might, and not allow it to influence her. She came back into the room, her legs bare beneath a shaggy red sweater. The sweater he had bought her for Christmas. Her nipples protruded like two small stones from under the loose wool. She opened the wardrobe and took out a pair of blue jeans and a grey corduroy skirt. He saw that she was on the point of asking him which he preferred. She stood in the unconsciously childish pose she assumed whenever she had a decision to make, however trivial: her feet apart, her head tilted to one side. He lay on his back watching her, his hands interlaced between the pillow and his head. He could feel the blood pulsing behind his ears but he kept his face impassive. She was studying her image in the mirror, eyes wide with anxious vanity. At last she dropped the jeans into the open case and began to pull on the skirt. Why? Was that what Helen would have chosen? What kind of look did she go for? Elegant, sexy, casual? But then they were not into looks—oh no, it was all on a higher, spiritual plane. Or was it? What did she admire in Martina anyway? Was it the same qualities as he saw, or something quite different, something hidden from him? Was she turned on by some reflection of herself or by some opposite trait, something lacking in her own character? He could not begin to guess. He knew so little about this woman Martina was abandoning him for. He had left it too late to pay her any real attention.

He had been struck by her the first night, he had to admit, meeting her in O'Brian's after that conference. He liked her body; the long legs and broad shoulders and something attractive in the sultry line of her mouth. A woman he might have wanted himself in other circumstances. If he had not been told immediately that she was a lesbian. Not that he would have guessed it; at least not at first glance. She was too good looking for that. But it did not take long to see the coldness in her, the chip on the shoulder, the arrogant, belligerent way she stood at the bar and asked him what he wanted to drink. But then she had every reason for disdain, had she not? She must have known already that his wife was in love with her. It had taken him a year to reach the same conclusion.

She sat on the bed to pull on her stockings, one leg crossed over the other. He heard her breathing—quick little breaths through her mouth. She was nervous then. He stared at the round bone of her ankle as she drew the black mesh over it. He followed her hands as they moved up the length of her calf. Her body was so intimately known to him he felt he might have cast the flesh on her bones with his own fingers. He saw the stretch marks above her hip. She had lost weight this winter. She looked well, but he preferred her as she used to be—voluptuous: the plump roundness of her belly and arms. He thought of all the days and nights of pleasure that they had had together. She certainly could not complain that he had not appreciated her.

He would always be grateful for what he had discovered with her. He would forget none of it. But would she? Oh no—she pretended to have forgotten already. She talked now as though she had been playing an elaborate game all these years – going through ritual actions to please him. When he refused to let her away with that kind of nonsense, the deliberate erasure of their past, and forced her to acknowledge the depth of passion there had been between them, she said, yes, she did not deny that they had had good times in bed but it had very little to do with him. He had laughed in her face. And who was it to do with then? Who else could take credit for it? She did not dare to answer but even as he asked the question he knew the sort of thing she would come out with. One of Helen's profundities—that straight women use men as instruments, that they make love to themselves through a man's eyes, stimulate themselves with his desire and flattery but that it is their own sensuality they get off on. He knew every version of their theories by now.

'Would you like some more coffee? she asked him when she had finished dressing. She was never so hurried that she could go without coffee. He shook his head and she walked out of the room, pulling a leather belt through the loops of her skirt. He listened to her light footsteps on the stairs. After a moment he heard her lift the mugs from their hooks on the wall. He heard her fill the percolator with water, place it on the gas stove and, after a while its rising heart beat as the coffee bubbled through the metal filter. He hung onto each sound, rooting himself in the routine of it, wanting to hide in the pictures they evoked. So long as he could hear her moving about in the kitchen below him busy with all her familiar actions, it seemed that nothing much could be wrong. Not that he believed that she would really go through with it. Not all the way. Once it dawned on her finally that indulging this whim would mean giving up Lisa, she would have to come to her senses.

Yes, she would be back soon enough with her tail between her legs. He had only to wait. But he would not let her see that he knew this. It would only put her back up—bring out all her woman's pride and obstinacy. He must tread carefully. Follow silently along this crazy pavement she had laid, step by step, until she reached the precipice. And when she was forced back, he would be there, waiting.

If only he had been more cautious from the beginning. If only he had taken it seriously, recognised the danger in time, it would never have reached this stage. But how could he have? How could any normal man have seen it as any more than a joke? He had felt no jealousy at all at the start. She had known this and been incensed, had accused him of typical male complacency. She had expected scenes, that was evident, wanted them, had tried to goad him into them. But for weeks he had refused to react with anything more threatening than good-humoured sarcasm.

He remembered the night she first confessed that Helen and she had become lovers: the anxious, guilty face, expecting God knows what extremes of wrath, and yet underneath it there had been a look of quiet triumph. He had had to keep himself from laughing. He was taken by surprise, undoubtedly, though he should not have been—with the way they had been going on—never out of each other's company; the all-night talks and the heroine worship.

But frankly he would not have thought Martina was up to it. Oh, she might flirt with the idea of turning on a woman but to commit herself was another thing. She was too fundamentally healthy, and too fond of the admiration of men. Besides, knowing how passionate she was, he could not believe she would settle for the caresses of a woman.

Gradually his amusement had given way to curiosity, a pleasurable stirring of erotic interest. Two women in bed together after all—there was something undeniably exciting in the idea. He had tried to get her to share it with him, to make it something they could both enjoy but, out of embarrassment, or some misplaced sense of loyalty, she had refused. He said to tease her, to draw her out a little, that he would not have picked Helen for the whip and Jackboot type. What did he mean by that, she had demanded menacingly. And when he explained that as, obviously, she herself could not be cast as the butch, Helen was the only remaining candidate, she had flown at him, castigating his prejudice and condescension.

Clearly it was not a topic amenable to humour! She told him that all that role playing was a creation of men's fantasies. Dominance and submission were models the women had consigned to the rubbish heap. It was all equality and mutual respect in this brave new world. So where did the excitement, the romance, come in, he wanted to ask. If they had dispensed with all the traditional props what was left? But he knew better than to say anything. They were so stiff with analysis and theory the lot of them it was impossible to get a straightforward answer.

Sometimes he had even wondered if they were really lesbians at all. Apart from the fact that they looked perfectly normal, there seemed something over-done about it. It seemed like a public posture, an attitude struck to provoke men—out of spite or envy. Certainly they flaunted the whole business unnecessarily, getting into fights in the street or in pubs because they insisted on their right to self-expression and that the rest of the world should adapt to them. He had even seen one of them at a conference sporting a badge on her lapel that read: 'How dare you presume I'm heterosexual.'

Why on earth should anyone presume otherwise unless she was proud of resembling a male impersonator? And so every time he had attempted to discuss it rationally they had ended by quarrelling. She condemned him of every macho fault in the book and sulked for hours, but afterwards they made it all up in bed. As long as she responded in the old manner, he knew he had not much to worry about. He had even fancied that it might improve their sex life—add a touch of the unknown. He had watched closely to see if any new needs or tastes might creep into her lovemaking.

It was not until the night she had come home in tears that he was forced to re-think his position. She had arrived in, half drunk at midnight after one of their interminable meetings, and raced straight up to bed without so much as greeting him or going in to kiss Lisa goodnight. He had followed her up, and when he tried to get in beside her to comfort her, she had become hysterical, screamed at him to leave her alone, to keep his hands away from her. It was hours before he managed to calm her down and get the whole story out of her. It seemed that Helen had told her that evening in the pub that she wanted to end the relationship. He was astonished. He had always taken it for granted that Martina would be the first to tire. He was even insulted on her behalf. He soothed and placated her, stroking her hair and murmuring soft words the way he would with Lisa. He told her not to be a fool, that she was far too beautiful to be cast aside by Helen, that she must be the best thing that had ever happened to her. She was sobbing uncontrollably, but she stopped long enough to abuse him when he said that.

At last she had fallen asleep in his arms, but for the first time he had stayed awake after her. He had to admit that her hysteria had got to him. He could see it had become some kind of obsession. Up to then he had imagined it was basically a schoolgirl crush, the sort of thing most girls worked out in their teens. But women were so sentimental. He remembered a student of his saying years ago that men had friendships, women had affairs. He knew exactly what he meant. You had only to watch them, perfectly average housewives sitting in cafés or restaurants together, gazing into each other's eyes in a way that would have embarrassed the most besotted man, the confiding tones they used, the smiles of flattery and sympathy flitting between them, the intimate gestures, touching each other's hand, the little pats and caresses, exasperating waiters while they fought over the right to treat one another.

He had imagined that lesbian love-making would have some of this piquant quality. He saw it as gently caressive—tender and solicitous. He began to have fantasies about Martina and Helen together. He allowed himself delicious images of their tentative, childish sensuality. When he and Martina were fucking he had fantasised lately that Helen was there too, both women exciting each other and then turning to him at the ultimate moment, competing for him. He had thought it was just a matter of time before something of the sort came about. It had not once occurred to him in all that while that they would continue to exclude him, to cut him out mentally and physically, to insist on their self-sufficiency and absorption. Not even that night lying sleepless beside her while she snored, as she always did after too many pints. It did not register with him finally until the afternoon he came home unexpectedly from work and heard them together.

There was no illusion after that, no innocence or humour. He knew it for what it was. Weeks passed before he could rid his mind of the horror of it; it haunted his sleep and fuelled his days with a seething, putrid anger. He saw that he had been seduced, mocked, cheated, systematically, cold bloodedly by assumptions she had worked carefully to foster; defrauded and betrayed. He had stood at the bottom of the stairs—his stairs—in his own house and listened to them. He could hear it from the hall. He listened transfixed, a heaving in his stomach, until the din from the room above rose to a wail. He had covered his ears. Tender and solicitous had he said? More like cats in heat! As he went out of the house, slamming the door after him, he thought he heard them laughing. Bitches—bloody, fucking bitches!

He had made it as far as the pub and ordered whiskey. He sat drinking it, glass after glass, grasping the bowl so hard he might have snapped it in two. He was astounded by the force of rage unleashed in him. He would have liked to put his hands around her bare throat and squeeze it until he'd wrung that noise out of it. Somehow he had managed to get a grip of himself.

He had had enough sense to drink himself stupid, too stupid to do anything about it that night. He had slept on the floor in the sitting room and when he woke at noon she had already left for the day. He was glad. He was not going to humiliate himself by fighting for her over a woman. He was still convinced that it was a temporary delirium, an infection that, left to run its course, would sweat itself out. He had only to wait, to play it cool, to think and to watch until the fever broke.

She came back into the room carrying two mugs of coffee. She set one down beside him giving a little nervous smile. She had forgotten he had said he did not want any.

'Are you getting up?' she asked as she took her dressing gown from the back of the door, 'there's some bread in the oven—will you remember to take it out?' Jesus! How typical of her to bake bread the morning she was leaving. The dough had been left as usual, of course, to rise overnight and she could not bring herself to waste it. Typical of her sublime insensitivity! He had always been baffled by this trait in her, this attention, in no matter what crisis, to the everyday details of life and this compulsion to make little gestures of practical concern. Was it another trick of hers to forestall criticism? Or did she really have some power to rise above her own and other people's emotions? But most likely it was just straightforward, old fashioned guilt.

'Fuck the bread,' he said and instantly regretted it.

She would be in all the more hurry now to leave. She went to the wardrobe and began to lift down her clothes, laying them in the suitcase. He watched her hands as they expertly folded blouses, jerseys, jeans, studying every movement so that he would be able to recapture it precisely when she was gone.

It was impossible to believe that he would not be able to watch her like this the next day and the day after. That was what hurt the most. The thought that he would lose the sight of her, just that. That he would no longer look on while she dressed or undressed, prepared a meal, read a book or played with Lisa. Every movement of her body familiar to him, so graceful, so completely feminine. He felt that if he could be allowed to watch her through glass, without speaking, like a child gazing through a shop window, he could have been content. He would not dare express it, needless to say. She would have sneered at him.

Objectification she would call it. 'A woman's body is all that ever matters to any one of you, isn't it?' And he would not argue because the thing he really prized would be even less flattering to her—her vulnerability, her need to confide, to ask his advice in every small moment of self-doubt, to share all her secret fears. God how they had talked! Hours of it. At least she could never claim that he had not listened. And in the end he had learned to need it almost as much as she did. To chat in the inconsequential way she had, curled together in bed, sitting over a glass of wine till the small hours, drawing out all the trivia of personal existence: the dark, hidden things that bonded you forever to the one person who would hear them from you. Was that a ploy too? a conscious one? or merely female instinct? To tie him to her by a gradual process of self-exposure so that he could not disentangle himself, even now when he had to because there was no longer any private place left in him, nowhere to hide from her glance, nowhere that she could not seek out and name the hurt in him. This was what had prompted her, an hour earlier, on waking, to make love with him: this instinct for vulnerability that drew her, like a bee to honey, unerringly to need and pain: this feminine lust to console; so that she had made one last generous offering—handing over her body as she might a towel to someone bleeding. And he had taken it, idiot that he was; accepted gratefully—little fawning lap-dog that she had made of him.

She was sitting at the dressing table brushing her hair with slow, attentive strokes, drawing the brush each time from the crown of her head to the tips of her hair where it lay along her shoulder. Was she deliberately making no show of haste, pretending to be doing everything as normal? It seemed to him there must be something he could say; something an outsider would think of immediately. He searched his mind, but nothing came to him but the one question that had persisted in him for days: 'Why are you doing this? I don't understand why you're doing this.' She opened a bottle of cologne and dabbed it lightly on her wrists and neck. She always took particular care preparing herself to meet Helen. Helen, who herself wore some heavy French scent that clung to everything she touched, that was carried home in Martina's hair and clothing after every one of their sessions. But that was perfectly acceptable and politically correct.

Adorning themselves for each other—make-up, perfume, eyebrow plucking, exchanging clothes—all these feminine tricks took on new meaning because neither of them was a man. Helen did not need to flatter, she did not need to patronise or idolise, she did not need to conquer or submit, and her desire would never be exploitative because she was a woman dealing with a woman! Neither of them had institutionalised power behind them. This was the logic he had been taught all that winter.

They told one another these faery stories sitting round at their meetings. Everything that had ever gone wrong for any one of them, once discussed in their consciousness-raising groups, could be chalked up as a consequence of male domination. And while they sat about indoctrinating each other with this schoolgirl pap, sounding off on radio and television, composing joint letters to the press, he had stayed at home three nights a week to mind Lisa, clean the house, cook meals, and read his way through the bundles of books she brought home: sentimental novels and half-baked political theses that she had insisted he must look at if he was to claim any understanding at all. And at the finish of it, when he had exhausted himself to satisfy her caprices, she said that he had lost his spontaneity, that their relationship had become stilted, sterile and self-conscious.

With Helen, needless to say, all was otherwise—effortless and instinctive. God, he could not wait for their little idyll to meet the adult world, the world of electricity bills, dirty dishes and child minding, and see how far their new roles got them! But he had one pleasure in store before then, a consolation prize he had been storing up for himself. As soon as she was safely out of the house, he would make a bonfire of them—burn every one—every goddamn book with the word woman on its cover!

She fastened the brown leather suitcase, leaving open the lock on the right hand that had broken the summer two years ago when they had come back from Morocco laden down with blankets and caftans. She carried it across the room, trying to lift it clear of the floor, but it was too heavy for her and dragged along the boards. She went out the door and he heard it knocking on each step as she walked down the stairs. He listened. She was doing something in the kitchen but he could not tell what. There followed a protracted silence. It hit him suddenly that she might try to get out of the flat, leave him and go without saying anything at all. He jumped out of bed, grabbed his trousers from the chair and pulled them on, his fingers so clumsy with haste he caught his hair in the zip.

Fuck her! When he rooted under the bed for his shoes, she heard and called up: 'Don't bother getting dressed, I'll take the bus.' She did not think he was going to get the car out and drive her over there surely? He took a shirt from the floor and pulled it on over his head as he took the stairs to the kitchen two at a time. She was standing by the stove holding a cup of coffee. This endless coffee drinking of hers, cups all over the house, little white rings marked on every stick of furniture. At least he would not have that to put up with any longer.

'There's some in the pot if you want it,' she said. He could see the percolator was almost full, the smell of it would be all over the flat now, and the smell of the bloody bread in the oven, for hours after she was gone.

'Didn't you make any tea?'

'No,' she said and gave one of her sidelong, maddening looks of apology as though it was some major oversight, 'but there's water in the kettle.'

'Thanks,' he said, 'I won't bother.'

He was leaning his buttocks against the table, his feet planted wide apart, his hands in his pockets. He looked relaxed and in control at least. He was good at that—years of being on stage before a class of students. He wondered if Helen would come to meet her at the bus stop, or was she going to have to lug the suitcase alone all the way up Leinster Road? He wondered how they would greet each other. With triumph or nervousness? Might there be a sense of anti-climax about it now that she had finally committed herself after so much stalling? Would she tell Helen that she had made love with him before leaving? Would she be ashamed of it and say nothing?

But probably Helen would take it for granted as an insignificant gesture to male pride, the necessary price of freedom. And suddenly he wished that he had not been so restrained with her, so much the considerate, respectful friend she had trained him to be. He wished that he had taken his last opportunity and used her body as any other man would have—driven the pleasure out of it until she had screamed as he had heard her that day, in his bed, with her woman lover.

He should have forced her to remember him as something more than the tiresome child she thought she had to pacify.

She went to the sink and began to rinse the breakfast things under the tap.

'Leave them,' he said, 'I'll do them,' the words coming out of him too quickly. He was losing his cool.

She put the cup down and dried her hands on the tea towel. He struggled to think of something to say. He would have to find something. His mind seethed with ridiculous nervous comments. He tried to pick out a phrase that would sound normal and yet succeed in gaining her attention, in arresting this current of meaningless actions that was sweeping between them.

And surely there must be something she wanted to say to him? She was not going to walk out and leave him as if she was off to the pictures? She took her raincoat from the bannister and put it on, but did not fasten it.

The belt trailed on one side. She lifted up the suitcase and carried it into the hallway. He followed her. When she opened the door, he saw that it was raining. A gust of wind caught her hair, blowing it into her eyes. He wanted to say, 'Fasten your coat—you're going to get cold.' But he did not and he heard himself ask instead:

'Where can I ring you?' he had not intended that, he knew the answer. He had the phone number by heart.

She held open the door with one hand and set down the case. She stared down at his shoes and then past him along the length of the hallway. Two days ago he had started to sand and stain the floorboards. She looked as if she was estimating how much work remained to be done.

'Don't ring this weekend. We're going away for awhile.'

He felt a flash of white heat pass in front of his brain and a popping sound like a light bulb exploding. He felt dizzy and his eyes for a moment seemed to cloud over. Then he realised what had happened. A flood of blind terror had swept through him, unmanning him, because she had said something totally unexpected something he had not planned for. He repeated the words carefully hoping she would deny them, make sense of them.

'You're going away for a while?'

'Yes.'

'Where to for God sake?' he almost shrieked.

'Down the country for a bit—to friends.' He stared at her blankly, his lips trembling, and then the words came out that he had been holding back all morning:

'For how long? When will you be back?'

He could have asked it at any time, he had been on the verge of it a dozen times and had managed to repress it because he had to keep to his resolve not to let her see that he knew what all this was about—a drama, a show of defiance and autonomy. He could not let her guess that he knew full well she would be back. Somewhere in her heart she must recognise that no one would ever care for her as much as he did. No one could appreciate her more, or make more allowances for her. She could not throw away ten years of his life for this—to score a political point—for a theory—for a woman! But he had not said it, all morning. It was too ridiculous—it dignified the thing even to mention it. And now she had tricked him into it, cheated him.

'When will you be back?' he had asked.

'I'll be away for a week, I suppose. You can ring the flat on Monday.'

The rain was blowing into her face, her lips were white. She leaned forward. He felt her hand on his sleeve. He felt the pressure of her ring through the cloth of his shirt. She kissed him on the forehead. Her lips were soft, her breath warm on his skin. He hated her then. He hated her body, her woman's flesh that was still caressive and yielding when the heart inside it was shut like a trap against him. 'Goodbye,' she said. She lifted the case and closed the door after her.

He went back into the kitchen. But not to the window. He did not want to see her walking down the road. He did not want to see her legs in their black stockings, and the raincoat blown away from her skirt. He did not want to see her dragging the stupid case, to see it banging against her knees as she carried it along the street. So he stood in the kitchen that smelled of coffee and bread baking. He stood over the warmth of the stove, his head lowered, his hands clenched in his pockets, his eyes shut.

She would be home anyhow—in a week's time. She had admitted that now. 'In a week,' she had said, 'ring me on Monday.' He would not think about it until then. He would not let himself react to any more of these theatrics. It was absurd, the whole business. She had gone to the country, she was visiting friends. He would not worry about her. He would not think about her at all, until she came back.

THE PRAM

Roddy Doyle

Roddy Doyle has written twelve novels, including *Paddy Clarke Ha Ha Ha*, for which he won the Booker Prize in 1993, *The Woman Who Walked Into Doors* (1996), *Smile* (2017) and, most recently, *Love* (2020). He lives and works in Dublin.

1.

Alina loved the baby. She loved everything about the baby. The tiny boyness of him, the way his legs kicked whenever he looked up at her, his fat – she loved these things. She loved to bring him out in his pram, even on the days when it was raining. She loved to sit on the floor with her legs crossed and the baby in her lap. Even when he cried, when he screamed, she was very happy. But he did not cry very often. He was almost a perfect baby.

The baby's pram was very old. Alina remembered visiting her grandmother when she was a little girl. She had not met her grandmother before. She got out of the car and stood beside her father in the frozen farmyard. They watched an old woman push a perambulator towards them. The pram was full of wood, branches and twigs and, across the top of the pram, one huge branch that looked like an entire tree. This old woman was her grandmother. And the baby's pram was very like the old pram she saw her grandmother push across the farmyard. Her father told her it had been his pram, and her aunts' and her uncle's, and even the generation of babies before them.

Now, in 2005, in Dublin, she pushed a pram just like it. Every morning, she put the baby into the pram. She wrapped him up and brought the pram carefully down the steps of the house. She pushed the pram down the path, to the gate. The gateway was only slightly wider than the pram.

—Mind you don't scrape the sides, the baby's mother had said, the first time Alina brought the pram to the steps and turned it towards the gate and the street.

Alina did not understand the baby's mother. The mother followed her to the gate. She took the pram and pushed it through the gateway. She tapped the brick pillars.

—Don't scrape the sides.

She tapped the sides of the pram.

—It is very valuable, said the mother.

—It was yours when you were a baby? Alina asked.

—No, said the mother. —We bought it.

—It is very nice.

—Just be careful with it, said the mother.

—Yes, said Alina. —I will be careful.

Every morning, she brought the baby for his walk. She pushed the pram down to the sea and walked along the path beside the sea wall. She walked for two hours, every morning. She had been ordered to do this. She had been told which route to take. She stopped at the wooden bridge, the bridge out to the strange sandy island, and she turned back. She did not see the mother or the father but, sometimes, she thought she was being watched. She never took a different route. She never let the pram scrape a wall or gate. She was drenched and cold; her hands felt frozen to the steel bar with which she pushed the pram, despite the gloves her own mother had sent to her from home. But, still, Alina loved the baby.

The little girls, his sisters, she was not so sure about. They were beautiful little girls. They were clever and lively and they played the piano together, side by side, with a confidence and sensitivity that greatly impressed Alina. The piano was in the tiled hall, close to the stained-glass windows of the large front door. The coloured sunlight of the late afternoon lit the two girls as they played. Their black hair became purple, dark red and the green of deep-forest leaves. Their fingers on the keys were red and yellow. Alina had not seen them play tennis – it was the middle of December – but the mother assured her that they were excellent players. They were polite and they ate with good manners and apologised when they did not eat all that was on their plates.

They were not twins. They had names, of course, and they had different ages. Ocean was ten years old and Saibhreas was almost nine. But Alina rarely – or, never – saw them apart. They played together; they slept together. They stood beside each other, always. From the first time Alina saw them, three weeks earlier, when she arrived at Dublin Airport, they were side by side.

The next morning, Alina's first working day, they came up to Alina's bedroom in the attic. It was dark outside. They were lit only by the light from the landing below, down the steep stairs. Their black hair could not be seen. Alina saw only their faces. They sat at the end of the bed, side by side, and watched Alina.

—Good morning, said Alina.

—Good morning, they said, together.

It was funny. The young ladies laughed. Alina did not know why she did not like them.

2.

Every morning, Alina brought the baby for his walk. Always, she stopped at one of the shelters at the seafront. She took the baby, swaddled in cotton and Gortex, from his pram and held him on her lap. She looked at the changing sea and bounced him gently.

She spoke to him only in English. She had been instructed never to use her own language.

—You can teach the girls a few words of Polish, the mother told her. —It might be useful. But I don't want Cillian confused.

The shelter had three walls, and a wooden bench. The walls had circular windows, like portholes. Alina held the baby and lifted him to one of these windows, so he could see through it. She did it again. He laughed. Alina could feel his excitement through the many layers of cloth. She lifted him high. His hat brushed the roof of the shelter.

—Intelligent boy!

It was the first time he had laughed. She lowered him back into his pram. She would not tell the mother, she decided. But, almost immediately, she changed her mind. She had the sudden feeling, the knowledge; it crept across her face. She was being watched.

She walked as far as the wooden bridge, and turned.

Every morning, Alina saw mothers, and other young women like herself. These women pushed modern, lighter baby-conveyances, four-wheeled and three-wheeled. Alina envied them. The pram felt heavy and the wind from the sea constantly bashed against its hood.

One thing, however, she liked about the pram. People smiled when they saw it.

—I haven't seen one of those in years, one woman said.

—God almighty, that takes me back, said another.

One morning, she pushed past a handsome man who sat on the sea wall eating a large sandwich. She kept pushing; she did not look back. She stopped at the old wooden bridge. She would never bring the pram onto the bridge. She looked at its frail wooden legs rising out of the sludge. The mutual contact, of old wood and old pram; they would all collapse into the ooze below. She could smell it – she could almost feel it, in her hair and mouth. She walked quickly back along the promenade.

The handsome man was still there. He held up a flask and a cup.

—Hot chocolate? he said. —I put aside for you.

He was a biochemist from Lithuania but he was working in Dublin for a builder, constructing an extension to a very large house on her street. They met every morning, in the shelter. Always, he brought the flask. Sometimes, she brought cake. She watched through the portholes as they kissed. She told him she was being watched. He touched her breast; his hand was inside her coat. She looked down at the baby. He smiled; he bucked. He started to cry. The pram rocked on its springs.

One morning in February, Alina heard her mobile phone as she was carefully bringing the pram down the granite steps of the house. She held the phone to her ear.

—Hello?

—Alina. It's O'Reilly.

O'Reilly was the mother. Everyone called her by her surname. She insisted upon this practice. It terrified her clients, she told Alina. It was intriguing; it was sexy.

—Hello, O'Reilly, said Alina.

—The girls are off school early today, said O'Reilly. —Twelve o'clock. I forgot to tell you.

—Fine, said Alina.

But it was not fine.

—I will be there at twelve o'clock, said Alina.

—Five to, said O'Reilly.

—Yes, said Alina.

—Talk to you, said O'Reilly.

—Your mother is not very nice, Alina told the baby, in English.

She could not now meet her biochemist. He did not own a mobile phone. She would miss her hot chocolate. She would miss his lips on her neck. She would not now feel his hands as she peeped through the porthole and watched for approaching joggers and buggy-pushing women.

She arrived at the gates of the girls' school at ten minutes to twelve. They were waiting there, side by side.

—But school ends at twelve o'clock, said Alina.

—A quarter to, said Ocean.

—We've been here *ages*, said Saibhreas.

—So, said Alina. —We will now go home.

—We want to go along the seafront, said Ocean.

—No, said Alina. —It is too windy today, I think.

—You were *late*, said Saibhreas.

—Very well, said Alina. —We go.

The biochemist waved his flask as she approached. Alina walked straight past him. She did not look at him. She did not look at the little girls as they strode past. She hoped he would be there tomorrow. She would explain her strange behaviour.

That night, quite late, the mother came home. The girls came out of their bedroom.

—Guess what, O'Reilly, they said, together. —Alina has a boyfriend.

3.

O'Reilly grabbed Alina's sleeve and pulled her into the kitchen. She shut the door with one of her heels. She grabbed a chair and made Alina sit. She stood impressively before Alina.

—So, she said. —Tell all.

Alina could not look at O'Reilly's face.

—It is, she said, —perhaps my private affair.

—Listen, babes, said O'Reilly. —Nothing is your private affair. Not while you're working here. Are you fucking this guy?

Alina felt herself burn. The crudity was like a slap across her face.

She shook her head.

—Of course, said O'Reilly. —You're a good Catholic girl. It would be quaint, if I believed you.

O'Reilly put one foot on the chair beside Alina.

—I couldn't care less, she said. —Fuck away, girl. But with three provisos. Not while you're working. Not here, on the property. And not with Mister O'Reilly.

Shocked, appalled, close – she thought – to fainting, Alina looked up at O'Reilly. O'Reilly smiled down at her. Alina dropped her head and cried. O'Reilly smiled the more. She'd mistaken Alina's tears and gulps for gratitude. She patted Alina's head. She lifted Alina's blonde hair, held it, and let it drop.

Alina was going to murder the little girls. This she decided as she climbed the stair to her attic room. She closed the door. It had no lock. She sat on the bed, in the dark. She would poison them. She would drown them. She would put pillows on their faces, a pillow in each of her hands. She would lean down on the pillows until their struggles and kicking ceased. She picked up her own pillow. She put it to her face.

She would not, in actuality, kill the girls. She could not do such a thing – two such things. She would, however, frighten them. She would terrify them. She would plant nightmares that would lurk, prowl, rub their evil backs against the soft walls of their minds, all their lives, until they were two old ladies, lying side by side on their one big deathbed. She would – she knew the phrase – scare them shitless.

—Once upon a time, said Alina.

It was two days later. They sat in the playroom, in front of the bay window. The wind scratched the glass. They heard it also crying in the chimney. The baby lay asleep on Alina's lap. The little girls sat on the rug. They looked up at Alina.

—We're too old for *once upon a time*, said Ocean.

—Nobody is too old for *once upon a time*, said Alina.

The wind shrieked in the chimney. The girls edged closer to Alina's feet. Alina thought of her biochemist, out there mixing cement or cutting wood. She had not seen him since. She had pushed the pram past the shelter. Twice she had pushed; three times. He had not been there. She looked down at the girls. She resisted the urge to kick their little upturned faces. She smiled.

—Once upon a time, she said, again. —There was a very old and wicked lady. She lived in a dark forest.

—Where? said Ocean.

—In my country, said Alina.

—Is this just made up?

—Perhaps.

She stood up. It was a good time for an early interruption, she thought. She carried the baby to his pram, which was close to the door. She lowered him gently. He did not wake. She returned to her chair. She watched the girls watch her approach. She sat.

—From this dark forest the wicked lady emerged, every night. With her she brought a pram.

—Like Cillian's? said Saibhreas.

—Very like Cillian's, said Alina.

She looked at the pram.

—Exactly like Cillian's. Every night, the old lady pushed the pram to the village. Every night, she chose a baby. Every night, she stole the baby.

—From only one village?

—The dark forest was surrounded by villages. There were many babies to choose from. Every night, she pushed the pram back into the forest. It was a dark, dark shuddery place and nobody was brave enough to follow her. Not one soldier. Not one handsome young woodcutter. They all stopped at the edge of the forest. The wind in the branches made – their – flesh – creep. The branches stretched out and tried to tear their hearts from their chests.

The wind now shook the windows. A solitary can bounced down the street.

—Cool, said Ocean.

But the little girls moved in closer. They were now actually sitting on Alina's feet, one foot per girl.

—Every night, said Alina, —the wicked old lady came out of the forest. For many, many years.

—Did she take all the babies? asked Saibhreas.

—No, said Alina. —She did not.

Outside, a branch snapped, a car screeched.

—She took only one kind, said Alina.

—What kind? said Ocean.

—She took only – the girls.

4.

—Why? Ocean asked.

—Why? Alina asked back.

—Why did the old lady take girls and not boys?

—They probably taste better, said Saibhreas.

—Yeah, Ocean agreed. —They'd taste nicer than boys, if they were cooked properly.

—And some girls are smaller, said Saibhreas. —So they'd fit in the oven.

—Unless the old lady had an Aga like ours, said Ocean. —Then boys would fit too.

Alina realised: she would have to work harder to scare these practical little girls.

—So, she said. —We return to the story.

The girls were again silent. They looked up at Alina. They waited for more frights.

—It is not to be thought, said Alina, —that the old lady simply *ate* the little girls.

—Cool.

—This was not so, said Alina.

—What did she do to them?

—You must be quiet, said Alina.

—Sorry, said both girls.

They were faultlessly polite.

Alina said nothing until she felt control of the story return to her. She could feel it: it was as if the little girls leaned forward and gently placed the story onto Alina's lap.

—So, she said. —To continue. There were none brave enough to follow the old lady into the dark forest. None of the mothers had a good night's sleep. They pinched themselves to stay awake. They lay on top of sharp stones. And the fathers slept standing up, at the doors of their houses, their axes in their hands, at the ready. And yet—

—She got past them, said Ocean. —I bet she did.

—Why didn't they have guns? said Saibhreas.

—Silence.

—Sorry.

—And yet, said Alina. —The old lady pushed the pram—

—Excuse me, Alina? said Saibhreas.

—Yes?

—You didn't tell us what she did with the babies.

—Besides eating them, said Ocean.

—You do not wish to hear this story?

—We do.

—And so, said Alina. —The old lady took all the baby girls. She carried every baby girl deep into the forest, in her pram. Until there were no more. Then she took the girls who were no longer babies.

Alina saw that Ocean was about to speak. But Saibhreas nudged her sister, warning her not to interrupt. Alina continued.

—She crept up to the girls in their beds and whispered a spell into their sleeping ears. The girls remained sleeping as she picked them up and placed them in the pram. She pushed the pram past the fathers who did not see her, past the mothers as they lay on stones. The wicked old lady took girls of all ages, up to the age of – ten.

Alina waited, as the little girls examined their arms and legs, wondering how the old lady had done this. She watched Ocean look at the pram. Above them, a crow perched on the chimneypot cawed down the chimney; its sharp beak seemed very close. The wind continued to shriek and groan.

—But, said Alina.

She looked from girl to girl. Their mouths stayed closed. They were – Alina knew the phrase – putty in her hands.

—But, she said, again. —One day, a handsome woodcutter had an idea so brilliant, it lit his eyes like lamps at darkest midnight. This was the idea. Every woodcutter should cut a tree every day, starting at the edge of the forest. That way, the old witch's forest would soon be too small to remain her hiding place. Now, all the men in this part of my country were woodcutters. They all took up their axes and, day by day, cut down the trees.

—But, Alina, said Ocean. —Sorry for interrupting.

—Yes? said Alina.

—What would the woodcutters do afterwards, if they cut down all the trees?

—This did not concern them at that time, said Alina. —They cut, to save their daughters.

—Did the plan work?

—Yes, said Alina. —And no. I will tell.

She waited, then spoke.

—Every morning, and all day, the old lady heard the axes of the woodcutters. Every morning, the axes were a little louder, a little nearer. Soon, after many months, she could see the woodcutters through the remaining trees.

She looked down at Ocean.

—One night she left. She sneaked away, with her pram. So, yes, the plan worked. But—

Again, she waited. She looked across, at the pram.

—She simply moved to another place. She found new babies and new little girls, up to the age of – ten.

—Where? said Saibhreas.

—You have not guessed? said Alina.

She watched the little girls look at each other. Ocean began to speak.

—You forgot to tell us—

—I did not forget, said Alina. —You wish to know why she took the little girls.

—Yes, please, said Ocean.

—Their skin, said Alina.

She watched, as the goose-bumps rose on the arms and legs of the little girls in front of her.

5.

It was dark outside, and dark too in the room. Alina stood up.

—But the story, said Ocean.

Alina went to the door and walked behind the pram. She pushed it slowly towards the girls. She let them see it grow out of the dark, like a whale rising from a black sea. She let them hear it creak and purr. She heard them shuffle backwards on their bottoms. Then she stopped. She stepped back to the door, and turned on the light.

She saw the girls squinting, looking at her from around the front of the pram.

—Tomorrow I will continue, said Alina.

They followed her into the kitchen. They stayed with her as she peeled the potatoes and carrots. They offered to help her. They washed and shook each lettuce leaf. They talked to fill the silence.

Alina left them in the kitchen, but they were right behind her. She went back to the sitting room, and stopped.

The pram had been moved. She had left it in the centre of the room, where the little girls had been sitting. But now it was at the window. The curtain was resting on the hood.

Alina heard the girls behind her.

—Did you move the pram? she asked.

—No, said Saibhreas.

—We've been with you all the time, said Ocean.

Alina walked over to the pram. She wasn't so very concerned about its mysterious change of position. In fact, she thought, it added to the drama of the interrupted story. The little girls lingered at the door. They would not enter the room.

Alina picked up the baby from the pram's warm bed. He still slept. O'Reilly would be annoyed.

—I pay you to keep him awake, she'd told Alina, once. —In this country, Alina, the babies sleep at night. Because the mummies have to get up in the morning to work, to pay the bloody childminders.

Alina walked out to the hall. She heard the car outside; she heard the change of gear. She saw the car lights push the colours from the stained-glass windows, across the ceiling. She felt the baby shift. She looked down, and saw him watch the coloured lights above him.

—Intelligent boy.

The engine stopped; the car lights died. Alina turned on the hall light. The little girls were right beside her.

—Your mother, I think, said Alina.

—Our dad, actually, said Ocean.

—How do you know this? Alina asked.

—Their Beemers, said Ocean. —Mum's Roadster has a quieter engine.

—It's the ultimate driving machine, said Saibhreas.

The lights were on, their daddy was home, and the little girls were no longer frightened. But Alina was satisfied. The lights could be turned off, and their fear could be turned back on – any time she wished to flick the switch.

She walked the next morning and thought about her story. She pushed the pram past the shelter and hoped to see her handsome biochemist. He was not there. She pushed into the wind and rain. Seawater jumped over the wall and drenched the promenade in front of her. She turned back; she could not go her usual, mandatory distance. She felt eyes stare – she felt their heat – watching her approach. But there was no one in front of her, and nothing. She was alone. She looked into the pram, but the baby slept. His eyes were firmly closed.

The little girls had their hair wrapped in towels when Alina continued her story that afternoon. They'd had showers when they came home from school, because they'd been so cold and wet.

Alina closed the curtains. She turned on only one small side-light.

The baby slept in the pram, beside Alina's chair.

—And so, said Alina.

She sat.

The little girls were at her feet, almost under the pram.

—Did the old witch come to Ireland? Ocean asked.

Alina nodded.

—To Dublin, she said.

—There are no forests in Dublin, Alina, said Saibhreas.

—There are many parks, said Alina.

—What park?

Alina held up her hands.

—I must continue.

—Sorry, Alina.

Alina measured the silence, then spoke.

—Soon, she said, —the squeak of the pram's wheels became a familiar and terrifying sound late at night as the old lady pushed it through the streets of this city. It was a very old pram, and rusty. And so it creaked and—

Beside them, the pram moved. It did not creak but it moved, very slightly.

The girls jumped.

Alina had not touched it.

The baby was waking. They heard a little cry.

Alina laughed.

—Strong boy, she said. —It was your brother.

Ocean stood up.

—Maybe O'Reilly's right, she said.

—Yes, said Saibhreas.

She crawled away from the pram.

—What did O'Reilly say? Alina asked.

—She said the pram was haunted.

Inside the pram, the baby began to howl.

6.

Alina stared at the pram while, inside, the baby kicked and screeched.

—Aren't you going to pick him up? said Ocean.

—Of course, said Alina.

But, yet, she did not move. It was as if she'd woken up in a slightly different room. The angles weren't quite right. The baby's screech was wrong.

She stood up. She approached the rocking pram. The movement did her good. The room was just a room.

She looked into the pram. The baby was there, exactly as he should have been. He was angry, red, and rightly so. She had been silly; the little girls had frightened her.

She turned on the light and the pram was just a pram.

—The pram moved today, said Saibhreas.

She said this later, in the kitchen.

—I should hope so, said O'Reilly. —It's supposed to bloody move. I pay a Polish *cailín* to move it.

Alina blushed; her rage pushed at her skin. She hated this crude woman.

—It moved all by itself, said Ocean.

Alina stared down at her chicken. She felt something, under the table, brush against her leg. Mr O'Reilly's foot. He sat opposite Alina.

—Sorry, he said.

—Down, Fido, said O'Reilly.

She looked at Alina.

—Lock your door tonight, sweetie.

—I do not have a key, said Alina.

—Interesting, said O'Reilly. —What happened the pram?

—The baby cried, said Alina. —And so, the pram moved some centimetres.

—And why, asked O'Reilly, —did Cillian cry?

—O'Reilly? said Ocean.

—What?

—The pram moved before Cillian cried.

—Yes, said Saibhreas. —It's haunted, like you said.

Alina sat as the little girls told their mother about the wicked old lady and her pram full of kidnapped babies, and how the wicked old lady had pushed the pram all the way to Ireland.

—Enough, already, said O'Reilly.

She turned to Alina.

—That's some hardcore story-telling, Alina.

—She takes the skin off the babies, said Ocean.

—Who does? said O'Reilly. —Alina?

—No, said Saibhreas. —The old woman.

—My my, said O'Reilly. —And look at the fair Alina's skin. How red can red get?

Alina stared at the cold chicken on her plate. She felt the shock – O'Reilly's fingers on her cheek.

—Hot, said O'Reilly.

The little girls laughed.

—We'd better call a halt to the story, Alina, said O'Reilly. —It's getting under your skin.

The little girls laughed again.

The following morning, Alina pushed the pram along the promenade. She had not slept well. She had not slept at all. O'Reilly's fingers, Mr O'Reilly's foot – Alina had felt their presence all round her. She'd got up and torn a piece of paper from a notebook. She'd chewed the paper. Then she'd pushed the pulp into the keyhole of her bedroom door. She'd lain awake all night.

She walked. The wind was strong and pushed against the pram. It woke her up; it seemed to wash her skin. It was a warm wind. Gloves weren't necessary. But Alina wore her gloves.

The pram was haunted. O'Reilly had said so; she'd told her little daughters. Alina did not believe it. She knew her folklore. Prams did not haunt, and were never haunted. And yet, she did not wish to touch the pram. She did not want to see it move before her fingers reached it. She'd put on her gloves inside the house, before she'd lowered the baby into the pram. She did not want to touch it. Not even out here, in bright sunshine, away from walls and shadows.

The pram was not possessed. A dead rat could not bite, but Alina would wear gloves to pick one up. That was how it was with the pram. Today, it was a dead rat. Tomorrow, it would simply be a pram.

She took off one of her gloves. She stopped walking. The pram stayed still. Alina put her bare fingers on the handle. She waited. Nothing happened. She felt the wind rock the pram on its springs. But the pram did not move backwards or forwards.

She removed her other glove. She pushed the pram. She pushed it to the wooden bridge, and back. She would continue her story that afternoon, despite O'Reilly's command. She would plant the most appalling nightmares and leave the little imps in the hands of their foul mother.

And then she would leave.

She pushed the pram with her bare hands. But, all the time, and all the way, she felt she was being watched. She put the gloves back on. She was watched. She felt it – she *knew* it – on her face and neck, like damp fingers.

—One night, Alina said that afternoon, —the old lady left her lair in the park and made her way to a tree-lined street.

—Our street has trees, said Ocean.

Outside, the wind cracked a branch. The little girls moved closer to Alina.

7.

Alina looked down at the little girls.

—The old lady crept along the tree-lined street, she said. —She hid behind the very expensive cars. The SUVs. This is what they are called?

The little girls nodded.

—And the Volvos, said Alina. —And – the Beemers.

Alina watched the little girls look at each other.

—She looked through windows where the velvet curtains had not yet been drawn.

Alina watched the girls look at the window. She had left the velvet curtains open.

She heard the gasp, and the scream.

—The curtains!

—I saw her!

Alina did not look. She leaned down and placed her hands beneath the little girls' chins.

—Through one such window, said Alina, —the old lady saw a bargain.

Alina held the chins. She forced the girls to look at her. She stretched her leg – she had earlier measured the distance from foot to pram – and raised her foot to the wheel.

—She saw *two* girls.

They heard the creak.

The little girls screamed. And so did Alina. She had not touched the wheel. The pram had moved before her foot had reached it.

Alina almost vomited. She felt the pancakes, the *nalesniki* she had earlier made and eaten, and the sour cream; she could taste them as they rushed up to her throat. Her eyes watered. She felt snails of cold sweat on her forehead. The little girls screamed. And Alina held their chins. She tightened her grip. She felt bone and shifting tongues. She could feel their screams in her hands. And the pram continued to move. Slowly, slowly, off the rug, across the wooden floor.

Alina held the faces.

—Two little girls, she said. —And, such was her wicked joy, she did not wait until they slept.

The pram crept on. It rolled nearer to the window. She heard the baby. She watched his waking rock the pram.

—The old lady found an open window, said Alina.

The baby screeched. And then other babies screeched. There was more than one baby in the pram.

The girls screamed, and urinated. And, still, Alina told her story.

—Through the window she slid. And through the house she sneaked.

The pram was at the window. The screeching shook the window glass.

—She found the girls quite easily.

The girls were squirming, trying to free their jaws from Alina's big fingers, and trying to escape from the wet rug beneath them. But Alina held them firm. She ignored their fingernails on her neck and cheeks.

—She had her sharp knife with her, said Alina. —She would cut the little girls. And she would take their skin, while their mother neglected them. Far, far away, in her Beemer.

But their mother wasn't far, far away in her Beemer. She was at the door, looking at her daughters and Alina.

—Hell-oh! she roared. —HELL-oh!

The pram stopped rocking. The little girls stopped screaming. And Alina stopped narrating.

O'Reilly stepped into the room. She turned on the light.

—She frightened us, said Ocean.

The girls escaped from Alina's grip. They shuffled backwards, off the rug.

—She hurt us, Mummy.

—We don't like her.

Alina took her hands down from her face. There was blood on her fingertips. She could feel the scratches, on her cheeks and neck.

She looked up.

The girls were gone; she could hear them on the stairs. She was alone with O'Reilly and the screaming baby. O'Reilly held the baby and made soft, soothing noises. She rocked the baby gently and walked in a small circle around the rug. The baby's screams soon lessened, and ceased. O'Reilly continued to make soft noises, and it was some time before Alina realised that, amid the kisses and whispers, O'Reilly was giving out to her.

—My fucking rug, she cooed. —Have you any idea how much it cost? There, there, good boy.

—I am sorry, said Alina.

—What the fuck were you doing, Alina?

Alina looked at the pram. It was against the wall, beside the window. It was not moving.

—The pram is haunted, said Alina.

—It's haunted because I said it's haunted, said O'Reilly. —I told the girls the bloody thing was haunted, to keep them away from the baby when he was born.

—But it *is* haunted, said Alina. —It has nothing to do with the lies you told your daughters.

—Excuse me?

—I saw it move, said Alina. —Here.

She stamped her foot. She stood up.

—Here, she said. —I saw. And I heard. More babies.

—Jesus, said O'Reilly. —The sooner you find a peasant or something to knock you up the better.

—I felt their eyes, said Alina.

—Enough, said O'Reilly.

—Many times, said Alina, —I have felt their eyes. I know now. There are babies in the pram.

—Look at me, Alina, said O'Reilly.

Alina looked.

—Are you listening? said O'Reilly.

—Yes, said Alina.

—You're sacked.

8.

O'Reilly wondered if Alina had heard her. She was facing O'Reilly, but her eyes were huge and far away.

—Do you understand that, Alina?

—Yes.

—You're fired.

Alina nodded.

—As of now, said O'Reilly.

—Yes.

—You can stay the night, then off you fucking go.

—Yes.

—Stop saying Yes, Alina, said O'Reilly.

But she wasn't looking at Alina now. She was searching for a phone number and balancing the baby on her shoulder as she walked over to the window and the pram.

—I'll have to stay home tomorrow, said O'Reilly. —So, fuck you, Alina, and life's complications.

She gently slid the baby from her shoulder and, her hands on his bum and little head, she lowered him into the cradle of the pram.

She heard the scream.

—No!

—Fuck off, Alina, said O'Reilly.

She didn't turn, or lift her face from the pram. She kissed the baby's forehead and loosely tucked the edges of his quilt beneath the mattress.

She stood up. She looked down at her son.

—There's only one baby in there, Alina.

She had the phone to her ear. She began to speak.

—Conor? she said. —It's O'Reilly. We have to cancel tomorrow's meeting. Yes. No. My Polish peasant. Yes; again. Yes. Yes. A fucking nightmare. You can? I'll suck your cock if you do. Cool. Talk to you.

O'Reilly brought the phone down from her ear at the same time that Alina brought the poker down on O'Reilly's head. The poker was decorative, and heavy. It had never been used, until now. The first blow was sufficient.

O'Reilly collapsed with not much noise, and her blood joined the urine on the rug.

Mr O'Reilly was inserting his door-key into the lock when Alina opened the front door.

—Alina, he said. —Bringing Cillian for a stroll?

—Yes, she said.

—Excellent.

He helped her bring the pram down the granite steps.

—Is he well wrapped up in there? said Mr O'Reilly. —It's a horrible evening.

—Yes, said Alina.

—And yourself, he said. —Have you no coat?

He looked at her breasts, beneath her Skinni Fit T-shirt, and thought how much he'd like to see them when she returned after a good walk in the wind and rain.

Alina did not answer.

—I'll leave you to it, he said. —Where's O'Reilly?

—In the playroom, said Alina.

—Fine, said Mr O'Reilly. —See you when you get back.

Alina turned left, off her usual path, and brought the pram down a lane that ran behind the houses. It was dark there, and unpleasant. The ground wasn't properly paved or, if it was, the surface was lost under years of dead leaves, dumped rubbish and dog shit. But Alina stayed on the lane, away from streetlights and detection. She pushed straight into darkness and terror. She held her arms stiff, to keep the pram as far from her as possible. And, yet, she felt each shudder and jump, each one a screaming, shuddering baby.

At the end of the lane, another lane, behind the pub and Spar. Alina stayed in this lane, which brought her to another. And another. This last one was particularly dreadful. The ground was soft, and felt horribly warm at her ankles. She pushed hard, to the lane's end and fresh air. The sea was now in front of her. Alina couldn't hide.

She knew what she had to do.

But now she wasn't pushing. The wind shook the pram, filled the hood, and lifted it off the ground. She heard the cries – the pram landed on its wheels, just a few centimetres ahead, and continued on its course. Alina had to run behind it, pulling it back, as the infant ghosts, their murderers or demons – she did not know – perhaps their spirit parents, she did not know, as all of them tried to wrench the pram from her. She heard the wails, and under, through them all, she heard the cries of the baby, Cillian. Her adorable, intelligent Cillian. Now gone, murdered by the murdered infants.

She refused to feel the cold. She didn't pause to rub the rain from her eyes.

She held onto the pram and its wailing evil, and she pulled and pushed the length of the promenade, a journey of two kilometres, to her goal, the wooden bridge, the bridge out to the strange island.

They found her in the sludge. She was standing up to her thighs in the ooze and seaweed. She was trying to push the pram still deeper into the mud. They found the baby – they found only one baby. The quilt had saved him. He lay on it, on top of the mud. The tide was out, but coming back. The water was starting to fill and swallow the quilt. They lifted the baby and the struggling woman onto the bridge. They left the pram in the rising water.

TEATRO LA FENICE

Christine Dwyer Hickey

Christine Dwyer Hickey has published eight novels, a short story collection and a full-length play. Her stories have been published in anthologies and magazines worldwide and have won several awards. Her eighth novel, *The Narrow Land*, is published by Atlantic UK (2019). She is a member of Aosdána. 'Teatro La Fenice' won the Observer Short Story Competition.

We walk together, Claire and I, across the lawn that leads down to the edge of the river towards the smooth stone steps that will take us there. We pass Mr Fleming, who keeps the grass laundered, ironing green stripes, light and dark, with the big yellow machine that goes before him. Behind him the house is tall and russet red. There are forty-two windows in all, most of which are the image of each other. Except for the window in the turret, which curves slightly towards the gable, and also the windows with the bars jammed into them, hidden under the hem of the house.

When we reach the steps, we stop for a moment, Claire organising her hand in mine. Then slowly we take them one at a time, one foot leading, the other joining and a little rest in between. Claire tells me this is because I am nervous, that I'm afraid I might fall on my face.

The grass is tougher here on the edge of the river, not so nice to the touch, and so Claire lays out a Foxford rug. She calls this 'our usual spot'. Guiding me down then to sit on one corner of the rug, moving my legs so that my knees face the centre, she then sits herself on the opposite corner in the same way, her knees facing mine. And that's how we are, Claire and I, two old biddies really. That's how you find us. Like a brace of old fairground ornaments on each end of a mantelpiece.

Claire's fingers begin to move, slowly clawing the back off an orange. When it's naked she hands it to me and I hold its body loosely on my palm. I wait for her to encourage me to eat and I am listening to the gnaw of my mouth on its flesh when Claire begins to speak.

'I suppose they were good enough to invite me. But at the same time, I'm not sure I feel like it – they've a nice garden though. Such a nice garden. And decking, if you don't mind.'

'Oh, decking – imagine that now?' I say.

'Yes. With a special place for cooking sausages in the corner. In the summer, like, a barbecue it's a bit like but, you know, much more sophisticated. Though by the time the sausages cook through, would it not be quicker to fry them on a proper cooker? Then bring them outside. Giving herself work, is what I say. It's a nice big garden all the same. Though, do you know, not a flower in it. And, I mean to say, what's a garden without flowers? I always insisted on looking after the flowers in our garden. No, Jack, I'd say, let the gardener see to the orchard and the lawn, but the flowers are mine. Jack used be livid.'

'Livid?'

'He liked me to look after my hands, you see.'

She stretches her fingers out and presses a plump, mauve hand into the sky.

'And there's my daughter-in-law with not a flower.'

'Not a flower?'

'Ah, daisies sometimes for a while. But she cuts them.'

'Cuts them?'

'Yes, cuts them.'

'Now! Imagine that!'

Claire continues about the garden. She only stops to dab juice away from my chin or to pull a cardigan that is already there across my shoulders. She is always fussing but it doesn't really bother me. And she doesn't demand much in return. Except my company and the odd little word or question just to show that I'm minding her.

And you'd have to be minding what Claire says. That memory – where she keeps it all! Down to the finest detail. I only see things in a block, one picture at a time. What comes before or what happens after – well, I'm just not in charge of the sequence.

The river is twitchy today. The river has come all the way from the city – Claire once told me that. In the city it's big and wide and stinking to the high heavens. By the time it gets to us it has sweetened. And shrunk. Twitchy and wrinkly and grey.

On the far side of the river, some distance away, is a thick tall wall made of random stone.

'That's the park over there,' Claire says, 'the Phoenix Park. That's where we're not allowed go, I hope you know that now.'

'Oh, yes, Claire, I do know that now.'

'I thought maybe, by the way you were staring up at it, that you'd forgotten, like.'

'Ah no. Ah no, Claire, not at all.'

'Well, that's good,' she says and goes back to the garden, her garden or her daughter-in-law's, I can't be sure which.

There are times when I might like to say more. To contribute to one of Claire's conversations. But I'm afraid to risk it. How can I say for instance, Yes, I was the same about my own garden, my own flowers? When I can't be quite sure if I had a garden at all, never mind flowers. And even if I was sure I ever had a garden, she'd be bound to trip me up. Bound to ask me name, rank and number of every last flower in the bed, and I'd never be able for that. Besides, she's happier with things as they are, her doing the talking, me doing the agreeing. I like her being happy too. We're great pals, Claire and I, great pals. Everyone says so.

'And do you know,' she continues, 'they don't even have a fry of a Sunday morning. And I do love a sausage and rasher of a Sunday morning, a nice bit of pudding too.'

'But I thought they had sausages on the boat?'

'Boat? What boat?'

'The deck-thing, you know. The thing that you said.'

'I said the decking. It's got nothing to do with a boat. It's attached to the house, for God's sake – will you ever listen?'

'Oh yes, that's right, of course. The house.'

Claire looks as if she might be going to sulk but then she changes her mind. 'I could never face the golf course until I'd a decent feed: a rasher and egg and that – you know, like? That's the worst about going continental, I always say. The breakfast. No fry. Oul' cake and a bit of jam.'

'A bit of jam.'

'Yes. And then there's mass. I know full well they never go except when I'm there. And, well, to tell you the truth I'm not that keen any more. All those strangers trying to shake your hand.'

'The Continentals?'

'Ah God, no. The church near where Gerard lives. Any church, really, nowadays. That sign of peace business. A way to pass germs is all that's good for. But they insist on going just because I'm there. I'd just as soon walk in the garden, talk to God in my own way, there amongst the flowers.'

'Except there aren't any.'

'What?'

'Flowers. There aren't any flowers.'
'Oh, yes, except for that.'

Now there, for example. I'd like to say something. Not about God, not about handshakes. Not so much about the rashers or anything else in the fry either. But, well, going continental. Claire is always talking about all the holidays she's had. And, for all I know, I might know just as much about it as she does. I see this picture of myself so often. Well, my hands really. Younger than now, of course, but the same ring is on the same finger and that's how I know it's me. And every time I look down on this part of the river and every time, I look over there and up at the big old stone wall of the Phoenix Park, I see it like it's on a screen. This big picture of a hand. The hand (the one that belongs to me) is holding another hand (that doesn't) – a hand with wider fingers and a sprig of black hair just under the knuckles. A man's hand. No doubt about it. And I really love it, that other hand. I just feel this huge gulp of love for it. For a hand! We are walking through streets so narrow that the hands have to split and my fingers creep up and crawl around his arm instead. We cross a bridge, a baby bridge, so small. And the sound of the water slapping and slurping and there's all these blobs of light crawling around on the stone like something under a microscope. Then we come out into a big square with tables and chairs and people and smells and it's all so... but how could I say that to Claire? How could I tell her that my hand is happy somewhere that might be foreign?

Oh, that would be lovely all right for her to take back to Matron.

'And supposing,' Claire says now, 'supposing the weather's bad? I'll be stuck indoors. Watching telly. They don't even go out of a Saturday afternoon. Would you believe it? She talks on her phone for about three hours walking around the house and garden so we all have to hear. And he? I don't know what he does be doing with himself. He's gone as fat as you like too. And the kids eat rubbish and lie on the floor watching the telly with me and, like, I'd have to watch whatever they want. And I used to love going out of a Saturday. A bit of shopping and then a stop off at Thompsons or the Green Door maybe for tea. Oh yes, the Green Door was the place. Best hat and gloves for the Green Door. Nothing less would do, you know.'

She turns slowly and stares into my face. 'Besides,' she goes, 'what will you do? If I take up their offer. All weekend. All on your own. Friday, Saturday and Sunday – you know, it's a long old time.'

'Me? Oh, don't worry about me. I'll be as right as a raindrop!'

*

The hands lock again. Then cross the square to steps on the other side. A big flight of steps. And they grow bigger the nearer they get. We climb. And then we're inside a marble hall and all you can hear are voices sort of purring, all the way up to the domed ceiling. More stairs now, but different this time, red as lipstick and polished brown wood at the sides. My hand (the one with the ring on) slides upwards and the man's hand follows it. And then. Oh then, the magnificence of it all! We come out into a place filled with rows of velvety seats. And we sit down on one on the edge of a tier halfway to the sky. Below us the hum and haw of an orchestra in preparation. Around us more voices talking and dresses crunching and perfume and aftershave. Above us angels. Fat little baby angels skirting a sky of blue and gold. And a thousand lights winking in chandeliers. And I feel like – well, I feel like a currant in a wedding cake! A great big blue and gold wedding cake. Imagine now, trying to say that to Claire?

Claire is so animated today. I know there'll be few moments of peace. She's been on about this weekend for such a long time. But of course, that's the thing – I can't be sure how long exactly. I seem to remember her speaking of it when the river was low. And it's full today. I also feel I've heard it when I was wearing my blue tweed coat and, yes, that skirt which she is now tucking around my legs is cotton red. Definitely red. Perhaps that was another week-end, one from a long time ago.

'You see the thing is,' she says, 'if I say yes then Gerard will have to drive all the way up from Cork to collect me. And he's so busy, 'twouldn't be fair. Though he has a beautiful car, I must say. Fifty-eight thousand it cost him. Fifty-eight.'

'Now. Imagine.'

'That's like twice what my own house cost that when we bought it. More maybe!'

'It must be very big.'

'Oh yes, even the boot is—'

'No, your house.'

'Oh yes. My house.'

She says nothing now for a while. I can hear the river whisper and mumble all sorts of secrets. Mr Fleming's machine wheezes back to it. And it's all so very pleasant, this conversation of sounds with no voices.

'He has a plug for charging his phone in the car,' she starts again, 'and a special clasp to put the phone in, so he can talk to it then when he's driving along, you see. And the kids, they all have their own phones too. Never off them in fact.'

*

Now what I think is this: if they have so many phones, why doesn't anyone ever ring Claire?

Even I get the odd phone call from – well, I don't quite know who. Not that I really want it, having to cross over to the phone with everyone grinning at me and making boyfriend jokes.

The next time whoever he is phones up I know what I'll say. I'll say, 'Would you like to speak to Claire? Ah do. She loves an old chat.' Yes, that's what I'll do.

Claire stands up and I know it's time for her foot-dip. She says there's nothing like river water for chilblains and corns. But we must never tell anyone about her dip. In a moment she'll walk to the end of the bank to the little ornamental bridge put in by a very important man who used to live here before Matron and her nurses took over. Claire will climb down to the little ledge near the bridge and sit herself down and dip her feet in, water curling around her legs and cuffing her ankles. Sometimes you can hear her giggling down there.

But first she has to get herself ready. And off they come, rolling down in little creases and turning her legs from brown nylon poles to purple gnarled ones. She's let the pants slip down as well by accident and I thank God Mr Fleming can't see this far, her bare bottom, like two big pork chops hanging down. And I noticed that, too, her pants are soiled. Oh, only slightly, but enough to cause shame. And I could easily do it too. Tell, I mean. I could easily say, 'Claire is not wiping herself properly.' After all, who told on me when I had that little accident with the sheets?

She stands before me now, pulling her skirt down carefully over her knees. 'No,' she says, 'I've decided. I'm not going. No, no. That's it. I've made my mind up.'

'Your mind?'

'Yes. At the end of the day, I just couldn't have it on my conscience leaving you all alone all that time. Well, supposing something were to happen to you. Or if you had one of your little accidents. Who'd cover up for you then? Sure you'd be lost without me. Anyone will tell you that.'

'Anyone?'

'Well, everyone then.'

*

Everyone says I'd be lost without Claire. But I wouldn't be lost, how could I? There's nowhere to get lost except for the Phoenix Park and I'd never be able to find my way there. I'd have to go out the front, through the main gate. Then through the little housing estate that leads to the main road and the West County Hotel. I'd have to turn left then and walk all the way down to the village. I'd have to cross the bridge and go up the row between the two shops and find the sneaky little turnstile gate in the wall beside the cottages. I'd have to get myself through the turnstile and then go left up a steep path with trees on one side, the wall on the other, steeper and steeper until I could see the river from the other side. Until I could see right across it, to the house, the turret, the riverbank and the Foxford rug with only Claire on it. Claire and the orange. And I wouldn't have a clue how to go about all that!

Why, even here in the house, I couldn't get myself lost. There are no more than three or four routes to be considered, anyway, and there's always someone you can follow if you find yourself getting confused. Not once in all the time I've been here have I forgotten. Not once. Except for – But that doesn't really count because that time I only pretended to be lost. Matron was so cross, I had to let her think it was an accident. The truth is I was just curious, that's all. That's why I followed her. I wanted to see what was behind the door that needs the two keys. It's a green door, too, but not Claire's green door. And what was behind it? Not gloves or hats anyway. Not pots of silver tea either – but Purgatory. That's what.

The name came into my head the minute I set eyes on it. 'Purgatory!' I said it out loud and the matron heard and that's how she knew I was there. Nobody belonging to this world or the next. People inside all crying and moaning, all trying to rock themselves back to this life or on to the next one in big cots like they were overgrown babies. And the smell! A smell of rabbits – that's what it was.

Claire says they're all in there on account of having eaten the aluminium off the bottom of the pans. Well, I ask you! They must have been mad in the first place – why else would they do such a thing? Luckily for Claire she never had aluminium in her house, only copper. Only copper would do.

Anyway, that day, the day Matron found me, she dragged my arm back into the main room and I followed it. And as I sat back down in my place, I made myself a promise. That I was never going to end up behind that door. And how was I going to do that? By keeping my mouth shut.

And was I glad to be back in our own main room? Our lovely own main room. They call it the Chinese Room because of the hand-painted designs on the wall. A very important man used to live in this house. Just him and his family – they had it all to themselves. He was the man who sold Parnell up the river. And you'd want to be very important to be able to do that.

It's a large room, the Chinese Room, each allotment of space taken up by a chair and on each chair a grey head like a jinny-jo nods away the time between meals.

'What a beautiful room!' That's what the people from outside always say, looking around it, up and down, all through their visit, as though they'll be asked to recite every inch of it before being allowed go home.

And silence, always silence. Here only the radio speaks. Except for, of course, when the doctor comes. Then it's a different matter. As soon as he walks through the door a chorus of 'doctor oh doctor' starts up and as he passes each one, the chorus reaches out and follows him. He's like Jesus walking among the lepers in the desert. When it's time for him to leave, he passes through the door and silence flies back in over his head like a bird then flits from chair to chair until all is quiet again. Unless the bells of the Angelus call out from a radio on top of the long-locked piano – then its 'pish-pish-pish declared onto Mary'.

Claire used to have a piano in her house too – same colour, only much bigger.

Claire pulls her cardigan like a shawl over her head. She holds it tightly with the hands Jack liked her to look after.

'Gerard will be furious. And it's not as if I'm not disappointed myself. And the kids? Well, they love their old granny, you know.'

Then I remember something. 'That's right, Claire – your granny flat!' I say, delighted with myself. 'What about your granny flat? Surely you want to see that!'

Well. You'd think I was after doing something terrible. You'd think I was the world's worst.

'I thought I told you never to mention that to me? What sort are you mentioning that to me? What sort of a—' she steps forward then and gives me such a puck in the arm that I topple over – 'bitch!'

And what did I say? What was it again? Granny flat. But I thought she'd like to see the granny flat they built her. Wasn't that why she sold her own house in the first place so that she could give them the money to buy a house with a big garden where they could build a flat for a granny?

Claire walks away from me, huffing with rage, and I stay lying with the hair on the Foxford rug sticking into my nose. Her funny long feet leave photos of themselves in the muck near the edge of the river. Soon she is there at the end of the bank. She tweaks the water with her toe but she doesn't sit down on the ledge. She stays standing, her back to me, her face towards the distant wall of the Phoenix Park.

Can she see pictures up there too, I wonder? A big piano, copper pots, the flowers that made her husband cross, the granny flat with no granny in it?

I would love to ask her. But I'm afraid her answer will tell me that the wall is only a wall. That there is nothing else there. No hands, no angels, no foreign voices. A big grey stone wall around a park that we're not allowed go into.

VIRGIN SOIL

George Egerton

George Egerton (1859–1945) was born Mary Chavelita Dunne Bright in Melbourne, but spent her life in Ireland. She wrote short stories and her best-known collections are *Keynotes* and *Discords*. Her work was political and feminist in outlook, and she was an integral figure in the New Woman literary movement.

The bridegroom is waiting in the hall; with a trifle of impatience he is tracing the pattern of the linoleum with the point of his umbrella. He curbs it and laughs, showing his strong white teeth at a remark of his best man; then compares the time by his hunter with the clock on the stairs. He is florid, bright-eyed, loose-lipped, inclined to stoutness, but kept in good condition; his hair is crisp, curly, slightly grey; his ears peculiar, pointed at their tops like a faun's. He looks very big and well-dressed, and, when he smiles, affable enough.

Upstairs a young girl, with the suns of seventeen summers on her brown head, is lying with her face hidden on her mother's shoulder; she is sobbing with great childish sobs, regardless of reddened eyes and the tears that have splashed on the silk of her grey, going-away gown.

The mother seems scarcely less disturbed than the girl. She is a fragile-looking woman with delicate fair skin, smoothly parted thin chestnut hair, dove-like eyes, and a monotonous piping voice. She is flushing painfully, making a strenuous effort to say something to the girl, something that is opposed to the whole instincts of her life.

She tries to speak, parts her lips only to close them again, and clasp her arms tighter round the girl's shoulders; at length she manages to say with trembling, uncertain pauses:

'You are married now, darling, and you must obey'—she lays a stress upon the word—'your husband in all things—there are—there are things you should know—but—marriage is a serious thing, a sacred thing'—with desperation—'you must believe that what your husband tells you is right—let him guide you—tell you——'

There is such acute distress in her usually unemotional voice that the girl looks up and scans her face—her blushing, quivering, faded face. Her eyes are startled, fawn-like eyes as her mother's, her skin too is delicately fair, but her mouth is firmer, her jaw squarer, and her piquant, irregular nose is full of character. She is slightly built, scarcely fully developed in her fresh youth.

'What is it that I do not know, mother? What is it?'—with anxious impatience. 'There is something more—I have felt it all these last weeks in your and the others' looks—in his, in the very atmosphere—but why have you not told me before—I——' Her only answer is a gush of helpless tears from the mother, and a sharp rap at the door, and the bridegroom's voice, with an imperative note that it strikes the nervous girl is new to it, that makes her cling to her mother in a close, close embrace, drop her veil and go out to him.

She shakes hands with the best man, kisses the girl friend who has acted as bridesmaid—the wedding has been a very quiet one—and steps into the carriage. The Irish cook throws an old shoe after them from the side door, but it hits the trunk of an elder-tree, and falls back on to the path, making that worthy woman cross herself and mutter of ill-omens and bad luck to follow; for did not a magpie cross the path first thing this morning when she went to open the gate, and wasn't a red-haired woman the first creature she clapped eyes on as she looked down the road?

Half an hour later the carriage pulls up at the little station and the girl jumps out first; she is flushed, and her eyes stare helplessly as the eyes of a startled child, and she trembles with quick running shudders from head to foot. She clasps and unclasps her slender, grey-gloved hands so tightly that the stitching on the back of one bursts.

He has called to the station-master, and they go into the refreshment-room together; the latter appears at the door and, beckoning to a porter, gives him an order.

She takes a long look at the familiar little place. They have lived there three years, and yet she seems to see it now for the first time; the rain drips, drips monotonously off the zinc roof, the smell of the dust is fresh, and the white pinks in the borders are beaten into the gravel.

Then the train runs in; a first-class carriage, marked 'engaged,' is attached, and he comes for her; his hot breath smells of champagne, and it strikes her that his eyes are fearfully big and bright, and he offers her his arm with such a curious amused proprietary air that the girl shivers as she lays her hand in it.

The bell rings, the guard locks the door, the train steams out, and as it passes the signal-box, a large well-kept hand, with a signet ring on the little finger, pulls down the blind on the window of an engaged carriage.

Five years later, one afternoon on an autumn day, when the rain is falling like splashing tears on the rails, and the smell of the dust after rain fills the mild air with freshness, and the white chrysanthemums struggle to raise their heads from the gravel path into which the sharp shower has beaten them, the same woman, for there is no trace of girlhood in her twenty-two years, slips out of a first-class carriage; she has a dressing-bag in her hand.

She walks with her head down and a droop in her shoulders; her quickness of step is due rather to nervous haste than elasticity of frame. When she reaches the turn of the road, she pauses and looks at the little villa with the white curtains and gay tiled window-boxes. She can see the window of her old room; distinguish every shade in the changing leaves of the creeper climbing up the south wall; hear the canary's shrill note from where she stands.

Never once has she set foot in the peaceful little house with its air of genteel propriety since that eventful morning when she left it with him; she has always framed an excuse.

Now as she sees it a feeling of remorse fills her heart, and she thinks of the mother living out her quiet years, each day a replica of the one gone before, and her resolve weakens; she feels inclined to go back, but the waning sun flickers over the panes in the window of the room she occupied as a girl. She can recall how she used to run to the open window on summer mornings and lean out and draw in the dewy freshness and welcome the day, how she has stood on moonlight nights and danced with her bare white feet in the strip of moonlight, and let her fancies fly out into the silver night, a young girl's dreams of the beautiful, wonderful world that lay outside.

A hard dry sob rises in her throat at the memory of it, and the fleeting expression of softness on her face changes to a bitter disillusion.

She hurries on, with her eyes down, up the neat gravelled path, through the open door into the familiar sitting-room.

The piano is open with a hymn-book on the stand; the grate is filled with fresh green ferns, a bowl of late roses perfume the room from the centre of the table. The mother is sitting in her easy chair, her hands folded across a big white Persian cat on her lap; she is fast asleep. Some futile lace work, her thimble, and bright scissor are placed on a table near her.

Her face is placid, not a day older than that day five years ago. Her glossy hair is no greyer, her skin is clear, she smiles in her sleep. The smile rouses a sort of sudden fury in the breast of the woman standing in her dusty travelling cloak at the door, noting every detail in the room. She throws back her veil and goes over and looks at herself in the mirror over the polished chiffonnier —scans herself pitilessly. Her skin is sallow with the dull sallowness of a fair skin in ill-health, and the fringe of her brown hair is so lacking in lustre that it affords no contrast. The look of fawn-like shyness has vanished from her eyes, they burn sombrefully and resentfully in their sunken orbits, there is a dragged look about the mouth; and the keynote of her face is a cynical disillusion. She looks from herself to the reflection of the mother, and then turning sharply with a suppressed exclamation goes over, and shaking the sleeping woman not too gently, says:

'Mother, wake up, I want to speak to you!'

The mother starts with frightened eyes, stares at the other woman as if doubting the evidence of her sight, smiles, then cowed by the unresponsive look in the other face, grows grave again, sits still and stares helplessly at her, finally bursting into tears with a

'Flo, my dear, Flo, is it really you?'

The girl jerks her head impatiently and says drily:

'Yes, that is self-evident. I am going on a long journey. I have something to say to you before I start! Why on earth are you crying?'

There is a note of surprised wonder in her voice mixed with impatience.

The older woman has had time to scan her face and the dormant mother-hood in her is roused by its weary anguish. She is ill, she thinks, in trouble. She rises to her feet; it is characteristic of the habits of her life, with its studied regard for the observance of small proprieties, and distrust of servants as a class, that she goes over and closes the room door carefully.

This hollow-eyed, sullen women is so unlike the fresh girl who left her five years ago that she feels afraid. With the quiet selfishness that has character-ised her life she has accepted the excuses her daughter has made to avoid coming home, as she has accepted the presents her son-in-law has sent her from time to time. She has found her a husband well-off in the world's goods, and there her responsibility ended. She approaches her hesitatingly; she feels she ought to kiss her, there is something unusual in such a meeting after so long an absence; it shocks her, it is so unlike the one she has pictured; she has often looked forward to it, often; to seeing Flo's new frocks, to hearing of her town life.

'Won't you take off your things? You will like to go to your room?'

She can hear how her own voice shakes; it is really inconsiderate of Flo to treat her in this strange way.

'We will have some tea,' she adds.

Her colour is coming and going, the lace at her wrist is fluttering. The daughter observes it with a kind of dull satisfaction, she is taking out her hat-pins carefully. She notices a portrait in a velvet case upon the mantelpiece; she walks over and looks at it intently. It is her father, the father who was killed in India in a hill skirmish when she was a little lint-locked maid barely up to his knee. She studies it with new eyes, trying to read what man he was, what soul he had, what part of him is in her, tries to find herself by reading him. Something in his face touches her, strikes some underlying chord in her, and she grinds her teeth at a thought it rouses.

'She must be ill, she must be very ill,' says the mother, watching her, 'to think I daren't offer to kiss my own child!' She checks the tears that keep welling up, feeling that they may offend this woman who is so strangely unlike the girl who left her. The latter has turned from her scrutiny of the likeness and sweeps her with a cold criticising look as she turns towards the door, saying:

'I *should* like some tea. I will go upstairs and wash off the dust.'

Half an hour later the two women sit opposite one another in the pretty room. The younger one is leaning back in her chair watching the mother pour out the tea, following the graceful movements of the white, blue-veined hands amongst the tea things—she lets her wait on her; they have not spoken beyond a commonplace remark about the heat, the dust, the journey.

'How is Philip, is he well?' The mother ventures to ask with a feeling of trepidation, but it seems to her that she ought to ask about him.

'He is quite well, men of his type usually are; I may say he is particularly well just now, he has gone to Paris with a girl from the Alhambra!'

The older woman flushes painfully, and pauses with her cup half way to her lips and lets the tea run over unheeded on to her dainty silk apron.

'You are spilling your tea,' the girl adds with malicious enjoyment.

The woman gasps: 'Flo, but Flo, my dear, it is dreadful! What would your poor father have said! *no wonder* you look ill, dear, how shocking! Shall I— ask the vicar to—to remonstrate with him?'

'My dear mother, what an extraordinary idea! These little trips have been my one solace. I assure you, I have always hailed them as lovely oases in the desert of matrimony, resting-places on the journey. My sole regret was their infrequency. That is very good tea, I suppose it is the cream.'

The older woman puts her cup on the tray and stares at her with frightened eyes and paled cheeks.

'I am afraid I don't understand you, Florence. I am old-fashioned'—with a little air of frigid propriety—'I have always looked upon matrimony as a sacred thing. It is dreadful to hear you speak this way; you should have tried to save Philip—from—from such a shocking sin.'

The girl laughs, and the woman shivers as she hears her. She cries—

'I would never have thought it of Philip. My poor dear, I am afraid you must be very unhappy.

'Very,' with a grim smile, 'but it is over now, I have done with it. I am not going back.'

If a bomb had exploded in the quiet, pretty room the effect could hardly have been more startling than her almost cheerful statement. A big bee buzzes in and bangs against the lace of the older woman's cap and she never heeds it, then she almost screams:

'Florence, Florence, my dear, you can't mean to desert your husband! Oh, think of the disgrace, the scandal, what people will say, the'—with an uncertain quaver—'the sin. You took a solemn vow, you know, and you are going to break it——'

'My dear mother, the ceremony had no meaning for me, I simply did not know what I was signing my name to, or what I was vowing to do. I might as well have signed my name to a document drawn up in Choctaw. I have no remorse, no prick of conscience at the step I am taking; my life must be my own. They say sorrow chastens, I don't believe it; it hardens, embitters; joy is like the sun, it coaxes all that is loveliest and sweetest in human nature. No, I am not going back.'

The older woman cries, wringing her hands helplessly:

'I can't understand it. You must be very miserable to dream of taking such a serious step.'

'As I told you, I am. It is a defect of my temperament. How many women really take the man nearest to them as seriously as I did! I think few. They finesse and flatter and wheedle and coax, but truth there is none. I couldn't do that, you see, and so I went to the wall. I don't blame them; it must be so, as long as marriage is based on such unequal terms, as long as man demands from a wife as a right, what he must sue from a mistress as a favour; until marriage becomes for many women a legal prostitution, a nightly degradation, a hateful yoke under which they age, mere bearers of children conceived in a sense of duty, not love. They bear them, birth them, nurse them, and begin again without choice in the matter, growing old, unlovely, with all joy of living swallowed in a senseless burden of reckless maternity, until their love, granted they started with that, the mystery, the crowning glory of their lives, is turned into a duty they submit to with distaste instead of a favour granted to a husband who must become a new lover to obtain it.'

'But men are different, Florence; you can't refuse a husband, you might cause him to commit sin.'

'Bosh, mother, he is responsible for his own sins, we are not bound to dry-nurse his morality. Man is what we have made him, his very faults are of our making. No wife is bound to set aside the demands of her individual soul for the sake of imbecile obedience. I am going to have some more tea.'

The mother can only whimper:

'It is dreadful! I thought he made you such an excellent husband, his position too is so good, and he is so highly connected.'

'Yes, and it is as well to put the blame in the right quarter. Philip is as God made him, he is an animal with strong passions, and he avails himself of the latitude permitted him by the laws of society. Whatever of blame, whatever of sin, whatever of misery is in the whole matter rests *solely* and *entirely* with you, mother'—the woman sits bolt upright—'and with no one else—that is why I came here—to tell you that—I have promised myself over and over again that I would tell you. It is with you, and you alone the fault lies.'

There is so much of cold dislike in her voice that the other woman recoils and whimpers piteously:

'You must be ill, Florence, to say such wicked things. What have I done? I am sure I devoted myself to you from the time you were little; I refused—dabbing her eyes with her cambric handkerchief—'ever so many good offers. There was young Fortescue in the artillery, such a good-looking man, and such an elegant horseman, he was quite infatuated about me; and Jones, to be sure he was in business, but he was most attentive. Every one said I was a devoted mother; I can't think what you mean, I——'

A smile of cynical amusement checks her.

'Perhaps not. Sit down, and I'll tell you.'

She shakes off the trembling hand, for the mother has risen and is standing next to her, and pushes her into a chair, and paces up and down the room. She is painfully thin, and drags her limbs as she walks.

'I say it is your fault, because you reared me a fool, an idiot, ignorant of everything I ought to have known, everything that concerned me and the life I was bound to lead as a wife; my physical needs, my coming passion, the very meaning of my sex, my wifehood and motherhood to follow. You gave me not one weapon in my hand to defend myself against the possible attacks of man at his worst. You sent me out to fight the biggest battle of a woman's life, the one in which she ought to know every turn of the game, with a white gauze'—she laughs derisively—'of maiden purity as a shield.'

Her eyes blaze, and the woman in the chair watches her as one sees a frog watch a snake when it is put into its case.

'I was fourteen when I gave up the gooseberry-bush theory as the origin of humanity; and I cried myself ill with shame when I learnt what maternity meant, instead of waking with a sense of delicious wonder at the great mystery of it. You gave me to a man, nay more, you told me to obey him, to believe that whatever he said would be right, would be my duty; knowing that the meaning of marriage was a sealed book to me, that I had no real idea of what union with a man meant. You delivered me body and soul into his hands without preparing me in any way for the ordeal I was to go through. You sold me for a home, for clothes, for food; you played upon my ignorance, I won't say innocence, that is different. You told me, you and your sister, and your friend the vicar's wife, that it would be an anxiety off your mind if I were comfortably settled——'

'It is wicked of you to say such dreadful things!' the mother cries, 'and besides'—with a touch of asperity—'you married him willingly, you seemed to like his attentions——'

'How like a woman! What a thorough woman you are, mother! The good old-fashioned kitten with a claw in her paw! Yes, I married him willingly; I was not eighteen, I had known no men; was pleased that you were pleased— and, as you say, I liked his attentions. He had tact enough not to frighten me, and I had not the faintest conception of what marriage with him meant. I had an idea'—with a laugh—'that the words of the minister settled the matter. Do you think that if I had realised how fearfully close the intimacy with him would have been that my whole soul would not have stood up in revolt, the whole woman in me cried out against such a degradation of myself?' Her words tremble with passion, and the woman who bore her feels as if she is being lashed by a whip. 'Would I not have shuddered at the thought of *him* in such a relationship?—and waited, waited until I found the man who would satisfy me, body and soul—to whom I would have gone without any false shame, of whom I would think with gladness as the father of a little child to come, for whom the white fire of love or passion, call it what you will, in my heart would have burned clearly and saved me from the feeling of loathing horror that has made my married life a nightmare to me—ay, made me a murderess in heart over and over again. This is not exaggeration. It has killed the sweetness in me, the pure thoughts of womanhood—has made me hate myself and *hate you*. Cry, mother, if you will; you don't know how much you have to cry for—I have cried myself barren of tears. Cry over the girl you killed'—with a gust of passion—'why didn't you strangle me as a baby? It would have been kinder; my life has been a hell, mother—I felt it vaguely as I stood on the platform waiting, I remember the mad impulse I had to jump down under the engine as it came in, to escape from the dread that was chilling my soul. What have these years been? One long crucifixion, one long submittal to the desires of a man I bound myself to in ignorance of what it meant; every caress'—with a cry—'has only been the first note of that. Look at me'—stretching out her arms—'look at this wreck of my physical self; I wouldn't dare to show you the heart or the soul underneath. He has stood on his rights; but do you think, if I had known, that I would have given such insane obedience, from a mistaken sense of duty, as would lead to this? I have my rights too, and my duty to myself; if I had only recognised them in time.'

'Sob away, mother; I don't even feel for you—I have been burnt too badly to feel sorry for what will only be a tiny scar to you; I have all the long future to face with all the world against me. Nothing will induce me to go back. Better anything than that; food and clothes are poor equivalents for what I have had to suffer—I can get them at a cheaper rate. When he comes to look for me, give him that letter. He will tell you he has only been an uxorious husband, and that you reared me a fool. You can tell him too, if you like, that I loathe him, shiver at the touch of his lips, his breath, his hands; that my whole body revolts at his touch; that when he has turned and gone to sleep, I have watched him with such growing hatred that at times the temptation to kill him has been so strong that I have crept out of bed and walked the cold passage in my bare feet until I was too benumbed to feel anything; that I have counted the hours to his going away, and cried out with delight at the sight of the retreating carriage!'

'You are very hard, Flo; the Lord soften your heart! Perhaps'—with trepidation—'if you had had a child——'

'Of his—that indeed would have been the last straw—no, mother.'

There is such a peculiar expression of satisfaction over something—of some inner understanding, as a man has when he dwells on the successful accomplishment of a secret purpose—that the mother sobs quietly, wringing her hands.

'I did not know, Flo, I acted for the best; you are very hard on me!'

Later, when the bats are flitting across the moon, and the girl is asleep—she has thrown herself half-dressed on the narrow white bed of her girlhood, with her arms folded across her breast and her hands clenched—the mother steals into the room. She has been turning over the contents of an old desk; her marriage certificate, faded letters on foreign paper, and a bit of Flo's hair cut off each birthday, and a sprig of orange-blossom she wore in her hair. She looks faded and grey in the silver light, and she stands and gazes at the haggard face in its weary sleep. The placid current of her life is disturbed, her heart is roused, something of her child's soul-agony has touched the sleeping depths of her nature. She feels as if scales have dropped from her eyes, as if the instincts and conventions of her life are toppling over, as if all the needs of protesting women of whom she has read with a vague displeasure have come home to her. She covers the girl tenderly, kisses her hair, and slips a little roll of notes into the dressing-bag on the table and steals out, with the tears running down her cheeks.

When the girl looks into her room as she steals by, when the morning light is slanting in, she sees her kneeling, her head, with its straggling grey hair, bowed in tired sleep. It touches her. Life is too short, she thinks, to make any one's hours bitter; she goes down and writes a few kind words in pencil and leaves them near her hand, and goes quickly out into the road.

The morning is grey and misty, with faint yellow stains in the east, and the west wind blows with a melancholy sough in it—the first whisper of the fall, the fall that turns the world of nature into a patient suffering from phthisis—delicate season of decadence, when the loveliest scenes have a note of decay in their beauty; when a poisoned arrow pierces the marrow of insect and plant, and the leaves have a hectic flush and fall, fall and shrivel and curl in the night's cool; and the chrysanthemums, the 'good-bye summers' of the Irish peasants, have a sickly tinge in their white. It affects her, and she finds herself saying: 'Wither and die, wither and die, make compost for the loves of the spring, as the old drop out and make place for the new, who forget them, to be in their turn forgotten.' She hurries on, feeling that her autumn has come to her in her spring, and a little later she stands once more on the platform where she stood in the flush of her girlhood, and takes the train in the opposite direction.

REVENGE

Anne Enright

Anne Enright was born in Dublin in 1962, and she lives there still. Writer of seven novels, essays, two books of short stories, collected as *Yesterday's Weather*, her work is widely translated and acclaimed. Her many awards and honours include the Man Booker Prize (2007), the Irish Book of the Year (twice) and the Laureateship for Irish Fiction (2015–2018).

I work for a firm which manufactures rubber gloves. There are many kinds of protective gloves, from the surgical and veterinary (arm-length) to industrial, gardening and domestic. They have in common a niceness. They all imply revulsion. You might not handle a dead mouse without a pair of rubber gloves, someone else might not handle a baby. I need not tell you that shops in Soho sell nuns' outfits made of rubber, that some grown men long for the rubber under-blanket of their infancies, that rubber might save the human race. Rubber is a morally, as well as a sexually, exciting material. It provides us all with an elastic amnesty, to piss the bed, to pick up dead things, to engage in sexual practices, to not touch whomsoever we please.

I work with and sell an everyday material, I answer everyday questions about expansion ratios, tearing, petrifaction. I moved from market research to quality control. I have snapped more elastic in my day etcetera etcetera.

My husband and I are the kind of people who put small ads in the personal columns looking for other couples who may be interested in some discreet fun. This provokes a few everyday questions: How do people do that? What do they say to each other? What do they say to the couples who answer? To which the answers are: Easily. Very little. 'We must see each other again sometime.'

When I was a child it was carpet I loved. I should have made a career in floor-coverings. There was a brown carpet in the dining room with specks of black, that was my parents' pride and joy. 'Watch the carpet!' they would say, and I did. I spent all my time sitting on it, joining up the warm, black dots. Things mean a lot to me.

The stench of molten rubber gives me palpitations. It also gives me eczema and a bad cough. My husband finds the smell anaphrodisiac in the extreme. Not even the products excite him, because after seven years you don't know who you are touching, or not touching, anymore.

My husband is called Malachy and I used to like him a lot. He was unfaithful to me in that casual, 'look, it didn't mean anything' kind of way. I was of course bewildered, because that is how I was brought up. I am supposed to be bewildered. I am supposed to say 'What *is* love anyway? What *is* sex?'

Once the fiction between two people snaps then anything goes, or so they say. But it wasn't my marriage I wanted to save, it was myself. My head, you see, is a balloon on a string, my insides are elastic. I have to keep the tension between what is outside and what is in, if I am not to deflate, or explode.

So it was more than a suburban solution that made me want to be unfaithful *with* my husband, rather than *against* him. It was more than a question of the mortgage. I had my needs too: a need to be held in, to be filled, a need for sensation. I wanted revenge and balance. I wanted an awfulness of my own. Of course it was also suburban. Do you really want to know our sexual grief? How we lose our grip, how we feel obliged to *wear* things, how we are supposed to look as if we mean it.

Malachy and I laugh in bed, that is how we get over the problem of conviction. We laugh at breakfast too, on a good day, and sometimes we laugh again at dinner. Honest enough laughter, I would say, if the two words were in the same language, which I doubt. Here is one of the conversations that led to the ad in the personals:

'I think we're still good in bed.' (LAUGH)
'I think we're great in bed.' (LAUGH)
'I think we should advertise.' (LAUGH)

Here is another:

'You know John Jo at work? Well his wife was thirty-one yesterday. I said. "What did you give her for her birthday then?" He said, "I gave her one for every year. Beats blowing out candles." Do you believe that?' (LAUGH)

You may ask when did the joking stop and the moment of truth arrive? As if you didn't know how lonely living with someone can be.

The actual piece of paper with the print on is of very little importance. John Jo composed the ad for a joke during a coffee-break at work. My husband tried to snatch it away from him. There was a chase.

There was a similar chase a week later when Malachy brought the magazine home to me. I shrieked. I rolled it up and belted him over the head. I ran after him with a cup full of water and drenched his shirt. There was a great feeling of relief, followed by some very honest sex. I said, 'I wonder what the letters will say?' I said, 'What kind of couples *do* that kind of thing? What kind of people *answer* ads like that?' I also said 'God how vile!'

Some of the letters had photos attached. 'This is my wife.' Nothing is incomprehensible, when you know that life is sad. I answered one for a joke. I said to Malachy 'Guess who's coming to dinner?'

I started off with mackerel pâté, mackerel being a scavenger fish, and good for the heart. I followed with veal osso buco, for reasons I need not elaborate, and finished with a spiced fig pudding with rum butter. Both the eggs I cracked had double yolks, which I found poignant.

I hoovered everything in sight of course. Our bedroom is stranger-proof. It is the kind of bedroom you could die in and not worry about the undertakers. The carpet is a little more interesting than beige, the spread is an ochre brown, the pattern on the curtains is expensive and unashamed. One wall is mirrored in a sanitary kind of way; with little handles for the wardrobe doors.

*

'Ding Dong,' said the doorbell. Malachy let them in. I heard the sound of coats being taken and drinks offered. I took off my apron, paused at the mirror and opened the kitchen door.

Her hair was over-worked, I thought – too much perm and too much gel. Her make-up was shiny, her eyes were small. All her intelligence was in her mouth, which gave an ironic twist as she said Hello. It was a large mouth, sexy and selfish. Malachy was holding out a gin and tonic for her in a useless kind of way.

Her husband was concentrating on the ice in his glass. His suit was a green so dark it looked black – very discreet, I thought, and out of our league, with Malachy in his cheap polo and jeans. I didn't want to look at his face, nor he at mine. In the slight crash of our glances I saw that he was worn before his time.

I think he was an alcoholic. He drank his way through the meal and was polite. There was a feeling that he was pulling back from viciousness. Malachy, on the other hand, was over-familiar. He and the wife laughed at bad jokes and their feet were confused under the table. The husband asked me about my job and I told him about the machine I have for testing rubber squares; how it pulls the rubber four different ways at high speed. I made it sound like a joke, or something. He laughed.

I realised in myself a slow, physical excitement, a kind of pornographic panic. It felt like the house was full of balloons pressing gently against the ceiling. I looked at the husband.

'Is this your first time?'

'No,' he said.

'What kind of people *do* this kind of thing?' I asked, because I honestly didn't know.

'Well they usually don't feed us so well, or even at all.' I felt guilty. 'This is much more civilised,' he said. 'A lot of them would be well on before we arrive, I'd say. As a general kind of rule.'

'I'm sorry,' I said, 'I don't really drink.'

'Listen,' he leaned forward. 'I was sitting having a G and T in someone's front room and the wife took Maria upstairs to look at the bloody grouting in the bathroom or something, when this guy comes over to me and I realise about six minutes too late that he plays for bloody Arsenal! If you see what I mean. A very ordinary looking guy.'

'You have to be careful,' he said. 'And his wife was a cracker.'

When I was a child I used to stare at things as though they knew something I did not. I used to put them into my mouth and chew them to find out what it was. I kept three things under my bed at night: a piece of wood, a metal door-handle and a cloth. I sucked them instead of my thumb.

We climbed the stairs after Malachy and the wife, who were laughing. Malachy was away, I couldn't touch him. He had the same look in his eye as when he came home from a hurling match when the right team won.

The husband was talking in a low, constant voice that I couldn't refuse. I remember looking at the carpet, which had once meant so much to me. Everyone seemed to know what they were doing.

I thought that we were all supposed to end up together and perform and watch and all that kind of thing. I was interested in the power it would give me over breakfast, but I wasn't looking forward to the confusion. I find it difficult enough to arrange myself around one set of limbs, which are heavy things. I wouldn't know what to do with three. Maybe we would get over the awkwardness with a laugh or two, but in my heart of hearts I didn't find the idea of being with a naked woman funny. What would we joke about? Would we be expected to do things?

What I really wanted to see was Malachy's infidelity. I wanted his paunch made public, the look on his face, his bottom in the air. *That* would be funny.

I did not expect to be led down the hall and into the spare room. I did not expect to find myself sitting on my own with an alcoholic and handsome stranger who had a vicious look in his eye. I did not expect to feel anything.

*

I wanted him to kiss me. He leant over and tried to take off his shoes. He said, 'God I hate that woman. Did you see her? The way she was laughing and all that bloody lip-gloss. Did you see her? She looks like she's made out of plastic. I can't get a hold of her without slipping around in some body lotion that smells like petrol and dead animals.' He had taken his shoes off and was swinging his legs onto the bed. 'She never changes you know.' He was trying to take his trousers off. 'Oh I know she's sexy. I mean, you saw her. She is sexy. She is sexy. She is sexy. I just prefer if somebody else does it. If you don't mind.' I still wanted him to kiss me. There was the sound of laughter from the other room.

I rolled off the wet patch and lay down on the floor with my cheek on the carpet, which was warm and rough and friendly. I should go into floor-coverings.

I remember when I wet the bed as a child. First it is warm then it gets cold. I would go into my parents' bedroom, with its smell, and start to cry. My mother gets up. She is half-asleep but she's not cross. She is huge. She strips the bed of the wet sheet and takes off the rubber under-blanket which falls with a thick sound to the floor. She puts a layer of newspaper on the mattress and pulls down the other sheet. She tells me to take off my wet pyjamas. I sleep in the raw between the top sheet and the rough blanket and when I turn over, all the warm newspaper under me makes a noise.

DISHONORING THE DEAD

Chiamaka Enyi-Amadi

Chiamaka Enyi-Amadi is a Lagos-born and Dublin-based writer, spoken-word performer and arts facilitator. Her work is published in *Poetry International 25*, *Poetry Ireland Review 129*, *RTÉ Poetry Programme*, the *Irish Times*, and *Writing Home: The 'New Irish' Poets* (Dedalus Press 2019), which she co-edited with Pat Boran.

By this evening my parents' bodies will be in the ground. Settling into the red soil. Embalmed in the elegance of the dead. The negotiation of my price has begun. We have all been here since dawn and my brothers are ready to put my husband in the ground. The sand is damp and the trenches of the freshly dug grave have gained a rich burgundy hue, boasting of how well it can drain the heavy September rains. Anything that is put into this Eastern ground stays here.

Is there any burden it cannot bear?

They say since he did not honor my parents when they were alive, he must find a way to repay the dead. He shared their daughter, now he will share their graves. He should have done the proper thing tradition expects of a man: Ask for my hand, offer a price, and wait for my father to finish chewing his kola-nut, to clear his throat so that his amused chuckle could be let out with earnest clarity.

Papa had lost all his teeth from age and gum disease. So, for most of his last days he'd numb his aching mouth with small gulps of dry gin from the bottle he tucked into the belly of his patterned wrapper. The bottle stayed cool against his abdomen and relieved the burning sensation that radiated from his hip and spread upwards into his greyed chest and arched back. My father was still a very handsome man at seventy-nine. His pupils glistened like the granite porch paving he often sat on to tease my mother when she refused to come out into the fresh morning air. Since losing control of her bowels she'd grown so frail that even the slightest breeze ate into her skin like mites burrowing into plywood. He'd ask the chicken and goats that roamed the small compound pecking at rotten yam peels to assemble into a unit and remove her from the rocking chair by their front window, where she sat tutting and shaking her head at her husband.

He would have stuck out his tongue and called his wife to sit by his side.

"Her mother knows her the best, she will decide her price."

Mama would feign a grumble and chastise my father for straying from tradition. Brideprice is a man's affair. But she was my heart and I was hers. And my father was a man who listened to his heart more than anything else.

Tradition is like bitter-kola. You are taught to bite into the hard coat, let the acrid taste fill up your mouth before you start chewing. Then you swallow with the knowledge that what you have eaten might displease your tongue but will be good for your blood. You do not taste kola and spit it out like a child spits out malaria medicine, or like the elders spit out the moistened chaffs from their chewing stick. It is wasteful and foolish.

My husband has been foolish.

Now that my parents are dead will he crawl into the earth, between their swollen limbs, to disturb their peaceful rest? Will he place the money on their heads and beg for blessings from broken bodies? These are dangerous thoughts.

The living have no use for what the dead have to offer and the dead have no use for what the living claim to offer. There is no use in throwing him in and asking him to sit on their heads and wait, wait for what, for the rot to begin and the stench to drive him out of his remaining senses?

I want to ask him all of this but the negation has begun, and this is a room full of angry men. My brothers, all seven of them, my uncles and my husband, all sat in a half moon, seething, filling the room with the stench of sweating bodies and the heat of untended pride. My children and I are seated in the corner of the room, closest to the front door. Our slippers are arranged on the foot mat. I can see out into the verandah through the netted cover of the front windows. The jacaranda trees have littered the yard with their purple flowers. I want to draw the imported royal blue velvet drapes hanging from silver railings, half-separating me from the outside world. All this beauty and elegance. All mine. He had begged me to make our house a palace fit for a king. Fit for him.

Now each tile is stained with red footsteps the shape of half-moons. My lips are cracked, almost bleeding. I bite down hard. I need to taste blood. Iron.

Strength. Memory. To remember that what is mine is also his, including this shame swallowing us. All ours.

He will settle my brothers first, there is no question of it.

"A man cannot come into our house and marry our only sister. Mba!"

"No. It can not be, not without proving that he can care for her the same way her family have or even better than we can…"

"And how long has he kept her in his house without paying his dues?"

Twenty-four years living with the man I love. Both of us learning each other's ordinary and peculiar ways and loving our children.

There is no betrayal quite like the accusation of invalidation. I feel it in my chest, the ugly sound unsettling my organs, rising up my throat like acid reflux, pushing my tongue aside, reaching for my lips to pull them apart, threatening to spill all over the room and soil the polished surface. Ruin his palace.

Twenty-four years of living with the man that I know inside out like any of our three children. I know him more than he knows himself, watching as he broke his promises; broke my will so that I would give him my money, and give him more children, before they cut me open to untangle our child from the noose he'd made out of the soft thing that joined him to my body. He made a tomb out of me.

Love died inside my body.

I begged my husband to ask the doctors to tie up all my tubes and burn all the ends to punish them for strangling my baby, to stitch me up tight so that I'd never come undone. I begged. I cried out. Cut. Tie. Cauterize. Wanting never to be opened again. He had kissed me and I tasted his tears and convinced myself that he loved me; that three precious children were enough for us.

When the anesthesia wore off, I woke to find my husband clutching pamphlets that showed the image of a couple smiling and half embracing a pregnant woman standing between them and I read, with aching eyes, the words *surrogacy made easy* on the front page. I know I have chosen my own misery to lie in bed with every day of my life, until I join my parents.

Igbo people say that children are their father's wealth, but a man who marries a kind and generous woman is the richest of them all. I married a man who built a thousand castles in his dreams but would rather sleep than work. He knew shortened paths to the field where he could scatter his desires like seeds on fertile soil.

This is how it feels to love someone who doesn't know what reciprocal love is. This is how it feels to love someone who is still not certain of who he is. This is how it feels to make yourself the means to a man's ends.

I feel myself coming undone. Is this what love does to the women who choose to believe in it? Does love oppress those who try to uphold its virtues? I suddenly feel my temples tightening into a migraine, my nerves recoiling against the sound that had filled the room, the incessant inquires hitting my head like small pestles grinding against the inside of my skull in this room full of men taking up all the space I need to mourn my parents, the space I need to love my children.

I get up to go check on the caterers preparing heaps of party jollof, rivers of soups full of an assortment of meat and seafood, in enormous cauldrons over open fire pits in the backyard. If there is one thing I am thankful for today it is duty, I know my role in all of this outdoor madness. I must take care of my guests. I am grateful for that. I know my parents would be happy if they could see that the people who had come to remember them, to show solidarity and respect, are looked after: well-fed, their spirits made merry with the overflow of palm wine, gin, whiskey, beer—no expense was spared in bidding my parents farewell. I'd spend it all for the people who'd raised me, loved me, spoiled me; put a good head on my shoulders; a generous spirit in my heart and a quick-fire tongue in my mouth, now gone. They chose to depart this world hand-in-hand and I choose to celebrate that. What else can I do? I cannot bring them back, even if I wanted to

the living have no use for what the dead have to offer
and the dead have no use of what the living claim to offer.

I see him from my peripheral vision. I could see him thinking about walking towards me, see him making the decision to do so, and now he is almost upon me and I feel ambushed. He has chosen to act as if he has forgotten what today is, like the rest of them, sitting in my house like Arthurian knights, discussing my family, portioning out love, weighing up ownership, identity, legitimacy. Which of my children look like my husband? Which ones look the most like my father? How much are they worth? Calculating rates, adding interest, dividing the profit between themselves. Deciding what my life and all the fruits of my labor are worth. Today of all days. But this is not the time or place for unraveling. I say to my husband

"There are things that need to be done."

"Your brothers are practically asking for my head." There is both panic and amusement hanging onto the end of his retort. As though he found the whole event to be one big joke, a tragic play to get him all fired up, to prick his reaction, excite his passions. All of this loss, shame, anger orchestrated for his delight.

"They can sit here till night falls if they like, shouting all kinds of nonsense, bargaining for a pound of your flesh, I don't care. It's up to them. It's up to you."

"All the things they are saying… I can't imagine what would call for all this animosity. Are we not all family?" His lips held a slight tremble, his almond eyes crinkled at the corners, "Is this what they have been thinking in their minds all these years? I can't understand how your brothers, your uncles, can be so backward—"

"Look I'm not having this conversation with you right now. I will say it once and only once. Today is not for them. Today is not for you" shaking my head, I feel the slight ease of tension slither down my neck. I gather all the air I can fit into my chest, straighten my back, tilt my head upward. I can look him in the eye now. He is biting the left side of his mouth, chewing it as though this whole thing is getting a bit too much for him. I forget sometimes that he is not even as old as the youngest of my brothers.

"I just thought you might want to go in and calm them down, I—"

"Me, do what? Go in and sit there like a zombie and calm them down. No oh. I have things to do ngwanu be going"

"Honey please it's really for your own good!"

"My own good?" I laugh. I can see his eyes widen, the slow blink, like a child seeking to be cajoled. He realises now he's had his fun. And that's it. No more. I will not humor him.

"Okay, maybe not, but I just don't have a lot more to say to your brothers"

"I'm glad. At least you have got it all off your chest finally isn't it? Now you're happy"

"Please, you know that's not it"

"Biko, please, no more for today. Let me just do what needs to be done"

"Okay just tell me what to do, I'll tell everyone to prepare to leave for the cemetery. Is everything ready out here?" he suggests.

I tell him I need to go through the menu once more with the caterers then I walk over to the event staff working at the back of the house.

I arrange for the handymen to begin their set-up. There are marquees, portaloos, speakers, tables, chairs, an altar, a stage to be assembled; two large canopies for the front and back yard and an additional four would be erected all the way down the street, so that all our neighbours, and even passersby that are drawn in by the festivities, would not be turned away. Everyone who turned up would feel loved and know that my parents were people deserving of a burial fit for royalty, in the village where they spent their whole life and raised their children.

My parents would rest well.

When I am done with the preparations, I go back into the house to check on the children and get them ready to leave for the burial. I want to gather them in my arms and tell them they are allowed to cry out, to make a fuss over everything. I want to nudge the stoicism out of them. I want to say *you are not visitors, this is your house too*. To ask Chioma "why are you sitting so still, are you now a statue?" and my Obinna, "big boy like you after all that Maltina you drank, you've not gone to toilet, aren't you pressed?" And little Ama, the most beautiful ornament of all, perched on the edge of the ottoman in the corner of the sitting room, furthest away from me… her face held in a stern gaze unlike any eight year old's I've ever seen…. I want to stroke their heads and tell them that their father will soon return to them from out of the lions' den. To promise them that soon we will be left alone, and it'll be just the five of us sitting at the dinner table. I would prepare my Sunday special; yam pottage and catfish pepper soup garnished with uhuru spices. And serve a generous helping the way my mother used to when she wanted to acquire my father's undivided attention, when she wanted no argument from the man. She'd use food as a weapon to disarm him, to seal his mouth. Then she'd offer a bowl of palm wine to quench the fire in his belly and spread some moss in his mind. Once she'd satisfied his appetite he had no means, no energy, no desire to fight her. But

tonight there would be no use for weapons.
Tonight there would be no war.
Only the aroma of my mother's uhuru spices
filling the house, lingering in the air, warming
our breaths, heralding another red dawn.

77 POP FACTS YOU DIDN'T KNOW ABOUT GIL COURTNEY

Wendy Erskine

> **Wendy Erskine** is a full-time secondary school teacher in Belfast. Her collection *Sweet Home* was published by the Stinging Fly Press in 2018 and Picador in 2019. It was longlisted for the Gordon Burn Prize and shortlisted for the Republic of Consciousness Prize and the Edge Hill Prize.

1. Gillespie Stanley John Courtney was born in Belfast on July 26th 1950. Also born on July 26th were Aldous Huxley, Jason Robards and Kevin Spacey.

2. Gil Courtney's mother, Elsie, registered him with her maiden name—Gillespie—as his Christian name. She initially said that this was done in error but in later years admitted that it was intentional.

3. Gil Courtney grew up at 166 Tildarg Street, Cregagh, Belfast. Some of the lyrics to the song 'Partial Aperture' on the first The Palomar album, *Golden Dusk*, are often said to have been inspired by the view from the back bedroom of this house. Visible beyond the rooftops are the Castlereagh Hills.

4. Palomar were known as The Palomar until 1975. Thereafter, they were known as Palomar.

5. The phrase 'taking drugs to make music to take drugs to', later used as the title of a Spacemen 3 album, was reputedly first coined by Gil Courtney during the recording of *Golden Dusk*.

6. The front room of the house at 166 Tildarg Street had a silver disc above the mantelpiece. (Although *Golden Dusk* only reached 21 in the UK charts, European sales ensured its silver status.) Gil recalled on a trip home one

time taking it off the wall and playing it. 'And what do you think it was,' he said when interviewed in 1972, 'but an Alma Cogan record dipped in silver paint. The paint just flaked off on my hands.'

7. It is likely that Gil Courtney's father was not Alec Courtney, husband of Elsie, and clerk at James Mackie and Sons, Belfast. Elsie was five months pregnant when they married. She was of the opinion that the father was most probably a merchant seaman, possibly Spanish, whom she met in Dubarry's Bar (now McHughs).

8. 166 Tildarg Street was on the market in 2012. The estate agent's description pointed out that it was in need of some modernisation. Photos showed empty rooms, bare walls and floorboards. Elsie Courtney's furniture and carpets had been removed to a skip some weeks earlier.

9. Gil Courtney's first instrument was the xylophone. At primary school a new teacher who introduced a musical half-hour on a Friday afternoon was surprised to see one of her pupils playing two xylophones at once. The young Gil Courtney said he was able to remember the tune of something he'd heard on the radio.

10. Miss Kathleen Hughes, a P7 teacher and church organist, gave Gil Courtney piano lessons in the school assembly hall. She later said that she had never encountered a child with such exceptional ability and whose sight-reading was so extraordinary. When Kathleen Hughes was unable to attend a funeral service owing to illness the eleven-year-old Gil took her place at the organ.

11. Gil Courtney's girlfriend, Simone Lindstrom, went on to have brief relationships with Neil Young and Terry Melcher, son of Doris Day. Dicky Griffin of Palomar described Simone as a 'high-maintenance kind of chick', while Elsie Courtney said she was 'Simone with the little turnip tits in the polo necks you could spit through.'

12. When Gil Courtney was fifteen he began playing with many of the showbands popular in Northern Ireland at the time. He played in groups including The Buccaneers, The Dakotas, The College Boys and The Emperors. Two or three gigs a week would have been common. Ronnie O'Hanlon, drummer in The Dakotas, recalled how they would travel across the province in the back of a van with the equipment: 'A lot of the roads were bad and you were thrown all over the place. A lot of these places were

in the middle of nowhere. The driver'd be thinking where in the name of God are we going down this dirt track and then all of a sudden, out of the dark there would be a dancehall, all lit up.'

13. Gil Courtney's music lessons with Miss Hughes always began with the removal of the boxes of sports equipment stacked on top of the piano.

14. The fourth song from Gil Courtney's solo album, *Volonte Blue*, was played by Stuart Maconie on his programme *The Freak Zone* on 6 Music on Sunday 16th October 2011.

15. In the Oh Yeah Music Centre in Belfast there is a small exhibition of Northern Irish pop memorabilia. There is a photograph of Gil Courtney and other members of The Palomar taken outside Gideon Hall's flat in London. They are dressed in the fashions of the time. To the left there is a photo of David McWilliams and to the right a snap of 60s Belfast psychedelic-blues group Eire Apparent.

16. Gil Courtney was educated at Harding Memorial Primary School and Park Parade Secondary School.

17. Gil Courtney used the Hohner Cembalet, the Hammond organ and the Wurlitzer electric piano.

18. Before its eventual closure in 1969, Gil Courtney and other members of both The Dakotas and The Emperors played Hamburg's Star Club. They were part of a group of musicians who briefly went to Germany to 'try their luck'; it was the first time that most of them had been outside Northern Ireland. Gil sent numerous postcards home and Elsie Courtney said that from the spelling and the grammar it was obvious this was a young man who had not spent long enough in school.

19. In *Uncut* magazine's April 2016 feature, 'The Quest for Rock's Great Lost Albums on Vinyl', Gil Courtney's album *Volonte Blue* was listed at number 13. At number 12 was Linda Perhacs' *Parallelograms*.

20. Alec Courtney, Elsie's husband, always used the name Stanley when referring to Gil.

21. In 1968 Gil Courtney moved to London to work as a session musician, supplementing his wages by joining the house bands at the Dorchester

and Park Lane Hotels. 'I never regretted any of my time spent playing in the *palais* bands,' Gil was quoted as having said. 'Many of those guys could really play and I learnt a lot.' During the time that Gil played at the Dorchester, Elsie Courtney and her sister Nan came to London. They stayed in a Dorchester suite, which Gil's connection in reception had managed to secure them *gratis*. 'It was all fine,' Elsie remembered, 'just as long as we always went in the back entrance and up the service stairs and didn't come down for the breakfast.' The sisters danced in the grand ballroom when Gil was playing. 'It was lovely,' Elsie said. 'All the crystal lights. There was a conductor. You should've seen the way the women were dressed. They were beautiful.'

22. The first twenty seconds of the song 'Under the Mountain' from *Golden Dusk* was used as the title music for an Argentinian football programme for five years in the 1980s. Gil Courtney had a co-writing credit on this and therefore received royalties, along with those for his contribution to several other songs on the record.

23. For a period of time 166 Tildarg Street was a popular destination for those bands who were playing Belfast and did not want to stay in a hotel. Elsie Courtney had fond memories of some of the people who stayed with her. Her favourite was Steve who could still sing the songs from *Oliver!*, the West End show in which he performed as a child. She said that he gave a rendition of 'Consider Yourself' in the kitchen, singing the final chorus up on the table.

24. Steve Marriott's band, The Small Faces, borrowed Gil Courtney's electric piano when they played the Floral Hall in Belfast. Ian McLagan's piano was not playing properly. The Floral Hall, an art deco ballroom over-looking Belfast, is now in disrepair and is used to store animal feed for the nearby zoo.

25. Gil Courtney was 6 feet 1 inch tall. His shoe size was 10.

26. Gideon Hall from Palomar published his autobiography in 2005. It was translated into nine languages.

27. Gil Courtney's work as a session musician brought him into contact with a drummer Kevin Heyward who had recently joined a band with two guitarists he had met through a mutual friend. Kevin Heyward invited Gil Courtney along to rehearse. This was the birth of The Palomar.

28. Gil Courtney rarely wore any colour other than black.

29. Alec Courtney did not approve of rock and roll, Gibs career or the guests who sometimes arrived at Tildarg Street. Elsie remembered him as an 'old stick in the mud who was happier down at the bible study'.

30. Gideon Hall was rather scathing about Elsie Courtney whom Gil would occasionally bring over for shows in London and Glasgow. 'God spare us all from the living embodiment of the oral tradition,' he was quoted as saying. 'What are the words guaranteed to strike most dread in me? *The motherfucking mother's here.*'

31. During breaks in session work, Gil Courtney would read paperbacks, usually either Agatha Christie or American sci-fi stories. 'Simone tried to get me into poetry, Ginsberg and so on, but I never really dug it.'

32. In his autobiography, Gideon Hall said of Courtney, 'I daresay it sounds harsh, perhaps it is, but really, was he anything more than a footnote? If even that? The myth of the beautiful loser. It's tired. It's tiresome.'

33. Gil Courtney went on a trip to Marrakech with a group of friends including Brian Jones of The Rolling Stones, shortly before the latter's death. Popular amongst the crowd was the local *kif*. Elsie couldn't remember whether Brian Jones had ever come to Tildarg Street, 'All these fellas, the girls might have had them on their walls but if they seen what I seen in the morning, dirty pants and them stinking of sweat and what have you, they might have thought different.'

34. *Golden Dusk* was described optimistically and ultimately accurately by Charles Shaar Murray as a 'prelude to greatness.' It received generally positive reviews in *Melody Maker* and *New Musical Express*, with critics particularly praising the Gideon Hall / Dicky Griffin-penned 'Goldline' and 'Damascus'. The songs on which Gil Courtney had co-writing credits were noted for their 'somewhat baroque excess.'

35. 'Goldline' was released as a single. It got to number 34 in the British charts but fared rather better in France. The band had a promo slot on a French television programme in 1972, the first one minute and twenty-three seconds of which can be viewed on YouTube, Gil Courtney for most of this time is just out of shot.

36. When Gideon Hall's autobiography was published it was selected by Eason's for inclusion on their roster for priority in-store promotion. Elsie Courtney was reprimanded by a member of Eason's staff in Donegall Place for moving some of the Gideon Hall books off the prominent display.

37. In January 1973 there was a drugs bust at Gil Courtney's Pimlico flat where a party was in progress. The raid allegedly discovered grass, cannabis resin and Mandrax tablets. Owing to Gil Courtney's apparent medical problems, a psychiatrist was able to make the case that he should receive a suspended sentence. It meant, however, that Courtney was unable to obtain a visa to tour overseas.

38. In a Q&A in *Pop Starz* magazine in the same year Gil Courtney answered the following: Favourite food? Ice cream and jelly. Favourite drink: tea. Favourite colour: yellow. Favourite way to spend a day: going for a walk in the park with friends. Favourite type of girl: nice.

39. In a 1993 interview, Van Morrison was asked if he could remember Gil Courtney. He said no.

40. Gil Courtney had a phobia of flying which he tried to alleviate through alcohol and drug use. Even a short flight would induce a panic attack. On a flight to France in 1972 he was unconscious when the group landed at Charles de Gaulle airport. He made the return journey by land and sea, arriving in London approximately two weeks later. Elsie Courtney said that she could never understand Gil's fear of airplanes. 'Well I don't know,' she said. 'What in the name of God's the problem? How could you not like it? I love getting on a plane. I love the drinks and the food in the little compartments and I love the air-hostesses and I love the duty-free.'

41. Gil Courtney failed to turn up for two concerts, one at Glasgow Barrowlands and the other at Manchester Free Trade Hall. The Palomar's manager at the time, Lenny Enlander, was dispatched to the Pimlico flat to tell Gil that he no longer had a place in the group. Enlander said later that 'It was hard to tell if Gil was actually there. Some guy I'd never seen before opened the door. It was like a *tabagie*. Smoke-filled, with blackout curtains on every window. I didn't want to tell him with other people there but Gil didn't want to leave and they didn't want to leave. I just said that's it, Gil, You can't go on. He didn't seem all that bothered. But then I didn't know if he entirely understood what I was saying, if you know

what I'm saying.' Lenny Enlander did not stay in music management. He ended up running a successful imports-exports business off the Great Eastern Road.

42. The web-based T-shirt business Avalanche Tees printed a limited run of T-shirts bearing the front cover of *Volonte Blue* after the feature in *Uncut*. These were available on Amazon and eBay later, at a reduced price. One of the T-shirts was sent to Texas.

43. Studio musicians who worked on *Volonte Blue* were unanimous in declaring the process tortuous. Courtney expected them to work up to twenty hours a day yet there were also periods when he would disappear for hours at a time and they would be left to their own devices. 'After the, what, fiftieth take, I was finished,' bass player Mac McLean said. 'I have worked with some picky bastards but the man was just insane. Charming for sure, but insane, "Play this like a peach being placed on a terracotta tile. In Marrakech." You know? Impossible.'

44. Gil Courtney and Simone Lindstrom were described in one magazine at the time as 'the most photogenic couple in London.' The magazine featured a photo of the pair in a sitting room with an ornately corniced high ceiling; Simone was in a filmy white dress and reclining on a sofa smoking a cigarette while Gil was crouched in front of her in a black suit. The picture could be regarded as a chilly version of Dylan's *Bringing It All Back Home* cover. The accompanying article profiled the couple in some detail and stated that Gil Courtney's imminent solo album was eagerly awaited.

45. The artwork for *Volonte Blue* features a striking image of an animal (non-specific) lying dead in the middle of a blue desert. Responsible for the cover was Peter Christopherson of the design group Hipgnosis and later of the band Throbbing Gristle.

46. The song 'Tint', the lead track on Side 2 of *Volonte Blue* was said by Gil to have been inspired by cellophane sweet wrappers.

47. When Alec Courtney died of a heart attack in 1975, Gil Courtney was unable to return home for the funeral.

48. The reception *Volonte Blue* received was lukewarm. Some critics praised the '*naif* charm' of some of its lyrics and others its 'loosening of formal

structures' but for many listeners it was characterised by incoherence and indulgence. Gil's health-related issues meant that the tour to promote the album had to be postponed, and then eventually cancelled.

49. The Palomar's second album, CCS, regularly makes it on to lists of the top 50 albums ever recorded. Gil Courtney, interviewed in *Melody Maker* in 1975, was asked if he had listened to CCS. After a pause he said, 'Yes, I have.' And then he was asked if he thought it was as good as everyone seemed to think it was. Gil took a long drag on his cigarette. And then he slowly exhaled. 'Yes,' he said. 'It's that good. What else can I say?'

50. In 1978 Gil Courtney played two shows with The Only Ones.

51. Gil Courtney returned to Belfast in 1980. It was no longer viable for him to remain in London. He travelled to Stranraer by train and got the ferry to Larne. Elsie Courtney met him at the station at York Road and was alarmed for several reasons. 'Well, first thing,' she said, 'he had no suitcase with him or anything like that, just a plastic bag with a few things in it.' She was also shocked by his skeletal appearance because at that point in his life he was eight and a half stone.

52. A three-second sample from 'Choler', the third song on Side 1 of *Volonte Blue* was used as a loop by the Dutch DJ Lars van Tellingen in 2001.

53. When Gil was a child, he and Elsie regularly used to visit the waterworks in North Belfast and feed the swans.

54. Gil Courtney had various food obsessions. Elsie Courtney stated that when he returned to Belfast he only wanted to eat food that was white. After a diet for some months of only potatoes, pasta and rice he then decided he only wanted to eat food that wasn't white.

55. In 1989 a student film society at the University of Leeds was making a vox-pop programme to be shown on student network television. The production team stopped random people in the street to ask them what music was important to them and why. The fifth person they filmed on a morning in April was a man, mid-thirties, balding, in a grey jacket. 'The music that means most to me,' he said, 'well, right then, the music that means most to me is without a doubt the music of Gil Courtney who played with The Palomar. His music is for me just, just transporting.' He paused but the camera was still pointed at him so he continued, 'It just,

what it does is, it just—penetrates to the heart of what it means to be lonely, or in love or to feel a failure and so, and so, at times I've found great comfort in his music, well, *Volonte Blue* is what I'm talking about really, not so much any of the other stuff he was involved with at all really, but other times you know I've found it exhilarating and a total affirmation of what it is to be alive. And I am not really overstating that, I do feel that. There's warmth there and there's strangeness there.' He paused again. 'That enough?' The man, embarrassed, laughed, blinked his eyes and put down his head. 'Right then, I think that probably is enough.'

56. For Christmas each year Elsie bought Gil a black merino wool crew-neck sweater.

57. When living again in Tildarg Street, Gil Courtney had a gramophone player and a few records that he played on very low volume. Elsie Courtney said that when you went into the room you wouldn't even have known anything was playing, if you hadn't seen the record rotating.

58. Elsie said that Gil never watched the television. He would only listen to the radio.

59. Gil Courtney used a EMS Putney VCS 3, generally regarded as the first portable analogue synthesiser.

60. A group of teenage girls were interviewed in 1971 for a German magazine's piece on the London music scene. Viv Vallely, 17, said, 'Of all the guys in all the bands the one I like the most is Gil Courtney from The Palomar. He's not like the singer or anything, he just plays the piano thing, but he's so handsome. And I love the way he speaks cos it's Irish and my granny is Irish. He spoke to me and my friends once when we was waiting outside.'

61. For fifty years the 'house next door', 168 Tildarg Street, was occupied by Arthur McCourt, who was quoted as saying, 'There is something to be said, I really do believe, for being ordinary and having no great talent at anything. I would really wonder if it would have been better for that fella to have gone into a job just like his father, gone to work at Mackie's or wherever, got married, had a couple of kids than go like a firework then nothing. In fact worse than nothing cos I saw the state of him. And for what? What's he got to show, some tunes nobody listens to?'

62. Late one evening in November 1990, as Gil was making his way to the Co-op on the Cregagh Road for cigarettes, he was the victim of robbery and assault. His wallet was stolen and he sustained a broken jaw and a four-inch cut to the side of his head.

63. From 1981 to 1996 Gil Courtney had a repeat prescription for opiate analgesics. Elsie Courtney, who was a patient at another GP practice, supplemented this with a supply of Tramadol, obtained despite her own very good health.

64. Gil Courtney was an aficionado of a magazine entitled *Seven Wonders of the Ancient World* that came out in 1994. Each monthly issue included a scale model of a particular construction. Issues one and two were The Great Pyramid of Giza and the Temple of Artemis at Ephesus. By issue three, however, few newsagents stocked the title, and Elsie Courtney visited numerous shops around Belfast to find that month's issue. The Lighthouse of Alexandria, issue 4, was found in the newsagent in Queen's Arcade, minus the model component.

65. Old bandmate Gideon Hall appeared on the *Sunday Times* Rich List in 2010, but did not feature in subsequent years owing to poor property-investments.

66. Neighbour Arthur McCourt said that when Gil Courtney died all the life went out of Elsie. 'That was it for her. She'd lived for the fella. There wasn't a lot of point for her after that.'

67. Gil Courtney never learned to drive.

68. The vox-pop filmed by the students from Leeds University, where a passer-by talked about Gil Courtney, did not make it to the final programme because a passing bus rendered the sound too poor in quality.

69. In the later years of his life, Gil Courtney would get up at dawn and walk to the centre of the town. When the buses bringing in students, schoolchildren and workers arrived at City Hall he would walk back home again.

70. The instruments on *Volonte Blue* were the following: harmonica, bass, violin, oboe, guitar, drums, organ, keyboards, synthesiser and mandolin.

71. In Gil Courtney's room he always wanted a bare light bulb. 'I would say to him there's nice lampshades in the town,' Elsie said, 'but he said no, he liked staring up at the filament. He liked the way it glowed.' She added, 'I'd rather have the place half decent but Gil was Gil.'

72. The first record Gil Courtney ever bought was 'Battle of New Orleans' by Lonnie Donegan.

73. When Gil Courtney received his diagnosis he opted not to receive any treatment, since chemotherapy would prolong life by only a few months. In the final days when Elsie could no longer look after him, he was moved to the hospice on the Somerton Road. On his windowsill at the place there was an amaryllis, just coming into bloom, Elsie remembered.

74. A journalist who interviewed The Palomar just after the release of *Golden Dusk* said, 'Tensions were pretty palpable. Gil was funny and intense and very likeable, but he was unpredictable and in some ways utterly clueless. They—Gideon and Dicky—they were very assured, public school background, with all that entails. Kevin was just the drummer. Gil was hardly the boy from the back streets but he was a destabilising element that they wanted to jettison. And Gil made it easy for them with the way he behaved. Gideon and Dicky, they might have the counter-cultural credentials, but on another day, with another roll of the dice, they could well have ended up in charge of ICI or BP. They were those sorts of people. The juggernaut that Palomar became would tend to bear that out.'

75. Gil Courtney's funeral took place in the Chapel of Rest on the Ravenhill Road. It was attended by only a handful of people, including a former member of The Dakotas and one of The Emperors. Elsie Courtney, in the belief that there would be a record player, had brought a battered and scratched copy of *Volonte Blue* but there was only a CD player available. Ronnie O'Hanlon had a couple of compilation CDs in his car, one of which was *Feelin' Good Vol. 2*, free with the *Daily Mail*. A decision on a track was quickly made. As they filed out of the chapel, 'Everybody's Talkin'' by Harry Nilsson was played, the music from *Midnight Cowboy*.

76. Gillespie Stanley John Courtney died in Belfast on February 2nd 2001. Fred Perry, Gene Kelly and Bertrand Russell also died on February 2nd.

77. Gil Courtney's favourite cigarettes were Chesterfields.

SOJOURN

Elaine Feeney

Elaine Feeney is a writer from Galway who teaches at the National University of Ireland, Galway. Feeney has written four collections of poetry, including *The Radio was Gospel* (2013) and *Rise* (2017), and a drama piece, WRoNGHEADED. Her debut novel *As You Were*, published in 2020 by Vintage, was chosen by the *Observer* as one of its Best Debut Novels for 2020.

I'm familiar with the sea. Throughout my girl summers I'd walk into her wet coughs, up to my knees, shiver, the cold water shocking my thighs, shiver, salting my darkened navel and over my nipples until it pooled in front of my sternum, shiver, shoulders dry, like a dipped portrait one now sees in a gallery, top of the head obscured with a cover of sorts, a masking tape or oily ebony paint that has been applied to obscure something, breasts or sternum, clavicle perhaps? Something bony and sharp.

Artists are inclined to obscure human portraits and it must be dependent on their mood or the mood of the weather, for the latter does furiously interact with one's spirits. But we can never quite get to root intentions of the artist, for I notice artists with brushes don't answer questions on motivation in the same way I must, in the way I constantly defend my work, especially to myself.

I had often entered the dank sea off the coast of England since my moving there, but lately, since the birthing of the two tiny humans, the sea was inducing a most unsettling sickness, which in turn unsettled me, the constant up and down of it, the back and forth, and moreover the thought of vomiting up in public without due warning, which would absolutely mortify me. The sea had begun to feel much like the mess under the stairs or the cramped scarlet bus I rode, though I ride it far less so now, as cadging around the two children is awfully bothersome. And the sea was inducing a movement that made no progress, much like the cooking a woman must do when she doesn't choose to.

And to that end, the motivation of artists who obscure a portion of their canvas must be surmised. I imagine they dip the canvas into paint to upset their subject long after they have finished it; perhaps the portrait preys on their mind, like humans do, all the insecurities of portraying someone other than oneself. I remain in constant obsession about this level of obscuration that comes from one's art, one's mistakes.

It was autumn, and decided that Husband and I would holiday on the West coast of Ireland for a brief sojourn and to visit a small island off the town of Cleggan, and the park where Yeats has a tree with names etched into it, of writers and dreamers. We were to be the guests of the poet, Richard. Husband said that I'd decided it, to get away from the squalling babies. I seem to remember it differently. But this is the way of us. Whatever the rationale, the trip was beginning to cause me much anxiety, after all that had been and gone, for now we had different abodes, Husband and I, and the unsettling came at me as a pulsing, not as sounds, but the accumulation of tiny vibrations, like the children's early vowels or cutting a beef tomato and the knife pulsing off the wooden plinth. I fear the power of knives, so I threw away the soft red tomato slice in the trash and left the knife down. Out of reach of the children.

Also, I do not like packing, especially for this particular trip, where I wasn't entirely sure in what capacity I was joining Husband, or even Richard, of whom we would be guests, given my letters with him. Perhaps it was indeed that Husband would accompany me in some guesthouse, but even this detail was uncertain. I berated myself, compared myself with my mother, who would have asked such questions, been quite certain of her rank and the order of things, before her departure.

I knew the island, Inisbofin, was sea-locked, without a bridge of any kind, and that set me to fretting about the water and if I would ever rediscover my sea legs. I found this alarming, another thing to add to an over-cluttered *to do list*, as though packing my suitcases and dressing myself accordingly weren't enough of an ordeal, now one must go and actually find something that isn't in the least tangible, *sea legs*. I grew increasingly concerned about the boat, a hooker named the Ave Maria, and so that by the time we arrived in Cleggan, I had indeed forgotten my physical self entirely.

Husband chatted about class on the trip, himself, Richard, the islanders; everywhere we went were long and rude conversations about the idiocy of people, ordinary people, women, writers. I always find the English, or the Anglo-Irish | English so obsessed about class and the mores of people. This must come from shallowness about oneself, for I am quite sure that Husband is mostly concerned about the ignorance of his broad tongue. Yet, despite the conversations, I don't know how the native Irish class determine themselves from the Anglo-Irish class, but I can easily spot the difference. Clothes on first encounter, or shoulders, and of course the broadened beautiful vowels.

Richard didn't have the appeal of an Irish voice that I liked, the timbre of which could excite me. His was rather slim and nasally.

After some time at Cleggan, awaiting Richard and the hooker to moor at Nimmo's Pier and take us off to Bofin, Husband, tiring of waiting and seeming unimportant in reflection of the vastness of the Atlantic Ocean, suggested we go get a drink in a public house with the locals, because this was an Irish custom before boarding a boat, and he was ever so polite with customs that were manly and existed in a bar. Also, they'd asked for his signature in their guestbook and I thought it might lift his spirits were he to leave his mark somewhere.

The pub was pleasant, if a little dark, and immediately upon stooping under the door, Husband went and signed their book, like one does in a boarding house, and I noted, to my upset, that he didn't use our address, the one we share with our children, and I was conflicted. I wanted to both fuck him and kill him that very moment, but this was our way, and for now, I thought rather haughtily, he could stay in Halifax and let Halifax mind him, for he needed so much minding, giving so much away to people we had never met, who would pore over his signature in the weeks to come and ask all sorts of questions. Of course, this village seemed far too real for the wants and whims of poets; perhaps they would think we had a holiday home and a fixed abode, and this settled me somewhat.

The strangers in the bar didn't seem happy with our being there, darting glances and quizzical wiry faces, and who could blame them? They dragged their tulip glasses full of black porter into themselves, as though they were cradling a baby, and guffawed at Husband, not that he'd care, for he was louder than anyone in the world when he wanted to be, and then he could be completely silent, and that presence was all-encompassing, like the shadows of rooks; it would come on him without any warning. He would go deadly quiet and contorted in his physical body, put his head down and stoop into his coat collars, and then, after some hiatus, rise out of it like a wise tortoise and talk and talk and talk, usually about other people, the way of them and less about their work, which infuriated me. But sometimes it was enjoyable, particularly if I was feeling low, or envious.

I said so much to him in the bar as I drank the warmest glass of Guinness, the black eel making his warm way up through the yellow froth. I found it hard to understand how a nation had built so much myth on this drink that tasted oddly like my own blood. Husband hardly looked up from his pint, for I was not in the least agreeable, all tense and fluttery, and though I nudged him hard so he might look at me in the eye, he only lifted his finger to the barmaid. I knew then it would have been best if I hadn't favourably recommended Richard's poetry, it drove Husband into himself, but the Cleggan Disaster was such a sad affair, and I liked him, Richard, and his poem about the sinking boat, well it blew me away in that way you get blown away when you're not expecting it, your mind is astray about beaches or money or a flower you saw once but never saw again, a deep violet one.

Husband lifted his finger to call the bar for another pint.

After we finished our drinks, we took our tentative leave. Husband ran his hand over the guestbook upon exit, perhaps to take some luck out with him. His face was ruddy now, and he was somewhat more jovial and in better spirits. But I was ever so flat-footed as we walked along down the street to the pier.

Nimmo's Pier was named after an adventure, though I find it difficult to figure out how anyone could decide to start an adventure here. That said, I imagine the situation was one where a boat simply crashed into the coast, for that's about the size of how most adventures begin, with a crash or by an accident. Even explorers just happen upon lands by fate, whichever way one sees it, though they pretend it's all been arranged prior; that's the way of the male, everything is planned, metre, form, rhyme, nothing is a stray word, or action, but of course it is, and we know it and keep it to ourselves, all the magic accidents that were planned as though Husband's work were like that of creating a bridge or laying rail track.

Of course it's not, it's not nearly that important.

The boat arrived with her big buffeting white sails and looked unsteady. The West of Ireland was billowing in a muted buffet of bleak colour, not in a Constable way, but in a different way, like how smoke might leave a gentleman's pipe and fingers yellow, and his eyes and cap grey, a grey tweed herringbone, I imagine, though the style of tweed was of no concern to the locals, who favoured oiled skins and fisherman's hats. I think they must be entirely practical rather than taking flights of fancy like we do. I cannot particularly remember the weather with any sort of decent specifics; it had that awfully grey hue, suffice to say, the mock-up of the day was a grey that matched the rock and the sea and the sky and Husband.

Back in Devon, the children aren't sleeping at night; they resemble Irish weather, grumbly. They're ever so unsettled since Husband took leave, and they miss his physicality about the place, and squawk at me all day long, no matter what I seem to do with them. I bring them out and they cry as it is so very cold, or perhaps that's just a freezing memory from last winter and all that entailed. Tiredness fuels empty thoughts, shiver, but not the same intense grey that the West coast of Ireland seems to have burled up in my face, and in Devon we stay in for a considerable amount of day, as long as I can bear without tearing out my eyelashes with boredom.

pluck, pluck, pluck...

I find my rearing of them does not resemble my mother's, and this is somewhat a tragedy. For one thing, my kitchen is so different to Mother's. One always assumes they'll follow their mother in some way, particularly in the way of her kitchen. Once or twice I tried, but it is difficult to settle yourself on domestic chores when words constantly reel inside your head, observations to be recorded. She had a terrifically big kitchen, which would scare me now. She would slice mangos on hot days, and prepare fish; it would all appear to be perfectly normal, these scenes, until I began to think more about it, Mother and the house and the sea and Father and the great man he was, and I can make out the husk of my memory shell, but little else besides. It's empty, and when I try to see it, it floats upwards, so furiously unreliable, like what happens to the dead when they're dead, and to bring it back to mind, I have to imagine myself walking upstairs, with my feet on the steps, and I count them out in German, but then I can't remember his face at all, it just ups and disappears from my memory...

eins zwei drei

But it doesn't matter, for in my dreams I cannot walk straight up a staircase. Firstly, I cannot seem to put my foot flat on the mahogany boards and then I lift upwards and outwards over the bannister and I must hold on very tight to it; and secondly, for I'm not a ferociously strong woman, but in a dream and especially a day-dream, I try to convince myself that of course I have power. But it is hard to be louder than Husband.

Richard stood on deck, skinny and hollow like a sailboat, and I remarked on it, as a woman remarks to make everyone feel a lot more comfortable and at ease, though I had made little else except to unsettle the whole darn lot, yet I said, rather unfortunately, that Richard looked a lot like Husband. I wasn't sure if it was a rugged handsomeness or that he looked out of place and kind of useless; if there was a storm on the way from Cleggan to Inisbofin, we would have to Mayday an islander or a man from the town of Cleggan and he'd have to come out and do something, as useless as these men looked.

The crossing had been uneventful, as I locked myself inwards and lay prone down on the floor of the boat, but nobody passed remarks. Richard and Husband were busy criticizing the work of other poets, mostly letters, and nonsense about publishers. We docked at the pier at Inisbofin; it was slippy as I alighted, and I remember some old rusty tin and the like, but the action hummed in such a way I thought I could most certainly die here, and that calmed me, although the thought was fleeting, and Richard took my hand as I walked from the boat. Husband had already begun walking off, up the pier with his hands behind his back—in that way a man walks and thinks at the same time.

I would have liked to have asked Husband to wait up, but I thought that I'd catch up later, and in any case, it wasn't worth making a fuss in a strange place before one had even settled into their lodgings and unpacked their clothes and toiletries and bits of ends, and asking a man to wait up when they hadn't remembered you in the first instance was *needy*, and I knew enough to know that now wasn't the time to be needy. No, now was the time to be needed and I had to figure this out, how to be needed. It was something I had never fully come to grips with, not in the way Mother had. I would think about it on the island, if we managed to remain solid and not succumb to our usual habit of becoming horny and self-destructive, as we did after wine and talk of beautiful phrases and things we had seen during our days.

I was hot and bothered by the time I arrived at the guesthouse. In the lodgings I was shown to my room, along a dark narrow corridor. The locker was ever so near the bed and the bed was covered in an eiderdown of plain cream. I noticed a jug and a bowl and became startled, for I'm never quite sure what to do when one finds oneself face to face with the past. But I asked the woman of the house for a little warmish water and she filled some into the jug, in that way a woman can predict another woman's needs, though might not always meet them. I was ever so grateful for it and poured it into the bowl and began to wash my face and neck with a cloth, the water soothing, in the way I had hoped, but I was terribly conscious of the fact that I'd have to redo my face make-up. I rationed this with myself and agreed the soothing was worth a possible reapplication. I had been so face-flushed on the boat and Richard kept on about it and in turn on about how he'd bought the hooker boat named as the Ave Maria off this man who loved it more than a woman, and I thought that's about right, because from everything I know of how a man loves a woman, this made the most sense. I lay down for a while and shoved my face into the cream eiderdown. I may have cried.

I slept. Upon my stirring, the woman of the house knocked gently and advised me of the hour and suggested I had a little time to myself, a polite way of putting my abandonment, before meeting up with my charges later that evening. She suggested a swim, and I agreed, that after the awful motion of the boat, being in the water may recalibrate the way I feel. She began to chatter about the disaster of that boat that had gone out and not returned and had left the fishermen to the sea, but then immediately she started fretting that she shouldn't have told me, as I gathered my swimming costume into myself and pawed it with my hands. But it was part of the reason I wanted to come here. I kept this to myself.

I left the house and walked out as far as the East Beach. I so wanted to go in for a swim, shiver, but I should like to test the water in advance, and all I could think of was the disaster; there was something about giving someone part of a story which was worse than not telling them at all, and far worse than giving the entire account. I have noticed that about the Irish, particularly the men—they talk a long time about very little, as though the topic is somewhere around the chatter, and it's your puzzle to find out.

I held my costume close into me and thought of the fishermen drowning and crying out, and I could hear Husband's voice, saying things to me, suggestions and chatter, but I couldn't concentrate on anything at all, especially recently what he was going on about. He didn't seem to want to be there, with me, in the same place as me, in the dark kitchen with me, or a garden, or walking along the street, and I wasn't entirely sure that us both leaving for another country was going to help us one bit; but men are far less concerned with long games anyhow, and are all far more impulsive.

I changed, feeling awkward as a couple ran a kite on the beach while their children played in the sand, one digging, the other building. The water was like a friend, helping, and it did what cold water does, made me feel awake. And for the first time in a long time, vibrant.

Later that evening, I returned to the lodging and fixed myself. I twisted my hair after braiding it, and my neck was tingling from the saltwater. I was giddy and unreliable.

The Bar was dark, and I was disappointed I hadn't bumped into Husband along the walk back from the East Beach. I didn't hassle the woman of the house as to his whereabouts, as women often do to each other, holding them accountable for the disappearance of a man.

The men were there, and I joined them. We started with a bottle of white wine and Richard tasted it and then looked like he had bitten into a lemon, though I found it quite pleasant, but a little too warm, like the earlier Guinness. I drank it very quickly until the flush rose on my breasts and up to my face and Husband shot me a look. I smiled at him. Richard was quoting Yeats and I wished they'd give over about apples.

I sat among them, blessed, and thought I'd like to light a long cigarette at this moment and escape. But I had none, so I poured myself another glass of wine and there was a moment of silence, but then all the men laughed, and I felt instantly angry.

I drank the wine and was feeling giddy, noting that Husband hadn't looked me in the eye since I sat down. The server woman came and smiled at me and stood at our table for some time and I asked after her family and she after mine, which brought them to the surface like boiling oil.

Of course something happened with Husband and I, in the way it always does with us, hidden and secret. Maybe I was inclined towards Richard. I think back on this and I am never certain or trustworthy of my recollection, of who touched who, but of course initiation is a futile mulling, for it's the aftermath that's always the more dramatic, and how inane it is to meet a man's leg under a table, and though I berated myself—please note I am also quite long-legged like a moorhen, as is Richard—sometimes I think that I was caressing the calf of Husband, and it was willing, hard, warm, so welcome, and I like this memory best. But then I think of *her*, with her dark hair and large lips, and I know it must be Richard I was seeking, or perhaps they were all seeking me, angrily, in the way men compete with each other. I had better stay on the sea like a portrait, remain there, dip myself down in the rainbow colours of the kites, bury myself alive in the child's bucket on the East Beach. I was self-destructive and seeking attention in the way I sometimes do, like Husband. Husband, noting my flirtation, or rouge, rose from the table, most irritated, and muttered about indigestion or a sharp pain in the bowels, lifted his collar up and over his chin.

I followed out into the night, after him, shiver, gathering my skin up and together, but couldn't catch up, shiver, and my shoes were now so tight they were melted on my hot feet, which began to swell. I took rest on the damp ditch, the dew falling as it did, without warning, more liquid than expected, enough to dampen me entirely, the back of my dress and my pants. I took off my shoes and curled my feet over the grass and the cold water began to bring the swelling down, faster than usual, and I could see the sinews in my feet, each bone that protruded into a toe, the baby toe, like the crowning heads of the children, and I rubbed them.

A dying corncrake cried out in the field behind the dry stone-wall that was precariously laid on the grass, bravely or stupidly, and I watched the corncrake move into the corner, like a rook returning back. I sat there to sing to it at first and to cool the toes, shiver, but I couldn't remember the words of any song.

I thought of the drowning men and the paintings with the faces dipped and I thought if I were to be a painting, I'd rather the face was covered in the blackest rook-black, and not in the cerise or the lemon sherbets, and that the painting should hang in the corner of a gallery, so no one sees it, like this dying corncrake, and its swalking swalking swalking, that I couldn't shut the damned thing out. Oh fuck, but so make me a rook in a gallery, blackened with only my breasts on show, although it's most unlikely I'd get any attention.

I hummed a little. I think it was Brahms, with the hard pianoforte banging after the violins, but the corncrake cawed out, louder and louder, my new friend, and I pulled my skirt down around my legs, taking my hair down and rubbing my arms fast with my hands. I took long deep breaths and watched the men bolt from the bar in his wake. In search of Husband, I went, but he was gone, far up the road as the corncrake cried out again, squalling, squalling, against the sea.

HUMP

Nicole Flattery

Nicole Flattery's story collection *Show Them A Good Time* was published by the Stinging Fly Press in Ireland and Bloomsbury in the UK. Her writing has appeared in the *LRB*, the *Guardian* and various anthologies. She was the recipient of the White Review short story prize in 2017. She lives in Galway.

At seventy, after suffering several disappointments, the first being my mother, the second being me, my father died. One evening he gathered the family in his room and asked if anyone had any questions. No one did. The next day he died. At the funeral everyone looked like someone I might sort of know. These strangers told anecdotes and made general health suggestions to each other. I passed out the sandwiches. The sandwiches were clingfilmed and oddly perforated, like they had been pierced again and again by cocktail sticks. I said 'Sambo?' to every single person in that room. It was a good word, a word I hoped would get me through the entire evening. I wasn't strong on speaking or finding ordinary things to discuss in large groups. The place was crowded with false grief, people constantly moving positions, like in A & E, depending on the severity of their wounds. I mentioned that I held his wrist when he passed and through the use of the phrase 'flickering pulse' I was booted up to First Class. My father told me he regretted not talking more. He felt the time others used for conversation, he filled with snooker or nodding or looking away. He surmised, through a mouthful of diabetic chocolate, that he had only spoke 30% of his life. It was a dismal percentage and I was familiar with what dismal percentages could do to a person. We were spending a lot of time together then, linking arms and being totally happy. I had this one trick I did for him. I'd curl up tight into his bed, under the starched sheets, and peep out at the nurses like I was an old lady. It was a scream. They said I was their youngest patient. I laughed and asked them to leave the pills in a tidy arrangement on the bedside locker. My antics gained me a certain level of recognition and infamy in the retirement home and, at times, I could feel my father almost bursting with pride. We both agreed it was the perfect trick for the occasion of his near-death. I was good at gestures, but it was only in that function room when I spoke my sad-but-true stories in my fragile tone, that I finally got the appeal of talking. I thought this is what I will be now: a talker. My job had taken a sinister turn and I had started to keep an eye out, like you do for a new lover, for other things I could try. There weren't many. All jobs seemed to contain one small thing I just could not do. It was maddening. I told a number of stories about my father that evening. I was there, but I wasn't. My mind was mainly preoccupied with what I could do in my new life as a talker: I would be both stylish and intelligent but also deeply affecting in my conversation. When that room of strangers looked up at me I did not know if I wanted them to cry or to clap.

It was in the shower where I found it first. I had moved into my father's old house, and sometimes would shower sitting-down on the stool that was installed for comfort or, if I was feeling up to it, I would stand. The bathroom was filthy with intermittent flashes of what looked like the colour peach. On sitting-down days, I often crawled from one side of the room to the other. I could get away with this because I lived alone. It must have been a standing-day as I realised I was a lot closer to the taps than I used to be. I was a lot closer to the hair on the taps. I was stooping over like I was playing Old Lady in a celebrated stage production, except I was all scrunched up and very naked. I pressed my fingers below my shoulders and felt it shifting, unfurling. The hard roundness of it—like a golf ball or a marble. I dressed myself quickly, being careful not to catch sight of it in the mirror. When I stood on the train that morning, my fingers gripping the rail above, I could feel it growing beneath my skin like a second layer of flesh.

I worked in an office outside the city and we all had the appearance of people who had been brutally exiled. We shed our city selves but, lacking imagination, we had nothing to replace them with. Between the forty of us, I think we could have made a complete person. I had been there six months and it was probably the longest position I ever held. None of it mattered but I liked to pretend it did. If someone came in I might say 'Come in!' That was it. That was the whole script. It wasn't exactly spiritually fulfilling. Often, I was so bored I couldn't hold a conversation. I walked around cubicles abandoning sentences. Whenever I entered the kitchen area, my colleagues left quickly and without warning. I think they were jealous because my desk got the most direct sunlight. I didn't understand them at all. I had a habit of thinking I was very unique and interesting.

My one friend spent her days on the phone to the refuse collection. There had been a dispute over the bins, no one knew who started it, but the rubbish had not been collected in six weeks and it was not a time for chit-chat, idle or otherwise. I wanted to tell Paula about my discovery, ask her had she noticed anything different about me, but all she did was place her hand over the mouthpiece of her phone and mutter 'Sorry'. She had married young and was squeamish about all sorts.

I used my mornings to investigate what was wrong with me. I opened several internet tabs, each one containing something possibly wrong, and explored them all. In the afternoons, my boss came and sat at the edge of my desk, like a hip teacher, and tried on being a thoughtful man. He was always trying to sell me things that were allegedly good for me—almond butter, aloe vera juice, himself. His face was stupidly handsome and so symmetrical it made me roll my eyes to the ceiling. He wasn't perfect though. I noticed he had a hidden aggressive streak and, at times, I suspected he was responsible for the absent bin men. Also, he was not someone I went to for love and affection and he was maybe better dressed than I would have liked. I had a lot of problems with him. He was obsessed with success. I felt I was under constant inspection, and he had a way of looking me up and down like I was a C.V. full of errors and misspellings. He was older, but it was hard to pin down anything precise. We went to a lot of dimly-lit restaurants. Anytime I thought I got a handle on his age, he ordered another bottle of wine and it was gone again. We talked mostly about the office, the flies that we couldn't get rid of, the people we disliked, how we physically had to wrench ourselves out of bed in the morning. Afterwards we would go back to his and he would attempt one of his two-and-a-half moves. He always fell asleep with both hands on my shoulders like we were in a conga line at a party. Conga, conga, conga. Honestly, I hated him.

At first, I worried about it a lot. The worrying made my food come up and up. I came to resemble my father in the early days of his illness; I was surprised when I caught sight of my concentration-camp legs. 'How do they support me?' I wondered. I had no idea but I got high and giddy on the engineering of it. At lunchtime, I ate outside with Paula. The smell of the office forced us into the cold and we sat together shivering over our lunchboxes. Paula's lunch was made up by her husband and always contained the correct amount of protein and carbohydrates. I can't describe the empty, whooshing feeling that went through me when I saw those food combinations. When I found the courage, I asked Paula if, at any stage of her life, she felt herself moving closer to the ground? If the chewing-gum stains on the street were any clearer to her than they used to be?

'I think I'm becoming a hunchback,' I confessed.

Paula was adamant that I was not a hunchback, that my fundamental problem was that I used people to feel attractive. Paula wasn't interested in turning heads. She didn't want men to look at her. Anytime a man looked at her she just picked up the phone and called the refuse collection. I think she was in love with the person on the other end of the line. Their conversations tended to be about Art and Beauty and not about bins at all. In a short space of time, Paula became quite a dangerous woman to know. Slowly, I moved my desk three inches away from hers.

At the weekends, I compensated by overeating. I went to nice places and flirted with the waiters. I bought books on pressure points from charity shops, some of which were highly complex pop-ups. I read these books or I rested them, two at a time, on my head and walked the length of my father's house. As soon as I moved in I realised this house was a mistake. It was too big for me and the stuff I owned shrank by comparison. It looked like I had a wardrobe of baby clothes in those giant, oak cupboards. If I couldn't sleep in one room I just moved to another. It wasn't as suffocating as I needed it to be. Sometimes, I just sat in a tiny space on the sitting-room floor and ran my fingers over those fake, 3D backs. It was like seeing a photo of myself with every flaw removed. Often, I played with my father's collectibles. It wasn't a large collection, just two ceramic children, a boy playing the flute, a girl smiling encouragingly, and a shell in which you could hear the sea. I moved the children around the mantelpiece and marvelled at their serenity. I turned them to face outwards; I turned them to face inwards. There wasn't much else to do. I listened to the seashell like it was my last hope.

My boss described the house as 'weird'. He said the whole set-up was 'weird.' Except me. I was cute and he liked to tickle me under the chin, and then take off his clothes. He guessed something was wrong with me lately, in the way I sipped my wines, the way I sat upright and desperately still. He raised the question of me making myself sick.

'Only during the week,' I said, cheerfully, touched by his concern.

We were giving up. Previously, he listed out my faults with amazing conviction and I truly thought that brought us closer together as a couple. I had no discernible direction in life, I didn't want anything, I was stupid and entitled. Suddenly, he acted as if he didn't care whether I knew these things or not. Instead, he said, 'Okay I'm going to make myself come now,'—as if removing me from the whole act was a sort of kindness. All that was left to talk about was what we'd do to the bin men if we ever found them. Our last night together I folded up my blouse and asked him to perform a thermal massage on my back and growing hump. He refused. Several weeks later, he called me into his office. There had been complaints from anonymous staff. I was never at my desk. He said it was imperative an assistant be at his or her desk.

'Where exactly are you?'

At home I was learning how to self-massage and was feeling pretty fulfilled. I had no interest in my job anymore but I tried. My concentrating face required more effort than genuine concentration. The organisation of the face, the setting up of the features, was exhausting. Afterwards, I often lay down on the cold tiles of the office bathroom floor and didn't move for hours. On normal days I did my job correctly, I counted and pointed and made pleasant popping noises with my mouth, but now there were no normal days. My boss suggested time off. To grieve.

He said I was a brilliant assistant but my father's death had affected me deeply. Take a holiday, he said. I muttered something about the restorative properties of the sea and went home to my sitting-room with its battered, springless couch. Before I left, Paula gave me one of those insincere half hugs. I smiled, thinking of the polite phrasing of the email that was probably sent around informing everyone of my departure.

Without work, I had hours and hours to fill. I performed difficult bending exercises. There was a futility and pointlessness to the whole procedure that I found particularly moving. These exercises had a sighing soundtrack I provided. I skimmed over articles on graceful posture: Pretend to be brimming with self-confidence. Pretend to be a movie star. Pretend to be a human being. At night, I tried to forget about it. I stayed out, alone. On the way home, drunk, I took bits of songs I heard in taxis and applied them to my own life. For the first time ever, I was meeting people. Full of my own brazen ugliness, I was just walking out into the night and finding them.

I considered myself pretty tolerant of people and open to new experiences and ideas. I didn't often seek out experiences but when they were presented to me I usually liked them. I took the new people out to meet college friends, beautiful sad girls who dressed like widows and claimed the world had crushed them, cruelly, like 'matchboxes'. Most of the new people were shy in their company. The men, usually men, often older, never joined in. They just looked at me like that was what they were supposed to do. It was unnerving. They smelled like crackers, sometimes crackers and cheese, sometimes crackers and another substance, but there was always a distinctive cracker smell in the air. My friends had their jackets on before they finished their drinks. I felt I was being thought of as 'inappropriate' and, in response, dug out dry skin from my scalp and discarded it on the floor beneath me. The men sat still and silent as dummies. 'What do you want from all this?' the girls asked. I didn't know. I was never a big dreamer. Maybe someone to wave at who feebly waves back? These women thought of me as typical: not tragic enough, but still capable of pulling stunts that lowered the calibre of their beauty. I counted the number of times I had touched them all, appraised their imperfections, cheered at their hickeys and sex bruises. It occurred to me that I could never ask any of these women to pour aromatherapy oils over my back, gently and without judgement. They would never rub their hands along my spine and check for signs of roundness whilst making soft reassurances. They were there for me in the ways they should be, at the funeral they formed a neat cluster and discreetly cried, but that was where it stopped. I wanted them to say: 'Thank you, thank you so much for everything you have done for us and our self-esteem.' I wanted them to cheer the fuck up. They didn't cheer up though and they didn't express gratitude. They just wafted out of the building and I straightened my back at them. The men continued to stare at me like I was an item of significant interest.

I needed these friendships to go somewhere. I made certain alterations to my lifestyle for these old men. I dusted, I tidied away my father's collection, I cleaned out my bathroom cabinet so it resembled the cabinet of a woman who had very little to worry about. I saw myself making these slight adjustments. I watched as if it was an instructive montage about how a person can take purposeful strides in their life. The music that accompanied these scenes was sassy and upbeat. I suddenly gave a shit and it suited me. My father used to ask if I cared about other people at all and the correct answer was 'Yes'. I did. I cared, I cared, I cared. I had healthy friendships in mind. Things should have been easier when I got the men alone but they never were. I wanted them to talk, to tell me everything, about their families, and the minor incidents that destroyed them, and maybe the moments they had ruined by doing or saying the wrong thing. What then, what then? But, nothing. Their eyes just roamed around like they were searching for something better beyond my head. Of course, they were all seized by a singular fear when I began my striptease. I guess it was because I was always more involved in the tease than the strip. I liked jokes, death jokes, single-girl jokes, and was shocked when these didn't lead naturally to a friendly situation. Sometimes, when the fingers were flying over the front of my blouse, I thought: 'This is hilarious. No, actually, this is an illness. This inability to take anything seriously. I should get money from the state.' Afterwards, I compensated by lying. I'd been let go. I'd been promoted, I do this, I do that, who cares? In a second of stupidity and weakness, I told one of them about my developing hump. I may have curled up on his chest and cried. I may have beaten his chest lightly with my fists. He promised that if we stayed together he would love me all the same. He wasn't begging but he nearly was. After he left the house, in the half-dark, I caught him on the street, kicking a taxi. It was an embarrassing situation.

The time came to return to work but I couldn't do it. It wasn't so much the job as the confusion and frustration that went with it. Standing and sitting and breathing in the stale air of people who despised me—I couldn't face it. I rang up HR and told them my boss made a pass at me. I said I hoped it accounted for some of my odder behaviour in the few weeks before my departure.

HR asked: 'What happened?'

I said: 'Well, he brought me into his office.'

HR said: 'Of course, he did. He's your boss.'

I said: 'He sat across from me at the table.'

HR said nothing.

I said: 'He leaned quite far across the table.'

HR said nothing.

I said: 'It was a very small table.'

I was granted a further two weeks holiday, fully paid. I decided to use that money to invest in my future. I visited various chemists and I had a lot of questions. 'Is it more politically correct to say: I have a hump or I am a hunchback?' The counter girls made funny clicking noises with their teeth and I pined for my own lost work noises. They prescribed yoga classes which promised to straighten my spine and make me wholesome at the same time. Things were too trippy for me in that tiny room and I found all the goodness smothering. Anything could happen in that blissed-out state and that seemed idiotic and negligent so I stopped going. A backscratcher appeared in my room, leftover from a previous life when back-scratching was something to look forward to. I slept beside it, and at night, it extended its long-armed sympathies towards me. When I woke up beside that disembodied hand, I didn't feel so bad. I went to a general store which felt illegal and like I was breaking a code—my friends and I were fonder of expensive, specific things. In the queue, fly-swatter in hand, I asked myself if I looked like a sophisticated person. I didn't. I closed my eyes and imagined hitting the hump downwards with tools and quiet prayers. In the lamplight of my luckless bedroom, I delivered fast, brisk strokes to the centre of my back. I found it hard to keep a straight face.

I saw a chiropractor. I made that choice. A solid man who searched his hands up and down my back as if looking for someone to blame. He was tall and boring and told me he went canoeing at weekends. I asked, 'How many tall men can you fit in a canoe?' which sounded like the beginning of something, a riff or an innuendo, but was a real and genuine query. The gap in my canoe knowledge was huge and overwhelming. I told him I imagined my hump would be a large square shape, like a heavy schoolbag full of difficult homework. He frowned and flipped me over. When I got closer, he didn't look like a chiropractor at all. He looked like a hippie, or a child's lazy drawing of a hippie. All he could offer was drugs and hand-holding, neither of which I wanted. Before I left, he gave me a tissue and said, 'In case, you get upset.' I would never get upset in that sort of room with that sort of man, but I stuck the tissue in my sleeve for safe-keeping. After that, there was nothing, just wide-open spaces, like the reception desk and the world. On the way out, I passed a girl with a neat bob and thought: That's me. I could be that girl. I could be a girl with a bob. She asked if I needed to make another appointment. I told her to schedule me in every month for the foreseeable future and to adopt an air of discretion when she greeted me at the desk. I did not expect to be treated vastly differently, I was a standard hunchback, but a smile or kind word might ease a burden. The bob put her hand over her mouth like a silent-movie actress. Where do they even find these women? She steadied herself on her chair as I shuffled away.

My life, and what I did with it, became a sort of mystery then. I studied the collection, I called Paula and heard the phone ring out and out, I took an aversion to the shower tray. I removed traces of my father from his own home. I needed it so that he wasn't my father, that I didn't know him, that I had never even heard of him. I wrote my boss a letter. It was titled: 'I'm Sorry'. Prompted by this letter he rang me and said he was sorry and let's meet, let's be two sorry people in the same room. I dressed up for it. I took my time. I wanted him to wait and I wanted to be the thing he was waiting for. In the lobby of the cinema he was nothing like I remembered; angrier, shorter. He looked like a small town I might live in and die. He told me there had been a confrontation with the bin men and he had been fired. His arm was in a cast. During the film, anytime he turned towards me, the cast rubbed off my face. Afterwards, we stood on the street and I thought he was going to kiss me or grab me or do something obvious. Instead, he pulled my hand and placed two of my fingers on his bare neck. 'Can you feel that lump? Right there?' I rubbed a small swollen mark from where the shirt of his collar had been closed too tightly. 'That's cancer, I think. It's cancer more than likely.' I agreed that it probably was cancer, that he had caught it early. He asked me if I wanted a drink and I said no, thank you. It was important to me that I was polite.

When I left him, I felt a happy relief. I thought of night classes, the sea, redecorating.

I DON'T

Lauren Foley

Lauren Foley is Irish/Australian, and queer. She also has Systemic Lupus Erythematosus (SLE) and is disabled, owing to this the majority of her writing is dictated. Credits include: *Overland*, the *Irish Times*, *Award Winning Australian Writing*, *Lighthouse*, *No Alibis* and *gorse*. Lauren was awarded a Next Generation Artist's Award in Literature from the Arts Council of Ireland, 2018–19.

Your husband fashions his beard to resemble Abraham Lincoln's, a little Amish, a lot wiry pig farmer. You say Adelaide really is not the place to be experimenting with avant-garde facial hair.

You get into one of your anti-creative moods—as you like to call them—and stop reading the endings to novels, you lay the unfinished novels in stacks of two perpendicular to your side of the bed, they then become rows of five broken up by volumes of French prose poetry and contemporary Latin-American short story collections.

Your GP says it very possibly could be a brain tumour. She asks your husband does he understand. She reiterates your symptoms to him slowly: constant head and body aches, fevers, vomiting, forgetting words, the order of tasks, getting lost, tripping over your feet, an inability to use a knife and fork, or write with a pen, mispronouncing words, constant fatigue, loss of bodily functions, aggressive behaviour, pain that medication cannot control. Not knowing why you are where you are. Hallucinations. She says, we also have to rule out MS. Encephalopathy. Brain lesions. Does he understand?

Your husband nods, and holds your hand.

Your soy-cappuccino flavoured vomit covers the heels of your court shoes, adjoining cubicle wall. You continue retching into the sanitary disposal bin inhaling students' week-old bloody iron. Bum cheeks rammed tight into the plastic rim. Gut and bowel churning. Reach down into blouse and lift right breast then left up and away from where they've stuck to the underside of bra. Bile. Frigid air. Pull wet wipes out of handbag, wipe down walls. Put lid back on sanitary disposal bin, wet wipe wash yourself, rinse out mouth in sink. Make up. Phone Janitorial Services: "Someone's thrown up in the women's toilets, Block C, Physics Building." Lean against the cold, cold wall. Shake hair loose. Pile hair on top of head. Secure with one bobbin and two pens. Walk across the university forecourt and back into your classroom. "Turn to page 25, and let's look at everyone's favourite: modal verbs." Your students groan. "It could be worse, it could be the passive…"

Your husband starts wearing folksy black ankle boots with Pilgrim-looking polished brass buckles.

You don't want to know what happens to the plot at the end of the novels; you feel the art might actually get broken in those spaces. And you can't stand to bear witness to this art getting hurt.

Your first specialist suggests changing your anti-depressant. He compliments the vibrant colours of your handbag in that way men talk to women, then talks to your husband about your anxiety. You tell him you are most certainly going to lose your good job if you cannot be helped. There are external factors contributing to why you are this stressed. All your harried breath is wasted, at first mention of historical mental illness the lights went out behind his eyes. He advises your husband to seek another psychiatric evaluation. Does he understand? Your husband nods, and holds your hand.

I stand just off the middle of the city square. All streets are moving upwards like external glass elevators lifting from the ground and sliding in and out. A 4D Tetris puzzle. You know you are going somewhere, it's two streets away, three. You don't know which way is left, or what left is. You know you are going to the yellow building with the stone door. You can't remember what it's called or why you're going there. You don't know if it's two streets away or three. You think you should go left. You don't know which way is left. You don't know what left is. You think you should go left. The streets keep lifting up around you and moving like a CGI earthquake in slow motion. You stand just off the middle of the city square trying not to cry.

Your husband invests in a steampunk-esque pocketwatch and researches Victorian-era waistcoats until 3am some nights on menstailoring.com.

That sensation of a kitchen knife blading deep into your chest and stopping just short of your stomach overtakes you if you read too close to the novels' ends. You want to offer the novelist's artistry to the unknownness of art, to some creative deity, or a Christian-type novel heaven where all their conceptually perfect endings could live.

Your second specialist tells your husband she has never had a patient unable to sit upright and stay awake for a consultation before. You sit there purposely spilling little pools of water from the floral glass tumbler their assistant brought you into the hollow in the palm of your left hand then wiping it across your eyes and face with your right, as you battle with your body to sit up and stop fucking slouching sideways. They order a hundred new tests. A thousand more. Your best friend IMs that you must have had every jesusing test in the world by now. LOL. Smiley face. You throw up in the disabled toilet sink while shitting an awful lot of blood from your excoriated arsehole down the loo. You might stand up soon. You ask your husband is it over yet? You need to lie down. A specialist says to your husband: "Your wife is very, very sick." Does he understand? Your husband nods. You hold his hand.

Your husband starts wearing skintight drainpipe black denim jeans with Rockabilly height turned-up ankle cuffs.

Endings never fail to make you cry.

Your psychologist reiterates how depression can feel like being sick. Depression can have physical symptoms.

Your husband emails you, do you understand?

"I would rather be dead than be sick and have no one believe me."

"Fucking fascists."

"Do you understand?"

Put on a mindfulness MP3. Take a walk. Watch some comedy clips on YouTube. Have a shower. Do some admin. Clean the house. Make the dinner. Remember the breath.

Your husband forgets to update his eyewear prescription at OPSM by the pre-specified date, and instead purchases a lorgnette at a Sotheby's auction in town.

Those opinions on themes and character stacked up and up and up like pillows around you while you lay on your marital bed draped in a silk kimono from Gilles Street Market and sherpa lining striped slipper socks from Target (said the French way) boutique.

The third specialist tells you he doesn't know what the outcome will be. The locum tells you it's in your lungs, the RN hangs her head, no one meets your eyes. Three-years max. The nurses come in and out of your room. Your liver's enlarged. Too high. Your blood pressure shrinks. Too low. Your thyroid's too big, too small. Big, big enough to eat you with, my dear. Your bladder. Lungs. Brain. Heart. Spleen. Bladder. Infection. Womb. Infection. Cervix. Infection. Ovaries. Infection. Babies. Infection. No babies. Infection. Babies? Infection. Sinuses. Infections. Stomach. Ear, nose, throat. Eyes. Hair falls out. Patchy eyebrows. Diet. Vitamin deficiencies. Your eyes. Blood red eyes. Yellow. All the better to see you with, my dear. Teeth. Toes. Knees swell up. Hands, fingers, elbows, ankles, toes. Head, shoulders, knees, and toes. Can't walk. Can't talk. Can't cut up your food. Can't use your hands. Glands. Muscles. Itchy skin. Glands. Muscles. Itchy skin. Rashes. Red rashes. Rashes. Itchy. Skin. Not kidneys. Red rashes. Itchy skin. A rabbit runs in front of your car. You scream. Your husband doesn't swerve. The rabbit, the rabbit. Its outline catches fire and its trail races out in front. Is it a fox? A wolf. Lupus! The engine explodes, your husband's face, his skin burns off, his skull his eyes. There's nothing there. There's nothing there. There's nothing there. Two external psychiatrists pull out of their hats: "Major Depressive Episode/PTSD."

Pain everywhere. Everywhere. Everywhere. My eyelashes, my eyelashes don't hurt.

Your husband buys a pet iguana from a travelling exotic-pet salesman he once met at a work conference in Auckland. He perches the pet iguana atop the right shoulder of his dress jacket and wears both to client meetings and the footy. Eventually the literature overtakes your household floorspace spreads outwards from the bedroom into the kitchen onto the verandah then down the hallway past the bathroom all the way out the back door and beyond. Your husband invests in a sturdy pair of wooden stilts so he can negotiate his way into and around the house of an evening—it's a bluestone turn-of-the century so the ceilings are pretty high. He starts wearing the stilts into work in the city and says he thinks his top hat is garnering more inadvertent recognition from passersby now. You put all the unfinished novels onto a newly assembled Regissör flat-pack bookcase you purchased via iPhone app and collected in-store from IKEA. The French prose poetry and Latin American short stories are now stacked like Duplo stick-a-brick houses tenement-high next to their shelved novel companions, but still the bottom one touches the floor.

Your husband's Abraham Lincoln beard grows all the way down to his clavicle. He says he just wants to be an individual, to do something no one else is doing. You take his hand in your hand, hold it there, and ask him earnestly can he see himself at all.

Other married women can walk their dogs, children, husbands outside. They walk around your block and up and down your oak tree-lined avenue. You hear one talking as she passes you by: "No, I'm just at the house where that mad book woman who never goes outside lives. The one with the happy marriage; yes."

THE LOVECATS

Patrick Freyne

Patrick Freyne is a writer of journalism, essays and short stories. He works for the *Irish Times* and his work has appeared in the *Dublin Review*, *Banshee* and *Winter Papers*. A collection of his essays will be published by Penguin Ireland in 2020.

One day I opened my door to a small, round man who said that our cats had to get married.

"What?" I said.

"Our cats are to wed," he said, again.

I looked down at Boris, who had crept up behind me and was looking up at our visitor with curiosity. The small round man moved his gaze down to him. "*He* knows what I'm talking about," he said.

"But what *are* you talking about?" I said. "Why must they be married?"

"My cat, Maybell, is with child," said the small round man, "and *he* must now do the honourable thing."

I turned to ask Boris about this before realising that this would be insane. "Who the hell *are* you?" I said instead.

"I am Mr Dermody," said the small round man. "I am your rear neighbour. I live on Curtin Street." This was the street parallel to mine. Boris did have a tendency to pop out an upstairs window on to an extension and over the back wall. "Our cats have become…" He paused with disgust. "*Friendly*. And now my cat is to bear kittens. The tom who sired the kittens…" He paused dramatically, looked at Boris again and pointed a finger. "Stands before us now."

For a moment I expected Boris to deny everything but he just stared up at me with his placid little face, inscrutable as ever. I shook my head at the small round man. "No, no. Boris was fixed. There is no way that that happened."

A week later I stood before the vet who said, "Boris is not fixed. He is perfectly capable of fathering kittens."

"But they said at the shelter that he was fixed!" I said.

"I don't know what to tell you," said the vet. "Sometimes mistakes are made."

Boris was a rescue cat. I knew very little about his background prior to his coming into my home, but over the years I felt like we'd become good friends. And this was at a time when I really needed friends. Now I felt like I didn't know him at all.

"Would you like me to arrange for him to have that operation?" said the vet.

"I... I need to think," I said. I picked Boris up – I'd meant to do this impatiently but he was so soft and pliant that touching him encouraged gentleness – and I put him into his carrier.

"Are you okay, Mr Dennehy?" asked the vet. She was a nice woman, but she didn't understand the dilemma I faced. For a week, I'd fended off Mr Dermody's letters and phone-calls and unannounced visits, and each time I'd staked my reputation on the fact that Boris was incapable of conceiving children. I looked down at Boris who looked up at me through the roof of his carrier. "Mew!" he said. Did he look... *guilty*?

I would have to change tack, I thought, as I pounded my way home, the cat carrier in my arms. I'd have to approach this problem another way.

"I accept that Boris may be the father of Maybell's unborn kittens," I said, while drinking sweet tea in Mr Dermody's tchotchke-filled sitting room. "But cats don't get married. There's no such thing as cat marriage."

I looked at the mantelpiece rather than meet Dermody's gaze. There was a puppy in a boot, an urchin chimney-sweep with disturbingly large eyes and, yes, two anthropomorphised cats in wedding costumes standing behind a heart that declared "Mew Love".

Maybell, who was a huge white ball of fluff, was lying in state on a nearby armchair on a big red cushion bearing the legend "Beddy-byes."

"I know a celebrant who specialises in just the thing," said Mr Dermody.

"Of course you do, you big nut," I thought, but I said: "But why would you want them to? They're cats."

"I need to ensure that little Maybell is provided for," said Mr Dermody. "While she's in the family way and beyond. I'm not a young man."

"Seriously?" I said. "I like Boris. He can be quite charming and he has a pleasantly philosophical outlook on life, but he's also an unemployed layabout. I mean, he won't be changing any nappies."

"Kittens don't wear nappies," said Mr Dermody stiffly.

"I'm glad you're aware of that, you crank," I thought but I said, "Do I have to do anything?"

Mr Dermody sniffed. "As the father of the bride I suppose the arrangements are down to me."

"I bet he *actually* thinks he's the father of the bride," I thought, but I said: "Fair enough. Make the arrangements and I'll make sure Boris is there."

I'm retired, what else was I going to do?

"Good," said Mr Dermody, clasping his hands together before looking at me with an arched eyebrow. "I'm surprised Boris isn't here today. It doesn't speak well of him."

"For the love of Christ," I thought and then I said it out loud. "For the love of Christ."

A couple of weeks passed before I got the invitation, a frilly doily daubed with blue ink. Dermody had lovely penmanship, I had to give him that.

"Mr Colin Dermody invites you to the marriage of Ms Maybell Dermody and Mr Boris Dennehy at the function room of the Royal Hotel, Clontarf, at 11am, Saturday February 4th. Black tie expected."

On the morning of the ceremony I couldn't find Boris anywhere. I'd been keeping him in the house after my meeting with Dermody but he looked at me so sadly that I felt cruel and I started letting him out. I watched him jump from the window to the extension and over the back wall. "Go off to your fancy woman," I said.

Boris always came back at night. The day of the wedding, however, he was nowhere to be found. I was in a panic. I jumped into my little car an hour early and zipped down the venue. I rushed through to the reception hall which was gilded with flowers, where an organist was practicing and Dermody was in a top hat and tails talking to a strikingly tall woman in a floral dress and a huge floppy hat. She towered over him.

"There's been a problem," I said, and then I realised that Boris was sitting on a little cushioned podium beside Dermody and beneath an archway of roses. He was also wearing a tiny top hat and a sort of half-tuxedo that covered his front legs but not his tail.

"You must be Christopher," said the woman in the huge floppy hat. "I'm Vanessa, Colin's sister."

I shook her extended hand weakly. "I'm also a cat groomer," she said. "So I took the liberty of giving Boris a bit of a makeover."

He did look quite distinguished.

"His lashes seem longer," I said.

"Falsies," said Vanessa, proudly. She was an impressive woman. She had a roman nose and a noble, patrician bearing.

"And you?" said Mr Dermody a little disdainfully. "Is that what you're planning to wear?"

I looked down at my crumpled suit. "Well, Yes."

"It's black tie," said Dermody.

"I thought that was a joke."

Dermody pinched his forehead with his fingers and said, "Oh God."

"Colin," said Vanessa. "Don't let little things spoil this big day."

I was so relieved to see Boris. I went to pick him up. "Watch his hat!" said Demody frantically.

Vanessa caught him by the shoulders. "Colin, relax. You'll overexcite yourself. Leave Christopher to me. Boris's hat will be fine. You go collect Maybell. She must be frantic with nerves."

Dermody straightened himself. "You're right Vanessa. As always." Then he walked from the room.

"Right," she said, looking me up and down. "Let's get a load of you." She straightened my tie and neatened my hair. "You'll be fine. Would you like a cup of tea? To help calm you down."

"I would," I said, feeling oddly grateful. She snapped her fingers and two cups of tea appeared. "It's always so difficult for the parents," she said. "Days like this."

"Yes," I agreed.

Boris was looking up at us from his little cushioned podium, not wandering around the room in terror as you'd expect from a cat in a new environment.

"Why is Boris being so compliant?" I asked.

"We've been bringing them up here to get them acclimatised," said Vanessa. "I work here. We've been doing it for weeks now."

"Seriously?" I said.

"Oh," she said, pushing her saucer of tea aside. "The guests are arriving."

I turned around to see a trickle of people in fancy frocks and evening suits. Some I recognised. The vet was here with her girlfriend. They waved over. Others, Vanessa introduced me to. "This is Michelle," she said. "She is the owner of Benjy."

My eyes were drawn to her feet where a white highland terrier gazed up at me.

"Benjy and Boris are basically frenemies," said Michelle. Benjy was now looking with hatred at Boris. Boris, who was at the other end of the room, was gazing back at Benjy with disdain.

"But I think they like each other really," she said.

"I think you might be misreading the situation," I said.

A group of small girls in party frocks came up and said, "Are you Pootle's owner?"

"Who's Pootle?" I asked.

"That's what we call *him*," said the smallest girl, pointing at Boris. "He's our favourite of the cats."

"I'm glad he's marrying Maybell," said the middle-sized girl. "I think it's very romantic."

The tallest girl shook her head. "Marriage is a patriarchal construct. Mam says that."

"But the heart wants what the heart wants," said the smallest girl. "Mam also says that."

"I suppose," said the tallest girl. "I hope she keeps her own name though."

"She will be doing nothing of the sort," said Vanessa, whooshing them away. She had come over with three people in tow. It was Mary, Simon and Andrea from work. I hadn't seen them since I'd retired.

"Oh, it's great to see you, Chris," said Andrea who was beaming. "When I got the invite, I thought. 'I never knew Chris had a son.' But then Mary said that Boris was your cat's name, and I thought, 'How lovely, a cat wedding!'"

Simon punched me on the shoulder playfully. "I just thought 'Classic Chris! He was always joking around in the office.'"

I really wasn't. I never joked around in the office. "Thanks for coming," I said and then Vanessa bustled them off to their seats.

"How did you know who to invite?" I whispered to Vanessa.

"Facebook," said Vanessa. A wave of panic overtook me and then someone tapped me on the shoulder. I knew before I turned who it was. It was Denis. I froze and I didn't know what to say.

"It's good to see you Chris," said Denis, shaking my hand warmly. "I'm glad you invited me."

"To my cat's wedding," I said, just to be clear.

"Whatever it is Chris, I'm just glad you got in touch," said Denis, and he meant it.

He hugged me. "Mam would be glad," he said. "She'd never have wanted us to be fighting." He leant down and gave Boris a kiss on the head. Then he went to sit beside his partner Marcia, who waved at me and smiled.

I waved back. Vanessa looked at her watch. "They'll be here anytime now," she said. "You'd better go have a word with the best man."

"The best man?" I said. She pointed to a toddler standing up near Boris.

"Puddy tat," said the toddler. His mother was standing beside him. "He just loves Boris," she said. "He's always trying to feed him things when he comes into our garden." She offered me her hand. "I'm Anne, by the way, I live next door to Colin. And this is Stanley. Did you know Boris likes crisps?"

"Puddy tat," said Stanley pushing both of his pudgy hands into Boris's fur. Boris, surprisingly, just purred contentedly.

"Puddy tat?" said Stanley looking up at me.

"Yes," I said. "Puddy tat."

Stanley nodded as though I'd said something very wise. And then I heard the sound of horse's hooves and a little gasp of expectation from the crowd. Dermody was in the doorway beaming with pride, holding Maybell in his arms. Maybell looked pretty blasé about the whole thing if I was to be honest. She was chewing at her veil. "Ah, doesn't she look lovely," said Vanessa. She looks ridiculous, I thought, but I said nothing. The crowd murmured approval. "Unna puddy tat!" said Stanley throwing his hands in the air.

Two other cats who looked very like Maybell were following her in a sort of cat-cage-cum-trailer that was pulled by a teenaged girl in a satin dress who looked very like Vanessa. They didn't look very happy, which may have had something to do with the purple crinoline frocks they were squeezed into. "Maybell's sisters," whispered Vanessa "Ethel and Brenda. They live with us."

"I'd have met them, I suppose, if I'd come to the rehearsal dinner," I said.

Vanessa looked at me gravely. "I thought you were taking this seriously."

I felt bad then and looking at the smiling congregation, I also felt very under-dressed. Something occurred to me.

"Hey, who's officiating?" I said.

"I am," said Vanessa. "I'm also a cat-wedding celebrant."

"What religion are they?" I asked, looking down at Boris.

"Don't be ridiculous," said Vanessa. "It's a multi-denominational ceremony. For those of all religions and none."

Dermody was up beside me now. He had tears in his eyes. Even my untidy unshaven person couldn't take this moment away from him. Maybell had most of the veil in her mouth. Boris was, embarrassingly, licking his soon-to-be-fixed parts on the podium. I suppose that was why they'd only fitted him with half a wedding suit. I picked him up so he sat placidly in my arms. He really was a good cat.

"Dearly beloved, we are gathered here today to witness the union of two of our friends in marriage," she began and then rattled through the ceremony. She is quite impressive, I thought.

Everyone contributed a little. Dermody sang Wind Beneath My Wings acapella. He had a lovely voice. It reminded me of his handwriting somehow. One of the small girls read from *The Prophet*. Denis got up and recited our mother's favourite poem, The Road Not Taken, by Robert Frost, and for a moment I remembered the two of us as small boys. He patted my shoulder as he passed. Stanley wandered off for his bit, so I've no idea what he was supposed to do but later on he was wandering around covered in ribbons so presumably it had something to do with ribbons.

At a key point in the ceremony Vanessa asked if anyone present knew of any reason why these two cats might not be joined in matrimony. There was a silence. Benjy barked and Dermody glared at me as if I'd planned for this, as though I'd bribed Benjy somehow – but everyone just laughed and when they did, Dermody laughed too.

And then, at the end, Vanessa pronounced them cat husband and cat wife. Maybell was coughing up bits of her veil, Boris was asleep but Dermody looked deeply moved. And I, to my surprise, found that I was moved too. We walked down the aisle together holding our alternatively slothful and gluttonous animals to a lyrical organ rendition of The Lovecats by The Cure.

Dermody, to be fair to him, put on quite a spread for the afters. I sat at a table with him, Vanessa, her daughter Jessica, Denis and Marcia. Boris was on my lap asleep. Maybell was on the table eating from a small plate of chicken. Dermody, who was across the table from me, looked at her adoringly. I felt a little bit bewildered by it all.

"Why did we just do all this?" I asked Vanessa. She was smoking an electronic cigarette. She made it look ladylike somehow, like it was a cigarette holder. She frowned slightly, gazed over at her brother and said: "I want to make him happy. We don't get much in this life, you know. I've got Jessica, I've got my cats and I've got him."

Behind us a DJ was playing cat-themed numbers – Cool for Cats, The Lion Sleeps Tonight, Phenomenal Cat, music from the musical *Cats* – an excited small dog was barking and three little girls were dancing around a laughing toddler throwing ribbons in the air.

"What a day eh?" said Denis. We talked for a long while. He told me about his job and about the renovations he and Marcia were undertaking on Mother's old house and about the time two years ago when Marcia got very sick. He wanted to call me then, he said. We weren't a demonstrative family, but at one point he squeezed my hand and I felt momentarily overcome. On my lap a small grey creature purred.

THE LADY, VANISHING

Mia Gallagher

Mia Gallagher is the author of *HellFire*, winner of the 2007 Irish Tatler Literature Award, *Beautiful Pictures of the Lost Homeland* (2016) and *Shift*, longlisted for the 2019 Edge Hill Short Story Award. Her short fiction has been widely published and anthologised. Mia is a contributing editor with the *Stinging Fly* and a member of Aosdána.

At dawn Tommy does it. The cows are lowing. Larksong in his ears. No bells chiming yet for the Easter Sunday Mass.

He gets her ready. He could leave her sleeping, curled up in her bed, but that wouldn't feel right, not for his princess of eastern promise.

Black shoes first. Shiny. Then the knickers, their favourite ones, the whitewhitewithblacklace. She's awake now. She watches; silent, eyes wide, as he pulls the flimsies up, lets the elastic snap around her waist. He's out of breath. Had to do everything himself. As usual. Because – god forgive him – she's so bloody helpless.

A sound. A sigh? Her mouth is open. Where are we—?

Surprise, Honey.

She's always loved it when he calls her that. *Oh, Honey, oh, Honey, my Honey, oh.*

He takes the red truck. The new woman in town likes that truck. Real cute, Tommy! You got some vision. Any room for a passenger there? She's from Chicago, the other end of the planet from Honey. She's not too old; she has money. And dark wild hair and a crackling laugh that runs down Tommy's spine, lifts his balls and squeezes, real slow.

They're at the ugly end of the harbour. Honey stares out. The slate cliffs cut brutal into the cobalt sky. A huddle of giant bins, filled with shattered glass, stinking sugar-crusted plastic, soggy paper.

He opens the door.

She looks surprised. What are you—?

Sshh, Honey.

A flicker. The breeze, catching her hair. He expects another question but she says nothing, just lets him lift her – so bloody helpless – out.

Gulls scream, wheel, lift on the wind.

Look!

He points west. At the ocean, cool blue in the dawn. At America beyond it and, in its heart, Chicago, invisible, where all his hopes lie.

Honey – look!

He forces her head around to the ocean. Makes her see. *This is why.*

What do they say in the agony columns? It's not you, it's me.

She's weightless in his arms. Cool. He touches her mouth, her shallow forehead, her staring eyes. She trembles. Her hands are warming up under his fingers. He traces the numb elegant length of her right leg from black patent toe to lonely-filling hole.

There's something wet in her eyes.

You got some vision, Tommy.

He could smash her first, break her, flatten her to an inch of his life, but that, he feels, would be cheating. So as he pushes her through the narrow mouth of the bin, she's still herself enough to resist, scraping at him with her hard fingertips. He's glad of that, in a way. She screeches when the rusted rim rips at her face. Hisses as it carves a pink gash down her cheek. There's blood on her nose. His? He recoils. Her hands snap loose, push at him. He bats them back, shoving her in until she starts to crumple again, sinking slow and sad into the broken glass.

Poor Honey, he starts to think, then stops himself.

Enough of that.

He twists the key; starts the ignition.

Mass first, then the full Irish. He's starving now, would eat the hands off of a skinny priest.

In the rearview mirror, he doesn't see her flattened foot in its black shoe uncoil, curling up from the mouth of the bin.

One more gasp at blown-up life—

put your lips together, honey, and

A gull swoops, pecks, punctures.

She sighs.

BADGER

Sarah Maria Griffin

Sarah Maria Griffin is the author of *Not Lost, Spare & Found Parts* and *Other Words For Smoke*. Her nonfiction has appeared in *Winter Papers*, *Guts*, the *Stinging Fly* and the *Irish Times*. She received the European Science Fiction Chrysalis Award in 2018 and was shortlisted for an Irish Book Award in 2018 and 2019. She tweets @griffski.

When your fist made contact with his nose and you felt it move beneath your knuckles, it was the biggest you'd ever been. It was the most right you'd ever done, the split second in which you became heroic – the moment in which you became legendary. You became a story to tell the grandchildren. Splitting bone and the protection of your sister was all that mattered, just then, in the dark outside the house, him hammered and screaming dark effigies of her name after trying to get her to open her window, now shut to him, indefinitely, after what he did.

Stupid boys and their greedy hands and their shallow threats would know better now – word would spread of what you did to him, how ugly you made him.

How you smashed his iPhone off the ground, told him *that's what he gets, that's what he gets.* The pieces of it shone in the night, sharp and cruel and money right there on the footpath. His nose a crumpled mess, his mouth drooling bright scarlet remorse. His pathetic skin matching his inside, at last, kneeling there, picking up pieces of his phone off the ground. Shards of expensive glass in his terrible fingers. You waited until he was done, waited until he got into his banger of a Toyota and drove away, the roar of his engine against the night still somehow pathetic. You and your sister haven't talked about it just yet.

This porch is wooden. It is old painted new: a schlocky turquoise now over the pine. It is where you and your sister sat in cool summers fighting over a sticky Gameboy that was only held together because of half a roll of Sellotape. It was always angled at ninety degrees or so, to help the light hit the screen just right so the pair of you could collect golden coins in LCD landscapes together. This porch is where you end up every summer you spend at home, trying to rekindle closeness, drinking cans, talking shite. Trying. She is blonde this year, it suits her.

The noise is newer than the paint, for sure. The noise hadn't been there last time you'd been home. The noise is fresh.

When the two of you were smaller you'd place tinny three quid headphones into plastic cups and hope they'd act as a speaker for the only tapes you had and the summer would get Cole Porter tender. Why there were so many Cole Porter tapes around nobody knew, but you both knew they sometimes had two-part songs and you'd De-Lovely to each other in the afternoon before the notes got too high or too low. The Walkman whirred old technology in the backdrop of the violins and serenades but you could sing over it then easy. The drone though, the new noise, that's harder to ignore.

It's usually summers that you're back rather than the grim cold of winter, the anxiety of Christmas. You swooping back over the nest you grew too big for, your wingspan an inconvenience. Your sister's wings are not that big just yet – she still fits perfectly here. You're jealous, but you don't say anything. Especially not now, not this minute, sitting out in the garden, eating an orange Sparkler ice-pop from the freezer that might have been there since last summer, or the summer before. It's too nice for anything serious just now. You are listening to her pick scales on the fat old guitar she's been learning to play.

Your mouth tastes of old ice and almost-orange. She's getting really good, but you don't say anything about that either. Her voice sounds older than she is and you wonder is that learned, is that what Cole Porter did – or did the boy just turn her more adult this year, has she grown Amazonian inside the body of a girl. Perhaps her voice sounds so huge because inside she is huge, because she has had to be, lately.

The noise from under the porch is what you've mostly talked about since you got back. It is an easy topic, rather than mundane catching up or heavy questions like *Why did he think he could come here* or *Do you know how much it's going to cost his family to fix his teeth* or *Do they ever think about me anymore?*

The noise under the porch was the first thing she told you about when you walked in the door from the airport, reeking of air conditioning, dry throated and teary-eyed with the gladness of being home. You dropped your bags and went to stand in the garden with her, your parents rolling their eyes, and you went, 'Yeah man, that is some unholy noise coming from down there.'

In the morning at the kettle she in her dressing gown said 'Jesus Christ I can hear it from in here!' and in the night after you got in from the pub you knocked on her bedroom door and whispered through the crack, 'Babes, I can hear it from my room, too!' Your parents insist that it'll go away in its own time and will not entertain conversation about it. Your sister keeps trying to bring it up, at dinner, at breakfast – but they just roll their eyes.

It's nothing, they insist.

It's *everything*, she replies.

As you washed his blood off your knuckles and your own from your mouth – you bit your tongue, he didn't have a chance to fight back – over the bathroom sink you could hear it still. The fucking noise of it. Even then, what you would have done for a moment of quiet.

It is louder than it was even yesterday and when your sister stops playing and goes, 'I don't think I can take it anymore,' you think she's about to bring up the lad but she doesn't, she goes, 'I have to see what's down there.' Her phone lies innocuously beside her, and chimes with a text message. That is the fourth time it's done that since you've been out here and she hasn't touched it. The light of the screen is so powerful that you can read it from here despite the glare of the sun – his name is four bad letters and anger is a strange thing, how quiet you can keep it, but how loud it feels in your gut, in your hands. You don't say anything. She ignores the phone, says, 'I think I'm going to go down and look.'

'No,' you say, 'I'll do it.'

You wonder will she check her messages while you are gone.

You get up and walk down the couple of steps to the grass, where the deck is raised a little, where there's a gap. You never thought much about going under the gap as a kid, seemed impossible then. Now it opens wide like a chasm, like c'mon down, don't you want to see? Your knees click as you lean, your hands are on the earth where the grass stops and under the house begins. Your sister is still strumming. The droning sound from under the house is different now that you're close to it, now that your face is right there, the darkness grazing your nose.

You begin to crawl forward, ducking your head low under the beams, your palms already beginning to tear against the grit. Your sister's swinging legs are behind you, to the left. You are not in the garden anymore, you are under the house. It smells like damp and concrete, like the week the deck was built is trapped under there, like the dust never really settled. The noise is texture now, against your eyes and ears. You hate it. You look around, neck craned, head scraping against the wood above you – you want to find the source of this terrible thing that has infected your home so you can stop it, so you can quell it—

You want to find the source until your eyes register it. At first you think it is a badger – four-legged, with a snout, kind of – but it is when you look for details there in the under house dark that you see it is all bees. Bees and broken glass on four legs with a hanging jaw, dripping something that smells sweet against the dust – honey, you think, it must be. The droning comes from every inch of it, a blur of black and gold and sharp. It opens a jaw and closes it again. It blinks. It is a terrible mess and the noise makes so much sense now, such awful sense. You think for a moment about taking a picture of it, shining a light on it from your phone, capturing even its image – but you don't do it. You think for a moment maybe you could punch it from here, maybe your fist, the fresh legend of it still strong, could maybe destroy this thing. It makes you feel sick but good, kind of. The noise is all over your body now.

You begin to back away. You cannot land your fist in the center of its terrible face, in the midst of the bees, the glass, the honey. You cannot just wrench its phone from its hands and shatter it on the pavement. There is nothing you can do to change things, maybe the noise will always be there. Maybe it will leave when it wants to, maybe it will find some other home to pollute with sound. You know this now. This lives under the house and that is just where it lives. It told you this, with its closeness. You back away, your hands dragging against the ground, useless now.

You do not turn your back on it, instead just slowly retreat into the light again. You can feel pebbles making their way under your skin on your palms, your nylons are torn for sure at the knees. You scrape your back against the lip of the decking as you come back out. You could have been there for an hour, a year, just looking at it. You miss it, in a strange way, almost immediately, but are glad you never have to be that near to it again.

The garden smells alive and clean. The sunset has coloured the sky pastel and girlish and great. Your sister is looking at you expectantly and you stand up, dust yourself off.

'Your tights!' she exclaims. Decimated cheap nylon. You wave it off.

'What was it?' she asks, not strumming the guitar anymore, just holding it, her long fingers around its neck. Her phone chimes.

'Nothing we can do anything about,' you say, 'just leave it.'

'Is it a wasps' nest?'

'I think so,' you say, lying, 'it doesn't matter.'

'Mam and Dad think it'll go away in its own time.'

'They're right.'

Her phone chimes again. Suddenly, without warning, she picks it up and throws it, hard, down on the little brick path. It audibly cracks.

You laugh. She laughs. The droning doesn't stop. Later, you wash the earth off your hands and open the bathroom window to hear it better. Over the rush of the water, it is almost music.

THE HOMESICK INDUSTRY

Hugo Hamilton

Hugo Hamilton is the German-Irish author of the best-selling memoir, *The Speckled People*. He has won many international awards, including the French Prix Femina Étranger and the Bundesverdienstkreuz, awarded by the German state. Hamilton is a member of the Aosdána and lives in Dublin. His latest novel is *Dublin Palms* (4th Estate, 2019).

I've got a job in the city now, in a company that manufactures Irish products, both for the home market and for export. Traditional music, language lessons, dancing records, tin whistles, Aran sweaters – the lot. I'm the distribution manager, so I can see these products being sent all over the world. Even as far away as China, there are homesick people who think of Ireland every day. People tearing the paper off to take out the books and start speaking Irish again like babies. People in tropical places like Cairns, Australia, sitting under palm trees in the heat with the sound of strange birds all around them, putting on the dancing CDs and working out the steps – one, two, three, one, two, three. For a moment, you get the impression that the whole world is homesick. I can see them up there in Alaska, wearing thick Aran sweaters under their parkas and holding small tin whistles to their frozen lips. Frozen fingers pressing out the first warped notes and bringing back the faraway feeling of home.

Nothing has changed very much and I sometimes get the impression that I am like my father when he was alive. I might as well be him. I get on the train every morning and sit down with the newspaper. I see the same people around me in the carriage, the same variation of faces, the same silence, the same glances avoiding each other. I get to the office and go into dream, drifting away to remote places.

People would say that's the way the world carries on from one generation to the next, father and son, into infinity. They will think I have just stepped into my father's shoes. Here he comes, they will say, carrying a cool, new shoulder-bag instead of his usual briefcase. He's looking younger, they might say, but apart from the shoes and the hair, apart from the general youthful swagger and the fact that I don't wear glasses like he did, nothing has moved on at all. I have the same forehead, the same hands, the same smile. I have the same history and I have become my father in every respect, which is what I had always hoped to avoid.

I have always refused to be like him. I wanted to be different, to travel, to forget where I come from. But sometimes when you try that hard, you just end up being the same without noticing it. You finally surrender to the songs like everyone else. Maybe you sometimes become what you fight against.

I suppose that's why they gave me the job as distribution manager, because they could see that I understood the idea of not belonging. They could see that I had inherited something from my father, in spite of the fact that I had always resisted it.

My boss calls me upstairs to his office one day and demands to know what has gone wrong. He's just like my father in many ways. He has that look of nostalgia in his eyes. His chin quivers when he speaks. He wears a pink shirt and the light on his desk keeps flickering and going out, so he has to tap it with his pen to get it going again. He looks at me under the arch of the light and shows his frustration. He says he hopes I'm not just in the job for the money and I laugh.

'What's that supposed to mean?' he asks.

'What?'

'That laugh?'

'Nothing,' I reply.

'You just laughed. I said I hoped you didn't just take on the job for the money and you just laughed. What's so funny?'

'I didn't mean to laugh,' I say.

He has something more substantial to talk about. He has ordered a skip which has been delivered outside at the front of the building so that a room at the back of the offices can be cleared. The room is to be used to store a new consignment of knitwear from the West of Ireland. Sweaters that women have been working on for weeks and weeks will shortly be arriving here, destined mostly for the export market. For tourists arriving in the summer, for airport shops and various outlets around the capital. In the meantime, we need to make storage space. He wants to streamline the knitwear operation, so that it's knitter to wearer in the shortest possible time.

But there is a problem, because my boss thinks I'm going to physically go in there with my staff and carry out all those dusty files and printing junk to the skip. He says it's urgent. He describes it as a crisis. A policeman on a motorbike has already called into the reception to ask how long it's going to take. The skip is taking up an entire lane of traffic. But I've refused to do this kind of work. It's not my duty. I will not be ordered to fill a skip. Skips are not my responsibility.

So here I am in his office once again, staring across his desk. He's wearing the same pink shirt as always, or else he must have a hundred pink shirts which he bought in one place because he likes them so much. He fiddles with the desk lamp again because he can't see me. He's blinded himself as if in self-interrogation.

'Are you afraid of work?' he wants to know.

'I'm not a labourer,' I reply.

He frowns when he laughs. He laughs when you think he should be getting angry. I want to ask him what's so funny, but he's already leaning across the desk, looking at me in the eye.

'If you could only see yourself,' he says.

He smiles. He slaps his desk and looks out the window. Then he looks back and starts shaking his head.

'I wish I had a mirror so you could see yourself,' he says.

I am the portrait of refusal.

Suddenly, he looks at the evening paper on his desk. He asks me what star sign I belong to, but I refuse to enter into this new game.

'Your birthday is this month, isn't it?'

I don't answer. I know this comradeship trick.

'Capricorn, right?'

He reads out the generic little piece of fortune-telling from the paper. 'You will find that your social life will improve dramatically later on this week.'

'Is that all?' I ask.

He smiles and tries to appeal to me as a friend. He's in a bit of a spot, he explains. Could I not make the exception for once? He tells me that he will never ask me to do anything like this again, that it's only because of the extreme urgency of the situation, the traffic outside. It's not the way he would have liked it, but the gardaí have been in a second time, demanding that the skip should be removed.

'I'm not doing it,' I say.

'Please,' he begs. 'Just this once.'

'You can find somebody else to do this kind of work.'

He stares at me across the table for a while longer. I can see his disappointment. He tries something else. He talks about moral responsibility, duty, dedication, laziness.

'Anarchy?' he suddenly shouts. 'Is that what you want?'

It descends into a political argument. He talks about a more equitable, a more socialist society, a fairer, Irish-speaking country. He doesn't let up. He wants a country like the Blasket Islands with nobody owning anything any more than anyone else.

'Nobody owning anything at all,' I say.

He leans forward to make his point. There was a shipwreck on the Great

Blasket once, he tells me, and some boys on the island found a casket full of brand new watches. They wanted to keep them for themselves and hid them in a cave. But they were not accustomed to owning anything or having any personal possessions, so by the end of the day, they had given them all away and everyone on the island was wearing a watch, even though they had no real use for them and nobody had any sense of time on the island.

He tries to fix the flickering desk lamp for good this time. He says it's not really socialism he's after at all but democracy. He says democracy is everybody doing their share regardless of what rank or position they hold. It's people paying their fare on buses.

'That's what democracy is,' he says. 'People respecting their country and working for each other.'

Suddenly he loses it. He burns his hand against the shade of the desk lamp. He gets up from his chair in a fury and flicks his wrist around the room. But it's only when he looks out through the window at the empty skip outside and all the cars snaking around it that he remembers why I had come to his office in the first place. Not a single thing thrown into the skip yet, while we're arguing about the solution for Ireland.

'I'll show you,' he says. 'Follow me.'

I follow him down the stairs, all the way down from the third floor, passing by people without saying a word all the way down to the offices at the back of the building. He takes off his tie and puts it into his pocket. He rolls up his pink sleeves and lifts up the rubbish in his hands, old files, printing materials, ink canisters. Out into the street he goes, carrying bits of junk and throwing them into the skip. I stand there and watch him, refusing to touch anything. He doesn't say a word. His hands are black. His pink shirt has gone grey and there are black streaks on his face from some old printing ink. He's sweating and breathing heavily.

I join in and start carrying things out with him. We work in silence, me carrying out the same amount as him, no more and no less, until the skip is full and we both go our separate ways, him back to his office upstairs and me back into the dispatch office in the basement. He doesn't give me those triumphant looks. He doesn't rub it in. If anything, he understands that I am hurt by this, and defeated.

A few minutes later the phone rings. I pick it up and wait. But there's nothing. It's the two of us listening to each other in silence. Then he finally speaks.

'I'll make it up to you,' he says.

But I've put it all behind me. By the following day it's forgotten. The Aran sweaters begin to arrive in big boxes. Larger consignments are on the way. We are overwhelmed by orders coming in and can hardly even keep up with the demand. Knitwear going out to addresses everywhere around the globe, Canada and the USA, France and Denmark, even Italy.

And one day not long after that, it's my birthday. My boss wants to show that he hasn't forgotten. He's a man who keeps his word and comes down in the afternoon with a gift. He and his secretary and two or three others from the department crowd around me in my office with a big parcel wrapped in blue paper. They clap and wish me a happy birthday in Irish.

'*Lá breithe shona dhuit*,' they say, all smiling, as they hand me the gift. They wait for me to open it, but I'm so surprised by all this kindness that I can only stare at the blue paper.

'Thanks,' I say.

'Aren't you going to open it?' my boss says.

I begin to take off the paper. I can smell what's inside before I can even see it. The familiar smell of rough wool is unmistakable. It's one of the hand-knit, Inishfree Aran Sweaters that I've been sending out to so many people abroad. And now, one of them seems to have come back to me as a birthday gift. A big brown, rope-patterned Aran sweater with a ringed collar.

'You shouldn't have,' I stammer.

For a moment, I ask myself if this is some kind of big joke they're playing on me, but they are all very serious.

'Are you going to put it on?' my boss says.

So I thank them again and again, and put it on out of politeness. I can smell the oily sheep's wool all over me and I suddenly feel suffocated. I used to wear one of these big sweaters as a boy. My father bought them for us. My father wore one himself. It's making me ill and I'm already thinking of what to do with it, how to get out of the building without them noticing that I've left it behind. When they finally leave, I wait for a moment before taking it off and replacing it in the plastic wrapper. I put it back with all the other jumpers waiting to go put in all directions, all over the world. Some days later it goes out by post to Spain, to an address in Madrid.

EGRESS

David Hayden

David Hayden was born in Ireland and lives in England. His writing has appeared in the *Stinging Fly*, *Granta*, the *Dublin Review* and *PN Review*, and *Being Various: New Irish Writing* (Faber). His first book of stories, *Darker with the Lights On*, was published by Little Island Press in the UK and in North America by Transit Books.

Many years have passed since I stepped off the ledge.

I had cleared my desk, and all that I wanted to keep was saved on a memory stick placed in my top pocket. Everything else – I deleted. I found a window that I could cut and cut again to make an opening through which I could step out onto a narrow ledge, and as I moved from there into the air I felt relief, a loss of weight. I began to observe the office building as if for the first time: the honey-coloured glittering skin of stone, the terracotta panels, smooth and grooved; the sheets of clean glass. My eye and mind moved with delight from the detail to the great mass of the building and back again. I felt joy to be outside forever.

I expected to be cold but the air was mild, the speed delicious, the fresh-ness vast and edible. I remember looking up briefly to see my fellow directors staring with alarm through the boardroom window. All except Andrew, who pinched his tie, smiled and waved.

I stopped of a sudden on the air, all my mass returned to me, seemingly in the pit of my stomach, my arms and legs flopped forward, and I gazed down to see a woman with a chestnut bob staring up – I was definitely too far away to tell it was a chestnut bob. She looked away, down at her feet or towards the door of the yellow cab that had just pulled in to the kerb, and I began falling again as quickly as before; and the cab door opened and, as she stepped in, she glanced at me again, and again I paused, juddered in the sky, and I heard the door thump closed – I was probably too far away to hear the door thump closed – and I began falling all over again with fresh delight. I sang, and the stale, old words tore away from my mouth and up towards where my life had been.

Pages flew up towards me. I caught one and read:

Forehand cross-court, faster than the eye can see and he's on his knees crying, and the crowd are cheering, they are on their feet, and he's still on his knees grasping his head as if to hold in the burst, the spraying contents, and his opponent has jumped the net and is standing close to, watching the victor weep. The winner's mother and coach appear and stand around him and the weeping continues until the crowd fall silent. The defeated man steps forward and places his hand on the victor's curly head and he calms, stills; his tears cease.

The page left my hand.

I had the idea that I should be falling at a more or less constant rate, varying a little depending on how much wind resistance I presented by increasing or decreasing my surface area; but I found that I was accelerating. And yet, after a few minutes, I could see that the ground was farther away from me than I could have expected it to be and, what is more, seemed to be receding faster than the rate at which I was falling. I rolled over and the building was peeling away to the side and I strained, against the blur, to look in through the windows to the brightly lit, open-plan floors and I saw people held in tension, faces desperate, smiling, empty, fear-struck, fulfilled, turned away. Everything was as it should be.

Many gathered coats and bags and headed for the exits. A moment later they were pushing out of three great revolving doors that face the street on the ground floor. Going home.

Homes are places made familiar through returning. Time is inside the fragrance of return, and it is not freshly-baked bread, not lemon zest, icy pine forest or mother's neck; it is not just stale coffee, stale smoke, stale sweat, the tang of detergents, or the rich, unnameable odours of the new, old, building reasserting themselves over, and through, the everyday fug; it is the substrate that we make, alone and together, out of the stew of chemicals that our skin encloses, out of the choices we make, or are made for us, about what we take inside, what appears outside, and everything that was there before us that still has a trace that can rise. The fragrance of return is all that we did, and was done, returning to us in a moment as the door opens.

Night happened without my consideration. The sodium orange street lights and palely fizzing moon appeared according to their different causes. On every floor were lone workers, spot-lit in their cubicles or at the desks of their private offices. My office, cool and comfortable, was up on high, towards the clouds. It was the perfect situation and moment and occasion for making money by making things happen. Each working hour like the beat of a heart, fast or slow, in sinus rhythm or bumpily asynchronous, entailed with all the others in apparent continuity, but each time gone and gone and gone and gone.

People like myself, whose long-settled routines determined their simplest choices, would be retiring to their beds and while I was tired it seemed risky or indecorous to fall asleep, to sleep while falling, and I resisted until the early hours when my eyes became the only part of my body to weigh, so far to say that I felt that they were pulling me to earth, orbs to orb. For a time, I was unconscious and dreaming – all useless things – and I woke in the dawn light reaching for a blanket that was not there, with a bladder big and tight inside my belly. I rolled over, unzipped and sprayed onto the street with relief, without regret. There was a larger movement inside me and I pulled down my pants and strained it out of me and watched the brown stuff fly away and thump into the street where, I imagine, it broke into turdy pebbles. It was only when I pulled up that I chastised myself for an unclean act, and then I didn't think about it again.

The workers were returning, many holding tall white tubes of coffee. They would join those who had stayed all night working on refractory problems, moving in minutely close or stepping back to a global distance to review risk or loss, to find resolutions that would cause money to leap free from wherever it was trapped: in bodies, components, minds or ore; in ideas, longings, irritations, bare possibilities. Everyone labouring to add more to the much.

The street was deep in snow: blank, then ridged and banked; grey and black and then clear. The bare boughs of the avenue trees sprouted curls of green that unfolded and spread wild, cloaking the wood, making buds and flowers and falling petals. The sun buried the city in heat; the star paled, lilac in dreams, scuffed yellow in the sky. The leaves turned sere, descended a scale of gold-orange-yellow-brown and flopped in fat, spicy drifts. Snow again and all was white, quiet, on the way back to green and gold and white. The smallest tremors of the sun on the air, the air pressing on the ground, the air pressing on itself – humidity from ash dry to falling ocean, heat searching and rising, swelling bodies and air. All days in one.

Cars appear bigger: shiny, brittle shells that move slowly, serried, similar amid their great variety; then smaller, faster, blips of light that never touch one another – then fewer and fewer until the avenue lies empty of all moving things except the occasional ancient bicycle – rider bent over the frame, face covered in a surgical mask.

I roll and smile to the sky. Birds with mighty, cloud-spanning wings gyre above, the sun flashes on their smooth bodies, and when I turn back I find I have dropped many floors and the ground is coming up fast. I close my eyes and count, running the numbers backwards. When I open them I find I have dropped many floors and the ground is coming up fast.

Many years have passed since I stepped off the ledge. All that I wanted to keep was saved.

REPRIEVE

Dermot Healy

Dermot Healy (1947–2014) was a novelist, playwright, poet and short story writer, best known for *A Goat's Song* and *The Bend for Home*. He published numerous short stories and several of his plays were staged. He was a recipient of the Hennessy Award and the Encore Award.

They took a taxi out of Birmingham to their modest lodgings. She sat so silent, it seemed her mind had slipped from her. Peter paid the driver handsomely. Then he argued with her in the room. "There is still time to go back on this," he repeated. She held her silence. She undressed and got carefully into bed. He kept talking away, fretting, worrying her. At this last moment he had ceased being the most generous man in the world.

Yesterday she had had the final consultation with the doctor. "It seems," he said, "that you have your mind made up." Sheila said: "I have." "I see no reason then for any delay," he replied. She had got up and crossed to the door, counting every step, trying to appear a confident, mature strong woman. She must, she had thought, show him. At the door she fainted. She blamed the heat in the room. She said: "Don't take this for weakness or anything like that." The doctor nodded.

Tonight, this man here, her confidant and financial adviser and lover, was having his moral fidgetings. At long last it came, what had been building up in her all night. From the first anxious strain at her heart muscles, from all the days moving between the cottage and the town, now it would happen. The tears burst out, oh just burst out of her eyes, streamed away from her. They came from her loins and wrists, happy life-giving tears and, God, it took the agony out of the room. He tried holding her, thinking his advice had won her. She let him. Then, as the crying subsided, she said, "Look what you're doing! Your boots, ruining the white bedspread!" That his untidiness should strike her just then was unbelievable. To have cared for a strange bedspread in a strange house where she would only spend two nights! But why should he lie there, turning his boots into the bedspread, talking so manfully of choices and life and marriage?

Morning, he dropped her off at the hospital. She was the youngest in the ward. Most were married women of about forty who didn't want any more children. A doctor came and gave her a spectacular shot in the arm. He said, "This will relax you!" There were an awful lot of women being pushed to and fro, and she among them, in wheelchairs. You waited about in wheelchairs for your turn. They chatted there in the corridor, high as sparrows on the morphine.

At last, it was after a day, she was pushed in on a trolley to an amazing place she had never been before. There was the great light-orchestration of the operating theatre, and the doctors in their green outfits moving about talking quietly.

"I want to tell you something, doctor," she said. "You're awful nice, but that injection you gave me. It was very good. But, you see I'm mad awake!" She laughed and laughed. "What has you so happy?" he asked, filling a new syringe, so thin and fine against the round tubular lighting. Of course, all she looked at was his eyes to see if he was a man or a boy. She couldn't tell him, but the flesh between her elbows and shoulders flushed with giddiness and happiness. They pulled back her single white covering, "I hope," she said, as he again lightly tipped the pinprick into the crook of her arm, "that this one works."

NINE YEARS IS A LONG TIME

Norah Hoult

Norah Hoult (1898–1984) published journalism, novels and short stories, and several of her books were banned. She published several story collections – *Poor Women!*, *Nine Years is a Long Time* and *Cocktail Bar*, which was republished in 2018 by New Island Books. Her novels include *Time, Gentlemen, Time!*, *Holy Ireland* and *There Were No Windows*, which was reissued by Persephone Books in 2005.

It wasn't until October was well under way that she began to wonder that she had had no word from him. Even then she didn't actually worry. He had probably gone on some business trip. Men in a good position, like he certainly was, often went away on business looking after their affairs. He might have gone to London: he was a member of some swell club there. That she did know, for he'd let out one day something about an important call being put through to his club in town, and he had had to return to Rotherfield sooner than he had expected.

All the same she found herself watching the posts, watching for the appearance of the telegraph boy—he usually wired. All the time she was watching. When she dusted the front room, or went to fetch anything from the cupboard, she would find herself come to a standstill in front of the window, and staring up and down the road. By the end of the month she admitted that it was a good piece over his usual absence.

Her husband thought it funny too. They had a talk about it one evening when their daughter, Irene, was out at her shorthand class.

She started the subject herself. She said: "What do you think about it, Harry? What's your real opinion? You can say right out what's in your mind, you know?"

They were sitting in the kitchen over the fire. He took up the poker, and knocked the coal about with it making a better blaze, before he answered. Then he said in a very thoughtful voice: "Well, of course, he might be dead."

She nodded her head. "I've thought of that myself."

So she had. But to have it put into words from him made it more real. Like hearing a thunder-clap when before you had just wondered if there mightn't be a storm about.

He added, leaning back in his chair, and looking at her out of small eyes blinking over their comfortable creases: "He could die sudden and you not a penny the wiser, seeing that you don't know his name or address or anything about him."

"I'll tell you this much," she said a little sharply, "if he did die, there'd probably be half a column at the least about him in the *Rotherfield Telegraph*. He'd be one of their leading citizens; there's no doubt about that. I wouldn't mind betting that he's the director of several companies."

"Well, what of it? You'd be none the wiser, since you don't know his name. There's several leading Rotherfield men died lately; about his age, too. I don't know that you'd do much good if you went over to Rotherfield, and looked up the papers. You wouldn't know, see, would you?"

She looked into the fire. "I suppose I wouldn't." She thought a little, then she said: "Tell you what. I wouldn't be surprised if his name started with a 'Mac'. He had a Scotch accent all right. Though he wasn't mean."

No, he wasn't mean. Three pounds a time came in very useful to help out. She was going to miss it, if it stopped. And so would Irene, and Mr Scott. Mr Scott was how she always thought of her husband.

He agreed with her this time. "Oh, no. I wouldn't say that he was mean. But reserved. Scotch people, of course, are like that. That was why he never let out a word about himself or his occupation."

The flames from the fire were beginning to scorch the front of her legs. She rubbed her hands up and down them. Then, crossing one leg over the other, she hazarded: "I often had the idea that ship-building was his line. Else, what brought him to Merseyhead so regular? I mean he came here before he met me."

"Very likely," said Mr Scott. "Quite likely. I'd say." He took out his pipe and his pouch, and began to press tobacco into the bowl.

She watched his red face bent forward with some hostility. If her Rotherfield friend didn't turn up soon, he'd feel it. He'd have to go without tobacco. All she had now was Irene's pound a week and about a pound profit on Miss Halpin, their paying guest, who had a good post as manageress of Bailey's, the big drapers. Two pounds a week didn't go far towards keeping them well fed, and with good fires. Seeing as he was the one who was out of a job, who didn't contribute nothing, it was only fair he should give up things.

"So that's what you think, that he's dead?" she asked, resuming the conversation, but as if she were attacking him.

He took a draw at his pipe, before answering. He was always one like that, one to take his time over things. It would annoy you if you didn't know him. It annoyed you when you did know him, too.

"I didn't say that he *was* dead, for I don't know. What I said was that he might he dead, for all you know, or that I know, or for all that we *would* know."

He stopped and looked at her, as if hoping that at last she had got the position clear. Deciding to take no risk he added patiently, "Because, you see, you are not in possession of his name, or of his address, or anything about him except that he lives, or lived, at Rotherfield. So that you can't find him, or satisfy your mind."

"I know that. I don't need you to tell me that."

"Well, then…"

"And I tell you, Mr Scott, you'll find it no bloody joke us losing three quid a month."

"I know that." His mouth pursed into lines of bitter resignation. "How long is this going on, I wonder?"

What he meant was, how long before his father kicked the bucket? Before their two minds was a picture of an old paralysed man. Just sitting in a big chair holding on grimly to life. When he died there'd be money coming to Mr Scott as his only son. *When* he died. All over the world there were people waiting for other people to die, and settle their financial problems for them. And it seemed like that the longer you waited, the longer you had to wait.

Mr Scott said what they'd each of them said many a time: "You'd think that with nothing to do, nothing to live for as you might say, he'd be glad to go. I'm sure I should in his place."

She nodded her head. But that topic was threadbare. Her mind went back to her own problem. Why didn't her Rotherfield friend wire? Wasn't she going to see him again ever?

The fire was too hot on her other leg now. So she reversed her position. Then she held out both legs in front of her. She used to have good legs; they were a little on the fat side now. She'd put on eight pounds this last year. Eleven stone ten was her weight.

"Do you think I've got to look much fatter lately?" she asked him.

Mr Scott looked at her indifferently, "I don't know. Maybe you have."

"My legs are fatter, aren't they?"

"You always had a good calf."

"Yes, but my ankles were slim. I used to be able to get my thumb and middle finger to meet round. Now I can't."

She showed him. There was a good inch of flesh-coloured stocking to spare over the squeezed flesh.

"Hmmm." He stared. Then he said: "Thinking of slimming or what?"

"Doctors say it's very bad for you. Besides, it wasn't as if I was a big eater. And heaven knows I get my share of exercise with all the housework."

"I'd leave it. I don't think it makes much difference. Nature intended there to be two kinds of women, big and small. I like the modern slim woman myself."

She had heard him say this till she was tired of hearing him. Whenever he came in from the pictures, he'd go on talking about some lovely slim little girl till you'd think he was daft. Getting into his dotage he was. Pinning pictures of girls up on his bedroom walls; just legs and scraps of lingerie. Sixty! An old man really. She could ask him, why he married her then? Of course she'd been slimmer then, but she'd always had a figure.

She said: "My Rotherfield friend said he always liked a woman with a figure. Something to get hold of."

"Some men do," he agreed, nodding his head in deep assent, so that you could see the thin hair brushed neatly across the top. "There was a time, I remember it well, when most men liked them big. Fashions change in women like they do in everything else. I think Edward liked them on the full-figured side. But I believe the Prince of Wales likes them skinny."

"Go on with you! What do you know about what the Prince of Wales likes in the way of women?"

"As much as anybody else, I suppose. Why, only the other day I walked back from the library with a man who knew someone who knew…"

"You told me that bit before. Anyone can pretend they know anything, can't they? Well, I'd better get Irene's supper."

She got up from her seat with a jerk. Anyhow it was no good worrying. Worrying never did any good. She might hear from him tomorrow.

But she didn't hear. Nor the day after. Nor the day after that…

A depression settled slowly and abidingly on her spirit. It was a bad time in the garden. You couldn't do anything with it just now, but prop up the chrysanthemums against the wind. And the daily housekeeping round, making the list for Mr Scott to go to the shops, cooking meals, washing clothes, ironing, dusting, and for diversion talking to Miss Halpin—who was as dull as ditchwater, and had probably never had a man in her life—hung heavily. When she lay down after clearing up from the one o'clock dinner, she didn't go to sleep, but her thoughts went round in a dull painful question. It seemed to rain every day, so that you had no heart in you to go for a bit of a walk or up to see the shops. It was a pity, because they said there was nothing like a walk or a change to take your mind off things—and walking reduced the weight too.

What she was really missing was the change her Rotherfield friend made, she decided. It had been a sort of holiday when she got his wire or letter. Then Mr Scott knew that he'd have to manage everything himself. She'd be the rest of the morning having a bath, and dressing herself with special care. The last touch was a drop or two of Coty's *Chypre*, that was too expensive to use for any but very special occasions. Then after a light lunch—no steak and onions—off to the Queen's where they always met. She liked sitting in the lounge of the Queen's, with well-dressed people about her, and having a drink and a chat, and then another drink before they went off to the hotel.

They were nearly always able to have the same bedroom, with the red curtains and the alabaster vases on the mantelpiece, so that it was really home-like in its familiarity. Mrs Weston always had the gas-fire lit for them ready.

It wasn't that her Rotherfield friend really attracted her in the way one or two men—no, really only one man in her life—had attracted her. But still a woman wanted to get into bed with a man now and then. It was only natural. She had always felt better in herself afterwards. Mrs Weston sent them tea up, or if they preferred they had it downstairs in the lounge. You'd see quite a good class of people having their tea, too; you'd be surprised. Mrs Weston knew some really famous theatrical people like the time when Daisy Allen had stayed with her. Handy, the place was. And central. Well Mrs Weston would be wondering what on earth had happened to her.

Almost every month—he'd missed now and again, of course—as regular as regular for nine solid years.

It *had* been a change. He went off pretty soon afterwards. Had some dinner engagement usually, he said. And she'd meet Irene coming out from the office, and they'd go off to the pictures, and have a little bit of supper somewhere afterwards. It always seemed to her that when she went into Spinetti's with Irene men used to look at her with increased attention. They looked at her a damn sight more than they did at Irene, pretty and slim and young as she was. Anyhow she always felt pleased with herself and warm and comfortable inside.

Now, if he never came to see her again, or if she never saw him again, life would just go on as if it were a wet November all the time.

She began to spend more time in front of her looking-glass. One morning she went out, and recklessly bought a special pot of expensive skin food. Irene saw it when she came back from the office.

"What's that? Is that yours?"

"Yes. I treated myself for a change. Mrs Rosenbaum was telling me that it's terribly good for the skin. Works marvels. So it should at the price."

"Well, I just hope to goodness, mother, you are not going to start making yourself up the way Mrs Rosenbaum goes on. I think it's disgusting. An old woman like that."

"She's not an old woman. She's only about fifty."

"Well, I do think there's nothing more repulsive than to see a woman of that age trying to make herself look young. They never do; they just look repulsive, revolting. Why should a woman when she's past forty go on fussing about herself?"

"I suppose you'd like me not to use powder or lipstick, even?"

"Well, I don't say I mind a little powder, but..."

She stopped, and shrugged her shoulders. Standing there scornful and young, with her smooth skin and hard eyes. She was always bossing her now. Last time they'd gone out together, she'd said: "Mother, you've got too much rouge and lipstick on," rubbed it off herself. And she wouldn't let her smoke on top of trams: when once she had wanted to light up—"Please don't, mother. If any of the girls at the office should get on!"

The whole thing was that she was beginning to put on airs and graces, to fancy herself. But Irene wasn't a bit like an ordinary girl, like she'd been when she was eighteen. She said she hated men. Once she had told her straight: "Well, if it hadn't been for some of my men friends, *you'd* have had a thin time when you were a kid, I can tell you. It wasn't your father supported you and him at the war."

Did her good to be told straight out. Of course, young people were like that, very intolerant. They thought no one should look nice but themselves. She said, and now there was anger in her voice: "Well, if you think I'm going to look dowdy just to please you."

"I don't want you to look dowdy. But if you have a lot of stuff on your face with your red hair—and honestly, mother, it suits you better if you'd stop henna-ing it so much—if you put on a thick cream and lipstick with your hair and big figure, it makes you look conspicuous, that's all."

"You're jealous. Because when we're out together more men look at me than they do at you."

"I'm not at all jealous..." Irene looked at her mother as if she were going to say hard words, then she went out of the room with her lips tightly pressed together.

Mrs Scott sat down in front of the fire, holding the skin food in her hand. There was a pain in her heart which she tried to banish by getting up quickly and putting a record on the gramophone:

"There's a lovely lake in London..."

"Pom pom pom-pom pom pom pom-pom," she hummed to herself defiantly, but her thoughts went on all the same. So Irene thought she was too old to bother about herself, that she looked fast when she took a bit of trouble with her appearance. She wasn't too old. She tried to cheer herself up thinking of the story her Rotherfield friend had told her about the old man who was asked at what age sexual desire had left him. But the smile faded, because it took her thoughts back to him again. Why *hadn't* she heard from him?

Had he got tired? Might as well face it. Irene thought of her as old and fast-looking. Had he come to think that about her? She got up and took down the oval mirror that hung over the mantelpiece and examined her face intently; then she held it farther away, so that it included the reflection of part of her figure as well.

She couldn't see that she looked so old. There was something cheeky and attractive about her face, especially when she made her eyes laugh. Experienced, of course. Well, why not? Well, wouldn't she be a fool at her age if she didn't look as if she had had something to do with men? Withering on the virgin thorn—somebody, not her Rotherfield friend, somebody else had used the phrase once, and she remembered it with satisfaction. That wasn't her line. Though it just about suited her lady lodger.

Of course she was on the plump side. That was upstairs. Her hips were still slim, and, thank God, she didn't stick out behind. And her friend had always said...

She heard Irene's steps in the hall, and replaced the mirror quickly. The hall door banged. She had gone back to work without saying "good-bye". Bad tempered. Not got over her buying something for herself. What she was going to do straight off was to go upstairs, and give her face a good massage with the skin food.

She came down to the afternoon cup of tea in a good temper. Her skin felt as soft as velvet to her touch, and the lines from nostrils to the corners of her mouth showed a lot less. Even Mr Scott noticed it.

He said: "You do look smart." He said that because she had on her best satin blouse, and men always liked satin. Satin or velvet. But he wouldn't have said anything, if she hadn't done her face up. They chatted amiably, and when he said: "Do you know Bessy Morris is on at the Palace: I wouldn't mind seeing her," she surprised herself by saying: "Let's go."

"But what about her ladyship's supper?"

"Let her have it cold for once. I'll do her up a nice salad and leave the coffee, so that it only wants heating."

"And Irene?"

"It just won't do that girl any harm to get her own eats for once. She's getting above herself."

"Haven't I said she puts on too many airs? Ever since she went to that office she's been a changed girl. And you always stick up for her."

"Well, I did stick up for her. But as a matter of fact you're right for once. She's getting to think there's no one in the world but herself."

"That's just what I've often said."

"I know that, and I'm agreeing with you. See?"

Pleasantly they set off for the Palace. It wasn't often that she went out with her husband. Not likely. It was treat enough for her to give him the money to go to the pictures. But he didn't look so bad when he was dressed nicely, with his hat brushed and everything. Irene would think she'd gone off her chump going out with him. It would show Miss Scott that she wasn't everybody.

She did it in style, too. At the interval, she slipped him half a dollar, and they went into the saloon, and had a Scotch and splash. He passed her back the change, and it warmed you up, so that you enjoyed the second half better.

Still, wasn't it funny, even in the Palace, a place he'd never be likely to go to, unless compelled by some business function, she found herself looking for her Rotherfield friend. Once she really thought she saw him, looked a bit like at the back, and her hand stiffened, ready to clutch Mr Scott's arm. But when the man turned, it wasn't a bit like him really.

Bessy Morris sang one of her old songs. She sang: "*I don't want to get old; I don't want to get old; I want to stay just as I am…*" Running furiously up and down the stage, and making everyone die laughing. "*I want to come home at half-past four and have a row with the woman next door, I don't want to get old…*"

She laughed a lot; and she also laughed loudly at the jokes of the comedian who followed. Thank God, she had a sense of humour and could enjoy a saucy story. A man in front, a very nice-looking, well-dressed fellow, too, kept looking round and trying to catch her eye. She didn't take any special notice: after all it wasn't playing the game to give a man encouragement when you were out with another—even if it happened to be only her husband, and she was paying for him.

All the same it just showed that she wasn't quite on the shelf whatever Irene thought. When they stood up for *God Save The King*, he just stared and stared at her. Mr Scott noticed it. He whispered: "Would you like me to slip away quietly?" but she shook her head. No, she didn't feel like it, and after all she had given all that up.

When they were sitting in the tram, she slipped out the mirror attached to her hand-bag, and was satisfied. There was a green light in her grey eyes that beckoned. Putting it back she hummed: "*I don't want to get old; I don't want to get old…*"

The next day wasn't so good. To begin with she had found herself with the definite expectation that she would hear from her friend that morning, and by twelve o'clock, when nothing had come—he was considerate; he always let her know before twelve—her spirits went down, plop, and she as definitely decided that it was the finish, and that she might as well face the fact. She stood at the window, and told herself so in good round language. Then she stared up and down.

It was one of those not infrequent days when without actually raining, it looked as if it were going to rain, that it would rain if the weather wasn't too indifferent and spiritless to be able to do anything so positive. It *should* rain. A grocer's van passed; the woman from two houses up went by on her morning's shopping. Mrs Scott's eyes followed her critically. What a way to go out, shoes all muddy, old mackintosh… oh, who cared! An errand boy wheeled by on a bicycle, whistling cheerfully. Let him whistle. He knew damn all about life.

Yes, he must be dead, and if he was dead, that was that, she couldn't do anything about it. Or he'd found another woman, younger and better-looking than she was. But that didn't seem reasonable. After all if he'd stuck to her for nine years, when he could have any girl he wanted, as any rich man could, why should he change now? Nine years showed that he was the faithful sort. Or he'd made it up with his wife; of course there was a wife somewhere; she knew that though he kept his mouth close. Perhaps she'd been in a lunatic asylum, and been let out cured. And he was sticking to her. That was another thing about married men. They might be ever so bitter about their wives, say they'd spoilt their lives, and all that stuff. And the very next thing, for the sake of his children, or for the sake of his home, or for the sake of his bloody position, or his bloody conscience, he'd turn you down as if you weren't flesh and blood at all.

Still, nine years was a long time, and she'd have thought he'd have done it before if he were going to do it.

Well, everything went in time, and it was no good moping about it. "The best of friends must part," as the old saying was. It wasn't as if she'd actually been in love with him, still you got used to having a man. At this very moment, she wouldn't mind… it was last night's outing, and being near her period. That was why she felt so depressed, too.

Depression or not, no good standing there, Mr Scott would be wondering when he was going to get his dinner: Dinnertime was what he spent all *his* morning waiting for. Like his blasted cheek, but there it was.

When they were sitting over a cup of coffee and Irene had gone back to work, Mr Scott said suddenly: "Do you know when I was coming back I saw a telegraph boy cycling up the road this morning, and I made sure he was going to turn in here. He just went a few doors on: I think it would be for Tilson's."

"Who the hell would be sending us a wire? The Sweep isn't on now. Did you think your father had died at last?"

"Not likely!" Mr Scott sniffed contemptuously through his nose. "No, *he'll* never die. I thought it was from your friend, of course."

"Well, you can give up thinking about him. It's over three months now." She put her cup on the table, and then turning towards him, raised her voice emphatically. "I shan't hear from him again. Not never. See?"

"I don't know. Christmas is coming. That might bring you something. Why are you so sure of a sudden?"

"I couldn't tell you why I'm so sure. I just know it today. I feel it in my bones. Somebody has been making mischief, saying that I'm a married woman, not a widow, like I told him, and my friend is so straight that he wouldn't go with a married woman. He told me that once, and I remember it now. Somebody might easily have seen me and him at the Queen's, and known us both. Or else he's dead. Or else... anyhow I just know I shan't see him again. So that's enough about that."

Mr Scott looked at her face. She was getting quite worked up about it. He sought for sympathetic words. "Well, no wonder you're upset. It must be—I was working it out in bed last night—must be a good nine years since you first ran into him—just by the Arcade, wasn't it?—and he turned out so lucky. Ah well, no use crying over spilt milk." He waited for her to speak, but as she said nothing he went on tentatively: "Dare say you could easily pick up someone else if you fancied?"

She gave him a hard look. "Could I? Well, I might. But you know damn well that having Irene going to an office, I can't do what I please. Besides, after being so regular with just the one man..." She stopped and her lips began to be unsteady. Horrified, she comprehended in a lightning flash that she had got the habit of being faithful. Why, if that chap last night had spoken to her, and she'd been on her own, she would have behaved like a silly kid and rushed away. She had just got out of the way of all that... pretty awful to think that she, Sally Scott, had dwindled into a Miss Prim and Steady for the rest of her life. Not a single man in her life, for you wouldn't count Mr Scott. Past work and past everything he was. She choked back a sob. That's what her Rotherfield friend had done to her. That's what a woman got for being so blasted loyal. She took out her handkerchief.

"Don't take on about it," said Mr Scott, rising uncomfortably. "'Course I can understand your feeling sore. Nine years is a long time."

"Oh, shut up, can't you? Don't you know any other words? Shut up, can't you?"

The tears were coming. She couldn't stop them. Aghast at herself, she got up, and turned her back, trying for self-control.

Mr Scott stood a few seconds contemplating her back, her downcast head. Her hair looked pretty when it caught the sun. It wasn't like Mrs Scott to give way. If it were Irene it would be different. She often threw fits about nothing at all. But, whatever her faults, Mrs Scott was generally a sensible cheerful woman. Why couldn't she see that she'd been lucky to keep her friend as long as she had done? Should he pat her shoulder? Better not. She might only fly out at him.

Mrs Scott put an end to his dilemma by saying: "Hadn't you better put the kettle on for washing up?"

"Right you are," said Mr Scott, and shuffled rapidly away into the scullery.

Mrs Scott replaced her handkerchief, and took out her flapjack. She dabbed her nose with powder, saying under her breath: "That's that." Then, moving briskly, she started to collect the dishes and bring them into the scullery.

STANDARD DEVIATION

Caoilinn Hughes

Caoilinn Hughes is the author of *Orchid & the Wasp* (2018), which won the Collyer Bristow Prize, and *Gathering Evidence* (2014), which won the Irish Times Shine/Strong Award 2015. Her short fiction has been awarded the Moth Short Story Prize and an O. Henry Prize in 2019. Her latest novel is *The Wild Laughter* (Oneworld, 2020).

There's the matter of girl or woman. There's the question of onus. Hers or anybody's or yours.

She appeared to be wearing two pendant necklaces, both with the same word in cursive. But if you got close you'd see that one was fake silver and the other was a green chain-shaped stain left on her blow-white skin. The word was Object. This would soon be a trend. Her friends would scour jewellery racks for nickel lettering to sully their décolletage. She couldn't help what she set in motion. The girl retied the rope-belt of her dress—white with navy pinstripes—and aligned her blue bra straps parallel with the dress's. A smile infused her cool expression in the restroom mirror. She'd accepted the trophy for 'Most Fashionable' at her High School graduation party a month prior, knowing full-well how silly-bitty such a moment was in relation to the life she was about to walk out to, when all the readying would pay off. Recalling so many green eyes on her like costume jewellery markings, chemicals were released in her brain or her womb or her groin—wherever chemicals came from. She hadn't decided upon a profession, but it would most definitely not be Lab Rat, so WGAFF vis-à-vis the origins of chemicals.

She pointed her phone at the restroom mirror, pulled a sceptical face and took a photo. Vis-à-vis. Voila. Décolletage. Touché. All the French. She must've been heeding Mrs. Lyons subliminally. The teenage brain was a fascinating organ. Muscle. Tissue. Limb. She opened Instagram and mouthed a possible caption: 'Too middle-aged nautical, pensez-vous? #perilsofprivilege #pearlsofprivilege'. She said the word hashtag aloud, ironically, because it was middle-agey. You had to balance wry self-deprecation, earnest self-appreciation and socio-political awareness. She dropped a pin in the haystack: Paris Gare du Nord.

As she tested what percentage of Perpetua filter to apply to the image, she caught sight of herself again in the mirror. Her belly was pilates-planked and her tongue was glued to her hard palate, to improve chin definition. She'd watched a YouTube tutorial on how to take a modelesque photo, out of sheer pragmatism because, in London, a scout can spot you on the tube and sign you for six figures. Imagining your shoulders being pulled apart pronounces your collarbones. Jutting your head forward casts a shadow around your face—lends you a jaw where you had none. Tilting your face down enlarges your eyes and makes a round face heart-shaped. But it made the girl look scalpy when she tried it. Alopecia wasn't accounted for in the #instagorgeous tips. Sneering at herself in the mirror, she let her belly swell like the hetero-fucking-sapien that she was. A bra strap slipped with her posture. The difference between desired and undesirable was *nothing*, the girl noted. The twitch of a muscle. Strategically-parted hair. And for what? And if the muscle wastes and the mark is unconcealable and the parting becomes parted?

She deleted the post and dropped her phone into her bag. Unclasped her necklace. The word was in English and she didn't want strangers to know her mother-tongue. It was an awkward time to be British in Europe. Not awkward like being... well, a lot of things. But still. She left the chain on the wet sink as a gift for some stranger, then dampened a wad of tissue to scrub the stain inscription from her skin. Like a hot towel taken to her smutty face.

On whatever pretence, the girl had hung back in London and departed after her friends. She'd wanted to feel this moment between one state of being and another, alone. To experience the flip side of independence: loneliness. She might stop off in Barcelona for a night. Eat tapas at a tablo-por-uno. Why not? She had a flexi-ticket. 'Your life is a flexi-ticket,' her brother's voice intruded. In her mind, his eyes were trained away from her body, bloodshot with the effort. He called her a spoiled twat, to which she'd said just because she *had* a spoiled twat didn't mean she *was* one. It was true that being a hot young female made the world more navigable, but she owed no one for that. It had its costs. A shiver surged from her sphincter to her scalp, then spilled onto the floor of her stomach. A shaken Pepsi bottle. Might she spew? She shifted on the plastic seat-bank. Scanned for a bin.

Evidently, she shouldn't have followed the instructions to be at the boarding area forty-five minutes before departure. The train probably wasn't even in France yet. Forty-five was a lot of minutes to be leered at. How many of these people would stay on for all eleven hours to Madrid? The hem of her nautical dress hauled thigh-ward when she crossed her legs. Her friends would have appreciated that her fishnet tights were satirical. To these people, they were slutty and, befitting their wearer, unimaginative. All they would see of such a girl, and see gladly, was the surface. Supposedly, she was duty-bound to contain it.

Lorde's 'Green Light' came through her earplugs. If Lorde made an album with Beyoncé, the girl mused, humans would reach peak music. She considered how this would play on various platforms. Twitter. Snapchat. Periscope. Yes, she was being frivolous, but there was only so much Save-the-NHS rhetoric a girl's circle could support and it was one hundred percent an aspect of patriarchy that frivolities were scorned in the first place. Obviously, there was everything to be fearful about and furious over. All a girl could do was take respite in a Portaloo amid the shitfest of Britain's problems.

Then, the girl's thoughts got derailed by a group of four drop-dead-gorgeous men awaiting a train to Milan in the next boarding area. They were talking with gusto, smiling widely, clutching one other's shoulders, so unlike the boys the girl knew, who brutishly bore one other's oppressive company. It wouldn't have surprised the girl if a queue formed around these men; if they used guitar cases to sign autographs or headshots. There was something spiritually uplifting about them. Their unabashed positivity. But one of the men—the handsomest one, according to the girl's qualitative-not-quantitative survey—looked very, very concerned, as if he'd lost something. As if what he'd lost was the girl.

A moment later, he was sitting beside the girl, facing her. Sharing in his concern, she met his gaze directly. His pale, round eyes were close-set. Like blown glass paperweights—swirling and suspended—made specifically to be rested upon something: upon her. The weight was perfectly-measured. They rendered her intelligible. He spoke heatedly in Italian, as if they knew one other, though he could see that her earplugs were in—she wouldn't be able to hear him. The earplugs had been engineered for her demographic, so they were pretty and shoddy and bled sound. 'Can you hear the violence?' Lorde sang. 'You'll feel it coasting.' A grin twisted the girl's mouth because the Italian man was so ridiculously animated and funny! His hands conducted a power ballad. Glisteningly white teeth flouted the espresso-culture stereo-type. No overpowering cologne, or BO like she was used to. If he smelled of anything, it was oatmeal. Tugging her earbuds free, the girl heard that he'd switched to English.

'… an other city. All the life depends on this. It's a tragedy!'

'What's a tragedy?' she asked.

The Italian man looked shocked. 'That I don't know you! That I am not your friend! That you are going this way and I am going that way!' The timbre of his voice was warm and grainy. 'I don't believe it. You are like nobody I ever saw. You are splendid. It is so rare. I hope that it's not offending. I know, is not usual, not at all, it can be crazy, and you can say no. I hope not. But of course it's possible. Only that the world it's so full of beauty we do not catch. You are more beautiful than a lily. A British rose.' His words tripped out, as if he couldn't say them urgently enough. 'Everything about you is *luminous*! Just look! How you sit. Not only how you look, but the energy coming from you, I feel it.' His words were lyrics filling in for the cut-off song. 'La ragazza più bella che abbia *mai* attraversato questa stazione, here you sit, listening to music. Not on Facebook, no, like the others, or writing a message to somebody. It's enough, your own mind. Da sola e magnifica. Bellissima sconosciuta.'

The girl laughed, only a tiny bit scathingly. At how peculiar it was, for any man—never mind one such as this—to be so effusive, unsarcastic, impassioned; risking so many witnesses to his rejection. He glanced back at the departure screen. 'I have to go. My friends, they think I am crazy. Forse è vero. It could be.' His shoulders were by his ears now in a stiff shrug and he faltered between smiling and frowning. 'But I must ask it. Not how you are called. What is your phone number. Or even your name, I don't ask it. Only to know if life can be like this. I want to know it, if it's possible. To kiss you.'

The Italian man made a prayer sign over his face—his fingers resting against his nose and his thumbs tucked under his jaw—awaiting retribution. As if he could barely watch; a distressed Caravaggio figure, modernized with designer stubble and two rings in the cartilage of his ear. Fellow passengers observed coolly, peripherally, as if the girl were a communal screen, displaying what's on sale, the weather forecast in adjacent territories, a trailer revealing far too much plot. A spoiler. 'Prêt … l'embarquement,' the announcement went, but no one stood or buttoned their coats. *Prêt,* the word was repeated. More vocabulary the girl unknowingly knew. There was that café franchise, Prêt a Manger. Or was it a chain? A handful of men had the controlling stake. British men? There were so many Prêt a Mangers in Europe, it took effort not to eat at one. The girl's breath quivered, as if her ribs were rail-lines, but it was only Lorde's monosyllables directed at her chest.

When she nodded, the Italian man's eyes lifted away from her. For a moment, she floated without the weight of them and lost her place in the story. His dense glass gaze returned to her mouth and she was distilled again as he leaned in. Then he turned and kissed—instead—the space between her cheek and ear. His stubble sounded of rain. His mouth, of a window opened onto it.

Had he meant only that? To kiss her cheek?

Was that all?

The girl grasped for air, as for full-body armour to delay mortification, but the Italian man was there to take her breath as she'd wanted it taken. He didn't hesitate to kiss her well. Now, with the thawing sensation of relief, she kissed him back. On her cheekbones, she felt him smiling. Tasted the sharp development of salt on her tongue. If there was only one organ in the skull, the brain wasn't it.

'It was a dream,' he said, after. 'Reality, it cannot be so pure. And beautiful.' He regarded the girl in the sorrowful-consuming way one regards the museum's prize painting as closing-time is announced. And he was gone. His friends had turned their backs, for privacy, and a queue finally subsumed them. All the trains had arrived and were leaving. Belongings were towed meaninglessly as shadows.

Still, passengers around the girl loitered, ogling her stubble-reddened mouth. If they watched, it would fade faster, the bliss in her body. Her uncouth pleasure. Her privileging the transient personal moment over the eternal political one. The impulse was to cover her body, but the girl was warm. Her skin was goose-pimpled and sweat-damp. 'Crabs are all you'll catch with fishnet stockings,' her father had said. Shirking the gaze was impossible, however she tried. Her actions would take place in a mise-en-abyme. She would flee, inside having fled, after fleeing. Behind her nod to a stranger was a larger nod to the greater stranger. The fault was recursive. Everything amplified and echoed, which may have been the effect of a life enlarging, or the distance between her own body and her grasp of it. Resolutely, the girl collected the fragments of her self and got them in line, obedient.

Hours seemed to pass before she was settled for the long journey. A seat at the end of the quietest carriage bought her space at the price of a foul stench from the toilet. It didn't matter. Finally, she could release what remained of the smile. Have her own response to her own actions. Girlishly, she traced her knuckles across her lips and tried to amber the memory—suspend it from its surroundings and keep it just as it was: a singular, dizzy, pressing thing.

The girl warped her smile into a yawn for the ticket collector, which felt like a Cirque du Soleil manoeuvre. Soleil. Sorry, she said drowsily. It took an age to brighten the screen of her phone for her ticket to be scanned. A cackle got caught in her throat. 'Excusez-moi,' she said to no one. Had it been validated? Was she not heard? Earplugs were in her ears, but nothing played through them. Melodrama was all sung out. She stared at the screen, blurry with notifications. What did all that surface approval matter, now that she'd kissed an Italian stranger in Paris Gard du Nord and her father would never find out. Maybe it was weird, and she felt it now, but that's how one learns. By doing. Nodding, an earbud fell from her ear and she pushed it back, in case a song would play. She was a fortunate person, so it stood within reason that music might just resound. *My* house. Under *my* roof. Hussy. Chez-moi. Voulez-vous. Blubber now, over what?

So dorky of her to have tissue in the corner of her mouth. How long had it been there? It was her chest, though, she'd scrubbed. So not her fault, entirely? She should have filled a bottle with water. L'eau. Hello? What's French for object? And mouth? She wiped the paper dreg and her hand flopped onto her lap. Her bottom lip pouted because the red icon on her phone meant battery low. If she napped, it might recharge. Fluky brat. Loose bitch. Enfant terrible. The girl wanted there to be another passenger, because it was quite unpleasant now. Aloneness. Sick, sinking tunnel blackouts. Patterns on the window. Outside smearing by, like a riverbank. She saw herself, then, in the Perspex, slumped. Imagine your shoulders pulled apart, she thought. Tilt your head forward and down—not so far. Not to your lap! If they saw you now. Most fashionable! LOL. ROFL. People coming, and a wheelchair. They set you upright. Swipe your weak chin dry. *Shhhh*. Fine, fine, sleep. It's understandable. When no one's serenading anyone. Make do with the warm, grainy background sounds. You can say something, but it's acronyms. It won't caption you. No one will follow. Hush now. Through slitted eyes, watch.

TRIO

Jennifer Johnston

Jennifer Johnston is better known as a novelist, but has contributed many short stories to many anthologies over the years. Her acclaimed work includes the novels *How Many Miles to Babylon*, *Shadows on Our Skin* (shortlisted for the Booker Prize) and *The Old Jest*, which won the Whitbread Book Award in 1979. In 2012, she was presented with the Lifetime Achievement Award at the Irish Book Awards.

In spite of the brilliant, sliding sun the evening was cold. Frank pushed his hands deep down into his pockets and stamped his feet uselessly.

'What a wind.'

Dust and an empty cigarette-box skeltered past their feet, down the hill past the waiting gateways and the neat hedges.

'West. It's from the west. That means rain. More rain. God, I'll be glad when this winter's over.'

Murphy pulled on his cigarette and let the smoke trickle slowly out through his nose. He was wearing a knitted hat pulled well down over his ears.

Frank shuffled his feet on the pavement again.

'I get chilblains,' he complained. 'Every bloody winter. There's nothing you can do about it. There was one year I didn't, that was the time I was working in London. It's the damp. So they say. Drive you crazy sometimes, so they would. Just that one year I didn't get them.'

Murphy sighed. Talkers. He was always lumbered with a talker. Voices always nagging away, nudging their way into his head, never letting him be at peace with his own thoughts. Silence was good. Golden, his mother used to say. He turned and squinted his eyes towards the setting sun. Golden, but you couldn't see with it dazzling in your eyes, even when you turned your head away again you couldn't focus for a moment or two. He walked back up the street towards the main road. With a bit of luck the sun would be behind the hill in about ten minutes.

'Did you ever suffer with chilblains?' asked Frank behind him.

'No.'

'You wouldn't know then what it's like at all.'

'No.'

They stood at the corner for a few moments, watching the cars go by. Behind them, below where they had been standing, a man sat, reading a book, in a parked car. Murphy dropped the butt of his cigarette on the pavement and then put his foot on it.

'What's the time?'

Murphy looked at his watch.

'Ten to.'

'He's late.'

They stared across the valley at the distant hills, the glitter.

'It'd be a great evening if it wasn't so cold. Maybe he'll not come.'

They turned and strolled back down the road again.

'He'll come all right.'

Patrick opened the door of his car and threw his briefcase over onto the back seat. Late. He got into the car and slammed the door. Meticulously he placed his thin white hands on the steering-wheel and stared at them. What does it matter anyway? Late or early. Nobody else worries. No one gets agitated. We all have our own obsessions. I like to treat time with care. He started the engine and sat listening to the comfortable sound of it. Like a cat by the fire. What precisely do I consider myself to be late for? The small preoccupations of domestic life. The kiss on the cheek. The careful arrangement of glasses on a tray. Clink, clink across the hall, taking care not to slip on the Persian carpet. Last shafts of sun and then pull the curtains, keep our privacy to ourselves. No dreams. No time for dreams. The stir and tumult of defeated dreams... who could have said that? From those years when I read books and nervously brooded on the meanings of things. I must tidy things up and have a break. I'm tired. He laughed and moved the car slowly forward across the yard. A break indeed. What happens I wonder when you, for a moment, realise the emptiness of the future, oh and God the past. The dreamlessness even of the past. Forget it. Impeccable safety.

'Good evening, sir.'

George, the security man, opened the gate into the street.

Patrick smiled and nodded.

'You're late tonight, sir. It's ten to.'

'Telephones should never have been invented.'

'Goodnight.'

'Goodnight, George. See you in the morning.'

'Of course he'll come.'

'But if he doesn't? What do we do?'

'We come back tomorrow.'

Murphy's voice was exasperated.

The wind was banging at their backs, pushing them firmly down the hill.

'I suppose we would.' Frank sighed. 'My sister's just been took into the hospital. Just there a few minutes before I came out. Her first. Ay. I know she'll be expecting me up to see her tomorrow.

The way of the world, thought Murphy, one goes, another comes. Apart from his own somewhat amazed arrival into the world, he had no close, touching experiences of either birth or death. It didn't do to look at the whole thing in a broad, emotional way. Achievement was what mattered.

'That is, if he comes...'

Murphy's cap had worked its way up on to the top of his head. He pulled it firmly, warmly down over his ears again.

The gate closed behind him. The traffic was edging slowly along between the high warehouses. Time, as usual, being wasted, maltreated. Then suppose, just suppose that I treated time as if it belonged to me. I am no longer time's servant. What then? It becomes at once a precious commodity. The only one worth having. Will I turn on the radio and listen to the news? Drown the sound of my own thoughts? I hate this street, the unpainted windows and the dirty walls. Hate is a word I haven't used since I was a child, and now, having used it, I feel myself filling with it, feel it burning inside me. It feels good. I must be having a little madness of some sort. I don't want to hold things together any longer. Not even at home. In the words of the immortal Greta Garbo. I want to be alone. Free. Me and my servant Time. Unobtainable, before it is too late. Christ. To have to watch yet again the great triumphal renewal of the earth as we ourselves decay. Break. I must break. My life in shreds.

'It's her first.'

'So you said.'

Mam went with her in the ambulance. Just to give her a bit of... well you know... moral support like. Sean's in England. That's her husband. She thought she'd like to have it here. At home. I suppose you're nervous with the first one. Mam went with her. I'd say she'd be all right, wouldn't you?'

'You're to cover me. That's all you're to do.'

'I'll try and get to see her tomorrow. That is...'

'Did you hear me?'

A small girl with a dog on a lead walked past them down the hill. She walked past the gate and the parked car and then crossed the road and went into a garden on the other side. Inside the gate she stooped and let her dog free. Huge clouds were beginning to pile up in the sky. The sun was almost gone. The hedge beside them smelt sweet.

'Whose child is that?'

'How the hell would I know whose child it is.'

They turned and walked slowly up towards the corner again. The man in the car put down his book and switched on the engine. Down the road a door banged. Frank groped in his pocket.

'Would you like a fag?'

'No. Did you hear what I said? You are to cover me. Nothing more. Just keep your eyes skinned.'

'I wonder will it be a boy or a girl.'

Only a golden line of sun. Rain was blowing from the west. It was going to be a stormy night.

So many wrong decisions I have made all the way down the line. I never searched for courage, never realised the possible need for it. Can I summon that neglected asset now, before it is too late? If... It's just nerves Mary would say. The situation is getting you down. You should take a break... pull yourself together. That's what I'll do. I'll go home and have a large drink and pull myself together. Face whatever it is she has arranged for me to face. It is unkind and totally unrealistic to throw the blame on her. Face my own music. Or else I could do the other thing.

He slowed down the car and pulled in to the side of the road.

I could. There is nothing to stop me. I could fill the car with petrol, I could... Commitments, aged commitments. Lack of courage. Worse, of hope. They would bring me back. I would blow it. He moved back into the mainstream of traffic.

I wouldn't mind what it was really. She'd like a wee boy. You want it to be all right. That's what really matters. You know, all right. One of my aunties had one that was... well... not quite right. That'd be always in your mind. He's grown up now. He's not too bad, just a bit soft, you know... but nice enough.'

Paining my head, all this talk. But maybe he's right, time is getting on. Maybe he's not coming.

Several large drops of rain, blown by the wind, scattered themselves on the ground.

Frank ducked his head into the collar of his coat.

'What did I tell you? Rain.'

Behind the clouds the sky was stained pink now.

'Red sky at night…'

'Oh, for Jesus' sake…'

'What's up, Murphy?'

They stood for a moment and then turned their backs on the west.

'Nerves?'

Slowly they moved down the street once more. Murphy felt in his pocket for a cigarette.

'Nerves got you?'

He put the cigarette into his mouth.

'I'd say you're right. He's not coming,' he said at last. His hand fumbled for the matches.

'It's late now. Too late.'

The car down the street revved its engine. Murphy dropped the cigarette on the ground.

'Just cover me,' he said. 'Don't do another bloody thing.'

Patrick slowed down and turned into the street. There was a car moving towards him and then past him as he swung the wheel to turn in the gate.

The spring will come and then the summer. I have no energy, no will. I will put on my smile. I will resume my role. I will wait.

He became aware of the two men walking down the path towards him. Quite casually they seemed to come, the guns raised in their hands.

How strange, how very, very strange…

There was no more time.

The echoing frightened some birds, who flew uneasily into the air. Far away a dog barked. The car accelerated and was gone. It was almost dark.

A LOVE

Neil Jordan

Neil Jordan's first book of stories, *Night In Tunisia*, won the Guardian Fiction Prize in 1979, and his critically acclaimed novels include *The Past, Shade, The Drowned Detective* and *Carnivalesque*. His films have won multiple awards, including an Academy Award (*The Crying Game*), a Golden Lion at Venice, A Silver Bear in Berlin and several BAFTAs. He lives in Dublin.

There were no cars in Dublin when I met you again, the streets had been cleared for the funeral of the President who had died. I remembered you talking about him and I thought of how we would have two different memories of him. He was your father's generation, the best and the worst you said. I remembered your father's civil war pistol, black and very real, a cowboy gun. It was that that first attracted me, me a boy beyond the fascination of pistols but capable of being seduced by a real gun owned by a lady with real bullets – I shattered two panes in your glasshouse and the bullet stuck in the fence beyond the glass-house shaking it so it seemed to be about to fall into the sea and float with the tide to Bray Head. Then you took the gun from me saying no-one should play with guns, men or boys and put the hand that held it in your blouse, under your breast. And I looked at you, an Irish woman whose blouse folded over and was black and elegant in the middle of the day, whose blouse hid a gun besides everything else. But except that you smiled at me with a smile that meant more than all those I would just have been a kid bringing a message from his father to a loose woman. As it was you walked over the broken glass away from me and I stepped after you over the broken pieces to where the view of the sea was and you began to teach me love.

And when we met again there were no cars and the headlines talked about love and guns and the man who had died and I wondered how different your memory of him would be from mine. It was a stupid pursuit since I had no memory of him other than from photographs and then only a big nose and bulging eyes and spectacles but I knew you would be changed and I knew I was changed and I wanted to stop thinking about it.

There were no cars but there were flowers in the giant pots on O'Connell

Bridge, there was a band somewhere playing slow music and there were crowds everywhere on the pavement, women mostly who remembered him as something important, women who clutched handbags to their stomachs and stared at the road where the funeral would soon pass. I could sense the air of waiting from them, they had all their lives waited, for a funeral, a husband, a child coming home, women your age, with your figure, they had loved abstractly whereas you had loved concretely with a child like me. That was the difference I told myself but it was probably only that I knew you and I didn't know them. But that had always been the difference, all women had been a mother to someone but you had been a lover to me. And I focused my eyes on the empty street with them and wondered had that difference faded.

I went into the cafe then and it smelt of Dublin, Ireland, the musty femininity of the women waiting on the kerb for the men to pass, dead, heroic, old and virginal. I sat by the plate glass window and looked at the shiny chrome expresso machine, a cloud of steam rising from it. A girl in a blue smock with an exhausted face brought me coffee and I felt for the first time that I was back somewhere. I tasted the coffee and got the cheap caffeine bite, details like that, the girl's legs, too thin so the nylons hung in folds around them. Outside I could hear the brass band coming nearer, louder like the slowed step soldiers use in funerals. I knew I was out of step, it was all militarism now, like air in a blister, under the skin, it was swelling, the militarism I had just learned of before, in the school textbooks. Then I remembered something else about him, the man who had died, he had been the centre of the school textbooks, his angular face and his thirties collar and his fist raised in a gesture of defiance towards something out there, beyond the rim of the brown photograph, never defined. And I wondered whether I'd rather be out of step here or in step in London, where the passions are rational. And I felt the nostalgia of the emigrant, but it was as if I was still away, as if here in the middle of it all I was still distant, remembering, apart from it. I shook myself but couldn't get rid of the feeling. Something had happened to me since leaving, something had happened to me long before I left, but then everything changes, I told myself and some things die. So I just looked out the plate-glass window and listened to the slow brass, swelling more all the time.

Then I saw someone looking like you coming down the street towards the cafe and as that someone came nearer I saw it was you, still you, your hair had got a little greyer but still kept that luxuriant brownness, your face had got thinner and fatter, thinner round the cheekbones, fatter round the jaw and neck. You hadn't seen me yet but I couldn't get myself to rise out of the seat so you would see me, I wanted to look at you like you were a photograph. I was remembering that letter of my father's, the only letter, that said you were sick and you did look sick, in the quiet way of bad sicknesses, cancer and the like. And then you opened the glass door and the brass music grew to an orchestra and the door closed and the music faded again and still I couldn't get up. And you were standing over me.

'Neil' you said!
   'Yes' I said.
   'Well' you said.
   'Yes' I said again.
   And then you sat down beside me, I was a child who isn't saying something, the thin girl came over to take your order. We were the only two in the cafe, you were talking, I was listening to you, quite natural, ordinary things after all. We were different, I was a young adult, you were an old adult, we both fingered coffee cups, mine cold, yours hot. I tried obscurely to remember, I had been an Irish boy with greased hair and a collarless leather jacket, you had been a single woman who kept a guest-house in a town called Greystones and now both of us were neither, my hair was dry and short, it came straight down my forehead and my forehead had a few lines, though people still told me sometimes that I looked sixteen, you were living in a house somewhere on the South Side, you didn't work now though the car keys you squeezed in your palm and the fur sleeves that hung dead from your wrists made you look well-off, in an extravagant, haphazard way.
   Then you mentioned the dead man outside.

And somehow it began to come right. I noticed the black silk blouse under the coat, the loose and mottled skin where your neck met your breast. I remembered the nights lying in your old creaking bed that looked out on the sea, our movements like a great secret between us, silent, shocking movements, our silence a guard against my father who had the room down below, our lovemaking a quiet desecration of the holiday town, of the church at the top of the hill, of the couples you fed so properly at mealtimes, of my embarrassed adolescence, the guilt you tried to banish in me, the country, the place, the thing you tried to hit at through me you taught me to hit through you. And all the time for me there was my father lying underneath, cold most likely, and awake and I wanted him to hear the beast I was creating with you, I wanted him to hear it scratching, creaking through to him from above, for your body was like the woman he must have loved to have me, I had seen her in those brown faded photographs with a floppy hat and a cane, in a garden, like you but fatter, with a lot of clothes that came off, the coloured dresses and blouses first, then the white underclothes, dampened under the armpits, between the legs. And when you undressed on the beach and I watched you from the road, watched each thing falling in a bundle on the sand, you could have been her, you could have been anyone's mother only you were naked with a belly that drooped a little and a triangle of hair underneath it. Only that when you saw me you didn't shy from my frightened stare, you smiled. That smile began it. But what perpetuated it was something outside, my mathematical father lying sleepless on his bed, your civil-war gun, rosaries, that rain-soaked politician with his fist raised, clenched. Against something. Something.

The brass band seemed much nearer now, going ahead of the same politician's cortege, ceremonial, thudding slow brass. I was watching you drinking your coffee. The brass music was cascading about you. I looked at the thin part of your face, you had no make-up on, your eyes looked almost ordinary. You were different and the same, I was different and the same, I knew that that is how things happen. And yet I'd met you because I wanted something more. We are all different threads, I told myself and once we had woven each other's threads into something like a bow. Once.

'Well'.

We were stuck on that word. Then I plunged.

'What are we going to do then, before I go back?'

'Back where?'

And I don't know whether you wanted to know, but I told you it all, about the hairdresser's in Kensal Rise, the women who tipped me pound notes if I touched their plump shoulders and told them they were too young for a blue rinse.

'Is that what you do'.

'Yes'.

And I told you about the cockney queen I shared a room with who I despised but who could be warm when—

'And don't you act now—'

And yes, I told you about the sweaty revues, revue being synonymous with theatrical sex, I told you about the empty stages where we rehearsed in our underwear and fingered each other's goosepimples, simulated copulation. Then I stopped, because you were drinking your coffee again and your unmadeup face looked sad, like an adolescent, the one I had been. And for a moment I was the experienced one, I clutched the gun, under my breasts, between the sheaves of my black blouse.

*

'We'll go to Clare. Lisdoonvarna'.

'Why there', I asked.

'I am past my prime. They are places for people past their prime'.

And I wondered should you say 'prime' or 'primes', I thought of all the hotels and guest-houses I had never been to. I knew middle-aged people went to those places and met men and took the waters and married maybe and drank sherries looking at the Atlantic, in bars that were probably closed now for De Valera's death.

'It's Autumn and everyone there will be past their prime. I want to see the bachelors court the spinsters. I want to take the waters. I want to drive in a Morris Minor past the Burren and look at the unusual flowers'.

There was an accusation in your voice as if you were trying to tell me something, something I didn't want to hear. I thought maybe you wanted to fit yourself, label yourself and I wondered would your conformity be as bizarre as my attempts at it had been.

You talked about happiness then, a murderous happiness that followed you round like a pet dog. And I looked at you, you had pressed your unpainted lips together, the blood had gone out of them and I saw the need for happiness that had ravaged you, I wondered what deity it was that would label you old maid or spinster when you had once pressed that happiness on me. Then I heard the band outside, so loud now, and the cortege was passing and the band was playing the old nationalist tunes to a slow tempo. I felt I was watching an animal dying through the plate-glass window, an animal that was huge, murderous, contradictory and I looked up at your face, not much older really than when I had last seen you and I looked out the plate-glass window again at the funeral of the man I didn't remember, the man you would have remembered. I wondered what your memories were, your associations. And I looked at your eyes, bare and washed clean and I somehow knew.

We walked outside then and the brass music became a deafening thud. We walked slowly down the street, we couldn't talk, the music was so loud. I bought a newspaper at the corner of Abbey Street and saw a headline about the funeral that was crawling along beside us. We passed a TV sales shop where a crowd of people were staring at a white screen, staring at the death being celebrated behind them.

As I remember you I define you, I choose bits of you and like a child with a colouring-book, I fill you out. The car-keys are swinging on your finger, your forefinger and thumb choose one, insert it in the lock and your whole hand tenses in the turning. Your car is like you said, a Morris Minor. It's grey and covered in dents and the chrome is rusty. Your hand turning is reddish, sunburnt, which accentuates more its many creases. Then a man-sized watch and the sleeve of your coat where the fur has rubbed off.

Once it was desire I filled you out with, not memory. You were a blown-up photograph to me, a still from a film. I brought the youthful sullenness I learnt from the hit songs to you. I ate chips before I came to you, my fingers stank of vinegar, my breath of nicotine. And you played with me, you let me fill you out, you played Ava Gardner to my James Dean. But I chose, I was arbitrary, I took what I wanted. Your brown hair, your anxious mouth, your bare feet – on the straw bedroom mat. I took some and left the rest, I didn't know what the rest meant, I didn't know what varicose veins meant or fallen arches or lace curtains, respectability, spinsterhood. I plead guilty but ignorant, I didn't know what woman meant.

'Can you drive?'

I said no. I said I would like to, I would like to feel machinistic and free but my father never drove so no-one taught me.

'What do you mean', you asked 'Machinistic—'

And I hadn't known what I meant, I got confused, I said something about the wheel driving, following the white line. Then you were quiet for a while, whether from tactfulness or not I don't know and then—

'I wasn't made for cars'.

I didn't believe you, you had shaped this car to fit you. You drove it like it fitted you, through the city that was empty, that had put its best side out for the man who had died. The streets were clean, the buildings were respectful, they seemed to curtsy before us as you drove. Then they got thinner and thinner and we were on the dual carriageway, driving west.

'I idolised him once'.

I meant to ask you about your sickness but the words wouldn't come. So you talked while you drove, abstracted talk.

'I was taught to idolise him, everyone was. I remember standing at meetings, holding my father's hand, waving a tricolour, shouting Up Dev. My father wore a cloth cap and a trenchcoat, everyone did then'.

Your eyes were squinted towards the road as if you saw what you were remembering on it.

'His face was like a schoolteacher's. Or maybe all schoolteachers tried to look like him. You could never see his eyes clearly because of his glasses. They were the first thing you noticed after his nose'.

We were passing Monasterevin. The town looped in a semi-circle round your car.

'Have you ever been to the West?'

'No', I said.

'You'll never understand this country till you have'.

Your voice sounded older, consciously older, something valedictory in it that made me remember the night my father took you out and me with him as his fifteen years old son, mature enough for adult company, my father being a lecturer in maths and a widower, a natural partner for you who was single, who kept the guesthouse he stayed in. We went to a variety in Bray where a Scottish comedian told Irish jokes and a youth with a guitar sang Lonnie Donegan songs and two girls with a ukelele sang George Formby and kicked their legs on either side of the stand-up mike. And afterwards we went for a meal in the Royal Hotel, we ate roast beef and drank sherry. I poured your sherry with the distance he had trained me in and I sat at the far end of the table while you both talked, he at length, you with many pregnant pauses. You talked about life, about friends in public life, who you knew of through your father, who he knew of through his work, he prided himself on both his aloofness from the world and his reserved contact with it. You were beautiful and intimidating in a navy dress and shawl and while in your silences you spoke to me, me in my greased hair and the suit I was told to wear, in your conversation you spoke to him and you managed the pretending so adroitly that in the end I was fooled and I screamed at you afterwards and it took three days for our mutual secret to build up again between us, for me to hold the you I wanted in my unwashed arms, selfishly and viciously, for you to tell me again about love and irreligion, about other countries where women are young at the age of thirty-nine and boys are men at fifteen.

'Are you happy?'

'Sometimes', I said.

'You used to be. You used to be very quiet, very joyful and very sullen'.

We were passing Portlaoise, the barbed-wire towers of the prison and the red wall of the mental hospital.

'It was all in your face', you said. 'In the way your snub-nose twitched—'

And we both laughed then, it sounded stupid but we laughed and your laugh was like a peal, you could have been standing in the broken pieces of glass again, beside the glasshouse, laughing. I tightened my nose like a rabbit the way I used to do, then I flushed in embarrassment doing it and that made you laugh louder, so loud that you began coughing and had to stop the car and wipe your mouth. There was blood on the kleenex you wiped it with.

'We're different', you said.

'Yes', I said. And you looked at me and giggled again. Like someone very young. Too young. You put your arms around me and kissed my face and I stayed very quiet, feeling you again, smelling you again. Your lips opened on my cheek and I could hear a tiny whistle off your breath.

'Aren't we?'

'Yes', I said, 'We're different' and I kissed you back so you could feel how different. But you stopped me.

'Don't try and change me'.

'How could I?'

'You could', you said, 'You could change me back'.

But you were happy then, weren't you? You began to drive faster, swerving gaily to avoid pigeons. You asked me about myself and my father and I answered both as well as I could. You still coughed every now and then and once you had to stop the car, your whole body tensed as if you were in pain. Your fingers clenched the wheel, they seemed to get even thinner and the bones on the backs of your hands were thin, leading like a scallop to the fingers. But you got over it then, you began to drive, you told me not to mind you, that you were only dying, it's a common complaint and you laughed like before and I laughed with you. Then we stopped in a pub for a drink and I drank a gin while you drank a pint of stout and the barman remarked on how it's normally the other way round.

When we were driving again we saw a fat girl standing by a petrol-pump following every car that passed her with her eyes and thumb. You wanted to stop but I didn't let you, I thought she'd come between us and the laughing. So we drove on and I had a clear view of the disappointment in her large blue eyes as she fumbled with her handbag, realizing the car wasn't going to stop after all. And I felt sorry for a moment but your mad peculiar gaiety filled the car again and stopped me feeling sorry.

When we came to Limerick you got quieter and I thought we were stopping since it was almost dark. But you said that you hated it there and you drove on till we came to a sign saying Lahinch and a street that was flanked by burrows and summer houses. You stopped. It was fully dark. We were on the street of a seaside town. I could see a beach at the end of the street, then sea, a different sea from the one we had left. But then all seas are the same, I thought and when we walked down to the beach and watched the tide sucking off the long strand I saw it was the same, like the one that had washed your guest-house.

I began to feel it all again, the seaside town, you beside me, wild and intractable and almost old, the bed and breakfast signs, the guesthouses. In the bars men stared at us, men that looked like weekend golfers but I didn't mind, you drank your guinness while I drank my gin, you talked about happiness so much that I had to tell you to stop.

And then we went to a guest-house and it was like yours, it had a grey granite front weeping from the seabreeze, like yours except that it was a man that signed us in, held out the guest book for us with large, country hands. You paid.

I went behind you up the stairs. Your breathing was so heavy that it sang in my ears. And then we were in the room and it was so bare, there were two beds, a wash-hand basin, a Virgin and a cinema poster, so seductively bare. You asked me to turn while you undressed. My face must have shown my surprise because before I could answer you turned. And I watched you, I saw your clothes form a little heap around your feet, I saw your shoulders that were very thin and your waist that was almost fat now and your buttocks and your legs. And your skin told me you were definitely older. When you were in your nightgown you turned.

'Come on', you said.

There was a knowledge burning through both of us, it was like the yearning that had been there years before, a secret, like blood. But it wasn't a yearning, it was a question and an answer. You knew that with every garment you took off you were stepping into a past self, a self that had that yearning and you could see from my face that I knew too.

'Come on', you said again.

And I took off my clothes and I wore the nakedness I had worn for you, I was a boy then, and I took off your nightdress so you could wear it too.

I didn't look at you, I put my arms around you, standing there, both of us were breathing, our chests touching. You stepped backwards towards the bed.

'Come on', you said.

And we were on the bed, the sea was breathing outside like a woman, we were moving together but I wasn't thinking of you, not you now anyway, I was thinking of you before, of the time he brought you out, the second time, the time after which something finished for me and for you and for him too maybe. He brought you to the Great Northern Hotel this time, and me, there were meal-tables there and a small space for dancing to a small three-piece band. And the meal was like before, you laughing with him and being silent every now and then and me pouring sherry for both of you, in good suit and greased hair. And when the meal was finished the reddish lights came on and the dancing began. The band played waltzes and both of you moved across the floor among other shapeless couples, you beautiful, him tall and supremely confident of something as he waltzed. And I sat there looking and saw him for the first time not as my father who wrote equations on sheets of paper into the night and knew a lot about things like sea-shells but as someone young and agile who had the same yearning for you as I had. And as I drank the sherry that you both had left I began to cry, I felt older than him, insanely older, I had the knowledge *of* you that made him dance so gracefully, that made that difference in him. Then I drank more sherry and saw his hands around your waist almost touching at the back and I knew people do that when they waltz but I began to hate him as I would hate someone my age. Then again I saw his eyes, distant and kind of hopeful, more hopeful than whenever he had looked at me and as I knew the yearning that was behind them I stopped my hate and felt baffled, sad, older than I could bear. The band was playing the Tennessee Waltz I remembered and I tried to catch your eye but you were looking the other way, looking strict, virginal, leonine. And then I felt the huge resentment, I couldn't do anything with it, my hands were shaking and I knew something was going to end. And you both came back and I pushed the bottle onto the floor with my hand so it would break, so nobody would know how much I had drunk, hoping it would look like an accident. But the crash was loud and everyone stared and he, my father, lost what he had had with you and went white, and shouted at me and you looked quickly at me and I felt I was a child, being chastened publicly. And later I lay in your bed with this huge resentment and hate. You were asleep when I heard him coming up the first floor landing and opening the toilet door. And I got up and you were still asleep, I took the gun from your drawer and went down and stood outside the toilet door. And when I heard the chain pull and I knew he was standing buttoning his fly I raised your civil-war gun and fired quickly four times into the door. And there were four bangs and four rapid thuds and I saw each shot wedging, hardly piercing the mahogany. And I ran upstairs knowing something had finished and I gave you the gun and cursed you quietly because it didn't work—

And then I stopped remembering, you were underneath me, I had come inside you in the room in Clare. Your arms were around my neck, hard, rigid and you said what I was remembering, 'It's finished', you said. And you kissed me tenderly and I kissed you back so you could feel how different we were. And I got from your bed quietly, you were exhausted, turning to sleep already. I lay in my own bed listening to the sea outside me, listening to your breathing. There was a luminous statue of the Virgin over you on the wall and a cinema poster. It said I WAS HAPPY HERE in bold letters and showed a woman in a romantic pose looming over a matchbox version of the town we were in. Then I looked at you and saw the eiderdown rising each time you breathed and your body clenching itself every now and then as if you were dreaming of pain. And I knew it had ended but I still thought to myself, maybe tomorrow—

And tomorrow you got up and drove, you drove to the town you had told me about, where the bachelors and the spinsters come, where you take the waters. We passed the fat girl again on the road but you didn't stop. And the town was like any other holiday town only more so, with its square of hotels and its peeling wooden verandas and old-fashioned cane chairs lining the verandas.

We stopped in the square. It looked strange to me, a holiday town that's inland. I said this to you, why no sea and you said 'There's the sulphur waters'.

We walked up the street a little. A man stared. I bought a guide-book in a shop. I thought of water and holidays, why they go together. Every building seemed to imply a beach, but there was none. It was as if the sea had once been here, but retreated back to Miltown Malbay, leaving a fossil. Somewhere a front door banged.

It was saying something to us, you were saying something, saying This is it, is me, always has been, the part of me you never saw, didn't want to see. And I believed it then, I knew you had always been coupled in my mind with hotels, with cane-chairs and ball-and-claw armchairs. And I crossed the square and bought a paper and read more about the President who had died, but in small print now.

We drove out to the Spa, to a building that looked like a Swiss hotel, but with a river that seemed to come from underneath it. You asked me did I want to come in and I said no, so you went through the two glass doors alone.

I sat in the car wondering whether you drank the waters or bathed in them. A couple passed, wearing suits that must have been too hot for the weather. I shouted at them 'Do you drink the water', I shouted, 'or swim in it'. The man looked at me and threw his hands up uncomprehendingly. I watched them going through the glass doors and imagined a room with a clean tiled floor through which flowed brackish, slow water. I imagined you taking your clothes off with a lot of older men and women and I watched from the side as you dipped yourself into the spa waters among people who had the minor complaints of middle-age to wash off, who had made the act of faith in water. But then, I might have been quite wrong, maybe you sat on a wooden bench in a line with other people and drank the brackish water from a tap.

And I knew it was definitely ending anyhow and that I should forget for your sake the peculiar yearning that sprang in me when my cock sprang to attention in my tight trousers that day you put the gun between your breasts into your blouse. You called it love, I remember. And it must have been.

EVELINE

James Joyce

James Joyce (1882–1941) is best known for his novel *Ulysses*, set in 1904, the year he left Dublin to live in Europe for the rest of his life. It was published in 1922. His debut publication was a collection of poetry, but his first fiction was the short story collection, *Dubliners*. His novels include *Finnegans Wake* and *A Portrait of the Artist As a Young Man*.

She sat at the window watching the evening invade the avenue. Her head was leaned against the window curtains and in her nostrils was the odour of dusty cretonne. She was tired.

Few people passed. The man out of the last house passed on his way home; she heard his footsteps clacking along the concrete pavement and afterwards crunching on the cinder path before the new red houses. One time there used to be a field there in which they used to play every evening with other people's children. Then a man from Belfast bought the field and built houses in it—not like their little brown houses but bright brick houses with shining roofs. The children of the avenue used to play together in that field—the Devines, the Waters, the Dunns, little Keogh the cripple, she and her brothers and sisters. Ernest, however, never played: he was too grown up. Her father used often to hunt them in out of the field with his blackthorn stick; but usually little Keogh used to keep *nix* and call out when he saw her father coming. Still they seemed to have been rather happy then. Her father was not so bad then; and besides, her mother was alive. That was a long time ago; she and her brothers and sisters were all grown up; her mother was dead. Tizzie Dunn was dead, too, and the Waters had gone back to England. Everything changes. Now she was going to go away like the others, to leave her home.

Home! She looked round the room, reviewing all its familiar objects which she had dusted once a week for so many years, wondering where on earth all the dust came from. Perhaps she would never see again those familiar objects from which she had never dreamed of being divided. And yet during all those years she had never found out the name of the priest whose yellowing photograph hung on the wall above the broken harmonium beside the coloured print of the promises made to Blessed Margaret Mary Alacoque. He had been a school friend of her father. Whenever he showed the photograph to a visitor her father used to pass it with a casual word:

"He is in Melbourne now."

She had consented to go away, to leave her home. Was that wise? She tried to weigh each side of the question. In her home anyway she had shelter and food; she had those whom she had known all her life about her. Of course she had to work hard, both in the house and at business. What would they say of her in the Stores when they found out that she had run away with a fellow? Say she was a fool, perhaps; and her place would be filled up by advertisement. Miss Gavan would be glad. She had always had an edge on her, especially whenever there were people listening.

"Miss Hill, don't you see these ladies are waiting?"

"Look lively, Miss Hill, please."

She would not cry many tears at leaving the Stores.

But in her new home, in a distant unknown country, it would not be like that. Then she would be married—she, Eveline. People would treat her with respect then. She would not be treated as her mother had been. Even now, though she was over nineteen, she sometimes felt herself in danger of her father's violence. She knew it was that that had given her the palpitations. When they were growing up he had never gone for her like he used to go for Harry and Ernest, because she was a girl; but latterly he had begun to threaten her and say what he would do to her only for her dead mother's sake. And now she had nobody to protect her. Ernest was dead and Harry, who was in the church decorating business, was nearly always down somewhere in the country. Besides, the invariable squabble for money on Saturday nights had begun to weary her unspeakably. She always gave her entire wages—seven shillings—and Harry always sent up what he could but the trouble was to get any money from her father. He said she used to squander the money, that she had no head, that he wasn't going to give her his hard-earned money to throw about the streets, and much more, for he was usually fairly bad of a Saturday night. In the end he would give her the money and ask her had she any intention of buying Sunday's dinner. Then she had to rush out as quickly as she could and do her marketing, holding her black leather purse tightly in her hand as she elbowed her way through the crowds and returning home late under her load of provisions. She had hard work to keep the house together and to see that the two young children who had been left to her charge went to school regularly and got their meals regularly. It was hard work—a hard life—but now that she was about to leave it she did not find it a wholly undesirable life.

She was about to explore another life with Frank. Frank was very kind, manly, open-hearted. She was to go away with him by the night-boat to be his wife and to live with him in Buenos Ayres where he had a home waiting for her. How well she remembered the first time she had seen him; he was lodging in a house on the main road where she used to visit. It seemed a few weeks ago. He was standing at the gate, his peaked cap pushed back on his head and his hair tumbled forward over a face of bronze. Then they had come to know each other. He used to meet her outside the Stores every evening and see her home. He took her to see *The Bohemian Girl* and she felt elated as she sat in an unaccustomed part of the theatre with him. He was awfully fond of music and sang a little. People knew that they were courting and, when he sang about the lass that loves a sailor, she always felt pleasantly confused. He used to call her Poppens out of fun. First of all it had been an excitement for her to have a fellow and then she had begun to like him. He had tales of distant countries. He had started as a deck boy at a pound a month on a ship of the Allan Line going out to Canada. He told her the names of the ships he had been on and the names of the different services. He had sailed through the Straits of Magellan and he told her stories of the terrible Patagonians. He had fallen on his feet in Buenos Ayres, he said, and had come over to the old country just for a holiday. Of course, her father had found out the affair and had forbidden her to have anything to say to him.

"I know these sailor chaps," he said.

One day he had quarrelled with Frank and after that she had to meet her lover secretly.

The evening deepened in the avenue. The white of two letters in her lap grew indistinct. One was to Harry; the other was to her father. Ernest had been her favourite but she liked Harry too. Her father was becoming old lately, she noticed; he would miss her. Sometimes he could be very nice. Not long before, when she had been laid up for a day, he had read her out a ghost story and made toast for her at the fire. Another day, when their mother was alive, they had all gone for a picnic to the Hill of Howth. She remembered her father putting on her mother's bonnet to make the children laugh.

Her time was running out but she continued to sit by the window, leaning her head against the window curtain, inhaling the odour of dusty cretonne. Down far in the avenue she could hear a street organ playing. She knew the air. Strange that it should come that very night to remind her of the promise to her mother, her promise to keep the home together as long as she could. She remembered the last night of her mother's illness; she was again in the close dark room at the other side of the hall and outside she heard a melancholy air of Italy. The organ-player had been ordered to go away and given sixpence. She remembered her father strutting back into the sickroom saying:

"Damned Italians! coming over here!"

As she mused the pitiful vision of her mother's life laid its spell on the very quick of her being—that life of commonplace sacrifices closing in final craziness. She trembled as she heard again her mother's voice saying constantly with foolish insistence:

"Derevaun Seraun! Derevaun Seraun!"

She stood up in a sudden impulse of terror. Escape! She must escape! Frank would save her. He would give her life, perhaps love, too. But she wanted to live. Why should she be unhappy? She had a right to happiness. Frank would take her in his arms, fold her in his arms. He would save her.

She stood among the swaying crowd in the station at the North Wall. He held her hand and she knew that he was speaking to her, saying something about the passage over and over again. The station was full of soldiers with brown baggages. Through the wide doors of the sheds she caught a glimpse of the black mass of the boat, lying in beside the quay wall, with illumined portholes. She answered nothing. She felt her cheek pale and cold and, out of a maze of distress, she prayed to God to direct her, to show her what was her duty. The boat blew a long mournful whistle into the mist. If she went, tomorrow she would be on the sea with Frank, steaming towards Buenos Ayres. Their passage had been booked. Could she still draw back after all he had done for her? Her distress awoke a nausea in her body and she kept moving her lips in silent fervent prayer.

A bell clanged upon her heart. She felt him seize her hand:

"Come!"

All the seas of the world tumbled about her heart. He was drawing her into them: he would drown her. She gripped with both hands at the iron railing.

"Come!"

No! No! No! It was impossible. Her hands clutched the iron in frenzy. Amid the seas she sent a cry of anguish!

"Eveline! Evvy!"

He rushed beyond the barrier and called to her to follow. He was shouted at to go on but he still called to her. She set her white face to him, passive, like a helpless animal. Her eyes gave him no sign of love or farewell or recognition.

ANTARCTICA

Claire Keegan

Claire Keegan has written *Antarctica*, *Walk the Blue Fields* and *Foster*. These stories are translated into 19 languages, have won numerous awards and been published in many publications and anthologies including the *New Yorker*, *Best American Stories*, the *Paris Review* and *Granta*.

Every time the happily married woman went away she wondered how it would feel to sleep with another man. That weekend she was determined to find out. It was December; she felt a curtain closing on another year. She wanted to do this before she got too old. She was sure she would be disappointed.

On Friday evening, she took the train into the city, sat reading in a first-class carriage. The crime novel didn't hold her interest; she could already predict the ending. She stared out beyond the window. A few lighted houses, fiery points, flashed past her in the darkness. She had left a dish of macaroni cheese out for the kids, brought her husband's suits back from the cleaners. She'd told him she was going shopping for Christmas. He'd no reason not to trust her.

When she reached the city she took a taxi to the hotel. They gave her a small, white room with a view of Vicar's Close, one of the oldest streets in England, a row of stone houses with tall, granite chimneys where the clergy lived. She sat at the hotel bar that night nursing a tequila and lime, but there was nothing doing. Old men were reading newspapers, business was slow, but she didn't mind; she needed a good night's sleep. She fell into her rented bed, into a dreamless sleep, and woke to the sound of bells ringing in the cathedral.

On Saturday she walked to the shopping centre. Families were out, pushing buggies through the morning crowd, a thick stream of people flowing through glass automatic doors. She bought unusual gifts for her children, things she thought they wouldn't predict. She bought an electric razor for her eldest son – he was getting to that age – an atlas for the girl, and for her husband an expensive gold watch with a plain, white face.

She dressed up in the afternoon, put on a short plum-coloured dress, high heels, her darkest lipstick, and walked back into town. A jukebox song, 'The

Ballad of Lucy Jordan', lured her into a pub, a converted prison with barred windows and a low, beamed ceiling. Fruit machines blinked in one corner and just as she sat on a bar stool a little battalion of coins fell into a shoot. On the next stool sat a guy in a leather jacket that looked like he should have given it to Oxfam years ago.

'Hello,' he said. 'Haven't seen you before.' He had a red complexion, a gold chain dangling inside a Hawaiian print shirt, mud-coloured hair. His glass was almost empty.

'What's that you're drinking?' she said.

He turned out to be a real talker, told her his life story, how he worked nights at the old folks' home. How he lived alone, was an orphan, had no relations except a distant cousin he'd never met. There were no rings on his fingers.

'I'm the loneliest man in the world,' he said. 'How about you?'

'I'm married.' She said it before she knew what she was saying.

He laughed. 'Play pool with me.'

'I don't know how.'

'Doesn't matter,' he said, 'I'll teach you. You'll be potting that black before you know it.' He put coins into a slot and pulled something and a little land-slide of balls knuckled down into a black hole under the table.

'Stripes and solids,' he said, chalking up the cue. 'You're one or the other. I'll break.'

He taught her to lean down low and sight the ball, to watch the cue ball when she took the shot, but he didn't let her win one game. When she went into the ladies' room, she was drunk. She couldn't find the end of the toilet paper. She leaned her forehead against the cool of the mirror. She couldn't remember ever being drunk like this. They finished off their drinks and went outside. The air spiked her lungs. Clouds smashed into each other in the sky. She hung her head back to look at them. She wished the world could turn into a fabulous, outrageous red to match her mood.

'Let's walk,' he said. 'I'll give you the tour.'

She fell into step beside him, listened to his jacket creaking as he led her down a path where the moat curved round the cathedral. An old man stood outside the Bishop's Palace selling stale bread for the birds. They bought some and stood at the water's edge feeding five cygnets whose feathers were turning white. Brown ducks flew across the water and landed in a nice skim on the moat. When a black Labrador came bounding down the path, a huddle of pigeons rose as one and settled magically in the trees.

'I feel like Francis of Assisi,' she laughed.

Rain began to fall; she felt it falling on her face like small electric shocks. They backtracked through the market-place where stalls were set up in the shelter of tarpaulin. They sold everything: smelly second-hand books and china dishes, big red poinsettias, holly wreaths, brass ornaments, fresh fish with dead eyes lying on a bed of ice.

'Come home with me,' he said. 'I'll cook for you.'

'You'll cook for me?'

'You eat fish?'

'I eat everything,' she said, and he seemed amused.

'I know your type,' he said. 'You're wild. You're one of those wild middle-class women.'

He chose a trout that looked like it was still alive. The fishmonger chopped its head off and wrapped it up in foil. He bought a tub of black olives and a slab of feta cheese from the Italian woman with the deli stall at the end. He bought limes and Colombian coffee. Always, as they passed the stalls, he asked her if she wanted anything. He was free with his money, kept it crumpled in his pockets like old receipts, didn't smooth the notes out even when he was handing them over. On the way home they stopped at the off-licence, bought two bottles of Chianti and a lottery ticket, all of which she insisted on paying for.

'We'll split it if we win,' she said. 'Go to the Bahamas.'

'Don't hold your breath,' he said, and watched her walk through the door he'd opened for her. They strolled down cobbled streets, past a barber's where a man was sitting with his head back, being shaved. The streets grew narrow and winding; they were outside the city lights now.

'You live in suburbia?' she asked.

He did not answer, kept walking. She could smell the fish. When they came to a wrought-iron gate he told her to 'hang a left'. They passed under an archway and came out in a dead end. He unlocked a door to a block of flats and followed her upstairs to the top floor.

'Keep going,' he said when she stopped on the landings. She giggled and climbed, giggled and climbed again, stopped at the top.

The door needed oil; the hinges creaked when he pushed it back. The walls of his flat were plain and pale, the sills dusty. One stained mug sat lonely in the sink. A white Persian cat jumped off a draylon couch in the living room. It was neglected, like a place where someone used to live; the rubber plant in the lounge crawled across the carpet towards a rectangular pool of streetlight under a high window. Dank smells. No sign of a phone, no photographs, no decorations, no Christmas tree.

A big cast-iron tub stood in the bathroom on blue, steel claws.

'Some bath,' she said.

'You want a bath?' he said. 'Try it out. Fill her up and dive in. Go ahead, be my guest.'

She filled the tub, kept the water as hot as she could stand it. He came in and stripped to the waist, and shaved at the handbasin with his back to her.

She closed her eyes and listened to him work the lather, tapping the razor against the sink, shaving. It was like they'd done it all before. She thought him the least threatening man she'd ever known. She held her nose and slid underwater, listened to the blood pumping in her head, the rush and cloud in her brain. When she surfaced, he was standing there in the steam, wiping traces of shaving foam off his chin, smiling.

'Having fun?' he said.

When he lathered a flannel, she got up. Water fell off her shoulders and trickled down her legs. He began at her feet and worked upwards, washing her in strong, slow circles. She looked good in the yellow shaving light, raised her feet and arms and turned like a child for him. He made her sink back down into the water and rinsed her off, wrapped her in a towel.

'I know what you need,' he said. 'You need looking after. There isn't a woman on the earth who doesn't need looking after. Stay there.' He went out and came back with a comb, began combing the knots from her hair. 'Look at you,' he said. 'You're a real blonde. You've blonde fuzz, like a peach.' His knuckle slid down the back of her neck, followed her vertebrae.

His bed was brass with a white, goose-down duvet and black pillowcases. She undid his belt, slid it from the loops. The buckle jingled when it hit the floor. She loosened his trousers. Naked, he wasn't beautiful, yet there was something voluptuous about him, something unbreakable and sturdy in his build. His skin was hot.

'Pretend you're America,' she said. 'I'll be Columbus.'

Under the bedclothes, down between the damp of his thighs, she explored his nakedness. His body was a novelty. When her feet became entangled in the sheets, he flung them off. She had surprising strength in bed, an urgency that bruised him. She pulled his head back by the hair, drank in the smell of strange soap on his neck. He kissed her and kissed her. There wasn't any hurry. His palms were the rough hands of a working man. They battled against their lust, wrestled against what in the end carried them away. Afterwards they smoked – she hadn't smoked in years, quit before the first baby. She was reaching over for the ashtray when she saw the shotgun cartridge behind his clock-radio.

'What's this?' She picked it up. It was heavier than it looked.

'Oh that. That's a present for somebody.'

'Some present,' she said. 'Looks like pool isn't the only thing you shoot.' She said this and laughed.

'Come here.'

She snuggled up against him, and they fell swiftly into sleep, the sweet sleep of children, and woke in darkness, hungry.

While he took charge of dinner, she sat in the couch with the cat on her lap and watched a documentary on Antarctica, miles of snow, penguins shuffling against the sub-zero winds. Captain Cook sailing down to find the lost continent, icebergs. He came out with a tea towel draped across his shoulder and handed her a glass of chilled Chianti.

'You,' he said, 'have a thing for explorers.' He leaned down over the back of the couch and kissed her.

'Can I do anything?' she asked.

'No,' he said and went back into the kitchen.

She sipped her wine and felt her throat opening again, cold sliding down into her stomach. She could hear him chopping vegetables, the bubble of water boiling on the stove. Dinner smells drifted through the rooms. Coriander, lime juice, onions. She could stay drunk; she could live like this. He came out and laid two places at table, lit a thick, green candle, folded paper napkins. They looked like small white pyramids under a vigil of flame. She turned the TV off, and stroked the cat. Its white hairs fell on to his dark-blue dressing gown that was much too big for her. She saw the smoke from another man's fire cross the window, but she did not think about her husband, and her lover never mentioned her home life either, not once.

Instead, over Greek salad and grilled trout the conversation somehow turned to the subject of Hell.

As a child, she had been told that Hell was different for everyone, your own worst possible scenario. 'I always thought Hell would be unbearably cold, a place where you stayed half-frozen but you never quite lost consciousness and you never really felt anything,' she said. 'There'd be nothing, only a cold sun and the Devil there, watching you.' She shivered and shook herself. Her colour was high. She put her glass to her lips and tilted her neck back as she swallowed. She had a nice, long neck.

'In that case,' he said, 'Hell for me would be deserted; there'd be nobody there. Not even the Devil. I've always taken heart in the fact that Hell is populated; all my friends will be there.' He ground more pepper over his salad plate and tore the doughy heart out of the loaf.

'The nun at school told us it would last for all eternity,' she said, pulling the skin off her trout. 'And when we asked how long eternity lasted, she said: "Think of all the sand in the world, all the beaches, all the sand quarries, the ocean beds, the deserts. Now imagine all that sand in an hour-glass, like a gigantic egg-timer. If one grain of sand drops every year, eternity is the length of time it takes for all the sand in the world to pass through that glass." Just think! That terrified us. We were very young.'

'You don't still believe in Hell?' he said.

'No. Can't you tell? If only Sister Emmanuel could see me now, fucking a complete stranger, what a laugh.' She broke off a flake of trout and ate it with her fingers.

He put his cutlery down, folded his hands in his lap and looked at her. She was full now, playing with her food.

'So you think all your friends will be in Hell too,' she said. 'That's nice.'

'Not by your nun's definition.'

'You have lots of friends? I suppose you know people from work.'

'A few,' he said. 'And you?'

'I have two good friends,' she said. 'Two people I'd die for.'

'You're lucky,' he said, and got up to make the coffee.

That night, he was ravenous, like a man leasing himself out to her. There was nothing he wouldn't do.

'You're a very generous lover,' she said afterwards, passing him the cigarette. 'You're very generous full stop.'

The cat jumped up on the bed and startled her.

'Jesus Christ!' she said. There was something creepy about his cat.

Cigarette ash fell on the duvet but they were too drunk to care. Drunk and careless and occupying the same bed on the same night. It was all so simple, really. Loud Christmas music started up in the apartment downstairs. A Gregorian chant, monks singing.

'Who's your neighbour?'

'Oh, some granny. Deaf as a coot. She sings too. She's on her own down there; keeps odd hours.'

They settled down to sleep, she with her head captured in the crook of his shoulder. He stroked her arm, petting her like an animal. She imitated the cat purring, rolling her 'r's the way they'd taught her in Spanish class while hailstones rapped the window panes.

'I'll miss you when you go,' he whispered.

She said nothing, just lay there watching the red numbers on his clock-radio change until she drifted off.

On Sunday she woke early. A white frost had fallen in the night. She dressed, watched him sleeping, his head on the black pillow. In the bathroom she looked inside the cabinet. It was empty. In the lounge, she read the titles of his books. They were arranged in alphabetical order. She walked back along treacherous pavements to check out of her hotel. She got lost and had to ask a troubled-looking lady with a poodle where to go. A huge Christmas tree sparkled in the lobby. Her suitcase lay open on the bed. Her clothes smelled of cigarette smoke. She showered and changed. The cleaning lady knocked at ten but she waved her off, told her not to bother, told her nobody should work on Sundays.

In the lobby, she sat in the telephone booth and called home. She asked about the children, the weather, asked her husband about his day, told him about the children's gifts. She would return to untidy, cluttered rooms, dirty floors, cut knees, a hall with mountain-bikes and roller-skates. Questions. She hung up, became aware of a presence behind her, waiting.

'You never said goodbye.' She felt his breath on her neck.

He was standing there, a black wool cap pulled down low over his ears, hiding his forehead.

'You were sleeping,' she said.

'You sneaked off,' he said. 'You're a sneaky one.'

'I—'

'You want to sneak off to lunch and get drunk?' He pushed her into the booth and kissed her, a long, wet kiss. 'I woke this morning with your scent in the sheets,' he said. 'It was beautiful.'

'Bottle it,' she said, 'we'll make a fortune.'

They ate lunch in a place with six-foot walls, arched windows and a flag-stone floor. Their table was next to a fire. Over plates of roast beef and Yorkshire pudding they got drunk again, but they didn't talk much. She drank Bloody Marys, told the waitress to go heavy on the Tabasco. He started on ale then switched to gin and tonics, anything to stave off the imminent prospect of their separation.

'I don't normally drink like this,' she said. 'How about you?'

'Nah,' he said, and signalled the waitress for another round.

They dawdled over dessert and the Sunday newspapers. The landlady came round and threw more wood on the fire. Once, while turning a page of the newspaper, she looked up. He was staring intently at her mouth.

'Smile,' he said.

'What?'

'Smile.'

She smiled and he reached over and pressed the tip of his index finger against her tooth.

'There,' he said, showing her a tiny speck of food. 'It's gone now.'

When they walked out on to the market-place, a thick fog had fallen on the town, so thick she could hardly read the signs. A straggle of Sunday vendors, out to win the Christmas trade, were demonstrating their wares.

'Done your Christmas shopping?' she said.

'Nah, got nobody to buy for, have I? I'm an orphan. Remember?'

'I'm sorry.'

'Come on. Let's walk.'

He gripped her hand and took her down a dirt road that led into a black wood beyond the houses.

'You're hurting me,' she said.

He loosened his hold but he did not say sorry. Light drained out of that day. Dusk stoked the sky, bribing daylight into darkness. They walked for a long time without talking, just feeling the Sunday hush, listening to the trees straining against the icy wind.

'I was married once, went off to Africa for a honeymoon,' he said suddenly. 'It didn't last. I had a big house, furniture, all that. She was a good woman too, a wonderful gardener. You know that plant in my lounge? Well, that was hers. I've been waiting for years for that plant to die, but the fucking thing, it keeps on growing.'

She pictured the plant sprawled across the floor, the length of a grown man, its pot no bigger than a small saucepan, dried roots snarling up over the pot. A miracle it was still alive.

'Some things you just have no control over,' he said, scratching his head. 'She said I wouldn't last a year without her. Boy, was she wrong.' He looked at her then, and smiled, a strange smile of victory.

They had walked deep into the woods by now; except for the sound of their footsteps on the road and the ribbon of sky between the trees, she could not have been sure where the path was. He grabbed her suddenly and pulled her in under the trees, pushed her back against a tree-trunk. She couldn't see. She felt the bark through her coat, his belly against hers, could smell gin on his breath.

'You won't forget me,' he said, smoothing her hair back from her eyes. 'Say it. Say you won't forget me.'

'I won't forget you,' she said.

In the darkness, he ran his fingers across her face, same as he was a blind man trying to memorise her. 'Nor I, you. A little piece of you will be ticking right here,' he said, taking her hand and placing it inside his shirt. She felt his heart beneath his hot skin, beating. He kissed her then as if there was something in her mouth he wanted. Words, probably. At that moment the cathedral bells rang and she wondered what time it was. Her train left at six but she was all packed, there was no real hurry.

'Did you check out this morning?'

'Yes,' she laughed. 'They think I'm the tidiest guest they've ever had. My bag's in the lobby.'

'Come to my place. I'll get you a taxi, see you off.'

She wasn't in the mood for sex. In her mind she had already packed up and left, was facing her husband in the doorway. She felt clean and full and warm; all she wanted now was a good snooze on the train. But in the end she could think of no reason not to go and, yielding like a parting gift to him, said yes.

They retreated from the darkness of the woods, walked down Vicar's Close and emerged below the moat near the hotel. The seagulls were inland. They hovered above the water fowl, swooping down and snapping up the bread a bunch of Americans were throwing to the swans. She collected her suitcase and walked the slippery streets to his place. The rooms were cold. Yesterday's dirty dishes lay soaking in the sink, a rim of greasy water on the steel. Remnant daylight filtered through gaps between the curtains, but he did not turn a light on.

'Come here,' he said. He took his jacket off and knelt before her. He unlaced her boots, undid the knots slowly, peeled her stockings off, eased her under-wear down around her ankles. He stood up and took her coat off, opened her blouse carefully, admired the buttons, unzipped her skirt, slid her watch down over her hand. Then he reached up under her hair and took her earrings out. They were dangly earrings, gold leaves her husband had given her for their anniversary. He stripped her as if he had all the time in the world. She felt like a child being put to bed. She didn't have to do anything to him, for him. No duties, all she had to do was be there.

'Lie back,' he said.

Naked, she fell back into the goose-down.

'I could go to sleep,' she said, shutting her eyes.

'Not yet,' he said.

The room was cold, but he was sweating; she could smell his sweat. He pinned her wrists back above her head with one hand and kissed her throat. A drop of sweat fell on to her neck. A drawer opened and something jingled. Handcuffs. She was startled, but did not think fast enough to object.

'You'll like this,' he said. 'Trust me.'

He bound her wrists to the brass bed-head. A section of her mind panicked. There was something deliberate about him, something silent and overpow-ering. More sweat fell on her. She tasted the tangy salt on his skin. He retreated and advanced, made her ask for it, made her come.

He got up. He went out and left her there, handcuffed to the headboard. The kitchen light came on. She smelled coffee, heard him breaking eggs. He came in with a tray and sat over her.

'I have to—'

'Don't move.' He said it very quietly. He was dead calm.

'Take these off—'

'Shhhhh,' he said. 'Eat. Eat before you go.' He extended a bite of scrambled egg on a fork and she swallowed it. It tasted of salt and pepper. She turned her head. The clock read 5:32.

'Christ, look at the time—'

'Don't swear,' he said. 'Eat. And drink. Drink this. I'll get the keys.'

'Why won't you—'

'Just take a drink. Come on. I drank with you, remember?'

Still handcuffed, she drank the coffee he tilted from the mug. It only took a minute. A warm, dark feeling spread over her and then she slept.

*

When she woke, he was standing in the harsh fluorescent light, dressing. She was still handcuffed to the bed. She tried to speak. She was gagged. One of her ankles, too, was bound to the foot of the bed with another pair of handcuffs. He continued dressing, clipping the studs of his denim shirt closed.

'I have to go to work,' he said, tying his bootlaces. 'It can't be helped.'

He went out, came back in with a basin. 'In case you need it,' he said, leaving it on the bed. He tucked her in and kissed her then, a quick, normal kiss, and turned the light out. He stopped in the hall and turned to face her. His shadow loomed over the bed. Her eyes were very big and pleading. She was reaching out to him with her eyes. He held his hands out, showing his palms.

'It's not what you think,' he said. 'It really isn't. I love you, you see. Try to understand.'

And then he turned and left. She listened to him leave, heard him on the stairs, a zipper closing. The hall light was doused, the door banged, she heard his walk on the pavement, footsteps ebbing.

Frantic, she tried her best to undo the handcuffs. She did everything to get free. She was a strong woman. She tried to disconnect the headboard, but when she nudged the sheet back, she could see the bed-head, bolted to the frame. For a long time she rattled the bed. She wanted to yell 'fire!' – that's what police told women to yell in emergencies – but she couldn't chew through the cloth. She managed to get her loose foot on the floor and thumped the carpet. Then she remembered granny, deaf, downstairs. Hours passed before she calmed down to think and listen. Her breathing steadied. She heard the curtain flapping in the next room. He'd left the window open. The duvet had fallen on the floor in all the fuss and she was naked. She couldn't reach it. Cold was moving in, spilling into the house, filling up the rooms. She shivered. Cold air falls, she thought. Eventually the shivering stopped. Chronic numbness spread through her; she imagined the blood slowing in her veins, her heart shrinking. The cat sprang up and landed on the bed, prowled the mattress. Her dulled rage changed to terror. That too passed. The curtain in the next room slapped the wall faster now: the wind was rising. She thought of him and felt nothing. She thought about her husband and her children. They might never find her. She might never see them again. It didn't matter. She could see her own breath in the gloom, feel the cold closing over her head. It began to dawn on her, a cold, slow sun bleaching the east. Was it her imagination or was that snow falling beyond the window panes? She watched the clock on his bedside table, the red numbers changing. The cat was watching her, his eyes dark as apple seeds. She thought of Antarctica, the snow and ice and the bodies of dead explorers. Then she thought of Hell, and then eternity.

DROWN TOWN

Colm Keegan

Colm Keegan was shortlisted for the Hennessy New Irish Writing Award and the Seán O'Faoláin Short Story prize. His debut play *For Saoirse* was nominated for the Fishamble New Writing Award in 2018. He is the author of two poetry collections, *Don't Go There* (2012) and *Randomer* (2018).

I've never felt more alive.

A big bass beat is thumping through the ground and into me from what might be the night's last song. The whole place is kicking, I'm drugged up and flying. My heart is going wild, buzzing off the energy of all the people as I cross the dance-floor. I'm with my mate Darin and he's flying too, sure I can nearly see his wings. Coolness comes off us like a ready-brek glow. It's in our eyes, in my gelled hair, in the ronnie Darin's trying to grow, and in our movement, the way we walk, half-dancing.

Darin points and shouts over the music.

'Let's go over there.'

I follow him up into the tiered seating. The air smells of grass. People have flipped down the blue plastic seats to stand on and dance. We get up as well and give it loads; our arms flying, legs not moving, wearing our best raver's faces and gurning to fuck. The song changes and a piano solo fills the air. I turn my face upwards and let the music pour over me, getting lost in the notes until someone taps me on the shoulder. A dancer on the seats behind waves a spliff in my face. I give a thumbs-up and take a drag off the joint. The smoke tickles my brain. I check out the dance-floor, a lake of bodies washed in laser green. I try to give the joint back but its giver closes his eyes and shakes his head back into the beat. I call to Darin.

'D'ya want this?' I wave the spliff and he takes it, but hands it back with a wink after one quick toke.

'We have to get down there.' I say. 'Get back into it.'

He does an okay sign with his hand and his grin widens. He hasn't got a clue what I'm saying, but it stops mattering. The joint has me gone all ripply.

I close my eyes and rise with the music, I see myself skimming along the Liffey, bridges rushing over me. I spiral up and around Liberty Hall and skip onto the top of the Custom House, seeing orange light streaking through the river like rocket trails from the buildings, or stilts keeping everything afloat.

Darin tugs at my t-shirt.

'You alright?'

'Yeah man, I'm sound.' He's all blurry, like he's behind dirty glass.

'We're gonna do it tonight,' he says. 'Arnotts, right?'

'Yeah, I'd say so, yeah.'

He's on about our deal. A promise we made ourselves one night on Henry Street.

'We have to. We will,' he's trying to convince himself.

'There's no panic,' I say again. 'We'll see what happens.'

I spot a perfect candidate for the spliff. A girl about my age in a purple lace dress that clings to everything walks by on the dance-floor, the lights pick out glitter on her tights, ultraviolet makes her trainers gleam and little freckles stand out on her cheeks. She stops and grabs a handrail and totters a bit, she's gorgeous, and she's out of it. I jump down off the chair and trot down to her in time to the beat. But then I can't think of anything to say. I just stand there with the music bashing my ears.

A big thick with his collar popped up comes over and grabs her by the waist, swings her around and tries to kiss her. She's having none of it but she doesn't squirm out of his grip either. I go over and offer him the joint.

'What the fuck is that?' he says, staring at the joint as if I've just flashed him.

'It's a J. Wanna toke bud?'

'I'm not your bud, Prick.' A frown tightens his big, spotty, angry head. I'd say in the daylight the hairs on his knuckles cast shadows. I can tell he would like to smash my face in, he's the type that would do it out of boredom. That's why I have a Stanley blade tucked into my sock, not that I'd ever cut anybody, but I bring it just in case. Everyone carries something.

'No bother man' I say, 'It's cool, more for me.' I take a big pull on the joint.

He moves away and tries to pull her with him into the crowd. She looks my way and stays still, their fingers play for a second, then he's floating alone. He reaches into his top and swigs from a bottle of Vodka before turning away with a grumble. She gives a little trickly wave and laughs.

'Bye-bye Vodka Boy.'

The girl wobbles again so I stamp out the joint and offer help. She drops into my arms, her head falls back, her hair goes across her face in strands but I can still see her eyes, the nicest I've ever seen. The DJ weaves classical music into the sounds.

'Hello there,' I say.

'Hello yourself,' she says.

Around us everybody is drowning in the swirl of violins, eyes closed, arms up, bodies swaying. I hold the girl's hips from behind and pull her body against mine. My little finger slides up her tights. We lean backwards together, arching our backs to send rushes up our spines. The beat builds up, the crowd moves quicker now. I let my lips get close to her ear, my chin feels the sweat on her neck. The floor starts shaking as the beat kills off the violins. The whole place jumps up and down. A roar swells up from the crowd. We separate and join the motion. I throw out a few two-fingered whistles. My buzz spills out onto my face in a big yoked-up smile. Everything is lovely, we're all moving together with the beat and I've never felt more alive.

The song stops. The lights go on. It's all over. I turn to grab her and kiss her but she's gone. I tell myself it's all good but the vibe is changing, something mean snakes through the place, infecting my belly. The magic is lost, it's all skaggy faces and people shouldering for space.

That time on Henry Street; me and Darin were on mushrooms, trippin' to bits, sharing his iPod and painting pictures with the tunes. It was sunny after raining and the streets were all glimmery. Outside Arnotts there was this homeless man warming a strip of cardboard, a smelly drunk fucker, all beardy and piss-stained with only cider cans for company. He waved us over. We just smirked and kept walking, but he got up and grabbed us, started screaming into our faces. Darin couldn't handle it and just broke his shite laughing. I laughed as well. Then the man gave me a full-force clatter in the face. I stood holding my cheek, pure silent as my buzz went all bogey. The tramp's gummy, reeking mouth became a black hole sucking me in. Darin saw me slipping, grabbed my shoulders and pointed up at the sky.

'We should dance up there!' he said.

'What?' I looked up, big tripped eyes blinking.

'Up there.' He was pointing at the top of Arnotts. 'Next week after the rave.'

When I realized what he was at I started laughing again, rescued.

'Yeah! That'd be fucking legend man.'

We walked off, talking real loud to let the dipso know he hadn't hurt us. He didn't know what was going on. We huddled close together over our new plan. All the way back to the flats we talked ourselves onto the buildings, imagining our arms in the air like the statues on O'Connell Street, but with headphones on, sparkling like the Spire, dancing over the empty streets as they swirled around us.

Some sap slips on the dance-floor and stumbles into me. I push back and we stare at each other. There's a shout from up in the chairs. Bouncers have a hold of the dancer that gave me the spliff. Vodka Boy is there as well, smirking. Darin's in the middle of it, his body language pleading to the listening bouncers. Whatever happened is done with until Spliffy loses it and starts swinging digs. I get up to Darin just as he side steps the scrap, smart enough not to get sucked in. But that Vodka muppet pushes the two of us flying. We lash into a bouncer and then everything takes off.

Vodka's laughing with a big spiteful grin on his face, crooked teeth showing in his half-cocked mouth. Darin manages to go for him. Vodka's buddy jumps on Darin, then I'm on the deck from a punch, getting kicked. I crawl clear. The whole tier is in uproar. People are falling off and over the chairs. Vodka's lashing Darin's head off the ground. I reach for the Stanley blade and give Vodka a boot that catches him lovely and then I slice at his face, missing on purpose. He backs off. Darin gets loose. Someone shouts about the knife. Space opens up around me and I'm free until the bouncers are on us again, bending our arms behind our backs and grabbing our hair. The knife disappears.

We're thrown out one of the emergency exits, let loose on the summer night. There must be about twenty of us but I don't know who's with who. Vodka appears in front of me and bashes his naggin into my head. The glass smashing makes me think of cash registers, my tooth chips, but I hardly feel it. Then it's blast off again, we're all punching and kicking, moving in circles. Everybody's night is ruined now, somebody is going to pay.

There's a fence of bouncers blocking people from joining in but some get through. We jostle out of the car park towards the Liffey. I touch my bleeding head and feel only a tiny little cut. We spill out onto the road. Outsiders get swallowed by the madness, trying to help or getting smart and getting attacked for getting too near.

The rave pours out more and more spectators, yelling and whistling, clapping even. I see the girl from the dance-floor with a gang of women high on the drama. Some are baring their teeth, nearly shouting at the sky. But she is still gorgeous though.

Darin runs from my side into the middle of the road shouting. He bounces through the mob, lashing at anyone in reach. Everything moves away from him like ripples from a stone. His top is all torn so he rips it off, his body is slick, the tendons stick out on his neck, for a second he's got control as if he owns the whole street. Then someone sees their chance and knocks him flying with a box. Everybody starts running.

A faux-hawked poser jumps at me and I level him with one punch. We zigzag through the traffic lights near the Custom House, the roads throb under our galloping feet, everything's tense. People are roaring and barking – deep round sounds that start in their ribcages. It's like the most you should ever want to do is scream. A car drives past, kicks batter its flanks, something smashes through the windscreen. The hairs prickle up on my neck. I've never felt more alive.

A raver in combats stands on the granite wall of the Liffey, lets out this huge fucking roar as people throng the edge of the swollen river. Whether he falls or jumps or gets pushed in I don't know. But someone else goes after him then another and another. Darin has someone in a headlock and is trying to force him over the wall, he grabs the belt of his enemy's jeans and manages to flip him in only for his neck to get grabbed. So he goes in as well. It's all yells and splashes as people enter the flow.

There's about fifty people treading water now in the river, laughing and calling others to leave the street behind. Fellahs acrobat through the air. Girls hand their things to friends and take the plunge in their minis and bras. People line the walls of the river clapping and cheering. I hear a young-one's voice and see my girl leaning over the edge. Now's the time to catch her and kiss her, but she climbs up and waves at me before jumping in with a splash.

Two shit-vans turn up, painting everything blue and making people scatter. I run for the wall. A girl Garda grabs for me but I dodge her and dive in head first.

The wind flies through my hair and then there are bubbles in my ears. I swim under the surface. I used to dream of playing in the Liffey when I was small. Football or kiss-chasing under Tara Street bridge. Loads of little eight-year-olds on water like glass. The cold brings my buzz back and it shoots through me in tingles. I stretch and float, wiggling my toes in my runners.

I swim around the edge of the crowd. The river is warm, the noise of it tickles my ears, the way it slides off my arms when I raise them from the water. Darin starts singing some song at the top of his voice, all the swimmers join in and so do I. A few of the police start laughing. I see my girl treading water over near the far wall. She waves again. Then I hear movement in the water behind me and it's Vodka with his face all stiff and he sort off hugs me hard and I feel something stick into my side. The pain of it gets me jumping and twisting like a fish on a line.

I manage one big shout and then I feel all dopey. Darin gets over to me and he can't tell what's wrong. My mouth won't work and I know that it's shock, and my hands are tight on my side and underwater Darin feels my stomach spilling into the river.

He shouts for help but nobody's listening, everybody's still having fun. Vodka's over at one of the ladders crawling up and out of the water. The Liffey is in my eyes and tears are coming out, everything's gotten nicer because I think I might be dying, all the streetlights are blurry and look like orange stars.

My girl comes over to help and I want to kiss her. Because I might sink and never come up if it wasn't for her, if it wasn't for the care in her eyes. I look above at all the people, at nobody giving a fuck and Darin screams so loud it's like his throat is tearing as the sound flies over the river.

The whole city turns to look at us. I'll never feel more alive.

THE INTRUDERS

Rita Kelly

Rita Kelly was born in Galway and writes poetry, fiction and drama criticism in English and Irish. She has won many awards and her work has been translated into various languages – the story included here is from her collection *The Whispering Arch*. Her latest work is based on letters the poet Máirtín Ó Direáin wrote to her thirty years ago.

Irish was always somewhat virginal. Prayers, poems, and Mass for St Patrick's Day. Shamrocks pinned to the full of our gymslips, crowding to greet the priest at the convent gate—*Dia duit, 'Athair. Fáilte romhat 'Athair.* And after communion and the sweet homily on the dear little snakes, we hymned mellifluously in the Saint's own sanctified language, *Aspal Mór na hÉireann.* Not a trace of the asp in *aspal,* though we hissed the *r's* with what we had been taught to be a Celtic sibilance which seemed to refute the claim for Patrick vis-à-vis the snakes. But *An tAthair* just smiled, or rather pulled his thick lips into that ingratiating grin which he seemed to adopt for us and for the good Sisters—*Bail ó Dhia orthu.* The sly glances across the aisle, row upon row, exposing quick teeth to a companion in our secret tiger's yawn, a glint of fang, before spitting out the regulated *r's* of the final verse.

The confessional was ideally makeshift so that *An tAthair* could hold our hands or touch our cheeks, part of the perks, as well as an invaluable practice for our oral examinations and the more seemingly *outré* the sin the more contact afforded. It was all so innocuous. *Sea, a chroí... inis dom arís... Beannacht Dé ort, a thaisce... agus ortsa, a Athair.* The *diabhal* never arose, there was no place for him in such an atmosphere. He did find mention, more than seemed necessary at times, in the conversation-pieces of the prescribed prose. But that was all native, and the *diabhal* had some kind of unexplained precedence in those Gaeltacht places. However, the word must be noted with its genitive form, but no one ever used it in an essay, and it was considered un-nice for conversation.

Even the Man who came with the *Fáinne* never used it. But then he never said much anyway, his brand of Irish was like himself: meagre and balding. The nun showed pain as he slurred his *r's,* making a whore of the slender endings. He wore an outsize *Fáinne,* gold and glistening, we got little silver ones, and the nun thought it would be a nice idea if he himself attached them to our gymslips when we had paid the money and said the necessary few words. He seemed a little worried at first, but the juniors encouraged him by their underdevelopment. He poked his way through us seniors, and some of us indeed were a handful, placing the *Fáinne* gingerly on the palpitating cleft. Privately we called him the Fanny Man, in public *An tUasal Ó Riain*. He began to teach us Irish dancing, at least that way he could keep us at a distance. We could dance already better than he could, but the nun felt, well after all he must be tolerated for the language, and he is doing his best, poor man. But he never got further than the 'Siege of Ennis', *ar aghaidh's ar gcúl ad infinitum*. So the nun talked him out of that, and he tried to talk her into camogie, and the amount of Irish to be learned from the rules. We tried it, broke some hurley-sticks, slashed some ankles, and gave it up, throwing the boots, which he had supplied at a reduced cost, into a press.

But his department appointed him to another town. We held a collection, bought him the new Irish Dictionary, a senior composed the dedication, she had thoroughly grasped the subjunctive mood and liked using it; a junior did the calligraphy in the antique script, where the M looks like a rake and there is a profusion of dots over everything. He came to give thanks, big the honour, not small the sorrow on leaving us, hope at God, hope at himself that we would all become in our mothers fecund and Irish, now that we were in our nice girls. He left many *sláns* at us, and we put many with him. Hope, of course, being at us, that everything would rise with him. What a hope.

Then there was the school-tour to the Gaeltacht, it was really the science department's idea, and they were not very interested in this Irish thing. Archimedes principle, they felt, is simply the same as *Prionsabal Archiméid*, something to be taught year in, year out. One clear diagram is more impressive than four pages of writing, so no need to be awkward about this language business, it is all so irrelevant anyway in the interest of science.

The bus travelled for hours. Even the juniors wearied of waving at young men on tractors. There were miles of sheep coming out of the indistinction, grazing, scurrying along mountain-paths, and slowly disappearing. Finally, the sea, and a secluded foreshore. Not a native in sight. We killed some jellyfish, put sea-anemones *in vitro* and watched them purple against the sun. We collected some clammy shells as the tide receded, noting the precise spot of the discoveries on our diagrams. Just one starfish, which we killed and dropped in stinking formalin for further study. Armfuls of *fucus spiralis* and *vesiculosus*, enough wrack to manure a potato-patch. Then we had tea and sandwiches among the rocks. But no swimming, because the bus-driver had us in full view despite his newspaper. Any kind of exposure in a public place was not the norm, it was even immodest to roll back the sleeves of our blouses. We came home with sand in our stockings, and hardly believing that the Gaeltacht was merely an acrid smell, a garage and a pub huddled together at intervals, bearing the sign *Tigh Mhicí Sheáin Pheaits* or *Tigh Pheaits Sheáin Mhicí* in most garish colouring; more sheep, a donkey or two, fatigue, and a sunset beyond imagination. We stopped in a village, and we all marched into the local convent to wash our hands. The bus jerked off again, casting an ungainly shadow until the light eked itself out of the sky. We disembarked at midnight, and the kitchen nun brought us warm milk and two plain biscuits to bring the Gaeltacht to an end.

Those who could not afford France went to this Gaeltacht during the summer, and brought their bicycles. They never brought back much, or so it seemed, other than harmless little stories about getting punctures in Irish, brushes with boys at the *céilí*, bullocks in fields, or the fact that their periods always came just when he said he'd see them on the beach. They picked up a phrase or two, so that they prefixed the most banal statement with *Craidhps, an dtuigeann tú bhfuil 's agat,* everything was *go cinnte dearfa* and happened in the *cianta cairbreacha* until the first hint of winter, hockey, and all was forgotten.

Then Cóilín came to produce our play, or rather rescue it. We had been doing so badly at the festivals that our drama-mistress became desperate, and word passed quickly round that a real native had come.

He was so—what we had not expected—sophisticated, a dark well-clipped beard, sunbrowned fingers slender and sensitive. Sea green eyes, a soft look in them, or was it mocking? No one called him an *tUasal*, quietly we said Cóilín, or else manoeuvered the vocative out of the sentence. To our great surprise we understood every word he spoke, his *r* was slender too, but subtly different, gently rippled, he didn't hiss. His speech was so distinct that all the difficult genitive-endings were clear, yet not unduly emphasized. And what he said always seemed significant, said with a desire to impart his feelings or elicit yours.

At once the play was the thing. So unlike our *comhrá* sessions when we attempted to outdo each other in knitting together a patchwork of ready-made bits of speech and idiom, and groped for a conversational structure in which to display them. And our *comhrá* pieces were always *cúrsaí reatha,* running affairs, and the weather. We were expected to be cognisant with pollution, education, religion, violence, party politics and lunar expeditions. We exhibited numerous nebulous ideas which were merely media clichés translated, and we shouldn't have cared in the least if everything connected with *cúrsaí reatha,* running affairs, found itself on a lunar expedition of no return. We had words for everything, spaceships, contraceptives, referenda, hijackings and abortions, all neatly underlined, giving declension, gender, person, number and case. But Cóilín simply never talked about these things. It was odd.

We heard him entranced, yet uneasy. His Irish was not just a language, in a curious way it was himself. Vibrant under one's gymslip. With him, none of us flashed our secret tiger's yawn across the class, except one of the denser girls who was surprised when it was not returned.

Then something happened to the play, it was no longer an excuse for a romp, and all about a bird and a tinker. It became something serious, interesting and slightly puzzling. We began to hear it and feel it, even into the girl's part Cóilín infused a life, a tone of voice, a character—she could be one of us in our private selves. One was slightly shocked to realise that one was really such an exuberant little tinker.

Then you changed too. Things were no longer so flippant, no longer a cause for adolescent giggling. Silences had meaning and import. Minute gestures of eye, of facial muscle. An ease and a reserve, a liveliness untainted by exaggeration or blatancy. You grew rather pensive, tended to avoid the after-tea chirrupy chatter and boisterous jump about. How attractive the outer garden by the river became. Those May evenings, the flit of wing through the plumtrees, their delicate blossom, not white, not red, so shortlived, from the moment of tenuous appearance to the touch of rust. This year you would not pick the fruit.

You'd be far from the eager hands which would pack it into a pillow-cover and hide it until midnight. Half-eaten plums flying across the beds, too much eaten too soon, and an overtired attempt to bring the feast to a climax. Passing the climax without knowing it and reaching a chaos of legs, nightdresses and stunted screams, until someone sees or imagines a light in the corridor, panic, and the feast deflates itself and all are supremely glad to sleep. No one comes, breathing becomes regular and soft, the dormitory is pervaded by a smell of crushed plums, childishly sweet…

You did hear a footstep, and Cóilín comes. Through the trees to where you are sitting on a discarded pew. You know that he ought to be at his tea, and you are embarrassed at finding yourself alone with him, it has never happened before, and there are so many mistakes that you could make, especially in the relative form.

His greeting is so natural, and though he must have said it many times to many people, it seems as if he had just composed it. He sits. He would. Now he can watch you, he talks on, the words are understandable in themselves, but the way they are combined and placed together gives something else not so readily understood, and the tone, difficult to name. It is friendly and easy, a little enthusiastic, but more.

You can see his hands, the vital fingers, the face is a blur of beard just out of focus; yes, *caint* is feminine so the adjective is aspirated. He says *drámaíocht* in the genitive, and *réalaíocht*. Must check, does it mean stars or reality? Those idioms, he could be saying one thing and meaning another, he probably is doing that. And very ordinary words have, well, have other meanings, which he must know though you do not. Of course, *nádúr* is first declension, stupid, politely he pretends not to notice. Politeness, or pretense?

You continue, trying to think less about grammatical distinctions. While you think about language, its links and articles, he has all the time possible to think of other things, to shape and dominate the conversation, push it this way and that, and worst of all, observe your difficulties and reactions. You have time for nothing except an endless and breathless debate on gender—so much depends on gender—you risk losing the primary meaning of his sentences, catch the beginning and the end of phrases, surmise the rest, of course you are doomed to make a faux pas, to blurt out *ó sea, sea* when it ought to be a decided negative. The whole thing begins to sound impossible, artificial. Why not admit defeat, excuse your Irish, surely he would go away rather than speak English. What was that? 'Am I boring you?' he said, and you answer automatically in Irish, turn, face him and get through at least three full-length sentences without a tremor. Now he falters, or seems to, his smile is so… and you quickly turn away. He continues, but the tone has changed, searching for words, or is he? And you finish a sentence for him, he repeats your addition, weighs it, accepts it as inevitably correct in the context. Is it a method for putting you at your ease, by seeming to adopt your problem of incoherence? Who knows.

He speaks of the drama-mistress, and says very flatly that she is *dóighiúil*, that could mean that he finds her 'good-looking', or it could mean 'generous', he does not insinuate which, but he must mean 'good-looking', after all the juniors have a crush on her, then he asks if you agree with him, you can only say 'perhaps', that is *b'fhéidir*. Now he praises her Irish. That needles you and you say if it were all that good why did she have to send into the wilds for him, and why was the play such a flop before his coming. He smiles, you are looking at him now, and notice the slight raising of an eyebrow. And you smile too, you are beginning to feel… but you can't be sure. He makes some joke about drama and mistresses and laughs, but its actual meaning is lost on you, and there is something disturbing about his laughter.

He rises, moves with deliberation towards one of the trees, turns, poses at an angle, hand on the bark, allowing his body to compose itself in contrast to the erect tree-trunk. A branch ruffles his hair and you notice, too suddenly, the tightness of his trousers. Now you don't know where to look, then you fix on the back of the school, like all town houses from the rear, it appears rather shabby. You imagine every room, every nook, know where every window opens, how much of the garden and river can be seen. Yet, it seems to distance, the desks, the chalk-dust, the waxed floors.

He is close by you again, sweet smelling, must be some male deodorant. He asks, can we be seen, and you say why, what matter and you are aware of grammar again. He is not thinking of kissing you is he? And you focus on his beard and blush. If only he would and… but he is talking about the river, yes, why not you think, over the stile, into the wilderness of osiers.

You run, and you know it's reckless, he is there right behind you on the stile, you pause, his hand touches yours, so close, you feel your nipples stiffen, and he says, *amach leat* just into your ear, and you are over.

Running blindly through the osiers you rip a stocking, what matter, even the trickle of blood on your skin, he is trying to get ahead of you. On and on through the heavy smell of mud and weed, jumping stumps of trees, through a tangle of undergrowth, squelching from footfall to footfall. He sits on a tree-stump, you return, stand over him unsteadily, quick, flushed breathing, shreds of phrases mocking and urging. And you are off again dragging him by the hand, you stumble and fall into a swamp of flowering-reeds, the blackamoors, feel the dampness seep through your blouse, and along your thighs, he simply looks down and laughs.

You are up, ignoring the mud and the wet, you pull up a blackamoor and explode it on his head, the brown flower-dust showers into his hair and beard—*I dtigh diabhail leat!* The phrase lingers. He is ruffling his hair to brush off the clinging particles, he pauses, and comes to help remove the mud from your blouse, and as he extends his hands you feel your throat constrict, and through a sticky spittle you shoot phrases out, you drag them up out of some boiling confusion, red and hot. The intent and fluency of them surprises you for a second merely. He seems to recognise the breathless, perspiring and fierce attack. Your Irish is charged as it never was before. He grins. You turn.

From the stile the school looks strange, foreign. A light is switched on in the study, how small, how distant, and the eagerness to put on your house-shoes, take your seat, and sink into the atmosphere of little noises, whispers, and pen-scratches, has suddenly deserted you. You are outside in a hint of dew and a fading light.

HUNGER

Louise Kennedy

Louise Kennedy grew up in Holywood, Co. Down. Bloomsbury will publish her debut collection, *The End of the World is a Cul de Sac*, in early 2021 and a novel, *When I Move to the Sky*, in 2022. She lives in Sligo.

The condolence book looks too heavy for the table it rests on, a desk-with-chair-attached from a classroom. A placard is propped nearby asking the mild folk who are beginning to move through this midland town to SUPPORT THE HUNGER STRIKERS.

Che Mc Garr is struggling to pin a crude black-and-white image of Bobby Sands to the front of the desk. A charge of early summer wind wraps it around his narrow hips. Che used to stand outside Mass selling month-old copies of the *Morning Star*. Now he's in Sinn Féin. I don't know where to look and wait until he has subdued the poster before taking the pen, one of those yellow biros that won't write unless you carve deep scores into the paper. Che Mc Garr's face is a breath from mine and this close I can see that his hair is thinning and he doesn't look remotely like Adam Ant.

I bend to the blank page. I etch my sympathies onto the paper in ornate pseudo-Celtic script. I hand the pen back.

Tiocfaidh ár lá, chicken, says Che, *our day will come*. I run down the steps and light a cigarette. In the window of Gogan's Hardware there is a tabby cat supine on a mat emblazoned with the face of John Paul II. It opens a green eye at me as I pedal home for breakfast.

My mother is standing at the ironing board beside a pile of wrinkled clothes, scratching at the taut skin on her belly. She is nine months and seventeen days pregnant. Her housekeeping has taken on a demonic quality. The pregnancy books call it nesting.

Have you thought any more about a name? I say.

I don't know what I'm going to call it. It's probably another bloody girl anyway, she says. She nods at a box of Bran Flakes. I pat my stomach as if I am full.

What's wrong with the name Bobby? Dad's grandfather was called Bobby, and you loved the Bobby Kennedy who got shot, I say.

Jesus Christ. Can I get through the delivery first? my mother says. She leans on the edge of the kitchen table and waves my grandmother's cigarette smoke out of her face.

Poor wee fella, all the same. 65 days he lasted, my grandmother says, putting her cigarette out and lighting another one.

Don't encourage her, my mother says, stretching her arms above her head.

I try again. You can still call it Bobby if it's a girl. Bobby McGee was a girl, I say. This might work. 'Me and Bobby McGee' is my father's favourite song. *Somewhere miscellaneous I let her slip away*, he sings at family parties. I haven't the heart to tell him the line is *Somewhere near Salinas*.

Thatcher's a bad article. She abolished the free school milk, my grandmother says.

I was the only person at the Town Hall. Nobody down here cares, I say.

Where we lived in the north, nobody cares either. We are not from Ballybloodymurphy, says my mother. Go to school.

I have no answer. The pretty north Down town we left two years ago is unlikely to be waking to the clanging of bin lids.

Language, says my grandmother. While she fills the kettle, I steal a dizzying gasp from the sopping cigarette she left in the ashtray.

In school, my day has come. I am the only northerner in the building and everyone wants to talk to me. My English teacher says that at least the hunger strikers have the courage of their convictions, even if this IRA is nothing like the old IRA.

The difference, Sir, is that you lot down here got your crappy Free State and left us as second-class citizens under a thinly veiled form of apartheid, I say. He gives me a warning.

At break-time an older girl I don't know very well pauses in front of me. She is holding a pink Cadbury's Snack bar, two bags of cheese and onion Taytos and a packet of Silvermints. The Silvermints will have their work cut out.

Hi, Attracta, I say.

I wish the rest of you murdering northern bastards would ever starve yourselves to death as well, she says.

After school, I climb the steps again and lean over the condolence book. There are about eight signatures now. Che Mc Garr's handwriting is more elaborate than mine. Jim the carpenter who never finished building our garden shed has signed his name. My father says Jim is an armchair republican and a workshy berk, but he underestimates him. In a few months, the Gardaí will stop a car near the Curragh and Jim will open the passenger door and come out with his hands up and a gun in his pocket. Elmer Fudd, Hong Kong Fooey and Deputy Dawg have signed their names too.

Che Mc Garr tells me that nature is calling and slinks into Mallon's pub, leaving me in charge of the book. I sit in the chair and watch a pigeon tap and tug at the wrapper of a spice burger. After fifteen minutes Che hasn't come back. I look at my own entry.

Ireland unfree will never be at peace. I love you, Bobby Sands, I have written. I feel ridiculous. A truckful of sheep spatters the town's only pedestrian crossing with hot, terrified shit and again I take the Town Hall steps, the poster snapping behind me. I pedal home as fast as I can. My sisters are doing their homework. My grandmother is fully dressed and not in her usual daytime ensemble of velour tracksuit, unfastened bra and quilted dressing gown. I run into the kitchen to look for my mother, to tell her I don't belong here, that I want to go home, but she has gone. My father has driven her to hospital. At three am on the morning of May 6th, 1981, twenty-three hours after the death of Bobby Sands, my mother gives birth to a baby boy. They name him John.

UNDER

Marian Keyes

Marian Keyes is the international bestselling author of fourteen novels including *Watermelon*, *Rachel's Holiday*, *Sushi for Beginners* and *The Break*. With a chatty, conversational style she explores themes including alcoholism, depression, addiction, cancer and domestic violence. Her novels have sold over 40 million copies and been translated into 36 languages. Her latest novel, *Grown Ups*, was published in February 2020.

I t's so peaceful down here. Muffled and calm, and empty, empty, empty. No-one but me. Countless fathoms of empty air above me is another world, the one I came from. I'm not going back.

Not that that's stopping them. My husband, my parents, my sister and my friends are determined to make me come round. Someone told them that people in a coma respond to stimulation, that hearing is the last sense to go, that music and conversation and the voices of my loved ones might haul me up from the depths.

They have me fecking well badgered.

They're nearly in competition over it, showing up at my hospital room, day and night, telling me the deathly dull minutiae of their day, from the dreams they had last night to how many red lights they broke on their way to work this morning, determined that they will be the first one to reach me. Or, worse still, playing music that they insist is my favourite but so isn't. It's the stuff they like. They can't help it; it's the rule; it's why people always buy presents for others that they'd like themselves.

The way Chris, my husband, insists I like Coldplay. I don't. He's the one who likes them, but persists in buying their CDs for me. But I see no need to disillusion him; it's only a small thing. The music I really love (seventies disco, for the record) is in my car because driving around on my own is the only time I can be myself.

My Dad, Mum and sister Orla have just arrived. Orla launches into a complicated account of a blowdrying disaster at the hairdressing salon she runs, where some woman said she was going to sue them for giving her whiplash of the eye with her fringe. Then Dad and Mum give me a blow-by-blow account of a film they've just been to see. I have a strange, sad little feeling that they only went so they'd have something to talk to me about – half-confirmed when Dad suddenly sighs, "Is there any point to this? Do you think she hears us at all?"

Yes Dad, I can hear you more than you'd think. It's coming from far away, like from a distant galaxy, but I can still hear you.

"We'll try a bit of James Last," he suggests. "She loves that."

You mean, you love it, Dad.

"We used to dance to it every Christmas," he said. "Me and her. She loved it."

Dad, I was six then. It's nearly thirty years ago.

A muzaky version of 'Waterloo' filled the room. Must be the Abba medley.

Christ, if they're wanting me to return to reality, they're going the wrong way about it.

Gratefully I slip below the surface, down, down, down, down, towards the fathomless bottom. It's so deeply restful here, like lying for a week on a beach on a perfect tropical island, with nothing to worry me, nothing to fear. Feeling nothing, nothing, nothing.

Chris, my husband, is here a lot. He sits very close to me and cries, Coldplay whining quietly in the background. He always smells nice and while he's here he triumphs over the decay and death of the hospital air. He talks incessantly, in a desperate voice. Today, he's saying, "Laura, remember the first time we met. On the flight to Frankfurt? And I wanted to sit by the window to see the Alps, and you wouldn't give up your seat? I thought you were the feistiest woman I'd ever met. And you said no matter how feisty I thought you were, you were still going to sit beside the window."

Yes, Chris, I remember.

"And remember when you took me shopping for my interview suit, and you got me in to all kinds of stuff I'd never have worn before. We had such a laugh."

Yes, Chris, I remember.

"Please come back, Laura, oh please come back." And then – I presume no one else was around – he whispered right in to my ear, "I'm so sorry, Laura, I love you so much, I'm so very, very sorry. I'll make it up to you, just please come back. I'll do whatever you want."

You could knock off the Coldplay for a while, I think.

But it doesn't matter. I'm going nowhere. I like it down here.

*

With a fright, I'm jolted out of my dark nothingness. My room seems to have filled up with irate Cockneys. Several of them shouting angrily: someone has slept with someone else, and the someone else thought the first person loved them but now they're going to effing kill them. Shouty voices and horrible aggression – what's going on? This business to stimulate me has gone too far! I want them out of my room.

My bed is shaking. Now what's happening? A Cockney-related earthquake?

"What on EARTH is going on here?" The voice of authority. Some sort of nurse, I'd be bound. "Mrs Coy and Orla Coy, get OUT of Laura's bed immediately."

More bed-shaking and my mum's mortified voice. "Sorry sister, we were trying to recreate watching *East-Enders* at home. When Laura comes over, we watch it snuggled up on the couch."

"But she's critically ill! Her head must not be moved! And you could have dislodged one of her tubes, that's the tubes that are keeping her alive, Mrs Coy."

I'm not sticking around for this. I sink back down, wafting slowly like a feather, waiting to be subsumed by dark comforting nothingness.

But something must have gone wrong when they invaded my bed because I'm not suspended in the balm of nothingness, I'm standing beside a river. This is new.

"Laura, Laura, over here, Laura!"

On the far bank is a collection of people, young and old and they're smiling and beckoning energetically. Who the hell are they? As I keep looking, some start to seem familiar; they look like my Dad, who is prone to roundy-facedness and high colour. Cousins of mine, they must be. And there's more. There's Aunty Irene, Mum's sister, who died when I was a baby, I recognise her from photos. And there are other Mum look-a-likes. I am related to these people.

The whole tableau was strangely familiar. It looked... actually... it looked exactly like a family wedding. They were all happy and red-faced as if they'd just been flinging themselves around some manky ballroom in their wedding finery to Let's Twist Again and Sweet Caroline. Any minute now it'll be time for the rubbery chicken. I shudder.

And then I clock Old Granny Mac, grim and upright in a hardbacked chair. In her hand was her blackthorn stick, the one she used to hit me and Orla on the ankles with when we were young. Well, fuck that, I'm not going someplace where someone else can hit me.

"Get in the raft, Laura." They called. "It's there, behind the rushes."

I take a look. The raft is a gammy, leaky-looking thing, more like a pallet, there isn't even sides to it. No way am I getting on. I might drown. Although from the looks of things, it seems I'm already dead.

"No!" I say loudly and it seems to boom in the sky overhead. "I'm not going."

A clamour of, "But you have to, it's your time. Your time is up!" Reaches me from the other bank.

"I don't give a flying fuck," I say, "I'm not going."

Family above me, family down here. I'm trapped.

"… heartrate stabilising…"

"We nearly lost her that time."

"She's a fighter this one."

"Oh yes? Might explain all those old bruises on her then."

Fiona's been here before, but I've only barely been aware of her. This time I can hear her clearly. "Laura," she's beseeching, "Don't die, Laura, just don't die and it'll be okay. I will help you fix it."

I can feel her desperation. She's suspected for ages. She hasn't actually said anything but there have been a lot of meaningful looks and coded suggestions. I should have told her, but I haven't. Haven't been able to. Even though she's my best friend. Because it's too shaming, you know?

Chris is back. The nice smell and the low, intense voice is beside me. "Laura, remember the time I was looking out into the garden and I said, "Laura look at the beautiful red poppy. But it wasn't a poppy at all, it was just a chipsticks bag. But because I wasn't wearing glasses, I thought it was a poppy. Remember how we laughed?"

Yes, Chris, I remember. And I remember what happened next.

Chris was back at my side. "Laura, remember the weekend we had in Galway and we saw the dolphins. Remember, there were loads of them, maybe twenty, playing with each other, jumping and diving, like they were putting on a show for us. Such a glorious day and had the whole beach to ourselves. Do you remember, Laura. We felt like we'd been personally chosen for a little miracle."

I remember, Chris, course I remember. Mind you, I remember better what happened next. Remember driving back to the guesthouse, we accidentally went the wrong way and somehow it was my fault and you swung your arm almost casually across my face, delivering such a blow to my nose and mouth, that blood spurted over the dashboard. Remember that, Chris? Because I do. I had to tell the people in the guesthouse I'd slipped climbing the rocks.

Remember that? And they marvelled at how unlucky I was, how only the day before I'd had that accident on the sailing boat that made my eye close up.

You'd never believe it to look at me, not even when I'm patterned with cuts and bruises. I wear high heels, I'm bossy at work and my hair is always nice (except when clumps of it have been torn out.) I manage to explain away my injuries on a sporty lifestyle which people buy because the truth would be so shocking. And, of course, everyone loves Chris. (Well, nearly everyone, I think Fiona has her doubts.) They say what a sweetheart he is. So devoted to me. So devoted that if I'm home ten minutes late, he dashes my face against the wall, or punches me in the kidneys, or discolates my shoulder.

Looking from the outside in, I should have left a long time ago. But the first time he hit me it was a one-off, a unique aberration. He was in the horrors, crying, begging for forgiveness. The second time was also a one-off. As was the third. And the fourth. At some stage the series of isolated incidents stopped being a series of isolated incidents and just became normal life. But I didn't want to see that.

I was too ashamed. Not just by the humiliation of being smacked and punched by the man I loved but because I had made such a big mistake. I'm a smart woman, I should have known. And once I'd known I should have legged it.

It complicated things that I loved him. Or had loved him. And, shallow as this may sound, I'd invested a lot of time and trouble in him being The One; seeing how wrong I'd been was hard to suck up.

Especially because we sometimes had our good days. Even now. There were times when he was like the person I'd first met. But I wasn't. My stomach was always a walnut of nerves, wound tight with anxiety, wondering what would happen to tip his mood. A telemarketer calling when he was having his dinner? A button missing from his shirt? Fiona ringing me?

The more he hit me, the less sure of myself I became. At times he almost had me convinced it was what I deserved.

I used to lie awake at night, my head racing, wondering if there was any way out of the trap. Perhaps he'd grow out of it and eventually stop? But even I could see he was getting worse, as he got away with more and more stuff. Go to the police? But they wouldn't help if I didn't press charges. And I couldn't do that. It would make my mistake, my shame, so horribly public and tawdry.

I could leave him, of course. Well, I'd tried that, hadn't I? And look where it had got me? Him going ballistic and flinging me down the stairs and fracturing my skull.

*

Down here, in the silence, everything seems calm and logical. Sometimes all you need is a little time out to see these things clearly. It's a bit like being on retreat. (Not that I've ever been on one, but I like the sound of them. Just not enough to submit to a weekend without telly and double-ply loo roll.)

Imagine, if I die, he'll have murdered me. He'll have done what he's threatened to do so many times. Although I never really believed him. In fact, I don't think he did either. He might have scared even himself with how badly he's injured me this time. Bottom line is, if I die, he'll be guilty of murder. But I'm the only witness. So if I die, he's in the clear.

But if I don't die…? Well, it's obvious: I will leave him. Even press charges. Why not? You can't go round hitting people and flinging them down flights of stairs. It's just not on.

But I might be too late, because down here something is changing… The darkness is filling up with white light. Not just ordinary white light, but super-intense, like it's being backlit with cleverly concealed halogen bulbs, the type they have in boutique hotels. And the light was forming itself into a shape – a roundy tunnel, with a pulsating circle of intense white light at its end. Suffused with intense wellbeing and serenity I am compelled to walk towards it. It's exactly like the stories in the *National Enquirer* from those near-death merchants!

I'm dying! Other than a small tinge of regret that I won't get to fix Chris, I'm, actually, excited.

I keep on walking towards the white light, which throbs hypnotically at me. And then… surely I'm imagining it… is the light fading a little… are the walls of the tunnel becoming more insubstantial? Yes, they are. They definitely are. Going, going, fast. Now there are only wisps, like dry ice, then they're entirely gone, the whiteness replaced with familiar darkness.

"Hey, what's going on?" My head calls.

"It's not your time," a voice booms.

"But I'm all set. I liked the feeling. Bring it on."

"It's not your time."

"Well make your bloody mind up!"

A pause. Had I gone too far. Then the boomy voice, sounding a little sheepish, murmurs, "Sorry. Administrative error."

I wait a little while, to see if the white light returns. Nothing. Nada. Rien. For a countless time, I eddy about in the silent nothingness, and for the first time since I came down here, I'm a little… well… bored. I watch carefully, alert to any signs that the light might return, any little chinks at all in the darkness. But there's nothing; it won't be back.

Well, I decide, if you're not going to let me die, I might as well live.

I take a deep breath and dive towards the surface.

THROUGH THE FIELDS IN GLOVES

Benedict Kiely

Benedict Kiely (1919–2007) wrote novels, short stories, autobiography and criticism. His story collections include *A Ball of Malt and Madame Butterfly* (1973) and he published ten novels, including *Proxopera*, *The Captain with the Whiskers* and *The Cards of the Gambler*. He was also a broadcaster who regularly contributed radio essays to RTÉ Radio's *Sunday Miscellany*.

He never will forget the face of the first of the sixteen girls he assaulted. Of the lot of them perhaps she appealed to him most. Light on her feet. Bouncing. Miniskirted. Minnehaha. Auburn hair in little kinky curls that looked as if you strummed them they'd play a tune. She was so surprised she couldn't say a sound. Her mouth opened in a perfect O. A perfect pink O, and little teeth showed and a flickering tongue, but no sound came out. Blue jacket with brass buttons. White silk flouncey scarf. White skirt, and so little of it that he had free play with her fragile legs. She raised her arms, hands drooping, as if she was about to fly. Her white small handbag fell to the ground and he was sorely tempted to grab it as a souvenir: there's nothing left for me of days that used to be, there's just a memory among my souvenirs. She wore no gloves. She was up on tiptoe for a while, really about to take off. But he flew instead, his work well done, her white skirt splashed with red. He could run like a hare, quick round the corner past the big, rich red-brick houses, high spiked iron railings, high privet hedges, a road on which you seldom met moving people. Then across the park by the lakeside walk, high hedges again, God himself can scarcely see what's going on down here. Out on the bank of the river, across the bridge by the bakery, down along the riverwalk: on the opposite side of the roadway a chain of small, poor cottages, a different world. No one would ever expect to find you in two such different places on the same day: then sit on a bench and watch the river widening towards the sea. A pity about the white handbag. The wife woulda loved it, even if she couldn't show it off. But perhaps it was safer that way. No evidence of his deed. No souvenirs. There's nothing left for me when Mama's had her tea, she eats as much in hours as I could do in years. He doesn't like that song. Some fellow who thought he was funny made up the words all over again and all wrong, just as if he knew about what wasn't his business.

As quiet here as in a church when there's nothing going on. There's a bit of a green park and a few benches. The river's very wide and slow now. Brown and green blobs of scum floating on it. A few ducks. A man said to him one day do you ever go up to evening devotions in that church in that convent in Drumcondra, you should you know, all the nuts in Dublin go there, who's a nut, but he meant no offence, all the nuts do go there, why he doesn't know, hopping from one foot to the other, sticking their thumbs in their mouths, but very quiet most of the time, that's the way to keep them: quiet. If the river and the city were not so dirty you could smell the salt from the sea.

The second girl was beautiful, but beauties can sometimes have no character, nothing you'd talk about or remember. Perfect complexion. Oh, a lot of bottles went into the making of that. Nose, a bit long. Long blonde hair. Light brown costume, a sort of fluffy hairy material. And nursing in her arms a packed plastic shopping-bag. So that she couldn't defend herself or her costume. She didn't scream. She said: Fuck you. You shit. Fuck you.

She was no lady. But he was gone like a flash before she could do fuck all about anything. It was oil that time.

The third girl: but how could you expect any man to remember everyone of sixteen girls. Or who would want to hear about them. But the fifth girl now was odd because she had a lame leg and ran after him and almost caught him. She could run like the black streak or the brown bomber or whoever it was. Something very abnormal about that and she lame. He felt sorry for her. In a sort of a way. She wasn't as well-dressed and fancypants and slim as the others.

Nobody to be seen in any direction but a few children playing by the edge of the water, and a wisp of a girl wheeling a pram, somebody else's pram, not her fault. A jet roars up from Collinstown, roars over the city, roars off to the south, roars and roars like a madman: at home, when they fly over, he can't hear his ears, or Martha whispering and sighing in her big chair, or Julia, who has goitre, rattling on forever about the Children of the Atom. They have a bloody nerve making that much noise. What he'd like to know is who gave them the right; packed full of slim bitches, that one still roaring, off south to Paris or Turkey or Torremolinos. He sweats at the thought of it, and shivers with the cold even though the sun is shining on the dirty water. The roar dies away. It's over Wexford by now: and he can again hear the children, little voices like birds. One of the Fatima ones was called Jacinta, but you don't say it like that, but with a hawk and a ha as if you were clearing phlegm. Julia and the goitre and the Children of the Atom. She can pronounce nothing. Some people were born with no brains.

Carefully he picks up his blue airlines zipper-bag: and walks home, thinking it's the funniest way to get to know people, women especially. You see them before. You see them during. You see them after: and sometimes you can even read what they say about you. He keeps the clippings, carefully hidden away. Poor Martha can't move and never would find them, but Julia's a curious hawk. And women get things wrong. And they tell lies. That one with the thin spike-heels, and pink pyjamas on her, out in the bright light of day: and a bundle of black hair, fuzzed out and blowing, and a face all painted, a bit of a tart and no better than she might be. When she saw the weapon she tried to run, but the left spike broke and down she went, and was at his mercy, covering her face with her hands and crying to the ground: and she was purple, hair and all, not pink, when he was finished with her. But the liar, she told the guards she fought like a tiger and might have marked his face. You couldn't trust their bible oath. Moreover she should have said tigress.

His cottage is number four in the last block of seven brown-brick cottages. Across the narrow roadway and over the low wall the tidal flow has held the greasy river to a standstill. Beyond number seven there's an acre of sparse salty grass, then sand and the flat sea. The sea-wind and sometimes even the spray or a flooding high-tide burn the grass. He turns to the right at number one, then left up the back laneway to the collapsing old garage at the rear of number four: his happy home. You could hide a corpse here, let alone a blue zipper bag: and if it didn't stink nobody would ever find it: old mattresses and old tea chests, the chassis of a dismantled motor, two broken lawnmowers, a discarded dresser. The landlord, who has houses out at rent all over the place, dumps everything here and removes nothing. But we can't complain, can we, he doesn't push for the rent, and he was always most considerate about Martha's misery, and he never minds us running the bit of a shop on the premises?

Here in an old wooden meat-safe that got woodworm is the perfect place for the bag of tricks, as secure as in the Bank of Ireland in College Green: Julia calls it the Bank of the Island, she can pronounce nothing. Nothing. Then out again and around the front of the cottages, approaching this time from the side of the sea: and down two stone steps and into the shop, alarm-bell ringing, and through the shop, Julia gulping with the goitre behind the scales and the counter: and into the kitchen behind the shop, and Martha in her chair, God help us all.

*

He lives on eggs most of the time, henfood out of their own shop. Julia isn't much of a cook and Martha can't rise out of the chair, a big rocking-chair that because of her weight won't rock. So he cooks his own eggs, boiled, fried, poached, scrambled, but not omelettes, he was never any good at omelettes, it's just as well that he doesn't like them: and the bin on the day before the dustbinmen call is always so full of eggshells that he fears that when he lifts the lid to put in more eggshells there'll be nothing more or less to be heard but chirping chickens. Martha lives on slops and milkfoods, stuff for toothless children, that Julia cooks for her, if you could call anything that Julia does cookery: and the bell rings from above the shopdoor, and Julia runs in and out, gobbling like a turkey, between the scullery and kitchen and the shop: mostly children sent out on messages by lazy parents, small orders, eggs, loaves, bottles of milk, tins of stuff, on and on long after the big shops have closed, the thin ones in white coats won't work after six, out walking with idlers who'll get them all in the family way and that'll fatten them. That's the advantage we have, charging high when the other shops are closed and the public can't get it anywhere else. He'd spoil their whiteness for them, only you couldn't very well go into a crowded shop in broad daylight on a commando: he had thought, off and on, of wearing white, white overalls like a painter, when he was out on a raid, but then you'd be too easily seen from a long distance, either advancing to attack or retreating, mission accomplished, in good order.

No, the best disguise was the old cloth cap, the old reliable: although he had thought of blackening his face like a paratrooper. The trouble was how would you get it washed again in time: in the lake in the park with the ducks quacking at you and the water thick as treacle from those Muscovy monsters? Too pass-remarkable. Once when he was a young fellow and sneaking out at night to try to pick up the dirty young ones that hung around a certain chip-shop on the Northside, Martha had always been a decent girl and hadn't hung around like that and look at the thanks the goodness of God gave her, he had walked right under the nose of his own father, and a fine long nose he had, he takes after his father in that, who didn't know him from Adam because he was wearing a cloth cap he always kept hidden in a secret place of his own in the house: nobody at home knew he had it and it wasn't much of a cap but it was as good as a mask. In Belfast, a plumber's mate once told him, they called cloth caps dunchers, neither he nor the plumber's mate who worked for a while for his own father with the nose, knew why: and in Glasgow, hookerdoons, because you hooked them doon over one eye. He often laughed to himself at that joke, Scotchmen were funny like Harry Lauder, when he was a boy he had seen Harry Lauder in the old Royal, laughed his sides sore.

*

Julia is sitting there as she always sits on the very rim of a round-bottomed cane chair, the sort you see in bootshops, always on the rim as if she hadn't enough backside to fill a chair: and reading out of the evening paper and saying Peter the Painter strikes again. Every time she reads out about Peter the Painter she tells over and over again what the Raid Indian did to the girl in Summerhill on the Northside, she means Red Indian, she never gets anything right. She says she knew the girl and the Raid Indian but with Julia, who's as thin as a broomstick except for the goitre God pity her, you never can credit a word.

The Raid Indian, she says, wasn't a proper Indian at all but a fellow from Ballybough on his way to a Francy Dress Ball in the Mansion House, and in Summerhill he stabbed a young one with a knife.

And Martha stirs and the chair strains and she says what did he want to do that for.

As if she hadn't heard it all before.

Julia says that the young one was sixteen and as bold as brass.

But why, Martha goes on, did he stab her.

He pays no attention. Julia's slim, fairenough, but it doesn't do her much good, she's able to walk but she's not out there on the streets, dressed to the ninetynines.

Julia says that the fellow was all dressed up you see for the francy dress, feathers on his head and things hanging out of him of all colours like the bend of the rainbow, and a knife in a bag, like the pictures, and two more with him, and a crowd after them, jeering, and the young one caught and pulled out a handful of his feathers and the next thing she knows a stab in the back.

Martha says the dirty brute.

Little she knows: but how would she know anything and she too heavy to get out of the chair and too afraid of choking to lie down. He could weep. And all those others free to come and go as they please.

But Julia says the judge said the fellow didn't mean it, and he was carried away and thought he was a real Raid Indian and the young one was tormenting and jeering and pulling his feathers. The cut was an inch and a half long and on the left side of her back bleeding and the fellow said he was doing a wardance and waving the knife and the young one hit against him and he didn't know he cut her until somebody told him, case dismissed. She had only two stitches.

Martha says that wonders never cease. She always says that.

Julia says pray, pray to Our Lady and the Children of the Atom, Russia will be converted and the sun started to roll from one place to another and changed colours, blue and yellow and everything, and came down nearly to the ground, and the people all crying and telling their sins out loud and there wasn't a priest anywhere, and then it jumped up again into the sky as cute as a coolcumber.

Julia's crazy: Julia says but this Peter the Painter must know he's doing it, he's done it before and he'll do it again.

Martha asks who was it this time, and points to the evening paper; and two of them, Julia says, photographs and all, they look as if they're pregnant: and the shopbell rings and Julia is up and out like a greyhound, so fast that he hasn't time even to ask her to bring him back a handful of eggs, all that running and excitement is good for the appetite, jogging.

Right well he knew but nearly too late that they were not pregnant. It was the funny clothes they were wearing. Julia never walks about on those swanky streets and roads, and knows nothing about the latest fashions. They looked like twins, short, bright, blonde hair, rimless glasses, little turneduppity noses: dressed like twins in blue-and-white smocks that made him make his mistake and use the spray, women who were up the pole couldn't run, spray one, spray two, red white and blue for England's glory, he mightn't have bothered about them only for that, red, white and blue like the Union Jack: and the way they looked at him as if he was of no account. But light white runner-shoes and bobbysox like John McEnroe and that should have warned him: took after him with the speed of light, saying nothing, just racing quiet like bad dogs, bitches, but no brains, no teamwork, no co-ordination. Tripped over each other and came down with a crash like a house falling, glasses flying east and west, and one of them was so winded that she couldn't get up or see where she was and the other stopped to help her, twins. The holy show of tangled legs and petticoats he saw when he looked back tempted him to give it another go and spray their legs so well that they'd be stuck together for a month of Sundays. But they might be only foxing, so he outfoxed them and vanished in the bushes.

But the lies they told. When Martha was asleep in the chair and Julia was busy in the shop with the late customers he cutely slipped the evening paper under his jacket so that later he could clip the clipping. Said he struck them and knocked them down, and that was a bloody lie because it was completely against his principles to touch a woman, slim or thin or fat or obese the doctors said, with his hands: and poor Martha, Julia says, has a gross of obesity. But, just like Julia, there never was a woman who could get anything right, except about the cap, in every clipping it said that Peter the Painter wore a cloth cap, but could never tell the colour, they didn't know he had three hookerdoons, that was as funny as Harry Lauder's red kilt, all three of different colours: and he'd buy a few more only it might be dangerous now to be seen in a shop looking for cloth caps: and they didn't know how easy it was to slip a cloth cap into a zipper bag and walk away, as cute as a coolcumber as Julia says, a tall bald man with a long nose. No woman or no clipping ever noticed that he had his father's nose but how could they since they had never known his father.

As he had known him when his father took him with him to help on jobs, and paid him a helper's wage, and he only a boy in short pants: his father was a decent man and fond of poetry. On the northside the father was a plumber, was no more, was long gone and resting in the faraway end of Glasnevin cemetery where all the patriots are buried. In the middle of the meadows, his father used to say, beside or behind Glasnevin or something, the corncrakes cry or creak all night long, or something like that, it was part of a poem: and his mother was a thin, quickwalking, brownfaced woman, hat pinned on one side, sixpence each way, never more and you couldn't have less, up and down the street all day long to the bookies, she could run like a hare: whatever happened to poor Martha to be there night and day like that in the chair: and the place that as a boy he liked best with his father was up on the roofs of the houses between the Strand Road and the northern railway, low houses and low roofs but with great gullies like mountain valleys and all sorts of treasures there that the kids would throw up from below, tennis balls, glassy marbles, yoyos, toys and once, believe it or not, a full-blown football: he had a world of his own up on those roofs and could think of all sorts of things: and the big black engine would go north on the same level as the roofs, and the people waving, and his father saying they'll be in Derry or Belfast before we're home for tea, and that you could write poetry and books about trains, the big wheels and the stories of all the people passing. Up on the lead of those gullies he learned to use the blowlamp, dead easy and the paintspray on the same principle, change the nozzle, one for paint, one for oil, and easy to come by for any man in the trade, and any God's amount of paint, he doesn't need much. As for poetry he was never much for that: but once in a pub, he could remember exactly when, because it wasn't often he darkened the door of a pub, redfaced bastards on whiskey and overdressed bitches drinking gins and tonics that cost the moon and sixpence, and a fat woman walked past to the loo as they called it nowadays and a drunk at the counter said why do you walk through the fields in gloves fat white woman whom nobody loves: and then said to the barman that that was a poem, as if anybody wouldn't have known, even if it wasn't much of a poem.

Misery Martha can't walk through the fields but she loves nice gloves.

She has lovely small hands, not too pudgy about the knuckles and how did that drunk know that nobody loved the fat woman who walked out to the loo?

Julia doesn't like Peter the Painter. Julia says that if a girl works hard and saves up to buy good clothes, she ought to be allowed to wear them in peace and not to have some madman spraying her with paint and easel oil. How does Julia know they work hard: and the worst thing is that Martha agrees with her, creaking in her chair and saying yes, wonders will never cease, to everything Julia says: and Martha says the dirty brute where does he get all the paint, and he thinks that's all the thanks he gets.

Julia's a sort of a farout cousin to Martha and not too clean, and, sitting with the two of them in the kitchen, he often thinks that she could make a better fist of keeping Martha comfortable in her chair: and if it hadn't been for Julia and her tongue going like a hambell Martha would lie down at night, much better than sitting all the time except for the usual, and he always leaves the house then, and the two of them to work it out between them. He would never have shown Martha in the paper about the case of the woman choking, but Julia, no, nothing, nothing could stop her, a forty-stone woman crushed to her death by her own bulk while firemen, all in the evening paper, tried to widen the doors of her home to take her to the hospital: and the doctor said that she had recently developed influenza and began lying down in bed, and that that wasn't good for her and the fat around her chest crushed her to death: and for years before that she had slept sitting up, and that way, the weight didn't press on her. Eight men carried her on mattress-covered plywood boards and a whole other slew of men sawing the doors wider but she died before she could be put in the pickup truck that was waiting in front of the house: and all that, faraway in sunny California, full of slim stars dressed to kill and married forty times. But one girl, now that he thinks of it or that the clippings remind him, and the only thing she said she noticed was that Peter the Painter had a long nose: but he can remember nothing at all about her.

Does Julia ever wonder why the evening paper vanishes every time there's a piece in it about Peter the Painter: you'd never know with Julia, and thin people are hell for curiosity, and he must remember to take the evening paper away all the time, and not just now and then.

This particular morning the first one he notices is a girl in red tights and a long red thing halfways between a jacket and a proper coat: not much sense in spraying her with red paint. That was a sort of funny, and he should have said miss, can you wait here for a while and I'll run home and change to white or green: the green above the red as the song says. The evening before that Martha was watching teevee and Julia getting ready to go out to her sodality and rattling on about the Children of the Atom: and about how Lucia, Looseyah Julia says, had asked the lady about two girls who had died recently, from some place with a funny name, and how the lady said that one of them was already in heaven but that the other one would be in purgatory until the end of the world: and that was a long time to be in purgatory or anywhere else: Looseyah mustn't have liked the other one: and the little boy, Francisco, said that he saw God and God looked so sad that Francisco said that he would like to console him, and Lucia said that many many would be lost: not much point in being God and lord of all if you have to lose so many and to look so mournful about it, although to have to listen to the like of Julia and to look at poor Martha like a mountain in the chair would put a long face on Harry Lauder, keep right on to the end of the road, keep right on to the end: and Jesus wept and would weep again if he saw the way Julia washes herself, a dip to the tips of her fingers and a stab of the comb to her hair, and the hat cocked on her head and trotting off to her prayers with a regiment of pious ones the like of herself. For himself he washes long and hard, not that he needs it but his father was a clean man and he likes to take after his father: as fancy as those slim ones are they mightn't be any better at the washing than Julia, and a spray of paint might do them a good turn by forcing them into the bathtub. He had worked in bathrooms in swanky houses and it wouldn't do you good to look at some of them: and working by night in the cellarage of some fancy lounge bars, you couldn't work there by day because you and the staff would be falling over each other, the rats were as big as cats or calves, if people only knew what they were drinking or where it was stored: and a man once told him that nuns never washed below the navel, it was the rule, but he supposes it would be a sort of a sacrilege to go in for spraying nuns with paint, or even oil.

But keep right on to the end of the road, keep right on to the end, though the way be long let your heart be strong, keep right on round the bend: and round the bend is bloody well right and you can say that again or sing it, and plenty more where that came from, and you're breaking my heart all over again oh why should we part all over again, and poor Martha used to love that song: and perhaps this is the day that he should pack it: for that one in the red tights gives him a very hard look but he goes on his way and pays her no attention. How can she know what he has in his mind or what he has in the zipper: and the next girl is a tall one with canary-yellow trousers and a blue sleeveless sweater, and the half-sleeves of a white blouse: all crying out for a splash of red. Thinfaced, redheaded, chewing, tightly pulled-in at the waist: her backside, though, when she falls and it's looking up at him, is fat and flabby and he feels that he may have made a mistake, and then he goes and makes a mistake for he stoops and hesitates and with one wipe she claws the cap off his head and nearly takes the head with it: and there he is, bald as a hoot as Julia says, and to make a bad job worse he isn't near the park that day but in a long quiet road at the back of the football grandstand and not a bush within miles: if you're tired and weary still journey on till you've come to your happy abode, and as he runs his feet hammer out the tune, and the road quiet and nobody to be seen: with a big stout heart to a long steep hill you may get there with a smile: freedom to run to the sound of your own hoofbeats like the bighorn sheep on the wild prairie and springtime in the Rockies on the teevee. Nobody to be seen but that one with the red tights fifty yards away along a side-road and waving her red arms at somebody in an upstairs window and shouting out allahakbar: he should have let her have it in the first place.

After that mishap he wears a hat: but some bloody burglar breaks into the old garage and breaks this and that and all round them, and steals the old mattress he keeps the clippings in. Julia says there are people around this place who would steal the grace out of the Hail Mary but, leaving all sides ajoke as she puts it, time it is and more than time that somebody put a stop to that Peter the Painter: and that one girl got a good look at him and that she had seen him before when he poured paint all over her, and that he was a bald man with a long nose. Martha says that wonders will never cease, it could be you, but he says I'm not the only one in the world: but, anyway, caution from now on and a nod's as good as a wink.

But the glooms and the restlessness when he looks at Martha in the chair and listens to Julia talking about Martha and Mary, and the Lord himself sitting in his chair, but well able to rise up out of it when he takes the notion, and ascend into heaven when the day comes round: and the Lord's Martha was able to move, not that she got much thanks for it, killing herself cleaning the house and Mary sitting on her ass at the Lord's feet getting all the kudos: a hell of a house it would be for the Lord or anybody else if Martha sat down and refused to get up and left the dishes in the sink.

On top of the hollum oak, says Julia to Martha, and Julia is always busy about many things and Martha, like Mary, sits and sits but not at the Lord's feet and, God of Almighty, she has not chosen the better part: on top of the hollum oak, the lady came from where the sun rises and places herself on top of the hollum oaktree, like the big trees in the park, that's what Francisco said when the Canon asked him: does she come slowly or quickly, she always comes quickly, do you hear what she says to Looseyah, no, do you ever speak to the lady, no, does the lady on the hollum oak ever speak to you, no I never asked her anything and she only speaks to Looseyah: and who does she look at, says the Canon, you and Jack Hinta or does she only look at Looseyah: no she looks at the three of us but she looks longer at Looseyah.

Whoever it was that robbed the old garage they wouldn't be able to make head or tail out of the clippings in the thin cardboard box in the old mattress, if they ever found them, or even, if they did find them, they'd just throw them away and never know that they were of any importance to anybody.

Martha says to Julia that the lady was very beautiful as if Martha was asking Julia a question and as if Martha hadn't heard this rigmarole twenty times over.

A hat isn't as good as a duncher or a hookerdoon: it doesn't sit so steady on the head.

Julia says that Francisco said that the lady on the tree was very beautiful, more beautiful than anybody Francisco had ever seen, with a long dress and over it a veil which covers her head and falls down to the edge of her dress which is all white except for gold lines, and she stands like somebody praying, her hands joined up to the height of her chin, and a rosary around the back of the palm of her right hand and hanging down over her dress, and the rosary as white as the dress: and if she had the misfortune to meet that Peter the Painter fellow she'd regret it.

He says before he can stop himself that Francisco never heard of Peter the Painter, and regrets that he said anything: but Julia, rattling on, has noticed nothing and is scattering the evening paper all around her, sheets all over the floor, and reading out about this man who owned a restaurant somewhere in England: and come from the east like the majors, Julia says, who came to King Herald who killed all the babies: or like the lady in white herself coming from the east to roost like a white bird on the hollum oaktree. But the wife of that man from the east could no more get out of the chair than Martha here, says Julia, and the poor man got depressed and made up his mind to burn the whole place down, and all in it: he went beresk, Julia says, and put the torch to the house and poured so much paraffin that he might have wiped out half the town except that it didn't catch right, and the floor was so slippy that when the eggspector of police walked in he slipped and measured his length and ruined his good uniform, and was so mad he hit the man: and the woman in the chair threw a bowl at the eggspector and cut his face, and it's all up in court, a holy show.

Oh lady, mother of Christ, on the hollum oaktree, get me out of here, away from the rattling-on of Julia, and Martha saying that wonders will never cease: and keep my head in the state of grace, that's what my mother used to say when the ways of the world were too much for her: and I'll say nothing lest I offend the Lord with my tongue. Then she would curse like a trooper and my father would laugh.

Great white gulls drift in the windy day, or strut like boxers on the seawall, like the white lady on what Julia calls the hollum oaktree. The hat does not sit easy, but it looks well and it looks different, and that's important, it isn't so easy to change your nose, that's funny: and he carries the machinery now in a white plastic shopping-bag with the name of the shop written on it: and he crosses the street if he sees a woman wearing anything red, a stitch in time saves nine. The playing children on the flat place by the widening river do not so much madden him as halt him, with not a pain exactly but a cold weakness, and memories of the happy days spent on the gullies of the roofs, treasure island, with his father: and the train with all the people puffing off to the north.

Sometimes he thinks as he walks across that flat place that burning the whole caboodle up or down might not be such a bad idea: the shop and Julia, and Martha in her chair, the garage and mattresses and all, and himself as well.

The park this day seems to have more children in it than he ever saw in one place in his life before. Where do they all come from? Not that he doesn't know. They congregate mostly in one corner around seesaws and swings and chutes and the like: and the big joke is that at that corner and just outside the red park-railings some cute builder has put up a block of fancy expensive flats, or apartments as they call them, or service flats who do they serve and with what, every modern this, that and the other, view of the park and the river and the mountains away faraway, alone all alone by the wavewashed shore, and not a bloody word about the view of the playground, and the children squalling all day long Maryanne outside your wide solar window. Crowd of crooks today in the building business, as much as a tradesman can do to get his money out of them: it wasn't that way in my father's time: but nothing now is on the mend: and Martha will never move out of that chair except to be carried, and crazy Julia can rattle on forever about the white lady and the Children of the Atom, and pray, pray, pray and Russia will be converted, and the sun jumped out of the sky, and the cow jumped over the moon, a likely story, if it jumped out there in Portugal it would have jumped out everywhere else, even here.

He does not come this way often: small streets of redbrick houses around the corner from the block of francy flats, he is beginning to talk like crazy Julia, and the sun jumped out of the sky: he doesn't like these streets, narrow, no gardens before the houses, the little windows too close to you, every

Tom, Dick and Harry, and Biddy and Bridget, and Jack, Sam and Pete, and Sexton Blake, and Buffalo Bill, and Laurel and Hardy, can see you little old lady passing-by: and there she is in a blue sweater with a Mickey Mouse on each breast, and black hair pulled back in a bun and parted distinctly up the middle, and tight blue levis as thin as sticks, and her little backside bouncing out, and as quick on her feet as a sparrow in a bush of bridesblossom or mock-orange: and he goes for the glasses and the dromedary Mickey Mice, for those bloody skintight levis would be no loss, one way or the other: and his hat blows off and the bloody street is full of Children of the Atom, and there he is as bald as a hoot, as Julia says, and dropping the shopping-bag and no time to pick it up, nor his hat even wherever it may be: and keep right on to the end of the road, keep right on to the end, though you're tired and weary, still journey on till you've come to your happy abode: and racing for the park and the bushes: and the children after him shouting, and he clips one of them on the ear: and across the grass of the soccer pitches, and a car in the park against all regulations, a bloody squadcar across the grass and no park-keeper to stop them: and the children around him like bluebottles, jeering: and he goes beresk, as Julia says, and kicks three of them and knocks another down with his fist: and so here we have you in the heel of the hunt, me bold Peter the Painter, says the fat man with the moustache as he leaps out of the squadcar, and two guards with him, and your painting days are over as the tattooed lady said when she killed her husband: and beyond the bushes there is Julia, darting like a rabbit.

For a minute he thinks it is his mother, hat cocked and pinned-on, and up and down the street, sixpence each way, never more and you couldn't have less: but no, it is Julia, and the children cheering, and the squadcar going back across the park and, swear to God, driving clean through a flowerbed: nothing these days is on the mend.

SARAH

Mary Lavin

Mary Lavin (1912–1996) wrote only two novels, *The House in Clewe Street* and *Mary O'Grady*, devoting herself to the short story, her collections including *Tales from Bective Bridge*, *In the Middle of the Fields* and *Happiness and Other Stories*. She was awarded the James Tait Black Memorial Prize, two Guggenheim Fellowships and the Katherine Mansfield Prize.

Sarah had a bit of a bad name. That was the worst the villagers said of her, although Sarah had three children, and was unmarried, and although, moreover, there was a certain fortuity in her choice of fathers for them. She was a great worker, tireless and strong, and several people in the village got her in by the day to scrub. Women with sons, and young brides, took care not to hire her, but oftentimes they were the very people who were the kindest to her. Not one of the children was born in the workhouse, and it was the most upright matron in the village that slapped life into every one of them!

"She is a good girl, at heart," said Mrs. Muldoon. "We are all born with a tendency to evil."

"How could the poor girl know any better?" said another neighbor. "Living with two rough brothers, without mother or sister!"

"And who ever remembers any talk of her having a father herself?" said Mrs. Muldoon.

If Sarah had been one to lie in bed on a Sunday morning, and miss Mass, the villagers would have shunned her, and crossed their breasts when they spoke of her. There was greater understanding in their hearts for sins against God than there was for sins against the Church. And Sarah found it easy to keep the commands of the servant of the Lord, even if she found it somewhat difficult to keep the commands of the Lord Himself. She did the Stations as often as anyone. She never missed Mass. And if there was a Lady Day, or a Holy Day, when the countryside gathered at the holy well in the next village, Sarah was always a credit to her own village, with her shoes off walking on the flinty stones, doing her penance for all the world like a holy nun. If any comments were made the other villagers, Sarah's neighbors, were quicker than Sarah herself to take offense. But with all this they tempered their charity with prudence on occasions, and when Kathleen Kedrigan, wife of Oliver Kedrigan and a newly married woman who had recently come to the village, spoke of getting Sarah in to keep the place clean for her while she was going up to Dublin to see a doctor, there wasn't a woman in the place who didn't feel it her duty to step across to Kedrigans' and offer a word of advice.

"I know she has a bit of a bad name," said Kathleen, "but she's a great worker. She can scrub a floor till it's as white as a piece of a rope! And she can bake better than anyone I ever knew, except my own mother!"

"All the same," said the neighbor, "I'd advise you to think twice before I'd leave her minding your house while you're away."

"She's only coming in for a few hours in the morning to give the floors a scrub, and to bake bread for Oliver. He's going to take his dinner across the fields at his brother's place."

"All the same," said another neighbor, "I wouldn't have her near the house atall, if I were you!"

"Who else is there I could get?"

"Why do you want anyone? You'll only be gone for two or three days!"

"Two or three days is a long time to leave the house in the care of a man."

"I'd sooner let the roof fall in, if I were you, than trust that brazen thing about the house."

"It isn't her I'd trust! It's Oliver," said Kathleen.

"It's not right to trust any man too far!"

Kathleen Kedrigan smiled and her pale papery face showed her contempt for the older women.

"Oliver isn't that sort!"

"She's a good-looking girl," said one woman, stung by Kathleen's smile.

"She has a secret way of looking at men," said the other woman. "I suppose you know your own business but I don't think it's right to trust any man, even the greatest saint that ever walked, with a woman like Sarah."

"I'd trust Oliver with every fancy woman in Ireland!"

"All right," said the two women, speaking at once. "It's your man, not ours. I don't know why we should worry about him!"

The women went out and Kathleen watched after them resentfully. She may not have been altogether serious about hiring Sarah Murray, but as she closed the door she made up her mind definitely. She was goaded on by a passionate pride in her own legitimate power over Oliver. She could trust him. And she'd let everyone see that she could!

The women went down the road and as they went they talked about Oliver Kedrigan.

"I don't know why he ever married that bleached-out doll. I wonder why she's going to Dublin? Isn't Dr. Deignan good enough for her? She doesn't look like a girl that would have a healthy child!"

As they passed Sarah's cottage they saw Sarah at the gate.

"She's expecting someone!" they said to each other, and as they went homeward they twitched their shoulders uneasily, filled with a strange uncontrollable envy of her youth and her brazen mind, and her slow leopardy beauty.

Sarah came over to Kedrigans' the morning Kathleen was going, and made her a cup of tea before she left. She carried her bag down to the bus for her as well, and so Kathleen didn't see the hired girl and Oliver standing in the sunlight, as the neighbors saw them an hour later, when he called her to hand him out the tin of sheep-raddle off the dresser. She handed it up to him as he sat on the blue cart and she laughed at the way the horse rattled his trappings restlessly.

They looked a far finer pair than Oliver and Kathleen had ever looked. Kathleen was anemic and thin-boned. Oliver and Sarah were peasants. They had the same quick gestures and warm coloring, and the same curious gold eyes. She handed him up the tin of raddle and Oliver looked down and laughed.

"Did you rub the raddle on your cheeks?" he said, when he saw the rough color that stained her face.

She put up a bare arm and wiped it across her face, the healthy red deepened with capricious temper. But she laughed again when he went down the road, and she watched him till the cart had rattled out of earshot, in the distance, where it looked no more than a toy cart, with a toy horse and a still young farmer made out of painted wood.

Kathleen came home on the following Friday. Her house was cleaner than it had ever been before. The boards shone white. The windows glinted. There was bread cooling on the window sill and the step outside the door was whitened with lime. She paid Sarah, and Sarah went home. Her brothers were glad to have her back again. She gave them the money. They were glad to have her cook good wholesome food again, and wash and scrub again.

Her children were glad to have her home again too. They were getting big and their uncles were making them work, piling turf, and running after the sheep like collie dogs.

Sarah worked hard for a few months, and one night, as she handed round the potato cakes at supper, her elder brother took a sharp look at her.

"For God's sake," he said to the younger brother, "for God's sake! Will you look at her!"

Sarah tossed her hair back and sat down. She ate her supper and drank two big cups of tea.

"I'm going out," she said, and went out the door into the wagon-blue evening light. Her going was nonchalant and independent, and her slow gait had a strange rhythmical grace.

When she was gone the brothers shuffled their feet and exchanged looks.

"Did you see her? Did you see her?" said Pat. "Holy God, but something has got to be done about her this time."

"Ah! What the hell is the use of talking like that? What's to be done? Tell me that! What's to be done? If the country is full of blackguards, what can we do about it?"

"I thought the talking the priest gave her the last time would put some sense into her. He said to me that a Home was the only place for the like of her, but I told him that we'd not have any part in putting her away. Wasn't that right? Wasn't that right? Sure my God, what would we do without her here? You must have a woman in the house. And the brats need their mother with them till they go to work, although that won't be long now. They're shaping into fine strong boys. Still, I must give the priest some answer."

"Tell him you can get no right of her atall, and let him tackle the job himself. I suppose it won't be long till he sees for himself. It's a good job the Kedrigans didn't notice her, or they'd never have given her an hour's work over there."

"How could they have noticed anything? Wasn't that over six months ago?"

"Pat...'

"Well?"

"Oh nothing, nothing. Nothing at all!"

"Can't you quit your hinting and speak out?"

"I'm only wondering... Who do you think is the father?"

"When you didn't know the father of the last one you're not likely to know the father of this one."

"The priest said that if she didn't tell him the name of the father he'd make the child able to talk, and make it name the guilty man."

"How well he didn't do it after all! Sarah was careful not to let him get a sight of the child till the whole thing was put to the back of his mind with the thoughts of laying the foundation-stone of the school! She can do the same with this one, then," said Pat, rising up and hitting his pipe against the chimney piece. "I'm going across to the quarry field to see if the heifer is all right. When Sarah comes back tell her to have the butter ready for Mick Grady to take up to Dublin in the morning."

"I won't mention anything else, of course?"

"What would you be mentioning? What is there to mention?" he said. "Won't it all be beyond saying in a few more weeks, when everyone in the village will see for themselves?"

"I suppose you're right. Well, come back and I'll give you a hand bringing in the heifer if she's in a bad way."

"Ah, the heifer'll be all right."

Sarah went out every night after that, when dusk began to crouch over the valley, and her brothers kept silent tongues in their heads about the child she was carrying. She worked better than ever before and she sang at her work. She carried the child deep in her body and she had a strange primitive grace in her rounded figure. She did not lose one shred of her tawny feline beauty, and she faced the abashed congregation at late Mass every Sunday. She walked halfway down the aisle and went to her usual place, in the fifth pew, under the third Station. Mrs. Kedrigan was expecting the long-delayed heir in a few weeks' time too, but she didn't go to Mass. The priest came to the house to her. She was looking bad, and she crept from chair to chair around the house, and at night she went out for a bit of a walk in the dark on the back road. She was bloodless and self-conscious. Her nerves were getting badly frayed and Oliver used to have to sit up half the night and hold her moist palms in his until she fell asleep; but she was frightened and petulant and, in bursts of hysteria, she called Oliver a cruel brute.

One evening she was drinking a drop of tea, made by a gossipmonger, who called in to inquire for her health. She had just had a bad scene with Oliver, and he had gone down to the Post Office to see if there was any letter from the Maternity Hospital in Dublin, where she had engaged a bed for the next month. When he came back he had a letter in his hand, but he waited till they were alone before he gave it to her. Before he gave it to her, he told her what was in it. It was an anonymous letter and it had named him as the father of the child Sarah Murray was going to bring into the world in a few weeks' time. He told Kathleen it was an unjust accusation.

Kathleen took the letter, and when she had read it, she threw it on the floor. Two unusual spots of color came into her cheeks.

"For God's sake, say something," said Oliver. "You don't believe the bloody letter do you?"

Kathleen didn't answer, and the red spots grew more hectic in her cheeks.

"You don't believe it, Katty? You don't believe it, do you?" And he went down on his knees and put his head in her lap. "What am I to do, Katty?"

"You'll do nothing," said Kathleen, speaking for the first time. "You'll do nothing. Aren't you innocent? Take no notice of that letter."

She stooped with a grotesque gesture and picked up the letter. She put it under a plate on the dresser and began to get the tea ready with slow tedious journeying back and forth across the silent kitchen. Oliver stood over the fire for a little while and once or twice he looked at his wife with suspicion and curiosity.

"I'll take the letter," he said at last, walking to the dresser.

"You'll do nothing of the kind," said Kathleen, and she took it out from under the plate. "This is where that letter belongs."

There was a sharp sound of crackling and a paper ball went into the heart of the flames. Oliver watched it burning and although he thought it odd that he didn't see the writing on it as it burned, he still believed that it was his letter that was curling into black scrolls in the grate.

The very next evening Sarah was sitting by the fire as Kathleen had been sitting by her fire. She was drinking a cup of tea and she didn't look up when her brothers came in. No one spoke and Sarah began to get up. Her brother Pat pushed her down on the chair again. The tea slopped over the floor. The cup shattered against the range.

"Is this letter yours? Did you write it?" said the older brother, holding out a letter addressed to Oliver Kedrigan that had gone through the post and been opened. "Did you write this letter?"

"What business is it of yours?" asked Sarah, trying to rise again.

"Sit down, I tell you," said Pat, pressing her back. "Can't you answer my question? Did you write this letter?"

Sarah stared dully at the letter. The yellow-brown eyes flickered fire.

"Give it to me," she snarled and she snatched it out of his hand. "What business is it of yours, you thief?"

"Did you hear that?" the younger man shouted. "Did you hear that? She called you a thief, did you hear that?"

"Shut up you," said Pat to the other man. "And answer me this you," said he, shaking the girl: "Is it true what it says in this letter?"

"How do I know what it says in the letter, and what if it is true? Is it any business of yours?"

"I'll show you whose business it is," Pat said, and he ran into the room, off the kitchen. He came out with an armful of clothes, a red dress, a brown coat, and a few odd garments. Sarah watched him, fascinated. He ran into the kitchen and looked at his sister and then he looked around the room in hesitation. Suddenly he saw the open door into the yard and he ran towards it. He threw out the armful of clothing and ran back into the room. He came out with a few more things in his arms and a red cap. He threw them out the door, too.

"Do you know it's raining?" said the younger brother.

"What do I care if it's raining?"

He went in again. He came out with a picture frame and a box of powder and a little green-velvet box stuck all over with pearly shells.

"Oh! Give me my box! Give me my green box." Sarah sprang to life after her long immobility.

The other brother was impelled into action too.

"Go after it if you want it," he shouted and pushed her out into the rain. She fell on the wet slab stone of the doorway and the brothers shut out the sight from their eyes by banging the door closed.

"That ought to teach her," said one. "Carrying on with a married man! No one is going to say I put up with that kind of thing. I didn't mind the first time, when it was a rich man like old Molloy, that could pay for his mistakes, but I wasn't going to stand for a thing like this."

"You're sure it was Kedrigan?"

"Ah, sure, didn't you see the letter yourself? Wasn't it her writing and didn't Mrs. Kedrigan herself give it to me this morning?"

"She denied it, Pat."

"She did and so did he, I suppose. Well, she can deny it somewhere else now."

"I suppose she'll go down to the Gilroys'?"

"Let her go where she bloody well likes and shut your mouth, you. If it wasn't for you wanting the money for the harness she wouldn't have gone near Kedrigans' in the first place. Keep away from that window. Can't you sit down? Sit down can't you!"

All this took place at nine o'clock on a Tuesday night. The next morning at eleven o'clock, Oliver Kedrigan came from a fair in another town, home across the fields. He called in across the yard to his wife.

"Kathleen, Kathleen! Hand me out the raddle. It's on top of the dresser."

Kathleen Kedrigan came to the door and she had the raddle in her hand.

"You won't be troubled with any more letters," she said.

Oliver laughed self-consciously. "That's a good thing, anyhow," he said. "Give me the raddle."

Kathleen held the tin of red marking in her hand, but she didn't move. She leaned against the jamb of the door.

"I see you didn't hear the news?"

"What news?"

"Sarah Murray got what was coming to her last night. Her brothers turned her out of the house, and threw out all her things after her."

Oliver's eyes darkened.

"That was a cruel class of thing for brothers to do. Where did she go?"

"She went where the like of her belongs—into the ditch on the side of the road!"

Oliver said nothing but his limbs stiffened with resentment. His wife watched him closely and she clenched her hands.

"You can spare your sympathy. She won't need it."

Oliver looked up.

"Did she stay out all night in the rain?"

"She did," said Kathleen, and she stared at him. "At least that's where they found her in the morning, as dead as a rat, and the child dead beside her!"

Her pale eyes held him. His own eyes stared uncomprehendingly into them.

She began to move back into the house away from his stare. He looked down at her hand that held the tin of red sheep-raddle.

"Give me the raddle!" he said, and before she had time to hand it to him he repeated it, again and again, frantically.

"Give me the raddle. Give it to me. Hurry, will you! Give me the God-damn' stuff."

THE VILLAGE BULLY

Sheridan Le Fanu

Sheridan Le Fanu (1814–1873) was an Irish novelist and short story writer, best known for his ghost stories and gothic fiction. His works include *Uncle Silas* (1864), the vampire novella *Carmilla* (1872) and his short story collection, *In a Glass Darkly* (1872), which features his most anthologised short story, 'Green Tea'.

About thirty years ago there lived in the town of Chapelizod an ill-conditioned fellow of herculean strength, well known throughout the neighbourhood by the title of Bully Larkin. In addition to his remarkable physical superiority, this fellow had acquired a degree of skill as a pugilist which alone would have made him formidable. As it was, he was the autocrat of the village, and carried not the sceptre in vain. Conscious of his superiority, and perfectly secure of impunity, he lorded it over his fellows in a spirit of cowardly and brutal insolence, which made him hated even more profoundly than he was feared.

Upon more than one occasion he had deliberately forced quarrels upon men whom he had singled out for the exhibition of his savage prowess; and in every encounter his over-matched antagonist had received an amount of "punishment" which edified and appalled the spectators, and in some instances left ineffaceable scars and lasting injuries after it.

Bully Larkin's pluck had never been fairly tried. For, owing to his prodigious superiority in weight, strength, and skill, his victories had always been certain and easy; and in proportion to the facility with which he uniformly smashed an antagonist, his pugnacity and insolence were inflamed. He thus became an odious nuisance in the neighbourhood, and the terror of every mother who had a son, and of every wife who had a husband who possessed a spirit to resent insult, or the smallest confidence in his own pugilistic capabilities.

Now it happened that there was a young fellow named Ned Moran—better known by the soubriquet of "Long Ned," from his slender, lathy proportions—at that time living in the town. He was, in truth, a mere lad, nineteen years of age, and fully twelve years younger than the stalwart bully. This, however, as the reader will see, secured for him no exemption from the dastardly provocations of the ill-conditioned pugilist. Long Ned, in an evil hour, had thrown eyes of affection upon a certain buxom damsel, who, notwithstanding Bully Larkin's amorous rivalry, inclined to reciprocate them.

I need not say how easily the spark of jealousy, once kindled, is blown into a flame, and how naturally, in a coarse and ungoverned nature, it explodes in acts of violence and outrage.

"The bully" watched his opportunity, and contrived to provoke Ned Moran, while drinking in a public house with a party of friends, into an altercation, in the course of which he failed not to put such insults upon his rival as manhood could not tolerate. Long Ned, though a simple, good-natured sort of fellow, was by no means deficient in spirit, and retorted in a tone of defiance which edified the more timid, and gave his opponent the opportunity he secretly coveted.

Bully Larkin challenged the heroic youth, whose pretty face he had privately consigned to the mangling and bloody discipline he was himself so capable of administering. The quarrel, which he had himself contrived to get up, to a certain degree covered the ill blood and malignant premeditation which inspired his proceedings, and Long Ned, being full of generous ire and whiskey punch, accepted the gauge of battle on the instant. The whole party, accompanied by a mob of idle men and boys, and in short by all who could snatch a moment from the calls of business, proceeded in slow procession through the old gate into the Phoenix Park, and mounting the hill overlooking the town, selected near its summit a level spot on which to decide the quarrel.

The combatants stripped, and a child might have seen in the contrast presented by the slight, lank form and limbs of the lad, and the muscular and massive build of his veteran antagonist, how desperate was the chance of poor Ned Moran.

"Seconds" and "bottle-holders"—selected of course for their love of the game—were appointed, and "the fight" commenced.

I will not shock my readers with a description of the cool-blooded butchery that followed. The result of the combat was what anybody might have predicted. At the eleventh round, poor Ned refused to "give in"; the brawny pugilist, unhurt, in good wind, and pale with concentrated and as yet unslaked revenge, had the gratification of seeing his opponent seated upon his second's knee, unable to hold up his head, his left arm disabled; his face a bloody, swollen, and shapeless mass; his breast scarred and bloody, and his whole body panting and quivering with rage and exhaustion.

"Give in, Ned, my boy," cried more than one of the bystanders.

"Never, never," shrieked he, with a voice hoarse and choking.

Time being "up," his second placed him on his feet again. Blinded with his own blood, panting and staggering, he presented but a helpless mark for the blows of his stalwart opponent. It was plain that a touch would have been sufficient to throw him to the earth. But Larkin had no notion of letting him off so easily. He closed with him without striking a blow (the effect of which, prematurely dealt, would have been to bring him at once to the ground, and so put an end to the combat), and getting his battered and almost senseless head under his arm, fast in that peculiar "fix" known to the fancy pleasantly by the name of "chancery," he held him firmly, while with monotonous and brutal strokes he beat his fist, as it seemed, almost into his face. A cry of "shame" broke from the crowd, for it was plain that the beaten man was now insensible, and supported only by the herculean arm of the bully. The round and the fight ended by his hurling him upon the ground, falling upon him at the same time with his knee upon his chest.

The bully rose, wiping the perspiration from his white face with his blood-stained hands, but Ned lay stretched and motionless upon the grass. It was impossible to get him upon his legs for another round. So he was carried down, just as he was, to the pond which then lay close to the old Park gate, and his head and body were washed beside it. Contrary to the belief of all he was not dead. He was carried home, and after some months to a certain extent recovered. But he never held up his head again, and before the year was over he had died of consumption. Nobody could doubt how the disease had been induced, but there was no actual proof to connect the cause and effect, and the ruffian Larkin escaped the vengeance of the law. A strange retribution, however, awaited him.

After the death of Long Ned, he became less quarrelsome than before, but more sullen and reserved. Some said "he took it to heart," and others, that his conscience was not at ease about it. Be this as it may, however, his health did not suffer by reason of his presumed agitations, nor was his worldly prosperity marred by the blasting curses with which poor Moran's enraged mother pursued him; on the contrary he had rather risen in the world, and obtained regular and well-remunerated employment from the Chief Secretary's gardener, at the other side of the Park. He still lived in Chapelizod, whither, on the close of his day's work, he used to return across the Fifteen Acres.

It was about three years after the catastrophe we have mentioned, and late in the autumn, when, one night, contrary to his habit, he did not appear at the house where he lodged, neither had he been seen anywhere, during the evening, in the village. His hours of return had been so very regular, that his absence excited considerable surprise, though, of course, no actual alarm; and, at the usual hour, the house was closed for the night, and the absent lodger consigned to the mercy of the elements, and the care of his presiding star. Early in the morning, however, he was found lying in a state of utter helplessness upon the slope immediately overlooking the Chapelizod gate. He had been smitten with a paralytic stroke: his right side was dead; and it was many weeks before he had recovered his speech sufficiently to make himself at all understood.

He then made the following relation: He had been detained, it appeared, later than usual, and darkness had closed before he commenced his homeward walk across the Park. It was a moonlit night, but masses of ragged clouds were slowly drifting across the heavens. He had not encountered a human figure, and no sounds but the softened rush of the wind sweeping through bushes and hollows met his ear. These wild and monotonous sounds, and the utter solitude which surrounded him, did not, however, excite any of those uneasy sensations which are ascribed to superstition, although he said he did feel depressed, or, in his own phraseology, "lonesome." Just as he crossed the brow of the hill which shelters the town of Chapelizod, the moon shone out for some moments with unclouded lustre, and his eye, which happened to wander by the shadowy enclosures which lay at the foot of the slope, was arrested by the sight of a human figure climbing, with all the haste of one pursued, over the churchyard wall, and running up the steep ascent directly towards him. Stories of "resurrectionists" crossed his recollection, as he observed this suspicious-looking figure. But he began, momentarily, to be aware with a sort of fearful instinct which he could not explain, that the running figure was directing his steps, with a sinister purpose, towards himself.

The form was that of a man with a loose coat about him, which, as he ran, he disengaged, and as well as Larkin could see, for the moon was again wading in clouds, threw from him. The figure thus advanced until within some two score yards of him, it arrested its speed, and approached with a loose, swaggering gait. The moon again shone out bright and clear, and, gracious God! what was the spectacle before him? He saw as distinctly as if he had been presented there in the flesh, Ned Moran, himself, stripped naked from the waist upward, as if for pugilistic combat, and drawing towards him in silence. Larkin would have shouted, prayed, cursed, fled across the Park, but he was absolutely powerless; the apparition stopped within a few steps, and leered on him with a ghastly mimicry of the defiant stare with which pugilists strive to cow one another before combat. For a time, which he could not so much as conjecture, he was held in the fascination of that unearthly gaze, and at last the thing, whatever it was, on a sudden swaggered close up to him with extended palms. With an impulse of horror, Larkin put out his hand to keep the figure off, and their palms touched—at least, so he believed—for a thrill of unspeakable agony, running through his arm, pervaded his entire frame, and he fell senseless to the earth.

Though Larkin lived for many years after, his punishment was terrible. He was incurably maimed; and being unable to work, he was forced, for existence, to beg alms of those who had once feared and flattered him. He suffered, too, increasingly, under his own horrible interpretation of the preternatural encounter which was the beginning of all his miseries. It was vain to endeavour to shake his faith in the reality of the apparition, and equally vain, as some compassionately did, to try to persuade him that the greeting with which his vision closed was intended, while inflicting a temporary trial, to signify a compensating reconciliation.

"No, no," he used to say, "all won't do. I know the meaning of it well enough; it is a challenge to meet him in the other world—in Hell, where I am going—that's what it means, and nothing else."

And so, miserable and refusing comfort, he lived on for some years, and then died, and was buried in the same narrow churchyard that contains the remains of his victim.

I need hardly say, how absolute was the faith of the honest inhabitants, at the time when I heard the story, in the reality of the preternatural summons which, through the portals of terror, sickness, and misery, had summoned Bully Larkin to his long, last home, and that, too, upon the very ground on which he had signalised the guiltiest triumph of his violent and vindictive career.

ME AND THE DEVIL

Eimear McBride

Eimear McBride is the author of three novels: *Strange Hotel*, *The Lesser Bohemians* and *A Girl is a Half-formed Thing*. She is the recipient of the Bailey's Women's Prize for Fiction, Goldsmiths Prize, James Tait Black Memorial Prize and Irish Novel of the Year Award. She held the inaugural Creative Fellowship at the Beckett Research Centre, University of Reading.

Three sheets to the wind I go to the rath where it stands against the night. Like birthing, blackthorns crown the stars across the planet sky. Below the ruck and pats of cows suck back my leather shoes til I curse the settled western dark that leads on to the coasts. There, for sure, the waters beat at stone and sand or cliff. There the birds cling, wail or sleep but don't do silent this: fall of owl beyond the trees then whoosh of screaming mouse. God. Oh God forsaken dark, me and the devil are with you now.

Even his pestiferous parishioners are turning out their lights, leaving the wind to bark up my back into righteous ridges of fright. Frigid fingers friggered the air beyond in the last breath he blew. I saw it and pondered – Father father – how that memory might crust for you.

We went east to the world when I was a child, although he turned my face from the sun. I the other, the unbeknownst but she, his secret one. And they hid the love between them or so I heard… so she said and what cause had I to disbelieve when I knew nothing better? Those first years when we lived far off, before the munificent lying began, I remember with much less cheerlessness than he gave me cause to again. He presented for hair-ruffling once a week, grim-faced to his silent sin and to her as well; the guilty vessel of whatever she'd brought out in him. Father I called him. Capital F. Father she called him too until after grace and Have you brushed your teeth? I was ushered up to my room. On that night, Fridays, I could not dream. There was no calling for or crawling to her bed. Even with phantoms plucking my ears I knew she'd not come, so not to expect. A little older and I'd lie in the dull of my bunk til the early shuffling out had died, then she'd wake me, insisting I'd never leave her alone. I'd swear it and never could quite recant.

Later on when we moved in in mock widowhood – she his housekeeper, me her lately fatherless son – I missed those weekends and her lonely warmth. What came afterwards made them glow like a taunt. I knew, you see, though no one said for years, it was him, he was my father, smaller 'f'. My blood taught me the truth of it when he was around. The very glamour of his attention flipped my stomach upside down – not that there was much attention. It was more a house of Get up to your room.

I don't know why we moved in and I can't believe he would have asked. She must have held me over him or maybe poverty brought it to pass. His stand-offishness soon peeled away making myth of his haughty before and, if it was some threat of hers that had forced his hand, he quickly repaid the favour. Panic I'd say was our home life, up there on his hill. Fine thick doors to keep her screaming behind. Fine big gates to block out the village. But who would have come there anyway? Who'd have questioned the parish priest? He always hit where blouses hid and what were a few handprints on me? Lucky little spoiled gurrier, sucking the Church's teat. Did they all know? How could they not have guessed? Maybe the vigorous thumpings were part of his ploy to keep them off the scent.

I wished all the time it was not him, for my real father to reappear, the one I'd conjure in my head for her. He – the real one – was, I was sure, the patient sort and kind. The pointer-out of rock formations, a namer of birds and clouds. She indulged it somewhat when I was young, dreaming families on her knee, but the older I grew her oftener answer was For God's sake give my head peace! So he died in me like all love would though I did not know that then. Instead it looked – love – for other ways in leaving me unprepared when it came.

Eight in a flurry across the yard to prod at my friend's pumping knee. Him hunkered and Ow-ing while I slopped his blood up turned me all the proverbial puppy. His glass eyes and grass stains, the gouge out of his skin, then the black finger-nailed fingers twisting my own as I dabbed There! And There! It's okay! Spikes sprung inside me, made of thrill, joining my kicked-dog self to him and he? Well… is why I'm here.

From then on I hung just around to make him laugh. Pushed myself into the frame of whatever he looked at. Asked and asked for him to stay the night so we could tent the sitting room and watch TV. Knowing it would lessen the slagging matches in our hall my mother encouraged every caller. And my adoration was held so far from my body that I hardly knew what it was, except real. My poor love in such short pants that dared not speak – or know – its name; not that any variety could have in our wasp swarm of a home. But others did, knew full well and how to beat it like a drum. The clouts I got for 'reluctant' confession box confessions about my mooning after O'Casey's son. Father father roaring I'll kill him, and purpling my mother's eyes to seal the deal, soon submerged me in a professional hate whose name I came to know too well.

Until fifteen I lived crushed up in my chest. Then came the wave that washed me out of myself, crashed me with feeling and real wants enough to be worth risking the do or die. That year I'd mostly been playing it straight, levering up skirts, drinking at the lake. I'd relinquished to form because there was no other way to make the years go peaceably by. But that choice made sensation an impregnable dream. Stood it snapped off at the root from my welter of feeling so I forgot to plan for the possibility of it coming. Then and oh, summer came.

In the hot of its depths – or as hot as it gets – with Father father in the US of A and mother at her spurious auntie's in Cork, sensibility blocked sense's way. *Fright Night* or something alone on our couch, a bottle of Smirnoff Blue, talk of the Leaving Cert, where we'd go after that, then my agony addled I'll miss you. Lunging – I still think with a shiver – so he'd barely room to draw back. Not that he tried and, in fairness, I'd say he was the first one of us to trousers off. He had been, all those years, my very best friend and I'm not sorry he was the first to be more. His mouth made me ripped down curtains and open blinds. Beyond that maw lay destruction, I knew and didn't mind. I never considered if he did either. That night he didn't and I still know that now. So away we went, bodies going riot. Afterwards, talk, then fits of quiet, then turning couch cushions over, then him out to the night and our quiet swears of more of this, much more of this and soon. As he walked down the path my brain went Tick! You are alive now! And I began readying myself for what had seemed far off but was suddenly present: body and brain syncing in time. In my mind's eye though I saw him – Father father – like the devil on a leash sniffing out my fragile secret. You better run, I thought Please let him come with me.

Tied we were, together, by our bodies after that. Stumbling down in ditches for a damp post-match or kissing in the cloakrooms like we could not be caught and neither were we either, right until we were. I remember it as sunny, that day the world eclipsed, scraping his thin back against the grey breeze-blocks and concrete, kissing half a second longer than I really knew was wise, but obliviously. The cubicle door. His face I remember and the fear it wore as the puck began to leach back from his lips. Sir… sir… it isn't what you think. And how could I, who loved him so be somehow jubilant that now our secret was out? He, four footballing brothers abreast and a Dad on the lash, had no romance about it.

First to the Principle: abomination rained on our heads, what we were, would become, but wouldn't, couldn't tell our parents. Instead, and for our immortal souls, he called the parish priest. In memory that day is now hard to breech. The sun on five pheasant feathers stuck in a jug. Weird decoration, was all I thought while Father father flayed me into hide. But the boy, my boy, he got underfoot. Stamping on and spitting shame, threatened naming from the pulpit. This I knew was empty but he did not and begged for the secret to be kept by us and God. I saw it start then but didn't know how to stop Father father untying him from life.

Two weeks ago I fell off Australia, so drunk I fell off the edge, which really was some achievement having gone there for the space. But I've never been a great one for dignity. Or not since those days of which I speak, when I was for advancing on Jerusalem and Oh O'Casey's son was the Friday night in every week. Since then there's been a lot more spewing down my front. A lot more box-springs squeaking loud to strangers' wants. More collapsing and failing than anyone could want but falling off Australia? Well… that was the last. The best too because it finally shook me clear of that notion of running I've been holding onto so dearly all of these past twenty years. There on the phone he was saying it Your mother is dead. Three in the morning. Peacefully in the end. I thought you should know. And he knew as I said I'm coming back, just what that meant. A blinder first though and then the sea. Bladdered I fell off the land I'd used to be free but when the waves warned Get up! that's what I did. Followed their instructions for Book yourself a ticket, and when I sat on the plane hearing Good luck with it, I thanked Australia then faced away.

Over oceans and lands I recalled my mother on her knees, begging, pleading, beseeching my mercy. The white I felt at what I'd seen and the rage required for what I planned to do. I held his fingers into the coals, enjoying the melt of his skin while I carefully roared I'm going to kill you for what you've done, believe me. I do, Father father screamed. My flaw was my indecision then. She, maddened, scratching up at my maddened face, reminding me of promises I made. You said you'd never leave me alone and I cannot live without him… promise me. And I loved her so I set him free. You are pathetic, I said. But you understand that, she agreed, which I did, which I hated more. That was the last moment I could have saved myself for the world, despite discovering that what lights must also burn. If I'd done it quick and done it then… But I dropped his burning sleeve and said instead You have the length of her life so take care of her and I'll see you again.

Crossways I have lived ever since. Making glass of my life while the globe got thick with words of acceptance that came too late. I always tell my secrets in the unrequited hope of laying the ghost who just one secret killed. It was so tiring at eighteen to run out of my skin, straight from the start to the end. I never stopped writing her though and she knew why. She never hid their address or refused to reply even when their scandal broke and he was fired and they slunk off to a private ignominy. But now Father father her body's not here to be a crutch for yours anymore.

Early this evening I knocked on his door. The past lit when he saw me but he knew not to run. I said Hello Satan I believe that it's time to go. Me and the Devil, walking side by side. Me and Devil heating by the fire. I'm going to dream of my love again now this debt is satisfied.

How were the years? I asked. Extra, he said Can I change your mind? I shook my head then asked if he remembered the boy on the floor. I do, he said And my heel, drawing it over his ribs while he lay there and cried. He carried all my life, I said. He said No… only some. You terrified him out of who he was, I accused but he just shrugged. Who do you think you're telling? he said You know what I was. We made our life of secrets, you betrayed it, me and your mother. Was it really that? I asked. It was, he said Except if he'd been a girl no one would have cared… I didn't want people looking at us and when he killed himself they looked the other way. Come with me, I said and out the door. The road hollowing beneath us as we made our way over to the dark rath and the quarry behind.

Me and Devil, walking side by side. Me and Devil eye becoming eye.

I said I will bury your body down by the deep water's side, then sit under the branch in the rath where O'Casey's son hanged and let the past be free. But I'm old now, he cried and I said He was young. But I am your father, he said. And he was my love. It is the worst sin, he said. I'm glad, I laughed Because only the best will do. Then I pushed him from the edge and out of the world. Or did I? I did say I was drunk at the start. No, how did I describe his fingers? Friggered.

Past tense.

So yes then, I did.

CANCER

Eugene McCabe

Eugene McCabe is a novelist, playwright, short story writer and award-winning writer who has worked as a farmer all his life. His work, including 'Cancer', *Heaven* and *Siege* deal with the Troubles in Northern Ireland. His plays include *Breakdown*, *Gale Day* and *King of the Castle*, and he is the author of two novels, *Death and Nightingales* and *The Love of Sisters*.

Today there was an old Anglia and five bicycles outside the cottage. Boyle parked near the bridge. As he locked the car Dinny came through a gap in the ditch: "Busy?"

"From the back of Cam Rock and beyont: it's like a wake inside."

For a living corpse Boyle thought.

"How is he?"

"Never better."

"No pain?"

"Not a twitch… ates rings round me and snores the night long." Boyle imagined Joady on the low stool by the hearth in the hot, crowded kitchen, his face like turf ash. Everyone knew he was dying. Women from townlands about had offered to cook and wash. Both brothers had refused. "Odd wee men," the women said. "Course they'd have no sheets, and the blankets must be black." "And why not," another said, "no woman body ever stood in aither room this forty years." At which another giggled and said, "Or lay." And they all laughed because Dinny and Joady were under-sized. And then they were ashamed of laughing and said "poor Joady cratur" and "poor Dinny he'll be left: that's worse." And people kept bringing things: bacon and chicken, whiskey and stout, seed cake, fresh-laid eggs, wholemeal bread; Christmas in February.

In all his years Joady had never slept away from the cottage so that when people called now he talked about the hospital, the operation, the men who died in the ward. In particular he talked about the shattered bodies brought to the hospital morgue from the explosion near Trillick. When he went on about this, Protestant neighbours kept silent. Joady noticed and said: "A bad doin, Albert, surely, there could be no luck after thon." To Catholic neighbours he said: "Done it their selves to throw blame on us" and spat in the fire.

It was growing dark at the bridge, crows winging over from Annahullion to roost in the fibrous trees about the disused Spade Mill.

"A week to the day we went up to Enniskillen," Dinny said.

"That long."

"A week to the day, you might say to the hour. Do you mind the helicopter?" He pointed up. "It near sat on that tree."

Boyle remembered very clearly. It had seemed to come from a quarry of whins, dropping as it crossed Gawley's flat. Like today he had driven across this border bridge and stopped at McMahon's iron-roofed cottage. Without looking up, he could sense the machine chopping its way up from the Spade Mill. He left the car engine running. Dinny came out clutching a bottle of something. The helicopter hung directly over a dead alder in a scrub of egg bushes between the cottage and the river. Dinny turned and flourished the bottle upwards shouting above the noise: "I hope to Jasus yis are blown to shit." He grinned and waved the bottle again. Boyle looked up. Behind the curved, bullet-proof shield two pale urban faces stared down, impassive.

"Come on, Dinny, get in."

He waved again: a bottle of Lucozade.

Boyle put the car in gear and drove North. They could hear the machine overhead. Dinny kept twisting about in the front seat trying to see up.

"The whores," he screeched, "they're trackin' us."

On a long stretch of road the helicopter swooped ahead and dropped to within a yard of the road. It turned slowly and moved towards them, a gigantic insect with revolving swords. Five yards from the car it stopped. The two faces were now very clear: guns, uniform, apparatus, one man had earphones. He seemed to be reading in a notebook. He looked at the registration number of Boyle's car and said something. The helicopter tilted sharply and rose clapping its way towards Armagh across the sour divide of fields and crooked ditches. Boyle remained parked in the middle of the road, until he could hear nothing. His heart was pumping strongly: "What the hell was all that?"

"They could see we had Catholic faces," Dinny said and winked. There was a twist in his left eye. "The mouth" McMahon neighbours called him, pike lips set in a bulbous face, a cap glued to his skull. Boyle opened a window. The fumes of porter were just stronger than the hum of turf smoke and a strong personal pong.

"It's on account of Trillick," Boyle said, "they'll be very active for a day or two."

"You'll get the news now."

Boyle switched on the car radio and a voice was saying: "Five men in a Land Rover on a track leading to a television transmitter station on Brougher Mountain near Trillick between Enniskillen and Omagh. Two BBC officials and three workers lost their lives. An Army spokesman said that the booby trap blew a six-foot-deep crater in the mountainside and lifted the Land Rover twenty yards into a bog. The bodies of the five men were scattered over an area of 400 square yards. The area has been sealed off."

Boyle switched off the radio and said: "Dear God."

They passed a barn-like church set in four acres of graveyard. Dinny tipped his cap to the dead; McCaffreys, Boyles, Grues, Gunns, McMahons, Courtneys, Mulligans; names and bones from a hundred townlands.

"I cut a bit out of the *Anglo-Celt* once," Dinny said, "about our crowd, the McMahons."

"Yes?"

"Kings about Monaghan for near a thousand years, butchered, and driv' north to these bitter hills, that's what it said, and the scholar that wrote it up maintained you'll get better bred men in the cabins of Fermanagh than you'll find in many's a big house."

Boyle thumbed up at the graveyard: "One thing we're sure of, Dinny, we'll add our bit."

"Blood tells," Dinny said, "it tells in the end."

A few miles on they passed a waterworks. There was a soldier pacing the floodlit jetty.

"Wouldn't care for his job, he'll go up with it some night."

"Unless there's changes," Boyle said.

"Changes! What changes. Look in your neighbour's face; damn little change you'll see there. I wrought four days with Gilbert Wilson before Christmas, baggin' turf beyont Doon, and when the job was done we dropped into Corranny pub, and talked land, and benty turf, and the forestry takin' over and the way people are leavin' for factories, the pension scheme for hill farmers and a dose of things: no side in any of it, not one word of politics or religion, and then all of a shot he leans over to me and says: 'Fact is, Dinny, the time I like you best, I could cut your throat.' A quare slap in the mouth, but I didn't rise to it; I just said: 'I'd as lief not hear the like, Gilbert.' 'You,' says he, 'and all your kind, it must be said.' 'It's a mistake, Gilbert, to say the like, or think it.' 'Truth,' he said, 'and you mind it, Dinny'."

He looked at Boyle: "What do you think of that for a spake?"

They came to the main road and Moorlough: "Are them geese or swans?" Dinny was pointing. He wound down his window and stared out. On the Loughside field there seemed to be fifty or sixty swans, very white against the black water. Boyle slowed for the trunk road, put on his headlights.

"Hard to say,"

"Swans," Dinny said.

"You're sure?"

"Certain sure."

"So far from water?"

"I seen it before on this very lake in the twenties, bad sign."

"Of what?"

"Trouble."

The lake was half a mile long and at the far end of it there was a military checkpoint. An officer came over with a boy soldier and said, "Out, please." Two other soldiers began searching the car.

"Name?"

"Boyle, James."

"Occupation?"

"Teacher."

"Address?"

"Tiernahinch, Kilrooskey, Fermanagh."

"And this gentleman?"

Boyle looked away. Dinny said nothing. The officer said again: "Name?"

"Denis McMahon, Gawley's Bridge, Fermanagh."

"Occupation?"

"I'm on the national health."

The boy beside the officer was writing in a notebook. A cold wind blowing from the lake chopped at the water, churning up angry flecks. The officer had no expression in his face. His voice seemed bored and flat.

"Going where?"

"Enniskillen," Boyle said.

"Purpose?"

"To visit this man's brother, he's had an operation."

"He's lying under a surgeont," Dinny said.

The officer nodded.

"And your brother's name?"

"Joady, Joseph, I'm next of kin."

The boy with the notebook went over to a radio jeep. The officer walked away a few paces. They watched. Boyle thought he should say aloud what they were all thinking, then decided not to; then heard himself say: "Awful business at Trillick."

The officer turned, looked at him steadily for a moment and nodded. There was another silence until Dinny said: "Trillick is claner nor a man kicked to death by savages fornenst his childer."

The officer did not look round. The boy soldier came back from the jeep and said everything was correct, Sir. The officer nodded again, walked away and stood looking at the lake.

Dinny dryspat towards the military back as they drove off. "'And this gentleman!' Smart bugger, see the way he looked at me like I was sprung from a cage."

"His job, Dinny!"

"To make you feel like an animal! 'Occupation' is right!"

Near Lisnaskea Dinny said: "Cancer, that's what we're all afraid of, one touch of it and you're a dead man. My auld fella died from a rare breed of it. If he went out in the light, the skin would rot from his face and hands, so he put in the latter end of his life in a dark room, or walkin' about the roads at night. In the end it killed him. He hadn't seen the sun for years."

He lit a cigarette butt.

"A doctor tould me once it could be in the blood fifty years, and then all of a shot it boils up and you're a gonner."

For miles after this they said nothing, then Dinny said: "Lisbellaw for wappin' straw, / Maguiresbridge for brandy. / Lisnaskea for drinkin' tay. / But Clones town is dandy... that's a quare auld one?"

He winked with his good eye.

"You want a jigger, Dinny?"

"I'll not say no."

Smoke, coughing, the reek of a diesel stove and porter met them with silence and watching. Dinny whispered: "U.D.R., wrong shop."

Twenty or more, a clutch of uniformed fanners, faces hardened by wind, rutted from bog, rock and rain, all staring, invincible, suspicious.

"Wrong shop," Dinny whispered again.

"I know," Boyle said, "we can't leave now."

Near a partition there was a space beside a big man. As Boyle moved towards it a woman bartender said: "Yes?"

"Two halfs, please."

"What kind?"

"Irish."

"What kind of Irish?"

"Any kind."

Big enough to pull a bullock from a shuck on his own Boyle thought as the big man spat at the doosy floor and turned away. Dinny nudged Boyle and winked up at a notice pinned to a pillar. Boyle read:

Lisnaskea and District Development Association
Extermination of Vermin
1/- for each magpie killed.

2/- for each grey crow killed.
10/- for each grey squirrel killed.
£1 for each fox killed.

Underneath someone had printed with a biro:

For every Fenian Fucker: one old penny.

As the woman measured the whiskies a glass smashed in the snug at the counter end. A voice jumped the frosted glass: "Wilson was a fly boy, and this Heath man's, no better, all them Tories is tricky whores, dale with Micks and Papes and lave us here to rot. Well, by Christ, they'll come no Pope to the townland of Invercloon, I'll not be blown up or burned out, I'll fight to the last ditch."

All listening in the outer bar, faces, secret and serious, uncomfortable now as other voices joined: "You're right, George."

"Sit down, man, you'll toss the table."

"Let him say out what's in his head."

"They'll not blow me across no bog; if it's blood they want then, by Jasus, they'll get it, all they want, gallons of it, wagons, shiploads."

"Now you're talking, George."

The big man looked at the woman. She went to the hatch, pushed it and said something into the snug. The loudness stopped. A red-axe face stared out, no focus in the eyes. Someone snapped the hatch shut. Silence. The big man spat again and Dinny said: "I'd as lief drink with pigs."

He held his glass of whiskey across the counter, poured it into the bar sink and walked out. Boyle finished his whiskey and followed.

In the car again, the words came jerking from Dinny's mouth: "Choke and gut their own childer. Feed them to rats."

He held up a black-rimmed nail to the windscreen.

"Before they'd give us *that*!"

"It's very sad," Boyle said. "I see no answer."

"I know the answer, cut the bastards down, every last one of them and it'll come to that, them or us. They got it with guns, kep' it with guns, and guns'll put them from it."

"Blood's not the way," Boyle said.

"There's no other."

At Eniskillen they went by the low end of the town, passed armoured cars, and the shattered Crown buildings. Outside the hospital there were four rows of cars, two police cars and a military lorry. Joady's ward was on the ground floor. He was in a corner near a window facing an old man with bad colour and a caved-in mouth. In over thirty years Boyle had never seen Joady without his cap. Sitting up now in bed like an old woman, with a white domed head and drained face, he looked like Dinny's ghost shaved and shrunk in regulation pyjamas. He shook hands with Boyle and pointed at Dinny's bottle: "What's in that?"

"Lucozade," Dinny said.

"Poison."

"It's recommended for a sick body."

"Rots the insides: you can drop it out the windy."

"I'll keep it," Dinny said, "I can use it."

Boyle could see that Dinny was offended, and remembered his aunt's anger one Christmas long ago. She had knit a pair of wool socks for Joady and asked him about them.

"Bad wool, Miss," he said, "out through the heel in a week, I dropped them in the fire."

She was near tears as she told his mother: "Ungrateful, lazy, spiteful little men, small wonder Protestants despise them and us, and the smell in that house... you'd think with nothing else to do but draw the dole and sit by the fire the least they could do is wash themselves: as for religion, no Mass, no altar, nothing ever, they'll burn, they really will, and someone should tell them. God knows you don't want thanks, but to have it flung back in your teeth like that it's..."

"It's very trying, Annie," his mother said.

And Boyle wanted to say to his aunt: "No light, no water, no work, no money, nothing all their days, but the dole, fire poking, neighbour baiting, and the odd skite on porter, retched off that night in a ditch."

"Communists," his aunt mocked Joady, "I know what real Communists would do with those boyos, what Hitler did with the Jews."

"Annie, that's an awful thing to say."

There was silence and then his aunt said: "God forgive me, it is, but..." and then she wept.

"Because she never married, and the age she's at," his mother said afterwards.

Joady was pointing across a square of winter lawn to the hospital entrance: "Fornenst them cars," he said, "the morgue." His eyes swivelled round the ward. "I heard nurses talk about it in the corridor, brought them here in plastic bags from Trillick, laid them out on slabs in a go of sawdust on account of the blood. That's what they're at now, Army doctors tryin' to put the bits together, so's their people can recognise them, and box them proper."

The old man opposite groaned and shifted. Joady's voice dropped still lower: "They say one man's head couldn't be got high or low, they're still tramping the mountain with searchlights."

"Dear God," Boyle said.

"A fox could nip off with a man's head handy enough."

"If it came down from a height it could bury itself in that auld spongy heather and they'd never find it or less they tripped over it."

"Bloodhound dogs could smell it out."

"They wouldn't use bloodhound dogs on a job like that, wouldn't be proper."

"Better nor lavin' it to rot in a bog, course they'd use dogs, they'd have to."

"Stop!"

Across the ward the old man was trying to elbow himself up. The air was wheezing in and out of his lungs, he seemed to be choking: "Stop! Oh God, God, please, I must go... I must..."

Boyle stood up and pressed the bell near Joady's bed. Visitors round other beds stopped talking. The wheezing got louder, more irregular, and a voice said: "Someone do something."

Another said: "Get a doctor."

Boyle said: "I've rung."

A male nurse came and pulled a curtain round the bed. When a doctor came the man was dead. He was pushed away on a trolley covered with a white sheet. Gradually people round other beds began to talk. A young girl looking sick was led out by a woman.

"That's the third carted off since I come down here."

"Who was he?" Boyle asked.

"John Willie Foster, a bread server from beyont Fivemiletown, started in to wet the bed like a child over a year back, they couldn't care for him at home, so they put him to 'Silver Springs,' the auld people's home, but he got worse there so they packed him off here."

"Age," Dinny said, "the heart gave up."

"The heart broke," Joady said, "no one come to see him, bar one neighbour man. He was tould he could get home for a day or two at Christmas, no one come, he wouldn't spake with no one, couldn't quit cryin'; the man's heart was broke."

"Them Probsbyterians is a hard bunch, cauld, no nature."

There was a silence.

"Did he say what about you Joady?... the surgeon?"

"No."

"You asked?"

"'A deep operation,' he said, 'very deep, an obstruction,' so I said 'Is there somethin' rotten, Sir, I want to know, I want to be ready?' 'Ready for what,' says he and smiles, but you can't tell what's at the back of a smile like that. 'Just ready,' I said.

"'You could live longer nor me,' says he.

"He hasn't come next nor near me since I've come down here to the ground... did he tell yous anythin'?"

"Dam' to the thing," Dinny said.

And Boyle noticed that Joady's eyes were glassy.

There was a newspaper open on the bed. It showed the Duke of Kent beside an armoured car at a shattered customs post. On the top of the photograph the name of the post read "Kilclean." Boyle picked up the newspaper, opened it and saw headlines: "Significance of bank raids"; "Arms for Bogsiders'; "Failure to track murderer"; "Arms role of I.R.A."

He read, skipping half, half listening to the brothers.

"In so far as ordinary secret service work is concerned, could be relied on and trusted... under the control of certain Ministers. Reliable personnel... co-operation between Army intelligence and civilian intelligence... no question of collusion."

"Lies," Joady said to Dinny, "you don't know who to believe." His voice was odd and his hand was trembling on the bedspread. Boyle didn't want to look at his face and thought, probably has it and knows. Dinny was looking at the floor.

"Lies," Joady said again. And this time his voice sounded better. Boyle put down the paper and said: "I hear you got blood, Joady."

"Who tould you that?"

"One of my past pupils, a nurse here."

"Three pints," Joady said.

Boyle winked and said: "Black blood, she told me you got Paisley's blood."

Joady began shaking, his mouth opened and he seemed to be dryretching. The laughter when it came was pitched and hoarse. He put a hand on his stitches and stopped, his breathing shallow, his head going like a picaninny on a mission box.

"Paisley's blood, she said that?"

"She did."

"That's tarror," he said, but was careful not to laugh again. Boyle stood up and squeezed his arm: "We'll have to go, Joady, next time can we bring you something you need?"

"Nothin'," Joady said, "I need nothin'."

Walking the glass-walled, rubber corridor Boyle said: "I'll wait in the car, Dinny."

Dinny stopped and looked at the bottle of Lucozade: "We could see him together."

"If you want."

The surgeon detached a sheet of paper from a file, he faced them across a steel-framed table: "In your brother's case," he was saying to Dinny, "it's late, much, much, too late." He paused, no one said anything and then the surgeon said: "I'm afraid so."

"Dying?"

"It's terminal."

"He's not in pain," Boyle said.

"And may have none for quite a while, when the stitches come out he'll be much better at home."

"He doesn't know," Dinny said.

"No, I didn't tell him yet."

"He wants to know."

The surgeon nodded and made a note on a sheet of paper. Dinny asked: "How long has he got, Sir?"

The surgeon looked at the sheet of paper as though the death date were inscribed: "Sometime this year... yes, I'm afraid so."

The Anglia and bicycles were gone now. It had grown dark about the bridge and along the river. Boyle was cold sitting on the wall. Dinny had been talking for half an hour: "He was never sick a day, and five times I've been opened, lay a full year with a bad lung above at Killadeas; he doesn't know what it is to be sick."

Raucous crow noise carried up from the trees around the Spade Mill, cawing, cawing, cawing, blindflapping in the dark. They looked down, listening, waiting, it ceased. "He knows about dying," Boyle said.

"That's what I'm comin' at, he's dyin' and sleeps twelve hours of the twenty-four, ates, smokes, walks, and for a man used never talk much, he talks the hind leg off a pot now, make your head light to hear him."

He took out a glass phial: "I take two of them sleeping caps every night since he come home, and never close an eye. I can't keep nothin' on my stomach, and my skin itches all over; I sweat night and day. I'll tell you what I think: livin's worse nor dyin', and that's a fact."

"It's upsetting, Dinny."

It was dark in the kitchen: Joady gave Boyle a stool, accepted a cigarette and lit it from the paraffin lamp, his face sharp and withered: a frosted crab. "Where's the other fella gone?"

"I'm not sure," Boyle said, "he went down the river somewhere." Joady sucked on the cigarette: "McCaffreys, he's gone to McCaffreys, very neighbourly these times, he'll be there until twelve or after."

He thrust at a blazing sod with a one-pronged pitch fork: "Same every night since I come home, away from the house every chance he gets." "All the visitors you have, Joady, and he's worried."

"Dam' the worry, whingin' and whinin', to every slob that passes the road about *me* snorin' the night long, didn't I hear him with my own ears…" He spat, his eyes twisting: "It's *him* that snores not *me,* him: it's *me* that's dyin', *me,* not him… Christ's sake… couldn't he take a back sate until I'm buried."

He got up and looked out the small back window at the night, at nothing: "What would you call it, when your own brother goes contrary, and the ground hungry for you… eh! Rotten, that's what I'd call it, rotten."

THOMAS CRUMLESH, 1960–1992: A RETROSPECTIVE

Mike McCormack

Mike McCormack is the author of two collections of short stories, *Getting it in the Head* and *Forensic Songs*, and three novels, *Crowe's Requiem*, *Notes from a Coma* and *Solar Bones*. In 1996 he was awarded the Rooney Prize for Literature. *Solar Bones* was awarded the Goldsmiths Prize, and in 2018 it received the International Dublin Literary Award.

My first contact with Thomas Crumlesh was in 1984 when he exhibited with a small artists' collective in the Temple Bar area of the city. His was one of the many fringe exhibitions hoping to draw the attention of the international buyers who were in Dublin for the official Rose Exhibition at the Guinness Hop Store. It was July, just four months after Thomas had been expelled from the National College of Art and Design for persevering with work that, in the opinion of his tutors, dealt obscenely and obsessively with themes of gratuitous violence.

His exhibition, *Notes Towards an Autobiography*, had been hanging less than three days and already word had got out and excited quite a bit of outraged comment. It consisted of four box frames with black silk backgrounds on which were mounted his left lung, the thumb of his left hand, his right ear and the middle toe of his left foot. Crumlesh was present also and easily recognizable – he was standing by the invigilator's desk with his head and left hand swathed in white and not-too-clean bandages. He was deathly pale and carrying himself delicately; like most young bohemians he was badly in need of a shave. After I got over my initial shock I ventured a few words of congratulations, more by way of curiosity than from any heartfelt belief in his work's merit. He surprised me with a lavish smile and a resolute handshake, contradicting completely his frail appearance. This was my first experience of the central paradox in his personality – the palpably gruesome nature of his work set against his unfailing good spirits and optimism. He surprised me further by telling me in conspiratorial tones that he planned to leave the country that very evening. Some criticism of his work had found its way into the national press and already a few people with placards had picketed the exhibition. He had even heard word that the police were pressing for warrants to arrest him under the obscenity laws. He confided further that what really worried him was that he might fall foul of Ireland's notoriously lax committal laws; he quoted an impressive array of statistics on secondary committals in the Republic.

I ended that encounter by buying his lung. His enthusiasm and verve convinced me of its worth and his whole appearance told me that he was in need of the money. Before I left he outlined the programme of work he had laid out for himself – a programme that would take him up to 1992, the year he hoped to retire. I offered to check his wounds – his bandages looked like they had not been changed in a few days. He declined the offer saying that he did not have the time, he needed to cash the cheque and he was afraid of missing the ferry to Holyhead. We shook hands before parting and I did not expect to see him ever again.

Our paths crossed again two years later. I was in London, attending a symposium on trauma and phantom pains in amputees at the Royal College of Surgeons. By chance, in a Crouch End pub, I picked up a flyer advertising the upcoming festival of Irish culture and music in Finsbury Park. Near the bottom of a list of rock bands and comedians was mention of a small exhibition of avant-garde work to be shown at a tiny gallery in Birchington Road. Thomas' name was mentioned second from the bottom. When I eventually found the gallery it was nothing more than two rooms knocked together on the third floor over a Chinese restaurant. Among the second-rate paintings and sculptures Thomas' work was not difficult to recognize. It stood in the middle of the floor, mounted on a black metal stand, a single human arm stripped of skin and musculature leaning at an obtuse angle to the floor. The bleached bones of the hand were closed in a half fist and the whole thing looked like the arm of some nightmare robot. As I approached it the arm jerked into life, the fingers contracted completely and the thumb bone stood vertical. It looked eerily like a ghost hitching a lift: from some passing phantom car. It was untitled but carried a price of two thousand pounds.

Thomas entered the room and recognized me instantly. I attempted to shake hands – an embarrassing blunder since I had to withdraw my right hand when I saw the stump near his shoulder. As before, he was in good spirits and he entered quickly into a detailed explanation of what he called his 'technique'. He had bleached the bone in an acid formula of his own devising to give it its luminous whiteness and then wired it to electrical switches concealed beneath the carpet which would be unwittingly activated by the viewer whenever he got within a certain radius – he admitted borrowing this subterfuge from the work of Jean Tinguely. He then circled the arm and put it through its motions, four in all. Firstly, a snake pose that turned the palm downwards from the elbow and extended the fingers fearsomely, then the hitching gesture, then a foppish, disowning gesture that swivelled the forearm at the elbow and threw the hand forward, palm upwards, and lastly and most comically an 'up yours' middle finger gesture that faced the viewer head on. He grinned like a child when I expressed my genuine admiration. I had no doubt but that I was looking at a postmodern masterpiece. I little suspected at the time that this piece would enter into the popular imagery of the late twentieth century, reaching iconic status through exposure on album covers, T-shirts and posters. I only regretted at the time that I had not the means to acquire it.

But Thomas was not without worries. He confided that he had found it extremely difficult to find a surgeon who would carry out the amputations, he had to be extremely careful to whom he even voiced the idea – the terror of committal again. It had taken him three months to track down an ex-army medic with shellshock who had been discharged from the parachute regiment after the Falklands War to where he ran a covert abortion clinic in Holloway. In a fugue of anaesthesia and marijuana Thomas had undergone his operation, a traumatic affair that had left him so pained and unnerved he doubted he would be able to undergo the experience again. This fright had put his life's work in jeopardy, he pointed out. He was looking me straight in the eye as he said this; I sensed that he was putting me on the spot. Then he came out straight with his request. What I need is a skilled surgeon I can rely on, not some strung-out psycho. He spoke evenly, without the least hint of hysteria in his voice. He will of course be paid, he added coyly. I told him that I needed time to think on it – it was an unusual request. He nodded his agreement, he understood fully the difficulties of his request and he would not blame me if I refused him outright. We shook hands before we parted and I promised to contact him the following day after I had given his request some thought.

In fact I had little to think about. I very quickly resolved my fundamental dilemma: the healing ethic of my craft set against the demands of Thomas' talents. One parting glance at the arm convinced me that I had encountered a fiercely committed genius who it seemed to me had already made a crucial contribution to the imagery of the late twentieth century. It was obvious to me that I had an obligation to put my skills at his disposal; the century could not be denied his singular vision on grounds of arbitrary scruples. My problem was how exactly I was to make my skills available. That evening in my hotel room I gave the problem much thought and I returned the following day with my plans.

I found Thomas in high spirits. The lead singer of a famous heavy metal band had just bought the arm and Thomas was celebrating with champagne, drinking it from a mug, trying to get the feel of his new-found wealth, as he laconically put it. He poured me a similar mug when I declared my intention to help him. I explained my plan quickly. Before every operation he should forward to me exact details of what he needed, then give me two weeks to put in place the necessary logistics and paperwork at the clinic where I worked. I believed I would be able to perform two operations a year without arousing suspicion. He thanked me profusely, pumping my left hand with his, telling me he could rest easy now that his future was secure. In a magniloquent moment that was not without truth he assured me that I had made a friend for life.

He contacted me for the first time in November of that year telling me that he planned to exhibit a piece during the Paris Biennale. He needed six ribs removed: when would be the most convenient time for me? I wrote in reply that I had pencilled in the operation for Christmas Eve and that he could stay with me over the festive season and into the New Year while he recovered. The operation itself, an elaborate thoracotomy carried out in the witching hour of Christmas Eve, was a complete success and when, on New Year's Day, I presented him with the bundle of curved, washed bones he was thrilled; it was good to be back at work, he said.

It was during these days of convalescence that our relationship moved onto a more intimate footing. Mostly they were days of silence, days spent reading or listening to music in the conservatory that looked out over Howth to the sea beyond. Sometimes a whole day would go by without any word passing between us. Neither of us was awkward in this. The looming, inexorable conclusion of his art ridiculed any attempts at a deeper enquiry into each other's past. He simply gave me his trust and I gave him his bones and internal organs. That was enough for both of us.

On the third of January he returned to London, he wanted to get to work as quickly as possible. Five months later he sent me a photograph from a gallery in Paris, a black and white close-up of a piece called *The Bonemobile*, an abstract, lantern-shaped structure suspended by wire. His letter informed me that although the piece had excited the inevitable outrage among the more hide-bound critics it had also generated some appreciative but furtive praise. Nevertheless, he doubted that any buyer would rise to the fifty thousand Franc price tag he had placed upon it. He understood the fear of a buyer ruining his reputation by buying into what some were already calling apocalyptic voyeurism. Still, he lived in hope.

That was the first of twelve operations I performed on Thomas between 1986 and 1992. In all I removed twenty-three bones and four internal organs, eighteen inches of his digestive tract, seven teeth, four toes, his left eye and his right leg. He exhibited work on the fringe of most major European art festivals, narrowly escaping arrest in several countries and jumping bail in four. In his lifetime he sold eight pieces worth a total of fifty thousand pounds, by no means riches, but enough to fund his Spartan existence.

Inevitably, by 1989 his work had taken a toll on his body. After the removal of a section of digestive tract in 1988 his body slumped badly and following the amputation of his right leg in 1989 he spent his remaining years in a wheelchair. Despite this his spirits never sank nor did his courage fail him; he was undoubtedly sustained by the tentative acclaim that greeted his work in avant-garde circles. For the first time also he was being sought out for interviews. He declined them all, pointing out simply that the spoken word was not his medium.

His deterioration could not go on indefinitely. In March 1992 he wrote telling me he planned to exhibit his final piece at the Kassel Documenta. He travelled to Dublin the following month and spent a week at my house where he outlined the procedure I was to follow after the operation. On the night of the tenth, after shaking hands with appropriate solemnity for the last time, I administered him a massive dose of morphine, a euthanasia injection. He died painlessly within four minutes. Then, following his instructions, I removed his remaining left arm and head – messy, dispiriting work. I then boiled the flesh from the arm and skull in a huge bath and using a solution of bleach and furniture polish brought the bone to a luminous whiteness. I fixed the skull in the hand and set the whole thing on a wall mount; *Alas, Poor Thomas* he had told me to call it. Then I sent it to Kassel at the end of the month, Thomas already having informed the gallery as to the kind of work they were to expect. In critical terms it was his most successful piece and when Kiefer singled him out as the genius specific to the jaded tenor of this brutal and fantastic century his reputation was cemented. This last piece sold for twenty-five thousand Deutschmarks.

When, as executor of the Thomas Crumlesh Estate, I was approached with the idea of this retrospective I welcomed it on two accounts. Firstly, it is past time that a major exhibition of his work be held in his native country, a country that does not own a single piece of work by her only artist to have made a contribution to the popular imagery of the late twentieth century – a prophet in his own land indeed. Secondly, I welcomed the opportunity to assemble together for the first time his entire oeuvre. My belief is that the cumulative effect of its technical brilliance, its humour and undeniable beauty will dispel the comfortable notion that Thomas was nothing more than a mental deviant with a classy suicide plan. The rigour and terminal logic of his art leaves no room for such easy platitudes.

Several people have speculated that I would use this introduction to the catalogue to justify my activities or, worse, as an opportunity to bewail the consequences. Some have gone so far as to hope that I would repent. I propose to do neither of these. Yet a debt of gratitude is outstanding. It falls to very few of us to be able to put our skills at the disposal of genius: most of us are doomed to ply our trades within the horizons of the blind, the realm of drones. But I was one of the few, one of the rescued. Sheer chance allowed me to have a hand in the works of art that proceeded from the body of my friend, works of art that in the last years of this century draw down the curtain on an entire tradition. His work is before us now and we should see it as an end. All that remains for me to say is, Thomas, dear friend, it was my privilege.

Dr Frank Caulfield
Arbour Hill Prison Dublin

HIGH GROUND

John McGahern

John McGahern (1934–2006) set much of his writing in his native Co. Leitrim. His novels – many of which were banned – include *The Barracks*, *The Dark*, *The Pornographer* and *Amongst Women*. He also wrote radio plays and short stories. He was awarded the Chevalier dans l'Ordre des Arts et des Lettres and one year before his death, published a memoir.

I let the boat drift on the river beneath the deep arch of the bridge, the keel scraping the gravel as it crossed the shallows out from Walsh's, past the boathouse at the mouth, and out into the lake. It was only the slow growing distance from the ring of reeds round the shore that told that the boat moved at all on the lake. More slowly still, the light was going from the August evening.

I was feeling leaden with tiredness but did not want to sleep. I had gone on the river in order to be alone, the way one goes to a dark room.

The Brothers' Building Fund Dance had been held the night before. A big marquee had been set up in the grounds behind the monastery. Most of the people I had gone to school with were there, awkward in their new estate, and nearly all the Brothers who had taught us: Joseph, Francis, Benedictus, Martin. They stood in a black line beneath the low canvas near the entrance and waited for their old pupils to go up to them. When they were alone, watching us dance, rapid comment passed up and down the line, and often Joseph and Martin doubled up, unable or unwilling to conceal laughter; but by midnight they had gone, and a night of a sort was ours, the fine dust from the floor rising into the perfume and sweat and hair oil as we danced in the thresh of the music.

There was a full moon as I drove Una to her home in Arigna in the borrowed Prefect, the whole wide water of Allen taking in the wonderful mysteriousness of the light. We sat in the car and kissed and talked, and morning was there before we noticed. After the harshness of growing up, a world of love and beauty, of vague gardens and dresses and laughter, one woman in a gleaming distance seemed to be almost within reach. We would enter this world. We would make it true.

I was home just before the house had risen, and lay on the bed and waited till everybody was up, then changed into old clothes. I was helping my father put up a new roof on the house. Because of the tiredness, I had to concentrate completely on the work, even then nearly losing my footing several times between the stripped beams, sometimes annoying my father by handing him the wrong lath or tool; but when evening came the last thing I wanted was sleep. I wanted to be alone, to go over the night, to try to see clearly, which only meant turning again and again on the wheel of dreaming.

'Hi there! Hi! Do you hear me, young Moran!' The voice came with startling clarity over the water, was taken up by the fields across the lake, echoed back. 'Hi there! Hi! Do you hear me, young Moran!'

I looked all around. The voice came from the road. I couldn't make out the figure at first, leaning in a broken gap of the wall above the lake, but when he called again I knew it was Eddie Reegan, Senator Reegan.

'Hi there, young Moran. Since the mountain can't come to Mahomet, Mahomet will have to come to the mountain. Row over here a minute. I want to have a word with you.'

I rowed slowly, watching each oar-splash slip away from the boat in the mirror of water. I disliked him, having unconsciously, perhaps, picked up my people's dislike. He had come poor to the place, buying Lynch's small farm cheap, and soon afterwards the farmhouse burned down. At once, a bigger house was built with the insurance money, closer to the road, though that in its turn was due to burn down too, to be replaced by the present mansion, the avenue of Lawson cypresses now seven years old. Soon he was buying up other small farms, but no one had ever seen him work with shovel or with spade. He always appeared immaculately dressed. It was as if he understood instinctively that it was only the shortest of short steps from appearance to becoming. 'A man who works never makes any money. He has no time to see how the money is made,' he was fond of boasting. He set up as an auctioneer. He entered politics. He married Kathleen Relihan, the eldest of old Paddy Relihan's daughters, the richest man in the area, Chairman of the County Council. 'Do you see those two girls? I'm going to marry one of those girls,' he was reported to have remarked to a friend. 'Which one?' 'It doesn't matter. They're both Paddy Relihan's daughters'; and when Paddy retired it was Reegan rather than any of his own sons who succeeded Paddy in the Council. Now that he had surpassed Paddy Relihan and become a Senator and it seemed only a matter of time before he was elected to the Dáil, he no longer joked about 'the aul effort of a fire', and was gravely concerned about the reluctance of insurance companies to grant cover for fire to dwelling houses in our part of the country. He had bulldozed the hazel and briar from the hills above the lake, and as I turned to see how close the boat had come to the wall

I could see behind him the white and black of his Friesians grazing between the electric fences on the far side of the reseeded hill.

I let the boat turn so that I could place my hand on the stone, but the evening was so calm that it would have rested beneath the high wall without any hand. The Senator had seated himself on the wall as I was rowing in, and his shoes hung six or eight feet above the boat.

'It's not the first time I've had to congratulate you, though I'm too high up here to shake your hand. And what I'm certain of is that it won't be the last time either,' he began.

'Thanks. You're very kind,' I answered.

'Have you any idea where you'll go from here?'

'No. I've applied for the grant. It depends on whether I get the grant or not.'

'What'll you do if you get it?'

'Go on, I suppose. Go a bit farther...'

'What'll you do then?'

'I don't know. Sooner or later, I suppose, I'll have to look for a job.'

'That's the point I've been coming to. You are qualified to teach, aren't you?'

'Yes. But I've only taught for a few months. Before I got that chance to go to the university.'

'You didn't like teaching?' he asked sharply.

'No.' I was careful. 'I didn't dislike it. It was a job.'

'I like that straightness. And what I'm looking to know is – if you were offered a very good job would you be likely to take it?'

'What job?'

'I won't beat around the bush either. I'm talking of the Principalship of the school here. It's a very fine position for a young man. You'd be among your own people. You'd be doing good where you belong. I hear you're interested in a very attractive young lady not a hundred miles from here. If you decided to marry and settle down I'm in a position to put other advantages your way.'

Master Leddy was the Principal of the school. He had been the Principal as long as I could remember. He had taught me, many before me. I had called to see him just three days before. The very idea of replacing him was shocking. And anyhow, I knew the politicians had nothing to do with the appointment of teachers. It was the priest who ran the school. What he was saying didn't even begin to make sense, but I had been warned about his cunning and was wary. 'You must be codding. Isn't Master Leddy the Principal?'

'He is now but he won't be for long more – not if I have anything to do with it.'

'How?' I asked very quietly in the face of the outburst.

'That need be no concern of yours. If you can give me your word that you'll take the job, I can promise you that the job is as good as yours.'

'I can't do that. I can't follow anything right. Isn't it Canon Gallagher who appoints the teachers?'

'Listen. There are many people who feel the same way as I do. If I go to the Canon in the name of all those people and say that you're willing to take the job, the job is yours. Even if he didn't want to, he'd have no choice but to appoint you...'

'Why should you want to do that for me? Say, even if it is possible.' I was more curious now than alarmed.

'It's more than possible. It's bloody necessary. I'll be plain. I have three sons. They go to that school. They have nothing to fall back on but whatever education they get. And with the education they're getting at that school up there, all they'll ever be fit for is to dig ditches. Now, I've never dug ditches, but even at my age I'd take off my coat and go down into a ditch rather than ever have to watch any of my sons dig. The whole school is a shambles. Someone described it lately as one big bear garden.'

'What makes you think I'd be any better?'

'You're young. You're qualified. You're ambitious. It's a very good job for someone of your age. I'd give you all the backing you'd want. You'd have every reason to make a go of it. With you there, I'd feel my children would still be in with a chance. In another year or two even that'll be gone.'

'I don't see why you want my word at this stage,' I said evasively, hoping to slip away from it all. I saw his face return to its natural look of shrewdness in what was left of the late summer light.

'If I go to the Canon now it'll be just another complaint in a long line of complaints. If I can go to him and say that things can't be allowed to go on as they have been going and we have a young man here, from a good family, a local, more than qualified, who's willing to take the job, who has everyone's backing, it's a different proposition entirely. And I can guarantee you here this very evening that you'll be the Principal of that school when it opens in September.'

For the first time it was all coming clear to me.

'What'll happen to the Master? What'll he do?'

'What I'm more concerned about is what'll my children do if he stays,' he burst out again. 'But you don't have to concern yourself about it. It'll be all taken care of.'

I had called on the Master three evenings before, walking beyond the village to the big ramshackle farmhouse. He was just rising, having taken all his meals of the day in bed, and was shaving and dressing upstairs, one time calling down for a towel, and again for a laundered shirt.

'Is that young Moran?' He must have recognized my voice or name. 'Make him a good cup of tea. And he'll be able to be back up the road with myself.'

A very old mongrel greyhound was routed from the leather armchair one side of the fire, and I was given tea and slices of buttered bread. The Master's wife, who was small and frail with pale skin and lovely brown eyes, kept up a cheerful chatter that required no response as she busied herself about the enormous cluttered kitchen which seemed not to possess a square foot of room. There were buckets everywhere, all sorts of chairs, basins, bags of meal and flour, cats, the greyhound, pots and pans. The pattern had faded from the bulging wallpaper, a dark ochre, and some of the several calendars that hung around the walls had faded into the paper. It would have been difficult to find space for an extra cup or saucer on the long wooden table. Plainly there were no set meal times. Two of the Master's sons, now grown men, came singly in from the fields while I waited. Plates of food were served at once, bacon and liver, a mug of tea. They took from the plate of bread already on the table, the butter, the sugar, the salt, the bottle of sauce. They spent no more than a few minutes over the meal, blessing themselves at its end, leaving as suddenly as they'd entered, smiling and nodding in a friendly way in my direction but making little attempt at conversation, though Gerald did ask, before he reached for his hat – a hat I recognized as having belonged to the Master back in my school days, a brown hat with a blue teal's feather and a small hole burned in its side – 'Well, how are things getting along in the big smoke?' The whole effect was of a garden and orchard gone completely wild, but happily.

'You couldn't have come at a better time. We'll be able to be up the road together,' the Master said as he came heavily down the stairs in his stock-inged feet. He'd shaved, was dressed in a grey suit, with a collar and tie, the old watch-chain crossing a heavy paunch. He had failed since last I'd seen him, the face red and puffy, the white hair thinned, and there was a bruise on the cheekbone where he must have fallen. The old hound went towards him, licking at his hand.

'Good boy! Good boy,' he said as he came towards me, patting the hound. As soon as we shook hands he slipped his feet into shoes which had stood beside the leather chair. He did not bend or sit, and as he talked I saw the small bird-like woman at his feet, tying up the laces.

'It's a very nice thing to see old pupils coming back. Though not many of them bring me laurels like yourself, it's still a very nice thing. Loyalty is a fine quality. A very fine quality.'

'Now,' his wife stood by his side, 'all you need is your hat and stick,' and she went and brought them.

'Thank you. Thank you indeed. I don't know what I'd do but for my dear wife,' he said.

'Do you hear him now! He was never stuck for the charm. Off with you now before you get the back of me hand,' she bantered, and called as we went slowly towards the gate, 'Do you want me to send any of the boys up for you?'

'No. Not unless they have some business of their own to attend to in the village. No,' he said gravely, turning very slowly.

He spoke the whole way on the slow walk to the village. All the time he seemed to lag behind my snail's pace, sometimes standing because he was out of breath, tapping at the road with the cane. Even when the walk slowed to a virtual standstill it seemed to be still far too energetic for him.

'I always refer to you as my star pupil. When the whole enterprise seems to be going more or less askew, I always point to young Moran: that's one good job I turned out. Let the fools prate.'

I walked, stooping by his side, restraining myself within the slow walk, embarrassed, ashamed, confused. I had once looked to him in pure infatuation, would rush to his defence against every careless whisper. He had shone like a clear star. I was in love with what I hardly dared to hope I might become. It seemed horrible now that I might come to this.

'None of my own family were clever,' he confided. 'It was a great disappointment. And yet they may well be happier for it. Life is an extraordinary thing. A very great mystery. Wonderful… shocking… thing.'

Each halting speech seemed to lead in some haphazard way into the next.

'Now that you're coming out into the world you'll have to be constantly on your guard. You'll have to be on your guard first of all against intellectual pride. That's the worst sin, the sin of Satan. And always be kind to women. Help them. Women are weak. They'll be attracted to you.' I had to smile ruefully, never having noticed much of a stampede in my direction. 'There was this girl I left home from a dance once,' he continued. 'And as we were getting closer to her house I noticed her growing steadily more amorous until I had to say, "None of that now, girl. It is not the proper time!" Later, when we were both old and married, she thanked me. She said I was a true gentleman.'

The short walk seemed to take a deep age, but once outside Ryan's door he took quick leave of me. 'I won't invite you inside. Though I set poor enough of an example, I want to bring no one with me. I say to all my pupils: *Beware* of the high stool. The downward slope from the high stool is longer and steeper than from the top of Everest. God bless and guard you, young Moran. Come and see me again before you head back to the city.' And with that he left me. I stood facing the opaque glass of the door, the small print of the notice above it: *Seven Days Licence to Sell Wine, Beer, Spirits.* How can he know what he knows and still do what he does, I say to the sudden silence before turning away.

'Do you mean the Master'll be out on the road, then?' I asked Senator Reegan from the boat, disturbed by the turn the conversation had taken.

'You need have no fear of that. There's a whole union behind him. Well, what do you say?'

'I'll have to think about it.'

'It's a very fine position for a young man like yourself starting out in life.'

'I know it is. I'm very grateful.'

'To hell with gratitude. Gratitude doesn't matter a damn. It's one of those moves that benefits everybody involved. You'll come to learn that there aren't many moves like that in life.'

'I know that but I still have to think about it.'

'Listen. Let's not close on anything this evening. Naturally you have to consider everything. Why don't you drop over to my place tomorrow night? You'll have a chance to meet my lads. And herself has been saying for a long time now that she'd like to meet you. Come about nine. Everything will be out of the way by then.'

I rowed very slowly away, just stroking the boat forward in the deadly silence of the half-darkness. I watched Reegan cross the road, climb the hill, pausing now and then among the white blobs of his Friesians. His figure stood for a while at the top of the hill where he seemed to be looking back towards the boat and water before he disappeared.

When I got back to the house everyone was asleep except a younger sister who had waited up for me. She was reading by the fire, the small black cat on her knee.

'They've all gone to bed,' she explained. 'Since you were on the river, they let me wait up for you. Only there's no tea. I've just found out that there's not a drop of spring water in the house.'

'I'll go to the well, then. Otherwise someone will have to go first thing in the morning. You don't have to wait up for me.'

'I'll wait,' she said. 'I'll wait and make the tea when you get back.'

'I'll be less than ten minutes.'

I walked quickly, swinging the bucket. The whole village seemed dead under a benign moon, but as I passed along the church wall I heard voices. They came from Ryan's Bar. It was shut, the blinds down, but then I noticed cracks of yellow light along the edges of the big blue blind. They were drinking after hours. I paused to see if I could recognize any of the voices, but before I had time Charlie Ryan hissed, 'Will you keep your voices down, will yous? At the rate you're going you'll soon have the Sergeant out of his bed,' and the voices quietened to a whisper. Afraid of being noticed in the silence, I passed on to get the bucket of spring water from the well, but the voices were in full song again by the time I returned. I let the bucket softly down in the dust and stood in the shadow of the church wall to listen. I recognized the Master's slurred voice at once, and then voices of some of the men who worked the sawmill in the wood.

'That sixth class in 1933 was a great class, Master.' It was Johnny Connor's voice, the saw mechanic. 'I was never much good at the Irish, but I was a terror at the maths, especially the Euclid.'

I shivered as I listened under the church wall. Nineteen thirty-three was the year before I was born.

'You were a topper, Johnny. You were a topper at the maths,' I heard the Master's voice. It was full of authority. He seemed to have no sense at all that he was in danger.

'Tommy Morahan that went to England was the best of us all in that class,' another voice took up, a voice I wasn't able to recognize.

'He wasn't half as good as he imagined he was. He suffered from a swelled head,' Johnny Connor said.

'Ye were toppers, now. Ye were all toppers,' the Master said diplomatically.

'One thing sure is that you made a great job of us, Master. You were a powerful teacher. I remember to this day everything you told us about the Orinoco River.'

'It was no trouble. Ye had the brains. There are people in this part of the country digging ditches who could have been engineers or doctors or judges or philosophers had they been given the opportunity. But the opportunity was lacking. That was all that was lacking.' The Master spoke again with great authority.

'The same again all round, Charlie,' a voice ordered. 'And a large brandy for the Master.'

'Still, we kept sailing, didn't we, Master? That's the main thing. We kept sailing.'

'Ye had the brains. The people in this part of the country had powerful brains.'

'If you had to pick one thing, Master, what would you put those brains down to?'

'Will you hush now! The Sergeant wouldn't even have to be passing outside to hear yous. Soon he'll be hearing yous down in the barracks,' Charlie hissed.

There was a lull again in the voices in which a coin fell and seemed to roll across the floor.

'Well, the people with the brains mostly stayed here. They had to. They had no choice. They didn't go to the cities. So the brains was passed on to the next generation. Then there's the trees. There's the water. And we're very high up here. We're practically at the source of the Shannon. If I had to pick on one thing more than another. I'd put it down to that. I'd attribute it to the high ground.

TRANSMISSION

Blánaid McKinney

Blánaid McKinney was born in County Fermanagh in 1961. She is
the author of the short story collection *Big Mouth* and the novel
The Ledge, both published by Phoenix House, London. Her work
has also appeared in numerous anthologies, including those by Faber,
Picador, Hennessey, Phoenix House and the *Paris Review*. She lives
in Enniskillen.

The best way to trash a car is from decoration to chassis, from accessory
down to frame, from light bulb down to skeleton. The opposite of the
way it was built, in fact. It becomes progressively more difficult, of
course, as the parts become bigger, tougher and apparently undentable. But
that's the most satisfying way of doing it. A crusher is lazy, burning too flashy
and neither involves much work or personal involvement.

If a car can be hand-built, it can be hand-trashed.

Michael went to the counter and paid for his purchases; a length of rubber
hose, a pack of cigarettes and a box of matches. He was in his mid-forties
and immaculately dressed, his high forehead giving him a patrician look,
that of a meticulous man who knows what he is about. He walked outside
and sat in the driver's seat of his beautiful 1993 BMW 53Si. Tracking it
down had not been easy; he had decided to find it months after the trial,
by which time it had been repaired, sold, sold again, given new papers and
even re-sprayed. But he found it and was amazed that there was no sign
whatsoever of either damage or repair. It was a lovely motor of dull, gunmetal grey.

He pulled out of the petrol station and drove south until he found the kind of
small town he was looking for. He cruised around its run-down streets, came
across a piece of waste ground and parked.

This car was not just a drive, it was a long, cool drink of water, a smooth,
wondrous ride that eased a man's spine and focused his mind. He let the

engine run idle for a long moment, then switched it off. He looked around. To the east was what looked like a big council estate, and to the south, a derelict factory. It was a hot, sunny day and the air hummed.

Michael felt calmer than he had in months and, at last, decisive. He got out, smoothed the lapels of his suit and combed his hair in the wing mirror. He wanted everything to be perfect. He stood back and looked at the car. There was a slight smear on the bonnet, which he carefully removed with a cloth handkerchief. Apart from that, the car was pristine.

He went to the boot, removed a heavy canvas bag and began to lay out the tools on the ground. Sledgehammer, hand mallets, various screwdrivers, hacksaw. In his beautiful suit and with his beautiful car, he had imagined that he would feel foolish, standing on a piece of waste ground in the middle of nowhere. But he didn't. He had a decent project here, a way to feel good again, and embarrassment had no place.

It was around noon and beginning to get uncomfortably hot. Michael removed his jacket, carefully folded it and placed it on a clean clump of the destroyed, goulash grass.

Then he removed his Rolex and his wedding ring, and put them both in his trouser pocket.

A long way off, a group of kids, shimmering in the heat, were kicking a football; their shouts carried to where he stood, again staring at the car.

He wanted to begin but hesitated at the absurdity of the moment. Very slowly he picked up one of the smaller hammers and walked the length of the car, scrutinising every inch of its burnished, gleaming surfaces. Then he took a deep breath and, very gently, tapped the right-hand sidelight with the hammer. Nothing happened. He hit it harder. It cracked and Michael knew then that he had begun and could not now stop.

He smashed it and moved on to the right front light and smashed that, then the left headlight: he broke all the lights, front, side and back, taking in the wing mirrors, and breaking off the centre grill valance and the wipers as he went. The glass made an almost musical sound. He was beginning to get into his stride. He took a tape from his pocket and slid it into the cassette player. He would leave that to last.

Copland's Clarinet Concerto filled the air and Michael got himself a bigger hammer.

*

He had moved on to the windows and was shattering the back windscreen when he noticed that the group of kids had moved closer and were watching him warily. They were joined by a toddler, probably a younger sister. Michael ignored them and, wiping the sweat from his face, brought the hammer down on the front windscreen. It webbed and crackled but didn't shatter cleanly, so he took the sledgehammer to it. At first he tried a fairly timid blow, then, with a knotted, arctic calm, he swung the hammer high over his head and put every ounce of strength into it. The screen was noisily obliterated and Michael found himself grinning and staring, surprised, at his own hands, with a kind of loveless relish.

He was beginning to enjoy himself. He wasn't into physical exercise, or working out, but he felt, trembling slightly, that he could do this. It would take time, but he could achieve this.

A couple of the older boys moved closer and stood about twenty yards away, fascinated by the spectacle of a well-dressed businessman destroying his car. And on their patch, too. They sported shaven napes and cautious, wetback expressions.

Michael was contemplating the side door panels when one of them shouted at him.

'Hey, mister! Is that your car?'

Michael, squinting in the sun, nodded.

'What's wrong with it?'

'Nothing. I just don't like it. You can give me a hand, if you want.'

The boys looked at each other, then sprinted forward and grabbed a hammer each.

Michael directed them to the rear panels, while he tackled the driver's door and the bonnet. For ten minutes, the three of them hammered and banged and whacked, creating a deafening cacophony, sending crumpled sheets of metal flying, whooping with exhilaration.

Michael was perfect management material; he enjoyed using his head, dealing with theories and abstractions, grappling with the ideology of business strategy. That was why repetitive, mechanical activities came as such a refreshing change. He had loved nothing more than cooking their weekend meals. Chinese food was perfect, since it involved hours of stripping, cleaning, peeling and chopping, a nicely mindless rota. And he was a good cook, too. She was proud of him for that, especially since she couldn't cook at all.

As he finally sent the buckled bonnet flying, Michael thought of how

Sundays were best. He would cook, sunlight would stream into the kitchen, and she would polish off a bottle of white and tell him her latest theories. He loved to listen to her talk; she could talk about anything and that simple arrangement made their days almost perfect. She talked, and he listened and chopped and laughed.

She had decided to read the dictionary and had got as far as the 'G's.

So, that last weekend, everything for her was gorgeous, great, gratuitous, grandiloquent, globular, geocentric and germinal.

He used to laugh a lot at the weekends, he thought, as he brought the sledge-hammer down on the roof as hard as he could. The boys were making good progress with the boot and rear doors so, taking a breather, they stood back to have a proper look.

The car looked hideous. All the doors were gone, lying battered nearby. The roof was stoved in, and the engine was exposed and naked to the world. Michael wasn't nearly finished. He was going to do this properly. He was going to dismantle this bastard completely. The boys looked at him expectantly.

'Take off the wheels,' he said, handing them the jack and wheel wrench.

'Cool!'

'Hang on a minute', said Michael.

It took at least fifteen minutes of steady battering but eventually he got the driver's seat loose and dragged it to one side. The boys set to work on the wheels and Michael sat down heavily on the seat, lit a cigarette and closed his eyes.

'Be careful of the glass!' he shouted, keeping his eyes closed.

The other kids, a young girl, a slightly older boy and the toddler, came closer, having decided that he might be mad but probably wasn't dangerous. Encouraged by the two apprentices, they picked up whatever tools were lying around and joined in.

Michael smoked his cigarette and listened to the livid, cheerful threnody, the combination of metal and giggle, the grating sounds of removal and childish squeals.

She had been childish in her enthusiasms. 'The out-takes of humanity' she called them, the interesting, peripheral things that hadn't yet been flattened by the tyranny of the mainstream.

Sometimes he understood what she was on about, sometimes not. He liked her idea of not shopping as being the only form of revolt we have left and, when she'd said she wanted to firebomb Mothercare, he had laughed until he cried.

On discovering that she was pregnant, the first thing she said was, 'I think I'll teach myself Latin.'

She showed him a piece of paper she had been carrying around for a little while.

It was the Creed.

'Et iterum venturus est cum gloria, judicare vivos et mortuos, cujus regni non erit finis' – 'And he will come again in glory to judge the living and the dead, and his kingdom will have no end.'

She was always bringing strangers home, tramps sometimes.

'The art of the dispossessed is the art of those who are, rather than those who have,' she would say.

One time, she invited a twenty-year-old homeless punk to dinner. He had the most amazing mohican Michael had ever seen. He was blind.

She announced that, if it was a boy, she wanted to christen him Theodore, after her hero, Theodor S. Geisel.

'Who?' asked Michael.

'Dr Seuss.'

She once went on a day trip to a nuclear power station, hoping to find something to scold about. She came home depressed and confused, because the absolute purity, stillness and utter immobility of the reactor rod cooling pond, the sheer perfection of that deadly water, was the most beautiful thing she had ever seen. It gave Michael a chance to pamper her for a week and to smother her with kisses every day.

Michael heard a noise beside him and opened his eyes. A young woman was standing looking at him, holding a child by the hand. He realised that he had tears in his eyes and looked away. The woman glanced at the swarm of children nibbling energetically and noisily at the shrinking, ruined motor, but didn't say anything. She wandered off to one side and sat down to watch. Michael stood up and took off his shirt. The sun beat down oppressively and he was afraid the heat might get to him. The children had stacked the wheels into a small tower and the girl was sitting on top, shouting proprietorially. The tubby toddler had produced a plastic hammer from somewhere and wobbled to the car, a breathless, tidy frame; as Michael approached, she tapped one bumper with it and ran off, shrieking with delight. They were all filthy.

*

Right, thought Michael. Down to business. Down to the M30, automatic guts of this beast. He contemplated the engine for a while, wondering if delicacy and patience, and a set of screwdrivers were what were required, or if the sledgehammer and his hurting muscles would be enough. For a moment he thought of a birthday cake he had been given as a child. It was in the shape of a car, and had been devoured in minutes.

One of the older boys was sucking on a carton of Ribena. Michael suddenly felt tired and thirsty.

'Can I have a drink?'

'Gimme a cigarette first.'

Michael blinked. The boy was about eleven. He tossed him the pack. It didn't matter. He got out the screwdriver and went back to work.

He worked all afternoon and into the evening. He unscrewed the valve cover and gave it to the boys, who fell upon it with hammers. Timing chains, sprockets, he removed them and flung them over his shoulder, and the children dismantled them even further. Intake and exhaust manifolds, camshaft, cylinder head and everything hiding beneath – he wanted to reach all of them. By now his hands were cut and blood trickled greasily down his forearms. He hadn't expected to get this far, to this degree of destruction, but having transformed things so much, he had to finish it. He couldn't stop, but there were so many factors, what seemed like a million components, all bolted and clinging together. He felt soft and weak, but he kept going. He took a breather after getting to the pistons and connecting rods, and let the children have another go.

After a few minutes of sitting in the sun, he was restless again and could feel the young woman's eyes on him.

He had unscrewed the drive plate and was grabbing for the oil pump when he thought of the expression on the defendant's face as sentence was passed. Twelve months for reckless driving. Suspended.

Michael remembered the way the courtroom had gone very quiet, as if everyone knew that something had gone dreadfully wrong, but was too afraid to comment. Michael was expecting the man to be jubilant.

Instead, he looked almost heartbroken and sat with tears pouring down his face, like someone who had been denied the punishment he felt he deserved.

Only three months pregnant.

But the baby managed to live for half an hour longer than she did.

*

Michael lost his patience trying to lever out the engine's rear plate, dropped the screwdriver and hammered insanely at the whole engine block. Shock waves vibrated up and down his arms, but he felt invincible. His sister had thought he was going mad. He didn't cry, or carry on, or anything; he simply worked and ate and slept, and refused to discuss his feelings, but inside he knew something would have to be done. He'd begun to have dreams in which he felt his hands around the man's throat, and he would wake up shaken and upset. If he could have identified with an inanimate object, it would've been the legally held shotgun that is always found nearby. He knew he had to do something. And that's when he'd decided.

Since he could not destroy the man, he would destroy the car.

He knew there wasn't any grand point to this wasteland circus.

It was just something he desperately needed to do.

There wasn't much more to be done. There are some things the human frame just cannot crack. The murderous impenetrability of the axles, the anti-roll bar, the driveshaft, the wheel-bearing housings' heartless iron stumps – no clever sophistication could deal with that. He was content with a draw. It had been reduced to a battered, ugly shell, but the kids were still howling, so Michael joined them all in one final trash. They banged and thumped and clanged on every inch of what was left of the car until everybody became tired and quietened down a little. Michael was covered in bruises and cuts, and he had blood on his arms and on his back, and every muscle in his body hurt, but he felt exhilarated and young again. He had destroyed and in doing so, somehow he had wiped out the other act of destruction. He felt creative. He felt useful. This thing was his spinal, vulgar nutrition.

As the sun began to go down, he organised his riotous creche in a tidying-up exercise. They ran around collecting all the panels and largish pieces of metal into one crooked heap, components and iron, unbreakable pieces into a second pile, and every bolt, nut and screw into a third.

Then Michael got out his length of rubber and, sucking on one end, he siphoned out as much petrol as possible from the fuel tank, into the toddler's plastic buckets. He poured the petrol all over the car, inside and out. One of the boys was rattling the box of matches and grinning at him. Michael hesitated for a moment, then rescued his Copland tape and said, 'Be my guest. But be careful, okay?'

*

They all settled down and sat around for a couple of hours in the dying, corrosive warmth of the sun, just enjoying the sight of a burning car. In thrall to the conspiracy of fire.

Staring into the flames, eyeing his blackened tyros and drinking a cold beer, which the young woman had unexpectedly and silently pushed into his hand, Michael remembered a news story from a few years ago. A motorist was trapped in a burning car in South Africa. And no one could get close because of the heat, so they were forced to stand around helplessly, listening to his screams. Then one man had walked up, taken out his pistol and shot the poor man in the head, before calmly walking away. Michael didn't know whether that was right or wrong. Maybe it wasn't a matter of right or wrong, but a question of what we permit ourselves, and others, to endure.

At that moment he felt like weeping and decided to have his sister over for dinner on Sunday, just so that he could do some cooking.

He was beginning to understand the necessity of crisis.

A few other people from the estate showed up with their children, and threw old pieces of furniture on to the flames. No one asked whose car it was. One elderly woman arrived with a crate of bottled beer and, as more rubbish was added to the flames, it was transformed from a bitter pyre into a bonfire.

People milled around, chatting quietly, while the children jumped up and down, and hamburgers appeared from somewhere. Infants yawned wetly.

And that was how they spent that particular evening, long and warm, doing nothing in particular, except watching a car die and the sun go down.

Enjoying life's visible beginnings and obvious endings.

The slow signals of recovery.

Michael was surprised no one had called the authorities.

THOSE THAT I FIGHT
I DO NOT HATE

Danielle McLaughlin

Danielle McLaughlin's short story collection, *Dinosaurs on Other Planets*, was published in 2015 by the Stinging Fly Press. In 2019 she won the Sunday Times Audible Short Story Award and was a recipient of a Windham Campbell Prize. A novel, *Retrospective*, is forthcoming in Spring 2021.

Ranelagh on a summer Saturday, the pavements scattered with blossoms, the air pulsating with the rhythmic thrum of lawn mowers. Kevin stood at the window of the Millers' living room, watching a dozen or so little girls pose for photos in the front garden. His own daughter was among them, her blonde curls straightened and pinned in a plait, so that at first, in the midst of so many other plaited heads, he hardly recognised her. The Millers lived in a Victorian red-brick near the church, and Fiona Miller had insisted on the party. It was no trouble, she told anyone who attempted to cry off. It would be a treat for the children, and she and Bob were happy to host it, knowing as they did that not everyone was as fortunate as themselves. The girls shrieked and giggled, buzzing with sugar and summer, and then, remembering themselves, they smoothed the skirts of their white dresses and raised small, careful hands to adjust veils and tiaras. 'Lovely, aren't they?' Kevin said, turning to the woman behind the drinks table. The woman frowned. She wasn't the caterer, but one of Fiona Miller's friends, perhaps even one of her sisters, and this placed her firmly in the ranks of people who hated him. 'Great that the rain's held off,' he said, because she could hardly find that objectionable, but she began to move bottles around the table as if they were chess pieces, taking them by the necks, setting them down in their new positions with unmistakeable hostility.

Sun angled through the slatted blinds, igniting the glitter of cards on the mantelpiece, bouncing off the guns of Bob Miller's favourite model plane—a WWI Sopwith Camel—displayed on a stand beside the door. Bob's great-grandfather had served in the London Irish Rifles, losing an arm at Flers-Courcelette. His uniform, and his cap with its badge of harp and crown, was displayed in a large glass case at the end of the Millers' hall. Also in the case were things belonging to other dead men: bullets, armbands and letters that Bob had purchased on the internet. Bob liked to joke that he'd been a military man in a previous life, though in this one he was senior actuary for an insurance company. Kevin turned again to the window. His wife was in the garden also, talking, he saw now, to the man who'd once been his boss. Earlier, he and the man had exchanged terse hellos in the hallway. He'd asked Kevin—and why did everyone feel obliged to ask?—if anything had turned up yet, and with that out of the way, had retreated to a suitable distance. Kevin watched the man rest a hand consolingly on his wife's arm, while she dabbed at her eyes with a hanky. He needed a drink. He'd hoped the woman at the table might have gone to join the others in the garden, but she remained at her post, arms folded across her chest. On his way out of the room, he touched a finger to the propellers of the little plane, sending the blades spinning into a blur of wood and metal.

He'd brought a naggin of vodka for this eventuality, stashed in the inside pocket of his jacket. But he'd been relieved of the jacket as soon as he'd arrived by Aoife, the Millers' older daughter. 'It's okay,' he'd said, 'I'll hold onto it, it's a bit chilly,' though it was late May, the day warm, the air thick with pollen and silky parachutes of dandelion seed that blew in white gusts down the avenue. Aoife—outraged at being on cloakroom duty—had man-handled the jacket off him anyway, and now he felt the missing naggin like a phantom limb. As he walked towards the kitchen, the front door opened and the small girls came hurtling down the hall, one of them with a parasol tucked under her arm like a bayonet. He flattened himself against the wall as they went by, a battalion of miniature brides, their white sandals clattering over the tiles. A veil brushed against his arm, the scratch of gauze surprisingly rough. At the end of the Millers' hall, before the glass case with the disembodied uniform, the girls veered left into the music room, and from there out to the garden to race in circles around the house, their cries rising and falling in Doppler effect.

Fiona Miller was in the kitchen squeezing oranges. She was a dark-haired, tanned woman a few years his senior. 'You shouldn't have come,' she said. She was using an electric juicer, feeding plump oranges in at one end, harvesting slow dribbles in a jug at the other.

'You invited me.'

'I had to invite you. But you shouldn't have come. What were you thinking, Kevin?'

She had always made him feel small; small and red-necked and lacking in etiquette. What about all that fucking we did, he wanted to say, where was the etiquette in that? Instead he said, 'Does Bob know?' knowing very well that Bob didn't.

'Don't do this to me, Kevin,' she said, 'because if you do, I'm warning you, you'll be sorry.' She picked up two more oranges and flung them into the juicer. She was wearing a low-cut black dress and he couldn't help thinking that her breasts were like two small oranges, and that the nipples pressing against the fabric were like little hard pips. He remembered how they used to feel in his hands, and when his eyes moved back to her face, he saw that she was watching him watching her, and he looked away, out to the hall where his wife was talking to one of the other mothers. She was holding several parasols, none of which belonged to their own daughter; his mother-in-law, who had paid for the outfit, thought parasols tacky. His wife glanced in his direction. It was one of the advantages of being with someone a very long time that he could tell instantly, even at a distance, that she was angry.

The juicer sputtered to a stop. 'I'm out of oranges,' Fiona said.

'I'll get some,' he said, sensing an opportunity, because there was an off-licence in the village.

'Aoife will get them. She can go on her bike. It won't take her a minute.' Fiona banged on the kitchen window. Aoife was sitting on a swing in the back garden, talking on her phone. She looked up and pulled a face at her mother, but didn't budge. Her mother banged on the glass again. Aoife slid slowly, insolently, off the swing and began to walk towards the house.

'How old is she now?' he said. 'Sixteen?'

'Eighteen next month. Which means we'll have to do this whole bloody thing all over again.'

'Well I won't come,' he said, 'so you needn't worry.'

'I'm not worried,' she said. 'You're not invited.'

Aoife arrived in from the garden, slamming the back door behind her. She snatched the ten euro note her mother handed her. 'Oranges,' Fiona said. 'Two nets, and make sure they're properly ripe.' Aoife rolled her eyes and left.

There came the sound of feet plodding down the hall, and a wet, wheezy sigh. Bob Miller was unlikely to take anyone by stealth. 'Beer, Kev?' he said, opening the fridge, and then, before Kevin could answer, 'I mean, Coke?'

'No thanks.'

Bob cracked open a can for himself. 'Long time no see,' he said. 'I was only saying to Fiona this morning: when was the last time we saw Kevin, and we couldn't remember, could we, Fiona?'

Fiona was slapping a wet cloth—randomly, it seemed to Kevin—over kitchen surfaces. Now she went to squeeze the cloth out in the sink, at the same time running fresh water noisily into a basin.

'So,' Bob said, 'what've you been getting up to?'

'Nothing much.'

'Anything turn up yet?'

'Not yet.'

'Have you tried Fás?'

A small, weeping child with a grazed knee came into the kitchen. She was followed by four other children who formed a circle as Fiona applied ointment—none too gently, Kevin noticed—and a plaster. No sooner had the children been dispatched outside, than Aoife arrived back, her cheeks flushed from the cycle, wisps of dandelion seed caught in her hair. She flung a plastic bag onto the kitchen island. 'These are mandarins,' Fiona said, peering into the bag, but Aoife had already flounced out to the garden to resume her position on the swing. Bob winked. 'The joys, eh Kev?' he said, and he flopped into a chair in the corner. Fiona took the oranges, or mandarins, to the sink and began to scrub them with a wire brush as if they'd been rolling around the floor of a nuclear waste facility. She piled them into a bowl, before proceeding to drop them one by one into the juicer, and the slow dribble started up again.

'Excuse me,' Kevin said, pretending to check his phone. 'I need to take a call.' Once in the hall, he went to the door of the living-room and looked in. The woman at the drinks table still hadn't moved from her station. She was busy now; the caterers had set out trays of salads and cold meats, and everybody had come in from the garden. He considered where Aoife might have put his jacket. He'd been in this house many times, mostly times when he shouldn't have been.

On the half-landing, he paused to inspect the photographs. He didn't recall noticing them before, but then before, his mind would have been on the curve of Fiona's hips as she climbed the stairs ahead of him. They weren't the usual snaps of sea-sides or birthdays, but black and white photographs of war. Biplanes rose from scorched airstrips, into skies black and hellish with smoke. Hollow-eyed soldiers in steel Brodie helmets lay on their stomachs in the mud. How he envied Bob Miller. He didn't envy him the photographs, ghoulish things that already had triggered the early stirrings of nausea. Nor did he envy him his wife, or his house, or his job, though there'd been a time when he'd envied all of these things. No, what he envied most was Bob Miller's want of imagination, a want that saved even as it failed, that allowed Bob to make a hobby of war, to gaze with complacency upon the horror of others, happy it hadn't come for him, certain it never would. Lucky, lucky Bob who knew so little pain that he must order it neatly packaged on eBay, to hang in lacquered frames on his wall.

In the spare room, the coats lay on the bed in a writhing mass of empty sleeves. Several had slid from the heap onto the carpet. He went through the ones on the bed first, lifting them, setting them aside until, halfway through, he found his jacket. When he picked it up, its lightness registered with him on some subterranean, animal level before the thought had even formed in his brain. The naggin was missing. He searched beneath the remainder of the coats on the bed, then started on the pile on the floor.

'All right, Kev?'

He was holding a ladies green blazer in his hands when he turned to see Bob in the doorway. 'Grand, Bob,' he said, 'I was just looking for my car keys.'

'You're not thinking of driving, Kev?'

'I need to get something from the car.' He floundered about, mentally, for something plausible. 'An inhaler. For my daughter.'

'Well then,' Bob said, 'we'd better find those keys,' and he bent to lift a man's navy overcoat from the floor.

Kevin had a sudden vision of Bob finding the naggin. 'Ta, Bob,' he said, 'but I've already found them, actually.' He patted the pocket of his jeans. 'They were under the valance.'

Bob straightened up. He looked confused. 'Right,' he said.

Kevin realised he was still holding the blazer, and tossed it quickly onto the bed. They stood in awkward silence for a moment, staring at each other, while through the open window came the shrill laughter of small girls playing tag on the Millers' driveway.

'I guess we can go back downstairs,' Bob said.

'Okay then.'

'Okay.'

Bob gestured for Kevin to exit the room ahead of him, and when they were both outside, he pulled the door shut and took something from his pocket. There followed the excruciating sound of the key turning in the lock. The men descended the stairs together, careful not to make eye contact, neither of them speaking. When they reached the bottom, Kevin didn't stop but kept on walking, down the hall and out the front door, across the cobble-lock drive to the pavement where his wife had parked their car by the kerb. He leaned against the garden wall and stared at the car. He didn't have the keys, his wife had them; these days, she was careful to keep them on her person at all times. He had a sense of somebody watching him, and knew that if he turned it would be Bob, but he didn't turn. Let him watch, he thought, because here on the street it was peaceful, the air clean and sweet-smelling, the only noise the yapping of a small dog further along the avenue. In the distance, beyond the village, beyond the city, he saw fields and hills, green un-peopled expanses not yet spoiled.

When he went back inside, a cake was being cut in the sunroom, a giant three-tiered confection, topped with a troupe of miniature white-iced girls in white-iced dresses. The real girls were seated around a trestle table, protective plastic covers over their clothes. His wife was at one end of the table, passing around slices of cake and plastic cutlery, but he didn't go in. Instead, he went to the living room where, with a heady feeling approaching joy, he found the drinks table deserted. It was a wasteland of empty bottles, wine, Pimms, prosecco, but in the middle of the debris was a bottle of vodka, practically untouched.

In the kitchen, he poured orange juice into a glass. Through the window he saw Aoife on the swing, her long legs dangling, the toes of her white Converse scuffing the dust. She was nothing like her father; Bob's genes had lost that particular skirmish. Instead, she was slim and dark and pretty, how he imagined Fiona must have been at that age. He watched her for a moment, then poured a second glass of juice and went out to the garden, taking the vodka and the glasses with him. The expression on her face bordered on a sneer, but she brightened when she saw the bottle. The day had remained fine, but there was something ominous in the stillness of the clouds, as if now that they had stopped moving, they might suddenly drop to earth. Aoife hopped off the swing. 'This way,' she said, indicating a gap in the hedge, 'they don't like it when I drink.'

'They don't like it when I drink either,' he said.

When she laughed it was her mother's laugh, uncouth with a hint of scorn, and her legs, when she settled herself beside him in the grass behind the hedge, were her mother's legs, long and tanned and small-boned. She giggled as he poured the vodka, and when she turned to smile at him, he noticed her eyes were slightly glazed. They were sitting in a wilderness of long grass and weeds, a narrow strip of no-man's land between the backs of the houses and a walled public green. Dog daisies and poppies grew wild and riotous, spilling petals and seeds onto the ground. He felt the jut of her hip as she edged closer to him, and as her long hair brushed against his arm, he caught a scent of vanilla and something else, something young and girlish, like apples or berries. He drank some vodka and looked up at the sky. The clouds seemed greyer and darker and were no longer still, but moved erratically, bulging against their casing of sky. It was as if something behind them was trying to break through, pushing them forward in a thick, billowing mass, so that they blew not like clouds, but smoke. As he watched, he saw in their depths quick and sudden flashes of silver. It might have been a final rallying of sun, but it reminded him of the light glinting on the metal guns of Bob Miller's model Sopwith Camel. And as he touched a hand to her cheek, he knew the sound he heard in the distance was not the hum of lawn mowers, but the drone of low-flying aircraft.

WALKING THE DOG

Bernard MacLaverty

Bernard MacLaverty has published five short story collections and five novels, the latest of which, *Midwinter Break*, won Novel of the Year in the Irish Book Awards 2017. Glasgow's *Sunday Herald* awarded him Writer of the Year in 2018. He has written versions of his fiction for other media – radio and television plays, screenplays and libretti for Scottish Opera.

As he left the house he heard the music for the start of the Nine O'Clock news. At the top of the cul-de-sac was a paved path which sloped steeply and could be dangerous in icy weather like this. The snow had melted a little during the day but frozen over again at night. It had done this for several days now – snowing a bit, melting a bit, freezing a bit. The walked-over ice crackled as he put his weight on it and he knew he wouldn't go far. He was exercising the dog – not himself.

The animal's breath was visible on the cold air as it panted up the short slope onto the main road, straining against the leash. The dog stopped and lifted his leg against the cement post.

'Here boy, come on.'

He let him off the leash and wrapped the leather round his hand. The dog galloped away then stopped and turned, not used with the icy surface. He came back wagging his tail, his big paws slithering.

'Daft bugger.'

It was a country road lined by hedges and ditches. Beyond the housing estate were green fields as far as Lisburn. The city had grown out to here within the last couple of years. As yet there was no footpath. Which meant he had to be extra careful in keeping the dog under control. Car headlights bobbed over the hill and approached.

'C'mere!'

He patted his thigh and the dog stood close. Face the oncoming traffic. As the car passed, the undipped headlights turned the dog's eyes swimming-pool green. Dark filled in again between the hedges. The noise of the car took a long time to disappear completely. The dog was now snuffling and sniffing at everything in the undergrowth – being the hunter.

The man's eyes were dazzled as another car came over the hill.

'C'mere you.' The dog came to him and he rumpled and patted the loose folds of skin around its neck. He stepped into the ditch and held the dog close by its collar. This time the car indicated and slowed and stopped just in front of him. The passenger door opened and a man got out and swung the back door wide so that nobody could pass on the inside. One end of a red scarf hung down the guy's chest, the other had been flicked up around his mouth and nose.

'Get in,' the guy said.

'What?'

'Get in the fuckin car.' He was beckoning with one hand and the other was pointing. Not pointing but aiming a gun at him. Was this a joke? Maybe a starting pistol.

'Move or I'll blow your fuckin head off.' The dog saw the open door and leapt up into the back seat of the car. A voice shouted from inside,

'Get that hound outa here.'

'Come on. Get in,' said the guy with the gun. 'Nice and slow or I'll blow your fuckin head off.'

Car headlights were coming from the opposite direction. The driver shouted to hurry up. The guy with the gun grabbed him by the back of the neck and pushed – pushed his head down and shoved him into the car. And he was in the back seat beside his dog with the gunman crowding in beside him.

'Get your head down.' He felt a hand at the back of his neck forcing his head down to his knees. The headlights of the approaching car lit the interior for a moment – enough to see that the upholstery in front of him was blue – then everything went dark as the car passed. He could hear his dog panting. He felt a distinct metal hardness – a point – cold in the nape hair of his neck.

'If you so much as move a muscle I'll kill you. I will,' said the gunman. His voice sounded as if it was shaking with nerves. 'Right-oh driver.'

'What about the dog?' said the driver.

'What about it? It'd run home. Start yapping, maybe. People'd start looking.'

'Aye, mebby.'

'On you go.'

'There's something not right about it. Bringing a dog.'

'On you fuckin go.'

The car took off, changed gear and cruised – there seemed to be no hurry about it.

'We're from the IRA,' said the gunman. 'Who are you?'

There was a silence. He was incapable of answering.

'What's your name?'

He cleared his throat and made a noise. Then said, 'John.'

'John who?'

'John Shields.'

'What sort of a name is that?'

It was hard to shrug in the position he was in. He had one foot on either side of the ridge covering the main drive shaft. They were now in an area of street lighting and he saw a Juicy Fruit chewing-gum paper under the driver's seat. What was he playing the detective for? The car would be stolen anyway. His hands could touch the floor but were around his knees. He still had the dog's lead wrapped round his fist.

'Any other names?'

'What like?'

'A middle name.'

The dog had settled and curled up on the seat beside him. There was an occasional bumping sound as his tail wagged. The gunman wore Doc Martens and stone-washed denims.

'I said, any other names?'

'No.'

'You're lying in your teeth. Not even a Confirmation name?'

'No.'

'What school did you go to?'

There was a long pause.

'It's none of your business.' There was a sudden staggering pain in the back of his head and he thought he'd been shot. 'Aww – for fuck's sake.' The words had come from him so he couldn't be dead. The bastard must have hit him with the butt of the gun.

'No cheek,' said the gunman. 'This is serious.'

'For fuck's sake, mate – take it easy.' He was shouting and groaning and rubbing the back of his head. The anger in his voice raised the dog and it began to growl. His fingers were slippery. The blow must have broken the skin.

'Let me make myself clear,' said the gunman. 'I'll come to it in one. Are you a Protestant or a Roman Catholic?'

There was a long pause. John pretended to concentrate on the back of his neck.

'That really fuckin hurt,' he said.

'I'll ask you again. Are you a Protestant or a Roman Catholic?'

'I'm... I don't believe in any of that crap. I suppose I'm nothing.'

'You're a fuckin wanker – if you ask me.'

John protected his neck with his hands thinking he was going to be hit again. But nothing happened.

'What was your parents?'

'The same. In our house nobody believed in anything.'

The car slowed and went down the gears. The driver indicated and John heard the rhythmic clinking as it flashed. This must be the Lisburn Road. A main road. This was happening on a main road in Belfast. They'd be heading for the Falls. Some Republican safe house. The driver spoke over his shoulder.

'Let's hear you saying the alphabet.'

'Are you serious?'

'Yeah – say your abc's for us,' said the gunman.

'This is so fuckin ridiculous,' said John. He steeled himself for another blow.

'Say it – or I'll kill you.' The gunman's voice was very matter-of-fact now. John knew the myth that Protestants and Roman Catholics, because of separate schooling, pronounced the eighth letter of the alphabet differently. But he couldn't remember who said which.

'Eh… bee… cee, dee, ee… eff.' He said it very slowly, hoping the right pronunciation would come to him. He stopped.

'Keep going.'

'Gee…' John dropped his voice, '… aitch, haitch… aye jay kay.'

'We have a real smart Alec here,' said the gunman. The driver spoke again.

'Stop fuckin about and ask him if he knows anybody in the IRA who can vouch for him.'

'Well?' said the gunman. 'Do you?'

There was another long pause. The muzzle of the gun touched his neck. Pressure was applied to the top bone of his vertebrae.

'Do you?'

'I'm thinking.'

'It's not fuckin Mastermind. Do you know anybody in the Provos? Answer me now or I'll blow the fuckin head off you.'

'No,' John shouted. 'There's a couple of guys in work who are Roman Catholics – but there's no way they're Provos.'

'Where do you work?'

'The Gas Board.'

'A meter man?'

'No. I'm an E.O.'

'Did you hear that?' said the gunman to the driver.

'Aye.'

'There's not too many Fenians in the Gas Board.'

'Naw,' said the driver. 'If there are any they're not E.O. class. I think this is a dud.'

'John Shields,' said the gunman. 'Tell us this. What do you think of us?'

'What do you mean?'

'What do you think of the IRA? The Provos?'

'Catch yourselves on. You have a gun stuck in my neck and you want me to...'

'Naw – it'd be interesting. Nothing'll happen – no matter what you say. Tell us what you think.'

There was silence as the car slowed down and came to a stop. The reflections from the chrome inside the car became red. Traffic lights. John heard the beeping of a 'cross now' signal. For the benefit of the blind. Like the pimples on the pavement. To let them know where they were.

'Can you say the Hail Mary? To save your bacon?'

'No – I told you I'm not interested in that kind of thing.'

The driver said,

'I think he's okay.'

'Sure,' said the gunman. 'But he still hasn't told us what he thinks of us.'

John cleared his throat – his voice was trembling.

'I hate the Provos. I hate everything you stand for.' There was a pause. 'And I hate you for doing this to me.'

'Spoken like a man.'

The driver said,

'He's no more a Fenian than I am.'

'Another one of our persuasion.' The gunman sighed with a kind of irritation. The lights changed from orange to green. The car began to move. John heard the indicator clinking again and the driver turned off the main road into darkness. The car stopped and the hand brake was racked on. The gunman said,

'Listen to me. Careful. It's like in the fairy tale. If you look at us you're dead.'

'You never met us,' said the driver.

'And if you look at the car we'll come back and kill you – no matter what side you're from. Is that clear? Get out.'

John heard the door opening at the gunman's side. The gunman's legs disappeared.

'Come on. Keep the head down.' John looked at his feet and edged his way across the back seat. He bent his head to get out and kept it at that angle. The gunman put his hands on John's shoulders and turned him away from the car. There was a tree in front of him.

'Assume the position,' said the gunman. John placed his hands on the tree and spread his feet. His knees were shaking so much now that he was afraid of collapsing. 'And keep your head down.' The tarmac pavement was uneven where it had been ruptured by the tree's roots. John found a place for his feet.

The dog's claws scrabbled on the metal sill of the car as it followed him out. It nudged against his leg and he saw the big eyes looking up at him. The gunman said, 'Sorry about this, mate.' John saw the gunman's hand reach down and scratch the dog's head. 'Sorry about the thump. But we're not playing games. She's a nice dog.'

'It's not a she.'

'Okay, okay. Whatever you say.'

The car door closed and the car began reversing – crackling away over the refrozen slush. In the headlights his shadow was very black and sharp against the tree. There was a double shadow, one from each headlight. From the high-pitched whine of its engine he knew the car was still reversing. It occurred to him that they would not shoot him from that distance. For what seemed a long time he watched his shadow moving on the tree even though he kept as still as possible. It was a game he'd played as a child, hiding his eyes and counting to a hundred. Here I come, away or not. The headlights swung to the trees lining the other side of the road. His dog was whimpering a bit, wanting to get on. John risked a glance – moving just his eyes – and saw the red glow of the car's tail lights disappearing onto the main road. He recognised where he was. It was the Malone Road. He leaned his head against the back of his hands. Even his arms were trembling now. He took deep breaths and put his head back to look up into the branches of the tree.

'Fuck me,' he said out loud. The sleeve of his anorak had slipped to reveal his watch. It was ten past nine. He began to unwind the leash from his hand. It left white scars where it had bitten into his skin. He put his hand to the back of his head. His hair was sticky with drying blood.

'Come on boy.' He began to walk towards the lights of the main road where he knew there was a phone box. But what was the point? He wouldn't even have been missed yet.

The street was so quiet he could hear the clinking of the dog's identity disk as it padded along beside him.

EXILE'S RETURN

Bryan MacMahon

> **Bryan MacMahon** (1909–1998) was a playwright, short story writer, novelist and memoirist. He also translated Peig Sayers' biography. His story collections include *The Red Petticoat* and *The Lion Tamer*, and he also wrote a memoir, *The Master*.

Far away the train whistled. The sound moved in rings through the rain falling on the dark fields.

On hearing the whistle the little man standing on the railway bridge gave a quick glance into the up-line darkness and then began to hurry downwards towards the station. Above the metal footbridge the lights came on weak and dim as he hurried onwards. The train beat him to the station; all rattle and squeak and bright playing cards placed in line, it drew in beneath the bridge. At the station's end the engine lurched uneasily: then it puffed and huffed, blackened and whitened, and eventually, after a loud release of steam, stood chained.

One passenger descended—a large man resembling Victor McLaglen. He was dressed in a new cheap suit and overcoat. A black stubble of beard littered his scowling jowls. The eyes under the cap were black and daft. In his hand he carried a battered attaché case tied with a scrap of rope. Dourly slamming the carriage door behind him, he stood glaring up and down the platform.

A passing porter looked at him, abandoned him as being of little interest, then as on remembrance glanced at him a second time. As he walked away the porter's eyes still lingered on the passenger. A hackney-driver, viewing with disgust the serried unprofitable door-handles, smiled grimly to himself at the sight of the big fellow. Barefooted boys grabbing cylinders of magazines that came hurtling out of the luggage van took no notice whatsoever of the man standing alone. The rain's falling was visible in the pocking of the cut limestone on the platform's edge.

Just then the little man hurried in by the gateway of the station. His trouser-ends were tied over clay-daubed boots above which he wore a cast-off green Army great-coat. A sweat-soiled hat sat askew on his poll. After a moment of hesitation he hurried forward to meet the swaying newcomer.

'There you are, Paddy!' the small man wheezed brightly, yet not coming too close to the big fellow.

The big fellow did not answer. He began to walk heavily out of the station. The little man moved hoppingly at his side, pelting questions to which he received no reply.

'Had you a good crossing, Paddy?' 'Is it true that the Irish Sea is as wicked as May Eve?' 'There's a fair share of Irish in Birmingham, I suppose?' Finally, in a tone that indicated that this question was closer to the bone than its fellows: 'How long are you away now, Paddy? Over six year, eh?'

Paddy ploughed ahead without replying. When they had reached the first of the houses of the country town, he glowered over his shoulder at the humpy bridge that led over the railway line to the open country: after a moment or two he dragged his gaze away and looked at the street that led downhill from the station.

'We'll have a drink, Timothy!' the big man said dourly.

'A drink, Paddy!' the other agreed.

The pub glittered in the old-fashioned way. The embossed wallpaper between the shelving had been painted lime-green. As they entered the bar, the publican was in the act of turning with a full pint-glass in his hand. His eyes hardened on seeing Paddy: he delayed the fraction of a second before placing the glass on the high counter in front of a customer.

Wiping his hands in a blue apron, his face working overtime, 'Back again, eh, Paddy?' the publican asked, with false cheer. A limp handshake followed.

Paddy grunted, then lurched towards the far corner of the bar. There, sitting on a high stool, he crouched against the counter. Timothy took his seat beside him, seating himself sideways to the counter as if protecting the big fellow from the gaze of the other customers. Paddy called for two pints of porter: he paid for his call from an old-fashioned purse bulky with English treasury notes. Timothy raised his full glass—its size tended to dwarf him—and ventured: 'Good health!' Paddy growled a reply. Both men tilted the glasses on their heads and gulped three-quarters of the contents. Paddy set down his glass and looked moodily in front of him. Timothy carefully replaced his glass on the counter, then placed his face closer to the other's ear.

'Yeh got my letter, Paddy?'

'Ay!'

'You're not mad with me?'

'Mad with *you*?' The big man's guffaw startled the bar.

There was a long silence.

'I got yer letter!' Paddy said abruptly. He turned and for the first time looked his small companion squarely in the face. Deliberately he set the big battered index finger of his right hand inside the other's collar-stud. As, slowly, he began to twist his finger, the collar-band tightened. When it was taut Paddy drew the other's face close to his own. So intimately were the two men seated that the others in the bar did not know what was going on. Timothy's face changed colour, yet he did not raise his hands to try to release himself.

'Yer swearin' 'tis true?' Paddy growled.

Gaspingly: 'God's gospel, it's true!'

'Swear it!'

'That I may be struck down dead if I'm tellin' you a word of a lie! Every mortal word I wrote you is true!'

'Why didn't you send me word afore now?'

'I couldn't rightly make out where you were, Paddy. Only for Danny Greaney comin' home I'd never have got your address. An' you know I'm not handy with the pen.'

'Why didn't you let me as I was—not knowin' at all?'

'We to be butties always, Paddy. I thought it a shame you to keep sendin' her lashin's o' money an' she to be like that! You're chokin' me, Paddy!'

As Paddy tightened still more, the button-hole broke and the stud came away in the crook of his index finger. He looked at it stupidly. Timothy quietly put the Y of his hand to his chafed neck. Paddy threw the stud behind him. It struck the timbered encasement of the stairway.

'*Ach!*' he said harshly. He drained his glass and with its heel tapped on the counter. The publican came up to refill the glasses.

Timothy, whispering: 'What'll you do, Paddy?'

'What'll I do?' Paddy laughed. 'I'll drink my pint,' he said. He took a gulp. 'Then, as likely as not. I'll swing for her!'

'Sssh!' Timothy counselled.

Timothy glanced into an advertising mirror: behind the picture of little men loading little barrels on to a little lorry he saw the publican with his eyes fast on the pair of them. Timothy warned him off with a sharp look. He looked swiftly around: the backs of the other customers were a shade too tense for his liking. Then suddenly the publican was in under Timothy's guard.

Swabbing the counter: 'What way are things over, Paddy?'

'Fair enough!'

'I'm hearin' great accounts of you from Danny Greaney. We were all certain you'd never again come home, you were doin' so well. How'll you content yourself with a small place like this, after what you've seen? But then, after all, home is home!'

The publican ignored Timothy's threatening stare. Paddy raised his daft eyes and looked directly at the man behind the bar. The swabbing moved swiftly away.

'Swing for her, I will!' Paddy said again. He raised his voice. 'The very minute I turn my back…'

'Sssh!' Timothy intervened. He smelled his almost empty glass, then said in a loud whisper: 'The bloody stout is casky. Let's get away out o' this!'

The word 'casky' succeeded in moving Paddy. It also nicked the publican's pride. After they had gone the publican, on the pretence of closing the door, looked after them. He turned and threw a joke to his customers. A roar of laughter was his reward.

Paddy and Timothy were now wandering towards the humpy bridge that led to the country. Timothy was carrying the battered case: Paddy had his arm around his companion's shoulder. The raw air was testing the sobriety of the big fellow's legs.

'Nothing hasty!' Timothy was advising. 'First of all we'll pass out the cottage an' go on to my house. You'll sleep with me tonight. Remember, Paddy, that I wrote that letter out o' pure friendship!'

Paddy lifted his cap and let the rain strike his forehead. 'I'll walk the gallows high for her!' he said.

'Calm and collected, that's my advice!'

'When these two hands are on her throat, you'll hear her squealin' in the eastern world!'

'Nothin' hasty, Paddy: nothin' hasty at all!'

Paddy pinned his friend against the parapet of the railway bridge. 'Is six years hasty?' he roared.

'For God's sake, let go o' me, Paddy! I'm the only friend you have left! Let go o' me!'

The pair lurched with the incline. The whitethorns were now on each side of them, releasing their raindrops from thorn to thorn in the darkness. Far away across the ridge of the barony a fan of light from a lighthouse swung its arc on shore and sea and sky. Wherever there was a break in the hedges a bout of wind mustered its forces and vainly set about capsizing them.

Paddy began to growl a song with no air at all to it.

'Hush, man, or the whole world'll know you're home,' Timothy said.

'As if to sweet hell I cared!' Paddy stopped and swayed. After a pause he muttered: 'Th' other fellah—is he long gone?'

Timothy whinnied. 'One night only it was, like Duffy's Circus.' He set his hat farther back on his poll and then, his solemn face tilted to the scud of the moon, said: 'You want my firm opinion, Paddy? 'Twas nothin' but a chance fall. The mood an' the man meetin' her. 'Twould mebbe never again happen in a million years. A chance fall, that's all it was, in my considered opinion.'

Loudly: 'Did you ever know me to break my word?'

'Never, Paddy!'

'Then I'll swing for her! You have my permission to walk into the witness-box and swear that Paddy Kinsella said he'd swing for her!'

He resumed his singing.

'We're right beside the house, Paddy. You don't want to wake your own children, do you? Your own fine lawful-got sons! Eh, Paddy? Do you want to waken them up?'

Paddy paused: 'Lawful-got is right!—you've said it there!'

'Tomorrow is another day. We'll face her tomorrow and see how she brazens it out. I knew well you wouldn't want to disturb your own sons.'

They lurched on through the darkness. As they drew near the low thatched cottage that was slightly below the level of the road, Timothy kept urging Paddy forward. Paddy's boots were more rebellious than heretofore. Timothy grew anxious at the poor progress they were making. He kept saying: 'Tomorrow is the day, Paddy! I'll put the rope around her neck for you. Don't wake the lads tonight.'

Directly outside the cottage, Paddy came to a halt. He swayed and glowered at the small house with its tiny windows. He drew himself up to his full height.

'She's in bed?' he growled.

'She's up at McSweeney's. She goes there for the sake of company. Half an hour at night when the kids are in bed—you'll not begrudge her that, Paddy?'

'I'll not begrudge her that!' Paddy yielded a single step, then planted his shoes still more firmly on the roadway. He swayed.

'The...?' he queried.

'A girl, Paddy, a girl!'

A growl, followed by the surrender of another step.

'Goin' on six year, is it?'

'That's it, Paddy. Six year.'

Another step. 'Like the ma, or... the da?'

'The ma, Paddy. Mostly all the ma. Come on now, an' you'll have a fine sleep tonight under my roof.'

Paddy eyed the cottage. Growled his contempt of it, then spat on the roadway. He gave minor indications of his intention of moving forward. Then unpredictably he pounded off the restraining hand of Timothy, pulled violently away, and went swaying towards the passage that led down to the cottage.

After a fearful glance uproad, Timothy wailed: 'She'll be back in a minute!'

'I'll see my lawful-got sons!' Paddy growled.

When Timothy caught up with him the big fellow was fumbling with the padlock on the door. As on a thought he lurched aside and groped in vain in the corner of the window sill.

'She takes the key with her,' Timothy said. 'For God's sake leave it till mornin'.'

But Paddy was already blundering on the cobbled pathway that led around by the gable of the cottage. Finding the back door bolted, he stood back from it angrily. He was about to smash it in when Timothy discovered that the hinged window of the kitchen was slightly open. As Timothy swung the window open the smell of turf-smoke emerged. Paddy put his boot on an imaginary niche in the wall and dug in the plaster until he gained purchase of a sort. 'Gimme a leg!' he ordered harshly.

Timothy began clawing Paddy's leg upwards. Belabouring the small man's shoulders with boot and hand, the big fellow floundered through the open window. Spreadeagled on the kitchen table he remained breathing harshly for a full minute, then laboriously he grunted his way via a *súgán* chair to the floor.

'You all right, Paddy?'

A grunt.

'Draw the bolt of the back door, Paddy.'

A long pause followed. At last the bolt was drawn. 'Where the hell's the lamp?' Paddy asked as he floundered in the darkness.

'She has it changed. It's at the right of the window now.'

Paddy's match came erratically alight. He held it aloft. Then he slewed forward and removed the lamp-chimney and placed it on the table. ''Sall right!' he said, placing a match to the wick and replacing the chimney. Awkwardly he raised the wick. He began to look here and there about the kitchen.

The fire was raked in its own red ashes. Two *súgán* chairs stood one on each side of the hearth-stone. Delph glowed red, white, and green on the wide dresser. The timber of the chairs and the deal table were white from repeated scrubbings. Paddy scowled his recognition of each object. Timothy stood watching him narrowly.

'See my own lads!' Paddy said, focusing his gaze on the bedroom door at the rear of the cottage.

'Aisy!' Timothy counselled.

Lighting match held aloft, they viewed the boys. Four lads sleeping in pairs in iron-headed doublebeds. Each of the boys had a mop of black hair and a pair of heavy eyebrows. The eldest slept with the youngest and the two middle-aged lads slept together. They sprawled anyhow in various postures.

Paddy had turned surprisingly sober. ''Clare to God!' he said. 'I'd pass 'em on the road without knowin' 'em!'

'There's a flamin' lad!' Timothy caught one of the middle-aged boys by the hair and pivoted the sleep-loaded head. Transferring his attention to the other of this pair: 'There's your livin' spit, Paddy!' Indicating the eldest: 'There's your own ould fellah born into the world a second time, devil's black temper an' all!' At the youngest: 'Here's Bren—he was crawlin' on the floor the last time you saw him. Ay! Bully pups all!'

'Bully pups all!' Paddy echoed loudly. The match embered in his fingers. When there was darkness: 'My lawful-got sons!' he said bitterly.

Timothy was in the room doorway. 'We'll be off now, Paddy!' he said. After a growl, Paddy joined him.

Timothy said: 'One of us'll have to go out by the window. Else she'll spot the bolt drawn.'

Paddy said nothing.

'You'll never manage the window twice.'

'I'll be after you,' Paddy said.

Timothy turned reluctantly away.

'Where's the...?' Paddy asked. He was standing at the kitchen's end.

'The...?'

'Yeh!'

'She's in the front room. You're not goin' to...?' Paddy was already at the door of the other room.

'She sleeps like a cat!' Timothy warned urgently. 'If she tells the mother about me, the fat'll be in the fire!'

Paddy opened the door of the front room. Breathing heavily he again began fumbling with the match-box. Across the window moved the scudding night life of the sky. The matchlight came up and showed a quilt patterned with candle-wick. Then abruptly where the bed-clothes had been a taut ball there was no longer a ball. As if playing a merry game, the little girl, like Jill-in-the-box, flax-curled and blue-eyed, sprang up.

'Who is it?' she asked fearlessly.

The matchlight was high above her. Paddy did not reply.

The girl laughed ringingly. 'You're in the kitchen, Timothy Hannigan,' she called out. 'I know your snuffle.'

'Holy God!' Timothy breathed.

'I heard you talking too, boyo,' she said gleefully as the matchlight died in Paddy's fingers.

''Tis me all right, Maag,' said Timmy, coming apologetically to the doorway of the room. 'Come on away!' he said in a whisper to Paddy.

'Didn't I know right well 'twas you, boyo!' Maag laughed. She drew up her knees and locked her hands around them in a mature fashion.

Another match sprang alive in Paddy's fingers.

'Who's this fellah?' Maag inquired of Timothy.

Timothy put his head inside the room. 'He's your... your uncle!'

'My uncle what?'

'Your uncle... Paddy!'

Paddy and Maag looked fully at one another.

Timothy quavered: 'You won't tell your mother I was here?'

'I won't so!' the girl laughed. 'Wait until she comes home!'

Timothy groaned. 'C'm'on away to hell outa this!' he said, showing a spark of spirit. Surprisingly enough, Paddy came. They closed the room door behind them.

'Out the back door with you,' Timothy said. 'I'll manage the lamp and the bolt.'

'Out, you!' Paddy growled. He stood stolidly like an ox.

Dubiously: 'Very well!'

Timothy went out. From outside the back door he called: 'Shoot the bolt quick, Paddy. She'll be back any minute.'

Paddy shot the bolt.

'Blow out the lamp, Paddy!' Timothy's head and shoulders were framed in the window.

After a pause Paddy blew out the lamp.

'Hurry, Paddy! Lift your leg!'

No reply.

'Hurry, Paddy, I tell you. What's wrong with you, man?'

Paddy gave a deep growl. 'I'm sorry now I didn't throttle you.'

'Throttle me! Is that my bloody thanks?'

'It was never in my breed to respect an informer.'

'Your breed!' Timothy shouted. 'You, with a cuckoo in your nest.'

'If my hands were on your throat...'

'Yehoo! You, with the nest robbed.'

'Go, while you're all of a piece. The drink has me lazy. I'll give you while I'm countin' five. One, two...'

Timothy was gone.

Paddy sat on the rough chair at the left of the hearth. He began to grope for the tongs. Eventually he found it. He drew the red coals of turf out of the ashes and set them together in a kind of pyramid. The flames came up.

The door of the front bedroom creaked open. Maag was there, dressed in a long white nightdress.

'Were you scoldin' him?'

'Ay!' Paddy answered.

'He wants scoldin' badly. He's always spyin' on my Mom.'

After a pause, the girl came to mid-kitchen.

'Honest,' she asked, 'are you my uncle?'

'In a class of a way!'

'What class of a way?' she echoed. She took a step closer.

'Are you cold, girlie?' Paddy asked.

'I am an' I am not. What class of a way are you my uncle?'

There was no reply.

'Mebbe you're my ould fellah back from England?' she stabbed suddenly.

'Mebbe!'

The girl's voice was shaken with delight. 'I knew you'd be back! They all said no, but I said yes—that you'd be back for sure.' A pause. A step nearer. 'What did you bring me?'

Dourly he put his hand into his pocket. His fingers encountered a pipe, a half-quarter of tobacco, a six-inch nail, a clotted handkerchief, and the crumpled letter from Timothy.

'I left it after me in the carriage,' he said limply.

Her recovery from disappointment was swift. 'Can't you get it in town a Saturday?' she said, drawing still closer.

'That's right!' he agreed. There was a short pause. Then: 'Come hether to the fire,' he said.

She came and stood between his knees. The several hoops of her curls were between him and the fire-light. She smelled of soap. His fingers touched her arms. The mother was in her surely. He knew it by the manner in which her flesh was sure and unafraid.

They remained there without speaking until the light step on the road sent her prickling alive. 'Mom'll kill me for bein' out of bed,' she said. Paddy's body stiffened. As the girl struggled to be free, he held her fast. Of a sudden she went limp, and laughed: 'I forgot!' she whispered. 'She'll not touch me on account of you comin' home.' She rippled with secret laughter. 'Wasn't I the fooleen to forget?'

The key was in the padlock. The door moved open. The woman came in, her shawl down from her shoulders. 'Maag!' she breathed. The girl and the man were between her and the firelight.

Without speaking the woman stood directly inside the door. The child said nothing but looked from one to the other. The woman waited for a while. Slowly she took off her shawl, then closed the door behind her. She walked carefully across the kitchen. A matchbox noised. She lighted the warm lamp. As the lamplight came up Paddy was seen to be looking steadfastly into the fire.

'You're back, Paddy?'

'Ay!'

'Had you a good crossin'?'

'Middlin'!'

'You hungry?'

'I'll see… soon!'

There was a long silence. Her fingers restless, the woman stood in mid-kitchen.

She raised her voice: 'If you've anything to do or say to me, Paddy Kinsella, you'd best get it over. I'm not a one for waitin'!'

He said nothing. He held his gaze on the fire.

'You hear me, Paddy? I'll not live cat and dog with you. I know what I am. Small good your brandin' me when the countryside has me well branded before you.'

He held his silence.

'Sayin' nothin' won't get you far. I left you down, Paddy. Be a man an' say it to my face!'

Paddy turned: 'You left me well down,' he said clearly. He turned to the fire and added, in a mutter: 'I was no angel myself!'

Her trembling lips were unbelieving. 'We're quits, so?' she ventured at last.

'Quits!'

'You'll not keep firin' it in my face?'

'I'll not!'

'Before God?'

'Before God!'

The woman crossed herself and knelt on the floor. 'In the presence of my God,' she said, 'because you were fair to me, Paddy Kinsella, I'll be better than three wives to you. I broke my marriage-mornin' promise, but I'll make up for it. There's my word, given before my Maker!'

Maag kept watching with gravity. The mother crossed herself and rose.

Paddy was dourly rummaging in his coat-pocket. At last his fingers found what he was seeking. 'I knew I had it somewhere!' he said. He held up a crumpled toffee-sweet. 'I got it from a kid on the boat.'

Maag's face broke in pleasure: ''Twill do—till Saturday!' she said.

The girl's mouth came down upon the stripped toffee. Then, the sweet in her cheek, she broke away and ran across the kitchen. She flung open the door of the boys' bedroom.

'Get up outa that!' she cried out. 'The ould fellah is home!'

SOMETIMES ON TUESDAYS

Janet McNeill

Janet McNeill (1907–1994) was a prolific author and playwright of over thirty works of fiction for adults and children. She explored life in Northern Ireland in works that include *The Maiden Dinosaur*, *Search Party*, *As Strangers Here*, *The Child in the House* and several short story collections for children.

He knew by the uneven rhythm of her typewriter that the letters she would offer for signature at half-past four would be a poor lot, falling far short of her usual standard. She had been upset all day, he'd tried to ignore it but it was impossible. This morning she had arrived at the office ten minutes late with an apology that was in effect a challenge, his cup of coffee was so cool she must surely have wept into it, when the telephone rang she wore a look of panic until the caller was identified, when it remained silent he knew she yearned with a desperate wish for it to ring. It seemed unreasonable that Meryl who shared with him a positive joy from work well done, so that a perfectly phrased letter, perfectly typed, became an act of creation, could be so vulnerable to the commoner anxieties.

Of course that husband of hers was to blame – that long-haired unchinned boy with the gentle face and the aggressive taste in shirts. When they had married two years ago he sent them a case of fish knives and his compliments, and felt confident that Meryl would tackle the intricacies of marriage with the same ease with which she handled her work at the office. Her vibrant happiness had startled him, her work had improved – if that was possible. The most complicated page of figures appeared lyrical, there was even a grace about the way she addressed envelopes.

It was six months ago that he had begun to notice a difference. It wasn't a general falling-off of skill but there were days when her mind seemed to wander. When in the evening he locked up his papers and put his coat on, the important part of his day had ended. For Meryl, twisting her hair in front of the mirror, holding a debate with her own reflection, the important part of the day was still to come.

"Goodnight, Meryl."

"Goodnight, Mr Fittleworth," and a final appraisal of her face in the glass, a mute appeal for guidance, before she tapped her way downstairs. He wondered what she was going home to, a passionate welcome, a row, a reconciliation, a contest in sulking, some kind of drama introduced over the evening meal, developed during the dish washing, brought to its inevitable climax in bed. Sometimes Mr Fittleworth was amazed by the thought that the same answer could be expected to solve so many problems. He was glad she had never confided in him or sought his advice on her private life. Meryl knew which side of the desk was hers.

The letters, when she brought them, were worse than he expected. He picked through the sheets.

"Some mistakes here, Meryl."

"Mistakes?" Her eye shadow had streaked and her face, which was usually as flawless as her letters, looked blotchy.

"This firm – surely they've moved to a new address."

"I'm, sorry, Mr Fittleworth."

"It should be 'concession' here, not 'progression'."

"Yes, Mr Fittleworth."

"And you were to get out a quotation for these people, weren't you?"

"Yes, I'm sorry."

"Better see to them, then."

She took the papers and went back to her desk with a touching meekness. Her damp scrap of a handkerchief lay beside the typewriter; sometimes she fingered it as if it brought her comfort. She looked such a child. He prided himself he had become accustomed to the long cinnamon-coloured columns of her thighs. He enjoyed the mild tenderness he felt for her.

Meryl's mistakes meant that he would be late in leaving the office, but since this was Tuesday he was content not to get away on time. Judith would be home before him, her vigil would be over, by the time he arrived she would know one way or the other, would have had a chance to take the hungry unbecoming look off her face. The pattern of the evening could proceed unthreatened – supper to the account of Judith's day at the Library and his own at the office, the newspaper for him while Judith busied herself with the dishes, after that the drugging world of telly, sharing its persuasive unreality with Judith in the way they had shared, thirty-five years earlier, the unreal world of the bedtime story before Mummy closed the book and turned out the light. Then the ritual of the cat and the milk bottles and the catches on the windows, and finally his own room to himself, hearing Judith's faint but accurate movements through the walls.

"Lucky you have a sister to look after you," his friends often told him, and he agreed that he was lucky. They had their disagreements of course. Judith was apt to be bossy. She took that from Aunt Florence, Mummy used to say so. He remembered that she had been bossy ever since childhood, bossy over shared toys, slices of cakes, turns on the swing. He didn't always allow her to get away with it. Differing from Judith was an integral part of their relationship; it carried no aftermath of guilt. No vows were broken, no post-mortems required, no reconciliations called for. Brothers and sisters expected to row, their closeness was something neither of them had chosen or could be held responsible for. Their lack of harmony didn't indicate an error of judgement. How impossible marriage must be in comparison!

And then there had come the Tuesday six months ago when he returned home and found Judith standing in the hall, preening herself critically at the mirror. She was wearing the pale suit she wore on Sundays, and even in the electric light her makeup looked too positive. The hall was full of perfume. He sometimes gave her perfume at Christmas, she seemed to appreciate it though it was out of character, and he often wondered what she did with it.

"Your supper's laid," she told him, talking sideways and still pushing her fingers impatiently into her hair, "and there's a casserole in the oven."

"Where are you going?"

"Out."

It wasn't their Choir night or her Girls' Club Night or the night when she went to the pictures with her school friend, Ethel.

"Out?"

She turned towards him, one hand on her hip, at the same time displaying and making a deliberate guy of herself.

"I've got a date."

Her coyness invited him to be amused.

"You've what?"

"I told you, George – a date."

He didn't know what to say. The date, apparently, was with Mr Harbinson, a man who came into the Library from time to time to do research. "You know – I've often spoken about him."

Still faltering for words, he was pleased to find a childhood tag handy. "'Very grand and handsome, I'm sure,' as the fox said to the rabbit." He was sure this was the right key, it would take the abnormality out of the situation, belittle the outing, unite Judith with himself before she went off. But Judith appeared not to have heard. She picked up her handbag, turned briefly and surprisingly to kiss his cheek, and left the house. Normally they kissed once a year, on Christmas Eve when they had decorated the tree.

This had been the pattern of Tuesday evenings for several months. It was always Tuesday. Judith explained that Mr Harbinson spent the week in the city and returned home to the Midlands at the weekend. George was uneasy. He tried to pretend that their life was the same as it had always been but it was a poor pretence. For Judith the days of the week now existed only so that Tuesdays could be one of them. She didn't talk about Mr Harbinson, but he seemed to intrude into their company when brother and sister spent the evenings together. Sometimes George studied her as she sat at the other side of the hearthrug. Her appearance hadn't changed except for a faint trace of complacency that he detected about her mouth. He decided it didn't suit her. Judith's features were severe in a handsome way, that was the Hamilton streak in her. He himself took after Grandfather Fittleworth. He tried to imagine her face, further softened, responding to Mr Harbinson across the dinner table. To imagine her transfigured by love was an indecency. He felt angry and betrayed.

One Tuesday when he reached home the hall was empty. He found Judith in the kitchen, wearing her apron, shaking lettuce leaves over the sink.

"You're going to be late," he said, and then she turned and he saw her face. The silent telephone was the most significant presence at the meal they shared. Afterwards, sitting with her, he felt filled with rage for the man. He remembered he used to feel like this when Judith came to Prefects' Dances at school and boys who were his friends bypassed her. The telly was useless. He brought out one of the old photograph albums and Judith responded, he blessed her for her good sense. Soon they were snugly established in the intricacies of family history, strangers were excluded.

"Here's Aunt Isobella again – she always inclined to be dressy."

"I'll say."

"Uncle Rupert – one for the girls, Mummy used to say. She said your hands are like his."

"I always mean to wear his ring. What's the use of having it if I don't wear it?"

"Take a look at this one, George! Me at the dancing display – a fairy I was, imagine!"

He remembered that display and in particular remembered Judith, taller than the other fairies, angular, completely without grace, telling her companions what to do. He had been embarrassed even then. Didn't she know? Did girls really not know?

There had been six empty Tuesdays since then. Over those weeks he thought Judith seemed to recover her poise and was grateful to her. He wondered if he should say something, but decided it would be better to let it go. What was there that he could say? The relationship hadn't been significant, or if it had he was glad she had got over it so successfully. It was beyond imagination that Judith's solid body could be racked with the same longings and raptures and indecisions as those Meryl suffered. Knowing Judith the way he did he was sure she couldn't make that much of a fool of herself.

On this, the evening of the seventh Tuesday, when he turned his key and went in there was no sign of Judith in hall or kitchen. Then he heard her voice on the telephone.

"Well, of course not! How could you? No, no – not at all! Yes, half an hour. Yes. Yes. 'Bye for now!"

Her face, as she came out of the room, shocked and startled him. He looked away from her at once and busied himself with the disposal of his coat and hat.

"Mr Harbinson, imagine!" he heard her declare, "he's in town. I'm going out for a meal with him."

If only she'd had the good grace to dissemble he might have given her his blessing, but she was trumpeting the news down the hall. There was something shameless about her, none of the Hamiltons had ever behaved like this, it was completely foreign to her inheritance.

"Lucky I'd made a salad. I had a sort of feeling he might ring," she rejoiced. So she'd been fooling him all these weeks, he remembered a succession of salads, Tuesday after Tuesday he had been deceived. He had only imagined the restored harmony between them.

He sat down to his solitary meal and listened to her upstairs, banging about from wardrobe to dressing table and back again. He was glad when at last the hall door closed behind her. He tried not to think of their meeting. Judith always hated to be touched, even when she passed him a plate she withdrew her fingers before they had brushed against his. Mummy used to scold her when she was a little child because she hid up the apple tree when visitors whose status entitled them to a kiss were taking their leave. There were difficult scenes when the sewing-woman paid her annual visit and clothes were altered and fitted. "She breathes at me! She breathes at my face!" Then Mummy's voice coming through the sewing-room door, pleading for toleration and co-operation. "Stand still, dear, stand still." "But she breathes!"

When he had eaten he found the empty house intolerable and went up the road to the local. He might find someone to talk to there. But he was unlucky. He was the only solitary customer, others were in pairs over their drinks. There was a young couple who reminded him of Meryl and her husband. The girl's neck was white and round above a soft fluffy jersey. The boy's knee was pressed against her, his hand encircled her wrist and his fingers had crept under the jersey's cuff. He knew they were enjoying the discipline which drinking together in a public house laid on them.

After a couple of drinks he went home and sat in his chair, miserable and impatient. He tried to prepare himself for what might come. How would she look when she came through the door? He wondered if she would look radiant without looking ridiculous and hoped for both their sakes that she could.

He wondered what he could find to say to her. He didn't dare to think of the changes which might take place in his own life. He knew well enough that the ease of his life with Judith had excused him from the complications of other relationships. He'd be at risk now, his friends would be good at telling him so. There would be a lot of funny stuff. Weddings were like that.

He was surprised to hear her key in the lock before the clock struck ten. Her step in the hall sounded brisk. "In there, are you, George? All alone in the dark?"

He murmured that he must have dozed off. She said, "I'll make a cup of tea," and he heard her going into the kitchen.

"Have a good evening?" he asked her as she passed him his cup.

"Oh yes, thank you. Very pleasant."

She stirred her tea and stared at the fire. Certainly there was no radiance about her but there was a difference. She had, he decided, the appearance of someone who passed unscathed through a kind of painful glory, and come out peacefully on the other side.

"Mr Harbinson well?"

"Very well, thank you."

He wondered if it would help if he used the childish phrase with which they winkled information out of each other in days gone by. "Come on, lets unbutton our bosoms," but he couldn't bring himself to say the words.

"Been out of town recently, has he?" he ventured.

"Yes. He's had commitments up north."

"But now he's going to be around again, is he?"

She sipped her tea before she replied. The sugar, dissolving, made bubbles in her cup. She fished for these with her teaspoon, secured them and swallowed them – she always did that, for luck, she said.

"No. He's just down settling up some business."

"And then?"

"He's been moved up north permanently."

"Oh." There seemed no other possible comment. He waited to be told that she was moving up north with him and braced himself to take it. Instead Judith said "Of course it's a much better arrangement, especially for his wife and family. All this travelling, never seeing them except at weekends…"

He was completely amazed. Wife? Family? Did she know? When had he told her? Was this the first she'd heard of it? Her appearance gave him no clue, she was unshaken. He felt he wanted to go down on his knees on the hearthrug out of gratitude and admiration for her. He wanted to ask for forgiveness for sins of suspicion that she didn't know he had committed. He wanted to find some way to celebrate her excellence. All his anger at Mr Harbinson's treachery was dissolved in his appreciation of this amazing sister of his.

She scraped the sugar from the bottom of her cup and said "George, you look tired."

"Do I?"

"Come on – bed!"

With profound thankfulness and a sense of continuity restored he went through the evening ritual as if he was celebrating a sacrament.

"Goodnight, George."

"Goodnight."

He closed his bedroom door and listened to her movements in the adjoining room. They were orderly and restrained, none of the wild abandon of a couple of hours ago.

As he turned back his bed and got between the sheets he thought briefly of Meryl, and wondered briefly whether her problems too had been resolved."

HOLLOW

Paul McVeigh

Paul McVeigh won the Polari First Novel Prize for *The Good Son* and has twice received the McCrea Literary Award. His short stories have appeared in Faber's *Being Various*, as well as in the *Irish Times*, the *London Magazine* and the *Stinging Fly*, on BBC Radio 4 and Sky Arts. He is co-founder of the London Short Story Festival.

1.

A couple lived on a farm, far away from the rest of the world and on their fertile land all crops flourished. They kept chickens that laid more eggs than they could eat, and, nearby, a stream jumped with fish to fry. They owned a well with a never-ending supply of water and, right at the edge of their land, a wood provided trees to chop for the fire.

The couple had everything their hearts desired except for one small thing.

On their wedding day, to mark the occasion, the couple had planted an apple tree at the entrance to the wood and, exactly five years later, it bore fruit for the first time, as though celebrating their anniversary.

"Surely, it's a sign," his wife said.

The farmer patted her stomach and smiled.

Years passed and the woman's belly showed no swell, and though love grew fat and rested deep within them, the couple stopped lying with each other.

The farmer took to going to the edge of the wood, at the end of his working day, to sit underneath the apple tree. At times, when he hadn't come home for supper, the wife would go looking for her husband only to find him sleeping against its trunk.

"See what you've done," she said, one evening, while helping her husband to his feet. "You've worn a dent in the tree with your back." She smiled through a sting of jealousy.

Later that night, being of a sensible nature, she shook her head and laughed at herself, returning to the calm she knew.

One day, when the man was tired from his work and felt the cool of the setting sun in his bones, he went to the wood and sat, leaning in the nook he had worn into the tree. This groove his body had made over the years seemed to welcome him. Before long he drifted off to sleep.

In his dream, he was exactly where he'd sat to rest but the world had become unbearably hot. He took off his shirt, then the rest of his clothes, and lay naked at the foot of the tree. Despite the heat, a blanket of cool damp leaves covered the earth, protected from the burning sun by the shade the tree provided.

I wish there was a breeze, he thought, and closed his eyes.

What felt like a cool breath, ran over him, making the fine, blonde hair of his stomach stand and his skin bump and tingle. When he opened his eyes, he saw the five-flowered blossoms on the apple tree trembling. The branches waved. He knew it wasn't the wind but the tree itself fanning him. The branches came toward him, wrapped underneath and around him, pulling him up and in until he was pressed against the trunk of the tree. He placed his hands on the bark and looked up at the dance of the branches above.

"How beautiful you are," he said, then kissed the tree tenderly. "How I've ignored you all this time. Have I been blind?"

The groove he had made with his back was now hip-height as he stood, and it yielded as he pressed against the tree. Leaves whispered in his ear and the smell of apple blossom filled his head and he became aroused. He made love to the tree in the way that dreams allow. As he came, the tree caved, and he sank deep inside the damp, darkness of its hollow.

When he woke, the farmer found he was lying naked on the earth. He tried to piece together what had happened, grasping at images from his dream, but, like snowflakes, they melted the instant he touched them. All that remained was a feeling of deep shame. He was cold and became self-conscious. Dressing quickly, he hurried home, his head thick with fog and full of fear and the sense of something important lost.

2.

The tree waited for the man to return. Every day, as the sun rose, the tree unfurled its leaves to the cottage in the distance. Every afternoon, the tree waited, hoping to see the man appear walking towards it through the long grass. But he was never again to rest himself on its bark.

As the days grew hotter, apples burst from its branches, tiny and sore. One, sprouting from the tip of the highest branch, caused the most pain. Within a week it had grown ten times the size of the others. It weighed the branch down until it rested on the earth. As the summer had its way, while the other apples matured and fell, the huge fruit stayed and did not stop growing.

One morning, as the tree opened for the sun, something was different. The large apple had disappeared. The branch that had held it now led inside the hollow that had been made so deep the last time the farmer had come. The tree pulled the branch to bring the fruit out, bark cracking from the effort. It called upon its deep roots to help. And with the strength of the earth itself, it strained until there was a cry. A human cry. Now the branch came easily. It rustled out from the hollow and with it a baby boy, the tip of the branch attached to the boy's belly.

The tree slid some branches under the baby and lifted it off the ground. The tree wept leaves and blossoms of joy at the sight. The boy screamed and cried. The tree curled a branch around a rock and bashed against its trunk until bark split. It brought the boy to the split and he drank the sticky sap.

The tree was devoted to the boy. It shaded him under its branches when he was hot and sheltered him in the hollow when he was cold. It let him drink his fill of its sap, held and rocked him till he slept. And the boy was content, playing among the roots.

The farmer never returned.

When the boy had been with the tree for seven years, and the autumn had painted them both brown and orange, a tiny figure appeared in the horizon and came towards them. The tree became frightened for the boy, ushering him into the hollow and concealing the entrance with its branches.

A little girl emerged from the grass swinging a tiny basket. She sat on the ground and picked the apples, throwing away the bruised and wrinkled but keeping the golden and shiny for herself. The girl began to sing. Clear, high and pure, her voice hung in the air like a sweet smell.

The tree resisted as the boy pushed at the branches to escape. The boy growled, a sound he'd never made before. The little girl jumped. The growling became a whimper. The girl looked at the tree, glanced back at the cottage in the distance, then stood. Flattening down her skirt, she tip-toed towards the tree trunk.

"Hello," she said, tugging at the branches that covered the hollow. The boy struggled on his side, too, and soon the two of them were face to face.

"Who are you?" she asked.

The boy reached out and touched her hair then felt his own. The girl spat on the hem of her skirt then wiped the earth from his face. The tree shivered at this, its leaves rustled a warning.

"That's better," the girl said.

The boy glanced back at the tree and then at the girl.

"I'm not supposed to come here," she said. "It'll be our secret." She held her finger to her lips. "I have to go, but I will come back," she smiled, picked up her basket, and off she skipped.

The boy ran after the girl until the branch that led from his belly to the tree snapped him back. He pulled at the branch. The tree felt those tugs deep in its sap. As the girl disappeared over the horizon, the boy dropped to the earth with a thump.

The boy didn't return to the tree straight away but sat watching the sun grow tired and heavy until it sank from the sky to rest. When the chill of the dark came to rouse him, the boy stood and, with his foot, made a circle of turned-up soil around the tree, mapping his boundary.

As the autumn darkened, the girl came to the tree every afternoon. She brought books with drawings inside and taught the boy about the world beyond the field. Even after he understood her talk, he would not speak back. He was ashamed of the rustling whispers that came out of his mouth when he practiced alone. The girl didn't seem to mind that he was always silent – except when he laughed. He couldn't keep the wet, sticky clacking sound inside.

The next summer, while the tree was busy bearing fruit, energy low, busy with so much life, the girl came all day, every day. The children started whispering. They were keeping secrets. When they did this, the tree would tickle them with leaves or drop apples on their heads. They'd laugh then move further away.

One dry, late summer's day, under the pale blue sky, the boy ran to greet the girl. This time they lingered at the very limit that his branch allowed. The summer had been a hot one, and the apples on the tree had grown heavy and begun to drop before their time.

When it happened, it was like an explosion. Every branch shook, every apple fell. When the surge passed, the tree saw the girl and the boy running across the field, hand in hand. In the girl's other hand, an axe glinted in the sun.

3.

The boy's bony fingers felt crushed by the girl's hand, he was sure he heard a snap, but he didn't mind. He barely touched the ground, pulled with such force by the girl, as she ran through the field, down and then up the hill. He'd never been outside of his little circle around the tree and the further he went the more frightened he became, but excited too. The girl didn't seem to notice. She pulled, dragging him on.

Ahead he saw a cottage, just like the pictures the girl had shown him. It was where people lived. People like him.

At the cottage, the girl rested the axe by the door, and said, "Wait here," kissing him on the cheek. He nodded and watched her go in. The door clicked but didn't catch, remaining slightly open. The boy was left alone for the first time in his life, he felt light headed and wondered if he had made a terrible mistake. He watched through the gap in the door.

"Daddy! I've brought my friend home," the girl cried.

"A friend? Where?" The father squinted at his daughter. "Don't leave the child outside."

"It's the boy I've been telling you about," she said, "the boy from the tree."

"The apple tree at the edge of the wood?" her mother asked. "That's your father's tree."

"I've told you to stay away from that tree," the farmer scolded. "And it's not my tree!" He glared at his wife. "No wonder her head is full of nonsense."

The girl ran out the door and grabbed the boy by the hand. He was stiff with fear, but she dragged him in and helped him onto a chair.

"See," she said, pointing at the boy.

The boy stayed silent, ashamed of the sound of his voice.

"Oh yes, he's a lovely boy, isn't he?" the farmer's wife said. "He looks a little familiar." She winked at her husband.

"Can we get him some clothes?" asked the girl.

"Don't be ridiculous," the farmer snapped.

"When I start school, he can come too," the girl continued, "We can say he's my brother."

The farmer slammed his fist on the table.

Her mother laughed. "He does have his father's eyes."

The boy remembered how still his mother was and hoped, if he sat like her, they might forget he was there.

"This is not a boy, it's a piece of wood," the farmer shouted and, at that, he jumped up, snapped the boy in half over his knee, and threw him on the fire. How the little girl cried in her mother's lap.

As he burned, as he screamed and spat crackles in the flames, the boy watched his father storm out of the cottage, pick up the axe at the door and head for the wood.

A SHIVER OF HEARTS

Una Mannion

Una Mannion is based in Sligo. She has won a Hennessy Award as well as the Doolin, Ambit, Cúirt and Allingham short story prizes among others. She has published in numerous journals and teaches at IT Sligo. Her debut novel, *A Crooked Tree*, will be published by Faber in 2021.

The Virgins look at me from blank eye sockets, their skin and robes chalky white after the kiln. A watery shaft of morning light falls diagonally on the casts, across a bent face, a heart, hands folded in prayer. Sometimes I think they are more beautiful before they are painted. Without colour, their protruding hearts are barely visible. Dympna says Mr Geoghan has a thing for bleeding hearts – all of his Virgin Marys have one, and the Christs and the Child of Pragues. I say they probably sell better.

I am two hours early and put on my apron. On the worktable, two rows of Virgin Marys silently await colour and incarnation; their quiet vacancy unnerves me. Dympna usually paints the under-colours, mantles, cloaks, robes, hair and skin. I apply the detail: eyes, lips, hearts, the gold-work. I use a gun to mist rosy cheeks. When they have dried, we roll the statues in corrugated cardboard and box them. If I work methodically, I will finish Dympna's work by eleven, mine by four when her bus gets back and before Mr Geoghan returns from deliveries.

It's Dympna who started referring to them as The Virgins. *Tess and I are painting The Virgins for the summer,* she says for ironic impact when we are drinking cans with some of the others in the park. She has shaved her head each side and teased up the rest. I tell her she looks like Cyndi Lauper dressed as Morticia Addams. She's beautiful, pale skin, jet black hair and big brown eyes that my uncle Martin says are like Celia Johnson's. I ask my uncle could there be a name for a group of Virgin Marys the way there is for other things he describes, like a clutch of eggs or a shimmer of hummingbirds. He looks it up in a dictionary; he can't find virgins, but a gang of nuns was once called a superfluity.

'Should've been a shower,' he says, 'if they're anything like the Sisters of Mercy.' I tell him there's a punk band called Sisters of Mercy in England.

In their kitchen where I spend my summers, my Uncle Martin and Aunt Violet speak like this, examining and weighing words, naming things, arguing: a deceit of lapwigs, a murmuration of starlings, a shiver of sharks, is Knocknarea the hill of the kings or the moon, or the executions. Words and places fall around me, mysterious and spectral. At night, I duck when I see a cloud of bats, the soprano pipistrelle, run past the Corpse Field near the Oyster Lane where they'd buried unbaptised babies and cross the road from three-cornered-garden, a triangular field where Martin once felt a ghost.

I take a brush from the jar, dip it in the tin of ultramarine blue and start on the mantle of Our Lady of the Immaculate Heart. I offered to go to the doctor with Dympna, but she said no. It would be easier alone. She just wants the pregnancy test and information about where to go in England. For the past two afternoons, she has slept curled on the worktop like a child.

It is my seventh summer in Ireland. In April, Dympna sent me a package to America, a large brown envelope with EIRE stamps arranged like a smiley face. She'd gotten us summer jobs in the religious statue factory doing brushwork. *The owner Ronnie Geoghan remembers your mother. Please say yes.* It's my first job if I don't count helping Martin and Violet in the dairy washing bottles. Martin is the last dairy farmer in Sligo still selling unpasteurised milk. At JFK my mother warned me again not to drink it.

'There's a reason they pasteurise milk. It's called disease.'

The first time I arrived in Shannon, I was ten and an Aer Lingus hostess walked me to the baggage claim and through the doors to arrivals. Which one's your uncle, she asked. I looked up at her. I had no idea what he looked like. A big man with long sideburns and red cheeks came towards us, his giant hand held out to shake mine.

'Tess Foley? I'm your Uncle Martin. Welcome home.' I almost corrected him. I soon realised it was an expression everyone used – *Welcome home, Tess, or home again Tess?* – and I would be bursting with how I belonged to where my mother was from.

When we arrived in Sligo, Violet was waiting outside. I was carsick and she told me to breathe in the sea air. White Hawthorn was in bloom along the stone walls of the fields that rushed down to meet the shimmering bay. The tide was in at every edge of the earth. It was like looking at a map, the land outlined by sea. At my back stood the mountain my mother had described, now purpled by the falling sun.

The paint fumes get to me, and I step outside the factory for fresh air. Mr Geoghan prefers us not to say factory, that we shouldn't think about it as a commercial enterprise, that what we do is sacred art. I say this to my mother on our weekly phone call that she makes to the payphone in the village hotel, and she can't stop laughing.

'I went to primary school with Ronnie Geoghan,' she says. 'Sacred art?' It's hard for me to believe that Mr Geoghan could be the same age as my mother. He looks old.

When I was younger I would ask her where my father was and she would say, *Somewhere in Ireland, I don't know.* A few summers ago, I began to worry. What if my father lived in Sligo or in our village? Maybe he had seen me walking or delivering milk with Martin and Violet and people would say that's Kathleen Foley's daughter home from America. Maybe he had seen me on the street. I asked her in the phone box in the hotel,

'Is my dad in Sligo? Does he know about me?' She paused.

'He knew. I don't know where he is now.' I don't ask her his name.

The Cathedral bells toll. Without Dympna, I work fast. I took to the brush-work quickly and Mr Geoghan has begun teaching me the detail. I've learned to mix the Judson's powder to the exact consistency turning it to liquid gold, deep and radiant on the virgins' crowns and halos, the fringes of their robes, on their wounded hearts.

I didn't go with Dympna to the CND concert which is a terrible pity, she says, because you and all your worrying would have prevented this trouble. She has been attempting levity, but I know she's scared. I'm not good in groups of Irish teenagers. I don't always get the wit. *You need to understand that slagging is a national pastime*, Dympna says. *They like you, so they tease you. Stop taking it so personally.*

Mr Geoghan disapproved when Dympna told him she was taking a day off for the concert.

'That's not about Sellafield or nuclear arms, it's about a piss-up,' he said.

'Mr Geoghan,' I said, 'I saw a Virgin Mary statue once that was burned by a nuclear bomb.'

'Did you? Where was that now?' He put down the brush and looked at me.

'When I was in elementary school we went to New York to see her. Outside Nagasaki there was a catholic cathedral with a painted wooden statue of the Virgin Mary. The morning the bomb was dropped, everyone in that village was instantly incinerated. After, when people went through the rubble they found her head, everything else was ash and stone. She was brought all over the world. I guess to protest nuclear arms.'

'What did she look like?' asked Dympna. The damaged head was seared in my memory.

'Sad and sort of terrifying. The heat disintegrated all the paint and her head and face were charred. But it's her eyes I remember most. They weren't there. Just big empty black sockets because her crystal eyes had melted from the heat. She looked out at us from these black hollowed spaces.'

'Maybe her eyes melted because of what she'd witnessed,' said Dympna. We stayed quiet for a minute, thinking and concentrating on the brushwork.

'Our Lady of Nagasaki,' I remembered. 'That's what she's called.'

The memory makes me shiver, and I go back in to start the hearts.

The Immaculate Heart of Mary is punctured by one sword and is surrounded by a crown of roses. It's easier to paint than the heart of Our Mother of Sorrows which is pierced by seven swords with blood dripping in the shape of tear drops.

'People buy these as house ornaments?' I asked that first day when Mr Geoghan brought out the templates with the colour codes.

'Mary has many devotees,' he said.

'It just seems a bit morbid.'

'See Mr Geoghan? The Yank says it's gruesome.' I reddened. Dympna nudged me. Her irreverence embarrasses me but it is also what draws me. Her honesty. *You don't have to be perfect like the bloody virgins, Tess. You can be real.* Dympna says the statues are creepy, how they're painted to be fake. The lips must always be thin, barely any flesh, and must never be smiling. The eyes should be emotionless with minimal paint. Their hearts sit outside their clothes; we don't see rib or sinew, we don't even see their necks. And I know that she is right about me, that I am never just me, that I am always trying to prove myself for my mother, prove us, in school, in Ireland, in America, at work, everywhere. Because my mother was sent away on account of me.

When I go back home, my mother sleeps in my bed for several nights, her chin on my shoulder like a child, asking questions. She doesn't let me unpack for days. She puts her head inside the suitcase, pulls the lid back over and breathes home.

'Why won't you go back?' I ask her. 'Martin and Violet keep asking when will you come home.'

'I just can't Tess. I can't go. I can't explain it, how much I hurt my mother.'

I want to say, but your mother's dead now.

Dympna never comes. I pack the statues and sweep. At home, there is no one in the kitchen or dairy. I go behind the house and look towards the bay. The tide is out. I can see the seals out on the far bank and a dark figure bent on the cockle strand. I go down to him. We pick until the tide is in around our knees and the sun has slipped behind the dunes.

'Now,' says Martin, 'that should do us,' and he hauls our bag over his shoulder. Coming back up through the fields, I see Dympna in the distance standing at the back of the house waiting for me. I ask Martin if we can spend the night in his chalet by the beach.

We have dinner first. Dympna eats and says very little and Martin and Violet are quiet, sensing something amiss. By the time we finish, it is dark. Martin puts the sleeping bags and pillows in the car with a box of food for the morning and drives us down to the chalet at the edge of the field, a few feet from the hightide line on the foreshore.

We sit on the beach looking out towards the bay, our backs cradled by the midden, and talk. The tide has turned, heading out again, and I have built us a small fire. Dympna never went to Longford. After work the day before she felt unwell and started to have stomach cramps. Later, she realised she was bleeding.

'Near midnight I woke my mother and told her.' She cups sand in her hands and lets it fall through her fingers.

'I didn't want to be alone. I started to think I could die. She said I wasn't going to die, that it was a miscarriage.' Dympna pulls her knees up to her chin and wraps her arms tight around her legs.

'And then she said I was a disappointment to her.' Above us, the moon moves to the corner of the mountain.

'And even when she said that, I still begged her not to leave me, to stay in the bathroom with me. But she left and shushed me from the other side of the door so my father wouldn't hear.'

I don't know what to say. I am used to Dympna knowing the right answers. The moon and the mountain are beside us. The marram grass moves at our backs. The fire casts shapes on her face, shadowing the hollows of her eyes. She looks smaller than herself. I wish I could hold her, that I could hold her and my mother in the palms of my hands, so that they knew how they were held. Against my skin, I'd feel their real hearts beating. We sit in the dark and say nothing.

ACCESS

Aidan Mathews

Aidan Mathews writes verse, fiction and drama. *Windfalls*, his first poetry collection, was published in 1977, and *Strictly No Poetry* – his most recent – in 2018. His short story collections include *Adventures in a Bathyscope*, *Lipstick on the Host* and *Charlie Chaplin's Wishbone*. Several of his plays have been performed, including *The Diamond Body*, *Saint Artaud*, *Exit-Entrance* and *Communion*.

And back be comes from the queue at the counter to the table where I'm sitting waiting, because he hasn't any cash, the same as last Saturday and in the same McDonalds too; but I say instead:

'Dad.'

I haven't called him Daddy for a long time. It was Dad by the time he left; it was Dad for ages before that, even. It just happens at a certain stage, ten, eleven, sooner for boys, I suppose, and you don't notice. First you stop saying Dadda, then you stop saying Daddy. Perhaps there's a point when you don't call him anything at all.

'I'm sorry, Wagsie,' he says. 'I'll go to the pass machine.'

And off he rushes, slipping in between all the other separated dads carrying trays ahead of their children, with his rolled-up newspaper jutting out of his pocket in the long navy coat that he wears when we meet at the weekend because I hate his anoraks that make him look poor.

I still haven't decided to tell him my news.

'Can I sit here?' says a mother, bossy with sundaes and tea bags, and I explain:

'My dad is sitting here. And my mum. My dad's gone to get money.'

'You can't reserve seats,' she says. 'It's not fair.'

She has hairs on her cheeks like sideburns. She smells of apple-flavour toilet freshener. But I say to her:

'My dad will be back in a minute.'

In fact, the pass machine isn't working and my dad has to traipse across the road with a bus beeping him, into the newsagent where he buys – this is true – a fart cushion for me and a copy of *Sugar* to get cashback for our Happy Meal.

'I don't want a Happy Meal,' I say to him. What I want is a cheeseburger, a caramel sundae and a medium diet Sprite.

'I'll have the happy meal,' he says. There's a character from *Lord of the Rings* in it. I thought you loved *Lord of the Rings*. We saw it twice.

'I'm too old for a happy meal,' I say. 'All the people getting happy meals are about two. I'm in sixth class. I have to read an article out of the *Irish Times* every week. Then I have to do bullets about it on the board.'

'Well,' he says, 'if you're so enormous, you can get the grub.'

He has shaved everywhere except around the psoriasis beside his ear, and he looks nice really without the scruffy beard. Also he has cut the bits of skin that stuck up around the moons of his fingernails. I watch him from the queue as he punches his newspaper out in the middle. And I wonder what he'd say if I did tell him. He would be over the moon, actually. He is not like other dads. My mother wishes he were. At least she wishes he had been.

'*Shay shay*,' I say to the Chinese man who hands me our lunch, because *shay shay* is the Chinese for thank you, and it must be nice for them to hear their own language.

'I am not Chinese,' he says. 'I am Korean American. But fair play to you.'

And I take my change from him, all the euro bits and pieces that come from other countries, Germany and Greece, places I am going to go to university in some day, and then I shove and push my way back to the table through the other waiting dads. Some of the other dads look younger than my dad does, because my dad hasn't shaved his head or bought slitty glasses like an eejit. He is not ashamed to say that he watched the first landing on the moon.

'Earth calling Dad,' I say, and I settle the tray.

'Listen,' he says, studying his paper like it was a treasure map. 'Do you remember that terrible train crash?'

'No,' I say. 'What terrible train crash?'

There is a Gandalf figure in the Happy Meal. A child would love it. I take it out and examine it a bit. Somewhere at home I have a model of Obelix, the funny fatso who carries huge boulders on his back, and it almost choked the dog and my mother had to boil it for ages afterwards in the kettle. But that was long ago. It has faded like Polaroids do.

'In this terrible train crash,' my dad goes on, 'there were dreadful casualties. People were burned to a cinder. There was one man they thought had been burned to a cinder, but he hadn't been. Instead, he survived the crash and slipped away before anybody noticed.'

'Why?' I say with my mouth full. The chips from the Happy Meal are pretty good, actually. I am hungrier than I thought I would have been.

'To start a new life,' says my dad. 'To begin again. To begin all over. To rise up from the ashes.'

'That is not so brilliant,' I say. 'What about his family?'

He thinks about that for a while, hunched over the paper and staring down at the leaky, wrecked ketchup sachet.

'He probably felt', my father says, 'that it was the best thing he could do for them.'

My dad always sounds like a priest when he says something unintelligible, so I knock back the Sprite too quickly and it soaks the collar of my sweater. But the lovely icy slush seeps through my train tracks onto my tongue.

'Would there be a coffin at a funeral if there was nothing left to go in it?' I say. 'Or would there be a jewellery box?'

'I don't know,' he says. 'You could bury a photograph. Or a change of clothes.'

'That's why Mum went mad,' I say. 'You say weird things in a priest's voice.'

My father stares through the window at the other dads in their shirtsleeves smoking outside in the carpark.

'How is she?' he says. 'How is Mum?'

'There was a diet on the radio and she lost weight. She lost five kilos.'

'I can't do kilos,' he says. 'I can do stones and things. I can do tons.'

'There is less calories in chocolate gold-grain digestives than there is in Weight Watchers,' I tell him. 'She was pretty pleased about that. She has gone back to dunking them.'

'Don't you worry about Weight Watchers,' he says. 'I work with women who wear their overcoats when the central heating's on, because they won't eat anything. Skin and bones, the lot of them. Skeletons in kindergarten smocks. Their breath is bad from the lack of food. Rocket and broccoli, and a half a stick of KitKat at the water cooler on payday.'

Sometimes it is pashminas and lemongrass, but today it is smocks and broccoli. The KitKat is completely new.

'I don't want you ending up anorectic,' he says.

'It's anorexic, I tell him. There's an X in it. I looked it up on Wikipedia.'

'What's Wikipedia?' he says. 'I looked it up in the *Oxford English Dictionary*.'

There is a streak of ketchup on the face of the girl on the cover of *Sugar*. He makes it worse for a while by scraping it with a fork. The daub becomes a doodle. He is not just thinking, you see. He is thinking to himself.

'And how's the boyfriend?' he says at last. 'How's Raymond?'

'Redmond is Redmond,' I say.

'Is he around?' says my dad.

'You know he is,' I say. 'When he is, I sleep with Mum. I sleep on your side. He sleeps in my room. Mum won't change my sheets afterwards, when I ask her. She says if I don't change them for a dachshund, she's not going to change them for a human being.'

'He's all right,' my dad says. 'He wears corduroy on his elbows of his jacket. Corduroy on the elbows of your jacket is cool.'

'Corduroy is all right,' I say. 'He wants you to think that he's a lecturer somewhere and not just a geography teacher in a school.'

But my dad hides behind the weekend supplement because someone he shared a room with in the alcoholics' unit in the hospital on the other side of the junction from the shopping centre has taken off a crash helmet at the counter.

Suddenly I decide to say it. There and then. Out of the blue. It wells up.

'He won't remember you,' I say. 'That was when you had the scruffy beard. Listen. Do you know what? I had a period.'

He comes out from behind the weekend supplement.

'No,' he says.

'I did.'

His face smiles and all the lines go out of it, except for the line from the stitches when he passed out in the taxi. Then he walks his fingers slowly across the table until they touch the charm bracelet on my wrist. His nail is still stained from cigarettes; but it will grow out.

'My little woman has become a big girl,' he says.

'It's really the other way round,' I say. His fingers climb up on my hand and hold it.

'If this was India, we'd have a feast,' he says. 'But it's only bloody Ireland.'

'We could go to *Lord of the Rings* again,' I say, 'and have popcorn.'

'We'll do better than that', he says. 'Much better. We won't have a feast, but we'll have a field trip. We'll go to the dolmen.'

And we get up and go, just like that, like we always do, while the man with the crash helmet is hiding his face from us with his gauntlet and the separated dads are taking the burger bread and breaking it and giving the pieces to their children.

Access to the dolmen is through a long passageway, a lane between wooden Americany houses with flat roofs and eucalyptus trees on a ridge that looks down over Dublin. You could stop and pick out the shopping centre, and listen to the low, throaty sounds of the motorway, but guard dogs growl at you as you go by and wedge their noses between the planks of the partition fences, so that you run past them. I am a bit too old to hold my dad's hand, but I hang on to the button of his coat sleeve.

'Imagine,' he keeps saying. 'My little woman has become a big girl.'

It has been a year at least since the last time we visited the dolmen, but it is still there, as quiet as ever, the shiny capstone long enough to play hopscotch on, and the two big, dogged uprights where a family sheltered during the Famine and where we ate a box of After Eights in the rain on my first Holy Communion. At the far end of the field where a metal plaque on a post reads Office of Public Works, a horse is rubbing its tail end against it. Drool is running from its mouth like a sort of yoghurt.

'I was always saying to the priest we should come here early on Easter morning and read the Resurrection stories,' says my dad. 'But he thought it'd be too cold.'

'Dad,' I say, 'I don't like the horse. Why is he rolling around in the nettles?'

My dad looks at him. You would think he was a vet, examining a specimen. 'He's a mare,' he says finally. 'He's having a foal. Look at how big he is.'

'Let's go back,' I say. 'Look at her dribbling.'

'We'll go round the other side,' Dad says. 'We'll circle her.'

But when we reach the dolmen at last and Dad goes into his druid mode, resting his palms on the side of the capstone, and then his forehead too, the horse straightens and stands up and looks at us. I do not think she is in search of a sugar lump.

'Dad,' I say. 'She's walking towards us.'

'There's room in the world for the three of us,' he says. 'Not forgetting the foal.' He's back in the days of picnics here and me squatting behind the trees when I had to.

'The people who raised these stones are still in our bloodstream,' he says. 'You can hear them with a stethoscope.'

Then the horse quickens towards us and lowers its head like a bull would. Like a bull it charges at us, and I let my father's coat-sleeve drop and I run away. I am running so fast I cannot hear my feet or my legs or my body, only the wind and the sky. When I stop, I hear the world again. I look back.

'Get out of the field, Wagsie!' my father shouts. 'Get out!' He's walking backwards between me and the horse, holding his hands up like a soldier surrendering. Then he trips and falls, and the horse rears up over him, whinny-ing, rolling its eyeballs, goo peeling like white of egg from its gums, and its mad hooves pedalling the air.

'Daddy,' I say. 'Daddy.'

The horse soars, stops, swerves to the side, and canters off. Midges are settling on my skin. My dad comes scrambling to me. His face is as red as if he had been drunk. And we do a sort of three-legged race to the car, the two of us, to the fart cushion and the magazine and all the empty takeaway cartons that are the middle of God.

'My little woman has become a big girl,' he says, but his breathing is still in ruins and his hands twitch on the steering wheel. I know that I am much older than he is and that he is already aged. I bleed for him. My big daddy has become a little boy. I walk my fingers slowly over his arm until they touch his watch-strap.

'We'd better not let your mum find out about this,' he says. 'The next thing you know I'd have to see you with a social worker.' The moon has come up on the left hand side of the car although the sun is still shining down on Saturday afternoon.

'I'll tell her we went to *Lord of the Rings*,' I say. 'For the third time.'

'For the third time,' he says. 'But she'll try to catch us out. She'll ask: "Which episode did you go to? Was it Episode 1 or Episode 2 or Episode 3?" She'd go and check the bloody CCTV.'

I rub the hairs on his hand backwards like a parent should. There is a bit of a hangnail on the moon of his left thumb, and a dent on the thumb where the French door slammed at the Holy Communion party. Once upon a time I used to suck his cigarette finger for the taste of it, the garden shed and summer evening of it. If I did that now, of course, they would come and take him away. So I rub the hairs on his hand forwards again.

'Dadda,' I say. 'Dadda.'

WOMEN ARE THE SCOURGE OF THE EARTH

Frances Molloy

Frances Molloy (1947–1991) was born in Dungiven, Co. Derry. Her 1985 autobiographical novel, *No Mate for the Magpie*, discussed her experiences growing up during the early years of the Troubles. Her short story collection, *Women are the Scourge of the Earth*, was published in 1998.

There's some people who will try to put the blame for what happened on to me but I'm not having that. I don't care what that note said. I don't care what the neighbours say. If they think I give a damn, then they're mistaken. That woman was unbalanced all her life. She'd been taking tablets for years from doctors for her nerves. Feared to let the wains out to play in case they got shot. Silly woman – I told her to catch herself on. If anybody wanted to shoot the bloody wains they could come into the house and do it.

I don't care what any of them try to tell you – I never lifted a finger to her in all the years I put up with her. Never mine what that hussy next door tries to make out. The stories I could tell you about her. You should see the odd assortment of characters that come and go there when he's out at his work, the poor bugger. There's no telling who or what fathered that crowd of cross-eyed brats of hers. I must say, it's always people like her who do the talking. I can't imagine what kind of a man he is at all to put up with it. She should be run out of the town. Many a better woman was tarred and feathered for far less. Shooting is too good for the likes of her.

That note that the missus left made out that I turned her mother and her sisters against her, but unbalanced and all as she was, she was fly enough not to mention why. Well, I'll tell you why, so you'll not be labouring under any illusions about her. She was carrying on with a fancy man. A friend of mine spotted the same car parked outside my house on the same day every week and gave me the wink. I soon put a stop to it I can tell you. I knocked his teeth right down his throat and let it be known that I would debollocks the bastard on the spot if he ever came snooking around my house again. I'll not be made a laughing stock of.

Her mother was fuming mad when I told her the way her precious daughter was carrying on. She said the missus was no daughter of hers and that she'd never darken her door again the longest day she ever lived and to give the woman her dues, she was as good as her word. All her sisters took my side in the matter too.

You would think that she would toe the line after that but by the blood of the crucified Jesus, God forgive me for taking the holy name, didn't she go more deranged than ever after that. She'd walk through the house in a stupor half the day, never even bothering to change from her night clothes. She was pining for him. You didn't need to be very clever to see that. All the time she kept pretending that it was her mother and her sisters that she wanted to see and she kept on asking me to go back to them and explain that she didn't have a fancy man, that he was only her friend. I told her that it was herself who had got into the mess and it was up to her to get herself out of it. I'm not going to be made a fool of.

I'm here to defend my good name, never mine your inquest. The woman was deranged, that's the long, the tall, and the short of it. I lived with her for fifteen years and I'm telling you now, she was never in her proper mine. I don't know what I was ever thinking about, having anything to do with the likes of her in the first place when I think of some of the women I could have had me pick of. I could have done a lot better for myself and married a good, strapping farmer's daughter with a bit of capital behind her. Indeed, I'll have you all know, I could have had any woman I wanted, just for the asking.

And here's another thing I want to draw your attention to, just when you're at it. A woman is supposed to obey her husband, is she not? She's supposed to do what he bids her, is she not? Isn't that what the law says? Isn't it? And isn't it wrote in the bible by the hand of the almighty Himself? Well, that woman never did my bidding in her life. Never once in fifteen years could I get her to do my bidding. For example, I told her to keep away from your woman next door. I didn't want no wife of mine consorting with the likes of her. But did she heed me? Like hell, she did. My friend seen that trollop from next door in having tea with her ladyship when ever I was out at my work. My blood still boils when I think of it – the likes of that trash sitting gossiping in my house and me out breaking my back to earn the money to entertain her. I soon put a stop to that, mine. I locked the outside doors to the house and took the keys with me to work for a week or so and made it known to the madam next door that if she wanted to visit my house she could try getting in and out the windows. I'll have you know, I won't be made a fool of.

And another thing she done you ought to know – she turned them five wains of hers against me. Not one of them has a decent word to say about their father now. That wee uppity lying bitch Una went away and told the doctors yarns behine my back. What do you think of that for respect then? Going away behine my back and in defiance of my orders, bringing doctors round the house to see the mother. That woman would be alive today if she'd seen far fewer doctors. It was all the fool tablets that she got from them that made her fall, that's where she got her bruises from, I never laid a finger on her in me life.

Una has turned into a right uppity wee brat and she would need to mine her step. She'll not always have the old grannie's skirts to hide behine. Just let her wait till all this fuss dies down. A man has a legal right to his own wains. I'll have her know before I'm through, who's the boss in our house. Who does she think puts the clothes on her back? Who does she think puts the food in her belly? Who does she think's been paying the rent all these bloody years? The beloved fancy man, Uncle Harry?

What do you think of that then, Uncle Harry? Uncle Harry, if you don't mine. She brought her dear Uncle Harry round to her old granny to poison her mine against me. Me and the mother-in-law had always got on well enough – I'm not saying that she wasn't a terrible old battle-axe, for she was, but as the man says, I didn't have to live with her. That woman has known me these eighteen years or more and still, she's prepared to take the word of a complete stranger before mine. What do you think of that for loyalty then? I suppose she thinks she's mixing in high-brow society now because he works in an office and dresses in pansy clothes.

But you haven't heard the best of it, no, not by a long shot. Wait till you hear the story the brave fellow is trying to put about. He's trying to make out that he met me missus at a meeting of some daft organization, what's this it's called now, let me think? It's for a lot of these people who has been let out of the funny-farm. 'Mental' or something, it's called. No, that's not right I think, nor was it called 'insane' either because it started with an 'm' I'm sure of that now. 'Mine', that's what it's called, it's for people that's out of their mines. 'Mine', 'Mine', that's what its name is, didn't I say it began with an 'm'. You see, I was right.

The bold uncle Harry told me mother-in-law that me missus was suffering from depression and that's why she joined this daft shower of freaks. He tries to make out that he was suffering from depression too and that's how the two of them met. According to his story, they were only friends and it helped them to meet for a chat and a cup of tea once a week. What do you think of that for invention? Isn't that very touching wouldn't you say? They were only good friends indeed. I'd say he must have been very hard up for a friend if he had to rely on her.

The old granny must be starting to dote, for didn't she swallow the whole story, lock, stock and barrel. You should hear her lamenting now about how she should never have doubted for a second the virtue of her lily-white daughter. All he called for was a chat and a cup of tea. What does he take me for, a real dodo? That's the kind of a story nobody but an old doting woman would fall for.

A quare lot she had to be depressed about I can tell you, with a mug like me out humping bricks on his back all day long to keep her in style. Carpets in every room, that woman had. When I think about it yet, my blood still boils. Me out slaving to provide grandeur for her to impress her fancy man with.

I'll tell you this now, she's the last woman I'll ever work for. Women, they're all the same – after what they can get out of you. There's only one thing a woman is useful for and that's on the broad of her back and nobody but a fool would marry a woman for that. There's plenty of that going free and no mistaking. Women are the scourge of the earth. I'm well rid of her. I've learnt my lesson. Once bitten, twice shy, as the man says.

HOME SICKNESS

George Moore

George Moore (1852–1933) was a novelist, poet, dramatist and short story writer. He published three poetry collections, several plays and novels, including *Spring Days*, *Sister Teresa* and *The Lake*. His six short story collections include *Celibates* (1895) and *The Untilled Field* (1903).

He told the doctor he was due in the bar-room at eight o'clock in the morning; the bar-room was in a slum in the Bowery; and he had only been able to keep himself in health by getting up at five o'clock and going for long walks in the Central Park.

"A sea voyage is what you want," said the doctor. "Why not go to Ireland for two or three months? You will come back a new man."

"I'd like to see Ireland again."

And then he began to wonder how the people at home were getting on. The doctor was right. He thanked him, and three weeks afterwards he landed in Cork.

As he sat in the railway carriage he recalled his native village—he could see it and its lake, and then the fields one by one, and the roads. He could see a large piece of rocky land—some three or four hundred acres of headland stretching out into the winding lake. Upon this headland the peasantry had been given permission to build their cabins by former owners of the Georgian house standing on the pleasant green hill. The present owners considered the village a disgrace, but the villagers paid high rents for their plots of ground, and all the manual labour that the Big House required came from the village: the gardeners, the stable helpers, the house and the kitchen maids.

He had been thirteen years in America, and when the train stopped at his station, he looked round to see if there were any changes in it. It was just the same blue limestone station-house as it was thirteen years ago. The platform and the sheds were the same, and there were five miles of road from the station to Duncannon. The sea voyage had done him good, but five miles were too far for him to-day; the last time he had walked the road, he had walked it in an hour and a half, carrying a heavy bundle on a stick.

He was sorry he did not feel strong enough for the walk; the evening was fine, and he would meet many people coming home from the fair, some of whom he had known in his youth, and they would tell him where he could get a clean lodging. But the carman would be able to tell him that; he called the car that was waiting at the station, and soon he was answering questions about America. But Bryden wanted to hear of those who were still living in the old country, and after hearing the stories of many people he had forgotten, he heard that Mike Scully, who had been away in a situation for many years as a coachman in the King's County, had come back and built a fine house with a concrete floor. Now there was a good loft in Mike Scully's house, and Mike would be pleased to take in a lodger.

Bryden remembered that Mike had been in a situation at the Big House; he had intended to be a jockey, but had suddenly shot up into a fine tall man, and had had to become a coachman instead. Bryden tried to recall the face, but he could only remember a straight nose, and a somewhat dusky complexion. Mike was one of the heroes of his childhood, and his youth floated before him, and he caught glimpses of himself, something that was more than a phantom and less than a reality. Suddenly his reverie was broken: the carman pointed with his whip, and Bryden saw a tall, finely-built, middle-aged man coming through the gates, and the driver said:—

"There's Mike Scully."

Mike had forgotten Bryden even more completely than Bryden had forgotten him, and many aunts and uncles were mentioned before he began to understand.

"You've grown into a fine man, James," he said, looking at Bryden's great width of chest. "But you are thin in the cheeks, and you're sallow in the cheeks too."

"I haven't been very well lately—that is one of the reasons I have come back; but I want to see you all again."

Bryden paid the carman, wished him "God-speed," and he and Mike divided the luggage between them, Mike carrying the bag and Bryden the bundle, and they walked round the lake, for the townland was at the back of the demesne; and while they walked, James proposed to pay Mike ten shillings a week for his board and lodging.

He remembered the woods thick and well-forested; now they were wind-worn, the drains were choked, and the bridge leading across the lake inlet was falling away. Their way led between long fields where herds of cattle were grazing; the road was broken—Bryden wondered how the villagers drove their carts over it, and Mike told him that the landlord could not keep it in repair, and he would not allow it to be kept in repair out of the rates, for then it would be a public road, and he did not think there should be a public road through his property.

At the end of many fields they came to the village, and it looked a desolate place, even on this fine evening, and Bryden remarked that the county did not seem to be as much lived in as it used to be. It was at once strange and familiar to see the chickens in the kitchen; and, wishing to re-knit himself to the old habits, he begged of Mrs. Scully not to drive them out, saying he did not mind them. Mike told his wife that Bryden was born in Duncannon, and when he mentioned Bryden's name she gave him her hand, after wiping it in her apron, saying he was heartily welcome, only she was afraid he would not care to sleep in a loft.

"Why wouldn't I sleep in a loft, a dry loft! You're thinking a good deal of America over here," said he, "but I reckon it isn't all you think it. Here you work when you like and you sit down when you like; but when you have had a touch of blood-poisoning as I had, and when you have seen young people walking with a stick, you think that there is something to be said for old Ireland."

"Now won't you be taking a sup of milk? You'll be wanting a drink after travelling," said Mrs. Scully.

And when he had drunk the milk Mike asked him if he would like to go inside or if he would like to go for a walk.

"Maybe it is sitting down you would like to be."

And they went into the cabin, and started to talk about the wages a man could get in America, and the long hours of work.

And after Bryden had told Mike everything about America that he thought would interest him, he asked Mike about Ireland. But Mike did not seem to be able to tell him much that was of interest. They were all very poor—poorer, perhaps, than when he left them.

"I don't think anyone except myself has a five pound note to his name."

Bryden hoped he felt sufficiently sorry for Mike. But after all Mike's life and prospects mattered little to him. He had come back in search of health; and he felt better already; the milk had done him good, and the bacon and cabbage in the pot sent forth a savoury odour. The Scullys were very kind, they pressed him to make a good meal; a few weeks of country air and food, they said, would give him back the health he had lost in the Bowery; and when Bryden said he was longing for a smoke, Mike said there was no better sign than that. During his long illness he had never wanted to smoke, and he was a confirmed smoker.

It was comfortable to sit by the mild peat fire watching the smoke of their pipes drifting up the chimney, and all Bryden wanted was to be let alone; he did not want to hear of anyone's misfortunes, but about nine o'clock a number of villagers came in, and their appearance was depressing. Bryden remembered one or two of them—he used to know them very well when he was a boy; their talk was as depressing as their appearance, and he could feel no interest whatever in them. He was not moved when he heard that Higgins the stone-mason was dead; he was not affected when he heard that Mary Kelly, who used to go to do the laundry at the Big House, had married; he was only interested when he heard she had gone to America. No, he had not met her there, America is a big place. Then one of the peasants asked him if he remembered Patsy Carabine, who used to do the gardening at the Big House. Yes, he remembered Patsy well. Patsy was in the poor-house. He had not been able to do any work on account of his arm; his house had fallen in; he had given up his holding and gone into the poor-house. All this was very sad, and to avoid hearing any further unpleasantness, Bryden began to tell them about America. And they sat round listening to him; but all the talking was on his side; he wearied of it; and looking round the group he recognised a ragged hunchback with grey hair; twenty years ago he was a young hunchback, and, turning to him, Bryden asked him if he were doing well with his five acres.

"Ah, not much. This has been a bad season. The potatoes failed; they were watery—there is no diet in them."

These peasants were all agreed that they could make nothing out of their farms. Their regret was that they had not gone to America when they were young; and after striving to take an interest in the fact that O'Connor had lost a mare and foal worth forty pounds Bryden began to wish himself back in the slum. And when they left the house he wondered if every evening would be like the present one. Mike piled fresh sods on the fire, and he hoped it would show enough light in the loft for Bryden to undress himself by.

The cackling of some geese in the road kept him awake, and the loneliness of the country seemed to penetrate to his bones, and to freeze the marrow in them. There was a bat in the loft—a dog howled in the distance—and then he drew the clothes over his head. Never had he been so unhappy, and the sound of Mike breathing by his wife's side in the kitchen added to his nervous terror. Then he dozed a little; and lying on his back he dreamed he was awake, and the men he had seen sitting round the fireside that evening seemed to him like spectres come out of some unknown region of morass and reedy tarn. He stretched out his hands for his clothes, determined to fly from this house, but remembering the lonely road that led to the station he fell back on his pillow. The geese still cackled, but he was too tired to be kept awake any longer. He seemed to have been asleep only a few minutes when he heard Mike calling him. Mike had come half way up the ladder and was telling him that breakfast was ready. "What kind of breakfast will he give me?" Bryden asked himself as he pulled on his clothes. There were tea and hot griddle cakes for breakfast, and there were fresh eggs; there was sunlight in the kitchen and he liked to hear Mike tell of the work he was going to do in the fields. Mike rented a farm of about fifteen acres, at least ten of it was grass; he grew an acre of potatoes and some corn, and some turnips for his sheep. He had a nice bit of meadow, and he took down his scythe, and as he put the whetstone in his belt Bryden noticed a second scythe, and he asked Mike if he should go down with him and help him to finish the field.

"You haven't done any mowing this many a year; I don't think you'd be of much help. You'd better go for a walk by the lake, but you may come in the afternoon if you like and help to turn the grass over."

Bryden was afraid he would find the lake shore very lonely, but the magic of returning health is the sufficient distraction for the convalescent, and the morning passed agreeably. The weather was still and sunny. He could hear the ducks in the reeds. The hours dreamed themselves away, and it became his habit to go to the lake every morning. One morning he met the landlord, and they walked together, talking of the country, of what it had been, and the ruin it was slipping into. James Bryden told him that ill health had brought him back to Ireland; and the landlord lent him his boat, and Bryden rowed about the islands, and resting upon his oars he looked at the old castles, and remembered the pre-historic raiders that the landlord had told him about. He came across the stones to which the lake dwellers had tied their boats, and these signs of ancient Ireland were pleasing to Bryden in his present mood.

As well as the great lake there was a smaller lake in the bog where the villagers cut their turf. This lake was famous for its pike, and the landlord allowed Bryden to fish there, and one evening when he was looking for a frog with which to bait his line he met Margaret Dirken driving home the cows for the milking. Margaret was the herdsman's daughter, and she lived in a cottage near the Big House; but she came up to the village whenever there was a dance, and Bryden had found himself opposite to her in the reels. But until this evening he had had little opportunity of speaking to her, and he was glad to speak to someone, for the evening was lonely, and they stood talking together.

"You're getting your health again," she said. "You'll soon be leaving us."

"I'm in no hurry."

"You're grand people over there; I hear a man is paid four dollars a day for his work."

"And how much," said James, "has he to pay for his food and for his clothes?"

Her cheeks were bright and her teeth small, white and beautifully even; and a woman's soul looked at Bryden out of her soft Irish eyes. He was troubled and turned aside, and catching sight of a frog looking at him out of a tuft of grass he said:—

"I have been looking for a frog to put upon my pike line."

The frog jumped right and left, and nearly escaped in some bushes, but he caught it and returned with it in his hand.

"It is just the kind of frog a pike will like," he said. "Look at its great white belly and its bright yellow back."

And without more ado he pushed the wire to which the hook was fastened through the frog's fresh body, and dragging it through the mouth he passed the hooks through the hind legs and tied the line to the end of the wire.

"I think," said Margaret, "I must be looking after my cows; it's time I got them home."

"Won't you come down to the lake while I set my line?"

She thought for a moment and said:—

"No, I'll see you from here."

He went down to the reedy tarn, and at his approach several snipe got up, and they flew above his head uttering sharp cries. His fishing-rod was a long hazel stick, and he threw the frog as far as he could into the lake. In doing this he roused some wild ducks; a mallard and two ducks got up, and they flew towards the larger lake. Margaret watched them; they flew in a line with an old castle; and they had not disappeared from view when Bryden came towards her, and he and she drove the cows home together that evening.

They had not met very often when she said, "James, you had better not come here so often calling to me."

"Don't you wish me to come?"

"Yes, I wish you to come well enough, but keeping company is not the custom of the country, and I don't want to be talked about."

"Are you afraid the priest would speak against us from the altar?"

"He has spoken against keeping company, but it is not so much what the priest says, for there is no harm in talking."

"But if you are going to be married there is no harm in walking out together."

"Well, not so much, but marriages are made differently in these parts; there is not much courting here."

And next day it was known in the village that James was going to marry Margaret Dirken.

His desire to excel the boys in dancing had aroused much gaiety in the parish, and for some time past there had been dancing in every house where there was a floor fit to dance upon; and if the cottager had no money to pay for a barrel of beer, James Bryden, who had money, sent him a barrel, so that Margaret might get her dance. She told him that they sometimes crossed over into another parish where the priest was not so averse to dancing, and James wondered. And next morning at Mass he wondered at their simple fervour.

Some of them held their hands above their heads as they prayed, and all this was very new and very old to James Bryden. But the obedience of these people to their priest surprised him. When he was a lad they had not been so obedient, or he had forgotten their obedience; and he listened in mixed anger and wonderment to the priest who was scolding his parishioners, speaking to them by name, saying that he had heard there was dancing going on in their homes. Worse than that, he said he had seen boys and girls loitering about the roads, and the talk that went on was of one kind—love. He said that newspapers containing love-stories were finding their way into the people's houses, stories about love, in which there was nothing elevating or ennobling. The people listened, accepting the priest's opinion without question. And their submission was pathetic. It was the submission of a primitive people clinging to religious authority, and Bryden contrasted the weakness and incompetence of the people about him with the modern restlessness and cold energy of the people he had left behind him.

One evening, as they were dancing, a knock came to the door, and the piper stopped playing, and the dancers whispered:—

"Some one has told on us; it is the priest."

And the awe-stricken villagers crowded round the cottage fire, afraid to open the door. But the priest said that if they did not open the door he would put his shoulder to it and force it open. Bryden went towards the door, saying he would allow no one to threaten him, priest or no priest, but Margaret caught his arm and told him that if he said anything to the priest, the priest would speak against them from the altar, and they would be shunned by the neighbours. It was Mike Scully who went to the door and let the priest in, and he came in saying they were dancing their souls into hell.

"I've heard of your goings on," he said—"of your beer-drinking and dancing. I will not have it in my parish. If you want that sort of thing you had better go to America."

"If that is intended for me, sir, I will go back to-morrow. Margaret can follow."

"It isn't the dancing, it's the drinking I'm opposed to," said the priest, turning to Bryden.

"Well, no one has drunk too much, sir," said Bryden.

"But you'll sit here drinking all night," and the priest's eyes went towards the corner where the women had gathered, and Bryden felt that the priest looked on the women as more dangerous than the porter.

"It's after midnight," he said, taking out his watch. By Bryden's watch it was only half-past eleven, and while they were arguing about the time Mrs. Scully offered Bryden's umbrella to the priest, for in his hurry to stop the dancing the priest had gone out without his; and, as if to show Bryden that he bore him no ill-will, the priest accepted the loan of the umbrella, for he was thinking of the big marriage fee that Bryden would pay him.

"I shall be badly off for the umbrella to-morrow," Bryden said, as soon as the priest was out of the house. He was going with his father-in-law to a fair. His father-in-law was learning him how to buy and sell cattle. And his father-in-law was saying that the country was mending, and that a man might become rich in Ireland if he only had a little capital. Bryden had the capital, and Margaret had an uncle on the other side of the lake who would leave her all he had, that would be fifty pounds, and never in the village of Duncannon had a young couple begun life with so much prospect of success as would James Bryden and Margaret Dirken.

Some time after Christmas was spoken of as the best time for the marriage; James Bryden said that he would not be able to get his money out of America before the spring. The delay seemed to vex him, and he seemed anxious to be married, until one day he received a letter from America, from a man who had served in the bar with him. This friend wrote to ask Bryden if he were coming back. The letter was no more than a passing wish to see Bryden again. Yet Bryden stood looking at it, and everyone wondered what could be in the letter. It seemed momentous, and they hardly believed him when he said it was from a friend who wanted to know if his health were better. He tried to forget the letter, and he looked at the worn fields, divided by walls of loose stones, and a great longing came upon him.

The smell of the Bowery slum had come across the Atlantic, and had found him out in this western headland; and one night he awoke from a dream in which he was hurling some drunken customer through the open doors into the darkness. He had seen his friend in his white duck jacket throwing drink from glass into glass amid the din of voices and strange accents; he had heard the clang of money as it was swept into the till, and his sense sickened for the bar-room. But how should he tell Margaret Dirken that he could not marry her? She had built her life upon this marriage. He could not tell her that he would not marry her… yet he must go. He felt as if he were being hunted; the thought that he must tell Margaret that he could not marry her hunted him day after day as a weasel hunts a rabbit. Again and again he went to meet her with the intention of telling her that he did not love her, that their lives were not for one another, that it had all been a mistake, and that happily he had found out it was a mistake soon enough. But Margaret, as if she guessed what he was about to speak of, threw her arms about him and begged him to say he loved her, and that they would be married at once. He agreed that he loved her, and that they would be married at once. But he had not left her many minutes before the feeling came upon him that he could not marry her—that he must go away. The smell of the bar-room hunted him down. Was it for the sake of the money that he might make there that he wished to go back? No, it was not the money. What then? His eyes fell on the bleak country, on the little fields divided by bleak walls; he remembered the pathetic ignorance of the people, and it was these things that he could not endure. It was the priest who came to forbid the dancing. Yes, it was the priest. As he stood looking at the line of the hills the bar-room seemed by him. He heard the politicians, and the excitement of politics was in his blood again. He must go away from this place—he must get back to the bar-room. Looking up he saw the scanty orchard, and he hated the spare road that led to the village, and he hated the little hill at the top of which the village began, and he hated more than all other places the house where he was to live with Margaret Dirken—if he married her. He could see it from where he stood—by the edge of the lake, with twenty acres of pasture land about it, for the landlord had given up part of his demesne land to them.

He caught sight of Margaret, and he called to her to come through the stile.

"I have just had a letter from America."

"About the money?" she said.

"Yes, about the money. But I shall have to go over there."

He stood looking at her, seeking for words; and she guessed from his embarrassment that he would say to her that he must go to America before they were married.

"Do you mean, James, you will have to go at once?"

"Yes," he said, "at once. But I shall come back in time to be married in August. It will only mean delaying our marriage a month."

They walked on a little way talking; every step he took James felt that he was a step nearer the Bowery slum. And when they came to the gate Bryden said:—

"I must hasten or I shall miss the train."

"But," she said, "you are not going now—you are not going to-day?"

"Yes, this morning. It is seven miles. I shall have to hurry not to miss the train."

And then she asked him if he would ever come back.

"Yes," he said, "I am coming back."

"If you are coming back, James, why not let me go with you?"

"You could not walk fast enough. We should miss the train."

"One moment, James. Don't make me suffer; tell me the truth. You are not coming back. Your clothes—where shall I send them?"

He hurried away, hoping he would come back. He tried to think that he liked the country he was leaving, that it would be better to have a farmhouse and live there with Margaret Dirken than to serve drinks behind a counter in the Bowery. He did not think he was telling her a lie when he said he was coming back. Her offer to forward his clothes touched his heart, and at the end of the road he stood and asked himself if he should go back to her. He would miss the train if he waited another minute, and he ran on. And he would have missed the train if he had not met a car. Once he was on the car he felt himself safe—the country was already behind him. The train and the boat at Cork were mere formulae; he was already in America.

The moment he landed he felt the thrill of home that he had not found in his native village, and he wondered how it was that the smell of the bar seemed more natural than the smell of the fields, and the roar of crowds more welcome than the silence of the lake's edge. However, he offered up a thanksgiving for his escape, and entered into negotiations for the purchase of the bar-room.

He took a wife, she bore him sons and daughters, the bar-room prospered, property came and went; he grew old, his wife died, he retired from business, and reached the age when a man begins to feel there are not many years in front of him, and that all he has had to do in life has been done. His children married, lonesomeness began to creep about him; in the evening, when he looked into the fire-light, a vague, tender reverie floated up, and Margaret's soft eyes and name vivified the dusk. His wife and children passed out of mind, and it seemed to him that a memory was the only real thing he possessed, and the desire to see Margaret again grew intense. But she was an old woman, she had married, maybe she was dead. Well, he would like to be buried in the village where he was born.

There is an unchanging, silent life within every man that none knows but himself, and his unchanging, silent life was his memory of Margaret Dirken. The bar-room was forgotten and all that concerned it, and the things he saw most clearly were the green hillside, and the bog lake and the rushes about it, and the greater lake in the distance, and behind it the blue lines of wandering hills.

DIVIDED ATTENTION

Mary Morrissy

Mary Morrisy is the author of three novels, *Mother of Pearl*, *The Pretender* and *The Rising of Bella Casey*, and two collections of stories, *A Lazy Eye* and, most recently, *Prosperity Drive*. She is Associate Director of Creative Writing at University College Cork and a member of Aosdána.

He rang first three months ago – at three in the morning. The phone blundered into my fogged brain and I lay in bed not sure if the burring was in my ears or the vestige of a dream phone. But then, phones in dreams ring, don't they? They're usually the old, black, Bakelite models – as if the fixtures in our dreams are awaiting modernization.

It continued for several minutes, not a demon of sleep but a whimpering child waiting to be picked up. Alarmed, I padded to the kitchen. It could only be death at this hour, death or bad news or… you. I shook the thought away. I was no longer a woman waiting for the phone to ring. I lifted the receiver.

"Hello?"

Silence.

"Hello?" I heard my own puzzled tone echo back at me.

Still nothing.

"Hello?" Mild aggravation now – I know that tone from the receiving end. "Who is this?"

The silence persisted. Why is it so disconcerting on the phone? Why does it yawn so? Minutes gape.

"Hello!"

There was a shifting sound. I got the impression of a large bulk wedged into a small space. Then an exerted breathing. It was laboured, distressed even. Was someone hurt, wounded in some way? I conjured up pictures of a street fight, or a mugging, a man stumbling into a phone box clutching a bloodied side and dialing the first number that came into his head. Was it someone I knew? Victor, I thought. A friend of mine, an asthmatic with a comic book name, prone to late night, melancholy drinking. You wouldn't know him. When he is distressed he makes this gnawing sound, a device to reassure himself that he will draw the next lungful.

"Victor, is that you, Victor?"

The breathing intensified, louder now, more protesting.

"Are you all right, Victor? Are you hurt? What's wrong?"

There was a harrumphing noise like a horse snorting and the breathing shite up a gear, quicker, more jagged. I heard in it, a rising panic, an urgency that had not been there before. And then, only then, I realized. This was an obscene call. I slammed the receiver down. I was shaking. The phone sat there, implacable. Flat as a pancake, the little square buttons in their serried rows, the receiver safely in its snug depression, the letter-box window stoutly declaring my number, the coy curl of its flex. How often had I sat staring at it, willing it to ring, cursing it for its refusal. But then it had been a co-conspirator, imbued with a delicious imminence as if it too was longing to hear from you. It was traitorous, sometimes, but never *this*, never spiteful. Now it had invited a pervert into my home. How could I ever trust it again?

You would have said, change your number, that's what you would have said. I know exactly the tone you would use – emphatic, overlaid with a professional concern. You managed that combination well. Go ex-directory, you would have said, like me. What a relief, you once said, no more crank calls. Precisely! You didn't know I had your number, did you? I got it by stealth. Oh, I looked in the directory hoping to find your name there carelessly among impostors. There were five who shared your name, all of whom could have been you, but I knew weren't. I pitied those who were not you. I pitied anyone who thought one of these frauds was you. But that was early on. It was only later I pitied myself.

It started innocently, I swear. I had not intended ever to use your number. Having it alone was enough. I carried it around in my wallet, taking it out from time to time and contemplating it, wondering what it would be like for this particular conjunction of figures to be familiar – oh let's not beat around the bush – to be *mine*. It soothed me to have it; it was connection, that's all, just connection. And it served as my lucky charm, like a rabbit's foot, which had the power to conjure you up and granted me an ownership, which you knew nothing about. As long as I had your number, I would be safe.

Celia told me to report the call.

"You must protect yourself," she said. Her stout face flushed angrily, her perm bounced. "The bastard!"

Much like what she said of you.

You once remarked that she had the sort of looks that would have won a bonny baby competition. Ruddy cheeks, plump arms, a stolid, ready smile, those curls. Can't you see her in bonnet and pantaloons, you said. Watch the birdie, Celia! I used to smile when I saw her and remembered that, a sly, complicitous smile, a smile for *you*. It was part of our language, the secret, mocking language of lovers. Now I look at Celia squarely in the face and think – she is here, you are not.

I didn't report it. I don't know why. Laziness, perhaps, embarrassment? But no, it was more than that. I was resisting this man, and his method of entry into my life. I didn't want him to force me into changing my number. I didn't want him to have the power to make me fear my own telephone. I didn't want the notion of him to make any difference to me – echoes, echoes. And anyway, I couldn't bring myself to describe the call. If I put it into words, it would sound flat and neutral. What was it but a series of silences punctuated by heaving and gasping? Who would understand the great gap between what it was and how it made me feel? Perhaps it *had* been Victor. He would ring soon and say shamefacedly "look, about the other night…"

But my biggest fear was that the policeman logging the call down in the large ledger of misdemeanours would look at me and know that I too have been a caller in my time.

I rang your number first as an experiment, simply to see if I could. And I was curious too, about your other life. The Wife, the Two Daughters, the Baby. *She* answered.

"809682, hello?"

I heard the sun in her voice; it spoke to me of gaiety and ease. I saw a blonde woman, hair scraped back in a workaday ponytail (that you might later loosen), a floral dress, bare legs and sandals. She was slightly out of breath as if she had run in from the garden. In the background a child was wailing. She said "excuse me" and put her hand over the mouthpiece.

"Emily," I heard her say, "give Rachel the teddy. You must learn to share."

"Hello?" she said again slightly crossly, returning to me.

I put the phone down swiftly.

Of course, it didn't stop there. Curiosity knows no boundaries. The first call had rewarded me with your daughters' names – you had always referred to them as The Children, an anonymous troop of foot soldiers. But then, I suppose my name was never uttered in your household.

I picked times when I knew you wouldn't be there. You see, it was not you I wanted, but your world. Sometimes, Emily – or was it Rachel? – answered. They would deliver your number in a piping voice before the receiver was taken away. I got to know the sounds of your house. Your doorbell has chimes.

Your hallway has no carpet – I have heard the tinny crash of toys falling on a hard surface. The television is in a room close to the phone. I have heard its muffled explosions, the clatter and boom of cartoons before your wife says: "Emily, *please* shut the door."

He rang again. Same time. He's a creature of habit. This time I was awake. I had come in from a party – yes, I'm getting out now, mixing, meeting people. I was making coffee. There was a vague drumming in my temples that would later become a hangover. I was still in my finery, or some of it. I had kicked off my shoes and was removing my earrings when the phone trilled. I lifted the receiver and knew immediately it was him. The quality of *his* silence is different; it is the silence of ambush. This time I said nothing, remembering with shame my response the first time, my babbling concern for Victor which had exposed me as a stupid woman who didn't recognize an obscene call even in the middle of it. I thought too that if I said nothing, *he* would be forced to speak.

As time went by, I got more adventurous, or desperate. I rang once at three a.m. – the witching hour! Nothing malicious, I promise; I simply wanted to hear your voice. You answered almost immediately. There must be another phone by the bed. You must have been awake. Perhaps you had just made love to her and you were having a cigarette, resting the ash-tray on your chest and blowing smoke rings into the air, your arm lazily around her shoulder. This, I know.

"Hello?" you said.

"Larry," I heard her whisper "who is it?"

Larry, she calls you Larry.

And then, there was another sound. The gurgling of a baby, the drowsy, drugged stirrings of a child suckling. The night feed.

"Don't know," I heard you say thoughtfully.

Was that suspicion in your voice?

I imagined you withdrawing your arm from around her

"Just a wrong number," I heard you say before the line went dead.

They say you should laugh at flashers. Cut them down to size, literally. But with a caller, my caller, it was more difficult. He operated on my imagination. I wondered what he did in the phone-box. (I always thought of him in a phone-box though he could have been ringing from the comfort of his own home.) I imagined him fumbling with his fly as I answered, then rubbing himself, abandoning himself to his own grim joy while I listened. He wanted me – anyone – to listen. And what did he get out of it? Horror, fear, abuse maybe. Perhaps that's what drove him on. That was another thing; he never seemed to reach a climax. Maybe he couldn't and that was his problem. Or maybe my silence, my intent listening inhibited him.

I remember once hearing my mother make love. She had been out and came home late. I heard the scrape of the key in the hall. The stairs creaked. The loose floorboard on the landing, which I knew how to avoid, groaned. My mother giggled. I imagined her leading someone by the hand, a blind man not familiar with the obstacles of our house – the low chest on the landing, the laundry basket that held the bathroom door ajar. He stumbled against something.

"Sssh," she urged, "the children!"

I lay, stiff with wakefulness, as they went into her room. A thin wall separated us. In the darkness I manufactured pictures. A skirmish in a cobbled square, her bed a high-sprung carriage rocked by a baying crowd. A cry! My mother's, sharp and high. Has someone hurled a stone?

The crowd sets to with more vigour, heaving pushing. She cries again but it is muffled as if she's being thrown against the coach's soft upholstery. I hear the tramp of boots on oily cobbles – left, right, left, right – the icy whip of bayonets, the vicious sheen of blades. A groan. He staggers; she cries out "no!". I hammer with my fists against the wall. Stop, stop!

I rang the night of the party. New Year. Tradition, you said, we always have a crowd in. You looked at me ruefully.

"I'd much prefer to be with you, you know that." You shrugged.

I called close to midnight. A guest answered. I felt safe to speak your name.

"Hold on," she said gaily, "I'll get Laurence. Laurence… phone for you."

The receiver was put down. For several minutes I was a gatecrasher at your party. Oh, how festive it sounded! There was a noisy crescendo of conversation, the ring of laughter, a male voice above the din calling plaintively "the opener, has anyone seen the bottle opener?"

I saw plates of steaming food being handed across a crowded room, glasses foaming at the rim, streamers trailing from your hair.

"Hello!" you cried triumphantly – several drinks on. "Excuse the noise. Party!"

I could have spoken then but I didn't. What would I have said? Happy New Year from a well-wisher. No, then you would have known the power I had over you, the power to betray *you*.

"Oops," I heard a woman cry, "careful!"

*

I didn't, of course, betray you. But knowing that I could changed things. I had to stop ringing for fear I would blurt it out – our secret. The snatched moments, the meetings in pubs, the subterfuge. Instead, I have to admit, I went to your home. Just once. Once was enough.

It was at night. I took the train. I crossed the metal bridge at your station imagining your gaze on its familiar struts. The stationmaster snoozed in his booth, his chin resting on his soiled uniform. He didn't check my ticket. This made me feel invisible, convinced me that I wasn't really doing this – making a pilgrimage to the shrine of your home. You see, even at the height of what I felt for you I realized how foolish I'd become. As I trod down the leafy passage leading from the station I heard the singing of the rails as another train approached, the train my sensible self would have boarded for the city. But it pulled away without her; there was no going back now. I picked my way through the quiet, darkening streets. It was late spring, fragrant after rain. Petals floated in the kerbside puddles. A fresh breeze soughed in the trees. I passed the lighted windows of other homes. Their warm rosy rooms were on display. Sometimes I glimpsed a family tableau. A father in an armchair, one child on his lap, another perched on the armrest. A granny with a walking frame and sagging face – a stroke victim, I guessed – being hauled to her feet by a young woman plump with goodness. Two blonde girls sitting cross-legged on a window seat plaiting one another's hair.

You live on a high, sloping avenue overlooking the bay. The lights of the city jostled on the skyline, beacons flooding the water with silent messages, mouthing like goldfish. I approached your house like a thief, with darting looks up and down the street. I cringed at the creak of the gate, slipping quickly around it to hide behind a large oak, the only tree in the garden. There was a muddied bare patch at its base as if it had sheltered others before me and I knew I would find hearts and arrows carved on its trunk. Your house stands on its own. Pleasing, symmetrical, five windows around an arched doorway. It was ablaze with light. I must have stood there for hours growing chilled and stiff as the night closed in, the sky turning to indigo. The swift stealth of the moon threw the garden into relief.

I was rewarded – finally. The front door opened. An orange beam of light flooded down the path. I peered from my fronds of shadow. And then your voice.

"… and then it's straight to bed!"

You were holding the hand of a dark-haired child of about five. Rachel, or at least I decided it was Rachel.

"Amn't I a good girl, Daddy, amn't I?"

"Yes, of course you are."

"Am I your favourite?"

A dog bounded down the garden. I froze. You never told me you had a dog. He frisked on the lawn and Rachel whooped delightedly.

"Look, Daddy, look at Brandy! (Brandy – what a name for a dog. Why didn't you go the whole hog and call it Hennessy?) Brandy trailed towards the gate.

"Brandy, Brandy," you called.

I stiffened, fearing the dog would smell the stranger in your midst and would expose me, panting victoriously at my feet. I imagined you finding me there, cowering in the undergrowth. How could I explain? There was no explanation except that I wanted to see you. I held my breath, terrified. You were close now. I could smell *you*, but it seemed that I had stood there for so long that my odour of fear and longing had been taken up by the very veins of the leaves and belonged now to the garden itself. Rachel saved me.

"Daddy," she wailed, "Daddy, where are you? I can't see you."

"It's all right, darling, I'm here."

"Daddy?"

"It's okay." You halted, a hair's breadth away. "I'm still here."

You turned away and walked into a sudden of shaft of moonlight. Seeing you thus, I ached to be discovered, to share in the tenderness you saved for this little girl. The dog scampered up the path ahead of you. Rachel rushed out of the gloom and clung to your waist. You lifted her up and carried her inside drawing the train of light in after you. The door closed.

I was alone, shut out where I belonged, in the pit of the garden.

I've told all this to my caller. I've named him Larry in your honour. I've had to battle against his groaning and heaving but I've persisted. He keeps ringing so it must do something for him. It's therapy for me, you could say. Therapy, indeed! I can see you wrinkle your nose disdainfully. I needed to tell someone. I needed to tell *you* but he's a good second best. I address the noisy static that is his frustration. I am happier that he is not listening exclusively to me. I could not bear undivided attention.

Last week I threw your number away. The paper on which it was written was yellowed and grubby and ragged along the folds. The ink had almost faded away. I found it had lost its power. Does this mean I'm cured? Of you, perhaps.

THE DESERTER'S SONG

Peter Murphy

Peter Murphy is a writer, spoken-word performer, musician and journalist from Wexford. He is the author of two novels, *John the Revelator*
and *Shall We Gather at the River.* He has released two spoken-word/
music albums with the Revelator Orchestra, *The Sounds of John the
Revelator* and *The Brotherhood of the Flood*, and currently performs
as Cursed Murphy Versus the Resistance.

*"When I deserted, when you found me here, you watched me come
through the woods. You thought, 'Who is this mad man?' You didn't know
I had deserted. That in the middle of the night I had left camp. Left my
rifle and my rations behind, wandered off. Left my fucking rations behind.
I stumbled along the path, you said, with my hands out. Like I was looking
for my mind."*

The Kill God – Eoghan Rua Finn

Now it so happened time's lightning forked, and there came to be the
time you know of and the time that you do not. My story happens in
the time that you do not. A bad time in our history, the land was torn
apart. Civil war had bared its jaws. Across the territories, unbelievers torching
churches, libraries, burning holy relics, fragments of our culture, remnants of
the past. Books and songs and painted pictures, microfilm, religious icons and
reliquaries. Compendiums. Illustrated manuscripts. Gold and silver rings and
torcs and ornaments. Every class of article that might proclaim our nation
sovereign among all the nations of the former West.

My name is Walter Ellison. I was the youngest in my crew, sixteen winters
borne the day I joined the fight against the philistine. Impressment sergeants
placed me with a reclamation squad. We were charged with excavating precious
artefacts, conveying them to refuge camps. I'd left my family in the hinterlands.
My father was an animal who brutalised me every hour I lived until the day
I told him he would never beat on me or Ma again. He came upon me, belt
pulled from its loops. I drew across him with my fist and down he went. Did
not rise again. Nor never would. I fled my home. My town. My mother's cries.
I hear them yet.

On a mission in the former border towns, a dig near Mangan's Hill, my fingers come on something in the dirt. I gouged it from the char. It was a half-burnt book. I called out to the sergeant and the sergeant came. Careful, near in wonderment, he took it from my hands and brought it to his tent. I followed in his footsteps. Sergeant bid me sit. He said this book was very old. He said this book was precious freight. What will we do with it? says I. He looked at me askance. Well, what? says I again.

My comrades stripped me to the waist. They took the book apart and corseted my middle with the disassembled pages, which they masked with bandages, and then they soiled the bandages with muck. Sergeant said we must have words alone. He instructed me to make my way towards the rebel camp north of Loch Cormorant. Three days by the crow. Confederate command had built an archive there. A sort of ark. Says the sergeant, if them heathens stop you at the tolls, you'll know what to say. You are this book's custodian now. Protect it with your blood. Then he called my comrades to my side and said our brother here is very brave. My comrades clapped me on the back and said I had the courage of a wolf.

The blood was heavy in my head that hour I set off on the track. A boy of sixteen year, abroad alone in a war-torn land. The highways swamped with muck. The sky gone black with birds in frenzy, circling for their carrion. I walked into the gloom of day, girded with resolve.

Maybe five clicks out I came upon a crossroads and I saw a raven pecking at a body in a ditch, pecking out its eye, swallowing its eye. I took so scared I retched. I took a slug of water from my canteen and I steeled myself and on I went. Soon after that I came upon a bombed-out shelter then I came upon a massive crater in a field then I came upon a shallow river and I crossed. Mire to my waist. Filthy. Slimy too. Rainbow-hued with oil. I scrubbed myself with grass and leaves and set off once again.

Presently I came upon a shanty sprawl, lean-to shacks of tin and plyboard huts. A tract of landfill heaped with burner phones, computer hardware, plastic waste, beggars hunting scrap. Bonfires crackled, smelting plastic from the precious metal detritus. Children dangled magnets tied to string, scavenging the last few bits of iron shavings overlooked.

Just beyond this shanty sprawl I saw a blockade on the way ahead. The heathens' crossing place. I joined the line. The roiling of my guts. The trembling of my hands. We shuffled through the checkpoint. Heathens ordered me to step out of the road. Questioned me. I told them what the sergeant told me to repeat, but like a fool I talked too long. On I prattled full of details of my injuries, the circumstances which involved the bombing of a tavern in the former bordertowns. Lord I could not stop my mouth. The heathen on the toll booth was about to let me pass only the other called me back. He cast his eyes over my person and commanded me to open up my pack. He rummaged through my personals. Unscrewed my flask and sniffed.

'Remove your shirt,' he said.

'Sir if it's all the same to you I'd rather not.'

He poked me with his Armalite. The leer of him. I'd barely balls enough to cup. I did as bid. He tugged my bandages. He said the dressing looked professional. What was the medic's name, he said, the one who treated me? I said I did not know his name I did not ask his name. 'Remove the bandage,' said the heathen, leering still. Everything was quiet as I peeled the bandage from my waist. But I was clever, see. I'd placed the pages of the book inside the lining of my flask to save them from the waters I had crossed.

'You're nothing much to look at, scut,' the heathen said. 'Be on your way.'

I put my flask back in my pack and walked into the afternoon, rattled but intact. Walked until the afternoon come dusk. Walked until I came upon a wood. There I sat upon a stump and rolled myself a smoke. Pondered on the road ahead. Thought about the rebel camp. How far it was. Drew deep upon my smoke. Then something detonated in my skull, and in its wake, pure dark.

I came to in a bombed-out chapel in the woods. My head felt halfway split. A throb behind the eyes. Before me, hunched over a fire, a man as burly as an ox and shaven bald. He wore a uniform and combat boots. My flask was at his feet. He'd taken it apart. What was he feeding to the fire but the pages of the half-burnt book. I hollered, Sir, that book is precious freight. Ye what, he said, as if in wonder at my insolence. That book is part of history, I said. He did not answer, only recommenced to feeding pages to the flames. Never mind this book, he said at last, when every page was burnt. History is lies. Nothing to be gotten from it, boy. The dead are parasites, leeching off the rest of us who walk the earth. Fuck the dead. It's time to write another book.

That's how I come to know the Butcher Colvin. I was yet a callow lad. Under his captaincy I came to be a man. He was like a father to me all the last days of the war I served in his command. Aye, but Colvin trained me well. Taught me to endure the freezing rivers. Taught me how to shoot. To kill. Made me run until I vomited. Cured me of my callowness and cauterised my heart. Aye, the Butcher Colvin made me hard as coal. Said that I would thank him should the heathen capture me and keep me in a cage. Said that I would thank him for the hatred he instilled in me, the poison that infused my veins.

The things we seen them times. Burned onto the retina. The starving people in the towns. The bodies rotting in the fields. Awful images. Pluck out my eyes.

I recall the day we came on Loftus Hall, an automated relay station for the comsat feed from generals in Kill. Nothing left inside but banks of static screens. Me and Colvin combed the debris, scavenging for salvage, copper, circuitry. Then he sent me down the bunker, underground, some class of storage cell, cool and dry. I strafed it with my light and then I saw them: human memory stems. Each stem was represented by a photographic avatar, a serial number and a name. But the avatars were melted, warped somehow. Twisted faces, screams encased in glass. Reminded me of foetuses in jars. Hideous perversions. Colvin called down: anything below?

'Nothing boss. Just junk.'

I raised my rifle, busted up them stems, got out of there as fast I could. Sunlight prickled on my skin like I was coming up on drugs. That night I dreamed of human souls trapped in an electronic hell.

Colvin did not give a fig for books or artefacts. He only cared for war, but when the fight against the philistine was lost he said that we must leave our warring ways behind. He said that we must find another way to serve our gods. We burned our uniforms. Rid ourselves of everything we owned. Even our names. Everything except that ring he wore. That ring, it was a precious article, he said, accorded him by generals in the war. I said I'll bear that ring my captain, give it to me, I will keep it safe. I kept my word. I wore it in a pouch around my neck. I bore his secret like a woman bears a child. I kept his true name in my mouth, under my tongue.

Sometimes Colvin left me tending camp for days. Sometimes weeks. One night in summer, I had been alone so long I thought I might go mad, I heard the heathens' drums strike up, the fear came on me bad. I knew they'd crucify me if they found our camp. I took so scared I fled the fire, left my rifle and my rations, all I had. Wandered through the woods. Out of my mind.

You saw me then. Stumbling, clawing at the air. You crept up on me like a girl would creep up on a hurted dog. You asked me who I was, from whence I came. I would not tell you, not at first. I kept my silence. But you held my hand and quieted my nerves. Offered me your name, Annie Cassidy. You asked me where my camp was situated and you led me there. Lay beside me 'til I slept. Fed me nuts and sloes and berries when I woke.

In time we grew familiar in those woods, like feral children, brother, sister, man and wife. And as the days went by I felt as though to keep a secret from you was betrayal of a kind, and this foolish notion loosened up my tongue, and God forgive me, I revealed the name of Butcher Colvin, and I made you swear never to tell. You swore upon your life you never would.

For a time we dwelled together happily enough, each contented in the other's company. I even dared to speculate the Butcher Colvin dead. Then one morning I awoke to see him standing by our campfire, wreathed in smoke, an apparition made incarnate before god, a figure from a myth, peering at us like some human owl.

'Take your ease,' he told me. 'She can stay. There's safety in the pack.'

Did he suspect you knew his name? I think he did. Maybe he reasoned it was best to keep you near. Times I saw him watching me, and watching you as well, out of the corner of his eye. He must've known. I'm certain of it, Annie, certain now, but hindsight is a cursed useless gift.

Then came the autumn day the Butcher Colvin took off to the hills to scout for game. We could not eat 'til he returned. That was his command, sovereign and sworn. We are kin, he said, and like a family we must eat together always. We must never eat alone. This is how we heal our tribe. We stitch humanity together, meal by meal.

God help me, I enforced his order to the word. Obeyed him like a soldier. That is what he trained me to become. A servile dog.

We waited but he never came. A day. Two days. A week. Two weeks. You begged me. Hunger drove us mad. I was hardy in my bones and you were slight. You were dying of starvation, Annie, and I watched you starve. I tried to comfort you. I talked about the house I'd build for us. I talked about the bread we'd bake. I said I'd keep you safe and warm. I told you we would never know the hunger nor the drought again. I told you I'd be with you always, and I promised he'd return, and he'd have food, and we'd eat together then.

He never came. I watched you weaken. Listened to you moan. I hear it yet. I hear your voice in every breath I draw. It haunts me day and night. This is what he made of me. From this day out I will not eat. Nor will I speak your name. I will not speak at all. I will only write this down. Cut out my tongue.

THE HUNGRY DEATH

Rosa Mulholland

> **Rosa Mulholland** (1841–1921) was a Belfast-born writer who published novels, novellas, dramas and poems, including *Narcissa's Ring*, *Marcella Grace*, *A Fair Emigrant* and *The Story of Ellen*. She wrote several short story collections, including *The Walking Trees and Other Tales*, *The Haunted Organist of Hurly Burly and Other Stories* and *Marigold and Other Stories*.

I

It has been a wild night in Innisbofin, an Irish island perched far out among Atlantic breakers, as the bird flies to Newfoundland. Whoever has weathered an ocean hurricane will have some idea of the fury with which the tempest assaults and afflicts such lonely rocks. The creatures who live upon them, at the mercy of the winds and waves, build their cabins low, and put stones on the roof to keep the thatch from flying off on the trail of Mother Carey's chickens; and having made the sign of the cross over their threshold at night, they sleep soundly, undisturbed by the weird and appalling voices which have sung alike the lullaby and death-keen of all their race. In winter, rain and storm are welcome to rage round them, even though fish be frightened away, and food be scarce; but when wild weather encroaches too far upon the spring, then threats of the "hungry death" are heard with fear in its mutterings.

Is any one to blame for this state of things? The greater part of the island is barren bog and rock. No shrub will grow upon it, and so fiercely is it swept by storm that the land by the northern and eastern coasts is only a picturesque wilderness, all life sheltering itself in three little thatched villages to the south. The sea is the treasury of the inhabitants, and no more daring hearts exist than those that fight these waves, often finding death in their jaws; but a want of even the rudest piers as defence against the Atlantic makes the seeking of bread upon the waters a perilous, and often an entirely impossible, exploit.

Bofin is of no mean size, and has a large population. Light-hearted and frugal, the people feel themselves a little nation, and will point out to you with pride the storied interest of their island. In early ages it was a seat of learning, witness the ruins of St. Coleman's school and church; in Elizabeth's day the queen, Grace O'Malley, built herself a fort on a knoll facing the glories of the western sky; and on the straggling rocks which form the harbour Cromwell raised those blackened walls, still welded into the rock and fronting the foam. The island has a church, a school, a store where meal, oil, soap, ropes, etc., can be had, except when contrary winds detain the hooker which plies to and from Galway with such necessaries.

Foreign sailors, weather-bound in Bofin, are welcomed, and invited to make merry. Pipers and fiddlers come and go, and, when times are pretty good, are kept busy making music for dancing feet. Even when the wolf is within a pace of the door laughter and song will ring about his ears, so long as the monster can be beaten back by one neighbour from another neighbour's threshold. But there comes a day when he enters where he will, and the bones of the people are his prey.

Last night's was a spring storm, and many a "Lord, have mercy on us!" went up in the silent hours, as the flooding rain that unearths the seedlings was heard seething on the wind; yet Bofin wakened out of its nightmare of terror green and gay, birds carolling in a blue sky, and the ring of the boat-maker's hammer suggesting peace and prosperity.

Through the dazzling sunshine a girl came rowing herself in a small boat that darted rapidly along the water. The oars made a quick pleasant thud on the air, the larks sang in the clouds, and the girl poured out snatches of a song of her own in a plaintive and mellow voice. The tune was wild and mournful; the words Irish.

Thud, thud, went the oars, the girl's kerchief fell back from her head as the firm elastic figure swayed with the wholesome exercise. Never was a fairer picture of health, strength, and beauty. Her thick, dark red hair filled with the sunshine as a sponge fills with water; her red-brown eyes seemed to emit sparks of fire as the shadows deepened round them in the strong light. Two little round dimples fixed at the corners of the proud curved mouth whis- pered a tale of unusual determination lying at the bottom of a passionate nature. There was nothing to account for her curious choice of a song this brilliant morning, except the love of dramatic contrasts that exists in some eager souls. Suddenly she shipped her oars, and sat listening to the waves lapping the edges of the seaweed-fringed cliffs. "I thought I heard some one calling me," she muttered, looking up and down with a slight shudder, but a bold gaze—"Brigid, Brigid, Brigid!" then, with a little laugh, she dipped her oars again, burst into a lively song, so reeling with merriment that it was wonderful how she found breath for it, and her boat flew along the glittering waves like a gull.

Above the broad, shelving, shingly beach within the harbour stood the school, the store, and some of the best dwellings on the island, and high and dry on the gleaming shingle the boat-maker was at work with a knot of gossips around him. The sky over their heads was a vivid blue; the brown-fringed rocks loomed against a sea almost too dazzling to look upon; the dewy green fields lay like scattered emeralds among the rocks and hollows.

"Lord look to us!" said a man in a sou'-wester hat, "if the spring doesn't mend. Half my pratees was washed clane out o' the ground last night."

"Whisht, man, whisht," said the boat-maker cheerfully. "Pick them up an' put them in again."

"Bedad," said an old fisherman, "the fish has got down to the bottom of all etarnity. Ye might as well go fishin' for mermaids."

"Aren't yez ashamed to grumble," cried a hearty voice, joining the group, "an' sich a mornin' as this? I tell ye last night was the last o' the rain."

"Ye have the hopes o' youth about ye, Coll Prendergast," said the old fisherman, looking at the strong frame and smiling bronzed face of the young man before him. "If yer words is not truth it's the sayweed we'll be atin' afore next winther's out."

"Some of it doesn't taste so bad," said Coll, laughing, "an' a little of it dried makes capital tabaccy. But whisht! If here isn't Brigid Lavelle, come all the way from West Quarter in her pretty canoe."

The sound of oars had been heard coming steadily nearer, and suddenly Brigid's boat shot out from behind a mass of rock, making, with its occupant, such a picture on the glittering sea that the men involuntarily smiled as they shaded their eyes with their hands to look. Resting on her oars she smiled at them in return, while the sunshine gilded her oval face, as brown as a berry, burnished the copper-hued hair rippling above her black curved brows, and deepened the determined expression of her full red mouth. Her dress, the costume of the island, was only remarkable for the freshness and newness of its material,—a deep crimson skirt of wool, with a light print bodice and short tunic, and a white kerchief thrown over the back of her head.

As she neared the shore Coll sprang into the water, drew her canoe close to the rocks, and, making it fast, helped her to land.

"That's a han'some pair," said the old fisherman to the boat-maker. "I hear their match is as good as made."

"Coll's in luck," said the other. "A rich beauty is not for ivery man."

"She's too proud, I'm thinking. Look at the airs of her now, an' him wet up to the knees in her sarvice."

"Ye'r' ould, man, an' ye forget yer coortin.' Let the crature toss her head while she can."

Brigid had proceeded to the store, where her purchases were soon made: a sack of meal, a can of oil, a little tea and sugar, and some white flour. The girl had a frown on her handsome brows as she did her business, and took but little notice of Coll, who busied himself gallantly with her packages. When all were stored in the boat he handed her in, and stood looking at her, wondering if she would give him a smile in return for his attentions.

"Let me take the oars, Brigid. Ye'll be home in half the time."

"No, thank ye," she answered shortly. "I'll row my own boat as long as I can."

Coll smiled broadly, half amused and half admiring, and again sought for a friendly glance at parting, but in vain. The face that vanished out of his sight behind the cliff was as cold and proud as though he had been her enemy. After he had turned and was striding up the beach the look that he had wanted to see followed him, shot through a rift in the rocks, where Brigid paused and peered with a tenderness in her eyes that altered her whole face. If Coll had seen that look this story might never have been written.

As the girl's boat sped past the cliffs towards home she frowned, thinking how awkward it was that she should have met Coll Prendergast on the beach. He must have known the errand that brought her to the store, and how dare he smile at her like that before he knew what answer she would give him? Coll's uncle and Brigid's father had planned a match between the young people, and the match-making was to be held that night at Brigid's father's house. Therefore had she come early in the morning in her boat to the store, to buy provisions for the evening's entertainment. Obedience to her father had obliged her to do this, but her own strong will revolted from the proceeding. She was proud, handsome, and an heiress, and did not like to be so easily won.

Brigid's father was sitting at the fire—a consumptive-looking man, with a wistful and restless eye.

"Father, I have brought very little flour. The hooker hasn't got in."

"Sorra wondher, an' sich storms. 'Tis late in the year for things to be this ways."

Brigid arranged her little purchases on the dresser and sat down at the table, but her breakfast, a few roasted potatoes and a tin mug of butter-milk, remained untasted before her.

"Father, isn't you an' me happy as we are? Why need I marry in sich a hurry?"

"Because a lone woman's betther with a husband, my girl."

"I'm not a lone woman. Haven't I got you?"

"Nor for long, avourneen machree. I'm readyin' to go this good while."

"But I will hold you back," cried Brigid passionately, throwing her strong arms around his neck.

"You can't, asthoreen. I'm wanted yonder, and it's time I was gettin' on with my purgatory. An' there's bad times comin', an' I will not let you face them alone."

"I could pack up my bundles and be off to America," said Brigid stoutly, dashing away tears.

"I will not have you wanderin' over the world like a stray bird," said the father emphatically; and Brigid knew there was nothing more to be said.

Lavelle's prosperity appeared before the world in a great deal of clean whitewash outside the house, and an interior more comfortable than is usual on the island. The cabin consisted of two rooms: the kitchen, with earthen floor and heather-lined roof, roosting-place for cocks and hens, and with its dresser, old and worm-eaten, showing a fair display of crockery; and the best room, containing a bed, a few pictures of sacred subjects, some sea-shells on the chimney-piece, an ornamental tray, an old gun, and an ancient time-blackened crucifix against the wall, this last having been washed ashore one morning after the wreck of a Spanish ship. This was the finest house in Bohn, and Tim Lavelle, having returned from seeing the world and married late in life, had settled down in it, and on the most fertile bit of land on the island. It was thought he had a stockingful of money in the thatch, which would of course be the property of his daughter; so no wonder if the handsome Brigid had grown up a little spoiled with the knowledge of her own happy importance.

As she went about her affairs this morning, she owned to herself that she would not be sorry to be forced to be Coll's wife in spite of her pride. True he had paid her less court hitherto than any other young man on the island, and she longed to punish him for that; but what would become of her if she saw him married to another? Oh, if they had only left the matter to herself she could have managed it so much better—could have plagued him to her heart's content, and made him anxious to win her by means of the difficulties she would have thrown in his way. Had Coll been as poor as he seemed to be, with nothing but his boat and fishing-tackle, she would have been easier to woo, for then eagerness to bestow on him the contents of that stocking in the thatch would have swept away the stumbling-block of her pride. But his uncle had saved some money, which was to be given to Prendergast on the day of his marriage with her. It was a made-up match like Judy O'Flaherty's, while Brigid's proud head was crazed on the subject of being loved for her love's sake alone.

"I'll have to give him my hand to-night," she said, folding her brown arms, and standing straight in the middle of the room she had been dusting and decorating. "I be to obey father, an' I'll shame nobody afore the neighbours. But match-makin' isn't marryin'; and if it was to break my heart an' do my death I'll find means to plague him into lovin' me yet."

Having made this resolve she let down her long hair, that looked dark bronze while she sat in the corner putting on her shoes, and turned to gold as she walked through a sunbeam crossing the floor, and having brushed it out and twisted it up again in a coil round her head, she finished her simple toilet and went out to the kitchen to receive her visitors.

The first that arrived was Judy O'Flaherty, an old woman with a smoke-dried face, who sat down in the chimney corner and lit her pipe. Judy was arrayed in a large patchwork quilt folded like a shawl, being too poor to indulge in the luxury of a cloak. But the quilt, made of red-and-white calico patches, was clean, and the cap on her head was fresh and neat.

"I give ye joy of Coll Prendergast," said Judy heartily. "Ye ought to be the glad girl to get sich a match."

"Why ought I be glad?" asked Brigid angrily. "It's all as one may think."

"Holy Mother, girl! don't be sendin' them red sparks out o' yer eyes at me! Where d'ye see the likes o' Coll, I'm askin', with his six feet if he's an inch, an' his eyes like the blue on the Reek afore nightfall?"

Brigid's heart leaped to hear him praised, and she turned away her face to hide the smile that curled her lips.

"An' yer match so aisy made for ye, without trouble to either o' ye. Not like some poor cratures, that have to round the world afore they can get one to put a roof over their heads or a bit in their mouths. It's me that knows. Sure wasn't I a wanderin' bein', doin' day's works in the mountains, and as purty a girl as you, Miss Brigid, on'y I hadn't the stockin' in the thatch, nor the good father to be settlin' for me. An' sore an' tired an' spent I was when one night I heard a knock at the door o' the house I was workin' in, and a voice called out: 'Get up, Judy; here's a man come to marry you!' Maybe I didn't dress quick; an' who was there but a woman that knew my mother long ago, an' she had met a widow-man that wanted somebody to look after his childer. An' she brought him to me, an' wakened me out o' my sleep for fear he'd take the rue. An' we all sat o'er the fire for the rest o' the night to make the match, and in the first morning light we went down to Father Daly and got married. There's my marriage for ye, an' the rounds I had to get it, an' many a wan is like me. An' yet ye'r' tossing yer head at Coll, you that hasn't as much as the trouble o' bein' axed."

The smile had gone off Brigid's face. This freedom from trouble was the very thing that troubled her. She would rather have had the excitement of being "axed" a hundred questions. As they talked the sunshine vanished, and the rain again fell in torrents. Brigid looked out of the door with a mischievous hope that the guests might be kept at home and the matchmaking postponed. Judy rocked herself and groaned:

"Oh, musha, the piatees, the piatees! O Lord, look down with mercy on the poor!" then suddenly became silent, and began telling her beads.

A slight lull in the storm brought the company in a rush to the door, with bursts of laughter, groans for the rain and the potatoes, shaking and drying of cloaks and coats, and squealing and tuning up of pipes. Among the rest came Coll, smiling and confident as ever, with an arch look in his eyes when they met Brigid's, and not the least symptom of fear or anxiety in his face. Soon the door was barred against the storm, the fish-oil lamp lighted, laughter, song, and dancing filled the little house, and the rotting potatoes and the ruinous rains were forgotten as completely as though the Bofin population had been goddesses and gods, with whose nectar and ambrosia no such thing as weather could dare to interfere.

"Faith, ye must dance with me, Brigid," said Coll, after she had refused him half-a-dozen times.

"Why must I dance with you?"

"Oh, now, don't ye know what's goin' on in there?" said Coll roguishly, signing towards the room where father and uncle were arguing over money and land.

"I do," said Brigid, with all the red fire of her eyes blazing out upon him. "But, mind ye, this match-makin' is none o' my doin'."

"Why then, avourneen?"

"I'm not goin' to marry a man that on'y wants a wife, an' doesn't care a pin whether it's me or another."

"Bedad, I do care," said Coll awkwardly. " I'm a bad hand at the speakin', but I care entirely."

But Brigid went off, and danced with another man.

Coll was puzzled. He did not understand her in the least. He was a simple, straightforward fellow, and had truly been in love with Brigid—a fact which his confident manner had never allowed her to believe. Latterly he had begun to feel afraid of her; whenever he tried to say a tender word, that red light in her eyes would flash and strike him dumb. He had hoped that when their "match was made" she would have grown a little kinder; but it seemed she was only getting harsher instead. Well, he would try and hit on some way to please her; and, as he walked home that night, he pondered on all sorts of plans for softening her proud temper and satisfying her exacting mind.

On her side, Brigid saw that she had startled him out of his ordinary easy humour, and, congratulating herself on the spirit she had shown, resolved to continue her present style of proceeding. Not one smile would she give him till she had, as she told herself, nearly tormented him to death. How close she was to keep to the letter of her resolution could not at this time be foreseen.

Every evening after this Coll travelled across half the island to read some old treasured newspaper to the sickly Lavelle, and bringing various little offerings to his betrothed. Everything that Bofin could supply in the way of a love-gift was sought by him, and presented to her. Now it was a few handsome shells purchased from a foreign sailor in the harbour, or it was the model of a boat he had carved for her himself; and all this attention was not without its lasting effect. Unfortunately, however, while Brigid's heart grew more soft, her tongue only waxed more sharp, and her eyes more scornful. The more clearly she perceived that she would soon have to yield, the more haughty and capricious did she become. Had the young man been able to see behind outward appearances he would have been thoroughly satisfied, and a good deal startled at the vehemence of the devotion that had grown up and strengthened for him in that proud and wayward heart. As it was, he felt more and more chilled by her continued coldness, and began to weary of a pursuit which seemed unlikely to be either for his dignity or his happiness.

Meanwhile the rain went on falling. The spring was bad, the summer was bad, potatoes were few and unwholesome, the turf lay undried, and rotting on the bog. Distress began to pinch the cheerful faces of the islanders, and laughter and song were half drowned in murmurs of fear. At the sight of so much sorrow and anxiety around her Brigid's heart began to ache, and to smite and reproach her for her selfish and unruly humours. One night, softened by the sufferings of others, she astonished herself by falling on her knees and giving humble thanks to Heaven for the undeserved happiness that was awaiting her. She vowed that the next time Coll appeared she would put her hand in his, and let the love of her heart shine out in the smiles of her eyes. Had she kept this vow it might have been well with her, but her habit of vexing had grown all too strong to be cured in an hour. At the first sight of her lover's anxious face in the doorway all her passion for tormenting him returned.

It was an evening in the end of May; the day had been cold and wet, and as dark as January, but the rain had ceased, the clouds had parted, and one of those fiery sunsets burst upon the world that sometimes appear unexpectedly in the midst of stormy weather. In Bofin, where the sun drops down the heavens from burning cloud to cloud, and sinks in the ocean, the whole island was wrapped in a crimson flame. Brigid stood at her door, gazing at the wonderful spectacle of the heavens and sea, looking herself strangely handsome, with her bronze hair glittering in the ruddy sunlight, and that dark shadow about her eyes and brows which, except when she smiled, always gave a look of tragedy to her face. She was waiting for Coll, with softened lips and downcast eyes, and was so lost in her own thoughts that she did not see when he stood beside her.

He remained silently watching her for a few moments, thinking that if she would begin to look like that he would be ready to love her as well as he had ever loved her, and to forget that he had ever wearied of her harassing scorn. At this very moment Brigid was rehearsing within her mind a kind little speech which was to establish a good understanding between them.

"I'm sorry I vexed you so often, for I love you true," were the words she had meant to speak; but suddenly seeing Coll by her side the habitual taunt flew involuntarily to her lips.

"You here again!" she said disdainfully. "Then no one can say but you're the perseverin'est man in the island!"

"Maybe I'm too perseverin'," said Coll quietly, and, as Brigid looked at him with covert remorse, she saw something in his face that frightened her. His expression was a mixture of weariness and contempt. He was not hurt, or angry, or amused, as she had been accustomed to see him, but tired of her insolence, which was ceasing to give him pain. A sudden consciousness of this made Brigid turn sick at heart, and she felt that she had at last gone a little too far, that she had been losing him all this time while triumphantly thinking to win him. Oh, why could she not speak and say the word that she wanted to say? While this anguish came into her thoughts her brows grew darker than ever, and the warmth ebbed gradually out of her cheek. They went silently into the house, where Brigid took up her knitting, and Coll dropped into his seat beside Lavelle. The bad times, the rotting crops, the scant expectations of a harvest, were discussed by the two men while Brigid sat fighting with her pride, and trying to decide on what she ought to say or do. Before she had made up her mind Coll had said goodevening abruptly, and gone out of the house.

The young fisherman's home was in Middle Quarter Village, a cluster of grey stone cabins close to the sea, and, to reach it, Coll had to cross almost the whole breadth of the island. He set out on his homeward walk with a weary and angry heart. Brigid's dark, unyielding face followed him, and he was overwhelmed by a fit of unusual depression. He whistled as he went, trying to shake it off. Why should he fret about a woman who disliked him, and who probably loved another whom her father disapproved? Let her do what she liked with herself and her purse. Coll would persecute her no more.

The red light had slowly vanished off the island, and the dark cliffs on the oceanward coast loomed large and black against the still lurid sky. Deep drifts of brown and purple flecked with amber swept across the bogs, and filled up the dreary horrors of the barren and irreclaimable land, which Coll had to traverse on his way to the foam-drenched village where the fishermen lived. The heavens cooled to paler tints, a ring of yellow light encircled the island with its creeping shadows and ghost-like rocks. Twilight was descending when Coll heard a faint cry from the distance, like the call of a belated bird or the wail of a child in distress.

At first he thought it was the wind or a plover, but straining his eyes in the direction whence it came he saw a small form standing solitary in the middle of a distant hollow, a piece of treacherous bog, dangerous in the crossing except to knowing feet. Hurrying to the spot, he found himself just in time to succour a fellow-creature in distress.

Approaching as near as he could with ease to the person who had summoned him, he saw a very young girl standing gazing towards him with piteous looks. She was small, slight, poorly and scantily clad, and carried a creel full of sea-wrack on her slight and bending shoulders. A pale after-gleam from the sky fell where she stood, young and forlorn, in the shadowy solitude, and lit up a face round and delicately pale, reminding one of a daisy; a wreath of wind-tossed yellow hair and eyes as blue as forget-me-nots. Terror had taken possession of her, and she stretched out her hands appealingly to the strong man, who stood looking at her from the opposite side of the bog. Coll observed her in silence for a few moments. It seemed as if he had known her long ago, and that she belonged to him; yet if so it was in another state of existence, for he assured himself that she was no one with whom he had any acquaintance. However that might be, he was determined to know more of her now, for, with her childlike appealing eyes and outstretched hands, she went straight into Coll's heart, to nestle there like a dove for evermore.

"Aisy, asthoreen," cried Coll across the bog, "I'm goin' to look after ye. Niver ye fear."

He crossed the morass with a few rapid springs, and stood by her side.

"Give me the creel, avourneen, till I land it for ye safe."

A few minutes, and the burden was deposited on the safe side of the bog, and then Coll came back and took the young girl in his arms.

"Keep a good hoult round my neck, machree."

It was a nice feat for a man to pick his way through the bog with even so small a woman as this in his arms. The girl clung to him in fear, as he swayed and balanced himself on one sure stone after another, slipping here and stumbling there, but always recovering himself before mischief could be done. At last the deed was accomplished, the goal was won.

"Ye were frightened, acushla," said Coll tenderly.

"I was feared of dhrownin' ye," said the girl, looking wistfully in his face with her great blue eyes.

"Sorra matther if ye had," said Coll laughingly, "except that maybe ye'd ha' been dhrowned too. Now which ways are ye goin'? And maybe ye'd be afther tellin' me who ye are."

"I'm Moya Maillie," said the girl; "an' I live in Middle Quarter Village."

"Why, ye'r' niver little Moya that I used to see playing round poor Maillie's door that's dead an' gone? And how did ye grow up that ways in a night?"

"Mother says I'll niver grow up," laughed Moya; "but I'm sixteen on May mornin', and I'll be contint to be as I am."

"Many a fine lady would give her fortune to be contint with that same," said Coll, striding along with the creel on his shoulders, and glancing down every minute at the sweet white-flower-like face that flitted through the twilight at his side. Thus Brigid's repentance would now come all too late, for Coll had fallen in love with little Moya.

How he brought her home that night to a bare and poverty-stricken cabin in the sea-washed fishing village, and restored her like a stray lamb to her mother, need not be told. Her mother was a widow and the mother of seven, and Moya's willing labour was a great part of the family support. She mended nets for the fishermen, and carried wrack for the neighbours' land, knitted stockings to be sent out to the great world and sold, and did any other task which her slender and eager hands could find to do. Coll asked himself in amazement how it was that having known her as a baby he had never observed her existence since then. Now an angel, he believed, had led her out into the dreary bog to stand waiting for his sore heart on that blessed day of days. And he would never marry anyone but little Moya.

It was impossible they could marry while times were so bad, but, every evening after this, Moya might be seen perched on an old boat upon the shingle, busy with her knitting—her tiny feet, bare and so brown, crossed under the folds of her old worn red petticoat, with a faint rose-pink in her pale cheeks, and a light of extraordinary happiness in her childlike blue eyes. Coll lay on the shingle at her feet, and these two found an elysium in each other's company. There was much idleness perforce for the men of Bofin at this time, and Coll filled up his hours looking after the concerns of the Widow Maillie, carrying Moya's burdens, and making the hard times as easy for her as he could. When people would look surprised at him and ask, "Arrah, thin, what about Brigid Lavelle?" Coll would answer, "Oh, she turned me off long ago. Everybody knows that she could not bear the sight of me."

In the meantime Brigid, at the other end of the island, was watching daily and hourly for Coll's reappearance. As evening after evening passed without bringing him, her heart misgave her more and more, and she mourned bitterly over her own harshness and pride. Oh, if he would only come once again with that wistful, questioning look in his brave face, how kindly she would greet him, how eagerly put her hand in his grasp! As the rain rained on through the early summer evenings there would often come before sunset a lightening and brightening all over the sky, and this was the hour at which Brigid used to look for her now ever-absent lover. Climbing to the top of the hill, she would peer over the sea-bound landscape, with its dark stretches of bog, and strips and flecks of green, towards the grey irregular line of the fishing village, the smoke of which she could see hanging against the horizon. Her face grew paler and her eyes dull, but to no one, not even to her father, would she admit that she was pining for Coll's return. She had always lived much by herself, and had few gossiping friends to bring her news. At last, unable to bear the suspense any longer, she made an excuse of business at the store on the beach;

and before she had gone far among the houses of that metropolis of the island, she was enlightened as to the cause of her lover's defection.

"So ye cast him off? So ye giv' him to little Moya Maillie?" were the words that greeted her wherever she turned. She smiled and nodded her head, as if heartily assenting to what was said, and content with the existing state of things; but as she walked away out of the reach of observing eyes, her face grew dark, and her heart throbbed like to burst in her bosom. Almost mechanically she took her way home through the Middle Quarter Village, with a vague desire to see what was to be seen, and to hear whatever was to be heard. She passed among the houses without observing anything that interested her, but, as she left the village, by the sea-shore she came upon Coll and Moya sitting on a rock in the yellow light of a watery sunset, with a mist of sea-foam around them, and a net over their knees which they were mending between them. Their heads were close together, and Coll was looking in her face with the very look which, all these tedious days and nights, Brigid had been wearying to meet. She walked up beside them, and stood looking at them silently with a light in her eyes that was not good to behold.

"Brigid," said Coll, when he could bear it no longer, "for Heaven's sake, are ye not satisfied yet?"

She turned from him and fixed her strange glance on Moya.

"It was me before, an' it's you now," she said shortly. "He's a constant lover, isn't he?"

"I loved ye true, and ye scoffed and scorned me," said Coll gently, as the gleam of anguish and despair in her eyes startled him. "I wasn't good enough for Brigid, but I'm good enough for Moya. We're neither of us as rich nor as clever as you, but we'll do for one another well enough."

Brigid laughed a sharp sudden laugh, and still looked at Moya.

"For Heaven's sake take that wicked look off her face!" cried Coll hastily. "Whatsomdever way it is betune us three is yer own doin'; an', whether ye like it or not, it cannot now be helped."

"I will never forgive either of you," said Brigid in a low hard voice; and then, turning abruptly away, she set out on her homeward walk through the gathering shadows.

II

All through that summer the rain fell, and, when autumn came in Bofin, there was no harvest either of fuel or of food. The potato-seed had been, for the most part, washed out of the earth without putting forth a shoot, while those that remained in the ground were nearly all rotted by a loathsome disease.

The smiling little fields that grew the food were turned into blackened pits, giving forth a horrid stench. Winter was beginning again, the year having been but one long winter, with seas too wild to be often braved by even the sturdiest of the fishermen, and the fish seeming to have deserted the island. Accustomed to exist on what would satisfy no other race, and to trust cheerfully to Providence to send them that little out of the earth and out of the sea, the people bore up cheerfully for a long time, living on a mess of Indian meal once a day, mingled with such edible seaweed as they could gather off the rocks. So long as shop-keepers in Galway and other towns could afford to give credit to the island, the hooker kept bringing such scanty supplies as were now the sole sustenance of the impoverished population. But credit began to fail, and universal distress on the mainland gave back an answering wail to the hunger-cry of the Bofiners. It is hard for any one who has never witnessed such a state of things to imagine the condition of ten or twelve hundred living creatures, on a barren island girdled round with angry breakers; the strong arms among them paralyzed, first by the storms that dash their boats to pieces, and rend and destroy their fishing gear, and the devastation of the earth that makes labour useless, and later by the faintness and sickness which come from hunger long endured, and the cold from which they have no longer a defence. Accustomed as they are to the hardships of recurring years of trial, the Bofiners became gradually aware that a visitation was at hand for which there had seldom been a parallel. Earth and sea alike barren and pitiless to their needs, whence could deliverance come unless the heavens rained down manna into their mouths? Alas! no miracle was wrought, and after a term of brave struggle, hope in Providence, cheerful pushing off the terrible fears for the worst—after this, laughter, music, song, faded out of the island; feet that had danced as long as it was possible now might hardly walk, and the weakest among the people began to die. Troops of children that a few months ago were rosy and sturdy, sporting on the sea-shore, now stretched their emaciated limbs by the fireless hearths, and wasted to death before their maddened mothers' eyes. The old and ailing vanished like flax before a flame. Digging of graves was soon the chief labour of the island, and a day seemed near at hand when the survivors would no longer have strength to perform even this last service for the dead.

Lavelle and his daughter were among the last to suffer from the hard times, and they shared what they had with their poor neighbours; but in course of time the father caught the fever which famine had brought in its train, and was quickly swept into his grave, while the girl was left alone in possession of their little property, with her stocking in the thatch and her small flock of "beasts" in the field. Her first independent act was to despatch all the money she had left by a trusty hand to Galway to buy meal, in one of those pauses in the bad weather which sometimes allowed a boat to put off from the island. The meal arrived after long, unavoidable delay, and Brigid became a benefactor to numbers of her fellow-creatures. Late and early she trudged from village to village and from house to house, doling out her meal to make it go as far as possible, till her own face grew pale and her step slow, for she stinted her own food to have the more to give away. Her "beasts" grew lean and dejected. Why should she feed them at the expense of human life? They were killed, and the meat given to her famishing friends. The little property of the few other well-to-do families in like manner melted away, and it seemed likely that "rich" and poor would soon all be buried in one grave.

In the Widow Maillie's house the famine had been early at work. Five of Moya's little sisters and brothers had one by one sickened and dropped upon the cabin floor. The two elder boys still walked about looking like galvanized skeletons, and the mother crept from wall to wall of her house trying to pretend that she did not suffer, and to cook the mess of rank-looking sea-weed, which was all they could procure in the shape of food. Coll risked his life day after day trying to catch fish to relieve their hunger, but scant and few were the meals that all his efforts could procure from the sea. White and gaunt he followed little Moya's steps, as with the spirit of a giant she kept on toiling among the rocks for such weeds or shell-fish as could be supposed to be edible. When she fell Coll bore her up, but the once powerful man was not able to carry her now. Her lovely little face was hollow and pinched, the cheek bones cutting through the skin. Her sweet blue eyes were sunken and dim, her pretty mouth purple and strained. Her beauty and his strength were alike gone.

Three of the boys died in one night, and it took Coll, wasted as he was, two days to dig a grave deep enough to bury them. Before that week was over all the children were dead of starvation, and the mother scarcely alive. One evening Coll made his way slowly across the island from the beach carrying a small bag of meal which he had unexpectedly obtained. Now and again his limbs failed, and he had to lie down and rest upon the ground; but with long perseverance and unconquerable energy he reached the little fishing village at last. As he passed the first house Brigid Lavelle, pallid and worn, the spectre of herself, came out of the door with an empty basket. Coll and she stared at each other in melancholy amazement. It was the first time they had met since the memorable scene on the rocks many months ago, for Coll's entire time had been devoted to the Maillies, and Brigid had persistently kept out of his way, striving, by charity to others, to quench the fire of angry despair in her heart. Coll would scarcely have recognized her in her present deathlike guise, had it not been for the still living glory of her hair.

The sight of Coll's great frame, once so stalwart and erect, now stooping and attenuated, his lustreless eyes, and blue cold lips, struck horror into Brigid's heart. She uttered a faint sharp cry and disappeared. Coll scarcely noticed her, his thoughts were so filled with another; and a little further on he met Moya coming to meet him, walking with a slow uneven step, that told of the whirling of the exhausted brain. Half blind with weakness she stretched her hands before her as she walked.

"The hungry death is on my mother at last. Oh, Coll, come in and see the last o' her!"

"Whisht, machree! Look at the beautiful taste o' male I am bringin' her. Hard work I had to carry it from the beach, for the eyes o' the cratures is like wolves' eyes, an' I thought the longin' o' them would have dragged it out o' my hands. An', Moya, there's help comin' from God to us. There's kind people out in the world that's thinkin' o' our need. The man that has just landed with a sack, an' giv' me this, says there's a hooker full o' male on its road to us this day. May the great Lord send us weather to bring it here."

"I'm feared—I'm feared it's too late for her," sobbed Moya, clinging to him.

They entered the cabin where the woman lay, a mere skeleton covered with skin, with the life still flickering in her glassy eyes. Coll put a little of the meal, as it was, between her lips, while Moya hastened to cook the rest on a fire made of the dried roots of heather. The mother turned loving looks from one to the other, tried to swallow a little of the food to please them, gasped, shuddered a little, and was dead.

It was a long, hard task for Coll and Moya to bury her, and when this was done they sat on the heather clasping each other's wasted hands. The sky was dark; the storm was coming on again. As night approached a tempest was let loose upon the island, and many famishing hearts that had throbbed with a little hope at the news of the relief that was on its way to them, now groaned, sickened, and broke in despair. Louder howled the wind, and the sea raged around the dangerous rocks towards which no vessel could dare to approach. It was the doing of the Most High, said the perishing creatures. His scourge was in His hand. Might His ever-blessed will be done.

That evening Moya became delirious, and Coll watched all night by her side. At morning light he fled out and went round the village, crying out desperately to God and man to send him a morsel of food to save the life of his young love. The suffering neighbours turned pitying eyes upon him.

"I'm feared it's all over with her when she can't taste the sayweed any more," said one.

"Why don't ye go to Brigid Lavelle?" said another. "She hasn't much left, poor girl; but maybe she'd have a mouthful for you."

Till this moment Coll had felt that he could not go begging of Brigid; but, now that Moya's precious life was slipping rapidly out of his hands, he would suffer the deepest humiliation she could heap upon him, if only she would give him so much food as would keep breath in Moya's body till such time as by Heaven's mercy the storm might abate, and the hooker with the relief-meal arrive.

Brigid was alone in her house. A little porridge for some poor creature simmered on a scanty fire, and the girl stood in the middle of the floor, her hands wrung together above her head, and her brain distracted with the remembrance of Coll as she had seen him stricken by the scourge. All these months she had told her jealous heart that the Maillies were safe enough since they had Coll to take care of them. So long as there was a fish in the sea he would not let them starve, neither need be in any danger himself. And so she had never asked a question about him or them. Now the horror of his altered face haunted her. She had walked through the direst scenes with courageous calm, but this one unexpected sight of woe had maddened her.

A knock came to the door which at first she could not hear for the howling of the wind; but when she heard and opened there was Coll standing before her.

"Meal," he said faintly—"a little meal, for the love of Christ! Moya is dying."

A spasm of anguish and tenderness had crossed Brigid's face at the first words; but at the mention of Moya her face darkened.

"Why should I give to you or Moya?" she said coldly. "There's them that needs the help as much as ye."

"But not more," pleaded Coll. "Oh, Brigid, I'm not askin' for myself. I fear I vexed ye, though I did not mean it. But Moya niver did any one any harm. Will you give me a morsel to save her from the hungry death?"

"I said I niver would forgive either o' ye, an' I niver will," said Brigid slowly. "Ye broke my heart, an' why wouldn't I break yours?"

"Brigid, perhaps neither you nor me has much longer to live. Will ye go before yer Judge with sich black words on yer lips?"

"That's my affair," she answered in the same hard voice; and then, suddenly turning from him, shut the door in his face.

She stood listening within, expecting to hear him returning to implore her, but no further sound was heard; and, when she found he was gone, she dropped upon the floor with a shriek, and rocked herself in a frenzy of remorse for her wickedness.

"But I cannot help every one," she moaned; "I'm starving myself, an' there's nothin' but a han'ful o' male at the bottom o' the bag."

After a while she got up, and carried the mess of porridge to the house for which she had intended it, and all that day she went about, doing what charity she could, and not tasting anything herself. Returning, she lay down on the heather, overcome with weakness, fell asleep, and had a terrible dream. She saw herself dead and judged; a black-winged angel put the mark of Cain on her forehead, and at the same moment Coll and Moya went, glorified and happy, hand in hand, into heaven before her eyes. "Depart from me, you accursed!" thundered in her ears; and she started wide awake to hear the winds and waves roaring unabated round her head.

Wet and shivering she struggled to regain her feet, and stood irresolute where to go. Dreading to return to her desolate home, she mechanically set her face towards the little church on the cliffs above the beach. On her way to it she passed prostrate forms, dying or dead, on the heather, on the roadside, and against the cabin walls. A few weakly creatures, digging graves, begged from her as she went past, but she took no notice of anything, living or dead, making straight for the church. No one was there, and the storm howled dismally through the empty, barn-like building. Four bare, whitewashed walls, and a rude wooden altar with a painted tabernacle and cross—this was the church. On one long wall was hung a large crucifix, a white, thorn-crowned Figure upon stakes of black-painted wood, which had been placed there in memory of a "mission" lately preached on the island; and on this Brigid's burning eyes fixed themselves with an agony of meaning. Slowly approaching it she knelt and stretched out her arms, uttering no prayer, but swaying herself monotonously to and fro. After a while the frenzied pain of remorse was dulled by physical exhaustion, and a stupor was stealing over her senses, when a step entering the church startled her back to consciousness. Looking round, she saw that the priest of the island had come in, and was wearily dragging himself towards the altar.

Father John was suffering and dying with his people. He had just now returned from a round of visits among the sick, during which he had sped some departing souls on their journey, and given the last consolation of religion to the dying. His own gaunt face and form bore witness to the unselfishness which had made all his little worldly goods the common property of the famishing. Before he had reached the rails of the altar Brigid had thrown herself on her face at his feet.

"Save me, father, save me!" she wailed. "The sin of murther is on my soul!"

"Nonsense, child! No such thing. It is too much that you have been doing, my poor Brigid! I fear the fever has crazed your brain."

"Listen to me, father. Moya is dying, an' there is still a couple o' han'fuls of male in the bag. Coll came an' asked me for her, an' I hated her because he left me, an' I would not give it to him, an' maybe she is dead."

"You refused her because you hated her?" said the priest. "God help you, my poor Brigid. 'Tis true you can't save every life; but you must try and save this one."

Brigid glanced at him, brightly at first, as if an angel had spoken, and then the dark shadow fell again into her eyes.

The priest saw it.

"Look there, my poor soul," he said, extending a thin hand towards the Figure on the cross. "Did *He* forgive His enemies, or did He not?"

Brigid turned her fascinated gaze to the crucifix, fixed them on the thorn-crowned face, and, uttering a wild cry, got up and tottered out of the church.

Spurred by terror lest her amend should come too late, and Moya be dead before she could reach her, she toiled across the heather once more, over the dreary bogs, and through the howling storm. Dews of suffering and exhaustion were on her brow as she carefully emptied all the meal that was left of her store into a vessel, and stood for a moment looking at it in her hand.

"There isn't enough for all of us," she said, "an' some of us be to die. It was always her or me, her or me; an' now it'll be me. May Christ receive me, Moya, as I forgive you." And then she kissed the vessel, and put it under her cloak.

Leaving the house, she was careless to close the door behind her, feeling certain that she should never cross the threshold again, and, straining all her remaining strength to the task, she urged her lagging feet by the shortest way to the Middle Quarter Village. Dire were the sights she had to pass upon her way. Many a skeleton hand was outstretched for the food she carried; but Brigid was now deaf and blind to all appeals. She saw only Coll's accusing face and Moya's glazing eyes staring terribly at her out of the rain-clouds. Reaching the Maillies' cabin, she found the door fastened against the storm.

Coll was kneeling in despair by Moya, when a knocking at the door aroused him. The poor fellow had prayed so passionately, and was in so exalted a state, that he almost expected to see an angel of light upon the threshold, bringing the food he had so urgently asked for. The priest had been there and was gone, and the neighbours were sunk in their own misery; why should any one come knocking like that unless it were an angel bringing help? Trembling he opened the door; and there was Brigid, or her ghost.

"Am I in time?" gasped she, as she put the vessel of food in his hand.

"Ay," said Coll, seizing it. In his transport of delight he would have gone on his knees and kissed her feet; but before he could speak she was gone.

Whither should she go now? was Brigid's thought. No use returning to the desolate and lonesome home, where neither food nor fire was any longer to be found. She dreaded dying on her own hearthstone alone, and faint as she was she knew what was now before her. Gaining the path to the beach, she made a last pull on her energies to reach the whitewashed walls, above which her fading eyes just dimly discerned the cross. The only face she now wanted to look upon again was that thorn-crowned face, which was waiting for her in the loneliness of the empty and wind-swept church. Falling, fainting, dragging herself on again, she crept within the shelter of the walls. A little more effort, and she would be at His feet. The struggle was made, blindly, slowly, desperately, with a last rally of all the passion of a most impassioned nature; and at last she lay her length on the earthen floor beneath the cross. Darkness, silence, peace, settled down upon her. The storm raved around, the night came on, and when the morning broke Brigid was dead.

Mildly and serenely that day had dawned, a pitiful sky looked down on the calamities of Bofin, and the vessel with the relief-meal sailed into the harbour. For many even then alive the food came all too late, but to numbers it brought assuagement and salvation. The charity of the world was at work, and though much had yet to be suffered, yet the hungry death had been mercifully stayed. Thanks to the timely help, Moya lived for better times, and when her health was somewhat restored she emigrated with Coll to America. Every night in their distant backwoods hut they pray together for the soul of Brigid Lavelle, who, when in this world, had loved one of them too well, and died to save the life of the other.

AWAY FROM IT ALL

Val Mulkerns

Val Mulkerns (1925–2018) was a novelist, short story writer and journalist. Her novels include *A Time Outworn*, *A Peacock Cry*, *The Summerhouse* and *Very Like a Whale*, and the story collections *Antiquities*, *An Idle Woman*, *A Friend of Don Juan*, *Memory and Desire*, and a memoir *Friends with the Enemy*.

'It's a public beach,' she said, amused at his annoyance.

'It's ours,' he insisted, stubbornly. '*They* are Trá na Fuinseoige people. They should go there and stay there.'

They were, of course, though it was no argument. It was a stiff climb over the rocks to get to this particular place and people with small children did not come here as a rule. You would sometimes find the odd lone camper here, like the French boy last year, but mostly only lovers came. If you found people in one sandy cove, you simply climbed over to the next one, and there you might have been at the world's end. It was she who had first shown him this remote western peninsula, her place of childhood summers. Now his air of outraged ownership both touched and irritated her.

'I know him by sight,' she said suddenly, raising herself on one elbow to peer through sunglasses at the fat father. The man was loud as well as large in an orange-striped T-shirt, and going bald like Timothy himself. It seemed strange for somebody of his years to have small children. Then suddenly she blushed to find herself putting words on that random impression. If Timothy and she married, Timothy and anybody for that matter, his children would be equally small playing on just such a beach.

'He's one of the O'Donnells,' she offered. 'Spent years over in Bradford or somewhere and learned all about wool. He's manager of the new factory now.'

'With an English wife,' Timothy said disapprovingly, as a sharp voice called to the children. Younger than her husband, she was fair-haired and passive, fully dressed still and knitting in the sun. The small boy and girl, already in swimsuits, were kicking a red ball to one another at the waves' edge.

'She looks nice,' Sarah said firmly. 'Happy.'

He turned restlessly over on the rug and grunted. 'Since *they* won't go away, why don't we? Over those rocks there's a beautiful empty beach just waiting for us. Come on, love. Have our swim there.' He was already on his feet, tugging at the rug, but Sarah felt stubborn and she did not approve of his disapproval.

'I'm staying here,' she said. 'You go over there for your swim if you like,'

'Alone?' His dependent eyes, the first of his features she had ever noticed, were full of sun and reproach. The thin top of his head was beginning to look angry so she rummaged out her sun cream.

'Bend down.' He did this obediently and she rubbed in the cream. Then he kissed her, mollified, and they lay back peacefully in the sun, but not for long.

'I must write to my mother,' he said. He searched in her straw bag where he had put a writing case among the sun oil and apples and togs. She knew he had been writing to his mother for all of the twenty years since the Department of Local Government had posted him to Dublin.

'What do you tell her every week?' she had often asked him, and lazily again now.

'Same old serviceable things,' he muttered, writing busily.

'She doesn't know about me, I suppose?'

'Good heavens, no.'

He had a selection of old-fashioned expressions – 'Goodness,' 'My dear girl,' 'Great Scott.' Two years ago when she had first taken him home, her own young sister had described him as 'Rather sweet really, but *un peu démodé*.' Perfect. It described the stuffy clothes, obstinately clung to when everybody else had long since abandoned good grey suits, the style of speech, the verbal courtesies, the dated blond charm of his face which reminded her of a British film star her mother had often enthused over. You saw other faces like that in Sunday night movies on Irish television. She never remembered the actors' names, but they mostly had faces like Timothy's and it always happened that ample nineteen fortyish brunettes fought one another bitterly for their favours. Sometimes she wondered if Timothy's resemblance to the heroes of her mother's youth was the reason why he had been welcomed so warmly right from the beginning – to family meals, to parties, even to Christmas dinners. Timothy's mother and sister went for Christmas to relatives in Cork, but Timothy had always preferred to stay in Dublin. Formerly he had treated himself to a hotel meal on Christmas Day; now for two years he had come to them. She found it odd to be remembering Christmas during a July heatwave.

'As I write,' she mocked him suddenly, 'the sun beats down on this jolly little beach and I wish you were here.'

'Wrong,' he said. 'Why should I wish she was here? I'd much prefer you.'

It was a glib compliment, and she had even asked 'for it, but it made her extraordinarily happy, as on the night when they were sitting in his flat before a decidedly dull television screen, with terrible reception. When he complained she said, 'You *might* have been at the office stag party. Why didn't you go?'

'Because I much prefer spending an evening with you.'

There were compensations, of course, when at last the talk died out and the pretence of watching television was mercifully over. But occasionally she would have preferred an evening out at the theatre, a restaurant, anywhere where they could be alone in a crowd. Timothy however didn't like crowds and hated the theatre. He said restaurants were dangerous places where one was likely to be poisoned unless exceptional luck prevailed.

'Yet I *did* see you one night at the St. Laurence Hotel in Howth,' she remembered, and said it aloud. 'That time Daddy suddenly took us all out to celebrate his Prize Bond.'

'Look,' Timothy said, alert, his letter laid unfinished in the breast pocket of his jacket. 'Sir Tycoon over there is about to sunbathe. Watch. Golly, he's fat.'

'You were with your sister,' Sarah remembered gently. 'I would have liked to know her.' For a second she brooded about the reason for this positive ache to know his family, his mother, his sisters, the people surrounding the unknown small boy who had been at school twenty years before she was born. He had made the introduction briefly, dutifully – 'Some good friends of mine' – but had shown no inclination for them to linger. They did not. He and his frowning oldish sister had left soon afterwards.

'Look,' Timothy said again. 'Where's the betting Mr. Man will not be left in peace for long?'

On the ebbing tide the red ball had bobbed a little out of reach of the two children, who apparently had no intention of getting too wet. The boy waded out once to his knees but the ball drifted just beyond him and he waded back, whereupon his sister whacked him with her spade. Immediately afterwards she screamed for her father, and her brother screamed at her.

'Told you so,' Timothy said. 'Now let's see what he'll do.'

'For somebody who resented the arrival of people, you're very interested in them.'

She didn't know why she felt mildly irritated with him until, made lazy by the sun, she forced herself to back-track into their exchanges, but slowly. Yes. This was something Timothy did very often. Distracted your attention when he didn't want you to question him. You might just think of asking why, if he could take his sister out to a meal, he couldn't take you too occasionally.

'Poor fellow,' he was saying now. 'Bad luck, sir.' She raised herself on one elbow again and Timothy patted her knee. She moved away, but went on watching the father and his children. The small boy and girl were frantically hopping about now, urging him on.

He had apparently been interrupted in the course of undressing because he still wore his T-shirt on top and a huge overstretched swim suit below. He stood uncertainly for a moment at the water's edge. His daughter tried to launch him, but without success. Timothy laughed delightedly.

'The ball's much further out now,' he said.

Quite suddenly Sarah found herself on the father's side. The water in the cove was icy, straight in from the Atlantic. The poor man probably had no intention of doing anything but sunbathe. She watched sympathetically as he waded out gingerly, pausing after every few steps to grip his hands under his arms. The children shrieked encouragement as he made a sudden grab at the ball, but it bobbed out of reach and he waded further in the direction of the rocky arm that divided this cove from the next. Quite suddenly, as they watched, he pulled the orange T-shirt over his head and emerged pale and pear-shaped. He turned to throw the shirt to his daughter, who didn't catch it. It floated at her feet but neither child paid any attention. Their father's movements had become crablike now in thigh-high water. He seemed at any moment about to wobble over.

'His feet are on the sharp stones now,' Sarah said, still concerned for him. 'Why on earth doesn't he swim for it?'

'He'll have to,' Timothy agreed, 'although if he doesn't get it quickly he's going to have most of his skin removed by the barnacles on those rocks. Look where the ball's going now.'

'Swim, oh swim,' Sarah said below her breath, but the children went on screaming and the man floundered on. Suddenly she understood why.

'He *can't* swim,' she said urgently. 'Look, it's absolutely certain, Timothy. He can't swim. We'll have to get it for them.'

'I'll go,' Timothy said without enthusiasm. 'You wanted to sunbathe for at least another hour before going in. I'd better go.'

Touched by his thoughtfulness, she watched him go down the beach with that loping boy's walk that belied his years. As the children cheered him she saw how he shuddered at the first touch of the water, then blessed himself as usual. Before going any further, he bent sensibly and picked up the father's T-shirt which he wrung out and gave to the small girl, pointing at her mother as an indication of what she should do. But the child stood clutching the T-shirt and Timothy waded out, after one expressive gesture in Sarah's direction concerning the coldness of the water. She waved to him and waited for the moment when he would strike out with his powerful crawl and recover the ball in no time. He continued to wade, however, though much more capably than the children's father with whom he was almost abreast.

Sarah saw the red ball bobbing closer and closer to the razor rocks, and at last touch them. She practically cried out in impatience then because Timothy could quite easily have had the ball back by now if he had started to swim at the right time. Instead he began an apparently long conversation with the children's father, gesturing at the rocks, at the ball, shrugging his shoulders, finally pointing to the ball's progress as though it no longer concerned him. They stood together in the sun, in the cold blue water, two middle-aged men in perfect agreement that nothing could be done. The small girl began suddenly to cry and hurled her father's garment further out as both men began to walk back together. Both children ran suddenly back to their mother, who had hardly suspended her knitting during the drama. Incredulous, Sarah watched as the father bent to pick up his soaked shirt and Timothy ran back to her up the beach, still shrugging and laughing. Before he reached her he turned an exuberent cartwheel on the soft sand.

'Golly, what a waste of good time!' he panted. Might as well have stayed cosily where I was, mightn't I?'

'Why didn't you swim out for the ball?' she asked, shocked by the contempt that suddenly overcame her.

'Because, my dear girl, you *saw* where it went. Hey, look at it now, firmly wedged between the spikes. Only a maniac would risk his entire coat of skin for a plastic ball whose cost is approximately forty new pence, or free with four washing powder labels.' He was laughing at her now, with all the good white teeth on display, entirely justified to himself.

There was plenty of time before it got so far,' she said. 'You just stood there, as though it didn't matter.'

'Well, does it?' he said reasonably. 'Do you think that the manager of the new wool factory is too poor to buy his brats another ball on the way home? For heaven's sake, love, what's got into you?' He towelled himself briefly and then lay down beside her, one hand on her warm leg. She shook it off stubbornly.

'It *does* matter,' she said. 'They didn't want another ball. They wanted that one, and you let them depend on you. Would you have been afraid to risk your skin if it had been one of the children? Would you?'

He laughed again, incredulous. 'Of *course* I wouldn't. You can't buy another child as easily as a red plastic ball.'

Sarah said nothing. Inexplicable tears stung her eyelids. She watched the ball as a twist of the tide carried it free of the rocks. The children ran cheering again down to the water's edge, and Timothy turned her face roughly to his. When he saw her eyes he began to laugh nervously again.

'Of all the baffling creatures—' he began, then stopped as he too saw the ball safely swept into clear water; 'So *that's* all it is. Pride. Little girl wanted a gallant princely rescue and was denied. But wait. Just watch this.'

He jumped up and this time raced away down the beach, urged on once more by the children. Sarah put a dress on rapidly over her togs and walked away up the stony track along which they had come. She wondered what on earth she would say to her mother if she arrived home a week early but she felt her young sister might understand.

LITERARY LUNCH

Éilís Ní Dhuibhne

> **Éilís Ní Dhuibhne**, from Dublin, has written almost thirty books, including six collections of short stories. Her most recent books are *Selected Stories* (Dalkey Archive, 2017) and *Twelve Thousand Days: A Memoir* (Blackstaff, 2018). Her work has won many awards. She is a member of Aosdána, an Ambassador for the Irish Writers' Centre and President of the Folklore of Ireland Society.

T he board was gathering in a bistro on the banks of the Liffey. "We deserve a decent lunch!" Alan, the chairman, declared cheerfully. He was a cheerful man. His eyes were kind, and encouraged those around him to feel secure. People who liked him said he was charismatic.

The board was happy. Their tedious meeting was over and the bistro was much more expensive than the hotel to which Alan usually brought them, with its alarming starched tablecloths and fantails of melon. He was giving them a treat because it was a Saturday. They had sacrificed a whole three hours of the weekend for the good of the organisation they served. The reputation of the bistro, which was called Gabriel's, was excellent and anyone could tell from its understated style that the food would be good, and the wine too, even before they looked at the menu: John Dory, oysters, fried herrings, sausage and mash. Truffles. A menu listing truffles just under sausage and mash promises much. We can cook and we are ironic as well, it proclaims. Put your elbows on the table, have a good time.

Emphasising the unpretentiously luxurious tone of Gabriel's was a mural on the wall, depicting a modern version of The Last Supper, a photograph of typical Dubliners eating at a long refectory table.

Alan loved this photograph, a clever, post-modern, but delightfully accessible work of art. It raised the cultural tone of the bistro, if it needed raising, which it didn't really, since it was also located next door to the house on Usher's Island where James Joyce's aunts had lived, and which he used as the setting for his most celebrated story, The Dead. In short, of all innumerable restaurants boasting literary associations in town Gabriel's had the most irrefutable credentials. You simply could not eat in a more artistic place.

*

The funny thing about The Last Supper was that everyone was sitting at one side of the table, very conveniently for painters and photographers. It was as if they had anticipated all the attention which would soon be coming their way. And Gabriel's had, in its clever ironic way, set up one table in exactly the same manner, so that everyone seated at it faced in the same direction, getting a good view of the mural and also of the rest of the restaurant. It was great. Nobody was stuck facing the wall. You could see if anyone of any importance was among the clientele – and usually there were one or two stars, at least. You could see what they were wearing and what they were eating and drinking, although you had to guess what they were talking about, which made it even more interesting, in a funny sort of way. More interactive. It was like watching a silent movie without subtitles.

A problem with the arrangement was that people at one end of the last supper table had no chance at all of talking to those at the other end. But this too could be a distinct advantage, if the seating arrangements were intelligently handled. Alan always made sure that they were.

At the right end of the table he had placed his good old friends, Simon and Paul (Joe had not come, as per usual. He was the real literary expert on the board, having won the Booker Prize, but he never attended meetings. Too full of himself. Still, they could use his name on the stationery). Alan himself sat in the middle where he could keep an eye on everyone. On his left hand side were Mary, Jane and Pam. The women. They liked to stick together.

Alan, Simon and Paul ordered oysters and truffles and pâté de foie gras for starters. Mary, Jane and Pam ordered one soup of the day and two nothings. No starter please for me. This was not owing to the gender division. Mary and Jane were long past caring about their figures, at least when out on a free lunch, and Pam was new and eager to try everything being a member of a board offered, even John Dory, which she had ordered for her main course. Their abstemiousness was due to the breakdown in communications caused by the seating arrangements. The ladies had believed that nobody was getting starters, because Alan had muttered I don't think I'll have a starter and then changed his mind and ordered the pâté de foie gras when they were chatting among themselves about a new production of A Doll's House, which was just showing at the Abbey. Mary had been to the opening, as she was careful to emphasise; she was giving it the thumbs down. Nora had been manic and the sound effects were appalling. The slam of the door which was supposed to reverberate down through a hundred years of drama couldn't even be heard in the second row of the stalls. That was the Abbey for you, of course. Such dreadful acoustics, the place has to be shut down. Pam and Mary nodded eagerly; Pam thought the Abbey was quite nice but she knew if she admitted that in public everyone would think she was a total loser who had probably failed her Leaving. Neither Pam or Mary had seen *A Doll's House* but they had read a review by Fintan O'Toole so they knew everything they needed to know. He hadn't liked the production and had decided that the original play was not much good anyway. Farvel, Ibsen!

In the middle of this conversation Pam's mobile phone began to play Waltzing Matilda at volume level five. Alan gave her a reproving glance. If she had to leave on her mobile phone she could at least have picked a tune by Shostakovich or Stravinsky. Ever mindful of his duty to the promotion of the national culture, he himself had a few bars by a young Irish composer on his phone. "Terribly sorry!" Pam said, slipping the phone into her bag, but not before she had glanced at the screen to find out who was calling. "I forgot to switch it off." Which was rather odd, Mary thought, since Pam had placed the phone on the table, in front of her nose, the minute she had come into the restaurant. It had sat there under the water jug looking like a tiny pistol in its little leather holster.

In the heel of the hunt all this distraction meant that they neglected to eavesdrop on the men while they were placing their orders so that they would get a rough idea of how extravagant they could be. How annoying it was now, to see Simon slurping down his oysters, with lemon and black pepper, and Paul digging into his foie gras, while they had nothing but *A Doll's House* and soup of the day to amuse themselves with.

And a glass of white wine. Paul, who was a great expert, had ordered that. A sauvignon blanc, the vineyard of Du Bois Père et Fils, 2002. "As nice a sauvignon as I have tried in years", he said, as he munched a truffle and sipped thoughtfully. "2002 was a good year for everything in France but this is exceptional." The ladies, much more interested in French wine than Norwegian drama, strained to hear what he was saying. Mary, who had been so exercised a moment ago about Ibsen at the Abbey, seemed to have forgotten all about both. She was now taking notes, jotting down Paul's views. He was better, much better, than the people who do the columns in the paper, she commented excitedly as she scribbled. No commercial agenda – well, that they knew of. You never quite knew what anyone's agenda was, that was the trouble. Paul was apparently on the board, because of his knowledge of books, and Simon, because of his knowledge of the legal world, and Joe, because he was famous. Mary, Jane and Pam were there because they were women. Mary was already on twenty boards and had had to call a halt, since her entire life was absorbed by meetings and lunches, receptions and launches. Luckily she had married sensibly and did not have to work. Jane sat on ten boards and Pam had been nominated two months ago. This was her first lunch with any board, ever. She was a writer. Everyone wondered what somebody like her was doing here. It was generally agreed that she must know someone.

One person she knew was Francie Briody. He was also having lunch, in a coffee shop called The Breadbasket, a cold little kip of a place across the river on Aston Quay. They served filled baguettes and sandwiches as well as coffee and he was lunching on a tuna submarine with corn and coleslaw. Francie was a writer, like Pam, although she wrote so-called literary women's fiction, chick lit for PhDs and was successful. Francie wrote literary fiction for anybody who cared to read it, which was nobody. For as long as he could remember he had been a writer whom nobody read. And he was already fifty years of age. He had written three novels and about a hundred short stories, and other bits and bobs. Success of a kind had been his lot in life, but not of a kind to enable him to earn a decent living, or to eat anything other than tuna baguettes, or to get him a seat on an arts organisation board. He had had one novel published, to mixed reviews; he had won a prize at Listowel Writers' Week for a short story fifteen years ago. Six of his short stories had been nominated for prizes – the Devon Cream Story Competition, the Blackstaff Young Authors, the William Carleton Omagh May Festival, among others. But he still had to work part time in a public house, and he had failed to publish his last three books.

Nobody was interested in a writer past the age of thirty.

It was all the young ones they wanted these days, and women, preferably young women with lots of shining hair and sweet photogenic faces. Pam. She wasn't that young any more, and not all that photogenic, but she'd got her foot in the door in time, when women and the Irish were all the rage, no matter what they looked like. Or wrote like.

He'd never been a woman – he had considered a pseudonym but he'd let that moment pass. And now he'd missed the boat. The love affair of the London houses and the German houses and the Italian and the Japanese with Irish literature was over. So everyone said. Once Seamus Heaney got the Nobel the interest abated. Enough's enough. On to the next country. Bosnia or Latvia or god knows what. Slovenia.

Francie's latest novel, a heteroglossial polyphonic postmodern examination of post-modern Ireland, with special insights into political corruption and globalisation, beautifully written in darkly masculinist ironic prose with shadows of l'écriture féminine, which was precisely and exactly what Fintan O'Toole swore that the Irish public and Irish literature was crying out for, had been rejected by every London house, big and small, that his agent could think of, and by the five Irish publishers who would dream of touching a literary novel as well, and also, Francie did not like to think of this, by the other thirty Irish publishers who believed chick lit was the modern Irish answer to James Joyce. Yes yes yes yes. The delicate chiffon scarf was flung over her auburn curls. Yes.

Yeah well.

I'll show the philistine fatso bastards.

He pushed a bit of slippery yellow corn back into his baguette. Extremely messy form of nourishment, it was astonishing that it had caught on, especially as the baguettes were slimy and slippery themselves.

Not like the home-made loaves served in the Gabriel on the south bank of the Liffey.

Alan was nibbling a round of freshly baked, soft as silk crispy as Paris on a fine winter's day roll, to mop up the oyster juice, which was sitting slightly uneasily on his stomach.

"We did a good job," he was saying to Pam, who liked to talk shop, being new.

"I'd always be so worried that we picked the wrong people," she said in her charming girlish voice. She had nice blond hair but this did not make up for her idealism and her general lack of experience. Alan wished his main course would come quickly. Venison with lingonberry jus and basil mash.

"You'd be surprised but that very seldom happens," he said.

"Judgements are so subjective vis-à-vis literature," she said, with a frown, remembering a bad review she'd received fifteen years ago.

Alan suppressed a sigh. She was a real pain.

"There is almost always complete consensus on decisions," he said. "It's surprising, but the cream always rises. I… we… are never wrong." His magical eyes twinkled.

Consensus? Pam frowned into her sauvignon blanc. A short discussion of the applicants for the bursaries in which people nudged ambiguities around the table like footballers dribbling a ball when all they want is the blessed trumpeting of the final whistle. They waited for Alan's pronouncement. If that was consensus she was Emily Dickinson. As soon as Alan said "I think this is brilliant writing" or "Rubbish, absolute rubbish" there was a scuffle of voices vying with each other to be the first to agree with the great man.

Rubbish, absolute rubbish. That was what he had said about Francie. He's persistent I'll give him that. Alan had allowed himself a smile, which he very occasionally permitted himself at the expense of minor writers. The board guffawed loudly. She hadn't told Francie that. He would kill himself. He was at the end of his tether. But she had broken the sad news over the phone in the loo, as she had promised. No bursary. Again.

"I don't know," she persisted, ignoring Alan's brush off. "I feel so responsible somehow. All that effort and talent, and so little money to go around…"

Her voice tailed off. She could not find the words to finish the sentence, because she was drunk as an egg after two glasses. No breakfast, the meeting had started at nine.

Stupid bitch, thought Alan, although he smiled cheerily. Defiant. Questioning. Well, we know how to deal with them. Woman or no woman, she would never sit on another board. This was her first and her last supper. I feel so responsible somehow. Who did she think she was?

"This is a 2001 Bordeaux from a vineyard run by an Australian ex-pat just outside Bruges, that's the Bruges near Bordeaux of course, not Bruges La Mort in little Catholic Belgium," Paul's voice had raised several decibels and Simon was getting a bit rambunctious. They were well into the second bottle of the sauvignon and had ordered two bottles of the Bordeaux, priced, he noticed, at 85 Euro a pop. The lunch was going to cost about a thousand Euro.

"Your venison sir?"

At last.

He turned away from Pam and speared the juicy game. The grub of kings.

Francie made his king-size tuna submarine last a long time. It would have anyway, since the filling kept spilling out onto the table and it took ages to gather it up and replace it in the roll. He glanced at the plain round clock over the fridge. They'd been in the there for two hours. How long would it be?

Fifteen years.

Since his first application.

Fifty.

His twelfth.

His twelfth time trying to get a bursary to write full time.

It would be the makings of him. It would mean he could give up serving alcohol to fools for a whole year. He would write a new novel, the novel which would win the prizes and show the begrudgers. Impress Fintan O'Toole. Impress Emer O'Kelly. Maybe even impress Eileen fucking Battersby. And the boost to his morale would be so fantastic… but once again that Alan Byrne, who had been running literary Ireland since he made his confirmation probably, had shafted him. He knew. Pamela had phoned him from the loo on her mobile. She had tried her best but there was no way. They had really loved his work, she said. There was just not enough money to go round. She was so sorry, so sorry…

Yeah right.

Alan was the one who made the decisions. Pamela had told him so herself. They do exactly what he says, she said. It's amazing. I never knew how power worked. Nobody ever disagrees with him. Nobody who gets to sit on the same committees and eat the same lunches anyway. As long as he was chair Francie would not get a bursary. He would not get a travel grant. He would not get a production grant. He would not get a trip to China or Paris or even the University of Eastern Connecticut. He would not get a free trip to Drumshanbo in the County Leitrim for the Arsehole of Ireland Literature and Donkey Racing Weekend.

Alan Byrne ruled the world.

The pen is stronger than the sword, Francie had learned, in school. Was it Patrick Pearse who said that or some classical guy? Cicero or somebody. That's how old Francie was, they were still doing Patrick Pearse when he was in primary. He was pre-revisionism and he still hadn't got a bursary in literature let alone got onto Aosdána, which gave some lousy writers like Pam a meal ticket for life. The pen is stronger. Good old Paddy O Piarsaigh. But he changed his mind apparently. Francie looked at the Four Courts through the corner window of the Breadbasket. Who had been in that in 1916? He couldn't remember. Had anyone? Thomas MacDonagh or Seán Mac Diarmada or some also ran whose name nobody could really remember. Burnt down the place in the end, all the history of Ireland in it. IRA of their day. That was later, the Civil War. He had written about that too. He had written about everything. Even about Alan. He had written a whole novel about him, and six short stories, but they were hardly going to find their mark if they never got published and they were not going to get published if he did not get a bursary and some recognition from the establishment and he was not going to get any recognition while Alan was running every literary and cultural organisation on the island...

At last. The evening was falling in when the board members tripped and staggered out of Gabriel's, into the light and shade, the sparkle and darkness, that was Usher's Quay. Jane and Mary had of course left much earlier, anxious to get to the supermarkets before they closed.

But Pam, to the extreme annoyance of everyone, had lingered on, drinking the Bordeaux with the best of them. They had been irritated at first but had then passed into another stage. The sexual one. Inevitable as Australian chardonnay at a book launch. They had stopped blathering on about wine and had begun to reminisce about encounters with ladies of the night in exotic locations; Paul claimed, in a high voice which had Alan looking around the restaurant in alarm, to have been seduced by a whore in a hotel in Moscow who had bought him a vodka and insisted on accompanying him to his room, she clad only in a coat of real wolfskin. Fantasy land. That eejit Pam was so shot herself she didn't seem to care what they said. Her mascara was slipping down her face and her blond hair was getting manky, as if she had sweated too much. It was high time she got a taxi. He'd shove her into one as soon as he got the other two out. He couldn't leave them here, they'd drink the board dry and if they were unlucky some journalist would happen upon them. He stopped for a second. Publicity was something they were always seeking and hardly ever got. But no, this would do them no good at all. There is such a thing as bad press in spite of what he said at meetings.

He paid the bill. There were long faces of course. You'd think he was crucifying them instead of having treated them to a lunch which had cost, including the large gratuity he was expected to fork out, 1200 Euro of National Lottery money. Oh well better than racehorses, he always said, looking at the Last Supper. Was it Leonardo or Michaelangelo had painted the original, he was so exhausted he couldn't remember. He took no nonsense for the boyos, though and asked the waiter to put them into their coats no matter how they protested.

Pam excused herself at the last minute, taking him aback.

"Don't wait for me," she said. She could still speak coherently. "I'll be grand, I'll get a taxi. I'll put it on the account."

She gave him a peck on the cheek – that's how drunk she was – and ran out the door, pulling her mobile out of her bag as she did so.

Not such a twit as all that. I'll put it on the account. He almost admired her, for a second.

With the help of the waiter he got the other pair of beauties bundled out to the pavement.

The taxi had not yet arrived.

He deposited Simon and Paul on a bench placed outside for the benefit of smokers and moved to the curb, the better to see.

Traffic moved freely along the quay. It was not as busy as usual. A quiet evening. The river was a blending delight of black and silver and mermaid green. Alan was not entirely without aesthetic sensibility. The sweet smell of hops floated along the water from the brewery. He'd always loved that, the heavy cloying smell of it, like something you'd give a two year old to drink. Like hot jam tarts. In the distance he could just see the black trees of the Phoenix Park. Sunset. Peaches and molten gold, Dublin stretched against it. The north side could be lovely at times like this. When it was getting dark.

The Wellington monument rose, a black silhouette, into the heavens, a lasting tribute to the power and glory of great men.

It was the last thing Alan saw.

He did not even hear the shot explode like a backfiring lorry in the hum of the evening city.

Francie's aim was perfect. It was amazing that a writer who could not change a plug or bore a hole in a wall with a Black and Decker drill at point blank range could shoot so straight across the expanse of the river. Well, he had trained. Practice makes perfect, they said at the creative writing workshops. Be persistent, never lose your focus. He had not written a hundred short stories for nothing and a short story is an arrow in flight towards its target. They were always saying that. Aim write fire. And if there's a gun on the table in act one it has to go off in act three, that's another thing they said.

But, laughed Francie, as he wrapped his pistol in a Tesco bag for life, in real life what eejit would put a gun on the table in act one? In real life a gun is kept well out of sight and it goes off in any act it likes. In real life there is no foreshadowing.

That's the difference, he thought, as he let the bag slide over the river wall. That's the difference between life and art. He watched the bag sink into the black lovely depths of Anna Livia Plurabelle. Patrick Pearse gave up on the peann in the end. When push came to shove he took to the lámh láidir.

He walked down towards O'Connell Bridge, taking out his mobile. Good old Pam. He owed her. Yet each man kills the thing he loves, he texted her, pleased to have remembered the line. By each let this be heard. Some do it with a bitter look, some with a flattering word. The coward does it with a kiss, the brave man with a gun. That wasn't right. Word didn't rhyme with gun. Some do it with a bitter look, some with a flattering pun. Didn't really make sense. What rhymes with gun? Lots of words. Fun, nun. Bun. Some do it with a bitter pint, some with a sticky bun, he texted in. Cheers! I'll buy you a bagel sometime. He sent the message and tucked his phone into his pocket. Anger sharpened the wit, he had noticed that before. His best stories had always been inspired by the lust for revenge. He could feel a good one coming on… maybe he shouldn't have bothered killing Alan.

He was getting into a bad mood again. He stared disconsolately at the dancing river. The water was far from transparent, but presumably the Murder Investigation Squad could find things in it. They knew it had layers and layers of meaning just like the prose he wrote. Readers were too lazy to deconstruct properly but policeman were probably pretty assiduous when it came to interpreting and analysing the murky layers of the Liffey. Would that bag for life protect his fingerprints, DNA evidence. He didn't know. The modern writer has to do plenty of research. God is in the details. He did his best but he had a tendency to leave some books unread, some websites unvisited. Writing a story, or murdering a man, was such a complex task. You were bound to slip up somewhere.

Perfectionism is fatal, they said. Give yourself permission to err. Don't listen to the inner censor.

He had reached D'Olier Street and hey, there was the 46A waiting for him. A good sign. They'd probably let him have a laptop in prison, he thought optimistically, as he hopped on the bus. They'd probably make him writer in residence.

That's if they ever found the gun.

A JOURNEY

Edna O'Brien

Edna O'Brien is an Irish novelist, memoirist and playwright who has published eight short story collections and novels, including *Night* and *A Pagan Place*. Her first novels, *The Country Girls Trilogy*, were banned in Ireland, but in 2019 were chosen as the Dublin One City One Book choice. She has won numerous awards, is a DBE and a Saoi in Aosdána.

February the twenty-second. Not far away was the honking of water fowl in the pond at Battersea Park. The wrong side of London some said, but she liked it and the pale green power station was her landmark, as once upon a time a straggle of blue hills had been. The morning was cold, the ice had clawed at the window and left its tell-tale marks – lines – long jagged lines, criss-cross scrawls, lines at war with one another, lines bent on torment. It was still like twilight in the bedroom and yet she wakened with alertness, and her heart was as warm as a little ball of knitting wool. He was deep in a trough of sleep, impervious to nudging, to hitting, to pounding. He was beautiful. His hair, like a halo, was arced around his head – beautiful hair, not quite brown, not quite red, not quite gold, of the same darkness as gunmetal but with strands of brightness. Oh Christ he'll think he's in his own house with his own woman she thought as his eyelids flickered and he peered through. But he didn't. He knew where he was and said how glad he was to be there, and drawing her towards him he held her and squeezed her out like a bit of old washing. They were off to Scotland, he to deliver a lecture to some students and later to men, fellow unionists who worked on the shipyards.

'We're going a-travelling,' she said almost doubtfully.

'Yes pet.'

At any rate he hadn't changed his mind yet. He was a great vacillator.

She made the coffee while he contemplated getting up, and from the kitchen she kept urging him, saying how they would be late, how he must please bestir himself. For some reason she was reminded of her wedding morning, both mornings had a feeling of unrealness, the same uncertainty plus her anxiety about being late. But that was a long time ago. That was over, and dry in the mouth like a pod or a desiccated cud. This was this. This man upstairs, why do I love him she thought. A working man, shy and moody and inarticulate, a man unaccustomed to a woman like her. They hardly talked. Not that speech was what mattered between people. She learnt that the very day she had accosted him in a train a few weeks before. She saw him and simply had to communicate with him, touched the newspaper he was scanning, flicked it ever so lightly with her finger, and he stared across at her and very quietly admitted her into his presence, but without a word without even a face-saving hello.

'I can't say things,' he had said and then breathed out quickly and nervously as if it had cost him a lot to admit. He was like a hound, a little whippet. It was like crossing the Rubicon. Also daft. Also dicey. A journey of pain. She had no idea then how extensive that journey would be. A good man? Maybe. Maybe not. She was looking for reasons to unlove him. When he came down he almost, but didn't smile. There was such a tentativeness to him. Is it always going to be like this she thought, spilling the coffee, slopping it in the saucer and then nervously dumping the brown granular mass from a strainer onto an ashtray.

'I have no composure,' she said. From him another wan smile. Would her buying the tickets be all right, would he look away while she paid, would it be an auspicious trip? She took his hand, and warmed it and said she never wanted to do aught else, and he said not to say such things, not to say them, but in fact they were only a skimming of the real things she was longing to say. Years divided them, class divided them, position divided them. He wanted to give her a present and couldn't in case it wasn't swish enough. He bought perfume off a hawker in Oxford Circus, offered it to her and then took it back. Probably gave it to his woman, put it down on the table along with his pay packet. Or maybe left it on a dressing table, if they had one. A tender moment? All these unknowns divided them. The morning that she was getting married, he was pruning trees in an English park, earning a smallish sum and living with a woman who had four children. He had always lived with some woman or another, but insisted that he wasn't a philanderer, wasn't. He lived with Madge, now, drank two pints of beer every evening, cuddled his baby and smoked forty cigarettes a day.

In the taxi he whispered to her, to please not look at him like that, and at the airport he spent the bulk of the waiting time in the gents. She wondered if there wasn't a barbers in there, or if perhaps, he hadn't done a disappearing act, like people on their wedding day who do not show up at the altar rails. In fact he had bought a plastic hairbrush to straighten his hair for the journey because it had got tangled in the night. Afterwards he put it in her travel bag. Did she need a travel bag? How long were they to stay? No knowing. They were terribly near and they were not near. No outsider could guess the relationship. In the plane, the hostess tried hard to flirt with him, said she'd seen him on television but he was shy and skirted the subject by asking for a light. He was very active with his union and often appeared on television debates; at private meetings he exhorted the members to rope in new ones. He had made quite a reputation for himself by reading them cases from history and clippings from old newspapers, making them realize how they had been treated for hundreds of years. He was a scaffolder like his father before him, but he left Belfast soon after his parents died. His brothers and sisters were scattered.

When they got to their destination he suddenly suggested that she dump the bag in a safety locker, and she knew then that she shouldn't have brought it, and that possibly they would not be staying overnight. Walking up the street of Edinburgh with a bitter breeze in their faces she pointed to a castle that looked like a dungeon and asked him what he thought of it. Not much. He didn't think much – that was his answer. What did he do – dream, daydream, imagine, forget. The leaves in the municipal flower-bed were blowing and shivering, mere tatters, but the soil was a beautiful flaky black. They happened to be passing a funeral parlour and she asked if he preferred burial or cremation but about that too he was tepid and indifferent. It made no matter. They should still be in bed, under covers, cogitating. She linked him and he jerked his arm saying those who knew him, knew the woman he lived with, and he would not like it to appear otherwise. They were halfway up the hill, and there was between them now, one of those little swords of silence that is always slicing love, or that kind of love.

'If Madge knew about this, she'd be immeasurably hurt,' he said.

'But Madge will know,' she thought, but did not say. She said instead that it was colder up North, that they were not far from the sea, and didn't he detect bits of hail in the wind. He saw the sadness, traced it lightly with his finger, traced the near tears and the little pouch under the lids. He said 'You're a terrible woman altogether,' to which she replied 'You're not a bad bloke,' and they laughed. He was supposed to have travelled by train the night before, the very night when he slept with her and had his hair pulled from the roots. How good a liar was he and how strong a man? He had crossed the street ahead of her and to make amends he waited for her across the road, waited by the lights, and watched her, admiring, as she came across, watched her walk, her lovely legs, her long incongruous skirt and watched the effect she had on others, one of shock as if she was undressed or carrying some sort of invisible torch. He referred to an ancient queen and her carriage.

'It's not that it's not pleasant holding your arm,' he said, and took her elbow feeling the wobble of the funny bone. Then he had to make a phone call, and soon they were going somewhere, in a taxi, and the back streets of Edinburgh were not unlike the back streets of any other town, a bit black, a bit drowsy and pub fronts being washed down.

'He's afraid of me,' she thought. 'And I'm afraid of him,' and fear is corrosive, and she felt certain that the woman he lived with was probably much more adept at living and arguing, would make him bring in the coal, or clean out the ashes or share his last cigarette, would put her cards on the table. For a moment she was seized with longing to see them together, and had a terrible idea that she would call as a travelling saleswoman with a little attaché case, full of cleaning stuffs so as she would have to go in and show her wares. She would see their kitchen and their pram and the baby in it, she would see how tuned they were to one another. But that was not necessary, because he was leaving because it had all gone dry and flaccid, between him and the woman it was all over. When he looked at her then it was a true felt look, and it was laden with sweetness, white, mesmerizing like the blossom that hangs from the cherry trees.

Before addressing the first batch of students he called on some friends. Even that was furtive, he didn't knock, but whistled some sort of code through the letter box. In the big, sparsely furnished room there was a pregnant cat, marmalade, and the leftovers of a breakfast, and a man and a woman who had obviously just tumbled out of their bed. She thought this is how it should be. When, through a crack in the kitchen door, catching a glimpse of their big tossed bed and the dented pillows without pillow-slips, she ached to go in and lie there, and she knew that the sight of it had permeated her consciousness and that it was a longing she would always feel. That longing was replaced by a stitch in the chest, then a lot of stitches, and then something like a lump in the back of the mouth, something that would not dissolve. Would he live with her like he said. Would he do it. Would he forsake everything, fear, respectability, safeness, the woman, the child? The questions were like pendulums swinging this way and that. The answers would swing too.

The woman she had just met was called Ita and the man was called Jim the Limb. He had some defect in his right arm. They were plump and radiant, what with their night, and their big breakfast and now a fresh pot of tea. They were chain smokers. Ita said her fur coat and the marmalade cat were alike, and he, her lover, said that probably that was a wrong thing to say. But there was no wrong thing as far as she was concerned. She just wanted them to welcome her in, to accept her. When they talked about the union, and the various men, and the weekly meetings, when they discussed a rally that was to take place later in London she thought, 'Let me be one of you, let me put aside my old stupid flitting life, let me take part, let me in.' Her life was not exactly soigné and she too had lived in small rooms and ridden a ridiculous bicycle, and swapped old shoes for other old shoes, but she seemed not to belong, because she had bettered herself, had done it on her own, and now that she was a graphic designer, she designed alone. Also these were towns-people, they all had lived in small steep houses, slept two or three or four to a bed, sparred, lived in and out of one another's pockets, knew familiarity well enough to know that it was the only hope. Ita announced that she was not going to the factory that morning, said dammit, the bloody sweatshop, and told him of two women who were fired because they had gone deaf from the machines and weren't able to hear proper. He said they must fight it. They were a clan. Yet, when he winked at her he seemed to be saying something else, something ambiguous, and saying 'I see you there, I am not forsaking you,' or was he saying, 'Look how influential I am, look at me.' A word he often used was big-shot. Maybe he had dreams of being a big-shot?

Just before the four of them left the house for the college he went for the third time to the lavatory and she believed he had gone to be sick. Yet when he stood on the small ladder platform, holding up a faulty loudspeaker, brandishing it, making jokes about it – calling it Big Brother he seemed to be utterly in his element. He spoke without notes, he spoke freely, telling the crowd of his background in Belfast, his father's work on the shipyards, his having to emigrate, his job in London, the lads, the way this fellow or that fellow had got nabbed, and though what he had to say was about victim-ization he made it all funny. When questions were put it was clear that he had cajoled them all, except for one dissenter, an aristocratic-looking boy in a dress suit, a boy who seemed to be on the brink of a nervous breakdown. Even with that, he dealt deftly. He replied without any venom and when the dissenter was booed and told to belt up he said 'Aach' to his friends who were heckling. The hat was passed around, a navy college cap into which coins were tossed from all corners of the room. She hesitated; not knowing whether to give a lot, or a little, and wanting only to do the right thing. She gave a pound note, and afterwards in the refectory to where they had all repaired, she saw a girl hand him ten pounds and thought how the collection must have been to foot his expenses.

Ita and Jim decided to accompany them to the next city, where he was con-ducting the same sort of meeting, in the evening, in a public hall. Getting on the station late as they did, he said 'Let's jump in here,' and ushered them into a first-class carriage. When the ticket collector came, she paid the difference, knowing that he had chosen to go in there because he felt it was where she belonged. At first they couldn't hear one another for the rattle of the train, the shunting of other carriages, and a whipping wind that lashed through a broken window. He dozed, and sometimes coming awake he nudged her with his shoe. The ladies sat on one side, the men opposite, and Ita was whispering to her, in her ear, saying when she met Jim how they went to bed for a week and how she was so sore, and finally had to have stitches. He looked at the women whispering and tittering and he seemed to like that, and there was a satisfaction in the way he rocked and dozed.

They were all hungry.

'Starving you I am,' he said to her as he asked a porter for the name of a restaurant.

'A French joint,' he decided. As they settled themselves in the drab and garish room, Ita tripped over the flex of the table lamp. Jim glowered with embarrassment, said this wasn't home, and to behave herself. They dived into the basket of bread, calling for butter, butter. He made jokes about the wine, sniffed it and asked if for sure it was the best vintage, and knowing that he was shy and awkward with his fingers she fed him her little potato sticks from her plate. He accepted them like they were matches, and then gobbled them down, and the others knew what they had suspected, that this pair were lovers, and Jim said they looked like two people in a picture and they smiled as if they were in a picture and their faces scanned one another as if in a beautiful daze. At the meeting he gave the same speech, except that it had to be shortened, and this he did by omitting one anecdote about a man who was sent to jail for speaking Gaelic in the northern province of his own country. There was a second collection and the amounts subscribed were much higher, because the bulk of the audience were working men, and proud to contribute.

Afterwards they repaired to a big ramshackle room, at the top of a big house in the north side of the city. In the hall there were hundreds of milk bottles, and in the back hall two or three bicycles jumbled together. He had bought a bottle of whiskey, and in the kitchen she heated a kettle to make a hot punch for him because his throat was sore. He came in and told her what a grand person she was, and he kissed her stealthily. The kitchen was a shambles and although at first intending to tidy it a bit, all she did was scald two cups and a tumbler for his punch. Some had hot whiskey, some had cold, whereas she had hers laced in a cup of tea.

In the ramshackle room they all talked, interrupting one another, joking, having inside conversation about meetings they'd been to, and other meetings to which they'd sent hecklers, and demonstrations that they were planning to have and all their supporters in France, Italy and throughout. She looked up at the light shade, crinkled plastic, as big as a beach ball, and with a lot of dots. She felt useless. The designs she made were simple and geometric and somewhat stark, but at that moment they seemed irrelevant. They had no relation to these people, to their conversation, to their curious kind of bantering anger. She remembered nights on end when she had striven to make a shape or a design that would go straight to the quick of someone's being, she had done it alone, and she had gruelled over it but these people would think it a bit of a joke.

The place was slovenly but still it was a place. Several brass rings had come off their hooks and the heavy velvet curtain gaped. He was being witty. Someone had said that there were more ways than one of killing a cat but he had intervened to say that it was 'skinning' a cat. That was the first flicker of cruelty that she saw in him. She was sitting next to him on the divan bed, she leaning back against the wall, slightly out of things, he pressing forward, positing the odd joke. He said that at forty he might find his true vocation in life, which was to be a whizz-kid. There was a rocking chair in which one of the men sat, and several easy chairs with stained and torn upholstery, their springs dipping down, to a variable degree depending on the weight and the colossal pranks of the sitters. Sometimes a girl with plaits would rush over and sit on her man's knee and pull his beard and then the springs dropped down like the inside of a broken melodion. If only he and she could be that unreserved.

Then he was missing, out on the landing using the phone. She knew they had missed the last plane, and long ago had missed the last train and that they would have to kip down somewhere, and she thought how awful if it had to be on a bench at a station or at a depot. Ita asked her if they were perhaps going to make a touring holiday, and she said no but couldn't add to that, couldn't gloss the reply with some extra little piece of information. When he came in he told her that a taxi was on its way.

'I don't know where we're heading for, Wonderland,' he said, shaking hands with Ita and then he said cheers to the room at large.

The hotel was close to the airport, a modern building made of concrete cubes, like something built by a child, and with vertical slits for windows. They might be turned away. He went in whistling. She waited, one foot on the step of the taxi and one on the footpath and said an involuntary prayer.

She saw him handing over money, then beckoning for her to come in. He had signed the register and in the lift, as he fondled her, he told her the false name that he had used. It was a nice name, Egan. In the bedroom they thought of whiskey, and then of milk and then of milk and whiskey, but they were too tired, and shy all over again, and neither of them was impervious enough to give an order, while the other was listening.

'I know you better now,' he said. She wondered at what precise moment in the day had he come to know her better, had he crept in on her like a little invisible camera, and knew that he knew her, and would know her for all time. Maybe some non-moment, when she walked gauchely towards the ladies' room, or when asked her second name she hesitated, in case by giving a name she should compromise him.

She apologized for not talking more, and he said that was what was lovely about her, and he apologized for giving the same lecture twice, and for all the stupid things that got said. Then he trotted around naked, getting his tiny little transistor from his overcoat pocket, studying the hotel clock – a square face laid into the bedside table – trying the various lights. He had never stayed in a hotel before, and it was then he told her that there would be a refund if in the morning they didn't eat breakfast. He had paid. His earnings for the day had been swallowed up by it.

'I'll refund you,' she said, and he said what rot, and in the dark they were together again, together like spare limbs, like rag dolls, or bits of motor car tyre, bits of themselves, together, so effortless, and so fond, and with such harmony, as if they had grown up that way, always were and always would be. But she couldn't ask. It had to come from him. He was thinking of going back home, leaving London, changing jobs. Well, wherever he went, she was going too. He had brought everything to a head, everything she had wanted to feel, love and pity and softness and passion and patience and insatiable jealousy. They went to sleep talking, then half talking, voices trailing away like tendrils, sleepy voices, sleepy brains, sleepy bodies, talking, not talking, dumb.

'I love you, I love you,' he said it the very moment that the hotel clock triggered off, and all the doubts of the previous day and the endless cups of coffee, and the bulging ashtrays were all sweet reminders of a day in which the fates changed. He said he dearly wished that they could lie there for hours on end and have coffee and papers sent up and lie there and let the bloody aeroplanes and the bloody world go by. But why were they hurrying? It was a Saturday and he had no work.

'I'll say good-bye here,' he said, and he kissed her and pulled the lapel of her fur coat up around her neck so that she wouldn't feel the cold.

'But we're going together,' she said. He said yes but they would be in a public place and they would not be able to say good-bye, not intimately. He kissed her.

'We will be together?' she said.

'It will take time,' he said.

'How long?' she asked.

'Months, years…' They were ready to go.

In the plane they talked first about mushrooms and she said how mushrooms were reputed to be magic, and then she asked him if he had wanted a son rather than a daughter, and he said no, a daughter, and smiled at the thought of his little one. He read four of the morning papers, read them, re-read them, combed the small news items that were put in at the last minute, and got printing ink all over his hands. The edges of the paper sometimes jutted against her nose, or her eye or her forehead and without turning he would say 'Sorry love'. To live with, he would be all right, silent at times, undemonstrative, then all of a sudden as touching as an infant. Every slight gesture of his, every 'Sorry love' tore at some place in her gut.

A bus was waiting on the tarmac, right next to the landed plane. He said they needn't bother rushing, and as a result they were very nearly not taken at all. In fact the steward looked down the aisle of the bus, put up a finger to say that there was room for one, and then in the end grumpily let them both enter. They had to sit separately, with an aisle between them and she began to revert to her cursed superstitions such as if they passed a white gate all would be fortunate between them.

At the terminus he had to make a phone call, and she could see him, although she had meant not to look, gesticulating fiercely in the glass booth. When he came out he was biting his thumb. After a while, he said he was late, that the woman had to stay home from work, that he was in the wrong again. She saw it very clearly, very cruelly, as clear and as cruel as the lines of ice that had claimed the window pane. Claims. Responsibility. Slogans. 'Be here be here.'

They walked up the road towards the underground station. No matter how she carried it the travel bag bumped against her, or when she changed hands, against him. He said she was never to tell anyone. She said she wasn't likely to go spouting it, and he said why the frown, why spoil everything with a frown like that. It went out like a shooting star, the sense of peace, the suffusion, the near-happiness. He asked her to hang on, while he got cigarettes, and then plunging into the dark passage that led to the underground, he saw her hesitate, and said did she always take taxis. They kissed. It was a dark unpropitious passage but a real kiss. Their mouths clung, the skins of their lips would not be parted, she felt that they might fall into a trance in order not to terminate it. He was as helpless then as a schoolboy, and his eyes as pathetic as watered ink. In some indefinable way, and whatever happened, he would be part of her for all time, an essence.

'If I must, if I must talk to you may I,' she said. He looked at her bitterly. He was like a chisel. 'I can't promise anything,' he said, and repeated it. Then he was gone, doing a little hop through the turnstile, and omitting to get a ticket. She walked on, the bag kept bumping off the calf of her leg; soon when she had enough poise she would hail a taxi. Would he go? Would he come back? What would he do? It was like a door that had just come ajar, and anything could happen to it, it could shut tight or open a fraction or fly open in a burst. She thought of the bigness and wonder of destiny, meeting him in a packed train had been a fluke, and this now was a fluke, and things would either convene to shut that door, or open it a little, or open and close it alternately, and they would be together, or not be together as life the gaffer thought fit.

TWO IN ONE

Flann O'Brien

> **Flann O'Brien** (1911–1966) was a novelist, journalist and playwright, best known for his humour and satirical work, including *At Swim-Two-Birds* and *The Third Policeman*. He wrote regular columns for the *Irish Times* and published work in Irish under the pseudonym Myles na gCopaleen.

The story I have to tell is a strange one, perhaps unbelievable. I will try to set it down as simply as I can. I do not expect to be disturbed in my literary labours, for I am writing this in the condemned cell.

Let us say my name is Murphy. The unusual occurrence which led me here concerns my relations with another man whom we shall call Kelly. Both of us were taxidermists.

I will not attempt a treatise on what a taxidermist is. The word is ugly and inadequate. Certainly it does not convey to the layman that such an operator must combine the qualities of zoologist, naturalist, chemist, sculptor, artist, and carpenter. Who would blame such a person for showing some temperament now and again, as I did?

It is necessary, however, to say a brief word about this science. First, there is no such thing in modern practice as "stuffing" an animal. There is a record of stuffed gorillas having been in Carthage in the 5th century, and it is a fact that an Austrian prince, Siegmund Herberstein, had stuffed bison in the great hall of his castle in the 16th century—it was then the practice to draw the entrails of animals and to substitute spices and various preservative substances. There is a variety of methods in use to-day but, except in particular cases—snakes, for example, where preserving the translucency of the skin is a problem calling for special measures—the basis of all modern methods is simply this: you skin the animal very carefully according to a certain pattern, and you encase the skinless body in plaster of Paris. You bisect the plaster when cast providing yourself with two complementary moulds from which you can make a casting of the animal's body—there are several substances, all very light, from which such castings can be made. The next step, calling for infinite skill and patience, is to mount the skin on the casting of the body. That is all I need explain here, I think.

Kelly carried on a taxidermy business and I was his assistant. He was the boss—a swinish, overbearing mean boss, a bully, a sadist. He hated me, but enjoyed his hatred too much to sack me. He knew I had a real interest in the work, and a desire to broaden my experience. For that reason, he threw me all the common-place jobs that came in. If some old lady sent her favourite terrier to be done, that was me; foxes and cats and Shetland ponies and white rabbits—they were all strictly *my* department. I could do a perfect job on such animals in my sleep, and got to hate them. But if a crocodile came in, or a Great Borneo spider, or (as once happened) a giraffe—Kelly kept them all for himself. In the meantime he would treat my own painstaking work with sourness and sneers and complaints.

One day the atmosphere in the workshop had been even fouler than usual, with Kelly in a filthier temper than usual. I had spent the forenoon finishing a cat, and at about lunch-time put it on the shelf where he left completed orders.

I could nearly *hear* him glaring at it. Where was the tail? I told him there was no tail, that it was a Manx cat. How did I know it was a Manx cat, how did I know it was not an ordinary cat which had lost its tail in a motor accident or something? I got so mad that I permitted myself a disquisition on cats in general, mentioning the distinctions as between *Felis manul*, *Felis silvestris*, and *Felis lybica*, and on the unique structure of the Manx cat. His reply to that? He called me a slob. That was the sort of life *I* was having.

On this occasion something within me snapped. I was sure I could hear the snap. I had moved up to where he was to answer his last insult. The loathsome creature had his back to me, bending down to put on his bicycle clips. Just to my hand on the bench was one of the long, flat, steel instruments we use for certain operations with plaster. I picked it up and hit him a blow with it on the back of the head. He gave a cry and slumped forward. I hit him again. I rained blow after blow on him. Then I threw the tool away. I was upset. I went out into the yard and looked around. I remembered he had a weak heart. Was he dead? I remember adjusting the position of a barrel we had in the yard to catch rainwater, the only sort of water suitable for some of the mixtures we used. I found I was in a cold sweat but strangely calm. I went back into the workshop.

Kelly was just as I had left him. I could find no pulse. I rolled him over on his back and examined his eyes, for I have seen more lifeless eyes in my day than most people. Yes, there was no doubt: Kelly was dead. I had killed him. I was a murderer. I put on my coat and hat and left the place. I walked the streets for a while, trying to avoid panic, trying to think rationally. Inevitably, I was soon in a public house. I drank a lot of whiskey and finally went home to my digs. The next morning I was very sick indeed from this terrible mixture of drink and worry. Was the Kelly affair merely a fancy, a drunken fancy? No, there was no consolation in that sort of hope. He was dead all right.

It was as I lay in bed there, shaking, thinking, and smoking, that the mad idea came into my head. No doubt this sounds incredible, grotesque, even disgusting, but I decided I would treat Kelly the same as any other dead creature that found its way to the workshop.

Once one enters a climate of horror, distinction of degree as between one infamy and another seems slight, sometimes undetectable. That evening I went to the workshop and made my preparations. I worked steadily all next day. I will not appall the reader with gruesome detail. I need only say that I applied the general technique and flaying pattern appropriate to apes. The job took me four days at the end of which I had a perfect skin, face and all. I made the usual castings before committing the remains of, so to speak, the remains, to the furnace. My plan was to have Kelly on view asleep on a chair, for the benefit of anybody who might call. Reflection convinced me that this would be far too dangerous. I had to think again.

A further idea began to form. It was so macabre that it shocked even myself. For days I had been treating the inside of the skin with the usual preservatives—cellulose acetate and the like—thinking all the time. The new illumination came upon me like a thunderbolt. *I would don his skin and, when the need arose, BECOME Kelly!* His clothes fitted me. So would his skin. Why not?

Another day's agonised work went on various alterations and adjustments but that night I was able to look into a glass and see Kelly looking back at me, perfect in every detail except for the teeth and eyes, which had to be my own but which I knew other people would never notice.

Naturally I wore Kelly's clothes, and had no trouble in imitating his unpleasant voice and mannerisms. On the second day, having "dressed," so to speak, I went for a walk, receiving salutes from newsboys and other people who had known Kelly. And on the day after, I was foolhardy enough to visit Kelly's lodgings. Where on earth had I been, his landlady wanted to know. (She had noticed nothing.) What, I asked—had that fool Murphy not told her that I had to go to the country for a few days? No? I had told the good-for-nothing to convey the message.

I slept that night in Kelly's bed. I was a little worried about what the other landlady would think of my own absence. I decided not to remove Kelly's skin the first night I spent in his bed but to try to get the rest of my plan of campaign perfected and into sharper focus. I eventually decided that Kelly should announce to various people that he was going to a very good job in Canada, and that he had sold his business to his assistant Murphy. I would then burn the skin, I would own a business and—what is more stupid than vanity!—I could secretly flatter myself that I had committed the perfect crime.

Need I say that I had overlooked something?

The mummifying preparation with which I had dressed the inside of the skin was, of course, quite stable for the ordinary purposes of taxidermy. It had not occurred to me that a night in a warm bed would make it behave differently. The horrible truth dawned on me the next day when I reached the workshop and tried to take the skin off. *It wouldn't come off!* It had literally fused with my own! And in the days that followed, this process kept rapidly advancing. Kelly's skin got to live again, to breathe, to perspire.

Then followed more days of terrible tension. My own landlady called one day, inquiring about me of "Kelly." I told her I had been on the point of calling on *her* to find out where I was. She was disturbed about my disappearance— it was so unlike me—and said she thought she should inform the police. I thought it wise not to try to dissuade her. My disappearance would eventually come to be accepted, I thought. My Kelliness, so to speak, was permanent. It was horrible, but it was a choice of that or the scaffold.

I kept drinking a lot. One night, after many drinks, I went to the club for a game of snooker. This club was in fact one of the causes of Kelly's bitterness towards me. I had joined it without having been aware that Kelly was a member. His resentment was boundless. He thought I was watching him, and taking note of the attentions he paid the lady members.

On this occasion I nearly made a catastrophic mistake. It is a simple fact that I am a very good snooker player, easily the best in that club. As I was standing watching another game in progress awaiting my turn for the table, *I suddenly realised that Kelly did not play snooker at all!* For some moments, a cold sweat stood out on Kelly's brow at the narrowness of this escape. I went to the bar. There, a garrulous lady (who thinks her unsolicited conversation is a fair exchange for a drink) began talking to me. She remarked the long absence of my nice Mr. Murphy. She said he was missed a lot in the snooker room. I was hot and embarrassed and soon went home. To Kelly's place, of course.

Not embarrassment, but a real sense of danger, was to be my next portion in this adventure. One afternoon, two very casual strangers strolled into the workshop, saying they would like a little chat with me. Cigarettes were produced. Yes indeed, they were plain-clothes-men making a few routine inquiries. This man Murphy had been reported missing by several people. Any idea where he was? None at all. When had I last seen him? Did he seem upset or disturbed? No, but he was an impetuous type. I had recently repri-manded him for bad work. On similar other occasions he had threatened to leave and seek work in England. Had I been away for a few days myself? Yes, down in Cork for a few days. On business. Yes… yes… some people thinking of starting a natural museum down there, technical school people—that sort of thing.

The casual manner of these men worried me, but I was sure they did not suspect the truth and that they were genuinely interested in tracing Murphy. Still, I knew I was in danger, without knowing the exact nature of the threat I had to counter. Whiskey cheered me somewhat.

Then it happened. The two detectives came back accompanied by two other men in uniform. They showed me a search warrant. It was purely a formality; it had to be done in the case of all missing persons. They had already searched Murphy's digs and had found nothing of interest. They were very sorry for upsetting the place during my working hours.

A few days later the casual gentlemen called and put me under arrest for the wilful murder of Murphy, of myself. They proved the charge in due course with all sorts of painfully amassed evidence, including the remains of human bones in the furnace. I was sentenced to be hanged. Even if I could now prove that Murphy still lived by shedding the accursed skin, what help would that be? Where, they would ask, is Kelly?

This is my strange and tragic story. And I end it with the thought that if Kelly and I must each be either murderer or murdered, it is perhaps better to accept my present fate as philosophically as I can and be cherished in the public mind as the victim of this murderous monster, Kelly. He *was* a murderer, anyway.

THE ROAD TO BRIGHTCITY

Máirtín Ó Cadhain

Máirtín Ó Cadhain (1906–1970) is one of Ireland's best-known Irish language writers of fiction. He published three novels, including the much-translated *Cré na Cille*, and many short stories in both languages. His short story collections include *An Braon Broghach*, *The Road to Brightcity*, *An Eochair / The Key* and *The Dregs of the Day*.

The cock crowing awakened Brid. She yawned and turned over, stretched and settled her head back again on the pillow. But her husband was awake too and shook her.

—The cock has crowed for the third time, he said. You'd better get up.

She was loath to leave the warm soft blankets, but having stretched her limbs again and rubbed the sleep from her eyes she jumped out. She had her new bodycoat on, the candle lit, and was raking live coals from the ashes before her husband arrived on the hearth.

—A wonder you bothered to get up, she said. You'd be time enough.

He made no answer awhile, went fumbling at the dresser.

—A right mess I made of it, he said, taking the little clock and shaking it close to his ear. —I was fully intent on winding it, still and all I went to sleep and forgot it. It's stopped at ten past two.

—May the deathrattle take it. It's four o'clock now.

—If not more.

—I'll have to be off as soon as I'm ready.

—You'd be time enough at five, leaving yourself four hours for the road. I'll slip down to Tomas's place and if young Taimin isn't up I'll wake him. He'd be great company for you, since neither Peige Sheamais nor any of the other village women is going to Brightcity.

—Taimin won't stir a foot for the next two hours most likely, since he happens to have a customer for the turf. I'll be home along with him if—

—If you don't get someone else.

—What I was going to say was, said Brid using the same wrangling tone as her husband, —if it should happen I'm ready to come home before he is and get the chance of another cart.

—A cart from the Currach. You seem to be sweet on the Currach people.

—I still know them better than I do the people of this village, she said serenely. I'm not five years here yet.

The husband was sorry to have given her that dig, small as it was.

—It's a nasty journey to Brightcity, for the little it's worth.

—What's worrying me is that it won't even be worth that much presently. In spite of all my care three of the hens stopped laying this week, and the fawn cow won't have what'll do the tea shortly. I'm afraid I won't have enough to chum again for a week—even in a fortnight's time I'll be hard put to it.

—A rest might do you no harm, he said, obviously not wishing to spell out what he meant. —You are worn out going to Brightcity one Saturday after another. It's a crucifying journey, since you can't take a jauntingcar like Maire Sheamais.

—It's crucifying enough. But there's no loss on me yet, she said offhand.

He was sorry for her, still he wasn't too pleased with her words. A strong active woman not yet past thirty! Not the way the women who had come before her used to speak. His own mother when she was a servantgirl with Liam Cathail used to go twice a day to the city with a tankard of milk, and no car to give her a lift home. Or his grandmother—she used be home from Brightcity before milking time with a hundredweight of meal on her back and with only two stops for a rest. But the women nowadays had only to go draw water from the well to be crippled with rheumatism the day after.

—I'll be alright if that woman in the Lawn laneway lets me alone, she said, deliberately disregarding his silence. Only for that I wouldn't be in nearly so much of a hurry—trying to get there before everyone else. It would hinder me on the way to market and it would be late evening when I got home.

—Don't be in any hurry home till you have the chance of a good lift. I'll see to the house.

—Like you saw to it last Saturday—the children would have been scalded by the kettle only Neil Sheamais came in. Unless you want the skin off your ears don't stir from the house till Neil comes. She said she'd be up about ten and won't need to go home till after dinner. I'll have to buy her some sort of a present for Christmas if God sends the pence. Haven't you sally rods to sharpen? Don't bother about anything else. Don't leave a pot where it's liable to topple anywhere about the house. And if Citin cries give her a sup of lukewarm milk in the bottle.

—I will, said the husband drily.

—And send the dash down to Peadar's with Neil, take care would you forget, she'll be churning today. And shift the calf from Glen Garth up to the Height—but for your life don't leave the house, not if prosperity were to knock at the door, without leaving someone to mind the children.

—I won't, he said, a shade stubborn.

—And I'll have to get ready immediately, she said gulping the last of her tea.

—Don't forget to bring a bite to eat.

—Devil a bite I'd need if the woman in Lawn Lane wouldn't delay me. She took me into the kitchen this day last week and gave me a cup of tea. Fine tea. Golden brown. A very kindly woman and not trying to get the better of a body like the rest of them. Her husband is a sergeant of Peelers. She's from Longford.

—I left a creel of turf at a Peeler's house along that road before I sold the horse. She was enticing me to have tea but I didn't go in. I hadn't enough English to deal with her.

—A palefaced woman and not very tall, was she?

—Devil the know I know now. Nearly four years ago.

He swallowed his tea and went out to the dooryard.

—There's still an hour of moonlight, he said when he came in. —I know by the stars of the Cluster that it's not a second past four o'clock. I imagine it'll be a fine morning, though the sky is rather overcast. Nobody seems to be going to Brightcity.

—Only the turfmen. The rest have exhausted their means. Don't you know it's the Dry of the Hens?

—I'll come to the head of the road with you. Or as far as Taimin Thomais till I wake him.

—Fine and early you're impatient to be out! You'd leave the house would you, not knowing—God between us and harm—what might happen the children?

—They're snoring. I won't be two ticks outside—

—Go back in there and sleep for another three hours. I'll be alright.

She went back into the room. The two children were in the small bed snoring softly, and the mother didn't disturb them except to shake a drop of holy water round the bed and sign the Cross on herself with it.

She lifted the strap of the butter-creel, prepared the night before, about her neck. The man settled her shawl over the top of the creel behind and she went out the door.

A rugged and dirty path led from the house to the village road. Water squelched under the soles of her boots and her left foot was already damp before she reached the firm cart-track. She was surprised that none of the village houses showed a light, she had thought that with the steady south wind there had been people would be up and out to snatch red kelp from the beach. Maire Sheainin showed no light either, but she'd be time enough up in another couple of hours since she could afford to take a jaunt on a sidecar.

No matter how often Brid had gone that way on the same errand at the end of night, she was always struck by the strangeness of the sleeping village. That cluster of houses wasn't nearly so bad on a blackdark night. Tonight there were shafts of moonlight sliced between the houses and byres and frightening straggles of shadow out from gable-ends. Needles of moonlight in the grain of the granite rocks glittered cold and hostile, snake's eyes, lying in wait. And the reign of the Moon that would have been so bright and blessed if it hadn't been distorted, was cast now as it were into a phantasma by the hosts of the Otherworld before their silent vanishing come cockcrow.

In that village which would be astir with sound and bustle in three or four hours' time, Tomas's housedog was now the only living voice. Nature's herald warning in a dark tongue that the Master—and his mistress Night—were still locked in sleep and not to be wakened. In a lull of the wind his angry bark rang back from the houses and the walled fields; the sound leaped over into the stony patches, thence to the craggy fens at the top of the townland, it went echoing birdlike from cliff to cliff, rockface to rockface extended it, until at last it died in a querulous whimper on the bare moorlands of the farthest heights.

A stream of shadow from Tomas's carthouse cut across the track. Brid glancing sideways saw the two forked sticks supporting the shafts of the cart loaded with turf, though there still wasn't a breath of smoke from the house. Of course she hadn't forgotten her husband's vexation when she wouldn't wait for Tomas's Taimin. As well as being a neighbour Taimin was also her husband's first cousin once removed. And if she was to wear out her tongue telling him, it still wouldn't stick in his mind that she didn't avoid Taimin from a sense of superiority, taking the chance of a lift home every Saturday on some cart from the Currach—her own village—five miles off on the other side of the parish. That of course was another sort of pride. Though she was five years married now she still felt all the village people to be strangers. She wasn't properly used to them, very likely she'd never get used to them, very likely she wasn't forthcoming enough to make free of people. Anyhow she had no wish for the company of Taimin Thomais. He had been at her matchmaking. She recalled clearly his flaring eyes as he gripped her fingers drinking her health. From that on she couldn't stand the look in his eye. He seemed to her always to have two looks in his eye, a dead-ash glaze, and behind it a flicker of passionate greed and rascality. She couldn't chat with Taimin Thomais without feeling glints of that hidden flame all the time aimed at her. She found it hard to explain, but she knew she felt as if there were sparks burning on her skin when he looked at her.

When she emerged from the village road on to the highway she stood for a moment listening. Nowhere the sound of cart or footstep. A bit early she thought. Else someone would be stirring. Still she had better get along, there were nine Irish miles before her to Brightcity, and better be early than late in getting there.

The moon had declined in the west above the Isles and long strands of her light touched millions of drops of quicksilver across the bay making, it might be, a bridge for the Fairy host to Little Aran. But brilliant as the moon was she had rather a look of melancholy in the empty sky, displaying all her trinkets to dramatise the weight of her despair. Brid longed for her setting. She would much rather be shawled in dark. She could make more free with the dark. By moonlight more than by the light of day a body might easily forget the eternal weft of one's being and think oneself part of the transient material world all round. Brid was happier in the dark, it gave her mind a chance to come to grips with life instead of having the brilliant extent of the view to distract her with thoughts of life's merciless hardship. She seldom had a chance to think, what with pressure of work, children peevishly demanding, or people in. Furthermore, she felt like shirking this journey today. Since she had to go she might as well go at her own pace and not in step with someone else. She could never bring herself to tell her husband that she wasn't so robust, nor anywhere near it, since having that last stillborn child, and lately the long walk was telling on her. And near Brightcity, if she was on her own, she would have a good chance of getting a lift from someone she knew and be saved the worst two or three miles of the journey.

If she was as far on to the east as the wood of Moyle, she thought, or close to it, before the sidecars began to overtake her, she'd have a good chance of a free ride the rest of the way, for by then the drivers would be so near the city that they wouldn't be on the lookout for further customers. But scarcely any driver would take up two, and if he did take one of a pair, which was unlikely, it would hardly be her. And to have a walking-companion taken up would leave her worse off than ever, having been within an inch of a lift. She was always worn out a mile or two farther from journey's end than she used to be, these days.

Wasn't it well for the women with small change enough to spend a few shillings on a jaunt. Maire Sheainin, for instance, up on a sidecar every single Saturday. But she musn't compare herself with Maire Sheainin who was coining money since the war came, and constantly getting handfuls from America as well. She herself had been at pains to spare every halfpenny last Saturday in order to lay a shilling for a jaunt halfway today, but the shilling went where all the other shillings had gone—into the till at the shop.

But if she wasn't clean out of luck she'd surely get a lift near journey's end. Her own neighbour, Mairtin Mor, who never had but the same three, would take her up. Didn't he take her up the Halowe'en Saturday? Or Sean Choilm. Of course if he had four he'd hardly be in the humour to put one more up on the box. Always mumbling about not liking to overstrain the horse. Anyway Peaid Neachtain wouldn't leave her on the road, he was in the habit of coming to play cards since the visiting season started. Coil Liam was the best on the road for a jaunt. She wasn't exactly in love with Mike the Shop—it was a great favour to get credit from him without expecting a jaunt as well. Sure enough, he usually had no more than himself and the brother's wife, apart from those he'd take up along the way, but he'd only take up a good pay, or else someone whose custom he was trying to attract away from the other shop. And Micil Pheige always passed her by. At one time he had been generous with a lift. None more generous. But something had got into him lately. He was infatuated with some crowd he called Sinn Feiners and anybody who wasn't a Sinn Feiner had no longer any hope of a lift. Brid often tried to puzzle out what sort of folk these Sinn Feiners were. Padraig Thomais Thaidhg was in them and had been taken up last year when there had been some kind of a skirmish up in Dublin and on the Plain. But the Earl, as he was called, got him out again. The Earl could save a man from the scaffold, though the Sinn Feiners were loud in their agitation against him. It was rumoured they were drilling with hurley sticks by night and were all set to make war on England. They had a meeting in Ballindrine lately and were at daggers drawn with the priest of that parish. But such doings were no affair of the poor. How should they have any inkling of them? The poor as always had to struggle on.

She went through the one-street town. Though there was light in one or two of the publichouses there wasn't a sinner to be seen apart from two policemen with their backs against the door of Geraghty's Yard, motionless. On the lookout for turfcarts without lights, maybe, though usually they didn't bother with them. Or maybe snooping on the publichouses? What were they talking of, thinking of? What would policemen have to think or talk about since they hadn't the hardship of strand, garth or bog, living in plenty and drawing their pay? Going by the Dunes she heard the noise of a car coming down the track from Ballydonagh, and she was undecided whether to wait for it or not. She had to face the hill of Ardfert. She saw from her by the light of the moon the slabs and pillarstones in the marshy ground on both sides of the road. Like heroes, half-risen, wakened by trumpet sound. —'Often the trumpet spoke, as often was the bloody work prolonged,' if old tales were true. But the woman who had to go to Brightcity often in the tailend of night, alone, at times unwillingly, must put ghostly things and fairy things out of her mind. Brid used to be afraid of these things at first, but she had mastered the fear and become so used to taking them lightly that her only reaction now was to quicken her step a little till she had cleared the hill of Ardfert.

But in that outlandish place there was nothing worse than Liam the Tailor and some young fellow she didn't know along with him. She recognised Liam's voice at once. She knew—the whole countryside knew—that he used often rip the silence of the night after drinking in the village; As soon as she recognised the voice she slowed up and stood stockstill. But there was no car to be heard, no one on foot, not even the car she had heard a while ago. She owed the tailor money, the price of the homespun suit he had made last year for her husband, and she had promised so often and failed to pay that she wouldn't for the world wish to overtake him now. But the pair were only strolling, and it was still a mile and a half to their own byroad. She greeted them.

—By the Lord, said Liam impudently to the fellow along with him, —when I was your age I'd not let my chance slip so easily. A fine young woman…

—I'm bespoke already, she said trying to laugh it off.

Liam let out a drunken guffaw. —Leave it to the Currach, he said, and started in on a long spiel about the quick wit of the Currach folk. Brid judged it best now to be making her way. She knew they weren't dangerous. In such cases she knew a woman was no more likely to be attacked and robbed than plundered in another way. But she was unwilling to linger and talk, especially since she'd be ashamed to mention the money again to the tailor. Yet she found it hard to dismiss him from her thoughts. A coincidence, to have met him of all people. —I wonder is he already telling his comrade about the money I owe him? But he wasn't that sort. Easy to deal with and kept his mind to himself. However, the drink was a peculiar thing. Well she'd have to pay him by Christmas no matter what. But what use was her pitiful few shillings to him? He had a good income without them, if he didn't leave every penny in the public-house and his wife and children at home pinching and scraping. It was a curious world.

She was fine and warm now having walked above two miles. It would do her no harm to take off her boots and carry them on her arm. One boot was letting the wet in, and grazing her foot a little. She threw the shawl back off her head on to the creel and walked more free. She was rightly into her stride now. The blood coursed through her veins like organ music. She didn't feel the road slipping by under her bare feet, the quick walk pleased her, a challenge to life.

After she passed the Leitir byroad there was light in every one of the few houses along the way, and turfcarts going the road. Sometimes five or six of them in a line and the drivers walking ahead in a group together. An odd one with the driver sitting on the spur of the front-board. Many women on the road too, with creels and baskets, in groups, in couples. Others walking among the turf-drivers. Brid knew most of them by sight only. Some of them were utter strangers come for the most part from places well to the east of the village, while she herself had been reared five miles west of it. She had never spoken much to them either, for up till today she had always had her own neighbours along with her. But the companionship of the road is free. Still she simply passed the time of day to each of them without getting involved in conversation. Not that she felt reluctant to talk, but she feared that some of them would be so eager to hold the 'stranger' in chat that she'd fail to get rid of them. It was the fashion for the groups to split up in pairs after the first stretch of the road, and whatever pleasure she'd take in the chatter of a group she was in no mood for a dialogue. The road being so long she was the less inclined for company. Nine miles she thought was a long way, too long to be caught in the ramifications of gossip.

Afraid too that a dialogue would become too intimate. There were dark ideas slinking at the edge of her mind, and bitterness to sting her feelings, but to her conscious mind the drag and drudgery of life never seemed anything to grumble at. Even Mike the Shop—it never occurred to her that he should be complained of and penalised for putting three different prices on the one article according to whether a body was badly in need of credit, or a safe bet, or able to pay on the dot. She was far from realising that man, not Providence, was answerable for the sea of troubles which confined her to struggle and skimp, sent her tramping every Saturday to Brightcity barefoot, left her worrying always, slaving all the time... She regretted that such things must be, part of the load to be carried in this Valley of Tears—tragic legacy of the Forbidden Fruit. But it never occurred to her that they might be a personal cause of complaint, no more than it might occur to her as an injustice that she rather than someone else had to put up with foul weather, misfortune, death, or the nightly absence of the sun. Though she understood the ideas 'luck', 'bad luck', 'misfortune', well enough, she was unable to give any precise sense to the notions of 'pleasure', 'joy of life'. But she knew she was far from being easy in her mind, far indeed. What she would most like to complain of was that her peace of mind was shadowed by the unrelenting pressure of external life, dulling the daylight, so that her irritations of spirit were trying to break out in spurts of bitterness... Now she couldn't go visit her own people on account of the two children, and the odd time anyone of them came to her, her inquisitive husband and prying neighbours put a private chat out of the question. She'd give a lot sometimes to be able to make free with some female acquaintance, though she knew well that chattering with the neighbours was no cure for her vexation of soul. Give them an inch, she knew, and they'd take an ell. They'd add a sequel to your story as if they weren't interested in hearing it or taking it in properly. Yet she knew it would be a great relief to her feelings to voice her complaint. And she'd prefer to do that with a stranger, someone from far-off, who would attend to it no more than to the sough of the wind, rather than an acquaintance who would treat it as an excuse to launch at length into her own story of her own hardships in plaintive detail, and as an item of gossip afterwards with the next door.

Today it was no comfort to her, as it had often been, to see there were many on the road as hard put to it as she. There were so many dark edges to her thoughts today she feared she mightn't be able to restrain herself if once she began complaining. Her ulcerated spirit was ready to break in bursts of bitterness. She was afraid she'd weep…

Easy enough pass out the ones she overtook. But there was a woman at the Ionnarba byroad and although Brid didn't even know her by sight it took her all her time to get out of her clutches. Having only a light basket the woman had no trouble keeping up with her. Brid had to quicken her step so that the woman would have to ask why the hurry and she could say she had to be in Brightcity for a customer who wanted the butter for breakfast at eight. Afterwards she more or less regretted leaving the woman behind, she seemed the kind that sought the company of a stranger, just like herself other Saturdays…

Gleneany. Ardnakill. Kylenahalla. The foaming stream at Sruthan. They floated towards her slowly as green-grass places to a traveller thirsting in the desert. She rested at Horsegap. And again on the Quarry Stone a little farther along. She had never felt so spent so soon. She had a sudden fear—'the fool's run soon finished'—if she dropped exhausted maybe after the first spurt? She'd die of shame if she had to be taking a rest at every turn when daylight came. What would they say? A fine lump of a young woman. And only two children yet. And what about women with twelve in family who were blithely making the journey?

She rested again. The strap of the basket was chafing her shoulder a little, for she had been drawing red kelp on her back during the week. But the moon had set, it was now the thick dark of the night's end. She'd do nicely, hardly anyone now would recognise her if she hurried past. Then she thought of bunching her nap skirt up about her thighs, it gave ease to her legs, they were streaming with sweat. It wasn't the decent thing for her to do—a young mother—she was glad it wouldn't be remarked on in the dark.

But soon again she was desperately struggling with herself trying to do without a rest till she'd have reached the top of the next rise. And she knew she'd soon be rambling in her mind again when she began guessing how many footsteps it was to the next rise after. She faced every slope up, slope down, every turn and twist of the road, with a child's cheeky impudence towards the stern looks of a father. Every foot of the way was a saga surpassing the feat of Watcher's Ford, the loyal boys of Ventry, Goll's patient suffering on the Rock, the black passion of sorrowful Deirdre. Brid, and many another Brid, felt each mile as a Via Dolorosa, each step a Gethsemene, each stone an Apple of Knowledge to be payed for in sweat, worry, hardship and humility…

At last she rested at the little bridge of Stonemasons. This was the halfway mark. Four Irish miles to go yet. She wondered how long she had been on the road. Bad luck to that tricksome clock. How long till daylight? But already the morning-star was rich in the east, losing its flush, clear now as wellwater, and a few early birds were astir.

She had never felt so spent at the halfway. Her body was hot from hard walking. Her feet were getting in each other's way and refusing to go forward. Every time she stopped to rest, her perspiring body shivered in the cold. And she felt her legs trembling, above the knees mostly, and stabbing pains deep down in her stomach. She was well aware what caused the pains… Heavy loads didn't suit her lately.

She attacked the road once more. Glad of the dark. Her shield. If she were to collapse the best thing to do would be to roll herself into the ditch by the grassy road-verge where she wouldn't be seen till morning. She thought of Neili Mhairtin found dead like that by the hedge at the butt of the Grove. It was said at the inquest that she had been two hours dead before she was discovered. The doctors stated that she died of hunger. One pitchblack morning with pelting rain, and the body found in a nook under the hedge. Still it was strange that none out of the scores that had gone by during that time had noticed her. And left a litter of children all of an age.

If that, God between us and harm, was to happen to herself wouldn't the house be in a queer fix. What would the two children do? If her man was put to the pin of his collar to manage them the one day of the week she was from home, how on earth could he cope with a seven-day week? Eibhlin near scalded herself with boiling water last Saturday though he had promised before she left that he wouldn't stir out to go pottering round till little Neili Sheamais came to take charge. Would he be on the same capering gadabout today? Might as well be talking to the wall. Were they awake yet and starting to cry? Often at it at the crack of dawn. And would he think to put a drop of warm milk in Citiri's sucking-bottle in place of the milk gone cold overnight...

She took a certain lively satisfaction in thinking how completely her man would fail to manage the children if she herself were to go. But he'd marry again. The children would have a stepmother. She'd neglect them, thrash them if they were cranky or got into mischief. She could expect nothing else from a stepmother, seeing how hard she found it herself by times to keep a hand off them. Children were a great hardship. The agony of giving birth. Two of her own stillborn. That's what robbed her of her young girl's shape, left her with the lazy bones of middle-age. Never the same since. Would she have another dead baby? God forbid. It would be the death of her. Yet welcome be the will of God. Suppose she never had any children at all? Would her man and herself be so intimate then? Or would the children's loud complainings be replaced by a cold surly silence of their own? Would he think it worth while to get up a morning like this to bid her goodbye on the road, if there were no children and he had no reason to say—doubtfully, like today—that he hoped he'd be able to manage them while she was away? She had only to look at Nora Anna and her husband. The pair of them like the lugs of a new tongs knocking no spark from each other, only a dull dead sound. Nothing for the couple to share but a carking solitude, if what was said was true. Brid didn't have carking and solitude to contend with, only the two cranky children.

Cranky. Always cranky or fool-acting. Kept her awake half the time. To make matters worse the whoopingcough and measles were going and the schools were closed. Misfortune seldom passed her door. If they were to get the whoopingcough or measles it'd be six long months before they'd have shaken it off, which would be no help to herself... Would she be able to give them schooling? She'd have to, they were due for America. They were saying on all sides that America would be opened up again if only the War was over. They'd have to shift for themselves since she had no dowry to marry them near home with. Hard to keep the older ones to school once they were able to give a hand at home, still they'd have to get a share of it even if it doubled her own work... Would they be quick in sending money home? Or would they be like her own sister who had promised to send her a bit in her fist three times a year and after the first year never sent a red halfpenny—unless she were to write this Christmas. A couple of pounds would be a great boon. There was good money to be got for everything, if one was in the way, but at the same time everything a body had to buy was four prices. Pigs fetched the best money, but just now her pigs were knocking against each other with the staggers. She wondered whether they might thrive on their own leavings...

This was Brid always, worrying all the time about the future, attending more to the trouble that might come than to the trouble here and now. It would be a great loss to them if anything happened the pigs. She was taking the bite out of her own mouth to fatten them for the big Christmas Fair in a month's time. They'd be fine and plump by then if she succeeded… She had a heavy bill at the shop, her shawl was threadbare, her boots letting in, grocery money to pay, tailor's money, manure money. On top of it all the cows were going dry and the hens ceasing to lay. In spite of her best efforts scraping and pinching to keep food in their mouths she'd soon have nothing to bring to the city. From now on the week's supply would have to do for a fortnight.

But these misfortunes were nothing, they were there, could be dealt with. They had shape and body, could be fought. People had wrestled with far more terrible misfortunes for hundreds of years. They would be fought with flesh and blood, with drudgery, careful management, and hope. But new twists threatening to come into the world, a new age, which had yet made no impact on the old traditions of this patient race, that was the prime cause of her unease. No telling what shape they'd take, how they'd appear, how severe they'd be. Life hung in the balance, no telling what might be. She heard old people say it was the end of the world. That the prophecy had come true—this was the 'War of the Two Strangers'. There was great talk of 'Conscription'. If her husband was to be taken from her and killed? So far everyone in that countryside who had gone to the War had been killed. And she was certain, if there was only one single shot to be fired, it was her own man would be struck. They were dogged by that kind of bad luck…

And times were becoming troubled even in Ireland. She heard there had been some sort of a commotion over beyond the other day. And it was becoming hard to get food even for money down. It was rumoured that no more tea would come in, flour, tobacco, nor even the brown sugar, and that the soldiers would seize the stock and crops next year if the War lasted.

In that case how long would she have to keep on going to the city? A year, two years, five years… twenty years… Till the eldest girl was fit to replace her. She herself would be middleaged by then and still more dependent on the journey. Would the look of her face then and the set of her body reveal to one and all her stonewall spirit, hard and defiant? Her back humped from the creel, her feet worn smooth and serviceable taking the long measured strides of a horse? Or walking at a fierce gait. Jawbone bleak as the beak of a currach. Leathery cheeks printed with crowfoot marks like the marks of a milestone. Eyes with a glint of pure steel. Such were the middleaged women she knew, their girls' features beaten ironhard by the weekly managing, the slaughtering Saturday walk.

And would her own children sup this sorrow? If they could find somebody to send them their passage-money from America they'd be well away. But like everything else, who could tell whether America would ever be opened up again. And for them to scrape a dowry together by their own drudgery, enough to get them husbands near home, that was the worst that could happen to them. Then they too would have the week's contriving to face and the Saturday walk. Yet who could tell? The world might have changed by then. In the beginning even the wealthy were without sidecars, but country boss-men had them now and the wealthy were tearing about in motors. Who knows, the day might come when countrymen too would have motors, just like the Earl. Only lately the bicycles began but some of the men had them already and an odd woman too. No matter. Bicycles weren't for married women in the country. But in this world it was wiser to say nothing. Who knows, by the time her own daughter was of age perhaps every woman would have a bicycle… But what good was a bicycle? No way a woman could carry a full creel or a basket on it, though she had seen messengerboys in Brightcity riding with even more awkward loads. But that was alright for short distances. A motor, that would be the best thing for a butterwoman. But she'd not see it in her own time. Nor very likely would her daughter see it. Nor her son's wife.

Her son's wife—that son yet unborn—would she be good to Brid? Would she bring her little dainties from town and her breakfast in bed? Or abuse her like Una Caitlin's daughter-in-law? She'd be nice enough, perhaps, till children came and were cranky. If her son were to marry, care and children and crankiness would start all over again—but then it would be the young woman's business. Still, it would be there, and she'd have to take her own share of it. But it would be a great standby to be getting the odd American pound from the rest of her children, and as well as that the old man and herself wouldn't make over the land and house entirely to the son until they themselves were getting the pension. She'd be independent again then. If she was displeased she could do what she liked with her money. There'd be a new generation in the house wrestling with the same things which she was wrestling with now. And no more than that to worry her, since she wouldn't herself have the responsibility. She'd have a chance to visit and chat. Spend long sessions in a neighbour's house. But in time she'd be unable to leave the house—or the bed maybe. She knew she'd be reluctant to have done with life. Death would come nonetheless… but she went no farther with that idea. Spite of the lively satisfaction she had in complaining and thinking of what she had to endure, she saw the 'final fields' far more clearly than she did the cursed crooked ways of life in the here and now…

Forge Hill. She stopped to rest. She had felt neither the way nor the weariness while she was thinking. But she was fairly crippled and ached with the hunger.

She began to eat her lunch, glad now she had brought it. Seldom had she been so hungry before reaching the outskirts of the city or thereabouts. The dark was thinning out, a grey sky whitening in the east, but there was a heavy mist, a touch of rain in the wind. She had a sudden fear the day might turn out wet, if it did she'd be wet to the skin before she got to Brightcity. What harm but she had to go to the market. Her clothes would dry on her skin and she was sure to get the devil of a dose. Still she wasn't quite so worried as she had been. She'd have as much of the road put by before daylight as on any previous Saturday. She was hardly a mile from the village of Moyle and that's where the sidecars overtook her always. But she'd have to get beyond it for if they had a seat to spare they'd still, as far as that village, be on the lookout for a woman with money. The slice of dry bread refreshed her, but she was taken with a hiccough, gulping in her throat as the tide's suck sounds in a hollow of rock by the shore.

She forgot the hiccough as she passed the byroad to Badgers' Peak, for she began to think of Larry the Peak. Dammit her father should have given her to Larry when he came asking—it would have shortened her road to Brightcity by about six miles. And she wouldn't have half the slavery. Or if she had married Paid Concannon from Derrypark, she'd be within call of the city with nothing to do but get up fairly early, milk the cows, sit up on her ass-and-cart and take the milk into town. But bad luck to him he was too old. Anyhow she wouldn't be keen on going in and out of the city twice a day—not once a week if she could help it. Pity she didn't go to America when she got the chance instead of giving in to the old folk at home.

A long loud roaring. Ship Rock. A sign of filthy weather, a woman from there told her one morning they walked together. A squall of wind whistled through the chinks in the loose-stone walls and screeched sharp and hoarse in the telegraph wires. She set herself silently to say the words of a song—Padraig Choilm's, *I am up since the moon was rising this night gone by.* But she had no more than two verses. Then she began on a story, 'The Knight of the Black Laugh', her uncle's story, Micil Mhairin, to cheer her bleak and lonesome state of mind. 'Hot it was and heavy. Hard they made the soft earth, soft the hard, till they caused the ground to tremble the length of nine furrows and nine ridges away, and forced wells of springwater up through the grey rock with the dint of their conflict.' She took pleasure in the reverberation of the words in the nooks of her memory. But she hadn't that story either. Strange she couldn't pick up things like that, for at school she hadn't been too bad. She must buy a newspaper today if she had a penny left over after laying by the price of a pint for the carter who would carry her home. She'd read it for her husband tomorrow and tell him how the War was shaping. But she doubted whether she would still be able to read it, it was so long since she had taken up a book or a paper. At least she'd be able to spell out the price of pigs, that's all he'd want.

When she reached the peak of Leana Hill the houses of Moyle appeared to her in strange distorted shapes through the foggy gloom. She was never too fond of going alone through that village by night, though she had done it once or twice. It had a reputation for robbery since the old days, though she hadn't heard of anyone being molested there for ages. Moyle had now been for two generations contrite and behaving well, but that wasn't enough to clear its name. Anyhow even if there were highwaymen there in hundreds it wasn't her sort they'd go for. The houses strung together and hung up above the roadway like a flock of eagles ready at any moment to swoop on their prey, that's what used to frighten her, and that was all.

The flow of her ideas was suddenly halted. There was someone in front of her on the road. A woman, a basket-woman. She had been so wrapped in her thoughts that this woman took her by surprise. She had come a long stretch of the road since she had last seen a human being. It was Peigin Nora from the village next her own, and she stood in the middle of the road waiting for her. No chance of shaking her off, a rabbit would more easily shake off a weasel. She felt helpless. Having avoided company all morning she had company now whether she liked it or not. And to think that the sidecars would be along any minute now. Peigin Nora of all women. All the women disliked her she was so loquacious. And disliked specially by the jaunting-car drivers. She often took a jaunt and quiffled the driver out of his fare. At least that's what Brid had been told. She was in a right fix now, no car would take up two, even if one of them wasn't Peigin Nora.

Against her will she listened while Peigin talked like the clappers of a mill. Grinding all sorts. The price of things. Price of transport. Conscription on the way. A big American liner sunk, laden with Christmas moneyletters, as well as tea and tobacco. The staggers and whoopingcough in the village at home since yesterday. And fever again in Lettergeeha. Mike the Shop to give no more credit to certain people unless they cleared their accounts this Christmas. A daughter of Tom Beg's coming home—it wasn't exactly known yet who the man was, but the priest tomorrow would be scarifying…

Passing the premises of Mairead the Pub Peigin asked her in, a halfglass of whiskey each would warm their hearts. But Brid knew she couldn't afford to call for a second round, and anyhow she never took a drop herself apart from an odd fingerwidth at a wedding or christening. Though she was inclined to think that a halfglass of punch would cheer her up if she had the price of it. She told Peigin to go in on her own, she'd wait for her. But Peigin wouldn't. She regretted having done Peigin out of her consolation, for she was well known to be fond of a drop. They tramped on in step together. Peigin now hadn't so much to say. Brid's thoughts were free to scamper like wild things through her mind. Her feet above all, nagging at her more than ever, would the last three miles knock her out altogether, she'd have to put on her boots again coming close to town, the worry was would they blister her feet on the last stretch. Getting wetter too, no wind, and a filthy drizzle fit to bedraggle and drench a body unawares. Looking back to see if there was a sidecar coming, only then did it occur to her to let down her bunched-up skirts, though she had intended to do it before reaching Moyle. Dark was fading bit by bit, daylight becoming distinct between her and the shawl of mist over Moyle Wood. Not a sough of wind in the wood today, silent and still as the breath of death under the bare trees, big wet drops fell from their tops in dirty splashes, angry 'bad luck' spits.

In Wood Valley farther on they were overtaken by the first of the side-cars—three one after another. Two of the drivers didn't even glance at them. Mairtin Mor in the middle one had looked as if he could hardly believe his eyes that there were two of them, studied them as if to resolve them into one to fit into the one empty seat he had up on the box behind him, winked at Brid towards the empty seat, and finally after some consideration shook the reins and set the horse to a trot up the rise. Next minute Coil Liam passed them with only two up. Brid knew he'd stand her a lift only for his intense loathing of her companion. Maire Sheainin was on this car. She barely nodded to Brid who'd swear she had a smile in her eye when it was clear Coil Liam had no intention of taking her up. Further along Micil Mor took up Peigin. Micil was the best in Ireland for a lift, and he'd prefer to take up Brid but, conscientious, thought the older woman more in need of it. —You are fine and strong and young enough for the road, he said. I'd take you if I could.

She came at length to the fork in the road. She knew if she took the road to the left she had a poor chance of a lift, nearly all the jauntingcars went to the right where there were more houses and they could make better headway. She lingered a good while in two minds about taking the righthand road, but the cup of tea she had got the week before, having gone to the left, banished every other idea. Nothing so refreshing as a cup of tea like that after a journey, it'd warm a person up wonderfully to start the day, instead of having to wait till one or two o'clock after doing the market and shops and then to be hardly able to drink it with hunger and weariness.

She hadn't gone far up the slope when she heard an ass-and-cart trundling behind her making a great effort. A cart from that district on the edge of the city, loaded with a variety of foodstuffs—potatoes, cabbage, root crops, a basket, a tankard of milk. A lone woman perched on the front shaft feet dangling and with every clout of the reins on the ass's rump drove him up the slope. Brid was on the point of asking her for a lift, but the woman had too much to attend to, hadn't time for a word or even a glance.

She met another ass's cart of the same locality, coming from the city having delivered the morning's milk, no need to spur the ass, he was trotting nicely of his own accord. A woman sat on an upturned empty milkcan, a longlimbed fullbreasted woman, obviously wellfed, bordering on forty. Brid didn't even know her by sight, but she thought at once of Paid Concannon's wife, the one he married when his offer for herself had been refused... Another sidecar coming. She was sorely tempted to look round, but was ashamed to. It was Sean Choilm, she recognised his growling 'hup' even before he came up with her. He'd certainly take her up, he had four passengers, but he'd hardly think it hardship on the horse to put another up on the box for the short bit of road left. But he passed her out without a word or a look... She was surprised to see him coming this lefthand road. But he had Cait Cheaite up, and she remembered telling Cait where the woman lived who had held her up last week. Cait was smart enough for anything.

She hadn't quite reached the top of the long rise when she heard another sidecar coming at an easy trot. She looked round in spite of herself and her heart jerked. Paid Neachtain. Many a time he had warmed himself well by her fireside since the cardplay season began, though she hadn't seen him for almost a fortnight. And he had only three up. It was hardly worth her while to take a lift now, only an Irish mile or so to go to Boherbwee. Still it was worth it, that mile was the worst, the hill was so long and monotonous. The horse was almost up with her, slackening on the slope. Paid merely shook the reins, flicked the horse setting it at full stretch passing Brid at a gallop up the hill. She nearly dropped where she stood, she wouldn't have believed it if she hadn't seen it with her own eyes. Now she wouldn't have wished for a fortune that she had looked back...

She trudged on uphill. She had to pull the shawl up over her head again, the thin mist was penetrating. Though the fog had lifted it was black and threatening to windward, it would likely come pelting any minute. She'd be saturated before she had her business done, bought her parcels and things and be ready for a cup of tea in the eatinghouse. And then maybe left to linger in her damp clothes until she'd find a carter to give her a lift home.

At long last she got to the top of the hill at College Wood within the suburbs, big commodious houses at hand, the first fringe of streets only a little farther on, Boherbwee but a quarter of a mile away. And nothing left but a downward slope to the city boundary. She set down the creel in a nook of a tall hedge. She'd have to put on her boots. Tying the laces she thought again of the cup of tea she'd get if the Peeler's wife delayed her. Somebody else might have got there ahead of her. Hardly likely. Pity she ever told Cait Cheaite. The world's best wheedler that same Cait. She'd try it anyway, the very first thing, though it'd bring her a good bit out of her way with maybe nothing but blisters to show for it. No use in delaying.

She slipped the cloth off the load in the little creel to make sure all was trim. There lay the pat of butter as innocent and pretty as Little Rushcoat when the Mettlesome Hero woke her from sleep. A waterdrop in the printmark and the butter fine and firm, unlike the mess summer butter makes. She unwrapped the eggs from the straw and paper and counted them again, yes, three score, scoured clean and pure, white, brown, pale blue. In no particular order, yet she knew the egg of each and every hen—the little grey pullet's, the speckled hen's one white with hardly the breath of a shell, and those of the crested hen brown and big as duckeggs, she was fond of those and would have liked to boil an odd one for herself since the Dry of the Hens came on only she didn't care to do it in secret. Strange poor creatures hens, God love them. But only for the care they got they'd have long ago died out. She wrapped up the eggs again and tidied the straw about them, drew the cloth over them and was ready to go once more…

The drizzle was over now and the air clean. Southeast, the sun. Scallopping with light the edge of a mass of raincloud, dark and threatening, breaking bright through it and beautiful, making the wet leaves in the wood and the raindrops on the road twinkle like jewels. As if the sun were rising upon the brink of victory, having endured and overcome the burden, the dangers, the disgrace and hardship of the night. Brid looked back along the road. Back along those nine crooked miles with which she had grimly struggled. She realised she must do them again, again and again. Do them till her jawbones showed bleak, her limbs weathered, the hard look came in her eyes. But she had them done for today and that was something. Her pulse throbbed, her heart sang. She was gamesome and happy, knowing the pure high-spirits of a young wild creature, and her body was as a scythe with a new edge to it eager for the swathe. She was ready again to take up her share of the burden of life. She gripped the strap of the buttercreel…

THE MAN OF THE WORLD

Frank O'Connor

Frank O'Connor (1903–1966) published two novels, but was best known as a writer of short stories, including *Guests of the Nation* and *My Oedipus Complex*. He was a poet and critic and edited various anthologies and a critical study on the short story.

When I was a kid there were no such things as holidays for me and my likes, and I have no feeling of grievance about it because, in the way of kids, I simply invented them, which was much more satisfactory. One year, my summer holiday was a couple of nights I spent at the house of a friend called Jimmy Leary, who lived at the other side of the road from us. His parents sometimes went away for a couple of days to visit a sick relative in Bantry, and he was given permission to have a friend in to keep him company. I took my holiday with the greatest seriousness, insisted on the loan of Father's old travelling bag and dragged it myself down our lane past the neighbours standing at their doors.

'Are you off somewhere, Larry?' asked one.

'Yes, Mrs Rooney,' I said with great pride. 'Off for my holidays to the Learys'.'

'Wisha, aren't you very lucky?' she said with amusement.

'Lucky' seemed an absurd description of my good fortune. The Learys' house was a big one with a high flight of steps up to the front door, which was always kept shut. They had a piano in the front room, a pair of binoculars on a table near the window, and a toilet on the stairs that seemed to me to be the last word in elegance and immodesty. We brought the binoculars up to the bedroom with us. From the window you could see the whole road up and down, from the quarry at its foot with the tiny houses perched on top of it to the open fields at the other end, where the last gas lamp rose against the sky. Each morning I was up with the first light, leaning out the window in my nightshirt and watching through the glasses all the mysterious figures you never saw from our lane: policemen, railwaymen, and farmers on their way to market.

I admired Jimmy almost as much as I admired his house, and for much the same reasons. He was a year older than I, was well-mannered and well-dressed, and would not associate with most of the kids on the road at all. He had a way when any of them joined us of resting against a wall with his hands in his trousers pockets and listening to them with a sort of well-bred smile, a knowing smile, that seemed to me the height of elegance. And it was not that he was a softy, because he was an excellent boxer and wrestler and could easily have held his own with them any time, but he did not wish to. He was superior to them. He was – there is only one word that still describes it for me – sophisticated.

I attributed his sophistication to the piano, the binoculars, and the indoor John, and felt that if only I had the same advantages I could have been sophisticated, too. I knew I wasn't, because I was always being deceived by the world of appearances. I would take a sudden violent liking to some boy, and when I went to his house my admiration would spread to his parents and sisters, and I would think how wonderful it must be to have such a home; but when I told Jimmy he would smile in that knowing way of his and say quietly: 'I believe they had the bailiffs in a few weeks ago,' and, even though I didn't know what bailiffs were, bang would go the whole world of appearances, and I would realize that once again I had been deceived.

It was the same with fellows and girls. Seeing some bigger chap we knew walking out with a girl for the first time, Jimmy would say casually: 'He'd better mind himself: that one is dynamite.' And, even though I knew as little of girls who were dynamite as I did of bailiffs, his tone would be sufficient to indicate that I had been taken in by sweet voices and broad-brimmed hats, gaslight and evening smells from gardens.

Forty years later I can still measure the extent of my obsession, for, though my own handwriting is almost illegible, I sometimes find myself scribbling idly on a pad in a small, stiff, perfectly legible hand that I recognize with amusement as a reasonably good forgery of Jimmy's. My admiration still lies there somewhere, a fossil in my memory, but Jimmy's knowing smile is something I have never managed to acquire.

And it all goes back to my curiosity about fellows and girls. As I say, I only imagined things about them, but Jimmy knew. I was excluded from knowledge by the world of appearances that blinded and deafened me with emotion. The least thing could excite or depress me: the trees in the morning when I went to early Mass, the stained-glass windows in the church, the blue hilly streets at evening with the green flare of the gas lamps, the smells of cooking and perfume – even the smell of a cigarette packet that I had picked up from the gutter and crushed to my nose – all kept me at this side of the world of appearances, while Jimmy, by right of birth or breeding, was always at the other. I wanted him to tell me what it was like, but he didn't seem to be able.

Then one evening he was listening to me talk while he leant against the pillar of his gate, his pale neat hair framing his pale, good-humoured face. My excitability seemed to rouse in him a mixture of amusement and pity.

'Why don't you come over some night the family is away and I'll show you a few things?' he asked lightly.

'What'll you show me, Jimmy?' I asked eagerly.

'Noticed the new couple that's come to live next door?' he asked with a nod in the direction of the house above his own.

'No,' I admitted in disappointment. It wasn't only that I never knew anything but I never noticed anything either. And when he described the new family that was lodging there, I realized with chagrin that I didn't even know Mrs MacCarthy, who owned the house.

'Oh, they're just a newly married couple,' he said. 'They don't know that they can be seen from our house.'

'But how, Jimmy?'

'Don't look up now,' he said with a dreamy smile while his eyes strayed over my shoulder in the direction of the lane. 'Wait till you're going away. Their end wall is only a couple of feet from ours. You can see right into the bedroom from our attic.'

'And what do they do, Jimmy?'

'Oh,' he said with a pleasant laugh, 'everything. You really should come.'

'You bet I'll come,' I said, trying to sound tougher than I felt. It wasn't that I saw anything wrong in it. It was rather that, for all my desire to become like Jimmy, I was afraid of what it might do to me.

But it wasn't enough for me to get behind the world of appearances. I had to study the appearances themselves, and for three evenings I stood under the gas lamp at the foot of our lane, across the road from the MacCarthys', till I had identified the new lodgers. The husband was the first I spotted, because he came from his work at a regular hour. He was tall, with stiff jet-black hair and a big black guardsman's moustache that somehow failed to conceal the youthfulness and ingenuousness of his face, which was long and lean. Usually, he came accompanied by an older man, and stood chatting for a few minutes outside his door – a black-coated, bowler-hatted figure who made large, sweeping gestures with his evening paper and sometimes doubled up in an explosion of loud laughter.

On the third evening I saw his wife – for she had obviously been waiting for him, looking from behind the parlour curtains, and when she saw him she scurried down the steps to join in the conversation. She had thrown an old jacket about her shoulders and stood there, her arms folded as though to protect herself further from the cold wind that blew down the hill from the open country, while her husband rested one hand fondly on her shoulder.

For the first time, I began to feel qualms about what I proposed to do. It was one thing to do it to people you didn't know or care about, but, for me, even to recognize people was to adopt an emotional attitude towards them, and my attitude to this pair was already one of approval. They looked like people who might approve of me, too. That night I remained awake, thinking out the terms of an anonymous letter that would put them on their guard, till I had worked myself up into a fever of eloquence and indignation.

But I knew only too well that they would recognize the villain of the letter and that the villain would recognize me, so I did not write it. Instead, I gave way to fits of anger and moodiness against my parents. Yet even these were unreal, because on Saturday night when Mother made a parcel of my night-shirt – I had now become sufficiently self-conscious not to take a bag – I nearly broke down. There was something about my own house that night that upset me all over again. Father, with his cap over his eyes, was sitting under the wall-lamp, reading the paper, and Mother, a shawl about her shoulders, was crouched over the fire from her little wickerwork chair, listening; and I realized that they, too, were part of the world of appearances I was planning to destroy, and as I said good-night I almost felt that I was saying good-bye to them as well.

But once inside Jimmy's house I did not care so much. It always had that effect on me, of blowing me up to twice the size, as though I were expanding to greet the piano, the binoculars, and the indoor toilet. I tried to pick out a tune on the piano with one hand, and Jimmy, having listened with amusement for some time, sat down and played it himself as I felt it should be played, and this, too, seemed to be part of his superiority.

'I suppose we'd better put in an appearance of going to bed,' he said disdainfully. 'Someone across the road might notice and tell. *They*'re in town, so I don't suppose they'll be back till late.'

We had a glass of milk in the kitchen, went upstairs, undressed, and lay down, though we put our overcoats beside the bed. Jimmy had a packet of sweets but insisted on keeping them till later. 'We may need these before we're done,' he said with his knowing smile, and again I admired his order-liness and restraint. We talked in bed for a quarter of an hour; then put out the light, got up again, donned our overcoats and socks, and tiptoed upstairs to the attic. Jimmy led the way with an electric torch. He was a fellow who thought of everything. The attic had been arranged for our vigil. Two trunks had been drawn up to the little window to act as seats, and there were even cushions on them. Looking out, you could at first see nothing but an expanse of blank wall topped with chimney stacks, but gradually you could make out the outline of a single window, eight or ten feet below. Jimmy sat beside me and opened his packet of sweets, which he laid between us.

'Of course, we could have stayed in bed till we heard them come in,' he whispered. 'Usually you can hear them at the front door, but they might have come in quietly or we might have fallen asleep. It's always best to make sure.'

'But why don't they draw the blind?' I asked as my heart began to beat uncomfortably.

'Because there isn't a blind,' he said with a quiet chuckle. 'Old Mrs Mac-Carthy never had one, and she's not going to put one in for lodgers who may be gone tomorrow. People like that never rest till they get a house of their own.'

I envied him his nonchalance as he sat back with his legs crossed, sucking a sweet just as though he were waiting in the cinema for the show to begin. I was scared by the darkness and the mystery, and by the sounds that came to us from the road with such extraordinary clarity. Besides, of course, it wasn't my house and I didn't feel at home there. At any moment I expected the front door to open and his parents to come in and catch us.

We must have been waiting for half an hour before we heard voices in the roadway, the sound of a key in the latch and, then, of a door opening and closing softly. Jimmy reached out and touched my arm lightly. 'This is probably our pair,' he whispered. 'We'd better not speak any more in case they might hear us.' I nodded, wishing I had never come. At that moment a faint light became visible in the great expanse of black wall, a faint, yellow stairlight that was just sufficient to silhouette the window frame beneath us. Suddenly the whole room lit up. The man I had seen in the street stood by the doorway, his hand still on the switch. I could see it all plainly now, an ordinary small, suburban bedroom with flowery wallpaper, a coloured picture of the Sacred Heart over the double bed with the big brass knobs, a wardrobe, and a dressing-table.

The man stood there till the woman came in, removing her hat in a single wide gesture and tossing it from her into a corner of the room. He still stood by the door, taking off his tie. Then he struggled with the collar, his head raised and his face set in an agonized expression. His wife kicked off her shoes, sat on a chair by the bed, and began to take off her stockings. All the time she seemed to be talking because her head was raised, looking at him, though you couldn't hear a word she said. I glanced at Jimmy. The light from the window below softly illumined his face as he sucked with tranquil enjoyment.

The woman rose as her husband sat on the bed with his back to us and began to take off his shoes and socks in the same slow, agonized way. At one point he held up his left foot and looked at it with what might have been concern. His wife looked at it, too, for a moment and then swung half-way round as she unbuttoned her skirt. She undressed in swift, jerky movements, twisting and turning and apparently talking all the time. At one moment she looked into the mirror on the dressing-table and touched her cheek lightly. She crouched as she took off her slip, and then pulled her nightdress over her head and finished her undressing beneath it. As she removed her underclothes she seemed to throw them anywhere at all, and I had a strong impression that there was something haphazard and disorderly about her. Her husband was different. Everything he removed seemed to be removed in order and then put carefully where he could find it most readily in the morning. I watched him take out his watch, look at it carefully, wind it, and then hang it neatly over the bed.

Then, to my surprise, she knelt by the bed, facing towards the window, glanced up at the picture of the Sacred Heart, made a large hasty Sign of the Cross, and, covering her face with her hands, buried her head in the bedclothes. I looked at Jimmy in dismay, but he did not seem to be embarrassed by the sight. The husband, his folded trousers in his hand, moved about the room slowly and carefully, as though he did not wish to disturb his wife's devotions, and when he pulled on the trousers of his pyjamas he turned away. After that he put on his pyjama jacket, buttoned it carefully, and knelt beside her. He, too, glanced respectfully at the picture and crossed himself slowly and reverently, but he did not bury his face and head as she had done. He knelt upright with nothing of the abandonment suggested by her pose, and with an expression that combined reverence and self-respect. It was the expression of an employee who, while admitting that he might have a few little weaknesses like the rest of the staff, prided himself on having deserved well of the management. Women, his slightly complacent air seemed to indicate, had to adopt these emotional attitudes, but he spoke to God as one man to another. He finished his prayers before his wife; again he crossed himself slowly, rose, and climbed into bed, glancing again at his watch as he did so.

Several minutes passed before she put her hands out before her on the bed, blessed herself in her wide, sweeping way, and rose. She crossed the room in a swift movement that almost escaped me, and next moment the light went out – it was as if the window through which we had watched the scene had disappeared with it by magic, till nothing was left but a blank black wall mounting to the chimney pots.

Jimmy rose slowly and pointed the way out to me with his flashlight. When we got downstairs we put on the bedroom light, and I saw on his face the virtuous and sophisticated air of a collector who has shown you all his treasures in the best possible light. Faced with that look, I could not bring myself to mention the woman at prayer, though I felt her image would be impressed on my memory till the day I died. I could not have explained to him how at that moment everything had changed for me, how, beyond us watching the young married couple from ambush, I had felt someone else watching us, so that at once we ceased to be the observers and became the observed. And the observed in such a humiliating position that nothing I could imagine our victims doing would have been so degrading.

I wanted to pray myself but found I couldn't. Instead, I lay in bed in the darkness, covering my eyes with my hand, and I think that even then I knew that I should never be sophisticated like Jimmy, never be able to put on a knowing smile, because always beyond the world of appearances I would see only eternity watching.

'Sometimes, of course, it's better than that,' Jimmy's drowsy voice said from the darkness. 'You shouldn't judge it by tonight.'

AILSA

Joseph O'Connor

Joseph O'Connor's novels include *Star of the Sea*, *Ghost Light* and *Shadowplay*, which won the 2019 An Post Eason Irish Novel of the Year Award. His story 'Ailsa' was made into a feature film in 1994, directed by Paddy Breathnach, starring Andrea Irvine and Brendan Coyle. It won the Euskal Media Prize at the San Sebastián Film Festival.

I drank far too much cheap gin last night. I can feel it all in my stomach now. When I walk around the apartment I can feel it swishing around. I'm feeling pretty damn precarious, I can tell you. I feel like I'm going to do something stupid. It was that cheap stuff, too. That's all you can get around here when you need a shot in a hurry. The guy who runs the shop next door, every time a customer says Jesus, he crosses himself. He's not exactly all there, if you ask me. Toys in the attic.

I've got a feeling in my head that just won't go away. This morning I lay in the bath with my head under the water and I listened to the sound of my breath. My tongue felt like velvet. When I spat in the sink I saw blood. I need to get my damn teeth seen to. Not to mention the rest. Sara made eggs but I just couldn't face them. She said but come on, so I got up and went out for a walk. I didn't even put on my jacket. She gets on my nerves when she gets pushy like that.

It made me have all these weird dreams, too, the gin, and every time I woke up I had to keep real still in case I got sick. Things were crawling over my body. Little things with legs. I was walking through this place in the rain, a park or something, where the trees had wings and I recognised it although when I woke up I couldn't remember. My brain felt like it was wrapped up in cotton wool.

Sara kept looking over at me and asking me if I was OK and I kept saying, yeah, yeah, I'm OK. She grinds her teeth when she's asleep. Sometimes she wakes up laughing. She kept telling me I needed a cup of hot sweet tea. Every time she said those words – hot sweet tea – I felt sick all over again. When I tell her she grinds her teeth, she goes all red and says she doesn't and laughs and tells me to stop kidding around.

At four o'clock this morning I went and sat on the toilet, stark naked with my head in my hands, hiccuping. Then I tried to drink a glass of water back to front but it spilled all over my chest. Cured me though. I sat in the room for a while reading some magazine article about fish or something, I don't know, but it got too cold. I lit a cigarette. Then I lit a match and held it against the tip of another match. The two matches stuck themselves together and I nearly set the damn ashtray on fire. When I got back into bed Sara moved her feet against mine.

A few months ago I fell in love with this woman. She lives down the stairs in the apartment nearest the front door. I don't know why I fell in love with her. I don't think I ever will.

Her name is Caitlin. That's her first name. Caitlin Rourke, funny name. It's a Scottish name, apparently. I looked it up and it's Scottish. Funny, because she isn't Scottish herself. She's from somewhere in America. Even if I didn't know that I could guess. She's just got this faraway thing about her. It's just a feeling. I can't put it into words. She's got long red hair, all down her back. She wears black all the time. I don't know what she's doing living here. But then I don't know what I'm doing living here. Sometimes I really don't. It just happened that way.

I don't know where she works. She's something in public housing or something but that's all I know. She gets this journal. It comes every Friday afternoon. Sometimes, if the weather's bad, it comes Saturday mornings. It's called *Housing Today*. I know because it comes in a clear plastic envelope so you can see the job advertisements on the back cover. There's a lot of jobs in housing, I'll tell you. That's all I know about her, really. And she pays her phone bills late. I know that because I do the same, and you know those little envelopes with the final demand? Well, hers always comes the same day as mine.

Sometimes she leaves her mail down there for days. It piles up. Or maybe she's not always home at night. I wouldn't know. It piles up for days and then suddenly one morning it's gone. I looked her up in the phone book but she's obviously ex. I got a copy of the electoral register in the post office, but it's still in the name of old Mr Johnson and it hasn't been changed yet. Nobody's told them what happened to him. I told the guy behind the counter. He kind of shrugged. Then he said the wheels turn very slowly but I made him take down a few notes just the same. I had to point out that it's people like me pay his wages, the fucking penpusher.

His son came by one day to collect all his old stuff. Old Mr Johnson's son, I mean. He seemed like a nice guy too. Big car full of kids, wife with cross eyes and very blue veins in her legs. They ran up and down the stairs all afternoon and Sara gave them cakes. He rang our doorbell and said he was looking for a Caitlin Rourke. Aren't we all, I thought. Although I didn't say that. Obviously.

One day she got a letter from some guy who signed himself 'Emperor'. What a sap he must have been, signing himself that. His name and address were on the envelope. 'University of Syracuse', it said. Damn intellectual. It was written in pencil. He wrote: I write this in pencil so it's easily erased. Just like me. What a sap. Other times she gets bank statements and stuff and brochures from the book club. And postcards from all over the damn world. She's got these friends who go skiing. The stuff they get up to over there, you wouldn't believe it. And how they put it all on the back of a postcard, when anyone could read it. That postman of ours, he mustn't be too easily shocked.

One morning when I was going out to work I found myself picking up one of her letters. Just like that. I just put it in my pocket. I hated myself later, but that's what I did. I just did it, I don't know, like I couldn't help myself. Walking down to the station I felt really unwell. Then I did it once or twice more, the next week, and then even more often the week after that. Then I did it a lot. Every week. I hate myself, but that's what I do. I open them on the train. I can't help it. See, in our house all the letters get left on this battered old chest that Vera the house loony found out in the back garden all covered in slugs. Vera's got more locks on her door than Fort Knox. She's crazy. She taped a note to the wall. Said: Is this anyone's? And if not/so does he/she mind if I use this for the letters?' – little arrow on the note pointing down at the chest. I mean, if anyone had owned it, what the hell was it doing in the back garden?

She's got a good bank balance. Caitlin, I mean. Better than mine, anyway. I started just taking her bills, but then sometimes I take her personal letters too and I open those. I read them in the toilet in the office. I go in there and light up a cigarette and read them. Then I tear them into tiny pieces and flush them away. Sometimes you have to flush twice. People look at me then, like maybe they know, though of course how could they? Sometimes I get this feeling the little bits are going to float back up the toilet or something, and I have to go check. Other times I save them for lunchtime. I read them on the bench in the park, when the weather's nice, eating my sandwiches. I sit there and run my finger through the envelope and unfold the paper real gently and then slowly I read.

One day I tore open one of her letters on the way down to the station and I threw the envelope on the ground. An invitation to a wedding. 'Ms Caitlin Rourke plus one', it said. Nice print too, with gold leaf on the edge. Must have cost a bit. That 'Ms' stuff really freaks me out, though. I have all kinds of arguments with Sara about things like that.

Anyway, I was half way into work when I got this idea that she was going to see the envelope lying on the ground. She would get off the train and walk across the bridge and, just my luck, see the damn thing on the ground. I came all the way back and looked around. The guy in the station asked me was I alright. I really didn't feel too good and it must have shown. It was cold, but my shirt was sticking to my body, and my heart was pumping. It took me an hour to find it and when I got into the office Mr Zimmerman wanted to see me.

She got a real stinker from the book club once, saying payment for her *Collected Dickens* was long overdue and they'd be having to resort to the unpleasantness of legal action soon. I sent them a draft under her name. Another time she got a thing that said if you filled this in you could win a million or a tropical island. You could take your choice. I filled in her name. I wrote 'MISS Caitlin Rourke', and I sent it away. Next day she got a note from the post office, said they understood her husband had reported that her name was missing from the electoral register. I ticked off the boxes and dropped it into the post office myself.

One day I came in and there was a note on the board. 'Someone's been stealing my mail,' it said, 'I would like to know WHO and more to the point I would like to know why. I am REALLY UPSET about this.' Sara said it was awful, and who would do such a thing? She looked up at me, held the phone between her head and her shoulder, took off her slipper, squeezed her foot.

'Probably Vera,' I said, 'you know how she is.'

Hello,' she said into the receiver, 'is anyone there?'

I went into the kitchen and splashed water on my face. Sara was speaking very slowly, the way people do with those answering machines.

At ten o'clock she stood up and said, 'I'm going to bed.'

'Go to bed,' I told her, 'I will be in soon.'

'OK,' she said, 'if you're going soon, I'll wait for you.'

I told her, 'Sara, for crying out loud.' She went to bed.

I've never said a single word to Caitlin Rourke. Once or twice we've met on the stairs, but always she just turns away. She has a long straight back. She looks kind of capable, like some women do. Like she wouldn't let you down. She looks like nothing could shock her. I've seen her down in the station too, getting off the same train, but she always lags behind so she won't have to talk to me. She stops and reads the timetables, that kind of thing. What's she reading the damn timetables for? I mean, she gets the same damn train every day.

One day I climbed the stairs behind her, looking up at her long black-stockinged legs. She gets the same train every day. I told you that, didn't I? Other times, she's fiddling with her keys in the doorway when I'm walking up the road. I pass by the gate and go get some cigarettes or, like last night, some gin. There've been house meetings but I've always got Sara to go. I couldn't stand it. Being in the same room as her would just kill me. I'd fall to pieces. As if things aren't bad enough.

One night Sara came back up and told me a funny story about Vera and something she said to Caitlin at the house meeting. I asked her if Caitlin had a boyfriend or anything. I had just finished doing the dishes and the skin on my hands was all wrinkled. I said has she got a boyfriend? I knew she wasn't married. Sara goes why? Are you interested?

That was our first really bad argument. It got out of hand, I admit it. I know she didn't mean it, but lately I've been feeling funny about stuff like that. I'm not myself any more, not since Mr Zimmerman let me go. It's all the sitting around. It just doesn't suit me.

I had to drive her to the hospital that night. We told the doctor she fell down the stairs. I wasn't sure if he believed us. She wanted me to see someone but I promised it would never happen again. I swore it wouldn't. That night she laughed in her sleep too. I couldn't bear to look at her the next morning, with her face like that. I asked her if she would be back tonight and she said she didn't know. Then she said she'd nowhere else to go, and she started to cry. I phoned her at the office at lunchtime and things were a little better. I promised it would never happen again. I said I don't know what's wrong with me. I think I have been working too hard. She said what do you mean working? and I said looking. Never mind, kid, she said, you'll find something soon. She calls me 'kid' sometimes. She told me that things would get better for both of us soon. She said you have to have a bit of belief in your life. I told her I loved her but she couldn't talk. Yeah, she said, I do too.

Sometimes in the night I get up and go for a walk. I don't sleep too easily. I stand outside her door in the dark, just listening, to see if I can hear anything. I stand there on the landing. Then I go down to the tracks and watch the night trains going by. I wonder where they all go to. You think the whole world is asleep but the trains just keep rolling. I stand on the bridge and look down. I spit over the side. It's cold down there, but you can see things more clearly. You hear the tracks kind of whining long before a train comes.

Sometimes when I'm here during the day I want to smash down her door and break her apartment to bits. I want to go into her bathroom and turn on all the water and let it soak through the floor. I want to take off all my clothes and lie between her smooth cold sheets. I want to search through her stuff. I want to take off my clothes and walk around her apartment. I want to open all her secret drawers.

One day I rang her bell. Then I rang every other bell in the house, but everyone was out so I was safe. I came back upstairs and tried my key in her lock. It didn't work. Thank God, I suppose.

A few months ago was the last time I saw her. She'd put on a little weight. She was looking so good, I almost said something to her. She buried her head in a magazine and when we got to our stop she didn't get off even though I knew that she had seen me. I stood on the platform and watched the train pull away. She never looked up but I knew alright.

It was Christmas, actually. I remember she said to Sara we should come down for a drink. I said I have a headache, you go. She said how come you always have a headache when people invite us. I told her she could go by herself. I said we didn't have to do every single damn thing together. I said you're getting too dependent. She said this morning she's too independent, now she's too dependent, she just can't win with me. That's it, I told her, turn it all into a game. She didn't go. She went down with a bottle of wine and said we had to go to Handel's 'Messiah' with this friend of her sister's.

She told me that Caitlin had put on a little weight. Oh, I said, has she, and what other news have you got if you're such a big deal. She said it's obvious the counsellor is doing you no good at all and I said, for God's sake, I'm warning you, don't start all that again.

That was Christmas, like I said. Last week I came in and there was another note. 'Caitlin and I have a baby girl!!' it said – 'and her name is Ailsa.' Signed by someone called Tony. Blue paper. Cheap.

I stood in the hall for a long time, just looking. Then I went upstairs. Sara didn't know who he was, but she said wasn't it so nice of him to write that, all the same. A lot of men wouldn't, she said. A lot of men are out of touch with their emotions. There were tears in her eyes when she said it. She went all quiet. She said it was just the onions in the casserole. There were tears in mine, too. Then she said it was just her hormones. She hugged me tight and told me she'd never realised I was so sentimental. It was a few days later when I found out she'd stopped taking the pill. Then she suggested we send a card, congratulations, just leave it downstairs on the dresser for her, with all her other mail. I said no. Yes, she said, that will be something for you to do. I said no, but she said yes, you know how you're supposed to take responsibility for things.

I lay in the bath this morning with my head under the water. I listened to my breathing and to the beat of my heart. I lay there perfectly still until the grey water went cold all around me.

SQUIDINKY

Nuala O'Connor

Nuala O'Connor lives in Galway and in 2019 won the *James Joyce Quarterly* competition to write the missing story from *Dubliners*, 'Ulysses'. Her fourth novel, *Becoming Belle*, was recently published to critical acclaim in the US, Ireland and the UK. Her forthcoming novel is about Nora Barnacle, wife and muse to James Joyce. Nuala is editor at flash e-zine *Splonk*.

Brine gets into your blood when you live beside the sea; it gets into your bones. You flow with a watery energy that carries you along. But you can become tough and unwieldy too, like salt-cured fish. I haven't always been a shore dweller but ending up here with Luke made me feel at peace. I live above Squidinky, my tattoo parlour, and at night I hear the sea shushing and the tourists who patter by, drunk on beer and each other.

Lying in bed I pluck sleep crystals from my eyes, stretch until my bones click, then heave myself up because my bladder is leading me to the bathroom. To my daily surprise the mirror above the sink tells me that I am old. Hovering in front of it I examine my shirred jowls and the yellow tinge to the waterlines of my eyes.

'Not too bad,' I announce, because if I say it enough it might be so.

Sunny days clang here: children beat buckets with spades, the ice cream van tinkles 'O Sole Mio', and parents whine and smile. There is such pleasure in letting all life take place outside my window, for those who come to the sea in search of happiness and escape. They are right to come here. This is the home of happy.

I won't open Squidinky today; the skins of a few more people can stay blank until tomorrow – things are slow in the spring anyway. This is a day for walking and relaxing; for air in the throat. After my porridge, I wrap my slacks into my socks and pull on rubber boots. Luke's green cape-coat will keep me cocooned if the wind is high.

Outside, the town is morning-quiet and there's a tang of fish-rot. I head along Walk and Run Avenue to the top of the terraces, planning to end up at the pebble beach. I pass the ghost hotel that sits on one wing of the town; there's a ghost estate on the other. Refugees from Nigeria and Ivory Coast used to live in the hotel, but they are gone now, taking with them their turbans and kaftans, their firm-faced children. They had a church service above the Spar every weekend and it oozed joy: they sang and clapped and shouted. I often stood outside to soak it in after buying my few messages. The people were moved, I think, to the direct provision centre in Athlone and, no doubt, they are the worse for it.

I continue along the avenue; pansies planted along the tops of stone walls curl their faces away from me like shy babies. I have the streets to myself and I savour the slap-and-echo of the soles of my boots on the footpath. The avenue feels long today but not in a bad way; it is uncluttered except for parked cars. I always relish that feeling of being queen of the town when I take an early walk. The sea glints through the gaps in the houses and I glance at it, anticipating the soothe of its blue expanse when I get to the beach.

The bench above the strand is occupied and I am put out. Who is this sitting on my seat? As I draw nearer, I see that the man on the bench is wearing socks and sandals. The first thing I always look at is people's shoes, don't ask me why. Socks and sandals, of all things. The man turns to me and raises his hand.

'Hello!' he shouts, as if we are friends. I nod and go to take the steps down onto the beach, but he pats the bench. 'Sit, sit. Come and take a seat here. Look at the view!' He tosses his hand at the bay as if he's responsible for it.

'I'll sit for a minute,' I say.

This *is* my bench. Well, it's Luke's bench; I put it here for him after he died, replacing a wooden one with fraying slats. On a cold day it is not as warm as the old seat, but the Council said steel would weather better. I am possessive about this bench, about its position overlooking the bay and the two lighthouses – Luke's favourite view. I sit at the opposite end to the man and stare out to sea. A messy cloud, like the aftermath of an explosion, hangs over the horizon.

'If you just looked at that little slice,' the man says, making a frame around the cloud with his fingers, 'you'd think all was not well.' He lowers his hands. 'But of course, all *is* well.' He looks at me, his worn face alive with smiles.

'Is it?' I say. 'What about the economy? Bankers? The hospitals?'

'What about the here and now?' he says.

A young mother in pink runners barrels past with a three-wheeled pram; she pushes her sunglasses up on her head. Her child, a portly toddler, looks backwards, up at the mother, and does the same.

'Sunglasses on a baby,' the man says, 'isn't it marvellous?' He rummages in a plastic bag at his feet. While he is distracted, I stand up. 'Have some fruit!' He hands me a red apple. 'It's a Jonaprince.'

I take the apple. 'Thank you,' I say and trot away.

He shouts, 'Cheerio!'

The man has tumbled my walk from its natural path and now I have to continue on into the marram grass and pretend that I don't mind. Soon I am tripping over the things the sea has belched up: plastic drums, lager cans, a wooden pallet. I stop walking and pull wind into my lungs then let it out. Ducks in chevron flight skim over my head and I watch them until they disappear. I veer down towards the beach where oystercatchers poke about in the sand.

In the ladies bathing shelter, I sit and look at the apple. I feel like tossing it away but instead I polish it with the hem of Luke's coat and bite into it. The skin is bitter, so I eat the flesh and spit the peels onto the ground. Luke's voice floats into my head: 'Spitting women and crowing hens will surely come to some bad ends.'

He always said that and I always answered, 'It's *whistling* women not spit-ting women.' Luke would shrug and we'd both smile. One of our shared rites.

I cannot even put a name on the feeling of missing Luke – it's too raw, too wide. All I know is that I am alone in a waiting room and the world has receded. My heart opens and closes like a mouth that wants to speak but can't form the words. The days carry forward in regular ways – I ink people, I eat, I watch television documentaries – but I push myself through weeks with a strength that seems to belong to somebody else. Mourning is hard work, it is long work; every twenty-four hours is a new lesson in learning the proper way to grieve. It's as though I am swimming through seaweed and, just as the water begins to clear, I whack into the hull of a boat.

I throw the apple butt onto the beach and the oystercatchers scatter then regroup. The rocks below the shelter are decorated with doughnuts of amber lichen; they bring colour to the grey. Between the rocks, shell caches lie in sandpits – mussels and winkles, empty of meat. I heave myself up and exit the bathing shelter. The man is still at Luke's bench but now he is standing. I take a wide arc to avoid him. He will think I'm rude but, sure, let him off.

'Ahoy!' he shouts, waving his arms like someone signalling from the deck of a ship.

'Jesus Christ.' I throw my eyes up in apology to Stella Maris who watches over the harbour from her plinth.

'Missus,' the man shouts, 'wait!' He putters up beside me. 'I'll walk with you.'

'I prefer to keep my own pace.'

'Not at all,' he says. 'You have "lonely" bobbing like a balloon over your head.'

I tut but he is undeterred. He comes with me, his plastic bag swinging at his side, all the way down Walk and Run Avenue to my door. We don't speak and I feel foolish and annoyed; foolish for being irritated – what harm is he doing? – but annoyed with him too for this disruption to my morning.

'Now,' I say, 'I'm home.' I fish my key from the coat's deep pocket.

'"Squidinky",' he says, craning to look at the shop sign. 'Well, if that doesn't beat all.' He sticks out his hand and I take it; he closes his other hand over mine and I see his knuckles are dotted with ink. 'Have a lovely day now, missus. Be good to yourself.'

Once inside the quiet of my hallway I feel I should be pleased as a peashooter to be on my own again, away from the pestering man, but I'm not. I am disarranged. I unpeel myself from Luke's coat and pop it onto its hook. It hangs like a collapsed cross and I twist it to press my face into the lining, searching for a whiff of him, the smallest scent. There is nothing there.

Luke would disapprove of all the time I spend alone now. It was he who kept up the friendships while I looked after the business. And because he was the one who rang people, who invited, greeted and mollycoddled them, once he was gone, I was forgotten. Our friends were his friends, it turned out.

In the morning 'O Sole Mio' drifts into my half-sleep. I think it is the ice cream van come a season early but it's someone whistling. The whistler trills the rising notes of the tune and drags them out; the sound is sweet wafting up to my bedroom. The words sing themselves in my head: *Che bella cosa una giornata di sole*. What a beautiful thing is a sunny day.

I peep out the window and see the man from Luke's bench standing outside. Gulls lunge around him, their cacophony hardly keeping up with their bawling beaks. The man whistles louder to drown them out, then throws his arms up in surrender. He laughs.

When I open the door to the parlour he is still outside.

'Hungry,' the man says, and I'm not sure if he is referring to himself, me, or the gulls.

'Can I help you?' I ask.

'I think so. I want to get a tattoo covered up.'

'Your knuckles?'

'No, no,' he says. 'Can I come in?'

I stand back and he walks past me, the same plastic bag rustling in his hand.

He takes a seat, removes his jacket and unbuttons his shirt. His story is revealed: he has been seaman, lover, convict. His chest is hairless and the nipples are two oxblood coins.

'So which one do you want covered?' I say, taking in the blurred lines of mermaids, and Sailor Jerry pin-ups, the lexicon of names: Mabel, Assoulina, Grace.

He stands and looks in the mirror, pushes his shoulders back to right the sag of his skin. 'Do you know what?' he says. 'Give me a new one altogether.'

I haul a book of flash from the counter for him to look through. 'Where do you want to place the new piece?' I say, my juices up at the idea of giving him something to blend with the cascade of ink on his chest. I hold out the book. 'Here you go.'

He puts his hands behind his back, refusing to take it. 'I don't want some readymade thing. I trust you.' He sits again, whistles a bar of 'O Sole Mio' and looks up at me.

'You trust me? You don't know me.'

'I know enough.' He slips off his shirt and shows his back to me; there are no tattoos. 'There's a man in Catalunya who collects tattooed skins. He says he'll buy mine when I'm done with it.'

'That's big in Japan,' I say. 'Well, maybe not big but they do it there.'

'I've been saving my back until I met the right artist. I want the sun – a great furze and orange ball of light. I want it to have a face.'

'I can do that.'

'I know you can. Like I said, I trust you.'

He comes every day after that and I work on his back; the sun's rays lick at his shoulder blades and armpits; its face frowns on the right side and smiles on the left. He asks me to put bones across the eyelids and a skull on each cheek.

'Everything has light and dark,' he says, 'even the sun. We'd be as well to keep that in mind as we go about our lives.'

My machine buzzes and he talks and talks. About his days as a seaman, about life in the belly of a ship. He tells me that Barcelona was his favourite port and how he misses the unpredictability of an onboard existence; the ferment of the uncertain.

I mention Luke, little snippets: our trips to India; his love of musicals, especially when Esther Williams was involved.

'It gave him such pleasure to watch that Esther swim,' I say. 'Luke was a merman, most at home around, in or on water. He taught me to love the sea.'

'I'm that way myself, half human, half fish,' the man says. 'You miss him, your Luke.'

'I do, of course.'

'How long?'

'A couple of years, nearly three.'

'Are you ready to let him go?' he asks.

Am I? This I don't know. I dip my needle and shade one of the skulls in the design on his back; it's benign, more Day of the Dead than Grim Reaper. Blood bubbles through the skin and I pat it away. *Will* I ever let Luke go? Do I have to? The absolute shock of his loss has eased, of course. That paroxysm that grief drags you down into swallowed me for the fat end of eighteen months. But I rose out of its depths somehow and found a plateau where I can exist, even if it is in a melancholic fug. I am lonely, it's true, but it's more than that – I'm alone.

I lift my finger off the machine and the room is quiet. 'I don't think you let go of the dead, exactly,' I say. 'You just place them into one of your heart chambers and open the door every so often. To invite them out.'

The man pushes himself up on his elbows and turns his head to face me. He nods and smiles and I am surprised to see his eyes are brimming, about to spill. He sits up and I hand him a tissue; I watch while he dabs at his face and lets whatever sadness has surfaced gust through him. It emerges on long sighs and cascades of tears.

'Are you all right?'

'Why don't we call it a day for today?' he says.

'If you're sure? All I've done is a bit of shading.'

'Let's go out for a walk. See what's to be seen.' He snuffles, blows his nose and exhales, vaporising whatever those thoughts were that upset him.

'A bit of air might do us both good, a little time out,' I say, peeling off my blue gloves and dropping them into the bin.

'Haven't we all the time in the world, the two of us?' he says.

He sits up on the side of the tattoo couch and I wash him down with cold water and rub emollient into his skin. I watch him put on his shirt; he does it deliberately, with care, unlike Luke who made a hurry of every small thing. I catch the scent of lemon off his clothes, that sweet freshness that always makes me feel hopeful and at ease.

We lock up the parlour and head along Walk and Run Avenue to the top of the terraces, past the ghost hotel and along the stretch where the residents have planted flowers on the tops of the stone walls. There are daffodils now, sweet and smoky and bright as the sun. We stop to sniff them and smile at each other, our noses bent into the flowers' yellow bells.

Once at the beach, we sit on Luke's bench and look out over the bay and the two lighthouses. Stella Maris watches over the water and the boats, her arms raised in an eternal blessing. I take my new friend's hand in mine and he throws his other arm around my shoulder; I lean my head against his head, feel the heat from his skin. He whistles a few bars of 'O Sole Mio'.

'Brine gets into your blood when you live beside the sea,' he says. 'It gets into your bones.'

We sit on, watching the oystercatchers and the ducks, the swoon of the marram grass. The bench grows warm beneath us. And the sea sways and shimmers under the awakened glow of a March sun.

THE GLASS PANEL

Eimar O'Duffy

Eimar O'Duffy (1893–1935) was a writer of fiction and satire but also wrote drama and poetry. His first book, *The Phoenix on the Roof*, appeared in 1915. His novels include *The Wasted Island* (1919), *King Goshawk and the Birds* (1926) and *Asses in Clover* (1933).

A sense of artistic propriety would make my friend Bradley a more interesting companion, and also a more capable detective, as this story will show. Those who are familiar with his record of well-earned successes will smile at this, and, referring to his latest case, demand if there was ever in the history of crime-detection a smarter piece of work than his handling of the Littlecroft Murder. Good! I accept the challenge. The Littlecroft Murder proves my contention to the hilt.

One bitterly cold evening in January, Bradley and I were ensconced in a pair of deep armchairs before a roaring fire in his sitting-cum-consulting-room, when the landlady announced Mr Jonathan Harbottle. I have an abominable habit, due, I suppose, to my occupation as a story-writer, of forming a complete mental picture of a person from his name; and Mr Jonathan Harbottle was at once presented to me as one of those hard-featured men who have done well out of the War, fifty-seven years of age with a full jowl and paunch. Judge of my chagrin when a handsome young fellow made his appearance at the door, tall and spare, with penetrating, observant eyes, and fine, nervous hands. He opened his business abruptly and without ceremony, jerking out the words as if he had held them in constraint longer than he could endure.

'What would you think, Mr Bradley, if in the midst of an absolutely uneventful country life you suddenly received a letter like this?' He gave my friend an envelope which he had held crushed up in his hand.

Motioning the young man to a chair, Bradley extracted the letter and read out its contents.

'"Here we are. Travellers' Rest, Southampton Docks. Don't fail this time, Shell out, or we'll come and see you."

'Short and to the point. No signature, I see. Cheapest quality paper, and uneducated writing. You don't recognise the hand, I suppose, Mr Harbottle?'

Our visitor shook his head.

'Posted on the fifth,' went on my friend, 'after having spent some time in an excessively dirty pocket. Well, Mr Harbottle, if you don't recognise the handwriting, and have no idea who could have sent it, and have led a perfectly uneventful life, I can't see what there is to worry about. The thing looks to me like a hoax.'

'So I thought myself,' replied our client, 'when the first one came.'

'You have had several?'

'This is the third I have received,' continued Harbottle. 'Unfortunately I destroyed the other two. This is the first I dreamt of taking seriously.'

'Were the others in the same hand?' my friend interrupted.

'Exactly. The first had an American stamp, and was posted in New York. It arrived about a month ago. I couldn't make much meaning out of it. As well as I remember, it said something about "shelling out," with a warning not to double-cross the writer. The second also came from New York, about a fortnight later. It simply repeated the message of the first, but in more threatening terms.'

'Have you informed the police?' asked Bradley.

'Yes: and they insist that it must be a hoax, though they have promised to make inquiries at Southampton. Mr Bradley,' went on the young man earnestly, 'I'm convinced that there's some mysterious but real danger threatening me. I live in the depths of the country, seven miles from the nearest village. You can understand what a difference that makes. My wife, who isn't at all nervous by nature, and treated the first letter as a joke, just as I did, has been thoroughly upset by this last one, and could hardly be persuaded to let me leave the house this morning.'

'You are not long married?' questioned Bradley.

'Only a year.'

'And your wife, I suppose, knows nothing about these letters either?'

'No more than myself.'

Bradley paused a moment, then said: 'Very well, Mr Harbottle, I shall look into this case at once. What is your profession, by the way—or your way of living?'

'I have no profession. I live on a small income derived from investments. If you have nothing more to ask me I'll leave you now. Here is my card. I am staying at the Euston Hotel for the night, and return home by the first train tomorrow.'

'I have nothing more to ask,' replied Bradley; 'but just one word to say. When you employ a doctor or a private detective, it is best to trust him and tell him *everything*. It tends to simplify the case.'

'I do trust you, and have kept back nothing,' protested his client; but I saw that his cheek reddened slightly.

'Very well, then,' said Bradley impassively, and held open the door.

*

'Our friend, of course, was lying,' observed the detective as he calmly relit his pipe after the young man's departure. 'His story is too thin altogether. You observed, of course, that the senders of the letter never signed their names, showing that they knew themselves to be known to the recipient. Then the allusiveness of their tone shows that they knew that the nature of the business would be familiar to him also. I'm afraid it's only too clear that our friend has been mixed up in some very shady transactions in the past. You must have noticed that they state their requirements and declare their whereabouts with complete faith in his direction—knowing that he cannot betray them without involving himself.'

'He betrayed them to us,' I objected.

'The greater fear sometimes expels the lesser. As I read it, our friend Harbottle has bolted with the spoils of some joint expedition, and his pals have tracked him down. It's none of my business to help him to keep them out of their share; but I shall certainly make some inquiries at Southampton—in the interests of those to whom the spoil originally belonged.'

I stayed at Bradley's rooms that night, and next morning we breakfasted early, with a view to getting to Southampton as soon as possible. We were just putting on our overcoats when we heard the hall doorbell ring: one long ring, then two shorter ones at decreasing intervals.

'Someone's in a hurry,' observed Bradley.

Next minute his landlady came in with an agitated young woman at her very heels.

'Oh, Mr Bradley,' gasped the latter. 'I'm so glad to have found you in,' and she almost collapsed on the nearest chair.

'Wouldn't give any name, sir,' apologised the landlady. 'She was too excited to say anything but just "Mr Bradley."'

'I am Mrs Jonathan Harbottle,' announced the strange young woman.

She was a beautiful creature, not more than twenty-two years of age, with dark hair and pale skin, flushed with the agitation of the moment. Her clothes were obviously of the most expensive kind, but must have been put on in the greatest haste.

'Mr Bradley,' she said, when the landlady had withdrawn, 'did my husband tell you everything yesterday?—I mean literally everything.'

'I regret to say that he did not, madam,' replied Bradley.

'Well,' said Mrs Harbottle, 'I won't keep the secret any longer. His life is more important than any secret, and I believe it's his life those dreadful men are after. There are two of them, Mr Bradley: two of the most dreadful-looking ruffians you ever saw.'

Bradley paid no attention to this. He was taking a cup and saucer from the china cupboard and laying a place at the table. Then, pouring out tea from the pot that had served us, and cutting some slices of bread, he said casually: 'Better have a little breakfast, Mrs Harbottle.'

The lady thanked him for his kindness, and admitted that she had had none before starting. She was steadied by the tea, and made a very good meal: indeed, she was a little shamefaced at her appetite. Bradley chatted with her urbanely as she ate, but as soon as she had finished he asked her for her story.

'But first,' he said, 'let me warn you that you do so of your own free will. My duty may compel me to use it against your husband.'

'It can do him no harm,' she said confidently. 'In the first place, you must know that his name is not Harbottle, but Wetheral—Walter Wetheral.'

'Not *the* Walter Wetheral?' I asked.

'Yes.'

Here was a quite unexpected revelation. Wetheral was the coming man in the English dramatic world. Indeed, he had all but arrived. Two of his plays were drawing crowded houses in London at that very moment.

Mrs Wetheral continued her statement.

'You may not know that my husband was years waiting for recognition, struggling along at hack work in Fleet Street, and often on the verge of starvation. It was at that period that I first met him and became engaged to him; and it was on my account that he took the step that so radically altered our lives. We were both eager to get married, and six months after our engagement recognition seemed as far off as ever. Then one day Walter put an SOS advertisement in the Agony Column of *The Times*, asking for work of any kind. To our surprise it received an immediate answer, a letter signed Jonathan Harbottle, asking Walter to come that night to the Carlton Hotel.

'Walter, of course, kept the appointment, and next day told me all that had occurred there. It appeared that this Mr Harbottle was an old bachelor without relatives of any sort, and was looking round for someone to leave his money to when he saw Walter's advertisement. He had previously been struck by some of his work in magazines, and decided that his money could not be better placed than in giving him a start in life. As a sort of preliminary test, Walter was to take over his country house for a year, with sufficient income to run it, while Mr Harbottle went to Madeira for his health. During that time he was to give up journalism, and devote himself entirely to literature. He was also to keep the whole transaction a secret.'

'What sort of man was this Harbottle?' asked Bradley, as the lady paused.

'I met him next day,' said Mrs Wetheral. 'He was one of those jolly old gentlemen, with a white beard and big beaming spectacles, and terribly amusing to talk to. He told us that he had already made his will. "But mind," he said, shaking his finger in comic admonition at Walter, "if you write one word of commercial stuff—one word that isn't real art—I'll cut you off with a shilling." It was on this occasion that he asked Walter to take his name. "Keep your own for literary purposes," he said. "But—well. I'd like to feel as if you were a sort of son to me." When he put it that way, of course, Walter couldn't very well object, and the whole thing was carried out in legal form a few days later.

'Not long after that, Walter and I were married, and Mr Harbottle at once went off to Madeira. When we came back from our honeymoon we took over the house he had lent us in Hertfordshire. It's in a lonely spot, right in the depths of the country, but the house itself is handsome and comfortable. Mr Harbottle had left his old butler in charge, and he had already got in new servants—two maids and a boy—in order to keep our arrangements a secret. The butler is a confidential old man who had been always in his employment, and, of course, knows everything.

'Well,' concluded Mrs Wetheral, 'there we've been living for the past year, ideally happy, until these dreadful letters arrived. And now you know the whole truth, Mr Bradley.'

'Your story certainly puts a very different complexion on the case,' said Bradley. 'Tell me, Mrs Wetheral, has it never occurred to you that these letters have been intended for the genuine Mr Harbottle?'

'Certainly. When the third one came, and we began to be afraid it wasn't a hoax, that solution occurred to us at once, and my husband wrote to him about it before coming to you. But of course it will take a long time for his letter to reach Madeira, and something happened which made me realise that it might be dangerous to keep his secret any longer.'

Long practice has given Bradley a professional impassivity, but at these words I could not help drawing my chair a little closer to our client.

'Yesterday afternoon I happened to be sitting at the drawing-room window, when I saw two men come walking up the avenue. They looked like seamen. One was very tall, the other quite short, but before I could observe any more they were hidden by an angle of the house, and next minute the hall doorbell rang. Instantly the words of the letter flashed into my memory. "Don't fail... or we'll come and see you," and I felt very thankful that Walter was away. I waited breathless at the window until, after what seemed like an age, the two men reappeared and retreated down the avenue. I rushed downstairs at once, and found the butler in the hall. He told me that the men had asked for my husband, but wouldn't state their business, so, putting them down as cadgers, he had sent them away. And what do you think, Mr Bradley?—he said one of them had an ugly-looking knife stuck in his belt.'

'You certainly did well to come to me, Mrs Wetheral,' said Bradley, 'and you may count on my wasting no time in getting on the track of these callers of yours. If you will take my advice, you will go straight home now and tell your husband all that has happened. I know that he intended to take the first train this morning, so you will probably find him there when you arrive. I have a few things to attend to here in town, but I shall follow you as soon as possible, and you may expect to see me at Willowdene either this evening or tomorrow morning.'

As soon as Mrs Wetheral had gone, Bradley caught up a railway guide and quickly ran through its pages.

'Excellent,' he said. 'She will catch the ten forty-five, and we can get another fifty minutes later. It wouldn't do at all if protectors and protected were to arrive on the same train. There may be tough work tonight, so, if you're coming, we'd better slip over to your rooms for your revolver.'

He took his own from a drawer as he spoke, and loaded its six chambers.

A two hours' run in a slow train brought us to Littlecroft, the station named on Wetheral's card. We at once sought out the less reputable of the two inns in the place, and went into the dining-room, where lunch was already being served. There were not many occupants of the room, and two of them caught our attention immediately. Both were obviously seamen, and equally obviously of criminal type. One was more than six feet in height, the other rather less than five. They were, in fact, our quarry, to the last letter of Mrs Wetheral's description.

When they had finished their meal they sauntered out to the bar, where they sat drinking and smoking the whole afternoon. Supper was served at six. Harbottle's dupes ate theirs quickly, then rose and went out. A minute later we heard them leave the inn and take the direction in which, we had learnt, lay Wetheral's house. Bradley waited to give them some start, then sprang to his feet saying: 'Come.'

It was quite dark outside, but we kept in touch with our quarry quite easily by the ring of their feet on the frozen road—the better to hear which, as well as for the concealment of our own movements, we walked on the grass by the wayside. Careful as we were, however, we could not avoid an occasional stumble, with the result that the suspicions of the pursued were aroused, and once they stopped to listen while we stood still and held our breath. We were obliged to keep farther behind after that, and, to make matters worse for us, a mist was beginning to rise. Where exactly we lost our way we never found out, but lost it we did. Alarmed after a while at hearing no sound ahead of us, we put on pace a little; then, as there was no sign of the quarry, we ran. We ran for nearly a mile before we realised that we had been given the slip.

We turned at once in our tracks and went back about a mile and a half to a likely-looking branch road, but after following that for twenty minutes we came to a crossroad that baffled us completely. What we did during the next six hours I cannot accurately remember. There were few houses to inquire at, and the sleepy-eyed inhabitants of one gave us directions that confused us worse than ever. Dread of what those two evil men might do would not, however, let us abandon the search. Yet it was by sheer chance that we finally came upon the house at about one o'clock in the morning.

I almost cried out with relief to make out the name on the gate: *Willowdene*. We walked up the avenue and rang at the hall door. Almost immediately a window overhead was opened, and a voice—Wetheral's—asked who was there. Bradley having announced our identity, Wetheral's head was withdrawn, and a minute later he opened the door. Briefly Bradley explained what had occurred; which Wetheral supplemented with the information that the men had arrived at about nine o'clock, that, on being refused admittance by the butler, they had gone the round of the house as if seeking another entry, and, failing to find one, had gone off after discharging a battery of bad language.

Wetheral offered us beds, and, for his sake as much as for our own, we accepted so far as to take a couple of couches and rugs in the drawing-room. Thoroughly exhausted by our long tramp, we were fast asleep in an instant.

A crash of breaking glass woke us to broad daylight. Instinctively we sprang from our couches, and rushed from the room and up the stairs. Two frightened-looking domestics stood on the landing above, and an old man, evidently the butler, came out to meet us from one of the rooms.

'I'm Bradley, the detective,' said my friend quickly. 'What has happened?'

'I'm afraid you're too late, sir,' said the butler. 'My master has been murdered in his sleep.'

At that moment a muffled female voice sounded from the room he had just left.

'That will be the mistress, sir,' said the butler. 'They must have locked her up.'

We followed him into the room, and, scarcely pausing to glance at the ghastly thing that lay on the blood-soaked bed, hastened to unlock the door communicating with Mrs Wetheral's room, the key being still in the lock. She knew nothing of what had occurred, having only just wakened, like ourselves; and though we broke the news to her as gently as possible, she immediately fainted. I helped the butler to carry her to another room, where, after applying restoratives, we left her in charge of the very capable maid, and returned to the scene of the crime.

It was now for the first time that I noticed the glass panels that formed the upper part of Wetheral's door. One of them was completely smashed—evidently the cause of our waking—and through it I could see Bradley, not, to my surprise, hunting about for clues, but quietly smoking a cigarette. As soon as we entered he turned to the butler.

'Do you remember, er——?'

'Wingate, sir,' said the old man.

Bradley acknowledged the name.

'Do you remember exactly what sort of knife that seaman was carrying yesterday?'

'Perfectly, sir. It was about as long as a table-knife, with a black leather sheath, and a horn handle.'

'Is that it, do you think?'

Wingate peered closely at the weapon which Bradley held towards him, examining it for quite three minutes before making up his mind. He was one of those ponderous old servants with a double chin and a great sense of personal importance. He took off his blue-tinted glasses twice, and polished them, before he could come to a decision. At last he said: 'It's certainly very like it, sir, but I couldn't swear to it without the sheath.'

'Very good, Wingate. Will you now be so good as to tell us exactly how the discovery of the crime took place?'

'Certainly, sir. It was Jane, the parlourmaid, sir, who discovered it first, indirectly. When she brought the master his shaving water, as usual, at seven o'clock, she could get no answer to her knock. So after a while she just tried the door, and found it locked. After that she came down to me, sir, to know what she should do. Of course I felt anxious at once, with those fellows hanging about yesterday, so I went up with her right away. I knocked at the master's door myself then, and of course there was still no answer, so I took the liberty of looking through the keyhole, and saw that the key was still in the lock. I immediately took off my shoe, sir, and broke the glass. Then I slipped my hand through, unlocked the door, and was just looking at the body when you gentlemen arrived.'

'I suppose you have guessed already, Wingate,' said Bradley, 'that these seamen are after your old master, the real Mr Harbottle.'

Wingate, thoroughly startled, began to stammer denials.

'Oh, that's no use with me, my man,' said Bradley. 'I know everything from Mrs Wetheral's own lips. But perhaps you might tell me if you know of any incidents in Mr Harbottle's life which might have set these fellows against him.'

Wingate drew himself up with dignity.

'Mr Harbottle,' he said, 'may not have been all he might have been. But a good master who pays good wages is entitled to good service, *and* discretion.'

'Excellent, Wingate,' said Bradley. 'I wish all servants were as loyal. Now, would you mind getting someone to take this note to the police station at Little-croft? The sooner they get on the tracks of those two scoundrels the better. '

'I suppose you're quite satisfied that they are the scoundrels,' I remarked when Wingate had set off on his errand.

'I don't see that there can be any doubt of it,' Bradley replied. 'We know all their movements up to a late hour last night. If you look out of that window you will see a ladder propped against the sill. I understand from the parlour-maid—whose story of the morning's events, by the way, completely confirms Wingate's—that it was kept in a shed in the garden, where they must have found it. You must have already observed the piece cut out of that pane by which they opened the window. Finally, there's the knife.'

'Yes,' I said. 'But don't forget this is a sort of blackmailing case, and it's most unusual for blackmailers to kill their victim—except as a last resort. Of course I grant you that this may have been the last resort, but, then, as you said just now, there's the knife. Did you ever hear of a murderer, not an absolute imbecile, who carried his knife about for days for everybody to identify, and then left it sticking in his victim's body?'

'He didn't, as a matter of fact. I found it near the window, where he might easily have dropped it in climbing out.'

'*Touché*,' I admitted. 'But if I were you I'd make some inquiries at the village whether anyone else than Wingate ever saw that knife.'

'You mean that Wingate——?'

'Wingate,' I said, 'is a most discreet and confidential servant. And while you're about it,' I added, 'just have a look at the footprints round the bottom of the ladder.'

Bradley darted downstairs in an instant, leaving me alone to frame into shape a sudden wild suggestion that had leaped to my mind when first I caught sight of Wetheral's door. I went out now to look at this again, and again the question asked itself: what on earth are those two glass panels for? It was their utter incongruity with their surroundings that had struck me at first and set me wondering. They were of that abominable patterned kind that one associates with city offices and railway stations, and they ruined the harmony of a landing, every door of which was of carved oak. Nobody with the smallest artistic sense would have perpetuated such a piece of vandalism even for a useful purpose: and what useful purpose did these things serve? Certainly they had not been put there for lighting's sake, for the landing was amply lighted without them. Then why?

The jagged hole in the left-hand panel stared at me like an evil interrogation mark; and even as the answer came to my mind, up the stairs came Bradley in the worst of humours.

'There are no footprints,' he admitted. 'But the ground is as hard as rock anyway, and if you think I'm going on a wild-goose chase after that knife, you're mistaken.'

'Quite right,' I said. 'It would be a waste of time. If these men did carry a knife, it proves they didn't mean murder. If they didn't carry one, our business lies with Wingate, who said they did.'

'You seem bent on dragging the most absurd complications into a perfectly simple case,' said Bradley irritably. 'If these two seamen didn't commit the murder, the whole thing becomes chaos. You say that blackmailers don't usually kill their victims. But how do we know they were only blackmailers? Those letters are altogether too vague to build on. Depend upon it, Harbottle knew his life was in danger, and counted on their killing his substitute and putting their own necks in the noose at the same time.'

'What an innocent a detective can be!' I exclaimed. 'I'm afraid, Bradley, you're a long way from having sounded the depth of human wickedness.'

'I think I've painted Harbottle fairly black,' remonstrated Bradley.

'No. Only a dirty grey. You see, he knew quite well that these men would *not* kill his substitute. That's why he had to kill him himself.'

Bradley's expression was one of blank astonishment. I hastened to enlighten him.

'Observe those panels. If you had any artistic sense you'd see that they are entirely out of place in this house; and even without it you must see that they are no earthly use. They were put there for one purpose, and for one purpose only.'

'Yes?'

'They were put there by Harbottle so that while on the landing he could slip his hand through and unlock the door from the inside. You see, he had the key in his hand when he broke the glass.'

'But Wingate——' began Bradley.

'Wingate wears close-cropped iron-grey hair, blue spectacles, and a shaven chin. Harbottle wore bushy white hair and a beard. The Wetherals never saw them together.'

'I do believe you've got it,' cried Bradley in great excitement. 'The astute scoundrel must have murdered his own substitute in order to get those other poor devils hanged. I think that the sooner we get in touch with the police the better.'

*

At the trial it turned out that this solution was correct. Harbottle had been concerned, years before, in a series of jewel robberies in the United States, with the two seamen as his accomplices—or rather his tools; for he was the brain of the enterprise—and when his catspaws were taken he escaped arrest and got away with the whole of the spoils. The seamen had done seven years in a penitentiary, and when their release became due he began planning to preserve his gains and rid himself of his enemies at one stroke.

Of course Bradley got all the credit for the arrest. Nobody could be expected to believe that it was my sense of artistic propriety that had run so desperate a criminal to earth. But if only Bradley had a touch of it, what a detective he would make!

A DEAD CERT

Seán Ó Faoláin

Seán Ó Faoláin (1900–1991) published novels, biography, non-fiction (including biographies of Constance Markievicz and Hugh O'Neill) and travel writing but is best known as a short story writer. He published several acclaimed collections, including *The Talking Trees, Foreign Affairs, and Other Stories* and *The Man Who Invented Sin.*

Whenever Jenny Rosse came up to Dublin, for a shopping spree, or a couple of days with the Ward Union Hunt, or to go to the Opera, or to visit some of her widespread brood of relations in or around the city, or to do anything at all just to break the monotony of what she would then mockingly call "my life in the provinces," the one person she never failed to ring was Oweny Flynn; and no matter how busy Oweny was in the courts or in his law chambers he would drop everything to have a lunch or a dinner with her. They had been close friends ever since he and Billy Rosse—both of them then at the King's Inns—had met her together twelve or thirteen years ago after a yacht race at the Royal Saint George. Indeed, they used to be such a close trio that, before she finally married Billy and buried herself in Cork, their friends were always laying bets on which of the two she would choose, and the most popular version of what happened in the end was that she let them draw cards for her. "The first man," she had cried gaily, "to draw the ace of hearts!" According to this account the last card in the pack was Billy's, and before he turned it she fainted. As she was far from being a fainter, this caused a great deal of wicked speculation about which man she had always realized she wanted. On the other hand, one of her rivals said that she had faked the whole thing to get him.

This Saturday afternoon in October she and Oweny had finished a long, gossipy lunch at the Shelbourne, where she always stayed whenever she came up to Dublin. ("I hate to be tied to my blooming relatives!") They were sipping their coffee and brandy in two deep saddleback armchairs, the old flowery chintzy kind that the Shelbourne always provides. The lounge was empty and, as always after wine, Oweny had begun to flirt mildly with her, going back over the old days, telling her, to her evident satisfaction, how lonely it is to be a bachelor of thirty-seven ("My life trickling away into the shadows of memory!"), and what a fool he had been to let such a marvelous lump of a girl slip through his fingers, when, all of a sudden, she leaned forward and tapped the back of his hand like a dog pawing for still more attention.

"Oweny!" she said. "I sometimes wish my husband would die for a week."

For a second he stared at her in astonishment. Then, in a brotherly kind of voice, he said, "Jenny! I hope there's nothing wrong between you and Billy?"

She tossed her red head at the very idea.

"I'm as much in love with Billy as ever I was! Billy is the perfect husband. I wouldn't change him for worlds."

"So I should have hoped," Oweny said, dutifully, if a bit stuffily. "I mean, of all the women in the world you must be one of the luckiest and happiest that ever lived. Married to a successful barrister. Two splendid children. How old is Peter now? Eight? And Anna must be ten. There's one girl who is going to be a breaker of men's hearts and an engine of delight. Like," he added, remembering his role, "her beautiful mother. And you have that lovely house at Silversprings. With that marvelous view down the Lee..."

"You can't live on scenery!" she interposed tartly. "And there's a wind on that river that'd cool a tomcat!"

"A car of your own. A nanny for the kids. Holidays abroad every year. No troubles or trials that I ever heard of. And," again remembering his duty, "if I may say so, every time we meet, you look younger, and," he plunged daringly, "more desirable than ever. So, for God's sake, Jenny Rosse, what the hell on earth are you talking about?"

She turned her head to look out pensively at the yellowing sun glittering above the last, trembling, fretted leaves of the trees in the Green, while he gravely watched her, admiring the way its light brought out the copper-gold of her hair, licked the flat tip of her cocked nose and shone on her freckled redhead's cheek that had always reminded him of peaches and cream, and "No," he thought, "not a pretty woman, not pretty-pretty, anyway I never did care for that kind of prettiness, she is too strong for that, too much vigor, I'm sure she has poor old Billy bossed out of his life!" And he remembered how she used to sail her water-wag closer to the wind than any fellow in the yacht club, and how she used to curse like a trooper if she slammed one into the net, always hating to lose a game, especially to any man, until it might have been only last night that he had felt that aching hole in his belly when he knew that he had lost her forever. She turned her head to him and smiled wickedly.

"Yes," she half agreed. "Everything you say is true but..."

"But what?" he asked curiously, and sank back into the trough of his armchair to receive her reply.

Her smile vanished.

"Oweny! You know exactly how old I am. I had my thirty-fourth birthday party last week. By the way, I was very cross with you that you didn't come down for it. It was a marvelous party. All Cork was at it. I felt like the Queen of Sheba. It went on until about three in the morning. I enjoyed every single minute of it. But the next day, I got the shock of my life! I was sitting at my dressing table brushing my hair." She stopped dramatically, and pointed her finger tragically at him as if his face were her mirror. "When I looked out the window at a big red grain boat steaming slowly down the river, out to sea, I stopped brushing, I looked at myself, and there and then I said, 'Jenny Rosse! You are in your thirty-fifth year. And you've never had a lover!' And I realized that I never could have a lover, not without hurting Billy, unless he obliged me by dying for a week."

For fully five seconds Oweny laughed and laughed.

"Wait," he choked, "until the lads at the Club hear this one!"

The next second he was sitting straight up in his armchair.

"Jenny," he said stiffly, "would you mind telling me why exactly you chose to tell this to *me*?"

"Aren't you interested?" she asked innocently.

"Isn't it just a tiny little bit unfair?"

"But Billy would never know he'd been dead for a week. At most he'd just think he'd lost his memory or something. Don't you suppose that's what Lazarus thought? Oh! I see what you mean. Well, I suppose yes, I'd have betrayed Billy. That's true enough, isn't it?"

"I am not thinking of your good husband. I am thinking of the other unfortunate fellow when his week would be out!"

"What other fellow? Are you trying to suggest that I've been up to something underhand?"

"I mean," he pressed on, quite angry now, "that I refuse to believe that you are mentally incapable of realizing that if you ever did let any other man fall in love with you for even five minutes, not to speak of a whole week, you would be sentencing him to utter misery for the rest of his life."

"Oh, come off it!" she huffed. "You always did take things in high C. Why are you so bloody romantic? It was just an idea. I expect lots of women have it, only they don't admit it. One little, measly wild oat? It's probably something I should have done before I got married, but," she grinned happily, "I was too busy then having a good time. 'In the morning sow thy seed and in the evening withold not thine hand.' Ecclesiastes. I learned that at Alexandra College. Shows you how innocent I was—I never knew what it really meant until I got married. Of course, you men are different. You think of nothing else."

He winced.

"If you mean me," he said sourly, "you know damned well that I never wanted any woman but you."

When she laid her hand on his he understood why she had said that about Billy dying for a week. But when he snatched his hand away and she gathered up her gloves with all the airs of a woman at the end of her patience with a muff, got up, and strode ahead of him to the leveling sun outside the hotel, he began to wonder if he really had understood. He even began to wonder if it was merely that he had upset her with all that silly talk about old times. A side-glance caught a look in her eyes that was much more mocking than hurt and at once his anger returned. She had been doing much more than flirting. She had been provoking him. Or had she just wanted to challenge him? Whatever she was doing she had maneuvered him into a ridiculous position. Then he thought, "She will drive to Cork tonight and I will never be certain what she really meant." While he boggled she started talking brightly about her holiday plans for the winter. A cover-up? She said she was going to Gstaad for the skiing next month with a couple of Cork friends.

"Billy doesn't ski, so he won't come. We need another man. Would you like to join us? They are nice people. Jim Chandler and his wife. About our age. You'd enjoy them."

He said huffily that he was too damned busy. And she might not know it but some people in the world have to earn their living. Anyway, he was saving up for two weeks' sailing in the North Sea in June. At which he saw that he had now genuinely hurt her. ("Dammit, if we really were lovers this would be our first quarrel!") He forced a smile.

"Is this goodbye, Jenny? You did say at lunch that you were going to drive home this evening? Shan't I see you again?"

She looked calculatingly at the sun winking coldly behind the far leaves.

"I hate going home—I mean so soon. And I hate driving alone in the dark. I think I'll just go to bed after dinner and get up bright and early on Sunday morning before the traffic. I'll be back at Silversprings in time for lunch."

"If you are doing nothing tonight why don't you let me take you to dinner at the Yacht Club?"

She hesitated. Cogitating the long road home? Or what?

"Jenny! They'd all love to see you. It will be like old times. You remember the Saturday night crowds?"

She spoke without enthusiasm.

"So be it. Let's do that."

She presented her freckled cheek for his parting kiss. In frank admiration he watched her buttocks swaying provocatively around the corner of Kildare Street.

Several times during the afternoon, back in his office, he found himself straying from his work to her equivocal words. Could there, after all, be something wrong between herself and Billy? Could she be growing tired of him?

It could happen, and easily. A decent chap, fair enough company, silent, a bit slow, not brilliant even at his own job, successful only because of his father's name and connections, never any good at all at sport—he could easily see her flying down the run from the Eggli at half a mile a minute, the snow leaping from her skis whenever she did a quick turn. But not Billy. He would be down in the valley paddling around like a duck among the beginners behind the railway—and he remembered what a hopeless sheep he had always been with the girls, who nevertheless seemed to flock around him all the time, perhaps (it was the only explanation he ever found for it) because he was the fumbling sort of fellow that awakens the maternal instinct in girls. At which he saw her not as a girl in white shorts dashing to and fro on the tennis courts, but as the mature woman who had turned his face into her mirror by crying at him along her pointing finger, "You are in your thirty-fifth year!" How agile, he wondered, would she now be on the courts or the ski runs? He rose and stood for a long time by his window, glaring down at the Saturday evening blankness of Nassau Street, and heard the shouting from the playing fields of Trinity College, and watched the small lights of the buses moving through the bluing dusk, until he shivered at the cold creeping through the pane. He felt the tilt of time and the falling years, and in excitement understood her sudden lust.

As always on Saturday nights, once the autumn comes and the sailing is finished and every boat on the hard for another winter, the lounge and the bar of the Club were a cascade of noise. If he had been alone he would have at once added his bubble of chatter to it. Instead he was content to stand beside the finest woman in the crowd, watching her smiling proudly around her, awaiting attention from her rout (What was that great line? *Diana's foresters, gentlemen of the shade, minions of the moon?*) until, suddenly, alerted and disturbed, he found her eyes turning from the inattentive mob to look out broodily through the tall windows. The lighthouse on the pier's end was writing slow circles on the dusty water of the harbor. He said, "Jenny, you are not listening to me!" She whispered crossly, "But I don't know a single one of these bloody people!" He pointed out the commodore. Surely she remembered Tom O'Leary? She peered and said, "Not *that* old man?" He said, "How could you have forgotten?"

Tom had not forgotten her, as he found when he went to the bar to refresh their drinks.

"Isn't that Jenny Rosse you have there?" he asked Oweny. "She's putting on weight, bedad! Ah, she did well for herself."

"How do you mean?" Oweny asked, a bit shortly.

"Come off it. Didn't she marry one of the finest practices in Cork! Handsome is as handsome does, my boy! She backed a dead cert."

Jealous old bastard! As he handed her the glass he glanced covertly at her beam. Getting a bit broad, alright. She asked idly, "Who is that slim girl in blue, she is as brown as if she has been sailing all summer?" He looked and shrugged.

"One of the young set? I think she's George Whitaker's daughter."

"That nice-looking chap in the black tie looks lost. Just the way Billy used always to look. Who is he?"

"Saturday nights!" he said impatiently. "You know the way they bring the whole family. It gives the wives a rest from the cooking."

It was a relief to lead her into the dining room and find her mood change like the wind to complete gaiety.

"So this," she laughed, "is where it all began. And look! The same old paintings. They haven't changed a thing."

The wine helped, and they were safely islanded in their corner, even with the families baying cheerfully at one another from table to table, even though she got on his nerves by dawdling so long over the coffee that the maids had cleared every table but theirs. Then she revealed another change of mood.

"Oweny! Please let's go somewhere else for our nightcap."

"But where?" he said irritably. "Not in some scruffy pub?"

"Your flat?" she suggested, and desire spread in him like a water lily. It shriveled when she stepped out ahead of him into the cold night air, looked up at the three-quarter moon, then at the Town Hall clock.

"What a stunning night! Oweny, I've changed my mind! Just give me a good strong coffee and I'll drive home right away."

"So!" he said miserably. "We squabbled at lunch. And our dinner was a flop."

She protested that it had been a marvelous dinner; and wasn't it grand the way nothing had been changed?

"They even still have that old picture of the Duke of Windsor when he was a boy in the navy."

He gave up. He had lost the set. All the way into town they spoke only once.

"We had good times," she said. "I could do it all over again."

"And change nothing?" he growled.

Her answer was pleasing, but inconclusive—"Who knows?"

If only he could have her in the witness box, under oath, for fifteen minutes!

In his kitchenette, helping him to make the coffee, she changed gear again, so full of good spirits (because, he understood sourly, she was about to take off for home) that he thrust an arm about her waist, assaulted her cheek with a kiss as loud as a champagne cork, and said fervently (he had nothing to lose now), "And I thinking how marvelous it would be if we could be in bed together all night!" She laughed mockingly, handed him the coffee pot—a woman long accustomed to the grappling hook—and led the way with the cups back into his living room. They sat on the small sofa before his coffee table.

"And I'll tell you another thing, Jenny!" he said. "If I had this flat twelve years ago it might very easily have happened that you would have become my one true love! You would have changed my whole life!"

She let her head roll back on the carved molding of the sofa, looking past him at the moon. Quickly he kissed her mouth. Unstirring she looked back into his eyes, whispered, "I should not have let you do that," returned her eyes to the moon, and whispered, "Or should I?"

"Jenny!" he ordered. "Close your eyes. Pretend you really are back twelve years ago."

Her eyelids sank. He kissed her again, softly, wetly, felt her hand creep to his shoulder and impress his kiss, felt her lips open. Her hand fell weakly away. Desire climbed into his throat. And then he heard her moan the disenchanting name. He drew back, rose, and looked furiously down at her. She opened her eyes, stared uncomprehendingly around her, and looked up at him in startled recognition.

"So," he said bitterly, "he did not die even for one minute?"

She laughed wryly, lightly, stoically, a woman who would never take anything in a high key, except a five-barred gate or a double-ditch.

"I'm sorry, Oweny. It's always the same. Whenever I dream of having a lover I find myself at the last moment in my husband's arms."

She jumped up, snatched her coat, and turned on him.

"Why the hell, Oweny, for God's sake, don't you go away and get married?"

"To have me dreaming about you, is that what you want?"

"I want to put us both out of pain!"

They glared hatefully at one another.

"Please drive me to the Shelbourne. If I don't get on the road right away, I'll go right out of the top of my head!" They drove to the Green, she got out, slammed the car door behind her and without a word raced into the hotel. He whirled, drove hell for leather back to the Club, killed the end of the night with the last few gossipers, drank far too much and lay awake for hours staring sideways from his pillow over the gray, frosting roofs and countless yellow chimney pots of Dublin.

Past twelve. In her yellow sports Triumph she would tear across the Curragh at seventy-five and along the two straight stretches before and after Monasterevan. By now she has long since passed through Port Laoise and Abbeyleix where only a few lighted upper-story windows still resist night and sleep. From that on, for hour after hour, south and south, every village street and small town she passes will be fast asleep, every roadside cottage, every hedge, field and tree, and the whole widespread, moonblanched country pouring past her headlights until she herself gradually becomes hedge, tree, field, and fleeting moon. Arched branches underlit, broken demesne walls, a closed garage, hedges flying, a gray church, a lifeless gate-lodge, until the black rock and ruin of Cashel comes slowly wheeling about the moon. A streetlamp falling on a blank window makes it still more blank. Cars parked beside a curb huddle from the cold. In Cahir the boarded windows of the old granaries are blind with age. The dull square is empty. Her wheeling lights catch the vacant eyes of the hotel, leap the useless bridge, fleck the side of the Norman castle. She is doing eighty on the level uplands under the Galtee mountains, heedless of the sleep-wrapt plain falling for miles and miles away to her left.

Why is she stopping? To rest, to look, to light a cigarette, to listen? He can see nothing for her to see but a scatter of farmhouses on the plain; nothing to hear but one sleepless dog as far away as the moon it bays. He lights his bedside lamp. Turned half past two. He puts out his light and there are her kangaroo lights, leaping, climbing, dropping, winding, slowing now because of the twisting strain on her arms. She does not see the sleeping streets of Fermoy; only the white signpost marking the remaining miles to Cork. Her red tail-lights disappear and reappear before him every time she winds and unwinds down to the sleeping estuary of the Lee, even at low tide not so much a river as a lough—gray, turbulent and empty. He tears after her as she rolls smoothly westward beside its shining slobland. Before them the bruised clouds hang low over the city silently awaiting the morning.

She brakes to turn in between her white gates, her wheels spit back the gravel, she zooms upward to her house and halts under its staring windows. She switches off the engine, struggles out, stretches her arms high above her head with a long, shivering, happy, outpouring groan, and then, breathing back a long breath, she holds her breasts up to her windows. There is not a sound but the metal of her engine creaking as it cools, and the small wind whispering up from the river. She laughs to see their cat flow like black water around the corner of the house. She leans into the car, blows three long, triumphant horn blasts, and before two windows can light up over her head she has disappeared indoors as smoothly as her cat. And that, at last, it is the end of sleep, where, behind windows gone dark again, she spreads herself under her one true lover.

Neither of them hear the morning seagulls over the Liffey or the Lee. He wakes unrefreshed to the sounds of late church bells. She half opens her eyes to the flickering light of the river on her ceiling, rolls over on her belly, and stretching out her legs behind her like a satisfied cat, she dozes off again. He stares for a long time at his ceiling, hardly hearing the noise of the buses going by.

It is cold. His mind is clear and cold. I know now what she wants. But does she? Let her lie. She called me a romantic and she has her own fantasy. She has what she wanted, wants what she cannot have, is not satisfied with what she has got. I have known her for over twelve years and never known her at all. The most adorable woman I ever met. And a common slut! If she had married me I suppose she would be dreaming now of him? Who was it said faithful women are always regretting their own fidelity, never their husbands'? Die for a week? He chuckled at her joke. Joke? Or gamble? Or a dead cert? If I could make him die for a week it would be a hell of a long week for her. Will I write to her? I could telephone.

Hello, Jenny! It's me. I just wanted to be sure you got back safely the other night. Why wouldn't I worry? About anyone as dear and precious as you? Those frosty roads. Of course it was, darling, a lovely meeting. And we must do it again. No, nothing changes! That's a dead cert. Oh, and Jenny! I nearly forgot. About that skiing bit next month in Gstaad. Can I change my mind? I'd love to join you. May I? Splendid! Oh, no! Not for that long. Say… just for a week?

He could see her hanging up the receiver very slowly.

THE DOCTOR'S VISIT

Liam O'Flaherty

Liam O'Flaherty (1896–1984) was a novelist and short story writer who was a native Irish-speaker but wrote mostly in English. His novels include *The Black Soul* (1924), *The Ecstasy Of Angus* (1931) and *Hollywood Cemetery* (1935). He wrote numerous short stores, which were collected in a three-volume set, and also published several books for children.

Maurice Dowling lay flat on his back in his little narrow bed. He gripped the bedclothes in his two hands and held his hands up under his chin. He lay so flat and he was so slim that his figure was barely outlined against the bedclothes. But his feet stuck up at the end of the bed because the blankets were too short. His feet, covered by a rather soiled white cotton sheet, pressed against the black iron support. A yellow quilt lay sideways across his body, all crumpled up in the middle. The hospital attendant had arranged it several times during the night and warned Dowling each time not to touch it again, but Dowling always kicked it away from his chest. He wouldn't touch it with his hands to throw it away and he wouldn't endure having it near his mouth. He had an idea that the quilt was full of fleas.

His head, half buried in the white pillow, was very thin. His hair was black and cropped close. But even though it was cropped close, it was not stiff and bristly as close-cropped hair usually is. It lay matted on his skull in little ring-letty waves. His face was deadly pale and his high cheekbones protruded in an ugly fashion from his hollow cheeks. His large blue eyes kept darting hither and thither restlessly, never stopping for a moment. And his large mouth also moved restlessly.

Dowling was terribly afraid of the patients who were with him in the hospital ward. He had just come in the previous midnight. This was his first morning in the ward. All the patients were awake now waiting for the doctor's visit at ten o'clock. Ever since it became light and he could see their faces he became seized with a great horror of them. During the night he had heard queer sounds, wild laughter, whisperings and bestial articulations, but he thought he was merely suffering from the usual nightmares and noises in his head. Now, however, that he could see them he knew that it could not be a freak of the imagination. There were about forty of them there. His own bed was in the centre of the ward, near a large black stove that was surrounded by wire netting on all sides. Then both sides of the ward were lined with low iron bedsteads, little narrow beds with yellow quilts on them. All the beds were occupied except two by the glass door in the middle of the left-hand side of the ward, the door leading on to the recreation lawn. And the two patients who slept in those two beds were sitting in their grey dressing gowns at a little bamboo table playing chess. At one end of the ward there was a large folding door and the other end was covered by a window through which the sun was shining brightly. Through the window, trees and the roofs of houses could be seen. Beyond that again, against the blue sky line, there were mountain tops.

Suddenly a patient began to cough and a silence fell on all the other patients. Tim Delaney had begun his usual bout of coughing preparatory to the doctor's visit. He did it every morning. The other patients enjoyed the performance. But Dowling was horrified by it. It gave him a nauseous feeling in his bowels, listening to the coughing. Tim Delaney was sitting up in bed, his spine propped against the pillow and all the bedclothes gathered up around his huddled body. He wore a white nightshirt with a square yellow patch between the shoulder-blades. His bed was only five yards away from Dowling on the right-hand side and Dowling could see his face distinctly. The face skin was yellow. The skull was perfectly bald. The eyes were blue and red around the rims on the insides. The whole head was square and bony like a bust of Julius Caesar's head. When he coughed he contorted and made a movement as if he were trying to hurl himself forward and downward by the mouth. His cough was hard and dry. Delaney had an idea that he was a cow and that he had picked up a piece of glass while eating a bunch of clover. According to himself the piece of glass had stuck in his throat and he could not swallow any solid food on that account. "That fellow must be mad," thought Dowling, as he looked at the queer way Delaney opened his jaws and bared his yellow teeth when he coughed. Dowling experienced the sensation of being gradually surrounded by black waves that presently crowded up over his head and shut out everything. A buzzing sound started in his ears and he forgot Delaney. He stared at his upright feet without blinking. A fixed resolution came into his head to tell the doctor everything. He decided that it was positively no use trying any longer to keep up the pretence of being ill. He was better off outside even if he died of starvation. He could not possibly endure the horror of being in such an environment. He had schemed to get into hospital in order to get something to eat and now that he was in hospital he could not eat. But then he had not expected to get into such a hospital, among these terrible wild-eyed people, these narrow sordid-looking beds, this dreary bare ward, with a big fat man in a blue uniform and a peaked laced cap, continually walking up and down, shaking a bunch of keys behind his back and curling his black moustache. And the food was so coarse. He had been given a tin mug full of sickly half-cold tea and a hunk of coarse bread without butter for breakfast. Naturally he couldn't touch it, desperate as his circumstances had been for the past six months. Instead of that he had expected to get into a hospital where there were pretty nurses, who smiled at a man and whose touch was soothing and gentle. He had expected quiet, rest, sleep, delicate food, treatment for the heaviness behind his eyes and his insomnia and the noises he heard in his ears. It was cruel torture to suffer from hunger, to starve in his tenement room, alone and without anybody to whom he could talk when he felt ill at night. But anything was better than this. He would endure anything if he could only be alone again. So he thought, looking at his feet.

Then the attendant came up to Delaney's bed and shook his keys in Delaney's face. Delaney stopped coughing. The attendant clasped his hands behind his back and marched slowly up the ward towards the folding door through which the doctor would enter at any moment. All the patients cast suspicious and lowering glances at the attendant as he passed them. The attendant examined each bed with a melancholy and fierce expression in his blue eyes. He seemed to be totally unconscious of the malicious glances directed towards him. In silence he would point a finger at a tousled sheet or a blanket or a piece of paper lying on a coverlet. The patient in question would tidy the place pointed at with jerky eagerness. Not a word was spoken. A deadly silence reigned in the ward. There was an air of suspense.

Suddenly the silence was broken by the sound of loud laughter coming from the outside of the folding door through which the doctor was to enter. Then the two wings of the door swung open simultaneously. The doctor and his attendant nurse appeared, each inviting the other to enter first. The nurse, a tall, slim, pretty, red-haired young woman of twenty-six, with a devilishly merry twinkle in her blue eyes, held her case sheets in a bundle under her right arm, while she held the door open with her left hand. The doctor, Francis O'Connor, was a middle-sized, middle-aged fat man, dressed in a grey tweed suit, with a gold watch-chain across the top button of his waistcoat. He waved his stethoscope at the nurse with his left hand, while the short fat white fingers of his right hand pushed back his side of the door. His jovial fat face was creased with laughter and little tears glistened in his grey eyes.

"Miss Kelly," he gasped, between fits of apoplectic laughter that shook his fat girth, "upon my soul there isn't a word of a lie in it. Go ahead. Ladies first."

Then he himself entered first, still laughing. The nurse followed him, coughed, took up the fountain pen that hung from her waistband and dabbed at her hair with the end of it. The attendant came up at a smart pace, saluted and whispered something to the doctor. The doctor's face became serious for a moment. He glanced in Dowling's direction. Then he began to smile again, rubbed his palms together and looked at the ceiling, at the floor, at the walls, at the windows, smelling everywhere.

"Upon my soul," he said at last, turning to the nurse "does my old nose – sniff, sniff, – deceive me or can I smell roses?"

The nurse nodded, swallowing her breath modestly. She pointed to the glass door that led to the recreation lawn. "It's from that bush that grows by the wall," she murmured, "I saw three there last night."

"Hm" said the doctor and he walked over to the first bed, throwing out his feet sideways without moving the middle of his body.

Dowling's heart had begun to beat wildly when the doctor entered the ward. He was delighted and relieved, for the moment, of all anxiety. Now everything would be all right. He could transfer all his worries to that jolly man, with the kind fat face. And what a pretty nurse! Though her face was rather hard. Dowling began feverishly to prepare his confessions. He would explain everything. Then they would discharge him immediately. And in all probability the doctor would take an interest in his case and find him employment suitable to an educated man of good family. He became absorbed in the contemplation of what would happen after that. With his pale cheeks flushed and the extremities of his limbs throbbing with excitement, his mind soared off into a day dream, building castles in the air.

The doctor pulled the clothes back off the first patient's chest. He put his stethoscope to his ears and bent down to listen without looking at the man's face. The patient, formerly a peasant farmer named John Coonan, lay perfectly still with his hands lying flat on his abdomen. He stared at the ceiling through little fiery grey eyes that were set close together with a little pointed yellow nose between them. He imagined himself to be hatching twelve eggs in his stomach and he insisted on lying perfectly still, lest he should disturb the formation of the birds.

The doctor's face gradually lost its merry creases as he listened here and there and tapped here and there. His eyes became sharp. Then they began to blink. Then his whole face looked cross and he straightened himself and cleared his throat. "Now my man…" he began absent-mindedly and then he stopped, puffing out his cheeks. He turned to the nurse and whispered to her, holding her arm as he walked to the next bed: "Now how can ye explain that? That man was getting better yesterday and today he's a foregone conclusion. Well, well. It's very queer." He went up to the next bed.

The patients in the ward had been silent and attentive until then, but suddenly they seemed unable to concentrate any longer on the doctor's presence. They began to practise with voice and limb the grotesque imitations of whatever their crazed imaginations conjectured themselves to be. Dowling was startled out of his reverie by the gradual renewal of insane sounds about him. Again the true fact of his environment became real to him. He began to tremble violently. The doctor was proceeding rapidly down the ward, casually examining the fairly healthy patients. Dowling could catch the doctor looking at himself now and again. Whenever he caught the doctor's eyes looking at him, the doctor turned away hurriedly. "He'll soon be here," thought Dowling excitedly, "and I can see he's interested in me already. He sees I'm different from the rest. Now how am I going to commence to talk to him?"

The doctor paused to look at the two old patients who were playing chess. The players never took any notice. Their gaze was concentrated on the board intently. One old fellow had his fingers on a black queen, making tentative excursions in all directions, and then coming back again to his starting point. He had his lips sucked far into his toothless mouth. The other man, clasping his dressing-gown about his withered body, looked on murmuring endlessly: "Five minutes' pleasure and I have to suffer a lifetime for it. Five minutes' pleasure and I…" The doctor walked away, followed by the nurse and the attendant.

They passed Dowling without looking at him. This irritated Dowling. He felt slighted. He ceased to tremble and his face darkened. The doctor went to the end of the ward and then came back rapidly up the other side. When he was just at the far side of Dowling's bed, he stood at the distance of a yard behind Dowling's head. He began to laugh and told the nurse a funny story about a greengrocer named Flanagan who had made a large fortune through contracts for the new government, in which he had relatives. This fellow Flanagan, a lean, stingy, mean, ignorant peasant, according to the doctor, went off from Harcourt Street Station every Sunday morning with his golf sticks, to play on his, Dr O'Connor's club links. He was a great joke, this fellow Flanagan. The doctor went on telling anecdotes about Flanagan, laughing violently in a subdued tone while he talked. But all the while he kept examining Dowling's head while he talked and laughed. Dowling's body was twitching in the bed with vexation.

The doctor finished his story and again he moved on and passed Dowling's bed without looking at Dowling. Dowling saw him pass and could restrain himself no longer. He called out angrily: "I say, doctor, I want to speak to you." The doctor turned about sharply and looked at Dowling seriously. The attendant came up to Dowling and whispered in his low passionless voice: "You must wait your turn." Then the doctor moved away again from bed to bed, talking, answering questions, examining the patients and joking with the nurse. Dowling watched him, boiling with rage. He decided that he would tell the doctor nothing. He wanted to kill somebody. Why should they persecute him like this? Could nobody in the world be kind to him?

At last the doctor reached the end of the ward and turned back. He came down towards Dowling hurriedly, his face creased in a smile. When he was within five yards of Dowling he held out his right hand and called out: "How are you, Mr. Dowling? Now I can attend to you." Dowling immediately became soft and good humoured and smiled, a wan smile. The doctor sat down on the bed, still holding Dowling's hot thin right hand in his own fat two hands. He was looking into Dowling's wild, strained, big blue eyes with his own little half serious, half merry, half sharp eyes. A mist came before Dowling's eyes. He swallowed his breath and then he began to talk rapidly, pouring a volume of words out without stopping for breath.

"This is how it happened," he began. The doctor bent down his head, he kept fondling Dowling's hand and listened. Dowling described how his mother died young while he was in his last year at college studying for the Indian Civil Service. His mother, a government official's widow, had an annuity that expired with her death. So Dowling, who had no other means of support, had to leave college and get employment as a newspaper reporter. That was eighteen months ago.

"I tell you," whispered Dowling, lowering his voice and almost shutting his eyes, 'that what got on my nerves was... er... a queer thing and it may appear silly but... you know I couldn't give expression to something that was in me... somehow... I don't know how to tell you... of course I'm not a genius... but every man you know... of a certain class, of course, doctor... I don't know your name... every man has some creative power... and reporting work is awful... telling lies and rubbish day after day... and nobody understood me... everybody seemed to think that I was cocky and thought myself, on account of my family and that sort of thing, you know, better than the others... so that I chucked it six months ago and knocked about since... and then, desperate, I pretended to be ill so that I could get into hospital..."

He had been talking at a terrific pace and stopped suddenly to draw breath. Speaking rapidly, the doctor interrupted him in the same jerky low tone. "And then, of course, you went to kill the editor, just to make people believe you were ill," murmured the doctor.

Dowling suddenly stiffened in bed. He dragged his hand from the doctor's two hands. He held his two hands clenched in front of his face. His face contorted into a demoniacal grin. His eyes distended and then narrowed to slits. His body began to tremble. Gibbering, he began to mutter. Then he became articulate.

"I'll kill the bastard yet," he screamed, "I'll kill him. Where is he? Where is he?"

Screaming he tried to jump out of bed, but the attendant's giant hands were about him. He felt himself pressed down into the bed, flat on his back.

Gibbering, he lay there trembling. Then another fit overcame him and he roared. The ward became filled with sound. All the other patients began to scream and cry and babble.

"Padded cell," murmured the doctor to the attendant. Then he sighed and walked away to the door.

UNDER THE AWNING

Melatu Uche Okorie

Melatu Uche Okorie is a writer and scholar. She was born in Enugu, Nigeria. She has an MPhil in creative writing from Trinity College, Dublin and is currently studying for a PhD. *This Hostel Life* is her first book. She is working on a new collection.

Everyone was already in as she had hoped. She sat on the first empty chair she saw, and when she had finished arranging herself – getting her pen and papers out, making sure her phone was switched off, zipping up her bag – she finally looked up and realised she was sitting directly opposite the leader. The large window behind him was slightly open. Outside, the weather was as unsettled as her disposition as if it was ruminating on whether to rain or not. The sun had also not bothered to come out, leaving the sky an unpleasant grey.

Today was her turn to present her work at the writers' group. The leader took a sip out of a paper cup on the table in front of him.

'Can you read us into your work?' he asked the girl, placing the cup back on the table.

'Where would you like me to start?' she replied, hoping he would want an extract only as he sometimes did.

'Why don't you read it all?' he said, looking enquiringly around the room like the thought had just occurred to him.

She bent her head and started to read, stuttering her words.

You stood under the awning outside the Spar shop, staring straight ahead, barely moving, a pink plastic folder tucked under your arm, waiting for the drizzle to stop. You felt uncomfortable not standing at the bus stop on the edge of the pavement because you knew that back home, life would not stop over 'this small rain'. The newspaper vendors would still blow their whistles in your face, with The Guardian, The News, *and* The National Enquirer *flapping in a transparent plastic bag on their arms. The hawkers would still walk around with trays on their heads, calling out 'Buy Akamu! Fresh corn with fresh coconut! Agege bread!' The blind beggars with plates in one hand and the other tucked into the hands of their small guides would still approach cars in traffic, singing blessings in pidgin English, Igbo, Hausa and Yoruba.*

Back home, rainfall meant other things to you rather than discomfort. It meant that the flat you shared with your mother's sister and her husband and your three cousins would not be stuffy. It meant that you wouldn't go to the well to fill the jelly-cans in the flat with water. It meant that there would be corn sellers lined up along your street selling your favourite fresh roast corn the next morning.

But here you were desperate not to stand out, so you stood with the young woman pushing a crying toddler in a stroller, and the two older women and an old man under the awning of the Spar shop, careful not to look directly at anyone, pretending not to be paying attention. You had observed it was the way of things here, so people were not made to feel uncomfortable, even though you could hear the woman with the stroller pleading with her wailing child to stop throwing her toys out of her pram, and the two women and the old man talking about the weather.

You got on your bus and after a while it filled up but the seat next to you remained empty although there were people standing in the small aisle. You stared out of the window, willing the bus to move faster. A few stops later, you felt someone sit beside you. It was a white-skinned woman, but when her phone rang, she answered in a language that was not English.

You got off at your stop and you immediately searched out the house with the little children who always shouted 'Blackie!' at you, but there was no one at the balcony, so you hurried past with relief.

You walked into the house in which you lived with your mother and your two siblings and saw your mother's friend, Aunty Muna, sitting on the sofa in the living room. 'Good Afternoon, Aunty,' you said, and she laughed, 'Haw haw haw,' before saying you were becoming the only African teenager she knew in the country who still said good afternoon and not hello. Her loud chortle made you remember and you went quickly to the window facing the small front garden and drew the curtains. You'd noticed that the family next door walked around rigidly and spoke to their children in really low tones, as if to say, 'this is how you should be behaving too', and you had noticed that their children would abandon their games and run inside if they saw that any member of your family was coming outside.

Your mother asked why you were late getting home from school and you said, without looking at her; that you had to wait for the drizzle to stop. She responded with a familiar answer, silence.

On the television a man was talking about how the new American President was his relative. Aunty Muna said to your mother that wasn't it interesting that the same people who were quick to claim this black man from America were the same people who said the black girl from London could not be a Rose of Tralee, at which your mother replied, is that so. To which

Aunty Muna then wondered aloud why she was even talking about the black girl from London when the African children born in this same country were not even accepted as Irish and do not hold the same passport as other Irish children. She told your mother how once in her daughter's school, all the children's pictures were put up on the wall with their countries of origin written above it and how the children with non-national parents had their parents' countries of origin. She said weren't children of any parentage born in Britain, British or those born in Australia, Australians. You asked her what children born here were called and she said, 'migrant children or children of non-nationals, depending on who their parents were.' She told your mother that she asked her daughter's teacher to change her daughter's country of origin, but the next day, all the pictures were taken down. It was Aunty Muna who had told you not long after you arrived that the people in the Western world liked Africans the way you enjoyed animals in a zoo; you could visit them, feed them, play with them, they must not be allowed outside their environment.

You sat curled up on the sofa Aunty Muna had been sitting on long after she had gone and you thought of the day you had received the phone call from your mother that her application for family re-unification had been granted and that you would be joining her and your siblings. You had imagined everyone would be like the pen pals your school principal had encouraged your class back home to have. People from Canada, Australia, England and America, that you wrote to unfailingly every Sunday about how hot and dry it was during the Harmattan, the leaves so dry they could cut your fingers quicker and deeper than any knife, and about your French teacher; Mademoiselle Jones, whom you mentioned just because she was the only person you knew who had a foreign name and wore short flowery dresses which made her look all the more exotic. You also tried to impress them with your taste in music and wrote that you liked Usher, Eminem, Britney Spears and Beyoncé, and you were astonished that some of them did not know who they were because they were not into 'that sort of music', and you had wondered what other kind of music there was. You sent them pictures of yourself at home and at school and they sent you their pictures, taken at school and at home. You were so excited to join your mother and had imagined she lived in a big house and drove a big car. Your aunt and your cousins had thought so too because of the money your mother sent every month for your upkeep. In the coming months, you would find out that your mother stacked shelves in a supermarket. She had been a manager at a telecommunications company before she left your father.

She had told you about her friend, Muna. This was at the time when you and she still talked. She said Muna was lucky to have a job in an organisation that looked after the welfare of migrants. Aunty Muna had told her that the organisation had the foresight to employ a migrant as that was the best way to really empower those migrants. She would also tell you other things Aunty Muna had told her; how the other staff in her organisation were polite to her, even though they excluded her in conversations amongst themselves, and when she made attempts to join in, they would quickly disperse.

You would find out your sister, who was almost nine, wanted her hair weaved long and flowing down her back and thought Peaches Geldof was cool for walking around barefoot and said she didn't want to visit Africa because Africans were poor and the African children shown on the television had no shoes. You would also find out that your eleven-year-old brother and his friends walked around with their trousers almost at their knees and rapped about everything.

In the college your mother enrolled you in to study travel and tourism, the girls wore a lot of make-up and looked so dark from their tanning, they confused you sometimes. They asked you where you learnt to speak English so well and if it were true Africans lived in trees and how they could never live in a hot country because they would melt. You muttered an empty response, desperate not to show your real emotions, but the sadness would still come when you got home and you would cry into your pillow.

But it was after you met Dermot that you started to write. He came to visit your mother four months after you arrived. He had been working in London for a few months, which was why you had never met him. Your mother introduced him as the nicest Irishman she had ever met. He told you eagerly that he had worked with a lot of charities in Africa and also did some work with Aunty Muna's organisation. He spoke about his experiences through his work with the openness your pen pal letters used to have, which made you like him even though he was old like your mother. And your smile reached your eyes for the first time in a long while because his were not guarded. He told you he hoped to get funding to run a project, helping migrant children and teenagers to integrate through football and dance. When your mother asked him from the kitchen, where she was preparing jollof rice with prawns for him, if one could be taught to integrate, you had jumped in and said you thought it was a great idea. He still responded to your mother's question and said he didn't think there were enough opportunities for people to integrate, to which your mother replied that the church, the school, the road, the shops and the playground should provide enough opportunities for people to integrate if they wanted to. Your mother glimpsed the look of impatience on your face and answered you back with silence.

You could tell him things you could not bring yourself to tell your mother, how you hurried with your shopping because the security men followed you around the shops blatantly and about the man who got on the same bus with you from school, and how he would wave and smile, and you would wave and smile back, until the day he told you he would give you €100 if you slept with him.

You had started with the small things first. And then you started telling him bigger things, about your father and how, in your head, you had blamed your mother for leaving. And how you had always struggled with the anger and guilt but couldn't talk about it because the first time you tried to say something, your mother had stood up from the bed and said, 'It always had to be about you,' and walked out of the room. You told him how for a long time you had felt as if all your family had died when your mother left you behind to travel with your siblings, both of whom were young enough to go with her on her passport. He had nodded his head repeatedly, as if he heard the things you were saying and the ones you left unsaid – that your mother leaving you behind was her way of punishing you.

He took you and your siblings to the cinema and you knew by people's reactions to you that they found it strange, the way their eyes slid away when you caught them looking. The old white couple who mumbled and scowled at him; the black man who looked at you with contempt before turning his back on you, his arms folded across his chest; the young woman with two little children who smiled at you and said too brightly, 'It's lovely today, isn't it?' You wondered if he felt as uncomfortable as you, but you couldn't read his expression. He started a conversation with the young woman but did not include you, so you walked away to look at the sweets until it was time to go in for the movie.

He got the funding for his project and you went with your mother and your nine-year-old sister to watch your eleven-year-old brother play on the migrants' team. There were little groups formed around the pitch; the black group, two white couples that spoke to each other in a foreign language and a large Irish group. Each group mostly ignored the other. When he came around later, he wanted to know if you thought the event was successful, but you dodged the question. You are yet to feel comfortable telling someone something was grand when you didn't think it was. He told you his dream would be to run more integration football and to go to schools to give anti-racism talks.

You told him then about the little children down the street, of perhaps the ages of five and six, who persistently shouted 'Blackie' at you whenever they saw you walking alone and how their parents talked amongst themselves like they could not hear. He told you not to bother about them. You also told him about the girls in your college who told each other to mind their bags or made so much about their purses being in their bags whenever they wanted to use the toilet. He told you he didn't think the girls meant anything by it. And you wanted to tell him about the woman at church who told you that a Traveller woman had said that Travellers were no longer the lowest class since the arrival of Africans. And you wanted to tell him about the bus driver who dropped you two bus stops away from your stop because there was nobody else apart from you still in the bus. And you wanted to tell him about the man who followed your mother to a supermarket car park and told her that he wanted a BJ, and how your mother told you she had felt bad she didn't have what he wanted until she realised what he meant. You wanted to tell him all these things but you didn't. You cried for a long time on your bed after he left, confused at how alone you felt with so many people around you and the next day, you went into this same Spar shop and bought a diary.

'Thank you,' the leader said, nodding encouragingly when she got to the end. He sifted through the papers in front of him, rearranging them, again and again before glancing around the room. 'So, what does everyone think of the work?'

A was the first to speak. 'I am surprised you wrote in the second person.'

The girl gave A an impassive smile. She wanted to show she could take any criticism.

B tucked her hair behind her ear before speaking. 'I think the story should have a bit of light and shade to it, so that it's not all bleak and negative.'

C – 'I'm not sure what it is, but there is something about writing in the second person that prevents me from caring about the character. I always know I'm reading a work of fiction.'

The leader – 'Why don't you think about breaking it up a little bit? Maybe give us a name somewhere.'

D – 'Why don't we ask her why she used the second person?'

She waited for someone to pose the question but all she saw were expectant eyes raised in her direction. 'I didn't want to personalise it by using a first person and giving the character a particular voice.'

The leader – 'Do you think you can break it up a little bit? Maybe use the second and third person?'

She gave him an 'I'll consider it' nod.

The leader – 'Another thing I would have preferred was for the reader to be the one picking up on the xenophobia like the incident on the bus.'

E – 'I saw it as a kind of paranoia on the part of the character. Like the scene at the cinema where a woman was being nice and she completely mis-read it.'

'That was exactly where I was going with the story.' The girl turned eagerly to E, glad someone had picked up on it. 'The character's paranoia.'

F – 'My only issue with the story was the lack of narrative thread.'

The comment irritated the girl. Does every story have to have the traditional plot trajectory? The girl wanted to ask F but didn't.

E – 'I think there is a narrative thread – the buying of the diary.'

F – 'I don't think that was enough.'

C – 'I liked the part where she was told by her aunt of how the West perceived Africans.'

A – 'I thought that was a little melodramatic.'

C – 'It might be harsh but the truth usually is.'

The girl nodded repeatedly to show both side of the argument made sense.

G – 'I think you should ground the narration in specific details so we can
understand why the girl feels such self-loathing and self-hatred.'

The girl felt a sudden urge to cry, so she scribbled on the paper she had
read from, 'self-loathing and self-hatred'.

The leader closed his note book and said, 'OK, that's all for today. Who is
presenting next week?'

F raised his hand.

Later that evening, the girl was alone, considering the story. Although she
wanted to keep the second person point of view rather than use it interchange-
ably with the third person, she still went ahead to make some changes.

*It was after meeting Dermot that you started to write. He came to visit
your mother four months after you arrived. He had been working in London
which was why you had never met him. Your mother introduced him to you
by saying, 'Didi, meet the nicest Irishman I have ever met.'*

*You felt an ache around your heart as you remembered the reasons you
were mad at him, so you tried to reason out his point of view in your head.
Your classmates who asked their friends to mind their bags were actually
not doing anything wrong; the bus driver who dropped you two stops away
from your bus stop could have done so due to road works; the man in the
supermarket who asked your mother for a BJ is just sick; and the children
who called out 'Blackie' at you whenever they saw you passing could just be
what they were, children.*

She emailed the changes to the others and it wasn't long before she started
to get their comments back.

B – 'I'm happy you kept the you voice, which really highlighted her
anonymity. Please don't change it. I did think it could be useful to still temper
the racism she experienced with examples of kind behaviour too. In places
there is so much bias, so much prejudice, that it almost swallows itself.'

F – 'If you can structure this piece around some kind of cohesive event or a
series of events beyond buying the diary itself, the writing will really stand out.'

D – 'Very strong. Admired your use of the second person. It worked very well. Clear straightforward narrative line. Work on the bleak picture. How you would do this, I don't know.'

A – 'I'm so glad you wrote this. I found it believable! You'll hate this suggestion, but… I'd actually be interested in seeing this rewritten in chronological order with the girl given a name.'

E – 'You are able to talk about difficult material without laying a heavy layer of judgment over everything. Also, I really think that the second person is powerful. I wouldn't change it.'

She dreaded G's response the most. She took her time to open it. 'Full of great details, but I would like you to a) lose the second person and b) observe chronology.'

C did not reply.

THE APPRENTICE

David Park

David Park is the author of ten novels and two short story collections. His work has received a range of awards and in 2019 his novel *Travelling in a Strange Land* won the Kerry Group Irish Novel of the Year.

It was very important to get the time right. Looking at the watch he had borrowed secretly from his sister, he saw that he was much too early. His anxiety to prove his reliability had prompted him to set out at least an hour too soon. Being early was both dangerous and foolish and would draw unwelcome attention. He looked at the watch again and knew he could not go to the spot marked out for him. Swinging his red sports bag into a more comfortable position on his shoulder, he allowed himself a glance at the open iron gate, then turned back the way he had come.

The afternoon was cold and he cupped his hands together in front of his mouth and blew warm breath into them. He wished he had worn his gloves. There were plenty of people about but he drifted from shop window to shop window without making eye contact with anyone. He turned up the black fur collar of his green jacket. Out of the corner of his eye, he saw a face he recognised, and huddled in a doorway until it had passed. He looked at the watch again and, unwilling to believe that only a few minutes had passed since his last glance, held it up to his ear and listened to its ticking. He had to put in time and he needed to do a better job than he was doing at that moment. There was a second-hand bookshop at the corner and he opened the door and went in. Thousands of second-hand paperbacks were stacked on makeshift shelves, classified into a multitude of subjects. Some of them looked ancient, their prices marked in old money and smelling musty and dead. Others were newish with garish covers where half-naked girls draped themselves over dishevelled beds or stroked the barrels of guns. Lifting one up, he read the blurb on the back. He thumbed the pages and, staring at the small print, knew it would take him a lifetime to read. There were no pictures, just pages and pages of the same small, black print. He wondered how anyone could be bothered to make such a physical effort and yet he was curious as he watched men browsing intently. He felt as if there was some kind of secret world enclosed between the covers – a world from which he was excluded. Then an elderly man with a small dog entered and deposited half a dozen books on the counter. After inspecting them, the owner of the shop handed over some money. An idea dawned on him. If he could gather up a clatter of books maybe he could make some money for himself. There were bound to be some lying about the house and perhaps he could extract some from school. No one would miss a few. It was a potential variation on lemonade bottles or scrap metal.

Not wanting to stay in the shop too long, he shouldered the bag and went out into the street. Involuntarily, his gaze went towards the iron gate. It was this gaze that prevented him from seeing the approach of one of his class-mates. The unexpected sound of his voice made him jump.

'What's up with you, Ricky? Rob a bank or something?'

'I didn't see you coming.'

'You nearly jumped out of your pants. What were you doing in the shop? Looking for porno books?'

Of all the people he could possibly have met, he could think of no one worse than Chick Kierney, but he tried to be calm and bluff it out.

'I was just looking around.'

'Books are no good – you have to read for ages before you find a good bit. It's not worth the effort. Mags are best. I can get you some if you've got the dough.'

'Naw, I'm not interested, Chick. Anyway, who needs mags when you can have the real thing?'

Chick smiled and thumped him playfully on the shoulder.

'Go on ye boy ye. Now you're talking.'

The conversation could have gone on forever. He had to extract himself. Looking deliberately at his watch, he said he had to go.

'Where're you going? What've you got in your sports bag?'

He silently cursed his classmate's insatiable curiosity, but forced himself into restraint.

'I'm going swimming in the leisure centre. Do you want to come?'

'In this weather? You must be joking. C'mon and we'll go round the town, and pick up a couple of good things.'

'Can't, Chick, I'm meeting someone,' he replied with a tone of finality, then turned and started to move off down the street.

'You're chicken, Ricky-dicky. Don't pee in the pool or you'll turn the water yellow!'

He clenched his fists at the insult, but kept on walking. He would settle that particular score at some later date. Crossing the street, he headed for the sports shop and mingled with the other young window-gazers. His eyes flitted over the expensive football boots and the kits of leading teams. He thought it was a con the way they changed them every year, so that no sooner had you bought your favourite team's kit than it was out of date. It was a racket. If ever he was rich, he would buy everything in the window – it all looked so new and fresh, with that clean, crisp smell that made you want to touch.

He walked on down the street and into the arcade. The smell of a hot dog stand curdled the air and reminded him that he was cold and hungry. Counting the change in his pocket, he found enough to buy one and loaded it with sauce and mustard until it dripped like an ice-cream cornet. He looked at his watch again and saw with some relief that time had started to pass. But it was still too early. Eating the hot dog, he crossed the road and went into the pet shop. Outside on the pavement were aquariums, dog baskets and kennels, a tank full of goldfish and an assortment of cages and equipment for pets. Inside, the fetid smell of animals flowed over him but he was indifferent to it, inspecting the stacked cages of birds in the order he always followed. First the budgerigars, vibrant in blue, yellow and green, then the canaries, zebra finches and Java sparrows. There was a mynah bird he hadn't seen before, and a new pair of lovebirds. White doves rustled and nestled together and he tapped the cage with his finger and cooed gently at them. Then, crouching down on his hunkers, he looked in at the rabbits, their doleful pink eyes staring impassively back at him. Further along were white mice, and breaking off a piece of bread, he fed them through the bars of the cage.

'Don't feed the animals son,' boomed a voice from behind the counter. 'They get fed enough and they don't need any more.'

He stepped back from the cage and stared at the sawdust floor.

'And by the look of that thing, you've probably given them and yourself a good dose of food poisoning.'

Embarrassed by the public chastisement, he sidled slowly up the shop and pretended to be studying a book on hamsters. After what he considered a suitable period of time, he casually ambled out the door and back on to the street. Looking at his watch, he calculated that if he walked slowly and went the long way round, it would be the right time to arrive at the gate. Suddenly a large hand clutched his shoulder.

'Long time no see, Ricky.'

It was James Fallon, the youth club leader. He felt the broad hand drawing him aside, away from the middle of the pavement, the man's height and size overshadowing him and trapping him in the doorway of a closed-down shop.

'Where've you been, Ricky boy? It's not like you to stay away for so long. What's wrong? Did somebody do something to you?'

'It's nothing like that, Mr Fallon. I've been busy recently. I wanted to come, but I wasn't able.'

'And what makes a young buck like you so busy then?'

He had talked himself into a dead-end and his brain scrambled to find some escape.

'Just things – you know how it is.'

'You're a real mystery man, Ricky. Father Logue's been asking after you as well, and the team's missing its centre-forward – we've had three replacements and they haven't scored a goal between them.'

He glanced at the boy's sports bag.

'You're not turning out for someone else, are you?'

'No, I'm going swimming at the leisure centre. I'll be coming back to the club all right. I'll probably be up tomorrow night.'

'That's good, Ricky, that's good. Have you heard from your brother yet?'

He wanted to look at his watch, but knew he could not. He fidgeted nervously from foot to foot, aware that time was moving on. Everything seemed to be going against him.

'He's not great at writing letters Mr Fallon, but we're going up to see him next month.'

'Well, tell him I was asking for him. Maybe I'll get to see him when he's feeling settled.'

'I'll do that. I have to go now because I'm meeting someone at the leisure centre.'

'You're a real busy lad, Ricky. I'll not keep you any longer – I wouldn't want you to be late.'

Smiling gently, he stepped aside, but before the boy could step out on to the pavement, he returned his hand firmly to his shoulder.

'Come back to the club, son. Run the streets and you'll end up in trouble. It's not worth it, Ricky.'

'Don't worry about it. I'm coming back. I'll be up tomorrow night.'

They parted, and as they walked in different directions, he glanced over his shoulder several times to check he wasn't being watched, and then, quickening his pace, he hurried towards the iron gate. Meeting two people he knew had been a piece of bad luck, but he had survived and it was now behind him. Proving himself reliable and trustworthy was all that mattered – he owed it to his brother. People walked past him, their faces pale and pinched with the cold, and he felt apart from them. As an old woman trundled a battered pram towards him, loaded with second-hand clothing, he crossed the road and, without looking right or left, walked through the gate that was a side entrance to the chapel. Once inside, he stepped off the path and stood with his back to the wall where he was unseen from the street. He was nervous now, and glanced repeatedly at his watch, knowing that the fifteen-minute waiting period had started. An old woman came through the gate heading towards the side door of the chapel, but she did not see him. Five minutes passed and no one else entered or left. He shuffled his feet and blew into his hands. Perhaps nothing would happen. Although he would not consciously admit it, part of him wished for the fifteen minutes to pass without his being needed.

His eyes flicked to the couple of stunted trees growing in the grounds of the chapel. They had shed most of their leaves and the few remaining fluttered lifelessly like tattered flags. Above, the sky was a strange blue-grey colour. Around his feet a spume of the previous day's confetti fluttered up in the wind. He looked at his watch again. Suddenly a man appeared at the end of the path – he was early. He tensed in readiness, but there was something wrong – the man was walking unsteadily, swaying from side to side. Something had gone terribly wrong. He felt the press of panic and thought of taking to his heels, but something stronger forced him to wait. By now the man had zigzagged close enough to be seen clearly and the panic was replaced by relief. It was a drunk. He pulled himself back into the shadow of the wall and dropped the sports bag to the ground, but his relief was short-lived. If the drunk had been walking at normal speed he probably would never have seen him, but as he drew close to the gate he stopped, and with flailing co-ordination attempted to light a cigarette.

'Hey son, can you help me a wee minute?'

He swayed off the path and lurched over to him, the smell of booze oozing out of every pore.

'Lend us a few bob, son. I want to light a candle for my wee boy. My wife died last year and now he's having a big operation. The doctors don't know if he'll make it or not.'

At that moment he would have given all the money he had in the world to be rid of this unwanted and dangerous distraction, but he knew without looking that his pockets were hopelessly empty. He had spent the last of his money in the arcade.

'My wee boy's all I've left in the whole world. Just a few bob to light a candle for him.'

The begging had become more insistent, and a shaking hand wiped away imaginary tears. He knew that he had to do something quickly. As one hand searched deliberately in his pocket, the other grabbed his bag and he side-stepped the drunk as if evading a tackle on the soccer field. Hurrying down the path towards the chapel he heard only a slurred, broken curse pursue him. Then from a safe distance he turned and watched the man stagger out through the gate, rehearsing his lines for the next audience. When he was sure he had gone, he returned to his original position and waited silently. A glance at his watch told him there were only five minutes left. Perhaps no one would come. Perhaps he would not be needed. Four minutes left. He cupped his hands again and blew into them. Suddenly, he tensed and tightened his grip on the shoulder bag – a man was running along the path towards him. A little cloud of breath preceded him, and by the way the distance between them was closing rapidly, it was obvious that he was running hard. So this was it. With a hand that shook a little, he unzipped the bag and held it open. The man was level with him now but they did not speak or look into each other's faces. He had stopped running but was still breathing heavily as he took it out of his pocket and dropped it into the boy's bag. Then he was gone, out into the street and away, a blur in the dusk, another face in the crowd. It was smaller and heavier than he had imagined and it felt warm as he carefully wrapped it in the towel and zipped up the bag. Then he too was gone, newly articled and proud, stepping out with the pride a young man feels on the first day of his first job.

MANNERS

Elske Rahill

Elske Rahill is an Irish novelist and short story writer. Her work includes the novels *Between Dog and Wolf* (2013, The Lilliput Press) and *An Unravelling* (Head of Zeus and The Lilliput Press, 2019) and the short story collection *In White Ink* (2017). She currently lives in Burgundy, France with her partner and four children.

The first time Adrian had seen the girls he thought they might be prostitutes. They both had crusty sores on their lips, which had been dabbed with flesh-coloured paste, then glossed over many times with candy-pink goo. Their nails were long and flaked with silver polish. One of them had a purple bruise on her neck. They wore thick gold earrings, tight sequinned jeans, and running shoes. They were his daughter's age, just turned women – buttocks full, hips pressing intently through the chafed denim. They had tight waists, bony wrists, wide, clear eyes and tough little jaws. He had expected them to get off at Stoneybatter, where a businessman could buy a lunchtime blow job for twenty euros. They might have been wearing flimsy nylon tops under their hoodies. They might have had slippery armpits under there, brothy sweat, more bruises, bites. But they had stayed on the bus until Grafton Street. As they disembarked one of them took the other's hand and whispered into her ear, grinning with the giddiness of a mischievous child. Then they waited quietly on the pavement for an older woman to get off the bus.

Adrian hadn't noticed the older woman until then. She was round, zipped into a too-small fleece jacket. She had the same jaw as them, the same dark, itinerant brows, but her skin had the look of granite, dense and pitted, and her coarse black hair was twisted into a plait that tapered all the way down to the cleft of her ass and swung there like a tail.

The girls weren't prostitutes. He should have seen that by the way they curved their shoulders – they didn't know they had two pairs of beautiful breasts in there under those hoodies. His own daughter knew only too well. It made him uncomfortable, the way Carla's clothes increasingly resembled underwear – bits of designer lace to decorate her cleavage and the tops of her thighs – and the way he paid for the privilege of seeing her walk out like that.

He was having a new credit card issued soon. He would keep the numbers from her.

He had been taking the bus to work for two months now. It had embarrassed his wife at first, and she had insisted on dropping him to the stop lest he be seen walking. Last weekend, though, he had heard her on the phone.

'Oh yes,' she had said, 'well, we're in the same boat. My Adrian sold the '07... who would have seen it coming? Grown men like ours, professionals, trudging to the bus stop...'

She still had the four-by-four. One car for a family of three was no great hardship, he told her, but Margaret savoured her horror at the loss of the Merc. He hadn't got much for it, but keeping it was an expense, he had explained – why pay insurance and petrol and parking fees, when he could as easily take the bus?

There were a few things that hadn't worked out. His girls needed to understand that.

He owned a vacant penthouse apartment in a half-built development surrounded by acres of flattened wasteland, a motorway without a pedestrian crossing, and the promise of a tram stop. Out of laziness or optimism, the large billboard saying HoneyHive Village: Work. Live. Succeed! had never been taken down. There was a crèche on the ground floor called Oxford Junior. It had a heart-shaped crest with a book in one chamber and a teddy bear in another. He had also bought one third of an unused warehouse.

Recently, in a cafe, he had overheard a conversation between a middle-aged man and his young lunch companion. The man spoke loudly, showing off. He told the girl that the word mortgage came from the French mort – death. It was a debt till death – that was the literal translation. That was why the French rented, the man had said.

He recognized the regular commuters now. Sometimes he found himself nodding at familiar faces, and they nodded back. It was nice, in a way, to see faces other than that of his secretary, the usual clients, and the man who worked at the coffee dock. There had been no new clients lately, no new stories, just follow-on cases – access reviews, maintenance reviews, fines for broken court orders.

He saw the girls once or twice a week. They always got on at the same stop – the Spar on the Foxborough road. He reckoned there must be a council estate around there. There were always skinny men loitering outside the shop. The woman with the plait usually chaperoned the girls. This time she sat beside Adrian at the back of the bus, facing them. She crossed her feet and folded her hands on her lap one over the other, like a lady. She pursed her lips, trying for pride, perhaps, or displeasure. It made him think of Margaret when she was young. When she was nervous she would straighten her back, fold her hands on her lap, survey the room, and swallow.

It was startling how easily he forgot what his wife had been like then – the way she pinned her shoulders back, the curve of her spine. He'd met her at a dinner party and wanted her immediately. It was the way she allowed her chair to be held for her as she seated herself at the table, the way she held her knees together. He had thought of making love to her, calling her 'good girl', the polite little moans she might make. They had driven him wild, those impeccable manners.

It took him two months. It was much as he had imagined it. She was sweet and mock-demure, hesitating with a grin before parting her legs. When prompted she sat daintily astride him as though riding a horse, brushed the hair from her eyes, left her underwear on with the crotch pulled aside, made small, dignified sounds and smiled triumphantly when he came. What made him start to love her a little, even on that first night, was the way that all of those manners fell away when she slept. She snored like a man, and muttered and scratched and kicked and drooled and fought with the pillow. In marriage he had hoped to access that part of her, to lose the politeness of words and waxed legs. He had looked forward to seeing her face scrubbed bare, to all the gore of pregnancy and birth, to sleeping curled together like animals.

Lately Margaret had taken to wearing an eye-mask to bed. He would come home some nights to find her lying on her back, her hands in cotton gloves to get the most out of her hand cream, and the black mask over her eyes with the word 'sleep' embroidered on it in silver thread.

One of the girls had tried to bleach her hair, but the peroxide had been no match for the thorough blackness of her mane. The hair had come out orange-pink, like a sunset, with two inches of roots. The other girl, slightly taller, with hair greased back in a tight ponytail, was beautiful. Her face was flat like so many of those traveller girls' – high, dented cheekbones like a form carefully beaten out of bronze. Her thick lips were both stoic and acciden-tally sensual, raw as a wound. It was the upper lip – the way it swelled a little over the plump lower one – that made her beautiful: the hurt she wore in her mouth, and the resignation, and something else as well – the wince at the edge of her eyes, as though she were tolerating something, resisting an urge to roar. He had noticed the colour before – emerald green shot through with glistening yellow shards like a shattered bottle.

The girls were each sipping a bottle of Lucozade and the sugar was already doing its job – they were becoming jittery and hyper, giggling and whispering. That must be their breakfast, he thought: a high-calorie drink designed for sportsmen, rich in glucose. He thought of Carla, battling already with her weight. Throughout sixth year she had been eating egg whites for breakfast, an apple for lunch, and turkey breast or white fish for dinner, grilled by Margaret on special fat-absorbing paper. Mother and daughter were both on the Special 8 diet now, which, as far as he could make out, meant that they ate nothing but bowls of cereal with fat-free organic yoghurt. If they could see this – two itinerant girls with perfect figures drinking Lucozade for breakfast...

Because she wasn't cooking for herself or Carla, Margaret had taken to filling the freezer with high-quality ready-made meals. She left one to defrost on the kitchen table for Adrian every afternoon. In the evening he was supposed to come home and put it in the microwave, but he was never hungry by then. He ate a lot during the day. Business had been quiet lately. Middle-class separations, with all the mess of joint bank accounts and properties, had kept Adrian in work for two decades, but things were different now. There was less money to fight over than there was to lose on legal costs, and no one could afford to live alone.

After greeting his secretary in the morning, and opening his post, Adrian had taken to sitting in an Italian cafe for an hour with coffee and a pastry and some folders. Sometimes he sat there until the afternoon. It was easier to deal with paperwork there, amongst walls of wine bottles, than in his brightly lit office. There were PhD students with laptops, women with babies, lovers with problems, ex-politicians. There were low-hanging amber lampshades and cheap paper placemats. There was good coffee. There was never such silence that you could hear the waste of energy hum in the plug sockets. At lunchtime he would order a plate of vinegar-drenched antipasto and eat it slowly.

He tried to tell Margaret what a waste of money the ready meals were – he ate so often during the day, he said, so many business lunches – but she insisted that since the recession had hit there were great deals on all these things. Marks and Spencer's wasn't even making a profit, she said. They were loss leaders, the three-for-two ready meals that she bought for Adrian. It would be a waste not to buy them, she said. She loved that expression, 'loss leaders'.

For the first years after they had married, she had cooked him elaborate dinners every evening. She went through phases. First everything was done in the pressure cooker, then the slow cooker. Then she began to grill things. For a time, it was their main topic of conversation – her cooking, and his eating. She always asked him what she might improve, and was there enough salt on it, and every Thursday she tried something new from the Living supplement of the Sunday paper. It had gone on like that for – how long? And when had it stopped?

Margaret took seriously her duties as wife. She had given up her job at the hotel. She had run the house like a good business, constantly striving for improvement. In the eighties they had needed a conservatory and an antique oak floor. In the nineties they had needed the conservatory taken out; in its place they needed decking, and a gazebo. Margaret had designed the gazebo herself, and had it custom made. That was her way of loving him. He knew that. He was no better.

He had started buying her chocolates and flowers. On her birthday he had bought a card that said 'To My Lovely Wife' on it. On the front was the outline of a woman. There was red silk stuck over it in the shape of a dress, and a string of tiny pearls glued at the neck. There was a time when she would have made a joke of that. Now, she was grateful. She kept the card on the dresser for six weeks. He was not the worst. There was no one who knew quite how to love anyone else. If family law had taught him anything, it was that. How many times, right before a settlement, at the end of a vicious dispute, after the poisonous accusations, the financial ruin, the custody battle, had he watched a client collapse in tears – 'I tried my best. I tried so hard to love...'

A few years ago he had paid a girl to piss on him. The girl was thin with brassy yellow hair. He could smell alcohol off her piss, and after it was done he couldn't remember why he had wanted so badly for Margaret to do it, why the thought had turned him on like that.

A boy sat himself down behind the girls. He had bum fluff on his chin – a colourless foam, like the mould that sprouts at the bottom of discarded tea cups – that nauseated Adrian. The three teenagers were talking in low, excited mumbles. The woman with the plait was scolding them continuously in that half-English language they spoke. Adrian couldn't decipher her words.

His grandmother used to bring dinner and worn blankets to Mrs O'Connor, a traveller woman with nine children who settled in a nearby field every summer. One day she had taken Adrian with her to the caravans. Bits of broken things lay discarded amidst patches of long, parched grass – half a bicycle, a crushed washing line and, in the black aftermath of a bonfire, a cluster of smashed bottles, green and brown and yellow. Adrian had seen a little boy with no trousers or shoes on straddling a shaggy horse, and Mrs O'Connor had shouted something at the boy in that language. Inside, the caravan was very clean and neat. There was a bedspread with large red flowers on it, and a skinny baby sleeping face down on a sheepskin. The sons had grown into thugs, his grandmother later told him, which was a terrible pity, because Mrs O'Connor had been a lady in her own way, and her long, black hair was always clean and glossy.

The woman was talking to the boy now. Adrian thought he could understand. 'When you get back don't go straight to sleep,' she said. 'Go for a walk first.'

Adrian checked his watch. Then he verified the time by checking his phone. It was 9.05. Carla would be picking up her results. How did it work? Did the students all queue up, the way they had when he was that age, and file into the principal's office to hear, after a summer of waiting, how they had done? Or were the results posted on a board, the way they were in universities? Or were they each handed a sealed envelope with their name on it? She wanted to do law like him, poor child. For a year the exams had taken over everything. Carla had tacked a study plan to the back of her bedroom door. Margaret had woken her every morning with a black coffee, and poached the egg whites while Carla did an hour of morning revision.

Was it he, or Margaret, who had chosen that crèche when Carla was tiny? The only one in Ireland to start Montessori classes at two years instead of three, which had a uniform that made the toddlers look like Victorian dolls, and taught them the violin when they could hardly walk. It had seemed to him, back then, that it would protect Carla to be armed with that education, that class. That's how it had seemed then.

Throughout sixth year, he and Margaret had been invited to the dinner parties of parents from the school. One night a father had cornered him in the kitchen.

'I hear Carla's getting straight A1s in higher maths? Martha says she's the best in the class. That's an advantage alright, isn't it? They get extra points for higher maths.'

'Yeah. I think she is. That's what she tells us anyway, hah! You never know, though, she says the girl who got the maths prize last year only got a C in the leaving. It all depends on the day, doesn't it?' The man eyed him suspiciously, and moved in closer.

'What grind does she go to? I won't mention it to anyone else. Please. Martha wants to do science. She needs a B in maths or she won't get into her course.'

He had told Carla yesterday, 'You know it doesn't matter how you do? Things will work out for the best. Your mother and I know you've worked hard. That's what matters.'

Things will work out for the best – what did he mean by that? He hoped she wouldn't get all those points. He hoped her fatnecked boyfriend would dump her. He hoped her life would be thrown off course now before it was too late. He wanted her to enjoy herself in college, to miss class sometimes, and get a job in a bar. He wanted someone to fall in love with her for real, not as an aspiration. He wanted her to sit on grotty couches and argue with other kids as though they all knew everything, and just talk, for God's sake, and laugh stupidly, and not keep striving into the future, as though there was something there for her.

Besides, Margaret had promised Carla, without consulting him, that she could have her own brand-new car if she got over 550. He couldn't afford that.

His phone was flashing and vibrating. He had forgotten to take it off silent. Six missed calls. Margaret and Carla had both been phoning. He picked up and Carla shrieked into the phone – 'Five-sixty-five, Dad! Five-sixty-fucking-five!'

In the background her classmates were shrieking too. The itinerant girls were looking at him. They could hear the shrieks. The green-eyed one had dimples twitching in her cheeks. She wanted to laugh at him. He was aware, suddenly, of his briefcase open at his feet. He hadn't closed it after taking out his phone. His wallet was lying mouth open on top of some thin files. There were two fifties and a five clearly visible, sandwiched between layers of fine Italian leather and silk. The girl saw him look at the wallet, and then at her, and he was too embarrassed to reach down and tuck it away, buckle up the briefcase. Carla was still screaming.

He didn't want to speak. The girl would hear his accent, and she would laugh. What would he say anyway?

'Well done, Carla. Well done, darling.'

'I have to go, Daddy. I have to ring Mark! Ahhhhh!'

The girls had lost interest in him now. They were messing with the boy behind them. The boy's ears were red. They were leaning around the seat, reaching into his pants with their lovely young hands – the rough palms, the filthy nails, the cracked metallic nail polish. It was electric blue today. The boy was hunched over his crotch, shrugging them away with increasing humiliation and anger. Poor kid. Adrian had the impression the boy might hit the girls if they didn't stop. The mother leaned over and slapped them each on the knees.

'I didn't raise you to be doin like that.' The girls turned around and sat on their hands, but they couldn't stop laughing. Then the taller, beautiful, green-eyed one said, 'Come on, Mammy. We're to be gettin off.' As the woman passed the boy, she clipped him on the ear. 'Go for a walk first,' she said.

Before dismounting, the mother took an old buggy from where she had left it by the side door. On the pavement she assembled the buggy with a deft flick of her foot, arranged some blankets to resemble a small baby, and covered the bundle with a rain protector. Then she handed each of the girls a paper cup, and fixed their hair.

A STRANGE CHRISTMAS GAME

Charlotte Riddell

Charlotte Riddell (1832–1906) wrote numerous novels and story collections. Her first eight novels were published under the name F.G. Trafford. Her works include *The Rich Husband*, *Fairy Water* and *A Struggle for Fame*. Her short story collections include *Frank Sinclair's Wife: And Other Stories*, *Weird Stories*, *Idle Tales* and *The Collected Ghost Stories of Mrs J.H. Riddell*.

When, through the death of a distant relative, I, John Lester, succeeded to the Martingdale Estate, there could not have been found in the length and breadth of England a happier pair than myself and my only sister Clare.

We were not such utter hypocrites as to affect sorrow for the loss of our kinsman, Paul Lester, a man whom we had never seen, of whom we had heard but little, and that little unfavourable, at whose hands we had never received a single benefit—who was, in short, as great a stranger to us as the then Prime Minister, the Emperor of Russia, or any other human being utterly removed from our extremely humble sphere of life.

His loss was very certainly our gain. His death represented to us, not a dreary parting from one long loved and highly honoured, but the accession of lands, houses, consideration, wealth, to myself—John Lester, Esquire, Martingdale, Bedfordshire, whilom John Lester, artist and second-floor lodger at 32, Great Smith Street, Bloomsbury.

Not that Martingdale was much of an estate as country properties go. The Lesters who had succeeded to that domain from time to time during the course of a few hundred years, could by no stretch of courtesy have been called prudent men. In regard of their posterity they were, indeed, scarcely honest, for they parted with manors and farms, with common rights and advowsons, in a manner at once so baronial and so unbusiness-like, that Martingdale at length in the hands of Jeremy Lester, the last resident owner, melted to a mere little dot in the map of Bedfordshire.

Concerning this Jeremy Lester there was a mystery. No man could say what had become of him. He was in the oak parlour at Martingdale one Christmas Eve, and before the next morning he had disappeared—to reappear in the flesh no more.

Over night, one Mr Wharley, a great friend and boon companion of Jeremy's, had sat playing cards with him until after twelve o'clock chimes, then he took leave of his host and rode home under the moonlight. After that no person, as far as could be ascertained, ever saw Jeremy Lester alive.

His ways of life had not been either the most regular, or the most respectable, and it was not until a new year had come in without any tidings of his whereabouts reaching the house, that his servants became seriously alarmed concerning his absence.

Then enquiries were set on foot concerning him—enquiries which grew more urgent as weeks and months passed by without the slightest clue being obtained as to his whereabouts. Rewards were offered, advertisements inserted, but still Jeremy made no sign; and so in course of time the heir-at-law, Paul Lester, took possession of the house, and went down to spend the summer months at Martingdale with his rich wife, and her four children by a first husband. Paul Lester was a barrister—an over-worked barrister, who everyone supposed would be glad enough to leave the bar and settle at Martingdale, where his wife's money and the fortune he had accumulated could not have failed to give him a good standing even among the neighbouring country families; and perhaps it was with such intention that he went down into Bedfordshire.

If this were so, however, he speedily changed his mind, for with the January snows he returned to London, let off the land surrounding the house, shut up the Hall, put in a caretaker, and never troubled himself further about his ancestral seat.

Time went on, and people began to say the house was haunted, that Paul Lester had 'seen something', and so forth—all which stories were duly repeated for our benefit when, forty-one years after the disappearance of Jeremy Lester, Clare and I went down to inspect our inheritance.

I say 'our', because Clare had stuck bravely to me in poverty—grinding poverty, and prosperity was not going to part us now. What was mine was hers, and that she knew, God bless her, without my needing to tell her so.

The transition from rigid economy to comparative wealth was in our case the more delightful also, because we had not in the least degree anticipated it. We never expected Paul Lester's shoes to come to us, and accordingly it was not upon our consciences that we had ever in our dreariest moods wished him dead.

Had he made a will, no doubt we never should have gone to Martingdale, and I, consequently, never written this story; but, luckily for us, he died intestate, and the Bedfordshire property came to me.

As for the fortune, he had spent it in travelling, and in giving great enter-tainments at his grand house in Portman Square. Concerning his effects, Mrs Lester and I came to a very amicable arrangement, and she did me the honour of inviting me to call upon her occasionally, and, as I heard, spoke of me as a very worthy and presentable young man 'for my station', which, of course, coming from so good an authority, was gratifying. Moreover, she asked me if I intended residing at Martingdale, and on my replying in the affirmative, hoped I should like it.

It struck me at the time that there was a certain significance in her tone, and when I went down to Martingdale and heard the absurd stories which were afloat concerning the house being haunted, I felt confident that if Mrs Lester had hoped much, she had feared more.

People said Mr Jeremy 'walked' at Martingdale. He had been seen, it was averred, by poachers, by gamekeepers, by children who had come to use the park as a near cut to school, by lovers who kept their tryst under the elms and beeches.

As for the caretaker and his wife, the third in residence since Jeremy Lester's disappearance, the man gravely shook his head when questioned, while the woman stated that wild horses, or even wealth untold, should not draw her into the red bedroom, nor into the oak parlour, after dark.

'I have heard my mother tell, sir—it was her as followed old Mrs Reynolds, the first caretaker—how there were things went on in these self same rooms as might make any Christian's hair stand on end. Such stamping, and swearing, and knocking about on furniture; and then tramp, tramp, up the great staircase; and along the corridor and so into the red bedroom, and then bang, and tramp, tramp again. They do say, sir, Mr Paul Lester met him once, and from that time the oak parlour has never been opened. I never was inside it myself.'

Upon hearing which fact, the first thing I did was to proceed to the oak parlour, open the shutters, and let the August sun stream in upon the haunted chamber. It was an old-fashioned, plainly furnished apartment, with a large table in the centre, a smaller in a recess by the fire-place, chairs ranged against the walls, and a dusty moth-eaten carpet upon the floor. There were dogs on the hearth, broken and rusty; there was a brass fender, tarnished and battered; a picture of some sea-fight over the mantel-piece, while another work of art about equal in merit hung between the windows. Altogether, an utterly prosaic and yet not uncheerful apartment, from out of which the ghosts flitted as soon as daylight was let into it, and which I proposed, as soon as I 'felt my feet', to redecorate, refurnish, and convert into a pleasant morning-room. I was still under thirty, but I had learned prudence in that very good school, Necessity; and it was not my intention to spend much money until I had ascertained for certain what were the actual revenues derivable from the lands still belonging to the Martingdale estates, and the charges upon them. In fact, I wanted to know what I was worth before committing myself to any great extravagances, and the place had for so long been neglected, that I experienced some difficulty in arriving at the state of my real income.

But in the meanwhile, Clare and I found great enjoyment in exploring every nook and corner of our domain, in turning over the contents of old chests and cupboards, in examining the faces of our ancestors looking down on us from the walls, in walking through the neglected gardens, full of weeds, overgrown with shrubs and birdweed, where the boxwood was eighteen feet high, and the shoots of the rosetrees yards long. I have put the place in order since then; there is no grass on the paths, there are no trailing brambles over the ground, the hedges have been cut and trimmed, and the trees pruned and the boxwood clipped. But I often say nowadays that in spite of all my improvements, or rather, in consequence of them, Martingdale does not look one half so pretty as it did in its pristine state of uncivilised picturesqueness.

Although I determined not to commence repairing and decorating the house till better informed concerning the rental of Martingdale, still the state of my finances was so far satisfactory that Clare and I decided on going abroad to take our long-talked-of holiday before the fine weather was past. We could not tell what a year might bring forth, as Clare sagely remarked; it was wise to take our pleasure while we could; and accordingly, before the end of August arrived we were wandering about the continent, loitering at Rouen, visiting the galleries at Paris, and talking of extending our one month of enjoyment into three. What decided me on this course was the circumstance of our becoming acquainted with an English family who intended wintering in Rome. We met accidentally, but discovering that we were near neighbours in England—in fact that Mr Cronson's property lay close beside Martingdale—the slight acquaintance soon ripened into intimacy, and ere long we were travelling in company.

From the first, Clare did not much like this arrangement. There was 'a little girl' in England she wanted me to marry, and Mr Cronson had a daughter who certainly was both handsome and attractive. The little girl had not despised John Lester, artist, while Miss Cronson indisputably set her cap at John Lester of Martingdale, and would have turned away her pretty face from a poor man's admiring glance—all this I can see plainly enough now, but I was blind then and should have proposed for Maybel—that was her name—before the winter was over, had news not suddenly arrived of the illness of Mrs Cronson, senior. In a moment the programme was changed; our pleasant days of foreign travel were at an end. The Cronsons packed up and departed, while Clare and I returned more slowly to England, a little out of humour, it must be confessed, with each other.

It was the middle of November when we arrived at Martingdale, and found the place anything but romantic or pleasant. The walks were wet and sodden, the trees were leafless, there were no flowers save a few late pink roses blooming in the garden. It had been a wet season, and the place looked miserable. Clare would not ask Alice down to keep her company in the winter months, as she had intended; and for myself, the Cronsons were still absent in Norfolk, where they meant to spend Christmas with old Mrs. Cronson, now recovered.

Altogether, Martingdale seemed dreary enough, and the ghost stories we had laughed at while sunshine flooded the room, became less unreal, when we had nothing but blazing fires and wax candles to dispel the gloom. They became more real also when servant after servant left us to seek situations elsewhere; when "noises" grew frequent in the house; when we ourselves, Clare and I, with our own ears heard the tramp, tramp, the banging and the chattering which had been described to us.

My dear reader, you doubtless are free from superstitious fancies. You pooh-pooh the existence of ghosts, and "only wish you could find a haunted house in which to spend a night," which is all very brave and praiseworthy, but wait till you are left in a dreary, desolate old country mansion, filled with the most unaccountable sounds, without a servant, with none save an old care-taker and his wife, who, living at the extremest end of the building, heard nothing of the tramp, tramp, bang, bang, going on at all hours of the night.

At first I imagined the noises were produced by some evil-disposed persons, who wished, for purposes of their own, to keep the house uninhabited; but by degrees Clare and I came to the conclusion the visitation must be supernatural, and Martingdale by consequence untenantable.

Still being practical people, and unlike our predecessors, not having money to live where and how we liked, we decided to watch and see whether we could trace any human influence in the matter. If not, it was agreed we were to pull down the right wing of the house and the principal staircase.

For nights and nights we sat up till two or three o'clock in the morning, Clare engaged in needlework, I reading, with a revolver lying on the table beside me; but nothing, neither sound nor appearance rewarded our vigil. This confirmed my first ideas that the sounds were not supernatural; but just to test the matter, I determined on Christmas-eve, the anniversary of Mr. Jeremy Lester's disappearance, to keep watch myself in the red bed-chamber. Even to Clare I never mentioned my intention.

About ten, tired out with our previous vigils, we each retired to rest. Somewhat ostentatiously, perhaps, I noisily shut the door of my room, and when I opened it half an hour afterwards, no mouse could have pursued its way along the corridor with greater silence and caution than myself. Quite in the dark I sat in the red room. For over an hour I might as well have been in my grave for anything I could see in the apartment; but at the end of that time the moon rose and cast strange lights across the floor and upon the wall of the haunted chamber.

Hitherto I had kept my watch opposite the window; now I changed my place to a corner near the door, where I was shaded from observation by the heavy hangings of the bed, and an antique wardrobe.

Still I sat on, but still no sound broke the silence. I was weary with many nights' watching; and tired of my solitary vigil, I dropped at last into a slumber from which I wakened by hearing the door softly opened.

"John," said my sister, almost in a whisper; "John, are you here?"

"Yes, Clare," I answered; "but what are you doing up at this hour?"

"Come downstairs," she replied; "*they* are in the oak parlor."

I did not need any explanation as to whom she meant, but crept downstairs after her, warned by an uplifted hand of the necessity for silence and caution.

By the door—by the open door of the oak parlor, she paused, and we both looked in.

There was the room we left in darkness overnight, with a bright wood fire blazing on the hearth, candles on the chimney-piece, the small table pulled out from its accustomed corner, and two men seated beside it, playing at cribbage.

We could see the face of the younger player; it was that of a man about five-and-twenty, of a man who had lived hard and wickedly; who had wasted his substance and his health; who had been while in the flesh Jeremy Lester. It would be difficult for me to say how I knew this, how in a moment I identified the features of the player with those of the man who had been missing for forty-one years—forty-one years that very night. He was dressed in the costume of a bygone period; his hair was powdered, and round his wrists there were ruffles of lace.

He looked like one who, having come from some great party, had sat down after his return home to play cards with an intimate friend. On his little finger there sparkled a ring, in the front of his shirt there gleamed a valuable diamond. There were diamond buckles in his shoes, and, according to the fashion of his time, he wore knee breeches and silk stockings, which showed off advantageously the shape of a remarkably good leg and ankle.

He sat opposite the door, but never once lifted his eyes to it. His attention seemed concentrated on the cards.

For a time there was utter silence in the room, broken only by the momentous counting of the game. In the doorway we stood, holding our breath, terrified and yet fascinated by the scene which was being acted before us.

The ashes dropped on the hearth softly and like the snow; we could hear the rustle of the cards as they were dealt out and fell upon the table; we listened to the count—fifteen-one, fifteen-two, and so forth—but there was no other word spoken till at length the player whose face we could not see, exclaimed, "I win; the game is mine."

Then his opponent took up the cards, sorted them over negligently in his hand, put them close together, and flung the whole pack in his guest's face, exclaiming, "Cheat; liar; take that!"

There was a bustle and confusion—a flinging over of chairs, and fierce gesticulation, and such a noise of passionate voices mingling, that we could not hear a sentence which was uttered. All at once, however, Jeremy Lester strode out of the room in so great a hurry that he almost touched us where we stood; out of the room, and tramp, tramp up the staircase to the red room, whence he descended in a few minutes with a couple of rapiers under his arm.

When he re-entered the room he gave, as it seemed to us, the other man his choice of the weapons, and then he flung open the window, and after ceremoniously giving place for his opponent to pass out first, he walked forth into the night air, Clare and I following.

We went through the garden and down a narrow winding walk to a smooth piece of turf, sheltered from the north by a plantation of young fir trees. It was a bright moonlight night by this time, and we could distinctly see Jeremy Lester measuring off the ground.

"When you say 'three,'" he said at last to the man whose back was still towards us. They had drawn lots for the ground, and the lot had fallen against Mr. Lester. He stood thus with the moonbeams falling upon him, and a handsomer fellow I would never desire to behold.

"One," began the other; "two," and before our kinsman had the slightest suspicion of his design, he was upon him, and his rapier through Jeremy Lester's breast.

At the sight of that cowardly treachery, Clare screamed aloud. In a moment the combatants had disappeared, the moon was obscured behind a cloud, and we were standing in the shadow of the fir-plantation, shivering with cold and terror. But we knew at last what had become of the late owner of Martingdale, that he had fallen, not in fair fight, but foully murdered by a false friend.

When late on Christmas morning I awoke, it was to see a white world, to behold the ground, and trees, and shrubs all laden and covered with snow. There was snow everywhere, such snow as no person could remember having fallen for forty-one years.

"It was on just such a Christmas as this that Mr. Jeremy disappeared," remarked the old sexton to my sister, who had insisted on dragging me through the snow to church, whereupon Clare fainted away and was carried into the vestry, where I made a full confession to the Vicar of all we had beheld the previous night.

At first that worthy individual rather inclined to treat the matter lightly, but when a fortnight after, the snow melted away and the fir-plantation came to be examined, he confessed there might be more things in heaven and earth than his limited philosophy had dreamed of.

In a little clear space just within the plantation, Jeremy Lester's body was found. We knew it by the ring and the diamond buckles, and the sparkling breastpin; and Mr. Cronson, who in his capacity as magistrate came over to inspect these relics, was visibly perturbed at my narrative.

"Pray, Mr. Lester, did you in your dream see the face of—of the gentleman—your kinsman's opponent?"

"No," I answered, "he sat and stood with his back to us all the time."

"There is nothing more, of course, to be done in the matter," observed Mr. Cronson.

"Nothing," I replied; and there the affair would doubtless have terminated, but that a few days afterwards, when we were dining at Cronson Park, Clare all of a sudden dropped the glass of water she was carrying to her lips, and exclaiming, "Look, John, there he is!" rose from her seat, and with a face as white as the table cloth, pointed to a portrait hanging on the wall. "I saw him for an instant when he turned his head towards the door as Jeremy Lester left it," she explained; "that is he."

Of what followed after this identification I have only the vaguest recollection. Servants rushed hither and thither; Mrs. Cronson dropped off her chair into hysterics; the young ladies gathered round their mamma; Mr. Cronson, trembling like one in an ague fit, attempted some kind of an explanation, while Clare kept praying to be taken away—only to be taken away.

I took her away, not merely from Cronson Park but from Martingdale. Before we left the latter place, however, I had an interview with Mr. Cronson, who said the portrait Clare had identified was that of his wife's father, the last person who saw Jeremy Lester alive.

"He is an old man now," finished Mr. Cronson, "a man of over eighty, who has confessed everything to me. You won't bring further sorrow and disgrace upon us by making this matter public?"

I promised him I would keep silence, but the story gradually oozed out, and the Cronsons left the country.

My sister never returned to Martingdale; she married and is living in London. Though I assure her there are no strange noises in my house, she will not visit Bedfordshire, where the "little girl" she wanted me so long ago to "think of seriously," is now my wife and the mother of my children.

WHERE DO I GO WHEN YOU DIE?

Keith Ridgway

Keith Ridgway is a Dubliner and Londoner. He is the author of the novels *Hawthorn & Child* and *Animals*, and other fiction.

What I needed at that moment was something inorganic, something that was elaborately machine-made and neat, metal cased, surprisingly heavy, matt finish, black or preferably charcoal, no markings, no lights. I wanted it to be about the size of a book, maybe a touch narrower, and about three centimetres thick. I needed it to connect wirelessly to my phone. I liked the idea of this connection causing my phone to behave in a completely different way to its usual condescending attitude of round-cornered helpfulness and its cheerful suggestions regarding time and place. I needed instead for my phone to appear, at least to a bystander, something sinister and perhaps even dangerous, the screen darkening suddenly, and a peculiar succession of small noises unrelated to anything in the natural world heralding an entirely new interface which offered no intuitive clue as to how to proceed. I wanted it to require of me an uncharacteristic discipline, to burden me with a profound and appalling responsibility, to demand of me a way of being in relation to it that brooked of no distraction. I would have to enter a complicated series of precise constructions in the form of esoteric symbols input using an on-screen keyboard unlike any other, the keys representing possibly a complete set of available symbols, but much more likely to represent, or to contain, symbol elements, which when combined as a sequence of key presses would create a symbol on the screen. I wanted it to be very complicated. So that with each key press the keyboard would reconfigure itself to present all available symbol elements which were possible to combine with that first keypress, and eliminating any symbol-elements which it was not possible to combine with the symbol-element just selected. Each touch completely altered the possible touches which could follow. Each decision wiped out the circumstances in which it was made, and would engender an entirely new set of circumstances, which would in turn disintegrate completely when I made the next decision. There would be no delete key. Furthermore.

Well, that was enough for now. These symbols, when created on screen, would look to the innocent eye, to the glancing eye, like they might be pictograms, related in some way to things in nature or in the shared human environment, but which would on closer examination be impossible to relate to anything. They would be uncannily familiar, suggesting perhaps – by virtue of the edges or sides or strokes they contained – numbers, or houses or vehicles or other items, or shapes in nature, or people or animals, or geometries of warning, or tags of composition or origin. But they would, to the passer-by who might lean over my shoulder for a closer look, turn out to be completely indecipherable. A non-correlating hieroglyphic system that apparently floated free of any signification whatsoever. What I would need also is not to know exactly what I was doing. Or, to know in some part of myself that was silent to other parts of myself. I would know what symbols were required, and how to produce them, but this knowledge would not be available to any articulate mechanism or instinct in my consciousness. The matt charcoal or black box would, after I had entered the correct series of symbols on my phone, open.

It would require an immense movement of people, a migration of many millions of people, moving in what looked at first like a random manner, but which over time clarified into a quite ordered sequence of discreet journeys which nevertheless involved all the connected land mass of Africa, Asia and Europe. That is what it would require. Or at least, the initiation of this is what it would require, to open the box. I do not like the term box. To open the device. In other words, there would be a delay between entering the correct symbols in the correct order on my phone, and the opening of the device. In that delay my phone would become inoperable. It would go dark, fizz a little as if cooked, and perhaps even exhale an acrid or even pleasant breath of vapour. A sweet puff of silver vapour, rushing up, gone. And my phone would at that point be useless. It might even shrivel up like foil, shrinking smaller and smaller in my hand until it was just a crumpled ball of densely packed glass and plastic and metal and whatever else goes into these things. A tiny flake of silver, shrinking. An alteration of scale that proceeds towards annihilation, a continual shrinking, a raising of possibly sweet vapour, continuing almost impossibly, continuing, continuing, etcetera like that and so on, just look at it, the same words, those words. And it would seem as if the device was watching while this happened, or was even causing it to happen through its attention, because the device would somehow appear to be paying attention, to be watching, though of course the device would be eyeless, lensless, matt and dark, making no sign at all that it was doing anything, unless it could be said that its design and presence created a sense of watchfulness, of operation, a sense of it being a device that was doing something, and perhaps that something would be, or at least would include, as an afterthought, as the least of the operations the device was carrying out, the complete and beautiful obliteration of my phone, which would finally, eventually, disappear on the skin of my palm, painlessly, evaporating, but leaving a tiny silver scar in the shape of the last symbol it communicated to the device, a sort of lozenge laid over a rectangle, or the rectangle over the lozenge, next to three very short vertical lines, each a little shorter than the one next to it, the longest line being the furthest from the main, if you could call it the main, part of the symbol, if you could call it a symbol, if you could call it a part, if you could call it.

The device then, the box, the device, opens. I would need at this point for it to open. To become open. Something would be underway on a vast scale, a global scale, involving the movement of almost unimaginable numbers of human beings, and the device, as it were being assured of this, perhaps through some communication not apparent in its surface, would alter that surface. The opening cannot be like an opening. It is not a box. It doesn't open like a box. It does not have a lid. This is not some stupid jack-in-the-box idiocy that pops open and surprises the passer-by, surprises me, with some grotesque revelation or with something like a message, a secret, an instruction or set of instructions that might achieve for us some better world. This is not about us. What I need just at the moment is for this not to be about us. By us I mean humanity. I mean us as a genus. All of us. By all of us I mean us-as-all, I mean us as a biological species. What I need to make clear is that this all-of-us and us-as-all does not necessarily include us-as-us, just us, you and me, that us, and this is about that us. It just is.

I need to explain myself better, obviously.

What I need at this moment is that the device begins to become open, begins, having been assured of the movement of vast numbers of people, to alter its relationship to its environment, to the world in which it exists. It is impossible to describe. But suddenly, a long suddenly, over a considerable period of time, in which nothing seems to happen, but suddenly nevertheless, we are inside the device.

It is important to state at this point that I am not responsible for anything. I am not responsible for the movement of almost unimaginable numbers of people. The symbols that I would have entered on my phone, as if almost in a trance, I do not know what those symbols mean, or what they do. I have no expectation regarding a specific outcome or result. I just see the people.

We are, as I say, inside the device. That what I need, right at this moment actually, I need for us to be inside the device, suddenly, just us, inside the device. In it. Well, in fact us and a limited number of other individual examples of the human being, of the genus. A few of us. But not enough, not in sufficient number or the appropriate configuration to be of any use. Just a handful. Whose hands? I don't know. I'm pretty tired now. A handful of us. Just me, and you, and a few of our friends. Well, mostly your friends, who I also love, but differently, mostly I love them because you love them, and the fact that they make you so happy makes me love them more, and I can see why they make you happy and why you love them, and I cannot conceive of a world where you would be cut off from what makes you happy and what you love, so here they are. And also some people I don't know but they are people that are here because of your kindness, the way it explodes and catches people and gathers them up and brings them, and some people also who are probably just here by accident because of some misunderstanding that one of us had when we were talking to someone at work or on the train or something, some odd little happenstance, peculiar things like that, nice people, laughing about it now, not upset about it or anything, not at all but here now, in here, with us, us and our friends and these few other people but mostly just us, you and me, our heads bowed towards each other, sitting side by side on something, some sort of thing we can sit on, comfortably, just you and me, holding each other's hands and just sitting there, our heads bowed, our heads touching, and honestly I don't know what we're doing or if we're talking to each other or laughing about something or whether we're kissing or just whispering our usual bullshit at each other, just the two of us, which is, I have to say it, the two of us is mostly you. You with your face, look at your face, and your shoulders, all that, just so beautiful and your face is always smiling, I think of it as always smiling, looking at me and smiling, and when I think of us I think of your face and inside that your smile and inside that I don't know, your love and your kindness and your patience, and your jokes, your laugh, your laughter, your smile, your love, all that, inside all that. Inside all that.

Inside all that.

That is basically what I need right now.

ROBBIE BRADY'S ASTONISHING LATE GOAL TAKES ITS PLACE IN OUR PERSONAL HISTORIES

Sally Rooney

Sally Rooney is the author of two novels. Her second novel, *Normal People*, was awarded the Costa Novel Prize and longlisted for the Man Booker Prize 2018. She was a Cullman Center Fellow at the New York Public Library for 2019–2020.

Conor calls her from an alleyway, near a plastic skip. It's going to eat his phone credit if she picks up, and he expects himself, in light of this, to hope belatedly that she won't pick up, but he finds himself, regardless, hoping that she does. And she does. She says hello in a crisp, amused voice, as if this phone call is already part of an ongoing joke between them.

Were you watching that? he says.

Oh, I was watching. The atmosphere in the stadium looked like fun.

It was good, yeah.

I envied you slightly, says Helen. I've been here looking at the memes for the last hour.

Relaxing now, he leans against the alleyway wall. It's late but still warm out in Lille, a humid heat, and he's been drinking since the late afternoon.

Memes about the match? he says. Are there ones already?

Oh yeah, it's like simultaneous. It's actually very interesting in the sense – well, do you want to hear my opinions about memes or are you busy?

No, go on.

Are there roaming charges?

I have free calls, he lies, implausibly and without really deciding to.

On the other end of the line, Helen doesn't question the plausibility of Conor having free calls while in France, mainly because she doesn't really register what he's said, beyond the sense that he has given her permission to talk about what she was already thinking about before. She's sitting on her bed, her back against the headboard. She sat this way for the duration of the Ireland–Italy match, which she streamed online and watched alone, eating a bowl of instant ramen noodles with disposable chopsticks while the light in her window faded from a bluish-white to a whitish-grey and finally to dark.

It's interesting to watch an event being recycled as culture in real time, she says. You know, you're watching the process of cultural production while it takes place, rather than in retrospect. I don't know if that's unique.

Yeah, I get you. And, uh. Well, I'm drunk so I'm not going to be at my sharpest here, but I want to say, you know, the disintegration of the idea of authorship.

Totally. That's sharp, you're very sharp. You don't even sound drunk.

I think about memes a lot, he says.

Helen lifts her laptop off her lap and on to the empty part of the bed, as a gesture of commitment to the conversation.

But what's tricky about the point you're making, she says, is that it becomes very difficult to locate power. And to analyse operations of power, culturally. I guess we're used to doing that through the hegemonic figure of the author, or at least through some identifiable power structure like a movie studio or an ad company.

Yeah, and now it's just happening through like, spontaneous mass participation.

I guess you could argue online spaces are gendered and classed in particular ways but like, are they even?

Let's never forget gender, says Conor. Gender everywhere, I would suggest. Are you hearing a lot of noise on the line?

A group of fans have just vacated the bar next to him and flooded on to the street cheering. In the lights over the bar their jerseys have that cheap-looking nylon sheen. They're singing something to the tune of the 1979 Village People hit "Go West". Almost all the chants, for some reason, are sung to the tune of "Go West", making the individual lyrics difficult to decipher in many cases, creative and redolent of spontaneous mass participation though they are.

A little bit now, she says. Are you somewhere busy? It was quiet before so I assumed you were back in the hostel.

No, still at the bar. With the, yeah – the legendary Irish fans.

That's you, you're a legendary Irish fan now. Are you wearing a jersey?

No, I'm kind of keeping my distance, he says. I'm trying not to sing too much or like, suck up to any cops or anything.

The sucking up to cops I must say is a global embarrassment.

French cops as well. The policemen of a country literally renowned for racism. But anyway, look, here we are.

Having said this, Conor realises that it sounded like an attempt to move the conversation on to some new destination. He can practically hear their sudden mutual awareness that he hasn't yet explained why he's calling her, that he has hollowed out a little well in the conversation now where this explanation should go, and yet he doesn't have one, or indeed anything further to say at all. He even considers hanging up, and emailing later to say the signal cut out.

He last saw Helen six weeks ago, at the beginning of May. He was visiting her in Cambridge for the weekend. After a long and tiresome day of travel and vague anxiety about currency, he arrived on Friday night. All day he'd been mentally converting sterling to euro in an attempt to keep track of how much money he was wasting on bus tickets and cups of coffee, and this minor but persistent cognitive effort had drained him and made him feel miserly and self-conscious. It was dark when he got off the bus. He remembers now the flat blue surface of the park beside the bus stop, picked out by streetlights, and the strange flavour of weather, the crisp quality of air, the cool winding-down of a day that might earlier have been warm. He saw Helen then, waiting in her little jacket and scarf, he was amused somehow by the sight of her, and he laughed and felt better.

They walked back to her apartment together, chatting about nothing really. He remembers the yellowish stone facade of her building while she rooted in her bag for the keys. Upstairs she made tea and laid out a little food. They talked until very late. Eventually, in her room, she undressed for bed. He sat on the sofa, where he had put his sleeping bag, and she was talking about something to do with her thesis, how much reading she had glanced at before and now had to do in earnest, and that it made her feel slightly fraudulent, and while she was saying this, she was standing at the wardrobe putting on her nightdress. She was partially, but it seemed not consciously, hidden by the wardrobe's open door. Still he could see her bare left shoulder, her slim white upper arm. She hung her blouse on a wire hanger, replaced it in the wardrobe, and without looking up said: are you watching me?

I'm looking in your direction generally, he said, but not "watching" as such.

She laughed then and closed the wardrobe door. It was a black nightdress, longish, with shoulder straps.

I was listening to what you were saying, he said.

Oh, I know. I'm very sensitive to losing someone's attention.

He found this remark pleasantly cryptic at the time. Now on the phone he waits for Helen to say something, though it is by the unspoken rules of ordinary conversation obviously his "turn" to speak, having just signalled that he has something to say.

Good match anyway, he says.

I wish I'd been there. Were you swept away on a tide of emotion?

I was swept a bit, yeah. I shed a tear.

She laughs. That's very sweet, she says. Did you really?

A tear came to my eye, I don't know if it was shed or not.

I was watching alone so I couldn't really experience the full range of emotions, she says. It's like when you go to see a film in the cinema, you laugh in places you wouldn't laugh if you were watching on your own. But it doesn't make the laughing false, you know. Being alone is just less enjoyable.

Are you lonely?

She pauses at this question, which is unusual to hear from Conor, and for the first time in the conversation, including the time when he earlier claimed to be drunk, she's struck by the possibility that he might actually be drunk.

I have to say, I don't like most English people very much, she says. So yeah, living in England, that becomes lonely. Maybe I'm just getting a bad impression of them with the referendum coming up.

Yeah, that looks rough. I think they will stay in, though.

I hope so. Either way it's brought out a lot of very ugly things.

I do feel for you having to live there, he says.

She, too, is thinking of the weekend he visited, the beautiful weather they had. On Saturday they woke up late, to a radiant blue sky powdered with tiny clouds. She made a pot of coffee, they ate toast and oranges. She tidied up the breakfast dishes while he showered, and she was comforted by the noise of the hot water tank and the rush of the taps. When he reappeared in the kitchen he was dressed, and she was still wearing her nightgown, with a cardigan wrapped over it. There was this moment of abrupt eye contact between them, which made her feel as if they hadn't really looked at one another since he arrived. Their eyes stilled the whole room. She thought about satirising this moment lightly to deprive it of its seriousness, maybe by doing something mock-flirtatious, but she couldn't rely on her flirting to seem comic to him rather than grotesque. Instead she turned away, flustered, and he just hovered there not saying anything.

It was a warm day out and Helen remembers what she wore: a flimsy white blouse, a pale ballet skirt, her flat shoes. She wasn't concerned, or doesn't remember being concerned, about her appearance in any real way, but she registered dimly that she would rather look bad than look as if she were trying to look good. They wandered around the Fitzwilliam Museum together in the afternoon, talking. After that they had lunch, and after lunch more coffee. Conor was telling some funny story about work and Helen laughed so much that she spilled coffee on her skirt, which pleased him. She knew that he relished her laughter. It seemed to give him some private, almost sheepish satisfaction, and while she laughed he would avert his eyes slightly, as if to look at her directly would be too much.

She's met a lot of very intelligent people in Cambridge, people who take a brittle pride in demonstrating how clever they are. She somewhat enjoys engaging them in conversation, little jousting exchanges, until the other party becomes defensive and irritable. But the enjoyment is ultimately feline, as if she's idly batting her interlocutor back and forth between her paws. There's something about their kind of intelligence which isn't lively or curious. Conor, who works in a call centre for a mobile service provider, is her ideal conversational partner, the person around whom she feels most clear-minded and least remote. They keep up with one another effortlessly in conversation, and maybe for this reason, or maybe out of a sincere and long-standing mutual affection, their discussions don't become competitive. Helen finds it philosophically sustaining that two people who agree on everything can still find so much to say to one another.

Most people are pretty liberal here, she says, and they're self-congratulatory about that. You can see they have a lot of contempt for normal people, who didn't go to Cambridge or don't have college degrees. And I think the contempt is actually part of what they congratulate themselves on.

Am I a normal person, to you?

Is that… you're objecting to my use of the phrase "normal people", or we're talking about our relationship?

He smiles. His eyes are tired and he closes them. The lids feel wet somehow. Well, I like to think I'm very special to you in some ways, he says. He can hear her laughing.

I am curious why you've called, she says. But I'm happy to be talking to you so I don't mind if there's no reason.

I'll be honest with you, I got carried away watching that match. The tide of emotion you were speaking about. And I felt an impulse to give you a ring. I wanted to tell you I love you, and all that.

For a few seconds he hears nothing at all. He can't tell what she's doing on the other end of the line. Then there's a faint noise like a laugh, and he realises it is a laugh.

I love you, too, she says. I was trying to think of something intelligent to say there about how we feel and express love through these communal cultural experiences like football, but then I thought, oh my god, shut up. I love you, too, I miss you.

He wipes at his eyes with the hand that isn't holding the phone. Her voice has a soft, wet quality to him, associated with the deepest consolation he has ever felt.

The weekend I stayed with you, I kind of thought something might happen, he says. But I don't know. Maybe it's good that it didn't. He swallows. I lied about having free calls, he adds. So I probably shouldn't stay on that long.

Oh, she says. Well, that's alright. Go and celebrate.

There's a final silence, in which they both feel the same nameless feeling, the same stirring impulse toward an unknown act, each in fact wanting the other to say again: I love you, I love you very much, but unable to say it again themselves. Despite this unexpected sense of irresolution, of something unfinished, they are each pleased at having managed to extract this new confession from the other, Helen thinking herself the more pleased because Conor said it first, and he thinking himself the more pleased because she didn't have the excuse of drunkenness. They say their goodbyes, distracted now. Conor slips his phone back into his pocket, stands up from the alleyway wall. On the main road a police car drives by, its siren revolving silently, and the fans cheer, for the police or for some other unrelated reason. Helen puts her phone on her bedside table with a soft clicking sound, glass on wood, and then pauses for a moment in stillness. She looks at the opposite wall as if a certain thought has only just now occurred to her. Absently she touches her hair, unwashed today. Then in one seemingly natural, thoughtless motion, she lifts her laptop back on to her crossed legs and taps the trackpad with two outstretched fingers to light the screen.

PHYSIOTHERAPY

Donal Ryan

Donal Ryan is a novelist and short story writer from Tipperary. He has won several awards for his work, which include the novels *The Spinning Heart*, *The Thing about December* and the short story collection *A Slanting of the Sun: Stories* (2015). He has twice been nominated for the Booker Prize. He teaches Creative Writing at the University of Limerick.

I squeeze the rubber ball three times and raise my arm so that my left hand meets his right and he always seems to smile as he takes the ball from me and grips it softly and I nod three times at him in time with his three squeezes. He reaches across himself with his good left arm and takes the ball from himself and repeats the exercise and I take it in my right and so on and so on and so on. The physiotherapist gave us a long-handled stick with a netted scoop at its end to retrieve the ball when we drop it the way we wouldn't be hauling ourselves up and out of our chairs and exhausting ourselves before we have our exercises done. Why don't you just give us a square ball the way it won't roll, I said to him, and he got a bit sour I think, and muttered something about the bones of our hands or some such. He reminded me of a nephew of mine I haven't seen for a long time. A curly-headed lad, long in the back and longer in the face, my sister Noreen's boy, gone off to London or somewhere but years and years. A lot of them get lost out foreign, they don't come back themselves.

We were married at twenty, Pierse and me. He was older by a week exactly. I wore a simple white dress my mother made for me, and he wore a navy suit borrowed from his father's brother who was about his size. We had our wedding breakfast inside in O'Meara's Hotel and only our families were there and my friend Theresa who was maid-of-honour and his friend Mossy who was best man. We went for a week to Galway on our honeymoon in a Volkswagen Beetle lent to us by the manager of the co-op, who was a friend of Pierse's father. He held my hand every minute of every day, hardly letting me go even while we ate. I sat on his lap in our narrow suite and he hugged me fiercely, and he kissed my mouth and face and eyes. We adventured up and down narrow streets and watched fishermen on the quays as they inspected their nets in the mornings and hauled their catches in the evenings and Pierse tried a few words of Irish out on a chap one day and the chap only smiled and didn't answer and Pierse smiled into the quayside stench and reddened so deeply I thought he'd burst.

Pierse got into auctioneering through another friend of his father's and he quickly gained a reputation for thoroughness and honesty and there was never a trace of sneakiness that was ever known about him, and people could see that in the first few instants of knowing him. He grew inches at an auction; it was the only place that time he seemed to fit, it was as though his gavel protected him from embarrassment, as though his practised ululations, inscrutable to me, threw up a wall of strength around him. Men as seemingly straight and quiet in their ways as him stood watching, nodding their bids, hardly seeming to care about the outcome. Pierse spoke slowly and clearly to potential buyers of houses, pointing out where work needed to be done, where things could be improved. He couldn't do the hard sell, he couldn't stretch the truth. Eventually there was a falling out and he came home one evening and sat after dinner for longer than he usually did and our son looked with concern at him as he excused himself and went looking for his hurley and ball and he told me after long minutes that he wouldn't be going back to Woodley and Woodley as there were underhand dealings going on and he couldn't be a part of them. He started to buy old rundown houses and renovate them and sell them for an honest profit and he made good money and seemed happy with his work, but it never made him as tall as he used to seem at his lectern, sweeping his gaze, am-bidding, gavel in hand.

I wonder what he thinks about all the day long. I should know, I suppose, or would, if I was any kind of a wife. Silence always suited him. That his silence now has been forced upon him by sickness hardly matters. I think a lot about the day he stole into the house through the back porch door and a present in his hand for me of a gold necklace with a heart on it and a diamond set in its centre and I sitting in the dining room at the table with James and his hand on mine and he gripping my fingers so tightly his knuckles were white. And a fool could know what was happening, what had happened, what had been about to happen. And he only punished me for that with silence. He left himself out through the front door and went down the avenue to his car that he had parked down there away from the house the way I wouldn't hear him coming in and he could surprise me, back early from his trip to the north, and the necklace boxed and bowed and held out before him like a thing being taken altarward in an offertory procession and the thorns of the rosebush opened the skin of my hand as I retrieved it from where he'd flung it and the salt of my tears seared in the tiny wounds.

I finished it with James that day and never took up with another man again.

Pierse ended his self-imposed exile from our bed after a few weeks but he got into the habit of staying up watching television at night, and drinking, never very much, but enough so that he'd sleep sedated and the smell of it would drift from his breath across to me. He was never bothered by the silence between us, only the loudness, when I'd burst out with something, to try to goad him, to wound him, to make him react in some way so that I could say there's the long and the short of it, there's what he feels; now I can know what I need to do to repay. But all debts are written off eventually, when it's clear no payment will ever be made, that restitution isn't possible and everything is then reset to nought.

Pierse took to holding my hand daily again after our son died. As though to stop the shaking in himself, he gripped me, and took both my hands in his, and squeezed his eyes closed and bared his teeth and his breaths would rush and heave from him like silent screams. He'd helped him buy his ticket to Australia; he'd even contacted some people he knew over there to arrange a few weeks or maybe months of work for him on building sites, and he'd driven him to the airport and hugged him awkwardly but tightly at the departure gate and showed no sign of letting go until Stephen pulled back gently laughing from him. He asked me did I want to stop somewhere for a bit to eat on the way home and I said yes and we stopped in Limerick and in a corner table of a darkened restaurant he'd sat in front of a plate of untouched food and said Christ, Maud, I think I'm after making an awful mistake. Letting him off like that. I should have persuaded him to stay here and work away with me. And not three weeks later our telephone rang in the early hours and he took my hand as we walked up the hall from our bedroom and a voice half a world away told us our Stephen was gone, scaffolding had collapsed under him and he had been killed.

There are days when it seems as though they are the only three things to ever have happened. I got married, I had a love affair, my son was killed. Someone now, some expert in the ways of human minds, looking from a cold distance at me and at the way I carried on, would say I was suffering then from some kind of depression or disorder or some such nonsense. But James stole in to my life smiling, and the sight of him, his presence in a room, caused the air to thicken, my mind to slow, my heart to quicken. I don't understand fully still to this day what came over me, or out of me, or what kind of a spell he cast on me, but I nearly drowned myself in foolishness and heat. The noise of those days, the burning joy, the wildness. He was a young widower; his wife had haemorrhaged in childbirth, his daughter was born to sadness and he told me these things in a soft voice, and he told me how he loved to talk to me, how he loved to look at my eyes, how he loved me. He kissed me and I lost my reason. When the church roof was mended and the fundraising committee we co-chaired was disbanded he came to our house and sat in the dining room and gripped this hand so hard it pained me and he asked me to come away with him and his teenaged daughter to England, and to bring little Stephen with me, and I nearly said yes until some gentle draught Pierse created in his effort to surprise me caused me to turn my head and see him there, at that doorway, with his gift for me on the palm of his trembling hand.

We're going well now, with our ball. The squeezing and passing from left hand to right hand to partner, and the wait to take it back, have fallen to an easy rhythm. Our knees are almost touching, I can feel the warmth of him. A strange, fortunate symmetry, that his left side was struck and my right, his within six months of mine. Mini-strokes, the doctors said. There'll be more, as likely as not. Tremors before the earthquakes. The ball falls from his hand; he sucks his teeth in crossness at himself. He looks at me, he stretches out his arm. He grips my hand and pulls lightly and I use the last of my fleeing strength to cross the space between us and turn myself so that I'm sitting on his lap. My necklace swings outwards, the little heart describes an arc and settles again on my chest. I'm seventy-seven and I'm twenty, my child is dead and he hasn't yet been born, there's a thickening of the air about me again in this dayroom, in this honeymoon suite, and my heart is slowing and my mind is quickening and the arms are tight around me and the breath and tears are on my face of the man I pledged to God to love and honour all my days.

RED EYE

Ian Sansom

Ian Sansom is a novelist, journalist and broadcaster. He is the author of more than a dozen books, including *The Truth About Babies*, *Paper: An Elegy*, *September 1, 1939*, and the Mobile Library and the County Guides series of novels.

I'm just trying to picture it. The day after the wedding. That was the real introduction. That was the real welcome.

The day after the wedding we watched it on video. It didn't do it justice, but we were more relaxed. People were drifting in and out, the whole family, neighbours. The man with the white quiff, in a grey cardigan, your neighbour, was singing 'Coward of the County'. I was talking to your granddad.

'If you know your English history you'll know that the long bow saved England on more than one occasion,' he said.

I tried to recall when the long bow had saved England.

'But remember,' he said, 'You're not in England now, son.'

'I know that,' I said.

'You want to grow your hair, then,' he said. 'You look like a squaddie. You don't want to look like a squaddie.'

He told me a story about what had happened to a squaddie who was living out, married to a local girl.

'See,' he said. 'You don't want to look like a squaddie.' He grabbed my arm. 'You're not undercover are yous?'

I said no, I wasn't undercover.

'You're sure?' he said.

'I'm sure,' I said.

'Good,' he said. 'We're a good family, and we don't want any trouble.'

'There'll be no trouble from me,' I said.

'Good man, good man. Welcome to the family,' he said. 'Welcome to Ulster.'

*

I needed a drink. It had been a dry wedding. Your mother had remarried a clean and sober man and he'd insisted on a dry wedding. There had been problems before, with the drink. Your aunts had brought mini bottles of vodka in their handbags and your nan had persuaded the barman to put aside a bottle of sherry for the older ones, but still. Tonight was the real celebration. Everyone who was anyone was there. All the family. All the neighbours. Welcome to Northern Ireland, they all said. Welcome to Ulster. Welcome to Belfast.

There was your neighbour with the moustache.

He said, 'Can I ask you, son, do you go to church?'

I said no, I didn't go to church, but I'd gone into town the day before the wedding and someone had given me a tract, the Reverend Ian Paisley's 'Even Lourdes Could Not Heal Cardinal Thomas O'Fee'.

I had it in my pocket. I was making conversation.

'Tomás Ó Fiaich to you,' he said, pronouncing it correctly. 'You ignorant English bastard. Go on, repeat it,' he said.

'Tomás Ó Fiaich,' I said.

'That's better,' he said. 'It's our culture too, you see. The language, everything. We have as much right to it as them.'

'Right,' I said. 'I'm sure you do.'

Paisley spent too much time in Strasbourg these days, apparently.

'But when's he back in Belfast I'll introduce you,' he said.

'OK,' I said.

'That'll be my wedding gift to you,' he said.

'Thank you,' I said.

'Your everlasting interests are at stake,' he said.

'OK,' I said.

'God gave us the world and what have we done with it?'

'Not a lot?' I said.

'Correct!' he said. 'Correct! Not a lot. You're not of the Catholic persuasion yourself?'

'No,' I said.

'Good,' he said, 'though I have nothing against them personally. It's just, I ask you, is the Pope expected to make any more infallible statements in the future?'

'I don't know,' I said.

'There we are,' he said.

'Where we are?' I said.

'I mean, it's illogical, isn't it. It can't be true. As a religion, I mean. You're not a Muslim either, are you?' he said.

'No,' I said.

'Good,' he said. 'Muhammad Ali, now he's a Muslim, isn't he?'

'I don't know,' I said.

'He is, sure. Muhammad Ali? And a word to the wise, son,' said. 'Round here we say Londonderry, not Derry.'

'Right,' I said.

'They want us to call it Derry,' he said.

'OK,' I said.

'But we won't.'

'Right,' I said.

'Welcome to Belfast,' he said. 'To think that song has been through Dolly's lungs…'

The man with the white quiff and the grey cardigan was singing 'Jolene'.

Then I was talking to your uncle, your dad's brother. He'd married a country girl. They farmed out near Millisle.

'Do you know much about cows?' he said. I knew nothing about cows. 'Sure, do you English know nothing?' he said.

'Not much,' I said.

'Aye, that's about right,' he said. He took his wallet from his jacket pocket and showed me some photos. 'What's that one there?' He pointed with his finger, like a cattleprod.

'I don't know,' I said.

'It's a Friesian!' he said. 'A Friesian! You at least know the difference between a heifer and a bull, boy, don't you? I hope so,' he said, 'for your wife's sake!' He slapped me on the back and gave me a fifty-pound note. 'Now, that's my gift to the two of you,' he said. 'You treat her right, yes?' he said. 'Her father may not be around, God rest his soul, but you'll still have me to answer to. Welcome to Northern Ireland.'

I went out into the yard. Walls, fences, the yellow cranes. Your cousin was pissing against the wall.

'Look at this,' he said.

'No, it's all right,' I said.

'This,' he said. He was wearing a medallion. It was a medallion that said 'I love you' when you breathed on it. He made me breathe on it.

'I tell you what,' he said. 'They fucking love that.'

'Do they?' I said.

'Are you taking the piss?' he said.

'No, no,' I said.

'Good,' he said. 'Because I tell you what,' he said, 'I've not got an O level to my name but I know what's what.'

'I'm sure you do,' I said.

'Dead on,' he said. 'Yous are dead on,' he said. 'The English, like. We are, we are, we are,' he said, 'we are the Billy boys! D'you know it?'

'I don't,' I said.

'Then you's a fucking cunt,' he said.

Back in the kitchen, the second baby's the worst, your sister was saying. 'Macaroni cheese was my thing,' she was saying, 'With the second. Six times a day I had to have it. More than sex. Funny thing is, if I'd have known I was going to want it all those times I could have made a big batch first of all. That's my top tip to you, brother-in-law,' she said. She gave me a drunken kiss. 'Make a big batch of macaroni cheese,' she said. 'When she's pregnant, that'll do you right.'

'Right,' I said.

'Plays havoc with your insides,' she said.

'The macaroni cheese?'

'The babies,' she said. 'Make the most of it now,' she said. 'While you can. These days, I don't know I've had a good night out until I've peed myself.'

'Peeled yourself?' I said.

'Peed,' she said. 'You know, peed. Piss.'

'You don't know you've had a good night out until you've peed yourself?'

'That's right,' she said.

'Jesus,' you said. 'Don't tell him that. Sure, let's have a look at the presents.'

'Welcome to the family,' she said. 'Welcome to Northern Ireland.'

The presents were on top of the telly. They included a bottle of sparkling cider, some mugs, and a garlic press from your aunt, who thought she was a cut above.

'But she's just a shell really these days,' you said. She'd had a hysterectomy. And she was married to an immoral man who liked to tell sexy jokes, you said, and sure enough, later he said to me, 'It's not the size of the bath, it's the water pressure that counts,' and then he said, 'What have you got? Eh? Bruno's no good. Gazza's no good. You're nothing now, you people. Nothing. You used to have an empire, but now what have you got? We've got Van Morrison. And George Best. You know George Best?' I said yes, I knew George Best.

'I don't know him, know him, but I know who he is,' I said.

'That'll do,' he said. 'I've been to Beachy Head.'

'Beachy Head?' I said. 'Why Beachy Head?'

'We were smuggling cigars.'

'Cigars?'

'Ten thousand Cuban cigars,' he said. 'Best in the world. We lost our shirt on that one.' He now ran a bar and grill in Donegal. 'A bar and grill' is what he called it. We had to visit, any time we were in Donegal. 'God's own country,' he said. 'This is. God's own country.'

We were eating the wedding cake: you didn't like fruit cake, so it was chocolate cake, with white chocolate icing.

'I'll take a slice of the cake, just to chase down the sandwiches,' he said. It was another uncle. He'd left in 1971. He didn't want anything more to do with the place. Was back for the wedding just. He was a gardener. Home counties. Cash in hand, no questions asked. He told people he was from the south, from the Free State, he said.

'Tell me,' he said, 'Is it possible to make a genuine mistake in life, do you think?'

'It's possible,' I said. 'Yes, of course it's possible to make a mistake.'

'A genuine mistake.'

'Absolutely,' I said. 'A genuine mistake is the best kind of mistake.'

'Some people don't believe in mistakes, but,' he said.

'That's true,' I said.

'They believe in Fate, or God, don't they?'

'They do.'

'Yes, that's right. But you think it's possible to make a genuine mistake?'

'I do,' I said.

'But you still have to live with the consequences of that mistake for the rest of your life, don't you?' he said.

'I suppose so,' I said.

'Well, there we are then,' he said. 'There we are then. Welcome,' he said, 'to Belfast.' And then he pulled me close. 'You're welcome to it.'

*

Then there was another uncle, who drove a lorry.

'Truck,' he said. 'We don't call them lorries. Trucks, we call them. D'you know what we call bus drivers?' he said. 'Ulsterbus drivers?'

'I don't,' I said. 'I don't know what you call Ulsterbus drivers.'

'Bus poofs,' he said. 'Or Wendys. Bus Wendys.'

'All right,' I said. 'Nice to meet you.' The man with the quiff and the cardigan sang 'I've Got You Under My Skin'.

There's only one photo of that night. This was before mobiles and camera phones and all the rest of it. Just one photo. I can't find it anywhere. All I remember is, all of us had red eye.

A RHINOCEROS, SOME LADIES AND A HORSE

James Stephens

James Stephens (1880–1950) was a writer of fiction and poetry. Much of his work was concerned with retelling of Irish folktales and myths. He published several works of fiction and poetry including *The Charwoman's Daughter* (1912), *The Crock of Gold* (1912), *The Demi-Gods* (1914) and *In the Land of Youth* (1924).

One day, in my first job, a lady fell in love with me. It was quite unreasonable, of course, for I wasn't wonderful: I was small and thin, and I weighed much the same as a largish duck-egg. I didn't fall in love with her, or anything like that. I got under the table, and stayed there until she had to go wherever she had to go to.

I had seen an advertisement—'Smart boy wanted', it said. My legs were the smartest things about me, so I went there on the run. I got the job.

At that time there was nothing on God's earth that I could do, except run. I had no brains, and I had no memory. When I was told to do anything I got into such an enthusiasm about it that I couldn't remember anything else about it. I just ran as hard as I could, and then I ran back, proud and panting. And when they asked me for the whatever-it-was that I had run for, I started, right on the instant, and ran some more.

The place I was working at was, amongst other things, a theatrical agency. I used to be sitting in a corner of the office floor, waiting to be told to run somewhere and back. A lady would come in—a music-hall lady that is—and, in about five minutes, howls of joy would start coming from the inner office. Then, peacefully enough, the lady and my two bosses would come out, and the lady always said, 'Splits! I can do splits like no one.' And one of my bosses would say, 'I'm keeping your splits in mind.' And the other would add, gallantly—'No one who ever saw your splits could ever forget 'em.'

One of my bosses was thin, and the other one was fat. My fat boss was composed entirely of stomachs. He had three baby-stomachs under his chin: then he had three more descending in even larger englobings nearly to the ground: but, just before reaching the ground, the final stomach bifurcated into a pair of boots. He was very light on these and could bounce about in the neatest way.

He was the fattest thing I had ever seen, except a rhinoceros that I had met in the Zoo the Sunday before I got the job. That rhino was *very* fat, and it had a smell like twenty-five pigs. I was standing outside its palisade, wondering what it could possibly feel like to be a rhinoceros, when two larger boys passed by. Suddenly they caught hold of me, and pushed me through the bars of the palisade. I was very skinny, and in about two seconds I was right inside, and the rhinoceros was looking at me.

It was very fat, but it wasn't fat like stomachs, it was fat like barrels of cement, and when it moved it creaked a lot, like a woman I used to know who creaked like an old bedstead. The rhinoceros swaggled over to me with a bunch of cabbage sticking out of its mouth. It wasn't angry, or anything like that, it just wanted to see who I was. Rhinos are blindish: they mainly see by smelling, and they smell in snorts. This one started at my left shoe, and snorted right up that side of me to my ear. He smelt that very carefully: then he switched over to my right ear, and snorted right down that side of me to my right shoe: then he fell in love with my shoes and began to lick them. I, naturally, wriggled my feet at that, and the big chap was so astonished that he did the strangest step-dance backwards to his pile of cabbages, and began to eat them.

I squeezed myself out of his cage and walked away. In a couple of minutes I saw the two boys. They were very frightened, and they asked me what I had done to the rhinoceros. I answered, a bit grandly, perhaps, that I had seized it in both hands, ripped it limb from limb, and tossed its carcase to the crows. But when they began shouting to people that I had just murdered a rhinoceros I took to my heels, for I didn't want to be arrested and hanged for a murder that I hadn't committed.

Still, a man can't be as fat as a rhinoceros, but my boss was as fat as a man can be. One day a great lady of the halls came in, and was received on the knee. She was very great. Her name was Maudie Darling, or thereabouts. My bosses called her nothing but 'Darling,' and she called them the same. When the time came for her to arrive the whole building got palpitations of the heart. After waiting a while my thin boss got angry, and said—'Who does the woman think she is? If she isn't here in two twos I'll go down to the entry, and when she does come I'll boot her out.' The fat boss said—'She's only two hours late, she'll be here before the week's out.'

Within a few minutes there came great clamours from the courtyard. Patriotic cheers, such as Parnell himself never got, were thundering. My bosses ran instantly to the inner office. Then the door opened, and the lady appeared.

She was very wide, and deep, and magnificent. She was dressed in camels and zebras and goats: she had two peacocks in her hat and a rabbit muff in her hand, and she strode among these with prancings.

But when she got right into the room and saw herself being looked at by three men and a boy she became adorably shy: one could see that she had never been looked at before.

'O,' said she, with a smile that made three and a half hearts beat like one, 'O,' said she, very modestly, 'is Mr. Which-of-'em-is-it really in? Please tell him that Little-Miss-Me would be so glad to see and to be—'

Then the inner door opened, and the large lady was surrounded by my fat boss and my thin boss. She crooned to them—'O, you dear boys, you'll never know how much I've thought of you and longed to see you.'

That remark left me stupefied. The first day I got to the office I heard that it was the fat boss's birthday, and that he was thirty years of age: and the thin boss didn't look a day younger than the fat one. How the lady could mistake these old men for boys seemed to me the strangest fact that had ever come my way. My own bet was that they'd both die of old age in about a month.

After a while they all came out again. The lady was helpless with laughter: she had to be supported by my two bosses—'O,' she cried, 'you boys will kill me.' And the bosses laughed and laughed, and the fat one said—'Darling, you're a scream,' and the thin one said—'Darling, you're a riot.'

And then… she saw me! I saw her seeing me the very way I had seen the rhinoceros seeing me: I wondered for an instant would she smell me down one leg and up the other. She swept my two bosses right away from her, and she became a kind of queen, very glorious to behold: but sad, startled. She stretched a long, slow arm out and out and then she unfolded a long, slow finger, and pointed it at me—'Who is THAT??' she whispered in a strange whisper that could be heard two miles off.

My fat boss was an awful liar—'The cat brought that in,' said he.

But the thin boss rebuked him: 'No,' he said, 'it was not the cat. Let me introduce you; darling, this is James. James, this is the darling of the gods.'

'And of the pit,' said she, sternly.

She looked at me again. Then she sank to her knees and spread out both arms to me—

'Come to my boozalum, angel,' said she in a tender kind of way.

I knew what she meant, and I knew that she didn't know how to pronounce that word. I took a rapid glance at the area indicated. The lady had a boozalum you could graze a cow on. I didn't wait one second, but slid, in one swift, silent slide, under the table. Then she came forward and said a whole lot of poems to me under the table, imploring me, among a lot of odd things, to 'come forth, and gild the morning with my eyes,' but at last she was reduced to whistling at me with two fingers in her mouth, the way you whistle for a cab.

I learned after she had gone that most of the things she said to me were written by a poet fellow named Spokeshave. They were very complimentary, but I couldn't love a woman who mistook my old bosses for boys, and had a boozalum that it would take an Arab chieftain a week to trot across on a camel.

The thin boss pulled me from under the table by my leg, and said that my way was the proper way to treat a rip, but my fat boss said, very gravely —'James, when a lady invites a gentleman to her boozalum a real gentleman hops there as pronto as possible, and I'll have none but real gentlemen in this office.'

'Tell me,' he went on, 'what made that wad of Turkish Delight fall in love with you?'

'She didn't love me at all, sir,' I answered.

'No?' he inquired.

'She was making fun of me,' I explained.

'There's something in that,' said he seriously, and went back to his office.

I had been expecting to be sacked that day. I was sacked the next day, but that was about a horse.

I had been given three letters to post, and told to run or they'd be too late. So I ran to the post office and round it and back, with, naturally, the three letters in my pocket. As I came to our door a nice, solid, red-faced man rode up on a horse. He thrust the reins into my hand—

'Hold the horse for a minute,' said he.

'I can't,' I replied, 'my boss is waiting for me.'

'I'll only be a minute,' said he angrily, and he walked off.

Well, there was I, saddled, as it were, with a horse. I looked at it, and it looked at me. Then it blew a pint of soap-suds out of its nose and took another look at me, and then the horse fell in love with me as if he had just found his long-lost foal. He started to lean against me and to woo me with small whinneys, and I responded and replied as best I could.

'Don't move a toe,' said I to the horse, 'I'll be back in a minute.'

He understood exactly what I said, and the only move he made was to swing his head and watch me as I darted up the street. I was less than half a minute away anyhow, and never out of his sight.

Up the street there was a man, and sometimes a woman, with a barrow, thick-piled with cabbages and oranges and apples. As I raced round the barrow I pinched an apple off it at full speed, and in ten seconds I was back at the horse. The good nag had watched every move I made, and when I got back his eyes were wide open, his mouth was wide open, and he had his legs all splayed out so that he couldn't possibly slip. I broke the apple in halves and popped one half into his mouth. He ate it in slow crunches, and then he looked diligently at the other half. I gave him the other half, and, as he ate it, he gurgled with cidery gargles of pure joy. He then swung his head round from me and pointed his nose up the street, right at the apple-barrow.

I raced up the street again, and was back within the half-minute with another apple. The horse had nigh finished the first half of it when a man who had come up said, thoughtfully—

'He seems to like apples, bedad!'

'He loves them,' said I.

And then, exactly at the speed of lightning, the man became angry, and invented bristles all over himself like a porcupine.

'What the hell do you mean,' he hissed, and then he bawled, 'by stealing my apples?'

I retreated a bit into the horse.

'I didn't steal your apples,' I said.

'You didn't!' he roared, and then he hissed, 'I saw you,' he hissed.

'I didn't steal them,' I explained, 'I pinched them.'

'Tell me that one again,' said he.

'If,' said I patiently, 'if I took the apples for myself that would be stealing.'

'So it would,' he agreed.

'But as I took them for the horse that's pinching.'

'Be dam, but!' said he. ''Tis a real argument,' he went on, staring at the sky. 'Answer me that one,' he demanded of himself, and he is a very stupor of intellection. 'I give it up,' he roared, 'you give me back my apples.'

I placed the half apple that was left into his hand, and he looked at it as if it was a dead frog.

'What'll I do with that?' he asked earnestly.

'Give it to the horse,' said I.

The horse was now prancing at him, and mincing at him, and making love at him. He pushed the half apple into the horse's mouth, and the horse mumbled it and watched him, and chewed it and watched him, and gurgled it and watched him.

'He does like his bit of apple,' said the man.

'He likes you too,' said I. 'I think he loves you.'

'It looks like it,' he agreed, for the horse was yearning at him, and its eyes were soulful.

'Let's get him another apple,' said I, and, without another word, we both pounded back to his barrow and each of us pinched an apple off it. We got one apple into the horse, and were breaking the second one when a woman said gently—

'Nice, kind, Christian gentlemen, feeding dumb animals—with my apples,' she yelled suddenly.

The man with me jumped as if he had been hit by a train.

'Mary,' said he humbly.

'Joseph,' said she in a completely unloving voice. But the woman transformed herself into nothing else but woman—

'What about my apples?' said she. 'How many have we lost?'

'Three,' said Joseph.

'Four,' said I, 'I pinched three and you pinched one.'

'That's true,' said he. 'That's exact, Mary. I only pinched one of our apples.'

'You only,' she squealed.

And I, hoping to be useful, broke in—'Joseph,' said I, 'is the nice lady your boss?'

He halted for a dreadful second, and made up his mind.

'You bet she's my boss,' said he, 'and she's better than that, for she's the very wife of my bosum.'

She turned to me.

'Child of Grace—' said she—

Now, when I was a child, and did something that a woman didn't like she always expostulated in the same way. If I tramped on her foot, or jabbed her in the stomach—the way women have multitudes of feet and stomachs is always astonishing to a child— the remark such a woman made was always the same. She would grab her toe or her stomach, and say—'Childagrace, what the hell are you doing?' After a while I worked it out that Childagrace was one word, and was my name. When any woman in agony yelled Childagrace I ran right up prepared to be punished, and the woman always said tenderly, 'What are you yowling about, Childagrace.'

'Childagrace,' said Mary earnestly, 'how's my family to live if you steal our apples? You take my livelihood away from me! Very good, but will you feed and clothe and educate my children in,' she continued proudly, 'the condition to which they are accustomed?'

I answered that question cautiously.

'How many kids have you, ma'am?' said I.

'We'll leave that alone for a while,' she went on. 'You owe me two and six for the apples. '

'Mary!' said Joseph, in a pained voice.

'And you,' she snarled at him, 'owe me three shillings. I'll take it out of you in pints.' She turned to me.

'What do you do with all the money you get from the office here?'

'I give it to my landlady.'

'Does she stick to the lot of it?'

'Oh, no,' I answered, 'she always gives me back threepence.'

'Well, you come and live with me and I'll give you back fourpence.'

'All right,' said I.

'By gum,' said Joseph, enthusiastically, 'that'll be fine. We'll go out every night and we won't steal a thing. We'll just pinch legs of beef, and pig's feet, and barrels of beer—'

'Wait now,' said Mary. 'You stick to your own landlady. I've trouble enough of my own. You needn't pay me the two and six.'

'Good for you,' said Joseph heartily, and then, to me—

'You just get a wife of your bosum half as kind as my wife of my bosum and you'll be set up for life. 'Mary,' he cried joyfully, 'let's go and have a pint on the strength of it.'

'You shut up,' said she.

'Joseph,' I interrupted, 'knows how to pronounce the word properly.'

'What word?'

'The one he used when he said you were the wife of his what-you-may-call-it.'

'I'm not the wife of any man's what-you-may-call-it,' said she, indignantly —'Oh, I see what you mean! So he pronounced it well, did he?'

'Yes, ma'am.'

She looked at me very sternly—

'How does it come you know about all these kinds of words?'

'Yes,' said Joseph, and he was even sterner than she was, 'when I was your age I didn't know any bad words.'

'You shut up,' said she, and continued, 'what made you say that to me?'

'A woman came into our office yesterday, and she mispronounced it.'

'What did she say now?'

'Oh, she said it all wrong.'

'Do you tell me so? We're all friends here: what way did she say it, son?'

'Well, ma'am, she called it boozalum.'

'She said it wrong all right,' said Joseph, 'but 'tis a good, round, fat kind of a word all the same.'

'You shut up,' said Mary. 'Who did she say the word to?'

'She said it to me, ma'am.'

'She must have been a rip,' said Joseph.

'Was she a rip, now?'

'I don't know, ma'am. I never met a rip.'

'You're too young yet,' said Joseph, 'but you'll meet them later on. I never met a rip myself until I got married—I mean,' he added hastily, 'that they were all rips except the wife of my what-do-you-call-ems, and that's why I married her.'

'I expect you've got a barrel-full of rips in your past,' said she bleakly, 'you must tell me about some of them tonight.' And then, to me, 'tell us about the woman,' said she.

So I told them all about her, and how she held out her arms to me, and said, 'Come to my boozalum, angel.'

'What did you do when she shoved out the old arms at you?' said Joseph.

'I got under the table,' I answered.

'That's not a bad place at all, but,' he continued earnestly, 'never get under the bed when there's an old girl chasing you, for that's the worst spot you could pick on. What was the strap's name?'

'Maudie Darling, she called herself.'

'You're a blooming lunatic,' said Joseph, 'she's the loveliest thing in the world, barring,' he added hastily, 'the wife of my blast-the-bloody-word.'

'We saw her last night,' said Mary, 'at Dan Lowrey's Theatre, and she's just lovely.'

'She isn't as nice as you, ma'am,' I asserted.

'Do you tell me that now?' said she.

'You are twice as nice as she is, and twenty times nicer.'

"There you are,' said Joseph, 'the very words I said to you last night.'

'You shut up,' said Mary scornfully, 'you were trying to knock a pint out of me! Listen, son,' she went on, 'we'll take all that back about your landlady. You come and live with me, and I'll give you back sixpence a week out of your wages.'

'All right, ma'am,' I crowed in a perfectly monstrous joy.

'Mary,' said Joseph, in a reluctant voice—

'You shut up,' said she.

'He can't come to live with us,' said Joseph. 'He's a bloody Prodestan,' he added sadly.

'Why—' she began—

'He'd keep me and the childer up all night, pinching apples for horses and asses, and reading the Bible, and up to every kind of devilment.'

Mary made up her mind quickly.

'You stick to your own landlady,' said she, 'tell her that I said she was to give you sixpence.' She whirled about. 'There won't be a thing left on that barrow,' said she to Joseph.

'Damn the scrap,' said Joseph violently.

'Listen,' said Mary to me very earnestly, 'am I nicer than Maudie Darling?'

'You are ma'am,' said I.

Mary went down on the road on her knees: she stretched out both arms to me, and said—

'Come to my boozalum, angel.'

I looked at her, and I looked at Joseph, and I looked at the horse. Then I turned from them all and ran into the building and into the office. My fat boss met me—

'Here's your five bob,' said he. 'Get to hell out of here,' said he.

And I ran out.

I went to the horse, and leaned my head against the thick end of his neck, and the horse leaned as much of himself against me as he could manage. Then the man who owned the horse came up and climbed into his saddle. He fumbled in his pocket—

'You were too long,' said I. 'I've been sacked for minding your horse.'

'That's too bad,' said he: 'that's too damn bad,' and he tossed me a penny.

I caught it, and lobbed it back into his lap, and I strode down the street the most outraged human being then living in the world.

A YOUNG WIDOW

Bram Stoker

Bram Stoker (1847–1912) was born in Dublin and is best known for his gothic vampire novel *Dracula* (1897). His novels include *The Primrose Path*, *The Snake's Pass* and *The Mystery of the Sea*. He wrote fairytales for children, and published the short story collections, *Snowbound: The Record of a Theatrical Touring Party* and *Dracula's Guest and Other Weird Stories*.

When I had dusted the little boy down and he had grown calm after his fright I lectured him on the danger of coasting down steep hills, until, at all events, he had acquired some mastery of the bicycle. He seemed duly penitent, and acknowledged in his boyish way that if I had not ridden after him and steered him he might have been killed. He was still tearful when he stammered out:

"I wish my mother could have thanked you!"

"Never mind, my boy!" I said; "You don't say anything at home unless you tell your father."

"Can't," he said, as his tears burst out afresh. "Father's dead years ago." I said no more, but left him at the house which he pointed out as that in which he lived. He told me that his name was Bobbie Harcourt, and he hoped he would see me again. "Why don't you call?" he added, as he ran up the steps.

As I rode home I thought to myself that the mother of such a pretty boy must be a sweet creature. A widow, too, I noted mentally. Young widowhood is always more or less a pleasing thought to a bachelor, especially when, like myself, he is beginning to notice his hair thinning on the top. I told Bobbie where I lived, so I was not altogether surprised when next day I got a letter in a lady's hand signed "Ada Harcourt," thanking me for what she deemed the great service I had rendered her and all her family. That letter, even after I had answered it, somehow impressed me, and every morning for a week, as I shaved myself and noticed the thin place "on top," my thoughts reverted to it. I always ended by taking it from my pocket and spreading it on the dressing-table in front of me.

Then I took my courage in both hands and called at Woodbine villa. The short time which elapsed between my knock, which began boldly and ended timidly, and the opening of the door was such as I am told drowning men experience, filled with a countless multitude of embarrassing memories. The trim maid, who opened the door, looked a little surprised when I asked if Mrs. Harcourt was at home; but with an apologetic "Pardon me a moment, sir," darted away, leaving the door open. She came down stairs again more slowly, and in a somewhat embarrassed giggling way asked me please to come in. "My mistress, sir," she said, "will be down in a few minutes, if you will kindly wait!"

I entered the pleasant drawing-room and tried, in the helpless way of embarrassed visitors, to gain some knowledge of my hosts by their surroundings.

Everything was pretty, but the faces of all the pictures and photographs were strange, so that it was as with recognition of an old friend that I came across a photograph of Bobbie, evidently done some two or three years before.

I was ill at ease, for manifestly my coming had in some way disturbed the household. Overhead there was rushing about to and fro, and the sound of drawers opening and shutting, and of doors banging. I thought I could hear somewhere afar off the voice of my friend Bobbie, but in a different and lighter vein than when I had listened to his tearful promises of amendment. Then I became gravely anxious; a full sense of my impropriety in calling pressed upon me, for light steps drew near to the door. There entered the room the most beautiful young woman I thought I had ever seen. Her youth, her dancing eyes, her pink cheeks suffused with blushes, and the full lips showing scarlet against her white teeth, seemed to shine through the deep widow's weeds which she wore, as rays of sunshine gleam through a fog. Indeed, the smile was multiplied as the gleam of golden hair seemed to make the "weeded" cap a solemn mockery. She advanced impulsively, and shook me warmly by the hand, as with very genuine feeling she thanked me for my heroic rescue of "dear Bobbie." At first she seemed somewhat surprised at my appearance; and, seeing with a woman's instinct that I noticed it, said frankly—

"How young you are! Why, from what Bobbie told me, I thought you were an old—a much older man!" The thin space seemed to become conscious as though a wave of either heat or cold had passed over it, and as I somehow seemed to recognise in the fair widow an "understanding" soul, I bent my head so that she could see the tell-tale place as I remarked:

"To children we grown-ups seem often older than even we are!" In a demure way, and in a veiled, not to say a smothered, voice she answered:

"Ah! yes, that is so. To us who have known sorrow time passes more quickly than to their light-hearted innocence. Alas! alas!" She stopped suddenly, and, putting her deeply-edged handkerchief to her face, gasped out: "Pardon me, I shall return in a moment," and left the room hurriedly. I felt more than uncomfortable. I had evidently touched on some tender chord of memory, though what I could not guess. All I could do was to wait till she returned, and then take myself off as soon as possible.

There was some talking and whispering on the stairs outside. I could not hear the words spoken, for the door was shut; but suddenly it opened, and Bobbie, red-faced and awkward, shot into the room. He was a very different boy now. There were no tears, no sadness, no contrition. He was a veritable mass of fun, full of laughter and schoolboy mirth. As he shook hands with me, he said:

"I hope mother has thanked you properly!" and turned away and stamped with some kind of suppressed feeling. The ways of boys are hard to understand!

When Mrs. Harcourt returned, which she did very shortly, now quite composed and looking more beautiful and more charming than ever, Bobbie slipped away. There was, somehow, a greater constraint about his mother. Some impalpable veil seemed to be between us; she was as if more distant from me. I recognised its import, and shortly made my adieux. As she bade me good-bye she said that we might perhaps never meet again as she was shortly going to take the boy abroad; but that she rejoiced that it had been her privilege to meet face to face his brave preserver. She used more of such phrases, which for days after seemed to hang in my memory like sweet music. The maid, when she let me out, seemed sympathetic and deferential, but there was in her manner a concealed levity which somehow grated on me.

For the next fortnight I tried to keep Mrs. Harcourt out of my thoughts—with the usual result. You can't serve ejectments on thoughts! They are tenants-at-will—their own will—and the only effect of struggling with them is that they banish everything else and keep the whole field to themselves. Working or playing, waking or sleeping, walking, riding, or sitting still, the sweet, beautiful eyes of Mrs. Harcourt were ever upon me, and her voice seemed to sound in my ears.

I found that my bicycle carried me, seemingly of its own will, past her door on every occasion when I had to use a lamp. Seeing clearly that her intention of foreign travel had not been carried out I ventured at least one day in an agony of perturbation to call again.

When I was opposite the house I thought I saw in the window the back of Ada's head—I had come to think of her as "Ada" now. I was therefore somewhat surprised when, after some delay, the maid, with a demure face, told me that Mrs. Harcourt was not at home. I felt almost inclined to argue the matter with the maid, who was now giggling as on the former occasion, when suddenly Bobbie came running out of the back hall and called to me.

"Oh, Mr. Denison, won't you come in? Ma is here and will be delighted to see you." He threw open the door of the drawing-room, which was the first room of the ground floor, and ushered me in, turning round and grinning at me as he said:

"Ma, here is Mr. Denison come to see you. Excuse me coming in!" With that he went out, shutting the door behind him.

I think she was as much startled and amazed as I was as she stood facing me with her cheeks a flaming red. She had discarded her widow's weeds and was now in a simple grey frock with pink bows at the neck and waist, which made her look years younger than even she had done before; her beautiful golden hair was uncovered. As I advanced, which I did with warmth, for it seemed to me somehow that the discarding of the widow's dress opened up new possibilities to herself, she bowed somewhat coldly. She did not, however, refuse to shake hands, though she did so timidly. I felt awkward and ill at ease; things were not somehow going as smoothly as I wished, and the very passion that filled me made its repression a difficulty. I couldn't remember a single thing which either of us said at that interview; I only recollect taking up my hat and moving off with mingled chagrin and diffidence. When I was near the door she came impulsively after me, and taking me by the hand said:

"This is good-bye, indeed, as I shall not be able to see you again. You will understand, will you not?" Her words puzzled me; but she had made a request, and such, though it entailed denial of my own wishes, could only be answered in one way. I put my hand to my heart and bowed.

As I walked away all the world seemed a blank space, and myself a helpless atom whirling in it, alone.

That night I thought of nothing but Mrs. Harcourt, and with the grey of the dawn my mind was made up. I would see her again, for I feared she would leave without even knowing my feelings toward her. I got up and wrote her a letter saying that I would do myself the honour of calling that afternoon, and that I trusted she would see me, as I had something very important to say. When I retired to bed, after posting the letter, I fell asleep, and when on dreaming of her, and my dreams were Heavenly.

When I knocked at the door in the afternoon the maid looked all demure and showed me without a word into the drawing-room. Almost immediately following her exit Mrs. Harcourt came in. My heart rejoiced when I saw that she was dressed as on the previous day. She shook hands with me gravely and sat down. When I had sat also, she said—

"You wanted to say something to me?"

"Yes," I answered, quickly, for the fervour in me was beginning to speak. "I want to tell you that—" With a gesture she stopped me.

"One moment! Before you say anything let me tell you something. I have a shameful confession to make. In a foolish moment I thought to play a joke, never thinking that it might reflect on my dear dead mother. Bobbie is not my son; he is my only brother, who has been my care since my mother died years ago. When he told me of the brave way you saved him, and when the kind letter you sent in answer to mine showed me you had mistaken our relationship, Bobbie and I laughed over it together, and I said what a lark it would be to pretend, if occasion served, to be his mother. Then you called, and the spirit of mischief moved me to a most unseemly joke. I dressed up in mother's clothes, and tried to pass myself off as Bobbie's mother. When I had seen you and recognised your kindness, I seemed in all ways a brute; but all I could do was to try that it might go on no more. Oh, if you only knew!" She put her pretty hands before her face and I saw the tears drop through them. That pained me, but it gave me heart. Coming close to her I took her hands and pulled them away, and looked in her brave eyes as I said;

"Oh, let me speak? I must! I must! I came here to-day to ask you to—Won't you—let Bobbie be my brother too?"

And he is.

BLACK SPOT

Deirdre Sullivan

Deirdre Sullivan is an award-winning writer from Galway. Her short fiction has been published in the *Dublin Review*, *Banshee*, the *Penny Dreadful* and the *Autonomy* anthology. Her sixth book for young adults, *Perfectly Preventable Deaths* (2019) was shortlisted for the Irish Book Awards. *Savage Her Reply* was published by Little Island in 2020.

You pass it always on your way to work. And there are flowers. Petrol station bouquets all in cellophane. Carnations, babies' breath and hot pink daisies. Sometimes there are roses from a garden. Or the wilder sort. Marigolds and buttercups and clover. Little bunches picked and wrapped in kitchen paper. Made at home.

Bunches added, never cleared away. Piles of them are rotting. Petals gone and stalks melted onto coloured rain with time. It makes you sad. It makes you sad to see the care and lack of care at once, all sellotaped together.

In your little Mazda with the heater blasting window mist at full cry. It ruins your skin. You moisturize but dryness it collects around the nose and when you scratch it's red, not raw, but sore. You look like you've been crying when you get to work a lot. In the face but never in the eyes.

You live far out the country, in a house you could afford. You drive when it is dark and arrive when it is getting bright. You leave work when it's dark and get home darker. You stay late most of the time. You have to. People never pick their children up on time and then there's tidying and sorting art supplies and things. Construction paper. Glue. You don't use glitter now. It is forbidden, it gets everywhere. Karen, the manager, found some in her knickers two Mother's days ago and said no more.

Karen's younger than you are. She hasn't worked in the creche for half as long, but when Michelle retired, she took the reins. You wonder if you'd spoken up, could you have. What you could have done to be that woman. The one who makes things happen for herself. You do not feel like that is ever you.

When Karen tells you to do things, you resent it sometimes and she feels it. You used to get on better. It's not that you don't listen. It's that she's younger.

It's that she doesn't always do her best. She expects you to do the grunt work and you don't get paid enough to like that.

Every morning, every evening. Flowers. You look at them. You always think, "One day I'll stop the car, get out and tidy." It would be a nice thing to do, but there are reasons not to get involved. You don't know who died here. You don't know who left flowers and for whom. You want a cup of tea. It's getting late.

Maybe in the summer, when it's nice again. Then maybe you could do it. When it's nice again. It has been years and still the flowers rot and you do nothing. 42 deaths changed to 43. Then 47. Accident Black Spot.

It has been a cold day. The storage heater on the wall at work made little difference. The walls are thin, when the children were indoors it was okay. Their bodies little stoves, wolfing down Ready Brek. Spaghetti hoops.

Sometimes their mothers drop them off at half seven, collect them after six. You give them breakfast, lunch and dinner, tea. You hug them when they cry. You're not supposed to now with child protection but you always do. Their shrivelled little faces full of woe. You have to give them love. They're hurting, hurting and you're not their mum but you are close and you are there.

You look after the pre-schoolers. Karen has the after-school club, she helps out different places and does paperwork till half past one. Laura has the babies, small and squat. The wee triangely things. You all help out each other, and there's Paula who is being trained and floats. Karen was like Paula once. You trained her up. She's good at what she does but so are you.

She wants to buy a house.

Don't bother you tell her. Time enough when you're a little older.

She doesn't roll her eyes but you can feel her wanting to. You wipe the desks down savagely, scratching them with nails through J-cloth fabric. Every little piece of crayon gone when you are done. Every daub of Pritt Stick.

It isn't enough. Work, home. It isn't enough and still it's all you have and you are tired. You do your make-up in the car on the way there. Cleanse your face each evening before bed with heavy hands. Scrubbing at the corners of your eyes. You do not wear an awful lot of make-up. Just enough to show you've made an effort. Taking pride.

It is November when it happens first. The morning dark and soft, the man on the radio joking about something and his voice is kind. You think he must be handsome in real life. Your hands on the steering wheel are tight. The skin on them is chapping. You should wear gloves. You should put on your gloves.

You're not sure when the beeping starts. You notice it before the little shop where you buy milk when you run out of milk. The light. The seat belt light. But yours is on, you fasten it each morning. Working with the children makes you safe. You wait for the green man, look right, look left. Rub in the soap and put your hands under the water rubbing for a count of ten, a count of ten again. Your hands are clean and you don't get knocked down. You set examples. The seat belt light is beeping.

It is strange. It passes three miles down the road, beside a little dormer bungalow with plywood in the windows and no door. You forget about it till tomorrow and the next day and the next.

It always happens on the way to work. The little seat belt light, all red and soft. It doesn't glare. It's like a little sunset. You go to the mechanic on day six. "It starts and stops," you tell him. "It's always different places."

He shrugs and charges you for being shrugged at. He did lift up the bonnet after all.

Work is softer for the next few weeks. The children come and go. You only hug them loosely round the shoulders. Wipe their noses, tears. Clean them up when they have little accidents. Sometimes they don't make it there in time. And that's okay. You have a box of gender neutral clothes that you put on them. Things you've bought and things the older children left behind. The dear departed. You miss them all a little. Wonder how they're doing.

The first ones that you had are almost grown now. You see them in the papers. One or two. Clare who got all A1s in the leaving. Norman who assaulted someone once. Poor Norman. You remember his sense of injustice. "She stoled my crayon" shrill across the room. You cut the pieces out and take them home and keep them. Your nieces and your nephews in Australia are in that shoebox too. Your brother's wife remembers you at Christmas. And once a year they clamber in your house, live up on you for weeks and leave you lonely and relieved at once. You love them but you also need your space.

When Mother was alive, you worried they would stop when she passed on. You assumed you would get stuck being her carer, moving into hers or she to yours. Nobody assigned you the role, but John lived far away and he had children. You were close. And you were all alone.

You could see it knitted in their eyebrows when they talked about the future and it percolated in your worried gut. But then she had two heart attacks and died. A big one first, a little one that killed her. And she was in the ground. And that was that.

It beeps till almost work one day. It punctuates the sunrise. You thought at first that it was something stuck. But still it comes and goes. You start to count them on the days they happen. Twelve. Fifteen. And nineteen. Thirty-six. Different places, houses, shops and flats. And sometimes fields. Just sometimes outside fields. The flowers still collect. The little tributes there still piling up. Hydrangeas. Blue. Pink. Purple. The same plant but grown in different earths, acidic, basic. You can put lime down to pink them if you want. You like the blue. You think you like the blue.

Madonna hates hydrangeas. You pick up nuggets, driving in the car. Little gossips. Stupid bits of news. You only sometimes read the papers. Sunday's one will do you for the week. There's online, but your connection's slow. When Lucy sends you pictures of the children they appear in rectangles from the top down, unpuzzling bit by bit.

You like real photos. Something you can hold. Can take to work and show them. You think sometimes they don't think you do things. Don't have a life. You do. You go for drinks, meet friends. Go to the cinema. Take long walks in the fields or on the beach. You like a glass of wine. You like The Beatles. People choose a lot of different things. And sometimes things just happen. Beep. Beep. Beep.

The number's higher now. A little boy. His name was Patrick. He was only twelve and walking home. They reckon that the driver was asleep. She was a junior doctor, young herself. "Her life's ruined now," says Karen. You agree and drink your Nescafé in plastic sippy cups for health and safety. You can't be drinking mugs around the kids. It doesn't taste the same. But coffee's coffee.

You wonder as the beeping punctuates the radio, if someone's there beside you. If maybe it is different sorts of people. Or the same thing, but going other places. The car feels different when the beeping's there. Not different bad. Just different.

The air is charged with something. You had assumed it was your own frustration. An inability to figure out what's going on and stop it. Why had you expected you could do that? You never could. You never did before.

Heavy's how you feel most mornings anyway. Your feet find it harder to step out of the car, to walk to work, unlock the door and turn on all the lights and start preparing. Flick on the heating. Make a cup of tea. The little chairs and all the little tables. You spend your whole day stooping, hurt your back.

The low thrum of the beep beep beep. You drive back to the spot, it doesn't stop. You drive away, you keep on driving till your petrol's down to dregs and gasps. The needle in the red you pull in to an Applegreens. Get a danish. Get a cup of tea and fill the tank. When you start up, the beeping's stopped again and you're relieved.

Is it someone, was it someone once? Can you feel anything beyond a beep? It isn't all that different. Colder maybe. You are always cold though. It is spring, but you still wear a scarf, a winter coat. The winter mild, the bitterness stings now at hands and feet through cheap acrylic gloves and sleeves and socks.

It's hard to sleep at night. The house is small but too big for one person. Getting out of bed to check locked doors, to switch off lights. It isn't that you're lonely. It's just a lot. Living is a lot of little jobs and big ones and sometimes they all coalesce in front of you. You can't see past them really. It's like a hill that's full of slippy mud and brittle rocks. You knew that it was big but now it's dangerous. You need to get some sleep. You wake up thinking thoughts.

Karen meets with you about a child. He's gluten-free and stealing others' sandwiches. She says it is a health risk. He's so quick though. Does it flying. Does it when your back is turned. His mother has complained. He's coming home with tummy pains a lot. He's only three. He doesn't have the sense to not be stealing. It's up to you to stop him doing that she says.

She writes it in her little yellow book and you want to ask her what she's writing down but you do not. It's about you. Collecting bits of you she doesn't like to offer up when you ask for a raise, ask for time off. You rarely ask for things but you still want them. You work so hard. You tell her you work hard she says I know.

Her hair is highlighted, her chin a little point like someone filed it. She has cheekbones Karen. Dresses well. Her earrings match her top. You hate your jeans. Your lap two draught excluders shoved together. Bulging as black pudding. Marked with stains. Fromage Frais and poster paint and sand. Her and Paula thick as thieves and you do all the work. You should be running the place. You almost do already. No one likes you. No one wants you here. And if you left, where would you go at your age?

After work, it's hard to start the car. Your hands keep shaking when you think of Karen's little voice. So diplomatic. Telling you these things as if you didn't know. You made a poster when the kids went home. Their little faces gathered all together, and a little stalk with green leaf poking out. A grape bunch of kids. You think it's funny. What if it is not? What if there's something in it you don't mean? You try to warp it, try to find an angle. But you can't. It doesn't mean she won't. It doesn't mean there isn't something there that she could use.

You loved your little house when you first moved. Because it was all yours. It wasn't pretty but you'd paint the walls. You'd put up pictures, pay a man to come and fix the bathrooms. Have a dado rail put in the hall. It suits you now, the shape of it. The colour. That doesn't mean you like it or it's nice. No beeping on the way home and you stop. Pull in beside the sign and slam on the emergency triangle.

A little photo of the little boy. A votive candle stand filled up with rain. So many flowers piled on top of flowers. Primroses and pansies, a baldy gang of hyacinths in a pot. You love the smell of hyacinths in the springtime. And maybe you could switch the button off. You wrap your legs inside the car again and turn the key and make your way back home. You boil some ravioli for your tea.

Your mother felt much better just before. She smiled at you. She asked about your brother. Where he was. He'd gone back to Australia you told her. It wasn't true. He was asleep in your guest bedroom, phone on loud and waiting for a call. You don't know why that lie came out your mouth. She smiled at you. At least I have my little girl, she said. My daughter. She held your hand. And when her eyes flicked closed again you rang him. She was dead before he hit the road.

Days pass and sometimes there is beeping. Sometimes not. You approach expecting it to start and when it comes it's almost a relief. It's happened and you don't need to be scared. Just wait it out. It will be over soon. You hold your breath a little as you near the sign. The text and the black hole. Proceed with caution. How else would you though? It's all you know.

You watch your soaps. You make enough lasagne for the week. Freeze half of it. It's handy to have in. Cooking for one person's hard they say but you don't think so. All you have to please is just yourself. And if you're tired you can leave the dishes.

Karen is engaged. A little nicer, showing off her ring and booking things, researching different venues, different looks. She doesn't want to leave it for too long. A year's the max, she says. The limit. It was buy a house or plan a wedding. So they'll stay put till they're good and married in their fancy apartment. Her fiancée's got some big finance job. They've been together since she was fifteen. You get the kids to make her paper cards. Blobs in dresses. Little soft red hearts. It's nice to do a kind thing for somebody. She posts the best one on her profile page.

In the car on the way home you turn the radio up, right up. The music's louder, louder than the news and than the weather. Louder than the rain upon the glass. There are loose chippings on the road this evening. You can hear them crunching underwheel like bone.

Shifting fifth to fourth and fourth to third and second for the turn. You learned to drive when you were just a kid. Your mother taught you, and she drove you mad. Telling you to look when you were looking. Rolling eyes as engines spluttered out. She wanted you to have your independence. And now you do. There's nothing tying you to anything. The house is just a house. The job's a job. The children would be fine, you know, without you. Horsing gluten in their hungry mouths.

The rain is hard and soft and all at once. It makes the night look fiercer. The trees are budding green and skeletal above the car. The little corpses on the motorway. Cats and rats and foxes. Hard when they're all squashed to tell what's what.

The beeping when it starts is low, insidious. You do not notice it until the turn, but as you do you're conscious that it's been there for a while. Since you passed by the spot. It took your mother just a week to die. But on the road it varies. Cars can do all kinds of things to bodies. Pulverize or dent them, scrape or scar. The impact of a human skull on things. On wheels and tarmacadam.

You heard about a man who lost his mind. Not the way you'd think. Acquired brain injury, you've heard it called. He had a wife and children and afterwards he couldn't count his fingers. An accountant. And he remembered what he was before. Why can't I do this now, he'd ask, why don't you like me? You think they later put him in a home. They'd have to do that surely. Nobody should live beside a ghost. Something asking questions out like that. Reminding you of things you should forget or put aside. Dead, but not yet dead. And always asking.

You're turning up your driveway.

Beep beep beep.

You're parking at your house.

It isn't stopping.

Gentle little light and beep beep beep.

You click your seatbelt off. You sit there for a long time, in the driveway between the house and road. Your hand is on the key in the ignition. The noise is there and still it isn't stopping. You do not want to turn the engine off. And then you do, and walk into the night.

You're not alone.

THE STORY

Cathy Sweeney

Cathy Sweeney's stories have been published in the *Stinging Fly*, the *Dublin Review*, *Southword*, *Icarus* and *Meridian*. Her debut collection of short stories, *Modern Times*, is published by Stinging Fly Press.

Last summer my wife and I, along with our young daughter, moved into a house recently vacated by a man called Albert Solberg. He vacated the house because he died. According to the inquest report, he died from asphyxiation. And so the Commission assigned the house to me. It is true that I was not at the top of the waiting list but I had a connection, through a distant cousin, with a prominent official in the Commission.

The house, when we moved into it, was filthy. My wife shovelled dirt from the floor and painted the walls with lime, but all the painting in the world could not get rid of the smell of fish. Solberg, it seemed, rarely ate anything else. All the neighbours said so, each in turn stopping to lean on the gate that stood a few yards from the front door, each telling the same story – about the fish and the smell and the dissolution – each putting a twist on the tale. Old Peters, who used to work in the mines, spoke of illicit material delivered to the door in packages tied up with ox tape. The widow testified to noises coming from the house in the cold hours of morning. Tanya, who had never married, spoke of cats in the garden and children who urinated in the yard.

I found the story a few weeks after we moved into the house. It was wrapped in newspaper and hidden behind the boiler in a cupboard in the kitchen. I had paid no attention to the boiler until winter came suddenly and we found that it didn't work. I wanted to hire a plumber but my wife said no – instead she read the manual while biting her fingers and shouting instructions at me. I followed my wife's instructions as best as I could, but whatever way I approached the boiler, I found in a matter of minutes that I felt like a boy pretending to be a man. All the while the spanner grew heavier and the instructions more strange. It was when my wife left the room to attend to the child that I found the story. I stretched my hand in behind the boiler and touched a bundle of paper. Immediately I knew I had found something, and that is why I did not tell my wife. The deeper a man gets into marriage the more he learns to keep something for himself.

A few days later, while my wife was out with the child, I retrieved the story from the back of the boiler and took it out to the shed. There I read it, a couple of pages at a time, whenever my wife was out at the market or visiting her mother. I also re-read snatches of it in the evenings while I smoked my pipe. My wife did not like me smoking a pipe and so there was an unspoken agreement between us that I smoke only in the evenings and only in the shed.

The plot of the story involved a girl and took place in the time when Solberg was a young soldier in the colonies. There was a sub-plot, but isn't there always. The girl in question was a maid in the house of the Governor, a house to which Solberg – though of humble origins – was often invited on account of a connection between the Governor and Solberg's mother. The story contained pages and pages of how Solberg took the maid: when, where, how; accounts full of great detail and description. There were also endless passages on Solberg's hatred of army life and his penury due to gambling and drinking, but I skipped over most of these. It is amazing how many words people use; words that require a third or fourth lifetime. It's as though they believe that words are immune to time.

My wife had another child and then another. The last child was a poorly one and that was that; I soon forgot about the story. The child could not walk and spent all day in a cart made from railway sleepers. Life was hard, but it was hard for everybody. Old Peters died of drink; he was found lying face down on his own kitchen floor. The widow went to live with her daughter in a one-room flat in the city and Tanya married a man with eight children. Over time my wife's face knotted like the branch of a tree and there was an unspoken agreement between us that there would be no more children. I gave up smoking my pipe. Each evening I carried the crippled child to bed and played my whistle for him – he took great pleasure in music – but, while still a boy, he died. I carried him to the doctor's house, but it was too late. His body, in my arms, felt like a large kitten, all knuckle and bone in a soft sack.

One night, a few months after that, I lifted the blankets to look at my wife as she lay in bed. Her soft susurrations had aroused my needs and I wanted desperately to see the shape of a woman. My wife awoke and, with her finger, drew an imaginary line down the middle of the sheet. I said nothing.

When spring came I started smoking again. I developed the habit of going out to the shed in the evenings to play my whistle and to read the newspaper, and this was when I found the story once more. It was in a wooden crate along with an old picture frame and a brass candelabrum that had been given to my wife by her step-father. The story was still wrapped in newspaper but I had forgotten what it was until I saw the familiar typeface of the front cover:

A Soldier's Story
By Albert Solberg

I opened the story without curiosity. I did not remember much of the detail, but I remembered its flavour, and it was one I had lost appetite for. I leafed through it and was about to wrap it up again in the newspaper when a single page fell out, one I had not noticed before. This is what it said:

LAST STATEMENT OF ALBERT SOLBERG

Only a rare individual can love another person in real time and so the next time I fell in love was twenty years after the events of this story. One afternoon last spring I sat on a park bench and fell in love with the maid that I knew when I was in my twenties and a soldier in the colonies; a woman that I cast off, as one does a winter coat when spring appears. The feeling was intense. I have nothing more to say. I despise the man who sets the past in print and calls it truth.

Dusk fell over the garden, and over the roof of the house and over the yellow streets beyond it and out over the hills and fields, but somewhere in a tree a blackbird was still singing. Go away, I felt like calling to the blackbird. Go to sleep. This day is now gone, as all days must go. Sing again tomorrow, if there is still a note that insists on being sounded. But that is not likely; it is more likely that you will wake in dawn's raw light and busy yourself seeking worms, and all too soon it will seem that there is nothing left to do in this world but eat and sleep and seek worms.

I have never loved a woman, but in that instant I too felt the loss of a woman I had once loved. How can that be? How can a heart be made sore by that which it does not know?

ONE MINUS ONE

Colm Tóibín

Colm Tóibín is the author of nine novels, including *The Master* and *Brooklyn*, and two collections of short stories, *Mothers and Sons* and *The Empty Family*. His books have been translated into more than thirty languages. He is Mellon Professor of Humanities at Columbia University.

The moon hangs low over Texas. The moon is my mother. She is full tonight, and brighter than the brightest neon; there are folds of red in her vast amber. Maybe she is a harvest moon, a Comanche moon, I do not know. I have never seen a moon so low and so full of her own deep brightness. My mother is six years dead tonight, and Ireland is six hours away and you are asleep.

I am walking. No one else is walking. It is hard to cross Guadalupe; the cars come fast. In the Community Whole Food Store, where all are welcome, the girl at the checkout asks me if I would like to join the store's club. If I pay seventy dollars, my membership, she says, will never expire, and I will get a seven-per-cent discount on all purchases.

Six years. Six hours. Seventy dollars. Seven per cent. I tell her I am here for a few months only, and she smiles and says that I am welcome. I smile back. I can still smile. If I called you now, it would be half two in the morning; you could easily be awake.

If I called, I could go over everything that happened six years ago. Because that is what is on my mind tonight, as though no time had elapsed, as though the strength of the moonlight had by some fierce magic chosen tonight to carry me back to the last real thing that happened to me. On the phone to you across the Atlantic, I could go over the days surrounding my mother's funeral. I could go over all the details as though I were in danger of forgetting them. I could remind you, for example, that you wore a white shirt at the funeral. It must have been warm enough not to wear a jacket. I remember that I could see you when I spoke about her from the altar, that you were over in the side aisle, on the left. I remember that you, or someone, said that you had parked your car almost in front of the cathedral because you had come late from Dublin and could not find parking anywhere else. I know that you moved your car before the hearse came after Mass to take my mother's coffin to the graveyard, with all of us walking behind. You came to the hotel once she was in the ground, and you stayed for a meal with me and Suzie, my sister. Joe, her husband, must have been near, and Cathal, my brother, but I don't remember what they did when the meal was over and the crowd had dispersed. I know that as the meal came to an end a friend of my mother's, who noticed everything, came over and looked at you and whispered to me that it was nice that my friend had come. She used the word "friend" with a sweet, insinuating emphasis. I did not tell her that what she had noticed was no longer there, was part of the past. I simply said, yes, it was nice that you had come.

You know that you are the only person who shakes his head in exasperation when I insist on making jokes and small talk, when I refuse to be direct. No one else has ever minded this as you do. You are alone in wanting me always to say something that is true. I know now, as I walk toward the house I have rented here, that if I called and told you that the bitter past has come back to me tonight in these alien streets with a force that feels like violence, you would say that you are not surprised. You would wonder only why it has taken six years.

I was living in New York then, the city about to enter its last year of innocence. I had a new apartment there, just as I had a new apartment everywhere I went. It was on Ninetieth and Columbus. You never saw it. It was a mistake. I think it was a mistake. I didn't stay there long—six or seven months—but it was the longest I stayed anywhere in those years or the years that followed. The apartment needed to be furnished, and I spent two or three days taking pleasure in the sharp bite of buying things: two easy chairs that I later sent back to Ireland; a leather sofa from Bloomingdale's, which I eventually gave to one of my students; a big bed from 1-800-Mattres; a table and some chairs from a place downtown; a cheap desk from the thrift shop.

And all those days—a Friday, a Saturday, and a Sunday, at the beginning of September—as I was busy with delivery times, credit cards, and the whiz of taxis from store to store, my mother was dying and no one could find me. I had no cell phone, and the phone line in the apartment had not been connected. I used the pay phone on the corner if I needed to make calls. I gave the delivery companies a friend's phone number, in case they had to let me know when they would come with my furniture. I phoned my friend a few times a day, and she came shopping with me sometimes and she was fun and I enjoyed those days. The days when no one in Ireland could find me to tell me that my mother was dying.

Eventually, late on the Sunday night, I slipped into a Kinko's and went online and found that Suzie had left me message after message, starting three days before, marked "Urgent" or "Are you there" or "Please reply" or "Please acknowledge receipt" and then just "Please!!!" I read one of them, and I replied to say that I would call as soon as I could find a phone, and then I read the rest of them one by one. My mother was in the hospital. She might have to have an operation. Suzie wanted to talk to me. She was staying at my mother's house. There was nothing more in any of them, the urgency being not so much in their tone as in their frequency and the different titles she gave to each e-mail that she sent.

I woke her in the night in Ireland. I imagined her standing in the hall at the bottom of the stairs. I would love to say that Suzie told me my mother was asking for me, but she said nothing like that. She spoke instead about the medical details and how she herself had been told the news that our mother was in the hospital and how she had despaired of ever finding me. I told her that I would call again in the morning, and she said that she would know more then. My mother was not in pain now, she said, although she had been. I did not tell her that my classes would begin in three days, because I did not need to. That night, it sounded as though she wanted just to talk to me, to tell me. Nothing more.

But in the morning when I called I realized that she had put quick thought into it as soon as she heard my voice on the phone, that she had known I could not make arrangements to leave for Dublin late on a Sunday night, that there would be no flights until the next evening; she had decided to say nothing until the morning. She had wanted me to have an easy night's sleep. And I did, and in the morning when I phoned she said simply that there would come a moment very soon when the family would have to decide. She spoke about *the family* as though it were as distant as the urban district council or the government or the United Nations, but she knew and I knew that there were just the three of us. We were the family, and there is only one thing that a family is ever asked to decide in a hospital. I told her that I would come home; I would get the next flight. I would not be in my new apartment for some of the furniture deliverers, and I would not be at the university for my first classes. Instead, I would find a flight to Dublin, and I would see her as soon as I could. My friend phoned Aer Lingus and discovered that a few seats were kept free for eventualities like this. I could fly out that evening.

You know that I do not believe in God. I do not care much about the mysteries of the universe, unless they come to me in words, or in music maybe, or in a set of colors, and then I entertain them merely for their beauty and only briefly. I do not even believe in Ireland. But you know, too, that in these years of being away there are times when Ireland comes to me in a sudden guise, when I see a hint of something familiar that I want and need. I see someone coming toward me, with a soft way of smiling, or a stubborn uneasy face, or a way of moving warily through a public place, or a raw, almost resentful stare into the middle distance. In any case, I went to J.F.K. that evening, and I saw them as soon as I got out of the taxi: a middle-aged couple pushing a trolley that had too much luggage on it, the man looking fearful and mild, as though he might be questioned by someone at any moment and not know how to defend himself, and the woman harassed and weary, her clothes too colorful, her heels too high, her mouth set in pure, blind determination, but her eyes humbly watchful, undefiant.

I could easily have spoken to them and told them why I was going home and they both would have stopped and asked me where I was from, and they would have nodded with understanding when I spoke. Even the young men in the queue to check in, going home for a quick respite—just looking at their tentative stance and standing in their company saying nothing, that brought ease with it. I could breathe for a while without worry, without having to think. I, too, could look like them, as though I owned nothing, or nothing much, and were ready to smile softly or keep my distance without any arrogance if someone said, "Excuse me," or if an official approached.

When I picked up my ticket, and went to the check-in desk, I was told to go to the other desk, which looked after business class. It occurred to me, as I took my bag over, that it might be airline policy to comfort those who were going home for reasons such as mine with an upgrade, to cosset them through the night with quiet sympathy and an extra blanket or something. But when I got to the desk I knew why I had been sent there, and I wondered about God and Ireland, because the woman at the desk had seen my name being added to the list and had told the others that she knew me and would like to help me now that I needed help.

Her name was Frances Carey, and she had lived next door to my aunt's house, where we—myself and Cathal—were left when my father got sick. I was eight years old then. Frances must have been ten years older, but I remember her well, as I do her sister and her two brothers, one of whom was close to me in age. Their family owned the house that my aunt lived in, the aunt who took us in. They were grander than she was and much richer, but she had become friendly with them, and there was, since the houses shared a large back garden and some outhouses, a lot of traffic between the two establishments.

Cathal was four then, but in his mind he was older. He was learning to read already, he was clever and had a prodigious memory, and was treated as a young boy in our house rather than as a baby; he could decide which clothes to wear each day and what television he wanted to watch and which room he would sit in and what food he would eat. When his friends called at the house, he could freely ask them in, or go out with them. When relatives or friends of my parents called, they asked for him, too, and spoke to him and listened avidly to what he had to say.

In all the years that followed, Cathal and I never once spoke about our time in this new house with this new family. And my memory, usually so good, is not always clear. I cannot remember, for example, how we got to the house, who drove us there, or what this person said. I know that I was eight years old only because I remember what class I was in at school when I left and who the teacher was. It is possible that this period lasted just two or three months. Maybe it was more. It was not summer, I am sure of that, because Suzie, who remained unscathed by all of this (or so she said, when once, years ago, I asked her if she remembered it), was back at boarding school. I have no memory of cold weather in that house in which we were deposited, although I do think that the evenings were dark early. Maybe it was from September to December. Or the first months after Christmas. I am not sure.

What I remember clearly is the rooms themselves, the parlor and dining room almost never used and the kitchen, larger than ours at home, and the smell and taste of fried bread. I hated the hot thick slices, fresh from the pan, soaked in lard or dripping. I remember that our cousins were younger than we were and had to sleep during the day, or at least one of them did, and we had to be quiet for hours on end, even though we had nothing to do; we had none of our toys or books. I remember that nobody liked us, either of us, not even Cathal, who, before and after this event, was greatly loved by people who came across him.

We slept in my aunt's house and ate her food as best we could, and we must have played or done something, although we never went to school. Nobody did us any harm in that house; nobody came near us in the night, or hit either of us, or threatened us, or made us afraid. The time we were left by our mother in our aunt's house has no drama attached to it. It was all grayness, strangeness. Our aunt dealt with us in her own distracted way. Her husband was mild, distant, almost good-humored.

And all I know is that our mother did not get in touch with us once, not once, during this time. There was no letter or phone call or visit. Our father was in the hospital. We did not know how long we were going to be left there. In the years that followed, our mother never explained her absence, and we never asked her if she had ever wondered how we were, or how we felt, during those months.

This should be nothing, because it resembled nothing, just as one minus one resembles zero. It should be barely worth recounting to you as I walk the empty streets of this city in the desert so far away from where I belong. It feels as though Cathal and I had spent that time in the shadow world, as though we had been quietly lowered into the dark, everything familiar missing, and nothing we did or said could change this. Because no one gave any sign of hating us, it did not strike us that we were in a world where no one loved us, or that such a thing might matter. We did not complain. We were emptied of everything, and in the vacuum came something like silence—almost no sound at all, just some sad echoes and dim feelings.

I promise you that I will not call. I have called you enough, and woken you enough times, in the years when we were together and in the years since then. But there are nights now in this strange, flat, and forsaken place when those sad echoes and dim feelings come to me slightly louder than before. They are like whispers, or trapped whimpering sounds. And I wish that I had you here, and I wish that I had not called you all those other times when I did not need to as much as I do now.

My brother and I learned not to trust anyone. We learned then not to talk about things that mattered to us, and we stuck to this, as much as we could, with a sort of grim stubborn pride, all our lives, as though it were a skill. But you know that, don't you? I do not need to call you to tell you that.

At J.F.K. that night, Frances Carey smiled warmly and asked me how bad things were. When I told her that my mother was dying, she said that she was shocked. She remembered my mother so well, she said. She said she was sorry. She explained that I could use the first-class lounge, making it clear, however, in the most pleasant way, that I would be crossing the Atlantic in coach, which was what I had paid for. If I needed her, she said, she could come up in a while and talk, but she had told the people in the lounge and on the plane that she knew me, and they would look after me.

As we spoke and she tagged my luggage and gave me my boarding pass, I guessed that I had not laid eyes on her for more than thirty years. But in her face I could see the person I had known, as well as traces of her mother and one of her brothers. In her presence—the reminder she offered of that house where Cathal and I had been left all those years ago—I could feel that this going home to my mother's bedside would not be simple, that some of our loves and attachments are elemental and beyond our choosing, and for that very reason they come spiced with pain and regret and need and hollowness and a feeling as close to anger as I will ever be able to manage.

Sometime during the night in that plane, as we crossed part of the Western Hemisphere, quietly and, I hope, unnoticed, I began to cry. I was back then in the simple world before I had seen Frances Carey, a world in which someone whose heartbeat had once been mine, and whose blood became my blood, and inside whose body I once lay curled, herself lay stricken in a hospital bed. The fear of losing her made me desperately sad. And then I tried to sleep. I pushed back my seat as the night wore on and kept my eyes averted from the movie being shown, whatever it was, and let the terrible business of what I was flying toward hit me.

I hired a car at the airport, and I drove across Dublin in the washed light of that early September morning. I drove through Drumcondra, Dorset Street, Mountjoy Square, Gardiner Street, and the streets across the river that led south, as though they were a skin that I had shed. I did not stop for two hours or more, until I reached the house, fearing that if I pulled up somewhere to have breakfast the numbness that the driving with no sleep had brought might lift.

Suzie was just out of bed when I arrived, and Jim was still asleep. Cathal had gone back to Dublin the night before, she said, but would be down later. She sighed and looked at me. The hospital had phoned, she went on, and things were worse. Your mother, she said, had a stroke during the night, on top of everything else. It was an old joke between us: never "our mother" or "my mother" or "Mammy" or "Mummy," but "your mother."

The doctors did not know how bad the stroke had been, she said, and they were still ready to operate if they thought they could. But they needed to talk to us. It was a pity, she added, that our mother's specialist, the man who looked after her heart, and whom she saw regularly and liked, was away. I realized then why Cathal had gone back to Dublin—he did not want to be a part of the conversation that we would have with the doctors. Two of us would be enough. He had told Suzie to tell me that whatever we decided would be fine with him.

Neither of us blamed him. He was the one who had become close to her. He was the one she loved most. Or maybe he was the only one she loved. In those years, anyway. Or maybe that is unfair. Maybe she loved us all, just as we loved her as she lay dying.

And I moved, in those days—that Tuesday morning to the Friday night when she died—from feeling at times a great remoteness from her to wanting fiercely, almost in the same moment, my mother back where she had always been, in witty command of her world, full of odd dreams and perspectives, difficult, ready for life. She loved, as I did, books and music and hot weather. As she grew older she had managed, with her friends and with us, a pure charm, a lightness of tone and touch. But I knew not to trust it, not to come close, and I never did. I managed, in turn, to exude my own lightness and charm, but you know that, too. You don't need me to tell you that, either, do you?

I regretted nonetheless, as I sat by her bed or left so that others might see her—I regretted how far I had moved away from her, and how far away I had stayed. I regretted how much I had let those months apart from her in the limbo of my aunt's house, and the years afterward, as my father slowly died, eat away at my soul. I regretted how little she knew about me, as she, too, must have regretted that, although she never complained or mentioned it, except perhaps to Cathal, and he told no one anything. Maybe she regretted nothing. But nights are long in winter, when darkness comes down at four o'clock and people have time to think of everything.

Maybe that is why I am here now, away from Irish darkness, away from the long, deep winter that settles so menacingly on the place where I was born. I am away from the east wind. I am in a place where so much is empty because it was never full, where things are forgotten and swept away, if there ever were things. I am in a place where there is nothing. Flatness, a blue sky, a soft, unhaunted night. A place where no one walks. Maybe I am happier here than I would be anywhere else, and it is only the poisonous innocence of the moon tonight that has made me want to dial your number and see if you are awake.

As we drove to see my mother that morning, I could not ask Suzie a question that was on my mind. My mother had been sick for four days now and was lying there maybe frightened, and I wondered if she had reached out her hand to Cathal and if they had held hands in the hospital, if they had actually grown close enough for that. Or if she had made some gesture to Suzie. And if she might do the same to me. It was a stupid, selfish thing I wondered about, and, like everything else that came into my mind in those days, it allowed me to avoid the fact that there would be no time anymore for anything to be explained or said. We had used up all our time. And I wondered if that made any difference to my mother then, as she lay awake in the hospital those last few nights of her life: we had used up all our time.

She was in intensive care. We had to ring the bell and wait to be admitted. There was a hush over the place. We had discussed what I would say to her so as not to alarm her, how I would explain why I had come back. I told Suzie that I would simply say that I'd heard she was in the hospital and I'd had a few days free before classes began and had decided to come back to make sure that she was O.K.

"Are you feeling better?" I asked her.

She could not speak. Slowly and laboriously, she let us know that she was thirsty and they would not allow her to drink anything. She had a drip in her arm. We told the nurses that her mouth was dry, and they said that there was nothing much we could do, except perhaps take tiny drops of cold water and put them on her lips using those special little sticks with cotton-wool tips that women use to put on eye makeup.

I sat by her bed and spent a while wetting her lips. I was at home with her now. I knew how much she hated physical discomfort; her appetite for this water was so overwhelming and so desperate that nothing else mattered.

And then word came that the doctors would see us. When we stood up and told her that we would be back, she hardly responded. We were ushered by a nurse with an English accent down some corridors to a room. There were two doctors there; the nurse stayed in the room. The doctor who seemed to be in charge, who said that he would have been the one to perform the operation, told us that he had just spoken to the anesthetist, who had insisted that my mother's heart would not survive an operation. The stroke did not really matter, he said, although it did not help.

"I could have a go," he said, and then immediately apologized for speaking like that. He corrected himself: "I could operate, but she would die on the operating table."

There was a blockage somewhere, he said. There was no blood getting to her kidneys and maybe elsewhere as well—the operation would tell us for certain, but it would probably do nothing to solve the problem. It was her circulation, he said. The heart was simply not beating strongly enough to send blood into every part of her body.

He knew to leave silence then, and the other doctor did, too. The nurse looked at the floor.

"There's nothing you can do then, is there?" I said.

"We can make her comfortable," he replied.

"How long can she survive like this?" I asked.

"Not long," he said.

"I mean, hours or days?"

"Days. Some days."

"We can make her very comfortable," the nurse said.

There was nothing more to say. Afterward, I wondered if we should have spoken to the anesthetist personally, or tried to contact our mother's consultant, or asked that she be moved to a bigger hospital for another opinion. But I don't think any of this would have made a difference. For years, we had been given warnings that this moment would come, as she fainted in public places and lost her balance and declined. It had been clear that her heart was giving out, but not clear enough for me to have come to see her more than once or twice in the summer—and then when I did come I was protected from what might have been said, or not said, by the presence of Suzie and Jim and Cathal. Maybe I should have phoned a few times a week, or written her letters like a good son. But despite all the warning signals, or perhaps even because of them, I had kept my distance. And as soon as I entertained this thought, with all the regret that it carried, I imagined how coldly or nonchalantly a decision to spend the summer close by, seeing her often, might have been greeted by her, and how difficult and enervating for her, as much as for me, some of those visits or phone calls might have been. And how curtly efficient and brief her letters in reply to mine would have seemed.

And, as we walked back down to see her, the nurse coming with us, there was this double regret—the simple one that I had kept away, and the other one, much harder to fathom, that I had been given no choice, that she had never wanted me very much, and that she was not going to be able to rectify that in the few days that she had left in the world. She would be distracted by her own pain and discomfort, and by the great effort she was making to be dignified and calm. She was wonderful, as she always had been. I touched her hand a few times in case she might open it and seek my hand, but she never did this. She did not respond to being touched.

Some of her friends came. Cathal came and stayed with her. Suzie and I remained close by. On Friday morning, when the nurse asked me if I thought she was in distress, I said that I did. I knew that, if I insisted now, I could get her morphine and a private room. I did not consult the others; I knew that they would agree. I did not mention morphine to the nurse, but I knew that she was wise, and I saw by the way she looked at me as I spoke that she knew that I knew what morphine would do. It would ease my mother into sleep and ease her out of the world. Her breathing would come and go, shallow and deep, her pulse would become faint, her breathing would stop, and then come and go again.

It would come and go until, in that private room late in the evening, it seemed to stop altogether, as, horrified and helpless, we sat and watched her, then sat up straight as the breathing started again, but not for long. Not for long at all. It stopped one last time, and it stayed stopped. It did not start again.

She was gone. She lay still. We sat with her until a nurse came in and quietly checked her pulse and shook her head sadly and left the room.

We stayed with her for a while; then, when they asked us to leave, we touched her on the forehead one by one, and we left the room, closing the door. We walked down the corridor as though for the rest of our lives our own breathing would bear traces of the end of hers, of her final struggle, as though our own way of being in the world had just been halved or quartered by what we had seen.

We buried her beside my father, who had been in the grave waiting for her for thirty-three years. And the next morning I flew back to New York, to my half-furnished apartment on Columbus and Ninetieth, and began my teaching a day later. I understood, just as you might tell me now—if you picked up the phone and found me on the other end of the line, silent at first and then saying that I needed to talk to you—you might tell me that I had over all the years postponed too much. As I settled down to sleep in that new bed in the dark city, I saw that it was too late now, too late for everything. I would not be given a second chance. In the hours when I woke, I have to tell you that this struck me almost with relief.

A HAPPY FAMILY

William Trevor

William Trevor (1928–2016) was a novelist, short story writer and playwright, whose works include *The Ballroom of Romance*, *Felicia's Journey* and *The Story of Lucy Gault*. He was awarded the Whitbread Prize, the Kerry Group Irish Fiction Award, and in 2014 was made a Saoi by Aosdána.

On the evening of Thursday, May 24th 1962, I returned home in the usual way. I remember sitting in the number 73 bus, thinking of the day as I had spent it and thinking of the house I was about to enter. It was a fine evening, warm and mellow, the air heavy with the smell of London. The bus crossed Hammersmith Bridge, moving quite quickly towards the leafy avenues beyond. The houses of the suburbs were gayer in that evening's sunshine, pleasanter abodes than often they seemed.

'Hullo,' I said in the hall of ours, speaking to my daughter Lisa, a child of one, who happened to be loitering there. She was wearing her nightdress, and she didn't look sleepy. 'Aren't you going to bed?' I said, and Lisa looked at me as if she had forgotten that I was closely related to her. I could hear Anna and Christopher in the bathroom, talking loudly and rapidly, and I could hear Elizabeth's voice urging them to wash themselves properly and be quick about it. 'She's fourteen stone, Miss MacAdam is,' Christopher was saying. 'Isn't she, Anna?' Miss MacAdam was a woman who taught at their school, a woman about whom we had come to know a lot. 'She can't swim,' said Anna.

Looking back now, such exchanges come easily to my mind. Bits of conversations float to the surface without much of a continuing pattern and without any significance that I can see. I suppose we were a happy family: someone examining us might possibly have written that down on a report sheet, the way these things are done. Yet what I recall most vividly now when I think of us as a family are images and occasions that for Elizabeth and me were neither happy nor unhappy. I remember animals at the Zoo coming forward for the offerings of our children, smelling of confinement rather than the jungle, seeming fierce and hard done by. I remember birthday parties on warm afternoons, the figures of children moving swiftly from the garden to the house, creatures who might have been bored, with paper hats on their heads or in their hands, seeking adventure in forbidden rooms. I remember dawdling walks, arguments that came to involve all of us, and other days when everything went well.

I used to leave the house at half past eight every morning, and often during the day I imagined what my wife's day must be like. She told me, of course. She told me about how ill-tempered our children had been, or how tractable; about how the time had passed in other ways, whom she had met and spoken to, who had come to tea or whom she had visited. I imagined her in summer having lunch in the garden when it was warm, dozing afterwards and being woken up by Lisa. In turn, she would ask me how the hours had gone for me and I would say a thing or two about their passing, about the people who had filled them. 'Miss Madden is leaving us,' I can hear myself saying. 'Off to Buenos Aires for some reason.' In my memory of this, I seem to be repeating the information. 'Off to Buenos Aires,' I appear to be saying. 'Off to Buenos Aires. Miss Madden.' And a little later I am saying it again, adding that Miss Madden would be missed. Elizabeth's head is nodding, agreeing that that will indeed be so. 'I fell asleep in the garden,' Elizabeth is murmuring in this small vision. 'Lisa woke me up.'

My wife was pretty when I married her, and as the years passed it seemed to me that she took on a greater beauty. I believed that this was some reflection of her contentment, and she may even have believed it herself. Had she suddenly said otherwise, I'd have been puzzled; as puzzled as I was, and as she was, on the evening of May 24th, when she told me about Mr Higgs. She sat before me then, sipping at a glass of sherry that I'd poured her and remembering all the details: all that Mr Higgs had said and all that she had said in reply.

She had been listening to a story on the radio and making coffee. Christopher and Anna were at school; in the garden Lisa was asleep in her pram. When the telephone rang Elizabeth walked towards it slowly, still listening to the wireless. When she said 'Hullo' she heard the coins drop at the other end and a man's voice said: 'Mrs Farrel?'

Elizabeth said yes, she was Mrs Farrel, and the man said: 'My name is Higgs.'

His voice was ordinary, a little uneducated, the kind of voice that is always drifting over the telephone.

'A very good friend,' said Mr Higgs.

'Good-morning,' said Elizabeth in her matter-of-fact way. 'Are you selling something, Mr Higgs?'

'In a sense, Mrs Farrel, in a sense. You might call it selling. Do I peddle salvation?'

'Oh, I am not religious in the least—'

'It may be your trouble, Mrs Farrel.'

'Yes, well—'

'You are Elizabeth Farrel. You have three children.'

'Mr Higgs—'

'Your father was a Captain Maugham. Born 1892, died 1959. He lost an arm in action and never forgave himself for it. You attended his funeral, but were glad that he was dead, since he had a way of upsetting your children. Your mother, seventy-four a week ago, lives near St Albans and is unhappy. You have two sisters and a brother.'

'Mr Higgs, what do you want?'

'Nothing. I don't want anything. What do you want, Mrs Farrel?'

'Look here, Mr Higgs—'

'D'you remember your tenth birthday? D'you remember what it felt like being a little girl of ten, in a white dress spotted with forget-me-not, and a blue ribbon tying back your hair? You were taken on a picnic. "You're ten years old," your father said. "Now tell us what you're going to do with yourself." "She must cut the chocolate cake first," your mother cried, and so you cut the cake and then stood up and announced the trend of your ambitions. Your brother Ralph laughed and was scolded by your father. D'you remember at all?'

Elizabeth did remember. She remembered playing hide-and-seek with her sisters after tea; she remembered Ralph climbing a tree and finding himself unable to get down again; she remembered her parents quarrelling, as they invariably did, all the way home.

'Do I know you, Mr Higgs? How do you manage to have these details of my childhood?'

Mr Higgs laughed. It wasn't a nasty laugh. It sounded even reassuring, as if Mr Higgs meant no harm.

On the evening of May 24th we sat for a long time wondering who the odd individual could be and what he was after. Elizabeth seemed nervously elated and naturally more than a little intrigued. I, on the other hand, was rather upset by this Mr Higgs and his deep mine of information. 'If he rings again,' I said, 'threaten him with the police.'

'Good-morning, Mrs Farrel.'

'Mr Higgs?'

'My dear.'

'Well then, Mr Higgs, explain.'

'Ho, ho, Mrs Farrel, there's a sharpness for you. Explain? Why, if I explained I'd be out of business in no time at all. "So that's it," you'd say, and ring off, just like I was a salesman or a Jehovah's Witness.'

'Mr Higgs—'

'You was a little girl of ten, Mrs Farrel. You was out on a picnic. Remember?'

'How did you know all that?'

'Why shouldn't I know, for heaven's sake? Listen now, Mrs Farrel. Did you think then what you would be today? Did you see yourself married to a man and mothering his children? Have you come to a sticky end, or otherwise?'

'A sticky end?'

'You clean his house, you prepare his meals, you take his opinions. You hear on the radio some news of passing importance, some bomb exploded, some army recalled. Who does the thinking, Mrs Farrel? You react as he does. You've lost your identity. Did you think of that that day when you were ten? Your children will be ten one day. They'll stand before you at ten years of age, first the girl, then the boy. What of their futures, Mrs Farrel? Shall they make something of themselves? Shall they fail and be miserable? Shall they be unnatural and unhappy, or sick in some way, or perhaps too stupid? Or shall they all three of them be richly successful? Are you successful, Mrs Farrel? You are your husband's instrument. You were different at ten, Mrs Farrel. How about your children? Soon it'll be your turn to take on the talking. I'll listen like I was paid for it.'

I was aware of considerable pique when Elizabeth reported all this to me. I protested that I was not given to forcing my opinions on others, and Elizabeth said I wasn't either. 'Clearly, he's queer in the head,' I said. I paused, thinking about that, then said: 'Could he be someone like a window-cleaner to whom you once perhaps talked of your childhood? Although I can't see you doing it.'

Elizabeth shook her head; she said she didn't remember talking to a window-cleaner about her childhood, or about anything very much. We'd had the same window-cleaners for almost seven years, she reminded me: two honest, respectable men who arrived at the house every six weeks in a Ford motor-car. 'Well, he must be someone,' I said. 'Someone you've talked to. I mean, it's not guesswork.'

'Maybe he's wicked,' said Elizabeth. 'Maybe he's a small wicked man with very white skin, driven by some force he doesn't understand. Perhaps he's one of those painters who came last year to paint the hall. There was a little man—'

'That little man's name was Mr Gipe. I remember that well. "Gipe," he said, walking into the hall and saying it would be a long job. "Gipe, sir; an unusual name."'

'He could be calling himself Higgs. He could have read through my letters. And my old diaries. Perhaps Mr Gipe expected a tip.'

'The hall cost ninety pounds.'

'I know, but it didn't all go to Mr Gipe. Perhaps nobody tips poor Mr Gipe and perhaps now he's telephoning all the wives, having read through their letters and their private diaries. He telephones to taunt them and to cause trouble, being an evil man. Perhaps Mr Gipe is possessed of a devil.'

I frowned and shook my head. 'Not at all,' I said. 'It's a voice from the past. It's someone who really did know you when you were ten, and knows all that's happened since.'

'More likely Mr Gipe,' said Elizabeth, 'guided from Hell.'

'Daddy, am I asleep?'

I looked at her wide eyes, big and blue and clear, perfect replicas of her mother's. I loved Anna best of all of them; I suppose because she reminded me so much of Elizabeth.

'No, darling, you're not asleep. If you were asleep you couldn't be talking to me, now could you?'

'I could be dreaming, Daddy. Couldn't I be dreaming?'

'Yes, I suppose you could.'

'But I'm not, am I?'

I shook my head. 'No, Anna, you're not dreaming.'

She sighed. 'I'm glad. I wouldn't like to be dreaming. I wouldn't like to suddenly wake up.'

It was Sunday afternoon and we had driven into the country. We did it almost every Sunday when the weather was fine and warm. The children enjoyed it and so in a way did we, even though the woods we went to were rather tatty, too near London to seem real, too untidy with sweet-papers to be attractive. Still, it was a way of entertaining them.

'Elizabeth.'

She was sitting on a tree-stump, her eyes half-closed. On a rug at her feet Lisa was playing with some wooden beads. I sat beside her and put my arm about her shoulders.

'Elizabeth.'

She jumped a little. 'Hullo, darling. I was almost asleep.'

'You were thinking about Mr Higgs.'

'Oh, I wasn't. My mind was a blank; I was about to drop off. I can do it now, sitting upright like this.'

'Anna asked me if she was dreaming.'

'Where is she?'

'Playing with Christopher.'

They'll begin to fight. They don't play any more. Why do they perpetually fight?'

I said it was just a phase, but Elizabeth said she thought they would always fight now. The scratching and snarling would turn to argument as they grew older and when they became adults they wouldn't ever see one another. They would say that they had nothing in common, and would admit to others that they really rather disliked one another and always had. Elizabeth said she could see them: Christopher married to an unsuitable woman, and Anna as a girl who lived promiscuously and did not marry at all. Anna would become a heavy drinker of whisky and would smoke slim cigars at forty.

'Heavens,' I said, staring at her, and then looking at the small figure of Anna. 'Why on earth are you saying all that?'

'Well, it's true. I mean, it's what I imagine. I can see Anna in a harsh red suit, getting drunk at a cocktail party. I can see Christopher being miserable—'

'This is your Mr Higgs again. Look, the police can arrange to have the telephone tapped. It's sheer nonsense that some raving lunatic should be allowed to go on like that.'

'Mr Higgs! Mr Higgs! What's Mr Higgs got to do with it? You've got him on the brain.'

Elizabeth walked away. She left me sitting there with her frightening images of our children. Out of the corner of my eye I saw that Lisa was eating a piece of wood. I took it from her. Anna was saying: 'Daddy, Christopher hurt me.'

'Why?'

'I don't know. He just hurt me.'

'How did he hurt you?'

'He pushed me and I fell.' She began to cry, so I comforted her. I called Christopher and told him he mustn't push Anna. They ran off to play again and a moment later Anna was saying: 'Daddy, Christopher pushed me.'

'Christopher, you mustn't push Anna. And you shouldn't have to be told everything twice.'

'I didn't push her. She fell.'

Anna put her thumb in her mouth. I glanced through the trees to see where Elizabeth had got to, but there was no sign of her. I made the children sit on the rug and told them a story. They didn't like it much. They never did like my stories: Elizabeth's were so much better.

'I'm sorry.' She stood looking down on us, as tall and beautiful as a goddess.

'You look like a goddess,' I said.

'What's a goddess?' Anna asked, and Christopher said: 'Why's Mummy sorry?'

'A goddess is a beautiful lady. Mummy's sorry because she left me to look after you. And it's time to go home.'

'Oh, oh, oh, I must find Mambi first,' Anna cried anxiously. Mambi was a faithful friend who accompanied her everywhere she went, but who was, at the moment of departure, almost always lost.

We walked to the car. Anna said: 'Mambi was at the top of an old tree. Mambi's a goddess too. Daddy, do you *have* to be beautiful to be a goddess?

'I suppose so.'

'Then Mambi can't be.'

'Isn't Mambi beautiful?'

'Usually she is. Only she's not now.'

'Why isn't she now?'

'Because all her hair came off in the tree.'

The car heaved and wobbled all the way home as Christopher and Anna banged about in the back. When they fought we shouted at them, and then they sulked and there was a mile or so of peace. Anna began to cry as I turned into the garage. Mambi, she said, was cold without her hair. Elizabeth explained about wigs.

I woke up in the middle of that night, thinking about Mr Higgs. I kept seeing the man as a shrimpish little thing, like the manager of the shop where we hired our television set. He had a black moustache – a length of thread stuck across his upper lip. I knew it was wrong, I knew this wasn't Mr Higgs; and then, all of a sudden, I began to think about Elizabeth's brother, Ralph.

A generation ago Ralph would have been called a remittance man. Just about the time we were married old Captain Maugham had packed him off to a farm in Kenya after an incident with a hotel receptionist and the hotel's account books. But caring for nothing in Kenya, Ralph had made his way to Cairo, and from Cairo on the long-distance telephone he had greeted the Captain with a request for financial aid. He didn't get it, and then the war broke out and Ralph disappeared. Whenever we thought of him we imagined that he was up to the most reprehensible racket he could lay his hands on. If he was, we never found out about it. All we did know was that after the war he again telephoned the Captain, and the odd thing was that he was still in Cairo. 'I have lost an arm,' Captain Maugham told him testily. 'And I,' said Ralph, 'have lost the empire of my soul.' He was given to this kind of decorated statement; it interfered so much with his conversation that most of the time you didn't know what he was talking about. But the Captain sent him some money and an agreement was drawn up by which Ralph, on receipt of a monthly cheque, promised not to return to England during his father's lifetime. Then the Captain died and Ralph was back. I gave him fifty pounds and all in all he probably cleaned up quite well. Ralph wasn't the sort of person to write letters; we had no idea where he was now. As a schoolboy, and even later, he was a great one for playing practical jokes. He was certainly a good enough mimic to create a Mr. Higgs. Just for fun, I wondered? Or in some kind of bitterness? Or did he in some ingenious way hope to extract money?

The following morning I telephoned Elizabeth's sisters. Chloe knew nothing about where Ralph was, what he was doing or anything about him. She said she hoped he wasn't coming back to England because it had cost her fifty pounds the last time. Margaret, however, knew a lot. She didn't want to talk about it on the telephone, so I met her for lunch.

'What's all this?' she said.

I told her about Mr Higgs and the vague theory that was beginning to crystallize in my mind. She was intrigued by the Higgs thing. 'I don't know why,' she said, 'but it rings a queer sort of bell. But you're quite wrong about Ralph.' Ralph, it appeared, was being paid by Margaret and her husband in much the same way as he had been paid by the Captain; for the same reason and with the same stipulation. 'Only for the time being,' Margaret said a little bitterly. 'When Mother dies Ralph can do what he damn well likes. But it was quite a serious business and the news of it would clearly finish her. One doesn't like to think of an old woman dying in that particular kind of misery.'

'But whatever it was, she'd probably never find out.'

'Oh yes, she would. She reads the papers. In any case, Ralph is quite capable of dropping her a little note. But at the moment I can assure you that Ralph is safe in Africa. He's not the type to take any chances with his gift horses.'

So that was that. It made me feel even worse about Mr Higgs that my simple explanation had been so easily exploded.

'Well,' I said, 'and what did he have to say today?'

'What did who say?'

'Higgs.'

'Nothing much. He's becoming a bore.'

She wasn't going to tell me any more. She wasn't going to talk about Mr Higgs because she didn't trust me. She thought I'd put the police on him, and she didn't want that, so she said, because she had come to feel sorry for the poor crazed creature or whatever it was he happened to be. In fact, I thought to myself, my wife has become in some way fascinated by this man.

I worked at home one day, waiting for the telephone call. There was a ring at eleven-fifteen. I heard Elizabeth answer it. She said: 'No, I'm sorry; I'm afraid you've got the wrong number.' I didn't ask her about Mr Higgs. When I looked at her she seemed a long way away and her voice was measured and polite. There was some awful shaft between us and I didn't know what to do about it.

In the afternoon I took the children for a walk in the park.

Mambi's gone to stay in the country,' Anna said. 'I'm lonely without her.'

'Well, she's coming back tonight, isn't she?'

'Daddy,' Christopher said, 'what's the matter with Mummy?'

*

I'm not very sure when it was that I first noticed everything was in rather a mess. I remember coming in one night and stumbling over lots of wooden toys in the hall. Quite often the cornflakes packet and the marmalade were still on the kitchen table from breakfast. Or if they weren't on the table the children had got them on to the floor and Lisa had covered most of the house with their mixed contents. Elizabeth didn't seem to notice. She sat in a dream, silent and alone, forgetting to cook the supper. The children began to do all the things they had ever wanted to do and which Elizabeth had patiently prevented, like scribbling on the walls and playing in the coal-cellar. I tried to discuss it with Elizabeth, but all she did was to smile sweetly and say she was tired.

'Why don't you see a doctor?'

She stared at me. 'A doctor?'

'Perhaps you need a tonic.' And at that point she would smile again and go to bed.

I knew that Elizabeth was still having her conversations with Mr Higgs even though she no longer mentioned them. When I asked her she used to laugh and say: 'Poor Mr Higgs was just some old fanatic.'

'Yes, but how did he—'

'Darling, you worry too much.'

I went to St Albans to see old Mrs Maugham, without very much hope. I don't know what I expected of her, since she was obviously too deaf and too senile to offer me anything at all. She lived with a woman called Miss Awpit who was employed by the old woman's children to look after her. Miss Awpit made us tea and did the interpreting.

'Mr Farrel wants to know how you are, dear,' Miss Awpit said. 'Quite well, really,' Miss Awpit said to me. 'All things being equal.'

Mrs Maugham knew who I was and all that. She asked after Elizabeth and the children. She said something to Miss Awpit and Miss Awpit said: 'She wants you to bring them to her.'

'Yes, yes,' I shouted, nodding hard. 'We shall come and see you soon. They often,' I lied, 'ask about Granny.'

'Hark at that,' shouted Miss Awpit, nudging the old lady, who snappishly told her to leave off.

I didn't quite know how to put it. I said: 'Ask her if she knows a Mr Higgs.'

Miss Awpit, imagining, I suppose, that I was making conversation, shouted: 'Mr Farrel wants to know if you know Mr Higgs.' Mrs Maugham smiled at us. 'Higgs,' Miss Awpit repeated. 'Do you know Mr Higgs at all, dear?'

'Never,' said Mrs Maugham.

'Have you ever known a Mr Higgs?' I shouted.

'Higgs?' said Mrs Maugham.

'Do you know him?' Miss Awpit asked. 'Do you know a Mr Higgs?'

'I do not,' said Mrs Maugham, suddenly in command of herself, 'know anyone of such a name. Nor would I wish to.'

'Look, Mrs Maugham,' I pursued, 'does the name mean anything at all to you?'

'I have told you, I do not know your friend. How can I be expected to know your friends, an old woman like me, stuck out here in St Albans with no one to look after me?'

'Come, come,' said Miss Awpit, 'you've got me, dear.'

But Mrs Maugham only laughed.

A week or two passed, and then one afternoon as I was sitting in the office filing my nails the telephone rang and a voice I didn't recognize said: 'Mr Farrel?'

I said 'Yes', and the voice said: 'This is Miss Awpit. You know, Mrs Maugham's Miss Awpit.'

'Of course. Good afternoon, Miss Awpit. How are you?'

'Very well, thank you. I'm ringing to tell you something about Mrs Maugham.'

'Yes?'

'Well, you know when you came here the other week you were asking about a Mr Higgs?'

'Yes, I remember.'

'Well, as you sounded rather anxious about him I just thought I'd tell you. I thought about it and then I decided. I'll ring Mr Farrel, I said, just to tell him what she said.'

'Yes, Miss Awpit?'

'I hope I'm doing the right thing.'

'What did Mrs Maugham say?'

'Well, it's funny in a way. I hope you won't think I'm being very stupid or anything.'

I had the odd feeling that Miss Awpit was going to die as she was speaking, before she could tell me. I said: 'I assure you, you are doing the right thing. What did Mrs Maugham say?'

'Well, it was at breakfast one morning. She hadn't had a good night at all. So she said, but you know what it's like with old people. I mean, quite frankly I had to get up myself in the night and I heard her sleeping as deep and sweet as you'd wish. Honestly, Mr Farrel, I often wish I had her constitution myself—'

'You were telling me about Mr Higgs.'

'I'm sorry?'

'You were telling me about Mr Higgs.'

'Well, it's nothing really. You'll probably laugh when you hear. Quite honestly I was in two minds whether or not to bother you. You see, all Mrs Maugham said was: "It's funny that man suddenly talking about Mr Higgs like that. You know, Ethel, I haven't heard Mr Higgs mentioned for almost thirty years." So I said "Yes", leading her on, you see. "And who was Mr Higgs, dear, thirty years ago?" And she said: "Oh nobody at all. He was just Elizabeth's little friend!"'

'Elizabeth's?'

'Just what I said, Mr Farrel. She got quite impatient with me. "Just someone Elizabeth used to talk to," she said, "when she was three. You know the way children invent things."'

'Like Mambi,' I said, not meaning to say it, since Miss Awpit wouldn't understand.

'Oh dear, Mr Farrel,' said Miss Awpit, 'I knew you'd laugh.'

I left the office and took a taxi all the way home. Elizabeth was in the garden. I sat beside her and I held her hands. 'Look,' I said. 'Let's have a holiday. Let's go away, just the two of us. We need a rest.'

'You're spying on me,' Elizabeth said. 'Which isn't new, I suppose. You've got so mean, darling, ever since you became jealous of poor Mr Higgs. How could you be jealous of a man like Mr Higgs?'

'Elizabeth, I know who Mr Higgs is. I can tell you—'

There's nothing to be jealous about. All the poor creature does is to ring me up and tell me about the things he read in my diaries the time he came to paint the hall. And then he tries to comfort me about the children. He tells me not to worry about Lisa. But I can't help worrying because I know she's going to have this hard time. She's going to grow big and lumpy, poor little Lisa, and she's not going to be ever able to pass an exam, and in the end she'll go and work in a post office. But Mr Higgs—'

'Let me tell you about Mr Higgs. Let me just remind you.'

'You don't know him, darling. You've never spoken to him. Mr Higgs is very patient, you know. First of all he did the talking, and now, you see, he kindly allows me to. Poor Mr Higgs is an inmate of a home. He's an institutionalized person, darling. There's no need to be jealous.'

I said nothing. I sat there holding her two hands and looking at her. Her face was just the same; even her eyes betrayed no hint of the confusion that held her. She smiled when she spoke of Mr Higgs. She made a joke, laughing, calling him the housewife's friend.

'It was funny,' she said, 'the first time I saw Christopher as an adult, sitting in a room with that awful woman. She was leaning back in a chair, staring at him and attempting to torture him with words. And then there was Anna, half a mile away across London, in a house in a square. All the lights were on because of the party, and Anna was in that red suit, and she was laughing and saying how she hated Christopher, how she had hated him from the first moment she saw him. And when she said that, I couldn't remember what moment she meant. I couldn't quite remember where it was that Anna and Christopher had met. Well, it goes to show.' Elizabeth paused. 'Well, doesn't it?' she said. 'I mean, imagine my thinking that poor Mr Higgs was evil! The kindest, most long-suffering man that ever walked on two legs. I mean, all I had to do was to remind Mr Higgs that I'd forgotten and Mr Higgs could tell me. "They met in a garden," he could say, "at an ordinary little tea-party." And Lisa was operated on several times, and counted the words in telegrams.'

Elizabeth talked on, of the children and of Mr Higgs. I rang up our doctor, and he came, and then a little later my wife was taken from the house. I sat alone with Lisa on my knee until it was time to go and fetch Christopher and Anna.

'Mummy's ill,' I said in the car. 'She's had to go away for a little.' I would tell them the story gradually, and one day perhaps we might visit her and she might still understand who we were. 'Ill?' they said. 'But Mummy's never ill.' I stopped the car by our house, thinking that only death could make the house seem so empty, and thinking too that death was easier to understand. We made tea, I remember, the children and I, not saying very much more.

THE APPLE

Una Troy

Una Troy (1910–1993), who later wrote under the pen name Elizabeth Connor, was born in Fermoy in Co. Cork. She wrote plays and published seventeen novels, including *Mount Prospect* (1936), *We Are Seven* (1955), *Maggie* (1958) and *A Sack of Gold* (1979). The short story that appears here was originally published in *The Bell* in 1942.

She had never used her mind for thinking, only for recording the thoughts of others. She was happy. She had always been happy. Walking now in the convent garden, her fingers staying automatically at the big, smooth beads of the Rosary that hung from her waist, her habit brushing on the bright June grass hedging the flower beds, she thanked God, with a simple, unsearching happiness, because the sky was blue, because the sun shone; she thanked Him, most fervently, for making this day, of all days, so fine and lovely, with no shadow of a cloud.

She was not afraid of being happy; she was used to it. Reverend Mother was coming down the path towards her. She was smiling as she came.

'Are you very excited, child?'

Mother Mary Aloysius blushed.

'A little Reverend Mother.'

Reverend Mother laughed.

'You're not the only one! They're like a pack of babies inside. I declare I've almost forgotten myself what the sea looks like.'

Forgotten the sea! Oh, but you couldn't! Even if you only saw it once in your life, you could never forget the sea. Today, it was blue – pale, pale blue, with no horizon but a misty curve far off where it sloped up to meet the sloping sky. I can see it, flowing over the roses there by the wall and the gulls' crying is loud above the blackbird's song…

'It's fifty years since I've seen it,' said Reverend Mother, and there was a gleam in her old eyes.

Mother Mary Aloysius saw the gleam and she kept her face tight and hard so that it wouldn't smile. Because Reverend Mother hadn't wanted to go at all – and now she was as bad as any of them. When the Bishop had altered the strict rule that forbade any member of the Order to set foot outside the

Convent grounds, Reverend Mother had been very angry. 'What was good enough for me when I entered,' she said, 'is good enough for me now, and she didn't speak at all kindly of the Bishop, who was only doing his best, poor man. 'I won't budge,' she said, and she didn't. She sent her nuns off on visits to the Convents at Michelstown, at Fermoy, at Kilkenny, and received them back with a sympathetic consciousness of her own firm virtue. But this year the Bishop himself had come and tackled her, like a brave man. She wasn't looking well, he said; the doctor prescribed a change; she needed the sea air. She was to take herself and four of her nuns off to the new house the order had bought at Youghal and she was to stay there for a month too. So, of course, Reverend Mother had to say 'yes' because Obedience was one of the Vows, but Mother Mary Aloysius was sure that she hadn't said it very meekly.

Mother Mary Aloysius had prayed for weeks that she would be one of the chosen. Oh, not because she wanted to be in Youghal – but because, if she went, they would travel the road by her own sea, her own rocks and cliffs, her own shining strand, her own home. 'Oh, please God,' she prayed, hoping hard it wasn't wrong to pray such a worldly prayer and telling Him if it was, not to grant it, 'please God, let Reverend Mother take me,' and God let her be taken, so everything was all right.

'It's thirty years since I saw the sea,' said Mother Mary Aloysius and kept on watching it flow beside her feet.

'Is it now, child? Well, well how times does go, to be sure! Who'd think it was that length since you came to us! It makes me feel an old woman,' said Reverend Mother, indignantly, glaring at her seventy odd years. 'Sure, you must be near fifty now?'

'Forty-nine,' said Mother Mary Aloysius.

Reverend Mother opened her mouth to speak and snapped it shut again with a click of her teeth. It was a disconcerting habit. But Mother Mary Aloysius knew it. She waited.

'I was thinking—' said Reverend Mother.

'Yes?' said Mother Mary Aloysius.

'We'll pass by your old home this evening, won't we?'

'Yes Reverend Mother.'

'Hm! I heard you talking about it in the Refectory. I was thinking— Would you like, now, if we stopped and you went and had a look at it? You know we still can't go inside any house, or even any other convent but our own Order's, but you could,' said Reverend Mother, you could walk around outside and you could,' said Reverend Mother, suddenly, 'you *could* look in through the windows.'

Mother Mary Aloysius gaped at her.

'Oh, Reverend Mother!' she said at last.

'Yes, child, yes,' said Reverend Mother.

'Oh, Reverend *Mother*!' said Mother Mary Aloysius.

'Yes. Well – we'll be leaving in half-an-hour,' said Reverend Mother, briskly, and was gone.

Mother Mary Aloysius hardly spoke at all in the car. She sat very straight and stiff between Sister Peter and Mother Mary Assumpta. She said yes, it would be very nice to see her home again after thirty years, and she said yes, that was a pretty view by those trees, and she said yes, that must be Waterford in the distance. And once Reverend Mother turned around from the front seat and smiled at her and Mother Mary Aloysius smiled back, but she smiled right through Reverend Mother.

She rode home from the hayfield on Susie, holding tightly on to Susie's mane, because her legs were very short and Susie was very very fat. Her father walked beside her; his hat was pushed on the back of his head and he carried a sprong over his shoulder. She dipped her fingers in the milk and held them out to teach the sucky-calves how to drink; she felt their rough, unaccustomed tongues drag at her hand. She scattered meal to the chickens and they came running. Chuck-chuck-chuck-chuck! She turned the wheel and blew the fire until it shone red in all their faces. She watched her mother put the cake in the pot-oven; it was special soda bread, with currants because it was her birthday. Tom and Mollie and Joe and she played hide-and-seek; the haggard was 'home'.

'Be a good girl and say your prayers and you'll be happy,' her mother said. 'Early to bed and early to rise,' said her father. 'That's my own girl,' said her mother, proudly, when she brought back the 'Extract from Literature' that she won at school. 'I declare to God, she's nearly as big as yourself, ma'am,' said Father O'Shea.

'It's a grand thing to be a nun,' her mother said. 'Such a happy life – and a person hasn't a care or trouble in the world. I'd be easy in my mind – of course, 'tisn't everyone that God gives the call to.'

All the same, her mother cried when she was leaving and the first weeks at the Convent were lonely ones. But they weren't unhappy – and the weeks after that, and all the weeks since, were happy as her mother had said they would be. Every hour was mapped our for you and you could see right on to the end, where God would take you to Himself and you'd meet Father and Mother again – and Moll that got a cold on the lungs – and the others that might be there before you – and you'd be there waiting to welcome the ones that were yet to come. They'd be all home together, loving one another like they used to be, and it would be home for ever and ever then…

*

She saw a familiar curving line of mountainy distance. With a jerk of the heart, she came back from yesterday and tomorrow to the living moment. She was looking out eagerly now, with wide hungry eyes. All at once, the road twisted to the left and beyond a field of young wheat was the sea.

'We're not so far now,' said Reverend Mother.

'Five miles,' she said. 'I know every inch of the way from here on. I used to come as far as this in the horse and trap to see my cousins!'

'Do they know at home you're passing?' Sister Peter asked and the look she gave at Mother Mary Aloysius had a lot of envy in it.

'No. There's only Paddy left at the farm. There used to be – ten of us it is that was in it long ago.'

There was an ache in her eyes, that were looking and looking at so much; there was an ache in her heart, too, there was loving and grasping at all that she saw.

Here's the village!' she said, and now she began to chatter because it helped to dull that odd feeling in her breast. 'That's Biddy Casey's – oh! of course she must be dead long ago – and there's a new name over the Post Office – Paddy didn't tell me – and that's old Mrs Graney's where I used to spend my penny on sweets. Pink ones I always bought. Isn't it queer how you remember things?'

Reverend Mother said gently: 'Maybe it is.'

She saw it. The car stopped. They were there. Her heart wasn't big enough to hold it all – Paddy standing by the car, and the thatch and pink walls, and the chip off the left pier of the gate. Everything the same – perhaps not so trim as it used to be but still just the same. It was crowding out her heart and hurting it. She must have a very small heart.

'Go around now, child, and have a look at things,' Reverend Mother said. She looked in through the front window. Everything was the same; Paddy had altered nothing. If he had had a wife, she would have made changes. She was glad, until she stopped herself, that he hadn't a wife. She was at the back of the house now, and alone. She couldn't even hear the voices at the gate. She laid her hand on the walls; she stroked them. She looked through the windows. The same – all the same. The back door was open; she looked through into the kitchen. The blue plates were on the dresser; the clock ticked on the wall; the fire was a smoulder of turf on the hearth. She looked up and, under the strawy eaves, saw the tiny window of her own room. So often she would kneel at that window and see, out beyond the fields, the sea under the sun or under the moon. The beams curved up oddly in the ceiling of that room; her bed was in the corner; on a shelf by the door were her books. Maybe they were still there…

'I wish—' she said softly. 'If I had a ladder—' and then laughed to imagine Mother Mary Aloysius climbing a ladder with her black skirts flapping around her, Mother Mary Aloysius perched on top, peering in through a little window at a little room.

The back door was open. There was one green pane of glass in the four cramped panes of that crooked window. When you looked through it, you looked into a new world where the sea had come in and covered everything and you were living safely, a mermaid on the sea-floor. There was a picture of a dog and a child hanging over your bed. The back door was open. A board was loose by the window; it squeaked when you stood on it; you could press it up and down with your foot and frighten yourself by pretending there was a mouse in the room. You weren't really frightened of that mouse. It was a pet one; its name was Florrie. The back door was open. There were three nails where clothes hung… The back door was open.

'If I go in,' said Mother Mary Aloysius, 'it will be a mortal sin.' She stood there rigidly.

'A mortal sin,' said Mother Mary Aloysius firmly, and went in. She went through every room in the house. Last of all, and longest of all, she knelt by the window of her own little bedroom and gazed across the pasture land and the gold cliff-tops at her own sea. The sun shone on it, and the moon; the frosty stars hung low over it; the sea-mist and the night hid it from all eyes but hers. When she came climbing down the narrow attic stairs, her habit clutched high in one hand, she carried the little room and all that was to be seen from it, safely in her heart. Her heart was so small that was all it could hold; and that fitted exactly into it as the egg to its shell. 'And now,' Mother Mary Aloysius said as she stepped out into the sunshine, 'I am in mortal sin.'

The delicate blades of grass growing through the crevice of the stones by the door were silver with lights; two shadows crossed the sun; a gull went calling towards the tide.

'My soul is black,' she said.

A poppy swayed at her from the hedge over the bohereen; a soft wind blew about her; her treasure, loveliest of all the loveliness of the day, was warm in her breast.

'Black…' she said.

But the poppy nodded; the breeze went rustling along; the grass and the birds flew into the sun.

And suddenly a dreadful thing happened to her. She could not understand it; she fought against it. 'But they told me so,' she said. 'They told me thus – and thus. They are right – they are always right.' She gripped at the beads of her Rosary; they slid from her blind fingers.

The world fell away from her, the world that others had fashioned for her with loving minds; and now she must strive for ever to refashion out of chaos the world of her own mind.

'It was no sin,' she said.

Her mind worked quicker and yet more quickly, as she hurried back to the car. As she ran she held her hand to her breast as if to keep her treasure secure but she did not yet realise how precious and how terrible was the price she had paid for it.

THE SEA'S DEAD

Katharine Tynan

Katharine Tynan (1859–1931) was born in Clondalkin, Dublin and become a prolific writer, publishing over 100 books of poetry, commentary, novels and short stories. *An Isle in the Water*, the collection from which this story featured, was published in 1896.

In Achill it was dreary wet weather—one of innumerable wet summers that blight the potatoes and blacken the hay and mildew the few oats and rot the poor cabin roofs. The air smoked all day with rain mixed with the fine salt spray from the ocean. Out of doors everything shivered and was disconsolate. Only the bog prospered, basking its length in water, and mirroring Croghan and Slievemore with the smoky clouds incessantly wreathing about their foreheads, or drifting like ragged wisps of muslin down their sides to the clustering cabins more desolate than a deserted nest. Inland from the sheer ocean cliffs the place seemed all bog; the little bits of earth the people had reclaimed were washed back into the bog, the gray bents and rimy grasses that alone flourished drank their fill of the water, and were glad. There was a grief and trouble on all the Island. Scarce a cabin in the queer straggling villages but had desolation sitting by its hearth. It was only a few weeks ago that the hooker had capsized crossing to Westport, and the famine that is always stalking ghost-like in Achill was forgotten in the contemplation of new graves. The Island was full of widows and orphans and bereaved old people; there was scarce a windowsill in Achill by which the banshee had not cried.

Where all were in trouble there were few to go about with comfort. Moya Lavelle shut herself up in the cabin her husband Patrick had built, and dreed her weird alone. Of all the boys who had gone down with the hooker none was finer than Patrick Lavelle. He was brown and handsome, broad-shouldered and clever, and he had the good-humoured smile and the kindly word where the people are normally taciturn and unsmiling. The Island girls were disappointed when Patrick brought a wife from the mainland, and Moya never tried to make friends with them. She was something of a mystery to the Achill people, this small moony creature, with her silver fair hair, and strange light eyes, the colour of spilt milk. She was as small as a child, but had the gravity of a woman. She loved the sea with a love unusual in Achill, where the sea is to many a ravening monster that has exacted in return for its hauls of fish the life of husband and son. Patrick Lavelle had built for her a snug cabin in a sheltered ravine. A little beach ran down in front of it where he could haul up his boat. The cabin was built strongly, as it had need to be, for often of a winter night the waves tore against its little windows. Moya loved the fury of the elements, and when the winter storms drove the Atlantic up the ravine with a loud bellowing, she stirred in sleep on her husband's shoulder, and smiled as they say children smile in sleep when an angel leans over them.

Higher still, on a spur of rock, Patrick Lavelle had laid the clay for his potatoes. He had carried it on his shoulders, every clod, and Moya had gathered the seaweed to fertilise it. She had her small garden there, too, of sea-pinks and the like, which rather encouraged the Islanders in their opinion of her strangeness. In Achill the struggle for life is too keen to admit of any love for mere beauty.

However, Patrick Lavelle was quite satisfied with his little wife. When he came home from the fishing he found his cabin more comfortable than is often the case in Achill. They had no child, but Moya never seemed to miss a child's head at her breast. During the hours of his absence at the fishing she seemed to find the sea sufficient company. She was always roaming along the cliffs, gazing down as with a fearful fascination along the black sides to where the waves churned hundreds of feet below. For company she had only the seagulls and the bald eagle that screamed far over her head; but she was quite happy as she roamed hither and thither, gathering the coloured seaweeds out of the clefts of the rocks, and crooning an old song softly to herself, as a child might do.

But that was all over and gone, and Moya was a widow. She had nothing warm and human at all, now that brave protecting tenderness was gone from her. No one came to the little cabin in the ravine where Moya sat and moaned, and stretched her arms all day for the dear brown head she had last seen stained with the salt water and matted with the seaweeds. At night she went out, and wandered moon-struck by the black cliffs, and cried out for Patrick, while the shrilling gusts of wind blew her pale hair about her, and scourged her fevered face with the sea salt and the sharp hail.

One night a great wave broke over Achill. None had seen it coming, with great crawling leaps like a serpent, but at dead of night it leaped the land, and hissed on the cottage hearths and weltered gray about the mud floors. The next day broke on ruin in Achill. The bits of fields were washed away, the little mountain sheep were drowned, the cabins were flung in ruined heaps; but the day was fair and sunny, as if the elements were tired of the havoc they had wrought and were minded to be in a good humour. There was not a boat on the Island but had been battered and torn by the rocks. People had to take their heads out of their hands, and stand up from their brooding, or this wanton mischief would cost them their dear lives, for the poor resources of the Island had given out, and the Islanders were in grips with starvation.

No one thought of Moya Lavelle in her lonely cabin in the ravine. None knew of the feverish vigils in those wild nights. But a day or two later the sea washed her on a stretch of beach to the very doors of a few straggling cabins dotted here and there beyond the irregular village. She had been carried out to sea that night, but the sea, though it had snatched her to itself, had not battered and bruised her. She lay there, indeed, like that blessed Restituta, whom, for her faith, the tyrant sent bound on a rotting hulk, with the outward tide from Carthage, to die on the untracked ocean. She lay like a child smiling in dreams, all her long silver hair about her, and her wide eyes gazing with no such horror, as of one who meets a violent death. Those who found her so wept to behold her.

They carried her to her cottage in the ravine, and waked her. Even in Achill they omit no funeral ceremony. They dressed her in white and put a cross in her hand, and about her face on the pillow they set the sea-pinks from her little garden, and some of the coloured seaweeds she had loved to gather. They lit candles at her head and feet, and the women watched with her all day, and at night the men came in, and they talked and told stories, subdued stories and ghostly, of the banshee and the death-watch, and wraiths of them gone that rise from the sea to warn fishermen of approaching death. Gaiety there was none: the Islanders had no heart for gaiety: but the pipes and tobacco were there, and the plate of snuff, and the jar of poteen to lift up the heavy hearts. And Moya lay like an image wrought of silver, her lids kept down by coins over her blue eyes.

She had lain so two nights, nights of starlit calm. On the fourth day they were to bury her beside Patrick Lavelle in his narrow house, and the little bridal cabin would be abandoned, and presently would rot to ruins. The third night had come, overcast with heavy clouds. The group gathered in the death chamber was more silent than before. Some had sat up the two nights, and were now dazed with sleep. By the wall the old women nodded over their beads, and a group of men talked quietly at the bed-head where Moya lay illumined by the splendour of the four candles all shining on her white garments.

Suddenly in the quietness there came a roar of wind. It did not come freshening from afar off, but seemed to waken suddenly in the ravine and cry about the house. The folk sprang to their feet startled, and the eyes of many turned towards the little dark window, expecting to see wild eyes and a pale face set in black hair gazing in. Some who were nearest saw in the half-light—for it was whitening towards day—a wall of gray water travelling up the ravine. Before they could cry a warning it had encompassed the house, had driven door and window before it, and the living and the dead were in the sea.

The wave retreated harmlessly, and in a few minutes the frightened folk were on their feet amid the wreck of stools and tables floating. The wave that had beaten them to earth had extinguished the lights. When they stumbled to their feet and got the water out of their eyes the dim dawn was in the room. They were too scared for a few minutes to think of the dead. When they recovered and turned towards the bed there was a simultaneous loud cry. Moya Lavelle was gone. The wave had carried her away, and never more was there tale or tidings of her body.

Achill people said she belonged to the sea, and the sea had claimed her. They remembered Patrick Lavelle's silence as to where he had found her. They remembered a thousand unearthly ways in her; and which of them had ever seen her pray? They pray well in Achill, having a sure hold on that heavenly country which is to atone for the cruelty and sorrow of this. In process of time they will come to think of her as a mermaid, poor little Moya. She had loved her husband at least with a warm human love. But his open grave was filled after they had given up hoping that the sea would again give her up, and the place by Patrick Lavelle's side remains forever empty.

ACKNOWLEDGEMENTS

Some of the stories here proved elusive to track down. I'm grateful to the following editors, publishers, writers and academics who helped me locate specific works, or offered advice or contacts.

Mariel Deegan of New Island Books, James Doyle of Turnpike Books, Jackie Lynam in Pearse Street Library, Deirdre McMahon in UCD, Declan Meade of the *Stinging Fly*, Professor Gerardine Meaney of UCD, Derek O'Connor, Dr. Tina O'Toole, University of Limerick.

Thanks also to the agents and editors of the writers in this collection, and to the authors themselves for allowing me to include their work.

With gratitude to Neil Belton for commissioning this book, and to Clare Gordon, Laura Palmer and Rachel Thorne for the arduous task of clearing permissions and dealing with contracts.

Thanks, as ever, to my agent Peter Straus.

EXTENDED COPYRIGHT

Bryan MacMahon: "Exile's Return" published in *Classic Irish Short Stories*, Oxford University Press, 1978. Reproduced by permission of the Estate of the author.

Janet McNeill: "Sometimes on Tuesdays" published in *The Belfast Telegraph*, 1971. Reproduced by permission of the Estate of the author.

Paul McVeigh: "Hollow," 2019, copyright © Paul McVeigh. Reproduced by permission of C&W Agency on behalf of the author.

Una Mannion: "A Shiver of Hearts," 2017. Reproduced by permission of the author.

Aidan Mathews: "Access" published in *Charlie Chaplin's Wishbone*, The Lilliput Press, 2015. Reproduced by permission of The Lilliput Press, Dublin.

Frances Molloy: "Women Are the Scourge of the Earth" published in *Women Are the Scourge of the Earth,* White Row Press, 1998. Reproduced by permission of the publisher.

Mary Morrissy: "Divided Attention" published in *A Lazy Eye*, Jonathan Cape, 1993. Reproduced by permission of the author.

Val Mulkerns: "Away From It All" published in *An Idle Woman and Other Stories*, Poolbeg Press, 1980. Reproduced by permission of the Estate of Val Mulkerns.

Peter Murphy: "The Deserter's Song," 2019, including a quotation from *The Kill God* by Eoghan Rua Finn, 2017. Reproduced by permission of both authors.

Éilís Ní Dhuibhne: "A Literary Lunch" published in *The Shelter of Neighbours*, Blackstaff Press, 2012. Reproduced by permission of the author.

Edna O'Brien: "A Journey" published in *A Scandalous Woman and Other Stories,* Weidenfield & Nicholson, 1974. Reproduced by permission of the author.

Flann O'Brien: "Two in One" published in *The Short Fiction of Flann O'Brien*, copyright © The Estate of Evelyn O'Nolan. Reproduced by permission of A.M. Heath & Co Ltd.

Máirtín Ó Cadhain: "An Bóthar go dtí an Ghealchathair" translated by Eoghan Ó Tuairisc. Reproduced by permission of Rita Kelly.

Frank O'Connor: "A Man of the World" published in *My Oedipus Complex*, Penguin, 1963. Reproduced by permission of Peters Fraser & Dunlop (www.petersfraserdunlop.com) on behalf of the Estate of Frank O'Connor.

Joseph O'Connor: "Ailsa" published in *True Believers*, Vintage, 1991. Reproduced by permission of Random House Group Ltd.

Nuala O'Connor: "Squidinky" published in *Joyride to Jupiter*, New Island Books. Reproduced by permission of New Island Books.

Seán Ó Faoláin: "Dead Cert" published in *The Talking Trees and Other Stories*, Jonathan Cape, 1971, copyright © The Estate of Sean O'Faolain. Reproduced by permission of the Estate c/o Rogers, Coleridge & White Ltd., 20 Powis Mews, London W11 1JN.

Liam O'Flaherty: "The Doctor's Visit" from *Irish Portraits*, Sphere Books. Reproduced by permission of Peters, Fraser & Dunlop (www.petersfraserdunlop.com) on behalf of the Estate of Liam O'Flaherty.

Melatu Uche Okorie: "Under the Awning" published in *This Hostel Life*, Virago, 2019. Reproduced by permission of Little, Brown Book Group Limited.

David Park: "The Apprentice" published in *Oranges from Spain*, Bloomsbury, 1990, copyright © David Park, 1990. Reproduced by permission of C&W Agency on behalf of the author.

Elske Rahill: "Manners" published in *In White Ink*, Apollo Books, 2017. Reproduced by permission of the publisher.

Keith Ridgway: "Where Do I Go When You Die?" 2019. Reproduced by permission of the author.

Sally Rooney: "Robbie Brady's astonishing late goal takes its place in our personal histories," copyright © 2017 by Sally Rooney. Used by permission of The Wylie Agency (UK) Limited.

Donal Ryan: "Physiotherapy" published in *A Slanting of the Sun: Stories,* Doubleday Ireland, 2016. Reproduced by permission of Random House Group Ltd.

Ian Sansom: "Red Eye" published in *Belfast Stories*, Doire Press, 2019. Reproduced by permission of the author.